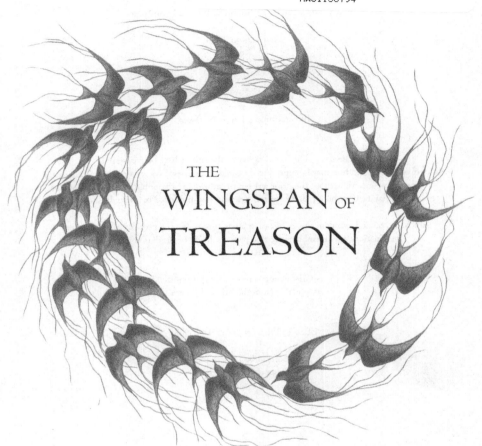

THE
WINGSPAN OF
TREASON

Book One of
THE STURMSINGER CHAIN

L. N. BAYEN

First published in Great Britain by Bregma Publishing

First edition 2024

Copyright © Lamia N. Bayen

Illustrations by Lamia N. Bayen

A CIP catalogue record for this book
is available from the British Library.

EPub ISBN: 978-1-7395098-9-7

Proofread by Ed Crocker
Typeset in Book Antiqua

BREGMA
PUBLISHING

London

This book is for every innocent
who has been touched by war;
who has felt its endless reverberations,
mourned its thefts,
known its myriad little griefs
and wept into the void –
there is hope.

The axe forgets; the tree remembers.

PROVERB OF THE ZIMBABWEAN SHONA TRIBE

MAPS

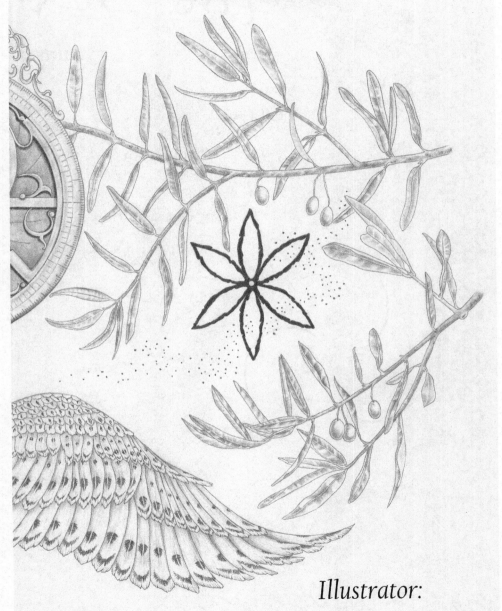

Illustrator:

L. N. Bayen

the SEV

AURELIA
PA

SILFREN
Part

FAR
NOREN

INVELMAR

ALTA

BLACK
LAVA
PLAINS

MORA

DERINDA

PENGA

P

AURELIAN
SEA

NORTH
ZMERRUDI
SEA

SE

ZENZEBRA

MORREGRAT

SI
P

KANEAN

DORENYA

UNGAL

NEKKE

PORVA

ZMERRUDI
PARE

SOUTH
ZMERRUDI
SEA

ORAO

BOLI

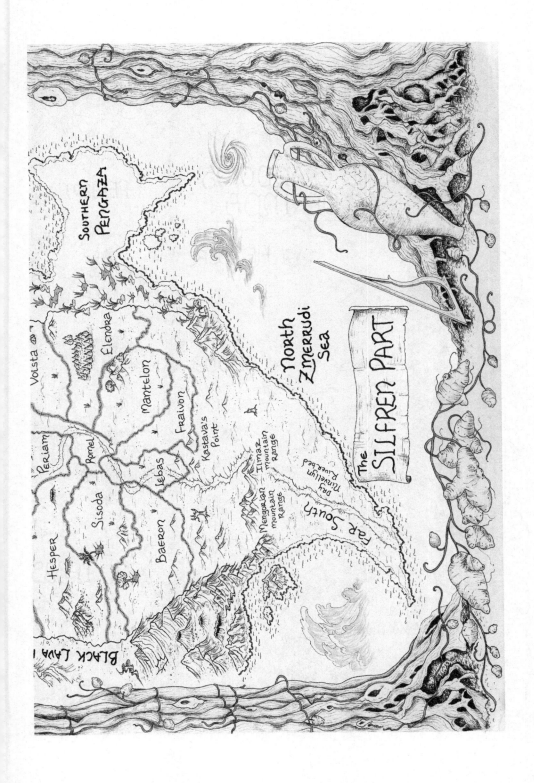

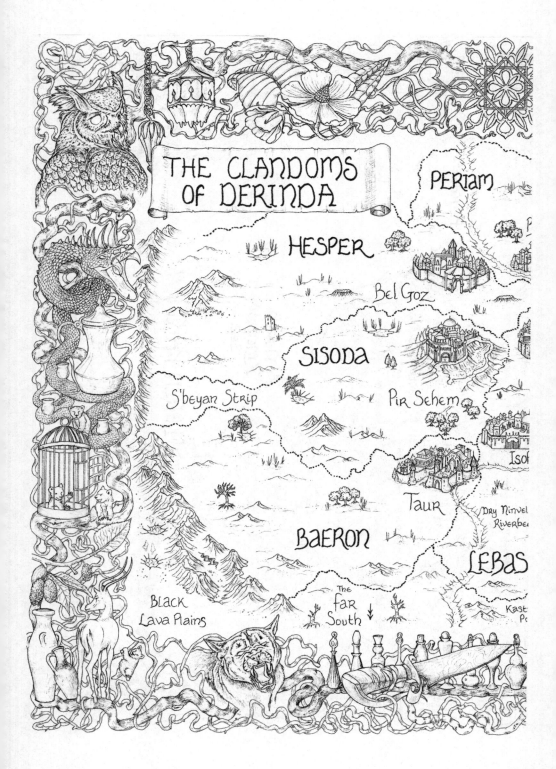

THE CLANDOMS OF DERINDA

PERIAM

HESPER

Bel Goz

SISODA

S'beyan Strip

Pir Schem

Iso...

Taur

Dry Ninvel Riverbe...

BAERON

LEBAS

Black Lava Plains

The Far South

Kast... Po...

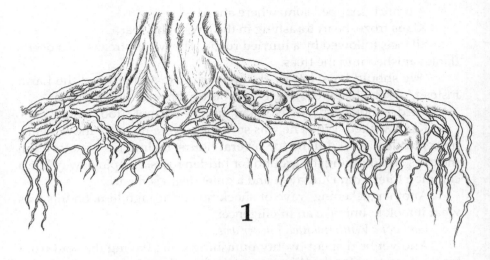

1

The Cuckoo's Nest

BEWARE, O INVELMARI, OF THE GLITTER OF YOUR BROTHERS' SILVER.
THE LOYALTY THAT BINDS YOU IS THE SACRED LEASH
YET PRESERVING YOUR FREEDOM.

SONNONFER: THE GREAT BLINDNESS

Klaus had often imagined death. It was an Intelligencer's truest companion. Insatiable thief; dark-eyed saviour. Not once had he imagined his death would be delivered by his own parents.

Run. For now, we run.

He had also dreamed of running, once. Years ago, before the barbed taproot of loyalty had finally reeled him home.

Until tonight. Tonight, at last, he ran.

Fog smudged the edge of darkness. The cast-iron breath of matted clouds smothered the stars, pitilessly blinding the night.

At dusk the forest had awoken as a feral creature, clutching at him with twisted hag fingers as he wove through the trees. If there was a moon, it had forgotten him. A meddling wind laden with ice-crystals pinched his face. Wolves mourned in the distance.

A branch snapped somewhere ahead.

Klaus froze, heart thrashing in the jaws of his fear.

Silence, followed by a hurried rustle. The white streaks on a deer's flank vanished into the trees.

'We should have left by the western gate and crossed the Larin instead,' Arik whispered. 'Fewer patrols on that side of Longtooth.'

Verdi shook his head. 'Not tonight. The current's too strong.'

Klaus waited. When he was sure there were no more movements, he continued as he'd done for several hours: feeling his way through the trees and nudging the ground for hidden roots; creeping away like a common thief from Dunraven and a quiet death sentence.

Another sickening wave of shock raked through him. So this was what it took to unmake an Intelligencer.

I am not a Wintermantel. I never was.

And yet he'd spent twenty punishing years flaying the soul from his flesh training for the Wintermantels, for a Form he'd never wanted.

Only the steel of that Form propelled him forward now.

Arik squeezed his arm as he pushed past him through the tangle of undergrowth.

On foot they were slow but better hidden. They'd stopped once to wait for a patrol to pass, but there had been no sign of pursuit. Not yet. Lady Wintermantel was hosting a meeting of Engineers that night; no one would have noticed them slip from the palace. It was morning Klaus was worried about.

'If we try to get to Andarsken Bridge –'

'No,' Klaus whispered. 'The Queen's expecting a party of Intelligencers back from Port Ellenheim. They'll return by the bridge.'

Verdi paled in the dark.

So they continued to where several trees had been felled over a narrow bend in the River Larin, crossing to its eastern bank. Then they hurtled through the night, borrowing as much time as they could from the cover of darkness. When dawn drew a grey finger across the sky, they finally stopped to rest. Everything was wet and heavy and cold. Verdi offered Klaus a strip of dried meat. He shook his head.

'Klaus…'

But even Verdi could scrounge no words of comfort.

Klaus lay down and drew around him the cloak Verdi had 'borrowed' from the servants' quarters. It smelled like a cellar that hadn't been opened in years.

'Why've they done this, Klaus?' Arik asked again. 'What happened?'

He'd held this question at bay, but it was insistent. *Why* had they done this – his own parents? *Only – they're not your parents.*

There had been no warning, nothing to stir even Klaus' suspicions, and he a bloody spy! It made this bewilderment all the more disabling.

He retreated behind the flint of his Form. 'Get some sleep. We'll need to move as soon as it gets dark.'

He should have been tired. He was acid and ice. Never had he dreaded sleep more than he did now. It was some time before it drew the executioner's cloth around his head, as restful as ever.

The ruins of these villages were no different to scores of disembowelled homes he'd seen before.

Far Northerners were more savage than the everwinter that scoured their ice plains of the very memory of mercy. Broken bodies littered the hamlet, intimately mutilated with a hatred that came from a primitive place as old as time. Smoke still hissed from burnt offerings to their heathen skylords.

Of the few survivors, only a dozen were strong enough to face the treacherous mountain passes of the Sterns on the journey home to Dunraven. The rest pleaded for death and were swiftly appeased. The living came with hollowed hearts, eyes sheltering in sockets as empty as those the Far Northern barbarians had gouged from the faces of their fallen brethren.

This had been Klaus' seventeenth nameday. It had changed little since his seventh. An Invelmari prince was quickly parted from tenderness.

'Courage.' Lord Wintermantel's order shook the snow clinging to the mountains like distant thunder. 'Grasp the courage of Sturmsinger. No Northern life shall go unavenged. Homes and lands await each one of you when we return.'

A long time before that would be of much comfort. But there was no insincerity in his father's promise. Invelmar's ruling Ealdormen had long learned that loyalty had to be earned and rewarded it as richly as disloyalty was harshly punished. Forgetting was the greatest mercy to have blessed the nature of man. Eventually even these wounds would heal. And then the cycle would begin again: Far Northern tribesmen, banished since the Second Redrawing to the northernmost white wastes beyond the Sterns, would regather to pinch the fatted haunches of Invelmar's northern outposts, ever hopeful their stings would seed a gangrene that might one day erode her defences.

It was only this struggle that had cured Klaus of the childish fantasies he'd once nurtured; of dreams of eschewing the court to travel the Seven Parts, to map the great unmapped swathes of Nékke and the Faire Isle and beyond. Now, at seventeen, the bitterness of this surrender had finally faded. Taking the Form of Intelligencer as Father had wished did, after all, grant him travel throughout the Parts. The intelligence he unearthed was a currency more prized than gold. And if rebel thoughts troubled him, Klaus only had to recall nights such as these, when charred babes buried their final screams in charred mothers' arms. Princely duty ceased to burden him then.

… And yet, just sometimes, following the sun's ascent from the curling palm of Northern valleys to daub with gold the snowdrifts draping the Sterns, it was impossible not to wonder how dawn might look from an untrodden hillside on the other side of the Parts.

'Only a week now, lord prince.' His Form Master for thirteen years now, Florian Arnander was also Father's closest advisor. Florian always seemed to know if that longing cast even the faintest shadow on Klaus' heart. A warning even hooved his words. 'Soon we will be in Dunraven.'

Before the next assignment, and the next. *Klaus quashed the renegade thought.*

Soon indeed they were in Dunraven, where Queen Adela compensated the survivors with parcels of rich farmland. The five families of Ealdormen led humble tribute to the fallen, laying wreaths of white rock-roses, first offerings of cold spring, to mark those whose bodies would never know graves.

It was then that Klaus saw him; a boy no older than seven, lone survivor of the ransacking of his family home. His arms were now full of those roses, child-eyes lustrous with tears held back by bravery beyond imagining, the sum of devastation itself eclipsed by his forbearance.

A hook slipped into Klaus' heart; a heart that no amount of flogging had truly turned.

Rebel longing tormented Klaus no more thereafter. Ealdormen's lives were forfeit to servitude, bound to the Sturmsinger Chain. Father was right; this had never been a choice. Especially for the likes of him, a Wintermantel, with Father next in line in the Chain to take Queen Adela's throne. How else was there to be any justice? It was the final stitch in his making as an Intelligencer.

Complete devotion came easily at last.

*

The cold woke him. A terrible, eviscerating cold. Even the endemic grip of the dreams that had plagued him all his life could not cocoon Klaus from a cold such as this.

He was frozen; it had been too risky to light a fire last night.

Last night. Memory assaulted all his senses at once, jerking his eyes open.

Dappled light swathed the hollow. Heart pounding, he re-digested the flurry of events that had forced their frantic departure from Dunraven.

There lay Arik to his right. Despite Klaus' pleading, the fool wouldn't stay home.

Thank the Lifegiver. One less piece left behind of the past he was quickly losing.

Across from him was Verdi, also still asleep. His boyish face was almost lost under a mop of black curls, peaceful despite their clumsy clipped-wing flight through the forest. Faithful Verdi, who despite his dreams would probably never leave his side.

Klaus reached under his cloak; the touch of his sword and his halberd were a cold comfort. His great crossbow was still slung across one shoulder, lying like a deadly lover beside him. But today even these extensions of himself provided little solace.

This was a numbing cold that paralysed his mind, maiming his thoughts and sending them tumbling over one another.

He had fled a royal house. He had betrayed the Blood Pact. He was not an Ealdorman. And he had taken a royal Form that had never been rightfully his but which was now so embedded into his being that it would forever hold him hostage to his treachery. He had betrayed the Ealdormen; he had betrayed the Sturmsinger Chain.

But have you? a bitter voice demanded. *Were you not the one betrayed first?*

It had been nine years since he'd laid eyes on that boy, laying rock-roses for his kin. Nine years since he'd conceded his soul to the Spyglass.

He sat up with a soft *crnshhh* of leaves. A weight tugged at his breast pocket. The others were still asleep; he pulled out the little package still wrapped in Elodie's silk handkerchief.

Inside was a round gold trinket box, the gems encrusting its lid scattering late morning sunlight. The clasp came open easily. It contained a small thick disc the colour of a stormy night, cool and smooth as though it had been fingered by a thousand hands. It was heavy, probably made of solid iron, and fit in his palm. Etched into the underside was a single stroke. He couldn't make out much else in the light of the hollow.

Something fluttered to his knee from the folds of the handkerchief: the scrap of parchment that had probably saved his life.

He couldn't bear to look again, and yet couldn't stop himself. He knew this elegant hand well. '*The cuckoo must fly this nest. 51°25′23′ N, 131°7′18′ W*'.

An old mooring post by the steps beneath the broken waterwheel on the overgrown bank of the Larin, submerged in water for all but two hours in the day when the river tide was at its lowest. That was where Elodie had hidden and waited after recognising the note was written in her mother's own hand, and where she had discovered their parent's greatest shame. *He* was the cuckoo, stolen from an unknown cradle and mislaid in the Wintermantels' nursery all those years ago. He had never been a Wintermantel prince.

So who the hell am I, then? And why had he been planted into an

Ealdorman's house?

He wouldn't throw it away, for one day he might need it to anchor him in case this memory ever faded – in case the anger became mellowed by time. He folded the note back into Elodie's handkerchief.

Klaus pulled out his crystal reading stone. The hemispherical lens magnified a jeweller's seal on the base of the trinket box. He found no other markings upon the iron disc.

A muffled sneeze broke his concentration, and he snapped the trinket box shut and stuffed it away. A ripple crept up Verdi's sleeve, punctuated by a tiny furry head poking out from under his collar. The silver-grey oceloe blinked at Klaus with enormous green eyes, one ear twitching.

'Don't wake him up,' Klaus whispered sternly.

'Too late,' Verdi mumbled, eyes still closed. But he burrowed into the leaves, pulling his coat tighter around him. Ravilion squeaked as the lapel dug into his ferret-like body, biting Verdi's ear. Verdi yelped and slapped his ear, sending leaves raining over the hollow.

When he'd finally stopped, the oceloe was poised on a branch overhead, haughtily licking his thick silver tail.

Arik sat up, wide awake and spattered with the forest floor. 'I don't think our trail was clear enough. Why don't you try a whistle?'

Klaus pulled an earthworm off his shoulder. 'I'm going to take a look around.'

He climbed up over the shelf of tree roots that had sheltered them. Feeble light trickled through half-dressed branches. Birdsong softened the quiet, but he was uneasy, half-expecting a patrol to step out from the trees.

A patch of stripped wood from a deer rub marked a nearby tree. They were still within hunting range and far too close to Dunraven

He returned to find Verdi trying to light a fire.

'It's too damp,' Arik grumbled. He offered Klaus a hunk of bread. 'Before it goes stale.'

Klaus shook his head. The numbness in the pit of his stomach left no foothold for hunger.

'You've got to eat something,' Verdi insisted.

'We have to move. We're still within the patrol perimeter. A couple of hours' hard riding is probably all that separates us from – from the citadel.'

His voice tripped. He'd almost said *home*.

Arik shook leaves from his cloak. 'Where to?'

'For you? Back to Dunraven,' Klaus told him. 'No one's trying to kill you.'

'No chance. All this time I've wasted looking for a way out of the Arm of the Court, and you've been my escape route all along ... I could have been chasing skirts.'

'You can't leave, you're an Ealdorman –'

'That's what they told you, too,' Arik joked, ignoring Verdi's grimace.

'They'll know you came with me. What will your uncles think?'

'They'll get over it.' Arik's voice hardened. 'Plenty of other Prosperes lining up to fill my boots. I've got my Form. Never wanted anything else from them.' He stretched. 'How do you know they'll even bother coming after you, anyway? The Wintermantels wanted to get rid of you and you've conveniently disappeared. They should be satisfied.'

'But they won't be,' said Klaus quietly. 'The Wintermantels won't compromise their succession. They'll want to make sure I can't come back and expose them. If any other Ealdormen discover they might have put an adopted imposter on the throne, the noose will be waiting.'

Of this, he was certain. It wouldn't matter that they'd planned to kill Klaus before that moment came. The deception would be enough. The five royal Ealdormen houses made every sacrifice necessary to uphold the Blood Pact that had protected the kingdom for over nine hundred years.

'And you.' Next Klaus turned to Verdi. 'Your apprenticeship with Mistress Berglund was near impossible to secure. You've wanted to be a physician longer than I can remember.'

His former servant's face filled with reproach. 'Do you really think there would still be a place for me amongst the Wintermantels now?'

It was an unkind but accurate truth. All that had stood between the little Derindin orphan and the prejudices of the palace had been the favour of the Invelmari prince.

'Well, then. East through Pengaza?' Arik suggested. 'Passage on a ship to Semra?'

'Port Ellenheim will be overrun with Isarnanheri.'

'We could cross the southern border,' Verdi offered tentatively. Ravi hopped down onto his arm. 'Hike through the Paiva and into the Derindin Plains. You'll be a stranger there.'

Arik shook his head, incredulous. 'And to think Klaus doesn't argue with *you* when you insist on tagging along. We'll stick out like a sore thumb between the Derindin. And we don't know a soul in Derinda.'

'*You'll* stick out anywhere,' Verdi retorted, drawing up his slight Derindin frame. Ravi yawned, ruining the effect. 'And there's my uncle Alizarin…'

'Do you know where to find him?' Klaus asked.

Arik choked on a mouthful of bread. 'Are you actually considering this madness?'

'All I know is his name,' Verdi confessed. 'But I'm sure we could track him down by clan.'

'And what do we do once we get there?' Arik demanded. 'Trek the Sourgrass Sea? Hide behind nomads and sand peasants? Sell our swords for small coin?'

'I don't know! We can figure that out if we make it across the border.' A measuring look crept over Verdi's face.

Arik cottoned on at once. 'I'm *not* going to wave my sword about to prop up rival nomads in the desert.'

'Why not? Soldiers are Invelmar's biggest export. You loan mercenaries –'

'Isarnanheri are not just *mercenaries*.'

'– to any Part that will pay – well, except Derinda –'

'Because no self-respecting swordhand goes to Derinda for work,' Arik snapped.

'Then neither you nor Klaus will have any trouble securing contracts. It's the best disguise.'

Arik's face reddened. 'I'm not slinking into the desert to pose as a second-rate mercenary.'

Klaus considered as they quarrelled. One sunrise ago he was a nobleman, a Wintermantel heir to the Invelmari throne and at the helm of a half-known destiny. Today he was unmade. Plucked from an unknown mother, disguised as a prince for twenty-six years, and now a fugitive from the North. His very name seemed alien to him, chosen as it was for a child ordained to preside over the greatest kingdom in the Seven Parts.

Why? Why've they done this to me?

Klaus throttled the question with Form. If he gave himself to it now, he would surely crumble. *For now, we just run.*

'Madness,' Arik repeated firmly. 'Madness.'

There was no question of hiding in Invelmar. Whoever he really was, Klaus' position in the Eye of the Court amongst Queen Adela's closest Intelligencers would be his death sentence now. The Far North was increasingly hostile to the Ealdormen's rule; they would find no friendship there. The tundra to the east was the main corridor for the Isarnanheri serving their contracts overseas, and they would be sure to cross paths with the Ealdormen Warriors who led them. And to the west, the Black Lava Plains were virtually impassable.

He knew little of the South. It was a great desert where long-lived clans bickered for power. There would be no Isarnanheri there, for Invelmar refused to loan her elite soldiers or sell her fabled steel to the neighbour they had once conquered. All Klaus' book learning couldn't hope to scratch beneath the surface of the desert's tempestuous past. Derinda's former glory had been reduced to miserly mention in the Sonnonfer, the sacred scrolls that chronicled the lore of Invelmar, or else to the romanticising of poets. In fact, much of what he did know of the

South had been cajoled from the bards. Now it was a place where the North imported such things as hunting birds, horse trainers and kahvi. None of the stories he had heard of its merciless winters and endless drought recommended it as a refuge.

But it was *unknown*, and he liked to know. And it was not the North.

'I'll follow you there,' he told Verdi. 'I've got nothing but the road.'

Verdi looked taken aback for a moment, then grinned. There was no hiding his excitement; Verdi had long dreamed of seeing his birthland. 'You don't have to come,' he told Arik mock-hopefully.

'Hilarious,' Arik fired back. 'Where you're heading, you'll need all the help you can get.'

Klaus consulted the compass he had not been without since the age of five. They'd barely cleared the farmlands that fringed Dunraven, with miles of patrolled forest remaining between them and the Paiva valley to the south.

'We'll stick to the forest for now,' he decided. 'At dusk we can risk following the river.'

'I don't like it,' Arik muttered. 'We should just leave this Part, go east through the Sourgrass Sea. We've got gold. You speak enough languages. We'll have our pick of ships.'

Klaus unfolded the single map he'd kept. He'd only recently begun making it, and hadn't yet plotted much beyond Sunnanfrost, the Wintermantels' palace in Dunraven. To leave the Silfren Part now altogether … the heart of him reeled all over again.

Quietly he replied, 'Maybe. But not yet.'

He ran his fingers lovingly over the ink. Two weeks' hard hike would take them into the wilderness of the Paiva. The Ninvellyn river would guide them through the valley to the market towns that huddled around the Ostraad dam marking the southern border of Invelmar. And south of the Ostraad was the great expanse of half-forgotten grassland that would eventually crumble into the barren desert of Derinda, where the sand had wings of devastating wind and rain was a stranger.

So there would be his calling: in the dirt dunes of the Derindin wastes. The cuckoo would fly south. Just then, stripped of everything but the memory of what he could have been, he could think of no better burial ground for Ulfriklaus Wintermantel, the man he had suddenly ceased to be and did not yet know how to replace.

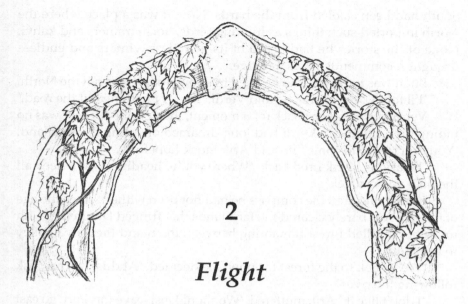

2

Flight

HAVE YOU FORGOTTEN THE BLINDNESS THAT REIGNED BEFORE
THE BIRTH OF INVELMAR? FROM FAR NORTHERN ICE-TOWERS
TO THE GREEN DELLS OF THE LOWER NORTH, WILD TRIBES
TORE THE NORTH INTO A THOUSAND THRONEDOMS.

SONNONFER: THE GREAT BLINDNESS

For Klaus, the days that followed would have passed in a daze were it not
for the threat of capture, keeping their senses sharp and their legs willing.

How could they have done this? Each step he took away from Dunraven
compounded his incoherent disbelief. *Why have they done this to me?*

Master Arnander had once been the Queen's Spyglass before the
fall from his horse that had forced his early retirement and had begun
training Klaus to the Form of Intelligencer from the clumsy age of four.
'*Make a box,*' he had said. '*Keep it in your bones, for that is where your matter
is least disturbed. Give it a name, for that makes it stronger. Give it a key, for
that gives you more power over it. That name must never pass any lips but your
own. Here you will banish all things that splinter your attention or cloud your
judgement. This box is how you will become a man, and this box is how a man
becomes a king.*'

And so into this box went all the anger, all the hurt, all the *bewilderment* of no longer being an Ealdorman, or a Wintermantel.

But what purpose did that leave him with now?

He put this problem into the box too, keeping only the salvageable portions of himself: scholar, soldier, spy. Then he closed Afldalr, for that was the box's name, and turned its key in a lock that had never been so tested. But Master Arnander was right. Afldalr made the days that followed bearable.

*

For now their road was clear: south, with the Ninvellyn.

Klaus updated his map whenever light permitted. A map, perpetually in the making, had been folded in his breast pocket for as long as he could remember. Usually it would have brought comfort; now his heart squeezed painfully against it.

He carried it in his mind's eye. Here were the Stern Mountains towering at Invelmar's northern peak; he'd retained their teeth and gaunt-cheeked faces and always marked the plateau where he'd fumbled through his first battle. From this deadly crown Invelmar unfolded south into the gentle Helftad mountain range that shaped her temperate heart. Strongholds and citadels followed the rivers meandering down from the Sterns.

And here was Dunraven, Invelmar's southernmost citadel and gleaming jewel. A city of great castles and sky-bridges; of jade and russet towers rising high over Longtooth Forest. The rivers Lune and Larin flanked its walls; sleeping lions that embraced along its southern perimeter to birth the great Ninvellyn river. Klaus knew their streams and tributaries like the veins of his forearm. Dunraven was as old as Sturmsinger's alliance of Northern tribes, conceived to rival the southern citadels the North had so envied. That was before the Second Redrawing, before the Northerners invaded the South and changed the land there forever.

Further south the land gently dimpled into the shallow bowl of the Paiva valley that swallowed the Ninvellyn into its wilderness. It was unfamiliar. As far-flung as Klaus' assignments had been, he'd had no duties in the valleylands. And duty had shaped everything.

'We would have been getting ready to leave for Frastlingen tomorrow,' said Arik, as though hearing his mind.

It had only been a month since their return from Kriselmark on the north-eastern Invelmari border, dismantling an armoury Far Northerners had quietly amassed. The simmering conflict the Far Northerners fostered against Invelmar was older than the Sonnonfer, but not for decades had their raids been as frequent as they'd been in the past sixmonth. No smoke without fire; Queen Adela's peace treaty with the Far Northern warlord Täntainen had collapsed a year ago upon the delivery of his dismembered remains to her gates. The investigation into his assassination had fallen to the lot of Lord Wintermantel, a master amongst the Eye's Intelligencers.

'Wouldn't you rather be with them?' Klaus replied quietly.

'Come off it, Klaus. Surely you're not feeling guilty. After the way they've used you?' When he made no reply, Arik dealt him a sharp look. 'Plenty of others to do our work.'

Klaus said nothing. Arik was definitely more committed to his Form of Warrior than to the Arm of the Court that led the Isarnanheri's campaigns. He poked Klaus in the rib.

'Don't you remember when you were fourteen, desperate to snap your bow in two and hide in the hold of a ship to Salussolia?'

'That was a long time ago.'

'Exactly.' Arik's eyes raked his back as they threaded their way through the trees. 'They broke you in good after that.'

A pair of lustrous child-eyes stared back at Klaus still, as devastating as they had been nine years ago: the moment that had turned his heart for good. Even before that deathblow, foolishness had been talked, cajoled, contemplated, and whipped out of him, day after day of perfecting his Form. Submission had been inevitable. Eventually the Blood Pact had eclipsed everything.

'The Chain won't turn itself, Arik. Three generations from now, the Prosperes will take the throne.'

'Not through me. Plenty of other Prosperes waiting to sire the next round if I drop dead.'

'But your uncles –'

'My cousin Fridolin will succeed them instead. He's no soldier and they hate his father.' Arik ducked under a low-hanging branch. 'Their pride could do with a battering.'

'Watch your voice. Extra patrols are still out looking for the Umari instrument.'

Arik snorted. 'It's been over a month. How long will they keep looking for a relic no one knows how to use?'

'For as long as it takes. The Queen won't stop until it's found.' The theft of the ancient instrument from the court library, now some months past, continued to cause uproar. Klaus had held it once, when he used to dream childish dreams of journeying as far as Ummandir from where hailed his bowmaster, imagining it had properties that would perfectly calibrate his maps even under alien stars. *Ha. Now you will have your wish.*

He banished the spiteful voice to Afldalr, to perish beside childish dreams.

They stayed back from the river, where merchant vessels sailed to and fro and nobles moored pleasure boats idly along the Ninvellyn's banks. Soon they would pass Oskar's and Taunsen's Confluences where the Ninvellyn received the Rivers Laithe and Lark from the west, bringing more river traffic. A fourth night's hike would take them past Fourwater Bridge and into the Paiva.

'It's not too late to turn back,' Klaus repeated when they stopped to rest. 'For both of you.'

'Put an end to that. Verdi, will you *stop* fidgeting? That blasted oceloe won't settle until you do. What's the matter?'

'He's restless.' Verdi snatched Ravi by the scruff of his neck. Even supper hadn't curbed his incessant scuttling. 'Oceloes have a nose for dangerous places. Or people. Living or dead...'

Arik's hand froze halfway to his mouth. 'You don't seriously buy into the horseshit the Derindin say about spirits haunting the Paiva?' The little Derindman looked away quickly, but his lower lip jutted out defiantly. 'Eisen's blade, you do...'

'Thousands died there during the Second Redrawing,' Verdi retorted. 'Whole bloodlands, buried in the valley. Why d'you think no one goes there? Even the Invelmari Guard keeps to the river –'

'Yes, because by land it's a jungle with nothing in it –'

'Deep down even Northerners *sense* it, that's why. The echo of something terrible.' Verdi raised his eyebrows at Arik. 'Clearly some more than others.'

'Load of rubbish. And all that rascal does is misbehave. The only thing he's got a nose for is whatever might fill his belly.'

Barely audible, Verdi murmured, 'He's just trying to stop so much ending up in yours.'

Tales of tormented spirits clinging to the overgrown Paiva had never troubled Klaus. He had learned to listen *through* the rambling of bards. Oftentimes the kernel of truth had to be scratched free from a mountain of dirt; sometimes a ballad or song was its only resting place. His Ummandiri bowmaster Kelselem Ousur'had had impressed that upon him. Besides, Klaus had no need of ghosts. He'd been haunted for as long as he could remember by the plague of dreams that had grown yet more vivid since his escape.

'Isn't this a relief?' Verdi timidly asked him once Arik was asleep. 'You never wanted to be king.'

This, at least, was true. He was *not* a spoke in the next turn of the Chain; this should have been the greatest relief. But what had paved his road here? Years robbed in service to the Ealdormen; a soul extracted by the Eye to perfect a Form he hadn't chosen – and had no right to have. A hoard of intelligence that made him too dangerous to be allowed a freeman's life.

Tersely Klaus replied, 'Not yet.'

*

Fifteen meant taking an oath that would be as inescapable as his shadow. Fifteen was when he was deemed to have mastered his Form. The ceremony he'd first dreaded, then grudgingly craved, was only hours away, and the healing gash on the back of his shoulder was still oozing. Gisla was not the gentlest of physicians, but without a fresh dressing his ceremonial robes would be ruined.

'Arik said Intelligencers don't live long,' Elodie worried. It was a big word, but as familiar to them as their own names, for they were Wintermantels. 'Or else have strange accidents.'

'Make yourself useful and fetch me that bowl of water, princess,' Gisla told her. 'Your brother has to be ready soon.'

'Arik likes to tease you,' Klaus reminded her. But there was plenty of truth to her words. Master Arnander had never spoken of what had caused the fall that had forced Queen Adela to release him from his Spyglass' duties leading her Intelligencers. At least he had survived.

Elodie carried the full bowl carefully in dimpled arms to the physician. A frown puckered her brow.

'Why must you do this?' She planted herself in front of where Klaus lay on his belly, her brown eyes brimming with reproach. 'You can still be an Intelligencer without joining the Eye of the Court.'

He kept still as Gisla removed the dressing, wincing at the touch of iodine tincture on raw skin.

'You promised not to get upset about this again, Elodie,' he admonished. 'This is a great honour. All the Ealdormen have to take a Form. Soon you will too.'

Her pout grew stubborn. 'I will be a Jurist.'

She was only six. She had no idea of the bitter wound that had been opened for him on this day, a wound that no amount of tincture would heal. It had only been a handful of years since he'd been brought to heel. At least she would get to choose.

'You will be the best Jurist that ever was seen in Invelmar.'

'What about Verdi? What Form will he have?'

Gisla's reply darted swiftly over his head. 'Fie! Viridian is a servant, princess – and Derindin! He can't take a Form.'

The little girl looked at her critically. 'He's better at that than you are.'

Klaus hid his smile, for it wouldn't do to upset the Thane's wife.

'Once the Queen swears you in to the Eye, will you have to become Spyglass one day, like Master Arnander used to be?' Fear furrowed her brow again. 'Will Father?'

Gisla put her irritation into the final bandage. Klaus refrained from gritting his teeth. Even this slight tensing of his jaw was too much freedom for an Intelligencer's face.

'No, and no,' Gisla rebuked. 'Have you been listening to anything Mistress Ulverston has taught you? When Queen Adela dies your father will become king, and your brother will be king after him. They can't be both king and Spyglass.'

Elodie ignored the physician, waiting instead for Klaus' reply. He sat up slowly, still stiff from the last campaign in the Sterns.

He had not chosen this Form. He had certainly not chosen to be promoted to the Queen's innermost circle of spies. In another life, his would have been a path of sea voyages and chronicling dying tongues and a study of stars. Once he'd finally shed those childish dreams, he too had wished to be a Jurist, and this too had been denied.

Fortunately there'd been one thing that had anchored him.

'We must all keep the Blood Pact, Elodie,' he said quietly. 'In different ways. And this is the way of most Wintermantels. Is that not worth the risk?'

'No.'

'Melodia!'

She was impervious to Gisla's appal.

He took her hands and twirled her on the spot until she burst out laughing, then steadied her.

'The Blood Pact has kept the kingdom safe for more than nine hundred years, Elodie. Nowhere else in all the Seven Parts has there been such a peace. When you see war, you will know how precious that is. And it is worth every risk.'

All children had to learn, paupers and princesses alike. It was the way of the North; the lifeblood of the Sturmsinger Chain. And it had been his anchor and would remain so always.

*

Arik crouched behind thick reeds on the Ninvellyn's eastern bank. 'The last patrol station is half a mile south of Oskar's Confluence, on the other side of the river. We should pass it in an hour.'

They waited for the changing of the guard, setting off with nightfall. Klaus couldn't remember the last time he'd felt warm. Damp cloaks did more to chill than warm them, but a fire was still too risky. Ravi had disappeared, keeping dry somewhere in Verdi's pack.

Verdi elbowed Klaus encouragingly. 'Still no sign of anyone coming after you.'

'I'm telling you, they're probably just happy to see the back of him,' Arik repeated. 'Once the patrol station's behind us, we can breathe easily.'

He'd barely spoken when a horse's neigh tousled the silence.

They froze. Klaus pricked his ears. Was it coming from across the Ninvellyn?

Torchlight glimmered through the trees behind them.

'They're on this side of the river,' Verdi breathed.

Stooping low in the undergrowth, they retreated back into the forest, away from the riverbank. The anticipation of capture crystallised into acrid fear. Voices accompanied the lights now. Did they have hounds? They'd have no chance against them.

Verdi stopped: a long narrow clearing lay ahead, cutting off the safety of the forest. Another step and they would lose the cover of the trees.

'Go south along the riverbank, then,' Arik hissed.

But a growing murmur of conversation had followed them from the riverbank.

Klaus risked the moonlight, darting across the clearing before it was too late. Arik cursed, following. An eternity later they were in dense forest again, still ahead of the approaching voices.

Klaus paused. They had surely been intermittently visible in the deepening twilight. But there was no commotion in their wake.

A horse stepped into the clearing behind them.

Klaus sank into the undergrowth.

The horseman stood still. Klaus' heart raced. *Did he see us?* A moment later torchlight filled the clearing as four others joined him, dismounting with grunts of relief.

'Make camp here,' said one. 'There are still a good few hours to the patrol station.'

Klaus recognised the voice immediately: Anselm Rainard, a retired Intelligencer of the incumbent ruling house and cousin to the Queen. The hair rose on his arms.

He ordered racing thoughts. Anselm had been with the party of Intelligencers expected to return from Port Ellenheim. His heart thumped; this meant something else –

'We'll be there for breakfast if we leave before sunrise.' Satisfied with whatever had stirred his suspicion in the forest, the first horseman also dismounted: Eohric Ealdwine, former Isarnanheri, Master of the Guard of Wintermantel.

Klaus' ears burned. Ealdwine had never warmed to him as a child, blocked many of Lady Wintermantel's plans to take Klaus on her travels, vehemently opposed Klaus' preferred Form of Jurist, and advised against his early graduation to the Eye of the Court. Klaus was convinced Ealdwine had only tolerated him out of fervent loyalty to Lady Wintermantel, to whom he was particularly devoted. Klaus had never understood what he'd done to earn the veteran soldier's disregard.

Even in their predicament, Arik grinned at him. Ealdwine had boxed *his* ears as a boy, but nothing matched Ealdwine's special resentment of the Wintermantel boy.

Maybe he knew all along.

Klaus dismissed the thought. Lady Wintermantel was the shrewdest woman he knew. She too had become an Intelligencer upon her marriage into an Ealdorman house. She wouldn't trust even Ealdwine with the secret of Klaus' sham birth.

Dread congealed in his veins. There'd be no escape if they were heard retreating into the forest.

He jerked his head east at Arik. But Arik tapped his ear.

Reluctantly, Klaus waited. These men had been away for weeks; they were unlikely to have heard of their disappearance. They'd started a fire now. The others were also Ealdormen: Lord Cenric of house Eldred, a high-ranking Intelligencer; Lord Berengar Prospere, Warrior general and a distant cousin of Arik. Klaus couldn't identify the youngest man, though his curly copper hair was familiar. Then he placed him: another Eldred, memorably missing most of his left ear.

Ealdwine sat facing the forest, the river at his back.

'She will not like this,' Cenric muttered.

Klaus couldn't help but strain to listen. They had travelled at Queen Adela's bidding, and he'd learned nothing of their mission.

'The mine is vast,' said Anselm. 'My spies say it spans the length of the mountain. But there's no trace of the spring.'

'Perhaps because it's not there,' Berengar Prospere remarked. 'A spring of that size, still hidden?'

'Can't afford not to find it, if it is. After all, the mine *was* there – just as the scrolls promised. It should run south, which is most troubling of all.'

'Then why've they not found the spring yet?'

'If it was sealed off at the Second Redrawing, as they claim…'

A snort. 'Impossible. Unless it's been buried underground.'

Ealdwine shook his head. 'And you think the Derindin have no idea it's there?'

'They're too busy land grabbing. And squabbling. That's all they're good at now.'

Klaus was thankful that Verdi had made it furthest into the forest, out of earshot.

'This wasn't always the Derindin way,' said Cenric Eldred. 'And there may come a time when they remember that.'

Berengar Prospere snorted again. 'It'll take a lot more than this rabble to remember.'

Ealdwine watched the fire. Rarely had Klaus been able to guess the man's thoughts – beyond his loyalty to Svanhilda Wintermantel and the Blood Pact.

'Well, we must know whether the Derindin have found it,' said Cenric.

'Unlikely.' Anselm threw away an apple core. 'Take the two clans who own the surrounding territory. They've been circling each other for decades like dogs in a ring. Had they set their sights higher, they could irrigate the whole Mengorian range with such a spring – an aqueduct watercourse would suffice. Instead they dig ditches and mine gems to sell to Zenzabrans so they can gild their citadels.'

'Then perhaps we should be grateful they're not better men,' said Berengar. 'They're certainly not ambitious.'

'It will be good men who will prove to be a thorn in our side,' Anselm replied, almost regretfully.

'We are safe from good men and clever ones both if those mines are merely full of gems,' said Cenric. 'But now this report suggests they've found deposits of iron ore.'

There was a pause filled with the sounds of eating, and the hiss and spit of damp wood resisting flames. Klaus hoped the smell hadn't woken Ravi, whose nostrils were bigger than his bottomless stomach.

'Iron is inferior to our steel,' declared the Prospere general.

'Undoubtedly. But iron and water both...'

'If it's there, the spring will make the southern wastes habitable ... cut a road south to the North Zmerrudi Sea,' Ealdwhine murmured.

'And that is the crux of the matter,' finished Anselm.

A cold shiver grazed Klaus' spine. *What on earth had these men been doing in Derinda?*

A single thud clapped in his chest: Eohric Ealdwine was staring directly at him.

The undergrowth was thick, the early moonlight barely penetrating the darkness under the trees. But he could have sworn that Ealdwine's eyes had momentarily locked with his.

And then Ealdwine looked away, face disappearing into a cup. The Ealdormen's talk moved on to the missing Umari instrument.

Klaus unfroze, hands trembling. He waited, but Ealdwine didn't look his way again.

He resumed Form, regaining control of himself. He crept deeper into the forest, measuring every step to avoid the snap of branches underfoot. *Better slow but certain.* Arik followed. When they caught up to Verdi, Ravi was wide awake and curled quietly around his neck. They detoured eastward, away from the river but safely out of the reach of the court.

'What was that all about?' Arik asked once they could finally risk speaking. 'Berengar's meant to be escorting Intelligencers back from Port Ellenheim. Doesn't sound like that's where they've been poking around.'

Klaus shook his head, just as bewildered. 'That was the official story.'

'Who was the redhead? Couldn't make out his face.'

'Clevenger Eldred. An Intelligencer.' Klaus knew very little of him. 'He was Spyglass Adelheim's squire, before he died, though he wasn't admitted to the Eye.'

Darkness brightened the whites of Verdi's eyes. 'What were they looking for?'

'A mine in the Derindin desert.' Klaus quelled another wave of unease. 'Nothing I was ever privy to.'

'And a spring,' Arik added. 'They're going by the scrolls.'

'There's no mention in the Sonnonfer of either a mine *or* a spring.' Of this Klaus was certain. No one studied the scrolls of the Sonnonfer more deeply than Intelligencers.

Verdi's eyes widened. 'Ealdormen, spying in the desert?'

'Don't worry,' Klaus reassured him. 'The Eye sends fewer spies to Derinda than all the Parts.'

Arik looked dubious. 'You really think Cenric went all the way down into the desert?'

'No. Cenric probably won't even go as far as the border towns now. Likes his comforts too much. Especially as the Derindin are suspicious and difficult to bribe.'

'I heard stories once from my uncles about underground lakes that Sturmsinger found during the Second Redrawing,' Arik mused. 'I thought they were legend.'

'Heard?' Verdi raised an eyebrow. 'Or *over*heard?'

'Perhaps that's what they wanted people to think,' said Klaus. 'To keep the water hidden.'

'Water *and* metal ore,' said Arik. 'Sturmsinger wanted to dry out the South, he wouldn't have overlooked a spring. Or a mine – any native metal will undercut imports from Invelmar. The Queen's probably worried about Derinda having metal that we can't tax.'

But Klaus sensed a more ominous threat. 'They're afraid of a Derindin road to the sea.'

Verdi gaped; Arik frowned. To the Northborn, the world was simple enough: impenetrable ice at one's back to the north, the lifeless Black Lava fields to the west, the steppe-savanna and swamp lakes that separated Invelmar from Pengaza and the Aurelian Part to the east, and to the south – sand. The endless and impassable sand of Derinda, through which it was difficult to imagine a road to the Zmerrudi Sea beyond; a salt barrier at the bottom of the Silfren Part.

So Klaus understood their silence. 'Derinda's been sand-locked to the south for centuries, without an ally in the world. Irrigation would open another road out of the desert. A sea crossing, south to the Zmerrudi Part and east to the Sirghen Part, bypassing Port Ellenheim. More routes out of this Part than Invelmar has right now, in fact. And iron, mined at home, with the water to do it and no Invelmari levy on trade through the North.' He glanced at Verdi. 'And the only thing preventing any of it is a huge waste of sand without water.'

Verdi stared back with fear and something else – a complex frustration, composed of layers of Derindin bitterness around a nucleus of loyalty to the benefactors who had raised him.

'You've a knack for collecting reasons to be executed these days.' Arik clapped Klaus's back. 'Side-stepping assassination wasn't enough. I applaud your knack for self-preservation, I really do.'

But thoughts of Adela's response to even the remotest of threats to Invelmar's hold on the South left no room for jesting. *Would I, too, have been ensnared in this web?* From this, at least, Klaus would be spared.

Fear frosted Verdi's voice. 'Maybe we should head east to Pengaza instead…'

'Excellent idea,' said Arik immediately. Verdi glared at him.

Klaus replied, 'We stick to the plan.'

His friends swapped increasingly wild theories about Southern uprisings and Northern retaliations, shaking off the fears of older men as they went. It was a distraction, at least. By the time they stopped to rest, mines and hidden desert springs were once again the stuff of rumour, and nothing seemed more distant in possibility than the idea of a fleet of Derindin ships on the North Zmerrudi Sea, trading with Morregrat or Zenzabra. They continued southward undeterred, for whatever lay ahead, a much more certain fate waited behind them.

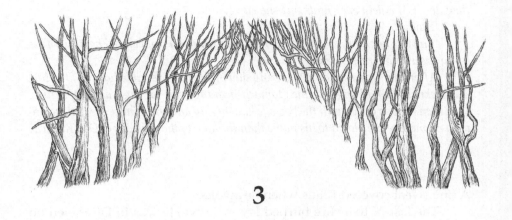

3

The Silenced Daughter

WARLORDS SLIT AND SUPPED ON THE FLESH OF THEIR BROTHERS,
WAGERED UPON THE STRETCH OF CHILDREN'S HUNGER
WHILE WIDOWS' TEARS WATERED THE FIELDS.
HAVE YOU FORGOTTEN?

SONNONFER: THE GREAT BLINDNESS

At first her words had no meaning, stumbling breathlessly over one another.

'Elodie, stop – slow down.'

She clutched both his wrists with icy fingers, her nails digging into his skin. Stark fear brightened her eyes, her face bone-white.

'There's no time – I've been waiting for you since morning – oh, Klaus, I learned something terrible – I'm so sorry, Klaus – I'm so sorry, it's because of me –'

It was there in the stables of Sunnanfrost that his world was torn apart. She sobbed into his chest: Mother's half-charred note, their parents' meeting under the old waterwheel of all places, the truth forged from their argument…

'Klaus, you have to leave – today, tonight –'

The sheer disbelief was paralysing. Even as ice set into his marrow, those words scorched him again and again – 'He's not of our blood! Elodie is of age…' Then a nausea that raised bile in his throat –

'Are you listening to me? They've already decided to kill you. And even if they don't, if Adela ever finds out she surely will –'

'Elodie...'

'She put her own cousin to the noose for being an undeclared bastard! This is – a thousand times worse –'

After that it was a loosely-strung day of the most terrible hours of his life. The sickness he had feigned; the stomach-heaving wait for dusk and departure. And then he was gone, with the box she had dug up and the trinket she had stolen, with no more of the North to his name than the dust of the road out of Dunraven...

A fine sweat covered Klaus when he awoke.

The last of their fire burned low nearby. He was in Dunraven no longer. He waited for his galloping pulse to settle and sat up to find Verdi watching him.

Elodie's weight in his breast pocket tugged as he moved, like the dragging of his heart.

He told Verdi, 'I'll take the rest of your watch.'

His oldest friend knew better than to argue, putting away the battered medicinal formulary he studied at every opportunity and settling down under his cloak. Ravi was already fast asleep, curled up as close to the fire as he could manage without singeing his fur.

Alone, the dreadful question waited: *why?*

Had they been so afraid that someone would snatch their true heir? Afraid enough to take an expendable child and put him up as decoy, keeping Elodie safe? Had someone threatened Wolfram Wintermantel, all those years ago?

From countless night watches, Klaus knew pre-dawn was the coldest segment of night. He stoked the fire and added more wood, though nothing seemed to warm him now. Once again he pulled out the iron disc, turning it in his hands. It was this Elodie had heard Svanhilda Wintermantel ask Lord Wintermantel to destroy: the only thing that *'came with the boy'*. The last evidence of their guilt. Perhaps the only clue to his true parentage.

Such an unremarkable and non-descript vessel, to hold so much. *Fitting*, a mean voice remarked inside him. Disheartened, Klaus put it away.

His mind drifted easily in the flicker of the flames.

Now he could begin to feel the other things he'd lost. His instruments, his maps, some of them years in the making; horses and huskies, blades ... Gerlinde. She had spurned him, but at least he had been able to see her amongst Adela's courtiers, could have tried again to woo her.

A knife twisted in his chest.

Arik thought it was no loss – at least, not yet. The Prosperes were mostly Warriors by Form, and Arik, heir to his house, recoiled from entrenchment in the War Council his uncles so ardently desired for him. Arik had seemed content enough leading the Isarnanheri into the Far North or across the Sourgrass Sea, as his mother had done, fulfilling Invelmar's contracts. But he despised the formalities of court as passionately as he revered the Blood Pact. For Arik, the Blood Pact was served not in a war room but on the open field, with a sword in his hand and a battle cry in his throat.

And Klaus – well. Once Adela was dead, Lord Wintermantel would be the next king in the Sturmsinger Chain. Klaus had been reminded of this every day he could remember. He'd been flogged once for likening this destiny to a living grave. He chose his words better after that.

I was never an ideal heir. He was not like Lord Wintermantel, who was towering of presence and undistracted by frivolities. Klaus was as restless as the rivers. He was drawn to unanswered questions, and things that called for a sure and steady hand. At five he fell in love with the maps that stretched across the walls of the War Rooms; maps that detailed with loving precision the great expanses of the once unknown and showed things as they were. He studied them until he could make them from memory and set to drawing his own. His tutors yet despaired, for his attention often strayed from algebra and taxation and into the lofty debates the Engineers were always having about the Lost Sciences; to spying on the scholars in the smoking room solemnly pondering the tenacity of the Blood Pact – the only place where such talk was permitted; to sneaking out of Sunnanfrost into the inns of Dunraven and imbibing the sly poetry of the bards.

And so for all his princely education, Dunraven had shaped him rather differently to how it had intended. The bards had more to tell of worth than all his tutors combined. They had license to speak of things others dared not. In the taverns he consumed greedily stories of the alchemists who had forged the fabled steel of Invelmar from equal parts heaven and hell, or of the El Nerian planetarium in Ummandir which contained every constellation named and nameless, or of *Simyerin* mapmakers who once lived south of the Paiva and commanded the earth with a forgotten language.

Much of it was taboo. He liked things to be seen in the light, and naturally recoiled from the guise of an Intelligencer. When he'd finally relinquished boyhood fantasies of ships and foreign shores, it was no surprise he'd wanted the Form of Jurist. Lord Wintermantel decided otherwise. They had hammered him into a deadly tool of their machinations, but he had never been a natural prince.

The Blood Pact, however, was another matter. The legacy of Ansovald

Sturmsinger, it bound the five houses of his allies together after his victory in the North had ended generations of bloody war. It was the single oath Klaus had spoken freely from the heart. *'Cometh the fall of the kingdom from destruction made if its fate be bartered for blood; to the dead we are bound and by our grace are the dead repaid.'* So long as the Sturmsinger Chain cycled the five Ealdormen houses on the throne that Sturmsinger had raised from warring tribes once as lawless as the Far Northerners, the Blood Pact would keep safe all that Klaus held dear. Since its inception there had been no true threat to Invelmar; the Ealdormen wielded their exceptional steel as a single fist. For this extraordinary peace, all Invelmari were beholden to the Blood Pact.

And now he had deserted it.

Forgive me, dear Sturmsinger. Let there be a place for me at your table even now.

It was far easier to shed the trappings of his old life behind than the shame of breaking this most sacred of bonds.

And always at the end of this dark tunnel of despair was that dreadful *why*: why had the Wintermantels needed him, and why did they decide to dispose of him now?

He forced these questions into Afldalr. Without answers, they would only thwart him.

'You're still awake,' he said quietly.

Verdi shifted under his cloak, head eventually reappearing.

'Can't sleep,' he mumbled.

Klaus knew it wasn't the hard ground or the cold keeping Verdi awake. 'Wanting to go home and actually going are two very different things.'

'I wasn't expecting it, that's all,' Verdi replied gruffly, disappearing again.

'It's not too late to change course.'

No reply came from beneath the cloak. Klaus knew better than to push. Brought to Invelmar in infancy to become servant to a prince, Verdi had made himself content enough in Dunraven. But he'd had as little choice in his path as Klaus had had in his.

Strange, that fate should have bound them together. A crowded silence carried them to another bleary dawn.

*

The Paiva valley spread southward from the riverland belly of Invelmar like a deep green kirtle. Superstition had kept the valley uninhabited by the Invelmari who'd claimed it at the Second Redrawing, and even patrols kept to the river. Or so it had been before their escape, Klaus reminded himself, taut as a bowstring in anticipation of pursuit.

Here they risked more travel by day, keeping out of sight of the river along which merchant ships and private vessels sailed between Dunraven and the border market towns. The valley was as fertile as it was wild. The Southern farmers who'd once tended it were driven south by Sturmsinger's forces at the Second Redrawing, sealing Invelmar's claim over the Ninvellyn waterway for good. Now their descendants overpopulated the market townships around the Ostraad dam. But their untended ancient orchards remained, providing a glut of apple and citron and yellow figs, sweet green nuts and meaty sour-root.

The Paiva cultivated its own thick solitude, enveloping them by day in humid warmth though Dunraven would now be glittering with winter's first frosts. Eventually there was even the simple pleasure of good hunting and the heady lure of the unknown, the world a clean page suddenly opened before them. The very last of summer loitered for them as long as she could, grudgingly giving way to evenings that grew longer and cooler. But settling down by the fire each night to chart another day's journeying on his map, Klaus couldn't shake the fear that this tranquillity had a storm on its heels.

'Verdi.' Arik picked up the firewood the Derindman had just dropped at the sound of a twig snapping. A rabbit's tail ducked into its burrow. 'If you don't get it together, I'm going to knock you out and throw you over my shoulder until we get out of the valley.'

Verdi scowled. His eyes hadn't stopped darting about, and he jumped at every hooting owl and night-forager.

'Are you seriously telling me you don't believe *anything* of what they say about this place?'

'I'd rather be haunted than hungry, and at this rate you're going to scare off everything we can eat.'

'Well, *I* believe.' Verdi shivered, drawing his cloak tighter around him. 'Oswald the librarian told me a story about a platoon of soldiers buried in the valley who never found rest. Slaughtered by a Prosperi army during the Second Redrawing, he said, and sworn to avenge their deaths. You of all people should be worried.'

'Rubbish,' said Arik, but he looked longer into the deep green shadows.

'Keep still,' Klaus murmured.

Verdi paled, but Klaus' eyes were fixed on a small antelope between the trees.

Arik breathed, 'Can you reach your crossbow?'

The creature sprang away before the words had left his mouth.

Arik cursed. 'Too fast. And too many blasted roots. How much more of this?'

'Another week at least.' It had been three weeks already since they'd left Dunraven. Were it not so risky, their journey would have been much faster by water.

Verdi froze. 'What's that?'

Something white glinted beyond the trees to their left. It looked bigger than an antelope. Klaus' hand hovered over the hilt of his sword.

They drew closer, stepping into a clearing. Standing in the middle above three shallow steps was a great arch of white stone.

Arik stopped in his tracks. 'What on earth?'

The clearing was empty. The forest was colder and quieter here; a pocket of stillness in the swarming Paiva. They walked around the arch. The white stone, greyed by time, was afflicted with climbing ivy and a patchwork of mosses. Despite this it was magnificent, towering over Arik. In the early twilight it glowed with a light of its own.

'There used to be hinges here.' Klaus brushed aside a tendril of ivy, revealing their crumbling sockets along one side of the arch. 'This was a doorway.'

Arik's eyes raked the surrounding forest. 'Who would build a doorway to nothing in the middle of nowhere?'

'Perhaps the question should be how a doorway that must have once led somewhere came to be in the middle of nothing.'

Verdi pointed to the top of the arch. 'There's an inscription under all that ivy.'

Ravi darted down from his shoulder and scuttled up the arch, stopping to sniff at crevices in the stone, his whiskers quivering with curiosity.

'Show off,' Arik muttered.

But he hurried down just as quickly, seeking refuge in Verdi's pocket. Verdi stepped back from the arch.

Klaus didn't recognise the script etched into the stone. The steps before the arch were worn smooth as though they had borne innumerable footfalls. An unspoken invitation beckoned to him up those mossy steps, and yet he found himself inexplicably repelled.

'The ancients built things that lasted.'

They spun around. Sitting on a tree stump on the fringe of the clearing was an elderly man feeding wood to a small fire. The soft crackle of the wood reached Klaus, the sweet smell of an unfamiliar herb diffusing from the flames.

Arik scanned the forest again, sword now in hand. How had they not noticed the man or his fire? His trimmed beard and the snowy hair grazing his shoulders were both clean, but his grey robes were grubby. He looked frail and yet sat with his back to three armed strangers, unworried.

'Who are you?' Verdi's voice was a little threadbare.

The old man set a small pot on the fire. 'I was once a man of the pen.'

Like the arch, there was something both alluring and discomfiting about him. Perhaps it was his stillness, as though the air could not circulate freely in his vicinity.

Klaus ran his hand over the moss-veined arch. 'Sir, what was this?'

The shadow of a smile hovered over the old man's lips. He was neither Derindin nor distinctly Northern. His eyes were startlingly pale, like a sky grey with the promise of rain.

'This used to be a place of learning,' he said, wistful. 'But cities are as mortal as men. Will you join an old man by his fire?'

They came closer, but remained standing.

'A fine specimen,' the man told Verdi, who looked confused. Ravi's ears twitched, emerging from Verdi's pocket with his head held high. The old man laughed.

Klaus watched the forest at their backs. 'What happened here?'

The man stirred the pot, now bubbling. 'A great flood. This doorway is all that remains of the city that stood here once.'

So deep in the Paiva, it was hard to imagine there had ever been anything here *but* its wild groves.

'I've never heard of any such place,' said Klaus, hearing at once how foolish this sounded.

'Not all things that should be remembered are.' The man offered them an empty cup. 'Tea to quench your thirst?'

They shook their heads. Verdi rummaged in his rucksack for a handful of apples. The man accepted one.

Klaus was far from satisfied. 'What's the meaning of the writing on the stone?'

The old man picked up a stick and scratched through the dirt at their feet in Invelmen:

'The greatest of debts shall hold prisoner
the lord and slave of the Silenced Daughter.'

When he finished he seemed oddly thinner, shoulders slumping. He threw a handful of earth over the fire, snuffing out his burning herbs. Then he stood; he was tall but not as imposing as he might once have been, like a towering tree that had seen an endless winter. 'And regretfully now we part.'

'Where will you go?' Arik looked around them. 'There's nothing here for miles.'

'Do not concern yourself, Master Invelmari. Many a recluse has come and gone in these parts without casting his shadow across the paths of men.' He picked up a staff that had lain against a tree; something else Klaus hadn't noticed. 'Sometimes the heart is lonely for things that cannot be found amongst the living.'

'Your brew...' Verdi began. But the pot was a gourd skin, its flesh now curled and smouldering.

The old man shuffled towards the arch, smiling over his shoulder. 'The tea was for you.'

'Your name, sir?' Klaus called out. 'I would be glad to know who you are.'

'A man so old that he has forgotten it. Well met, travellers.'

He walked around the empty doorway. *Would he have vanished, if he'd passed through it?* Klaus ridiculed himself for the notion. The man paused, his last look reserved for Klaus.

'You will come to know this tongue well.'

It was a voice that held the flutter of a thousand pages. Then he vanished into the trees, the sweet scent of his fire dissipating in his wake.

Nobody wanted to loiter in the clearing. They continued south along the river. Klaus couldn't help feeling as though something precious had slipped through his fingers.

'I told you,' Verdi breathed, fear fraying his voice. 'Told you –'

'What, that the valley's haunted? I'm going to cuff your ears.' But Arik hadn't resheathed his sword. 'He's likely a vagrant with nowhere to go. Probably banished, which means he's been up to no good. He won't last these winters long.'

'Then he's a ghost,' said Verdi firmly.

Arik nearly tripped on a root. 'If you say one more thing about ghosts –'

'Most likely he has a boat moored nearby,' Klaus interrupted. 'The nearest market town is only a couple of days away by river.'

Verdi's shoulders relaxed. 'What about this city he mentioned?'

'Nobody's lived in the Paiva for over nine hundred years. Not since the Second Redrawing.'

Klaus glanced over his shoulder. The arch had vanished between the trees, and the beating of the Paiva's unruly heart was restored. He almost wanted to go back, to prove it was still there. *I should have checked my compass.* But irrationally he suspected he wouldn't find it again. And, truth be told, he'd rather not know if he couldn't.

*

Why now? How long had they planned this? What had happened, twenty-six years ago?

'Maybe they feared Svanhilda Wintermantel was barren,' said Arik, oblivious to Verdi's grimace. 'Lord Wintermantel would have been desperate for an heir. And then it might have been too suspicious to remove you right after Elodie was born.'

Klaus turned their catch of a pair of guinea fowl over the fire. His friends were eager to swap theories, keeping silent only out of compassion. Sometimes he heard their murmured musings when they thought him asleep. But such deceit could only be ignored so long. A hundred tormented questions seethed in Afldalr every night, holding him captive.

Barrenness was the Ealdormen's greatest anxiety, it was true; the Sturmsinger Chain needed to turn. Elodie, barely seventeen, had been continually sought after in marriage since she was ten. Quietly, in the back of Klaus' mind, a dim memory spoke; whispered rumours on Dunraven's streets of *the damaged queen* ... Adela had once even had a peddler swing from the noose for speaking such dishonourable words about Svanhilda Wintermantel, a thane's daughter and a noblewoman even before her marriage into an Ealdorman house. Klaus had been very young then. Malicious idle-talk of jealous rivals, Lord Wintermantel had griped, unusually tolerant on that occasion of Adela's heavy-handed response.

But had Lady Wintermantel struggled to conceive, or did she simply bear a child of great deformity or disease? Did they conspire to conceal the secret death of a sickly trueborn, rather than expose their shame to the other Ealdormen? *What about Elodie?* Admittedly, *she* was a fairer-haired likeness of her mother. Klaus was Northern in a nondescript way; darker-eyed than both Wintermantels, golden-brown headed unlike either. Or had Lord Wintermantel confessed to an infidelity that could not one day taint the throne in contravention of the Blood Pact?

If he summoned the man and woman he had known as his parents, a dark red sound drowned out rational thought, and the betrayal and bewilderment were more than he could bear.

Finally he replied, 'If so, I can't imagine they ever intended to keep harbouring an imposter son at Sunnanfrost indefinitely, once Elodie was born.'

'Maybe they did,' said Arik. 'They raised you properly and you turned out well. They placed you in the care of a retired Spyglass – and then in the Queen's closest circle, even though they knew that one day you could betray them.'

'Most likely they had reason to believe that someone would harm their heir and force them to relinquish succession to another Wintermantel.' Klaus threw a twig into the fire. 'It hardly matters now.'

'Who would have known they were bigger scum than my uncles all this time?' Arik's voice hardened. 'It's not just how they treated you, Klaus. They've committed the highest treason. They would have –' Arik stopped short. 'If Elodie hadn't been born, they would have put a stranger on the throne. What might have happened to the Blood Pact then?'

Though Klaus knew Arik's outrage was not rooted in any contempt for common blood, it was still difficult to swallow. The integrity of the Blood Pact rested on the continuation of the Sturmsinger Chain in eternal penitence for the wars waged by Sturmsinger's armies. Breaking the Pact, wittingly or unwittingly, would ruin Invelmar. His life was certainly not above that of the kingdom.

'Then they were confident they would see me dead first,' he said. 'And here we are.'

'But what changed?' Arik pressed. 'Why remove you now?'

'Elodie's almost gained her Form,' Verdi reminded him.

'Elodie's seventeen, they've had years to change course. Something must have happened.'

The same thought nagged at Klaus, but it was too entangled with raw emotion, like all his questions. His friends meant well, but for now he wished for nothing more than to forget.

'Do you think anyone else knows the truth?' Arik asked.

'No,' said Verdi at once. 'The Wintermantels would never give anyone such a hold over them.'

Klaus glanced at his closest friend. The little Derindman became his shadow as soon as he was old enough to walk.

'Elodie isn't a child anymore,' Klaus repeated. 'Perhaps they realised it was time to prepare her.'

Unlike the revulsion summoned by thoughts of Wolfram and Svanhilda Wintermantel, it was still just as easy to think of Elodie as the sister he adored – stubborn as steel, sharp-witted like her mother, yet sweeter than honey. Meanwhile, *he* had fallen far from the tree – he had none of the ambition or the ruthlessness of Wolfram Wintermantel, nor the deadly beguilement of his wife.

'Maybe you're right.' Arik held out a scrap of bird meat to Ravi, who was possibly going to explode if he kept eating but darted forward anyway.

Verdi offered Klaus an unconvincing smile. 'Once we're somewhere safe, perhaps you can track down your real parents.'

How? We're leaving the North. Klaus reached into his coat for the small parcel. He hadn't meant to hide the trinket box from his friends. But it would arouse yet more questions he wasn't ready to ask.

'When she told me, she gave me this.'

Arik unwrapped Elodie's handkerchief and gave a long whistle.

The stones encrusting the box glittered in the firelight.

'Open it.'

Arik's large fingers struggled with the clasp. He gave it to Verdi who delicately unhooked it, picking up the disc inside.

'What's this?'

'I think it's just a weight. But they were afraid it would give my real identity away. Elodie dug it up before they could destroy it.'

'Then you have a clue to where you came from,' said Arik encouragingly.

'Perhaps. It certainly sounded like it could prove who I'm *not*.'

'And the box? These gemstones could probably buy a small kingdom.'

'Lady Wintermantel's. Elodie only stole that to help us on our way.'

'You're sure that's all it is?'

'It's stamped with the court jeweller's seal. There's nothing special about it.'

Arik returned the disc. 'Well, there's nothing special-looking about *this*. Maybe it was left with you by accident.'

Verdi disagreed. 'The Wintermantels believed it would reveal their deception. That guarantees it means something.'

Arik grinned after a moment. 'Good old Elodie. She looted the Wintermantels!'

'She's braver than them both,' Verdi declared. Arik rolled his eyes. Even Ravi seemed to gag before spitting out an apple pip.

'I just hope no one finds her out,' Klaus murmured, rubbing the healing cut on his wrist made by a dead man's ring.

He thought of her with a terrible ache. Elodie Wintermantel had saved his life and ensured their future, wherever it unfolded, might be comfortable. But no measure of gold could buy a fugitive his freedom. And what good were material comforts if he were to be perpetually hunted?

*

It was a pleasure boat of the most lavish kind. Everywhere was carved Zmerrudi ivory and tapestries years at the loom. Garlands of lanterns festooned the decks, adorning the dark night-serpent flank of the river with a tangle of captive stars.

Of the three merchants dining, only one, the goldsmith Robert, was Invelmari, though he spent more time away from Invelmar than within it. The other two, Semrans who frequented Dunraven selling prime smokeleaf, had no ties to the Blood Pact to revere.

'I heard the chambers of Wintermantel's palace are two walls thick, like

the Queen's torture chambers.'

Klaus poured wine into the glass of Mazard Sem-Sendri, who ought to have stopped drinking several hours ago. Adela's interrogation rooms were thin-walled and within earshot of her dungeons.

His countryman Terelmez Sem-Kandar smirked. *'I heard it was because Lord Wintermantel's pleasures run feral.'*

'Wouldn't yours? That wife of his…!'

'More likely they need to hide the demon locked in their closet.'

'Demon?'

'The Far Northern demon that haunted the very first Wintermantel when he ditched their idols to join Sturmsinger's table. A demon made of rage that took a liking to Wintermantel blood.' Mazard took a gulp and let drink dribble over his jowls, mock-rabid. Terelmez spluttered with vulgar laughter. *'Wild dogs, Wintermantels become when the demon takes hold.'*

'Careful, Mazard,' warned Robert, not so estranged from home after all. *'You'll lose your head for blasphemy. And I'd rather not lose my ears for listening.'*

It was the first sensible thing anyone had said. But Klaus wasn't there to trap wine-loosened tongues, though they'd twice insulted his house. His subject was their guest, Nokla Laferniere; a Pengazan ambassador whose vices evidently could not be satisfied within the guest quarters of the Queen's palace, and who was in possession of a disastrous piece of knowledge.

'Tell us, then, Master Laferniere,' said Terelmez. *'Will there be a wedding or not?'*

Laferniere had enough sense to limit his drink, but Klaus had already slipped a disinhibiting stimulant into his glass that was as potent as the sum of what the others had consumed in wine.

'Of course. Why should there not be?' Laferniere was holding up to the drug well, but his real weakness was his contempt: for Invelmar, the kingdom that had his own by the throat, though the Sturmsinger Chain had not lately threatened Pengaza with invasion. There was no need. Pengaza wisely indulged the whims of the North; an Invelmari conquest in all but name.

Mazard leaned forward, bloodshot eyes glinting. *'Only I heard something on my ship to Port Ellenheim. Glimpsed the lovely Genevieve myself, glowing in Haimric's rubies … heard her rather enjoying a taste of Invelmari stock before the banquet. Couldn't wait for the main meal at Dunraven, evidently.'*

The ambassador stiffened. The Pengazan princess had made that crossing into Invelmar to marry Alasdair Haimric, heir of the third Ealdorman house in the Chain. *'Impossible.'*

'What, royal blood never goes into heat?' Mazard scoffed. Klaus smirked, and the Semran took his bait. *'Why, even the servant thinks otherwise. You, man. What do you say?'*

Klaus smoothed his face. *'I say a taste of royal fruit is sweetest on the wrong side of the blanket, sir.'*

Nokla remained stony amidst the gales of their laughter, determined to protect both his ward's honour and the long-awaited nuptial agreement with Dunraven. It was this that gave the truth away. He caught Klaus' wrist as he refilled his glass. The chiselled jewel set into his ring cut into Klaus' skin, drawing blood.

'I'll have the tongue out of your head,' he told Klaus coldly. 'You've no idea whom you slander.'

Klaus bowed. 'Forgive me, sir. Only I know that steward. Never known him not to have his way.'

'Ha!' Mazard slapped his thigh. 'Pour this man a glass. Don't deny it, Laferniere. I know what I heard. A girl with fine appetites, I say. Not afraid to eat below stairs. More wine!'

Klaus bowed and left to fetch another bottle, then swung himself over the side of the boat and slipped into the river. He accepted dry clothes from the guard waiting on the riverbank and rode back into Dunraven past the salute for a Wintermantel prince.

Tomorrow, three merchants would die on a stake outside Adela's gates. The Invelmari steward who'd bedded the princess had already swung from the noose, as had everyone who'd had the misfortune of hearing him brag of his private Pengazan conquest.

He joined the Queen in her private skygarden the following evening, where he watched through an eyescope as the guards nailed their corpses to the posts of Gireht Square. She had exercised brevity. She'd had them killed first.

'The ambassador tried to hide it, though he knew it was true. He has honour.'

'Shame he didn't keep a better eye on her, then. You're quite sure of when the Semran boarded that ship?' Adela was meticulous. She applied her Form of Jurist with lamentable precision. 'Three weeks ago?'

'Without any doubt. One of my spies was on the same vessel.'

'Then we shall have to delay the handfastening for ten weeks more. If she's with child, we'll know then for certain.' She paused. 'Six months. That's as long as I'll give her. She'll fall from her horse after that.'

'Why not call off the marriage altogether?'

'We need to strengthen our position in Port Ellenheim. A Pengazan union every few cycles of the Chain has always ensured that. The wedding will flatter them, even if it doesn't last. But once a whore, always a whore. I'll not taint the Chain.'

Klaus held his tongue. They had no need of more power in Pengaza. Invelmar's only port near the border they shared with Pengaza was vital to Invelmar's trade in steel and soldiers, but it was already untouchable. Adela sensed his dissidence anyway.

'It's not enough to hold them in the palm of your hand, my dear.' She smiled; gently fatal benevolence. 'They must feel cherished. You'll only earn their loyalty when you gain their hearts.'

'What about after she is dead?'

'Her cousin is almost your sister's age. She is fit to share the throne itself. Why did you think I refused her hand for Alasdair Haimric?' Adela plucked at the air. 'Yeraldine will be yours.'

Klaus frowned behind his Form. Elodie was seventeen, nine years his junior.

'Dearest Ulfriklaus. It is terrible, the curse of peace.' She sighed. 'To have the power to take whatever you wish from the world, but always be held back.'

'The Blood Pact only prohibits war within our borders, not beyond.'

'But not all the Ealdormen agree that we should conquer new pastures. I won't risk their dissent. No matter. Each time anyone hires our soldiers, we discover their weakness. Then there is the invaluable work of your noble Form, my dear ferret. How many times have we held our enemies hostage to their own secrets?'

How many times indeed. He may not have chosen this Form, but once he'd succumbed, he had given himself to it completely.

'See to it that the ambassador sickens after his meal tonight,' ordered the Queen. 'No one can know that Genevieve's linen is stained. But let him go quietly, he is husband to the king's aunt.'

Nokla Laferniere had denied the princess' infidelity. Klaus had hoped the man's decorum would have spared him. But Klaus was in no position to argue. He chose strycnos enriched with perepfan; it would stifle him softly in his sleep. Klaus delivered it in the lip-paint of Nokla's mistress, in case Nokla had already sought confidence in her arms. This assignment was his alone. In six months, he would ensure that Genevieve's neck broke during the fall she would have from her horse.

No loose ends, the Queen had instructed. Of the four royal Forms, loose ends fell to the lot of Intelligencers. And so Invelmar continued to silently conquer the world.

Father couldn't take the throne soon enough.

4

Iron and Ink

AND IN THE FAR NORTH DWELT THE FOULEST SCOURGE: BARBARIANS
WHO BECKONED DEMONS WITH DARK WORSHIP;
WHO THREW DAUGHTERS TO THE WOLVES
TO BESEECH THEIR IDOLS FOR SONS.

SONNONFER: THE GREAT BLINDNESS

As they finally approached Noisy Tree four weeks after fleeing Dunraven, Verdi wished he had never suggested coming.

For all his dreams of the South, Invelmar was all he knew. The tradition of sending poor Derindin boys north in search of better fortunes had begun as soon as the dust of war had settled after the Second Redrawing. He had arrived in the Wintermantel household before he could walk, only two years younger than his future master. Though he'd been treated well enough, Invelmar was more than one household, and Southerners were still its chattel.

But it was familiar.

Even after Lady Wintermantel awarded Verdi his apprenticeship with the chief physician at Sunnanfrost, he was still defined by his differences. He'd had few hopes of outgrowing those differences in Dunraven. But

Klaus was the closest thing to family he had. And then there was Elodie.

A foolish thought, of course.

Klaus' assignments hadn't taken him southward, thus Verdi had only glimpsed the South through the eyes of other Derindin servants, like horsemaster Rigo Firefin. Their memories of *home* were seductive: the secret speech of horses; odes around night-fires to immemorial golden ages; clan-kinship and cousins beyond counting. The comfort of mini-beasts. But the Derinda that Northerners mocked daunted and dismayed him: deep divisions, impoverishment, perpetual unrest.

'Are you sure?' Arik asked again. 'Derindin clans are constantly warring over something or other. You *sure* you want to wade into a bunch of petty bird fanciers' infighting?'

'When did you become an authority on the South?' Verdi retorted.

'Please. The desert may be a mystery, but *that* much everyone knows – because it hasn't changed in a thousand years.'

'Then hopefully they'll be too busy to notice us much.' Klaus picked up a stick. 'Most of the Derindin living around here belong to clan Akrinda.' He drew in the dirt, outlining the border towns: Noisy Tree, Whimsy, TipToe, Appledor. 'Of all the clans, Akrindans are the most friendly and the least trustworthy. They're the only Derindin who can be talked into schemes serving Invelmari interests, though even they stop short of spying for us outright. But they're the most likely to send word north if we stir their suspicions.'

Arik flicked a twig at Ravi. 'I feel better already.'

Verdi was growing queasy. 'What about the Isarnanheri?'

But Arik waved a dismissive hand. 'I've only brought Isarnanheri here to escort the Engineers for their annual inspection of the dam. Or to oversee repairs. But the Guard keeps a base in Appledor.'

Verdi raised an eyebrow. 'So the Guard's too scared to patrol the valley, but happy enough keeping a base on the other side of it?'

Arik ignored this. 'A light vessel can sail here in just days from Dunraven. News of us must have arrived in the market towns by now. We'll need to be careful.'

Verdi looked Arik up and down. 'There's really no way to disguise *you*.'

Really, that was true for both his friends, but Arik was particularly hard to miss. Tall even by Invelmari standards and distinctly yellow-haired, he'd be a banner for the North amongst the Derindin, who were dark-haired, light-eyed and more modestly built.

'Maybe we could shave your head,' Verdi suggested.

Anyone else might have crumbled under the withering look Arik gave him. Verdi had plenty of practice.

Klaus would also dwarf the Derindin, though his colouring might draw less attention from a distance. He told Arik, 'Perhaps you should stay outside the town.'

'Rubbish. The towns are full of Invelmari traders, we'll mix right in.'

'At least keep your hard head hooded,' Verdi murmured, after first carefully stepping out of the reach of Arik's arm.

Verdi gazed downriver again. He had no real resentment for the North. If anything, the North had a clear shape and a known nucleus. Not so the leaderless South. Odes to golden ages were poor substance for survival.

But maybe it could deliver, at last, a feeling of being *home*.

It was even warmer now, as though they'd stepped back through the season. The Ninvellyn here was busy with merchant boats, the river patrol, messenger vessels. They continued through the Limpra Hills rising above the eastern bank of the Ninvellyn, gaining a good view of the road below. They could yet hear the full-throated rush of the river racing towards the Ostraad dam, so great was its body. Near the town it was crossed by two bridges before stretching so wide into its terminal reservoir that at times Verdi lost sight of its western bank. Ravi ran through low-hanging branches overhead, occasionally and not entirely accidentally, according to Arik, kicking down the odd broken branch or over-ripened fruit.

They reached Noisy Tree before dusk. They made camp in the hills above the vast reservoir lapping at the Ostraad, gleaming like a silver-blue pearl cupped by the forests overlooking its shores.

'It's beautiful,' Verdi murmured, before yelping in pain; Ravi had bitten his knee. The oceloe was cranky. No one had produced anything to show for the smells drifting from nearby cooking fires, and his whiskers hadn't stopped twitching all evening.

Arik kept a resentful distance from Ravi. 'For once, I agree with *him*.'

The town clung to the eastern bank of the reservoir. Small brightly-painted buildings sprang up amongst the trees like wildflowers. Humble cabin homes stood back cautiously from the road like half-hearted watchmen. Plumes of smoke drifted above the reservoir shore, which had several jetties and a marina where a fleet of assorted riverboats bobbed gently. The western shore was a dark thread in the distance. To the north-west, Appledor was a grey smudge nestled in the woods.

And there it was to the south of the reservoir, Sturmsinger's deathblow and the fatal conclusion of the Second Redrawing: the Ostraad dam, hulking like a fallen great-hammer across the Ninvellyn in its brutal chokehold.

Verdi was reminded of the spill of blood at the foot of an executioner's block. A shudder nipped the back of his neck.

Arik frowned. 'It looks busy.'

'Probably thanks to the last big markets before winter.' Verdi scratched Ravi's head. 'And full of wonders. Horsemaster Rigo said it's the only place outside of Derinda where the Derindin sell their minibeasts.'

Arik eyed the oceloe balefully. 'I wouldn't boast too much about that.'

Klaus folded away the parchment on which he'd been noting more of his incessant navigations. 'Until we find out what news has arrived from Dunraven, we shouldn't be seen together in the town.'

'That could be days,' Arik protested.

Verdi rubbed his knee, still sore from Ravi's teeth. 'Why don't we see what they're saying on the Babble?'

Arik scowled. 'That lot? Load of tripe, their "news". Nothing but rumours and gossip.'

Verdi suppressed laughter. The Babble, an inconstant chain of street urchins and wandering peddlers who passed around word of whatever they deemed newsworthy, had at one time in Dunraven spent some months circulating, embroidering and reviving the romantic exploits of Arik Prospere – at least, when they were sure they were out of his hearing.

'How do we go about tracking down your uncle?' asked Klaus.

'Rigo mentioned he's from clan Elendra, but not much else. We could look for him in Noisy Tree, or else make for his clandom.'

Arik's frown deepened. 'You've really never heard from him?'

Verdi shook his head, doubt churning his stomach. But Derindin from all over the Plains oversummered in the market towns to sell their wares and restock for winter. Someone was bound to have crossed paths with his uncle.

'We should assume he may have got wind of your disappearance,' Klaus warned. 'He may even be looking out for you already.'

Verdi looked away. 'Doubt he's been keeping an eye out, if he's never bothered to find me before.'

Dreams of returning South seemed terribly foolish now. *This was my idea.* He had no one else to blame but himself.

Sundown set the water ablaze as the last of the fishermen came ashore. Lanterns bloomed on gently rocking rows of moored boats and barges in the marina. They finally agreed on new identities for themselves. Arik would be a blademaster, and Verdi his squire.

'Try to pretend you know something about steel,' Arik told him darkly.

Klaus hardly needed to feign being a war chronicler, drafting notes for his map until it was too dark to see. Then he withdrew into himself again, eating little and speaking less.

If Arik noticed he didn't show it, vengefully tormenting Ravi instead. Truthfully, Verdi had been happy enough in Klaus' service in Dunraven. Perhaps he was more willing to admit that here, now that he was on the doorstep of his kin. And the Wintermantels had been kind to him. In fact, Verdi would never have believed their deceitful treatment of Klaus had their crime not been discovered by Elodie herself.

Elodie. He swallowed around the lump in his throat.

Were the people who had sent him away in his basket any better than those who'd given Klaus to the Wintermantels in his? *At least I might know them now.* Verdi had wished for this more times than he knew, never thinking it would bring more dread than excitement.

*

Alone in the market square the following morning with his hood raised over his head, Klaus could have been on one of his many secret haunts of Dunraven's taverns, listening to the preaching of clerics and the grumbling of wives and the soft conspiring of the bards.

The great cobbled square in the heart of the town bustled with brightly coloured stalls. There were carts laden with cheeses and cured meats and caskets, farmers herding cattle, women juggling baskets of nuts and bread and warm pastries. Stall-owners kept watch over barrels piled high with olives and spices, gems in locked cases, rolls of richly embroidered silk and brocade … jars filled with preserves of fruits Klaus couldn't name. Cages contained an astonishing array of birds, for the Derindin were reverent of winged beasts. Songbirds greeted him sweetly, startling and delighting passers-by in turns. Great falcons perched on gloved forearms. Even in Invelmar, the best-trained birds had been bred by Derindin falconers. Every so often he caught sight of the Derindin's famed diminutive beasts: oceloes with luxurious tails and tiny sleepy fox-stoats and bearlings, and even, on one proud arm, a full-maned silver tigon.

He picked out an inn, a post house, several apothecaries, a bathhouse and a stable yard, where he spotted Arik and Verdi conferring with a horsemaster. Verdi was a natural species here – slender, dark-haired and olive-skinned, with the startling eyes of the Derindin and the ever-present oceloe that had marked him an outsider in Invelmar. *Perhaps some good for the little Derindman would come with this turn of the tides.*

The markets brought together local folk – Derindin, Invelmari – and merchants from far-flung places. Slight and secretive Nékkei, distinct in their white patterned kaftans; honey-complexioned high-browed Semrans, lustrous pearls adorning their braided hair. Klaus even spied a woman of Zenzabra, statuesque and proud, a burgundy sash half-drawn across her handsome ebony cheeks. He spotted a handful of Invelmari metal traders, far from their towns along the Northern iron trading highroad of Kaldistazvegr: tall thick-armed Invelmari miners offering contracts on the lower grade ores that Invelmar permitted them to sell to the South. Klaus trod warily. All sales would be strictly vetted and closely monitored. Ealdormen Blacksmiths were known to make unannounced inspections here, tipped off by Intelligencers about black market sales of prized ironstone.

At least there was no such embargo on the Invelmari grain upon which Derinda relied to supplement its own drought-restricted reserves. Northern farmers from Rainsthwen and the pasturelands of Invelmar's Barrvegr network of grain routes stood over sacks of wheat, oats and barley. In return, the Derindin bartered kahvi and olives, fine cloth and rare emeralds, rose oil and jasmine water, mechanicontraptions and spidersilk.

Klaus kept to Form, wary of the colourful braying of trade. At the first sight of the dark green uniforms of the Invelmari Guard, he turned casually down a street lined with shuttered shops.

'Milk!' A boy nudged his elbow. 'Fresh milk, sir?'

Klaus shook his head. The boy had no time to wheedle him. He moved on, his shrill cry mingling with the raucous chorus of the market.

Hot grease and fresh bread seasoned the air, but Klaus' belly stopped grumbling when he saw it: a shabby yet magnificent brass-wrought shutter, part-drawn over a shop door.

He crossed the street. The panel was engraved with riders fleeing a great domed building, horns raised to their lips. Soldiers. No – they bore not weapons, but words; books, great tomes, scrolls, gathered in their arms and strewn underfoot. A narrow script flowed around the scene in letters of brass.

'Can I help you?'

A middle-aged man stood in the shop doorway. His face was empty, his short beard sprinkled with grey. His Invelmen held hues of the more full-bodied dialect of the Plains, thicker than that of the market towners; the accent of one raised on Derindask. Klaus cursed his momentary lapse. *I might have just as easily been noticed by the Guard.*

Klaus bowed. A distinctly Invelmari gesture; Derindin did not bow. 'What's your fare?'

'Parchment. Instruments.' The Derindman's face was guarded. 'Collector, are you?'

'Chronicler. Just passing through.'

Klaus stepped inside the shop and into the musty embrace of books. Shafts of grainy light streamed in through the windows, illuminating floating shoals of dust. A thrill darted through him. As well as quills and ink-horns and writings on every subject, there were rows of astronomical and mathematical instruments: astrolabes and sextants, compasses, nocturnals and all manner of clocks. Other instruments he didn't recognise.

The golden eyes of a falcon glowed like beacons on a high shelf, tucked deep between books.

His eyes fell on a glass dome standing on a wooden plinth amongst stacks of parchment. Beneath the glass lay a small black cylinder, burnished so that it glinted even in this dim light. As though it exerted a lodestone's pull on him, Klaus drifted towards it.

He heard himself ask, 'What's that?'

He sensed rather than saw the shopkeeper's curious look. 'That is an unlading pen, one of just a few survivors of its kind.'

An odd name for a pen. 'Is it made of stone?'

'Close.' The shopkeeper lifted the dome and picked it up. 'The outer shell is made of rock from the Black Lava Plains, though it has a nib of tungsten. But its genius is inside. It contains an intricate machine made of three hundred and twenty parts, perfectly balancing its action.' He indicated the slim barrel. 'This dial winds up a spring and pulley mechanism that draws ink into its reservoir, and simultaneously filters out any impurities from the ink. A magnetic sensor measures the particles for filtration as it writes.' He held it up into the light. 'But it can only be used with *racono* ink, which is made from a pigment found in only one or two quarries to a recipe now lost. Anything else clogs the mechanism.'

'Why do you call it "unlading"?'

'It is said that it relieves its user of burdens.'

The ink barrel was slimmer than Klaus' index finger and twice as long, and yet could boast such a brain. The Derindman placed it on his palm; it was surprisingly light, the rock shell very cold.

'Was it made in the South?'

The Derindman gave Klaus a thin smile. 'By an artisan of what you Invelmari call the Lost Sciences.'

'Then does it still work?'

'There are many reasons why it shouldn't.'

This was no deterrent. 'Is it for sale?'

A wind chime tinkled as the door closed, and a slight figure entered the shop. Her face was buried in the hood of her cloak and a sand-mask was drawn over her face, but her voice carried her scowl.

'Does the North believe it can steal the past from us as well as the future?'

Her contempt was scalding. Klaus could only just make out the reflection of light on a pair of cold Derindin eyes. He returned the unlading pen before bowing towards her.

'I am indeed guilty of being interested, I'm afraid.'

'It would be better for us all if you weren't.' She set a parcel on the cluttered counter, nodding at the shopkeeper. 'From Master Ristowin. I promised to run it over before my caravan leaves.'

She left as abruptly as she had entered.

'No,' the shopkeeper replied, as though nothing had passed. 'It's priceless, and neither is it mine to sell. I'm minding this shop for a friend. In any case, it's useless without the ink, and no one's made any for centuries.'

'Is there no chance of making more?'

'A question better put to an alchemist. Or Ristowin, for that matter, for it was a metalsmith who made the first ink. But it's unlikely. And what use would you have for a pen that doesn't work?'

When Klaus couldn't immediately answer this, the Derindman smiled humourlessly again. 'There is danger in the desire to possess things that have no purpose any longer.'

Preferring his interest to be mistaken for Northern vanity than to foolishly confess the strange pull of the pen, Klaus bowed and turned to leave.

'The sacking of Gelengahal by Invelmar.' The shopkeeper jerked his head to the shutter that had drawn Klaus to the shop. 'In case you were wondering, chronicler.'

The shopkeeper did not look sorry to see him go.

He spent his only smallcoin on a pot of kahvi in the corner of a cantina busy with locals and visitors alike. The freshly roasted beans were better than any he'd had at home. Klaus allowed himself to fade into his surroundings, to become invisible as every Intelligencer was taught: shoulders slouched, cloak hanging drab and partially drawn over his head, weapons concealed, idle movements feigned, distance glazing his eyes, rate of breathing indolent, and a dozen other little things besides. His Form became grey.

For over an hour he hunched over some lines of poetry he wrote idly on a scrap of parchment, forcing his Form to hold when the Guard looked in to take sweetmeats. Some Derindin became stony around the Guard, averting their eyes, while others sat to simpering attention. No sign of the Babble, though there was talk of intensifying fighting in the Far North, and of the death of an elderly Ealdorman of house Haimric. Customers griped about the bandits who'd been particularly active that season across the desert, stealing with impunity. Between the striking of bargains and accounts of desert raids, there was no mention of a missing prince.

Something's off. What story had the Wintermantels told to mask the disappearance of not one but two Ealdormen, one of them heir to the throne? How had they convinced Adela not to mount a massive search?

He was on the hunt for another tavern when he passed a forge. An idea struck him.

'Good day,' he greeted one of the workmen, slightly clipping his words in the speech of north-eastern Invelmari. 'Is Master Ristowin hereabouts?'

'Further down, near the apothecary.' To his retreating back the man added sourly, 'And don't forget he's not the only metalsmith in town!'

A master craftsman, then. Klaus found him in a smaller workshop; a sun-weathered man whose cheeks resembled leather softened by overuse. He crouched over a crowded workbench, alone.

Klaus waited in the doorway until the metalsmith looked up through the pair of spectacles perched on the end of his nose.

'Well?' he said. 'Are you coming in?'

Klaus entered, leaving the door slightly ajar.

'Good morning, sir.' He hesitated.

'Yes?'

Now that he was here, the idea seemed foolish. Klaus would have taken his leave were it not for the Derindman's patience. He extracted the weight from his pocket, keeping the trinket box concealed

'I wondered whether you can tell me anything about this.'

Ristowin set down a pair of callipers and pushed his spectacles up his nose. He wiped his hands on a rag before taking the disc. Klaus followed the way he felt all around it, with eyes first open and then closed. He fingered its surface, cupped it in his hands, even raised it to his nose to sniff, running it over one cheek. Finally, he examined it under a magnifying glass.

When he had finished, he set it down on the workbench between them.

'It's a weight,' he said.

Klaus blinked, quelling a reflux of frustration with Form. 'I know.'

Ristowin placed it on the pan of a scale on another counter, balancing it with a weight of his own, then another. He frowned, dissatisfied. 'Though it is imprecise.'

Completely useless, then.

Ristowin peered up at Klaus. His eyes were coal black; unusual for a Derindman. 'What is it you wish to know about it?'

'Can you tell where it's from?'

'It was made before the First Redrawing from the iron ore of a mine now depleted in a place the ancients called Ettsrakka,' Ristowin replied with absolute confidence and no hesitation. 'Now I have told you both where and when it is from. There is otherwise nothing special about the weight itself.'

'Ettsrakka,' repeated Klaus. 'That's a bloodland recorded in the Sonnonfer.'

'It is. At least that is what your people, the sons of the Forge, came to call it. It is also the place where the mystics say a great starfall struck the Silfren Part before men walked the earth, untold years ago. Where that was exactly, I wouldn't know.' The metalsmith raised the weight. 'You see, iron is not native to the Seven Parts of this world. It is a visitor from the heavens that stayed amongst us. But some iron is even more celestial than the rest.'

Klaus stared at the weight. Invelmar founded the greatest forges in the Seven Parts and owed its fortune to the steel perfected by generations of Northern blacksmiths. But he had never met one who spoke to substance as did this wafer of a Derindman.

'How can you tell where this metal is from?'

'Every element of the visible world has a unique signature. It can be detected if one listens closely enough, though not with an ear of flesh. Substance possesses a precise pattern of vibrations or ripples that can be deciphered, if you will. All materials do this, for those who know how to listen.'

'What do you mean, the "visible" world?'

Ristowin smiled. 'Is that all?'

It was the only question he hadn't answered.

Something made Klaus not want to leave. He almost asked about the racono ink that animated the unlading pen, but held his tongue.

'Now I will ask you a question in return,' said the metalsmith. 'Where did you come by it?'

'It was entrusted to me while I was in the North.' This was strictly true.

Ristowin paused. 'Most people requesting an evaluation of an object wish to know its value.'

Klaus shrugged. The thought hadn't entered his mind.

'Then I will tell you it is of absolutely no use to any except those who wish to remember.'

What little hope Klaus had stoked of the disc providing some clue about his true parentage all but evaporated as he left.

Questions stormed his mind. What had a lump of iron to do with his family, and what did *they* have to do with a bloodland? Ealdormen had defeated Far Northern rebels in Ettsrakka, somewhere in the colossal range of the Sterns. A battle fought so long ago, its location was now forgotten. The Sonnonfer didn't distinguish Ettsrakka for anything more than hosting another Northern victory. Were his parents Northern warriors, then, or even spies? Loyal servants, eager to make the ultimate sacrifice to serve a barren Ealdorman's house with the offering of their own child? Or were they dead – making it easier for the Wintermantels to take a child none remained to claim?

He drifted between market stalls, picking out threads of useful talk from the idle. Much of an Intelligencer's work was slow and painstaking and pedestrian. He was pretending to inspect a waterskin when the lightest of touches brushed his side.

He whipped out his hand and caught the thin wrist of a boy, no older than six or seven, whose fingers were creeping towards the pocket containing Elodie's heavy trinket box.

'Aaaah!' the boy yelped, squirming.

Klaus gripped his arm. The boy stopped wriggling and glowered up at him, clearly more disappointed than ashamed at being caught. His ankles were dirty under long-outgrown trousers, his tunic torn in more places than it had been darned. Tired sandals were barely hanging on to his feet. His eyes were the palest aquamarine, and the dark hair on his head grew with abandon.

Klaus pulled out the pear he'd been saving, tossing it to the boy as he let him go. Likely more used to a whelping than a reward, the boy darted off just as instinctively as he caught the pear, but stopped once safely out of reach to look back, giving his young age away with round-eyed curiosity. Then he scarpered off, disappearing into the crowd with his prize.

Klaus set off in search of an inn. His departure was not unnoticed. Neither was his little act of kindness. In the marketplace, where a man wrote out the sum of his true self for the world to see, every small portion of him counted.

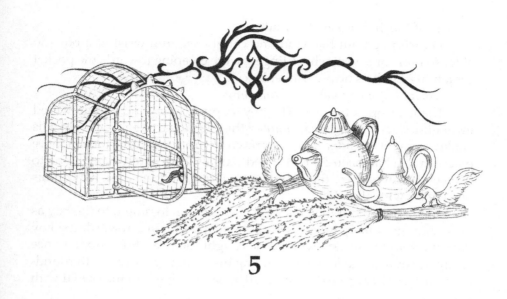

5

Noisy Tree

THEIR HORDES SPILLED DOWN FROM THE STERNS INTO THE LOWER
NORTH, SWELLING OUR RIVERS WITH BLOOD AND SOILING
OUR BANNERS WITH THE TAINT OF BASTARDS.
HOW COULD LIGHT PIERCE SUCH DARKNESS?

SONNONFER: THE GREAT BLINDNESS

'Lord Gautselin Haimric died,' said Klaus. 'There's no other news from
Dunraven.'

They regrouped on the hill over fresh bread, roast chicken and
steaming vegetables fragrant with unfamiliar herbs. The food was quickly
devoured, the bird stripped to its bones. Ravi polished off the titbits
clinging to the carcass before pelting up a tree where he began to lick
himself.

'Thanks,' Arik said in disgust to the hind leg raised high above Ravi's
bottom. 'I told you, maybe the Wintermantels would rather forget the
whole business and let you go.'

Verdi kept one eye on his oceloe. 'Or they want us to feel safe so

46

we become careless.'

Klaus had no reply. How had they explained his absence? Dispatched him on a sensitive assignment, perhaps? And what about Arik?

Arik was unconcerned. 'Let's go back and find an inn. See how many Invelmari are here? No one's going to notice two more. Maybe we can track down Verdi's uncle.'

But five inns later, Klaus had still not found one with an empty bed. At the sixth Arik and Verdi were already there, speaking to the innkeeper.

Klaus pulled up a stool in the inn's busy cantina. A serving girl hardly spared him a glance when he took a cup of kahvi from her tray as she passed. He sipped, listening.

'There'll be no beds for days,' the innkeeper told his friends. 'More folk are held up in the border towns this summer.'

'Why?' Verdi asked.

'Waiting for safe passage south with the bigger caravans. What with these bandit raids, no one'll risk travelling in small groups.'

A tin cup flew across the room and bounced off the back of Verdi's head.

'Ow!'

Verdi turned, rubbing his head. Ravi's ears flattened, eyes growing to green baubles.

Coarse laughter broke out across the cantina. Within a moment, Arik had crossed the room to haul a thick-set Derindman from his seat.

A hush filled the cantina. The man's companions – all four of them – sprung to their feet, knives drawn and laughter snuffed out.

The man in Arik's grasp sneered. Arik lifted him until his collar rode up against his neck. He began coughing, face turning red.

'Put me down, you great oaf,' he spluttered in thick Invelmen.

Arik eyed the man's companions. 'I'll snap his neck if you come any closer.'

'You're outnumbered, Invelmari scum,' growled one. 'Have they never told you a Derindman can skin a man alive before the blood in him's gone cold?'

Not if he can't see. But before Klaus could load his crossbow, Arik hurled the offender at his friends.

A moment later, five furious Derindmen had kicked away the table and chairs to advance on Arik – halting when he drew his sword. Gawping diners gathered by the door, blocking their escape.

'Out of my way!' The innkeeper elbowed into the fray. 'Fools! Which one of you idiots is going to pay for this?' He brandished a broken chair leg, though he gave Arik a wide berth.

Another Derindman stepped between Arik and the mob. Klaus recognised the shopkeeper who'd shown him the unlading pen.

'Peace, Gisane,' he told the innkeeper. 'Lower your sword, Invelmari. There'll be no brawling here.'

To Klaus' surprise, the men obeyed and left with a minimum of muttering, though doors slammed behind them. People turned back to their food and drink.

The innkeeper glowered. 'If there's trouble in these parts, you can be sure there's always an Invelmari hand in it.'

Arik raised an eyebrow. 'What, the Derindin never brawl?'

'Perhaps you should leave,' said the shopkeeper. 'Seek your board elsewhere.'

Gisane bristled. 'Now look here, Suman. Unless you'll be chasing those oafs, someone needs to be paying for wrecking my inn.'

The man called Suman replied, 'It will be seen to.'

Arik and Verdi left.

Suman followed them out, conceding his humourless smile when Klaus joined them outside a moment later. 'There's a small inn ten minutes from here, near the marina. Try for a bed there. Tell them Suman sent you.'

Arik resheathed his sword. 'Why should we trust you?'

Suman's smile didn't reach his eyes. 'I could ask you the same. You are not merchants.'

But it was Verdi to whom Suman's eyes drifted. Ravi clung to Verdi's shoulder, watching the inn with his tiny teeth bared.

Klaus pressed coin into Suman's hand. 'For the damage.'

Suman accepted it without protest.

They were already walking away when Verdi hesitated, turning back. Suman was still watching them. 'Do you know anything of a man called Alizarin Selamanden?'

The triumphant gleam in Suman's eye was so brief, Klaus almost missed it.

'Are you looking for him?' Too surprised to reply, Verdi gaped. 'I'll be sure to let him know where you'll be.'

With that, Suman returned to the inn.

'What did you do that for?' Arik asked, furious.

'I don't know!' Colour rising, Verdi folded his arms. 'Why *not* him? We have to start somewhere and he helped us once already.'

'We'll have to leave in the morning,' said Klaus, resigned. 'Whether we find your uncle or not, someone will remember us now. And if anyone realises who you are...'

If just one person recalled that Alizarin Selamanden's nephew had been the servant of the missing Wintermantel heir, their long-winded escape would have been for nothing. *We should leave tonight.* But Klaus had gathered hair-raising stories of the perils of night travel in the Derindin Plains.

'I'm sorry,' said Verdi, now aghast. 'I didn't think –'

'Let's try this inn,' said Klaus evenly. *If we're found out, I don't think it'll be because of this man, Suman.*

It was a well-tended place near the marina. The stoic innkeeper offered them the use of an empty barn after informing them he had no beds for the night. His face gave nothing away at the mention of Suman's name.

'Some token,' Arik grumbled as they settled down between bales of fresh hay. It was dry and, after weeks of hard ground, luxurious.

'He didn't charge us for the use of his stable,' Klaus pointed out.

And it was warm. Not just the dark-thickened warmth of the balmy southern dusk the frosts hadn't yet vanquished, but warm too with the energy of *possibility* shimmering in the air. Klaus lay under an open shutter in the roof, counting stars bloom shyly in a velveteen night. Somewhere beyond the Ostraad was a road where no one was likely to follow him.

It was a bittersweet comfort. It would be a road out of the land he loved and, for all his childhood fancies, had never in his wildest dreams thought to leave without hope of return. But beyond was also the promise of the undiscovered – a return to those childhood fancies, perhaps. To go back to a child's heart and what *might have been*, before his soul had been claimed for the Crown – would that be so terrible? The knot in his stomach loosened for the first time since leaving Dunraven.

It was the first time he had seen Lord Wintermantel truly angry. Ten years it had taken; the man had the patience of stone.

'But I don't want to be trapped here,' Klaus protested, finally braving the words he'd nursed every night since Master Arnander had taken possession of his life. 'I want to be a wayfarer like Magnhild Youngwater, and travel the Parts all the way to the Utter East...'

He had often heard it said that a Wintermantel's rage was the foundation of the Sterns; unlikely to avalanche, but colossal if ever it should – but he'd assumed this rage had died with Grandfather. Lord Wintermantel's face broke with the darkness of storm clouds erupting.

'You are not a freeman to choose your path,' he thundered. He grabbed the scruff of Klaus' neck and pulled-shoved-strode him to the balcony. '"Trapped?" All this, and you want more? All this, and you think you will not be satisfied?'

Below them, the splendour of Dunraven stretched all the way to the horizon: towers and castles and jewel-hued rooftops; a thousand markets; countless streets and alleys; untold riches. The ringing of a hammer on anvil channelled its soul. In the pre-dusk it glowed from within, perhaps with the sheen of the Invelmari steel which had made it surely the greatest citadel in all the Parts.

Lord Wintermantel's rage ebbed away as quickly as it had broken.

'You will travel,' he said flatly, and for a moment Klaus thought he'd imagined the ghost of regret in his grey eyes. 'So long and far that you will long for the scent of your wife and child, and wonder whether they were not merely remembered from a dream. You will lead the Isarnanheri throughout more of the world than you ever wished to see. There. Until you are crowned, you will know more roads than men.'

But they voyage only to fight! Only to serve! *More protests rose in Klaus' throat, but he didn't dare provoke the man again.*

Whatever had tempered Lord Wintermantel's anger, it was a complex creature that must have forced upon him the weight of the world to iron him back to such evenness.

'All cubs wish to roam, to discover, even when they don't know the inside of their own den.' When Father looked at him like that, Klaus found it difficult not to listen. 'How can you seek to know strangers in the distance, when the fate of a whole nation rests upon your own?' Lord Wintermantel's gaze became lost somewhere down there amongst the anthills of the citadel. 'Millions of lives, each a whole world, entrusted to you to protect and to serve – men and women who wish to be given purpose, who wish to be known. Every belly that sleeps hungry will be your responsibility. Every discontented heart is a fist waiting to strike against the Blood Pact. If you wish to travel, go down there and know them. They are the bricks and mortar of this palace, these streets. It will be a longer and more difficult journey than anything you could map.'

'Yes, my Lord.' The trouble was, once Klaus started listening to Lord Wintermantel, he usually imbibed deeply, until the fervour of his fancies was dulled, and he was ashamed of whatever his own feelings had been. 'I'm sorry I overlooked my duty.'

'You are my son, Ulfriklaus. You will be king when I am gone. You will be the arbiter of their happiness, and their happiness is the resin that binds the Blood Pact. And if you are to make anyone happy, you must first know them.' Lord Wintermantel's eyes, the colour of smoke, always seemed to sift straight through Klaus, to trickle into all the cracks and fill them with his will. His Form was magnificent. 'Let that be your voyage, and it will last the rest of your life.'

You are my son, Ulfriklaus … you are my son … you are my son…

The words taunted him as he woke, breaking into scornful laughter, cackling like birds: *You will be king!* The back of his neck felt bruised.

An owl hooted in the dark. The smells of the barn filled his nostrils, followed by the scratchy discomfort where a clump of hay had dug into the back of his head as he slept.

'Nightmare?'

Klaus turned towards Arik's voice in the dark, rubbing his neck. It was unusual for anything to keep Arik awake. 'Can't sleep?'

He heard Arik twisting around in the hay.

'They shouldn't get away with it,' Arik said eventually. 'I'll bet my sword arm the Wintermantels told no one what they did. No one will ever know their treachery.'

The haze of sleep cleared. However fond and protective he was of Verdi, Arik would never speak within the Derindman's earshot against the Ealdormen.

Klaus' stomach writhed. Arik had chosen him over the Ealdormen. But the Blood Pact came before all things; it was the lifeblood of Invelmar. How heavily would it weigh upon Arik to let the Wintermantels' crime go unpunished? How long would it be before the pull of the Blood Pact overcame Arik's desire to spite his uncles' ambitions for him?

'How can you bear it?' Arik asked. 'Are you not angry? If it had been me…'

Klaus stared up through the open shutter in the roof. A fleet of clouds intermittently obscured the moon, blunting the starlight. Was he angry? Something rattled distantly in Afldalr. He was angry, but more than that, he was numb. And that was merciful.

'What good will anger do? If I let myself feel it, I'll go straight to Adela and tell her what they've done.'

'Never.' Arik's reply was immediate. 'She would kill you and lose no sleep over it.'

'But she would ensure the Wintermantels were punished.'

'And you along with them. No.'

Relief prickled Klaus' eyes. 'Maybe she wouldn't kill me. She might consider it a great service if I deliver her the truth.'

'You would be a loose end. She would consider it your duty to be tied off to protect the Blood Pact, and she'll cut your throat herself if necessary. You're lucky Verdi's not awake to hear you. Put it out of your mind.'

It was his turn to lay awake long after Arik finally fell asleep. Afldalr rattled again. For as long as he could, he would cling to the numbness.

*

Suman Traistrom poured another kahva at the inn. The tavern was full for supper, but Gisane the innkeeper was still too busy grumbling about his broken chairs to be glad for the custom. He checked his pocket watch. He'd sent Petra out an hour ago, and she was the most efficient falcon he'd trained.

A lute began playing. A woman's voice joined it in an oft-told Derindin sorrow-song. That was all they were good at cultivating now: sorrow. In the South it was everywhere, however fair blew the wind, watering the land in place of rain.

Moments later, a man sat beside him. He didn't lower his hood. Suman pushed the pot of kahva towards him; he shook his head.

'You don't mean to stay?'

'No. Still seeing to the repairs on the water wagons.' They listened to the singer for a few moments. 'Did you pay the tumblers?'

'I did. They played their part well.' Suman shook his head when Alizarin reached into his cloak. 'No need. They already paid for the damage.'

His companion said nothing.

'Who are the two Northmen?' Suman asked.

There was a pause. 'We will find out.'

'They'll see that he's safe, at least,' Suman conceded. 'It's true, what they say of Invelmari. Hard as their mountains.'

'Perhaps.'

Suman finished the kahva. 'What will you do?'

A much longer pause. 'He wasn't expected yet. It's too soon.'

This time, Suman didn't hesitate. 'Is it?'

His companion made no reply. There were some matters upon which they had always disagreed. They listened to the rest of the sorrow-song. Then they parted, for they each had much upon which to reflect, and time was short.

6

Alizarin

KNOW THAT THE LIFEGIVER HEARS ALL PRAYERS, EVEN
THE MURMURINGS OF ANTS UNDERFOOT. PERHAPS IT WAS
IN A BROKEN FARMER'S LAMENT FOR HIS SCORCHED FIELDS,
OR IN THE ANGUISH OF A WOMAN GRIEVING FOR HER PILLAGED
WOMB, BUT ONE PRAYER ROSE ON WHITE WINGS AND TOUCHED
THE HEAVENS. AND THE LIFEGIVER SENT DOWN HIS MERCY
INTO A CRADLE HIGH IN THE STERNS…

SONNONFER: THE GREAT BLINDNESS

When he turned into the next street, he became another creature completely. He rounded the curvature of his spine, losing height; dropped his arms to realign his posture. Cast down his eyes, feigned the slightest stiffness – just a hint of paralysis in one leg. Looked this way and that, scattering attention from himself to where he directed… His target, Alfrid, was leaving the tavern. A young merchant's son, lately pursuing a blacksmith's daughter far beneath the pull of his own good looks. Klaus twisted a cap in his hands; an irritating distraction.

'G-Good evening, sir,' he stammered. 'Spare any smallcoin for an old potion maker who those f-f-fancy apothecaries drove out?'

'Go away, old man.' The youth paused, reconsidering. 'Potion maker, you

say?'

By the time they parted, Alfrid had relieved Klaus of a tiny vial of finest grade surrwyrte, the most reliable of all contraceptives. Klaus stepped into the tavern with a little less gold than the vial was worth, dropping his hunch and his outer cloak as he entered. Beneath were the trappings of a well-to-do gentleman. A tunic of embroidered cloth, though not with gold; fine enough to betray wealth but not frivolity. The dirt of a thriving farm flecked his nails, but his index finger had now gained a good sapphire ring. The stammer vanished. His next target was dining within.

'Master Baxter.' Smithies were afforded every courtesy in Invelmar; Klaus bowed low at the table of this one. 'I'd hoped to ask after your daughter...'

Several weeks of work had already softened the smithy's resistance to Klaus' courtship. Today, a gift of silver, generous enough to intimate the good living awaiting his daughter. Smithy Baxter was already unconvinced of Alfrid's courtship. Eventually, Klaus dropped subtle mention of his rival's gambling weakness, while conceding that Alfrid managed to find gold enough for regular purchases of surrwyrte. Smithy Baxter was suitably alarmed. His daughter had little interest in Klaus' advances, of course; she'd been thoroughly seduced by her better-looking flatterer. And what was a farmer next to a merchant's son? But she was not amongst Klaus' targets.

That night her father's displeasure would hasten the elopement plans with which the couple hoped to force his blessing. Tomorrow, Klaus would be waiting to overhear the ramblings Alfrid teased out of her in the best room of a grand inn, the keys to which Alfrid had won at a game of cards with a forgettable stranger. In her ramblings would be the confirmation that this fraudster had used their courtship as a means of searching her father's forge for papers of experimental chemistry – papers he'd not yet stolen. That was where Klaus' soldiers would arrest him.

'Dull work for you, perhaps, but well done.' The Mistress of the Forge was pleased. An Ealdorman of house Haimric, she had offset barrenness with her Form of Blacksmith. Arik claimed she killed her lovers for fear they might have overheard her speak of the steel's secrets in her sleep. 'Shame about the smithy, he was clever with his head as well as his hands. But what use is that if he's so careless?'

Because, of course, Adela didn't stop at executing the thief. Her Spyglass – the first unnamed appointee in decades, after three named predecessors – had deemed it necessary. Smithy Baxter had to go, along with wife and daughter. Those hadn't been the terms of Klaus' assignment, but it was the result he had delivered nonetheless.

A fine sweat clung to Klaus' skin. The sun wasn't yet up, but nothing seemed less appealing than more of such sleep.

There was fresh bread, a cup of dark honey and a jug of foaming milk at the barn door. After breakfast they tried their luck again with the innkeeper, who shook his head before the question had even left Klaus' lips. He asked them no questions of his own, not even how long they might stay in his barn.

'Thought you wanted to leave,' said Arik.

'It won't do any harm for anyone watching to think we mean to stay longer.'

Verdi asked, 'What about my uncle?'

'One afternoon to let him find us,' said Klaus. 'He has the advantage over us now. Then we leave.'

They returned to the market to buy supplies for the desert crossing: storm hides for the horses, water canteens, sand-masks. It took the better part of ten minutes and the purchase of a decoy sausage to tear Ravi away from a stall selling cured meats.

Arik watched him devour it in disbelief. 'He's no bigger than a pigeon. Where does he put it all?'

Verdi tickled Ravi's head as he sat nibbling on his shoulder, the meat in a death-grip between his paws. 'At least if he's eating I know where he is.'

'Yes, for about five minutes...'

The Invelmari Guard's station was empty, Invelmar's dark green banner hanging limp from its tower. The white starblossom of Invelmar in its centre was torn, its five petals severed – a punishable crime, for this symbol of the five ruling houses was sacred. *It must have been deliberately allowed to remain so.*

'What on earth?'

A wizened little man appeared in the square, garbed in deep burgundy robes over a patchwork tunic. He carried a long container across his back, shaking a fistful of tambourines. A crowd quickly clustered around him. He began pouring a dark ruby-red liquid from the container into small tin flagons hooked onto his belt, which he then passed around. More flagons were threaded around his neck, clattering like cymbals.

Ravi darted forward and disappeared into the crowd around him.

'Ravilion!'

Klaus glimpsed the oceloe standing on his rear legs at the seller's feet, front paws digging into his booted shin.

'I'm sorry!' Verdi hurried forward, face beet-red.

The seller chuckled and held out a flagon. 'Mulberry water? A delicacy in these parts. Try.'

The fragrant sweet drink was delicious. Klaus was still lowering a flagon from his lips when Ravi's head appeared on his arm, sniffing at the rim.

The seller poured another. 'Oceloes can't resist it.'

'What's in it, oceloe opium?' Arik raised his flagon high but needn't have worried; Ravi was lapping away at Klaus', who considered himself lucky to have managed to steal a sip first.

The seller bowed theatrically after Arik flipped him coin for their drinks. 'Water tokens before we part, travellers? I will give you a good price.'

Klaus smiled. 'No need.'

They had to fish Ravi's head out of a flagon in order to return it, Verdi dragging him away by the back of his neck. He hung in the air looking slightly dazed, ruby droplets dripping from his whiskers.

Arik waited until they were out of earshot. 'What in the world is a water token?'

'Not heard of them,' said Klaus. 'There's been permanent drought for years in the Plains. Maybe they're rationing water.'

Arik glanced at him hopefully. 'Rethinking going south?'

'No. But we should find out if these tokens are something we'll need.'

They stopped at a tavern for news: still nothing.

Why's there no word of our disappearance yet?

Anything at all ... even gossip? Klaus could then at least try to guess the Wintermantels' intentions and plan accordingly. *And they know this.* Lord and Lady Wintermantel were both Intelligencers. They would keep him in the dark.

Verdi tried to reassure him. 'Surely they can only explain away your absence for so long.'

'What am I, offal?' Arik mock-grumbled.

'Your uncle will realise,' Klaus told Verdi. 'He must know that you've been in the Wintermantels' house all this time. He'll work out who we are.'

Verdi frowned, trying to find a reason to disagree. 'Only if your disappearance is announced. And it hasn't been, yet.'

They returned to their inn for supper. A maid was scrubbing the wooden floorboards. A man sat half-hidden in the corner of the empty cantina.

His table was bare, and he had clearly been waiting.

Klaus knew him immediately. His eyes were the same cobalt blue. Black hair curled to the nape of his neck and, though more sun-worn, he had the same dramatic face as his nephew.

The maid had vanished.

Wide-eyed, Verdi stepped forward. 'Uncle Alizarin?'

Alizarin Selamanden rose. He was taller than his nephew, and broader. He had the hands of a man who'd had to carry a sword.

'Your return has long been awaited, sister's child.'

His voice was as rich and many-layered as aged wine. Alizarin laid a hand on Verdi's shoulder. Verdi stared back, speechless. It was as though a mirror was reflecting upon itself along a slope through time. Klaus couldn't help but wonder how beautiful Verdi's mother must have been.

Verdi's voice shook. 'I didn't realise I was expected.'

Alizarin looked up at the two Invelmari flanking his nephew. Scoured of that brief glimpse of emotion, his face became unreadable. Klaus was certain, then: Alizarin had known his nephew had disappeared from Dunraven four weeks ago; had probably always kept a watch over him from the distance. He knew exactly which household had raised his nephew.

'Who have you brought with you, Viridian?'

'Friends,' Arik replied.

'"Friends",' Alizarin repeated. A hundred more years of dust on Arik's cloak would have failed to disguise the Ealdorman's imperial poise.

Klaus' heart raced, though he'd planned this gamble. 'Playmates, once. Then classmates. But I think you know already who we are.'

Alizarin's face remained empty. 'What do you hope to achieve, sister's child, by bringing with you an Ealdorman and the heir to the North?'

Verdi looked around the dining room nervously. They were still alone; probably no accident. 'We want to travel into Derinda. I thought...'

His uncle fixed his blazing eyes on Verdi. 'Yes?'

'He thought you might help,' Arik finished. He cocked an eyebrow at Verdi. 'I told you this was madness.'

Determination and disappointment wrangled on Verdi's brow.

But Alizarin wasn't finished with Arik and Klaus. 'What drives two Ealdormen into hiding?'

Verdi glanced at Klaus, though they'd agreed on this too. 'Only one Ealdorman. There was … a terrible lie. Klaus is not a Wintermantel. That's why we have to leave.'

A very deep silence.

'Have you considered the danger you could bring upon us, just for harbouring you?' Alizarin finally asked.

Quietly, Klaus replied, 'Of course.'

'You know nothing of the Plains. Of its hardships, its black storms, its droughts. Winter is near and it's like nothing you've seen in the North. Don't be fooled by the mild air here at the border, that's the valley's doing.'

Verdi insisted, 'We'll learn.'

'And what then?' Alizarin looked at Klaus. 'If your masters allow you to live in exile, will you be contented hiding in the desert? Among Derindin?'

To this Klaus had no honest answer.

'What about you?' Alizarin asked Arik. 'Does house Prospere not follow Wintermantel in succession in three generations' time? Yes, we follow the cycle too. It's difficult to escape.'

Arik didn't balk. 'I'll follow my friends across the Lava Plains if that's where they go.'

'Admirable. But *you* –' Alizarin finished upon his nephew. 'You needn't be a fugitive.'

Verdi lifted his chin stubbornly. 'We go on together or not at all.'

A bee buzzed at the window in the late afternoon sun. Shadows played across Alizarin Selamanden's face. Finally he pulled out a chair.

'Then you had better sit down.' A dour smile toyed with the corner of his mouth. 'No use talking on empty bellies, there'll be plenty of that soon enough.'

The maid returned. Supper appeared. The dining room was permitted to fill again. A serving boy brought an earthen pot of stew and a rosy loaf still hot from the oven.

'We leave at dawn,' Alizarin warned. 'I only delayed our departure when I heard of your arrival.'

'Where are you going?' asked Verdi.

'Romel. With a favourable wind, that'll take three weeks through open desert after crossing the grasslands. From Romel we go to Samsarra, home of clan Elendra.'

'So soon,' murmured Verdi, giving Klaus a sidelong glance.

I must flee the North. But the moment, now it had finally arrived, was still crippling.

'We can't risk more delay; the first windstorms are probably a week behind us.' Alizarin's dour smile returned. 'Have you ever known a Plains wind, Masters Invelmari?'

They ate in silence. Apprehension stifled Klaus' hunger. Alizarin ate little, watching his nephew. Ravi leaned against the salt dish, happily chomping through a serving well beyond even his usual stomach capacity.

'How do you plan to go about concealing yourselves?' Alizarin asked.

A small commotion stirred amongst the diners behind them.

Alizarin stiffened. 'Don't turn around.'

From the corner of his eye, Klaus glimpsed a scruffy Derindin youth in a ragged travelling cloak. His reedy voice cut sharply through the chatter. An assortment of passers-by trailed in after him, hanging on to his words.

'Heard it with my own ears,' he announced. The sing-song cadence to his delivery raised gooseflesh on Klaus's arms. *The Babble.* 'From the Wintermantel palace, no less – from Sunnanfrost. A week ago now. The Wintermantel prince, and another Ealdorman too – a Prospere. Bodies found in the forest. Half-mauled by wolves!'

The breath seized in Klaus' airway.

'But where?' Diners shushed each other to listen.

'West of Dunraven. Fools out hunting alone at night. Pups too keen to run like dogs. Arrogant, like all Northerners.' Scornful laughter rumbled through the cantina. The Babble, probably not yet sixteen and very much a pup himself, preened at his handiwork.

Alizarin's eyes narrowed. 'Couldn't an old hand have brought this story in?'

Arik murmured, 'If he doesn't stop babbling soon I'll be happy to show him a mauling right now.'

'Trouble's afoot up north,' someone muttered. 'All the rioting in the Sterns, that missing Umari instrument … now Wintermantel's heir. You mark my words.'

'What's that instrument got to do with anything? They don't know how to use it anyway. Minds like mud.' Another round of laughter.

'What's it to us if there's trouble up north? Serves them right. They can have their trouble and keep it!'

'Because it'll spill down through the Part, you fool,' said the first speaker, but he was hushed by his fellows.

'So what now?'

'Well, Wintermantel's got the girl left, don't he?'

The Babble leaned against the door, watching his news take.

'A mere seedling,' another diner remarked. 'And only one.'

'Not much to bank on. A slip of the hand could pluck her in a flash from Sunnanfrost, and then what'll happen to the Sturmsinger Chain…?'

More laughter. Verdi paled, fists clenched under the table. Arik's face was wooden. Such talk was punishable by death in Invelmar.

'Good riddance, I say,' chipped in another. Gradually, chairs twisted back to their tables and the clink of cutlery was restored. There was plenty to talk about now. The Babble watched in satisfaction, his work done. He hung around the innkeeper, waiting for his reward for bringing a crowd into the inn. Klaus kept his head low; a Babble was as much a greedy pair of eyes and ears as a blaring horn. Fortunately, he didn't linger – not with such choice news to spread while cantinas were full for supper. He left, followed by a gaggle eager to hear more.

Verdi and Arik looked at Klaus.

Dead. With just a few words he had been killed, his entire existence erased.

Tentatively, Verdi told him, 'At least now there won't be an open hunt for you with a price on your head…'

'And luckily he's got a few details wrong,' Arik added. 'They said we went missing only a week ago. Even if someone doesn't believe we're dead, they won't expect us to have made it here already.'

They were both right. It would be harder to stay hidden if the Wintermantels had circulated a story that kept him alive. He would have been sought relentlessly, like the Umari instrument. Now any search for him would be hampered by secrecy. But he had also been erased. He'd become nothing.

Any sliver of doubt he might have had in the otherworldly dead of night... Elodie had *not* been mistaken. *It really was all a farce.*

Klaus summoned back the iron cocoon of Form. He met Alizarin's eyes. Dozens of thoughts passed between them – of bounty hunters, of never-ending subterfuge, of the cold, hard bed of a fugitive on the ground.

'Well, Ulfriklaus,' said Alizarin. 'You had better choose a new name for yourself.'

Klaus threw his hood over his head, rising. The cantina was now full. Someone had taken up a lute.

Arik stood. 'We'll collect our horses and meet you at dawn.'

'Have a care,' Alizarin warned. 'Your amnesty is over.'

Klaus stepped out into the night, dragging deeply on cool air. They returned to the barn and readied their packs. Ravi was already asleep in a nook in the rafters when they settled down between the bales of hay.

'He knew we'd gone missing even before the Babble came in,' said Arik.

Klaus made no reply.

Eventually, his friends stopped tossing and turning. Klaus was less fortunate. On the eve of the hardest road he had ever taken, the strength had finally drained from him, like rainwater into a gutter. But he couldn't sleep. Tonight, Afldalr could not help him. This was pain he could not understand.

Tomorrow, Afldalr would be locked again, its bowel lined with fury; stronger than before, colder than ever. For now, it smouldered.

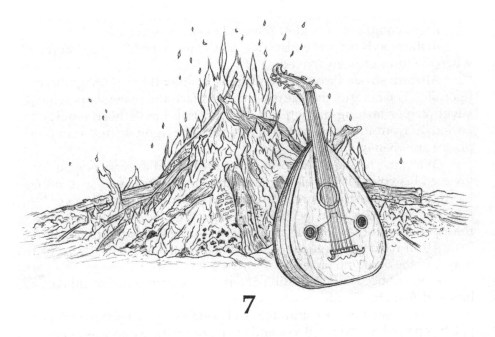

7

Into the Plains

AND FROM THIS HUMBLE CRADLE GREW THE GREATNESS OF ALL THE
NORTH: A BLACKSMITH'S SON, POLISHED ON A LOWLY FORGE; FATHERED
BY BARBARIANS YET BLESSED WITH SUCH JUDGEMENT AND MIGHT THAT
HE WOULD SEE THROUGH THE BLINDNESS AND COMMAND THE STORM.

SONNONFER: THE BIRTH OF ANSOVALD STURMSINGER,
LORD OF ALL THE NORTH

By morning, news of the two dead Ealdormen was common knowledge.
There was a blessed inconsistency of facts. One Babble insisted three
bodies had been recovered, one a woman's. Another told of a party of
four. All agreed that one of the dead was the Wintermantel prince, but
few mentioned Arik and none identified a Derindin servant. Curiously,
the reports were united on *where* they'd died – west, through the stone
quarries towards the city of Yelzberg, in the opposite direction to the road
they'd taken out of Dunraven.

Klaus could only wonder. *They don't want us found.*

In the woods beyond Noisy Tree, a hush fell over Alizarin's caravan when the three of them arrived.

Alizarin strode through the wagons to greet them. A magnificent tigon stood on his arm, the size of a small cat, face and mane snow-white, silver stripes lashing her white body and tail. Ravi's head emerged curiously from underneath Verdi's collar. The tigon spared him one glance and then ignored him.

'Welcome, nephew.' Alizarin's greeting carried to every wagon. He lowered his voice. 'It is widely known that my nephew was sent to the North, but not exactly where. I'd keep that knowledge to yourselves.'

Dozens of eyes raked them: hostile, inquisitive, indifferent. Gradually, the Derindin returned to their preparations, curiosities far from satisfied.

Alizarin led them into the camp. 'Whatever the North has done, you may find the South no haven.'

Klaus noticed the Derindin's interest was stirred not so much by him and Arik, but Verdi.

'You'll need this.' Alizarin stopped beside a wagon. Its roof had been patch-repaired in several places and the paint on the wood was peeling, but it looked sturdy.

'Thank you,' Verdi mumbled. 'We should pay you for it –'

'It's not for sale.'

Red spots blossomed on Verdi's cheeks.

'Master Viridian!'

A man approached, his arms spread wide. His short-cropped beard was greying, his sun-beaten face beaming. Suman trailed him, bearing a very large falcon on his gauntlet.

'Welcome!' The man enveloped Verdi in a bear hug. 'Here you are at last. Welcome back, young man. A happier surprise I couldn't have imagined. Who are your friends?'

'This is Meron, plant scholar and curator of Elendra's Arboretum,' said Alizarin. 'You've met Suman Traistrom of clan Mantelon.'

They were interrupted by a small cheer at the arrival of two men and a boy carrying several pails.

'Fresh milk will be a luxury for a while,' said Meron. 'Have you eaten?'

The boy was quick to spot the newcomers. He skipped towards them – once his share of milk was secured in a battered tin cup in one hand, along with a hunk of bread in the other – and Klaus recognised the street urchin who'd tried to pick his pocket in the market.

'These guests are travelling with us, Fibbler,' Alizarin told him as he walked away. He added over his shoulder, 'Hands to yourself!'

'So it's Fibbler, is it?' said Klaus. The boy gave them a toothy grin.

Evidently, he hadn't forgotten Klaus either.

'Are you from Invelmar?' he demanded. 'Only I heard there's an Invelmari prince missing and they've found his body, all eaten by worms. And there was more people besides. Mebbe you heard something up north?'

'Sounds horrible,' said Arik. 'Where d'you hear that?'

The boy sat on a tree stump and chased a mouthful of bread with a slug of the milk. 'It's all over the Babble.'

'The Babble, eh?' said Verdi. 'Must be true. Well, it sounds like you know more than we do.'

Fibbler swallowed, appraising them suspiciously, bright-eyed as a bird. 'And they said there were three others with him. Sure you didn't hear anything more?'

'How long did the Babble say they'd been dead?'

'Ohhh, not two weeks ... you could still make out their faces,' Fibbler calculated confidently. 'Can't have been much longer'an that if you can still see their faces, and besides the tigers would have got them.'

Verdi suppressed a smile. No one had the heart to tell him there were no tigers roaming the North.

'We left long before then, I'm afraid,' said Klaus. 'Sounds like we missed all the excitement.'

Fibbler nodded, apparently satisfied.

'Wotcha doing here, then?' he said thickly around another bite of bread.

'Marcin is a swordsman, and I'm a war chronicler,' said Klaus. 'We came to see the South with Verdi. He's Alizarin's nephew.'

Fibbler stopped chewing and gaped at Verdi in stunned silence.

'Let's have a look at the wagon,' said Verdi quickly, hurrying towards it.

It was practical, if bare: two built-in bunks, an empty crate serving both as storage and a table, and a pile of neatly folded blankets. Dusty light streamed in through two small windows. An oil lamp hung from the roof, paned with coloured glass.

Fibbler hopped up into the seat with the familiarity of one who had done so many times before. 'This is Alizarin's old wagon.'

A roar came from behind them. '*Fibbler!*'

The little boy froze, then stuffed the last of his crust into his mouth. He jumped down and darted off away from the voice.

Alizarin's caravan comprised some twenty wagons and perhaps twice as many passengers and horses. A Derindman silently helped them harness their horses to the wagon; he spoke almost no Invelmen at all.

'I'll call him Silverflank,' Arik declared, admiring the grey stallion he'd purchased in Noisy Tree.

'You can't change his name!' Verdi told him indignantly. 'Derindin never change a horse's name. Its bond to a new master degrades each time its name is changed.'

His words rang a little too loudly; the entire camp had fallen quiet.

Verdi blushed, but the Derindin had gathered and faced north – towards the river. A woman let loose a long ululating cry that rippled on the wind. One by one, the Derindin joined her in a rolling lament that tugged at the heart. Klaus had never heard a sound more mournful. Even Ravi froze mid-squirreling all over his new wagon, clinging to a shutter like a spider to listen. Then the Derindin mounted their horses, and wagon wheels began to turn southward.

Something squeezed painfully in Klaus' chest as he turned his back on the North.

'Go back,' he told Arik quietly. 'You've seen me safely to the border. If you board a boat from Noisy Tree to Dunraven, you'll be there within a week –'

'What are you talking about?'

'You've not considered what you're forsaking.' Klaus glanced at Verdi. 'Lady Wintermantel has always been fond of you, she would keep you under her protection –'

'Lady Wintermantel would assume I knew the truth and kill me on sight.'

Arik took the reins. 'Let's go, Klaus.'

And so they went.

The Limpra Hills rose steeply above Noisy Tree. Theirs was a wide dirt road fashioned by the footfalls of countless Derindin caravans crossing the border. Klaus committed every detail to memory for his map. The Paiva crept up on the north-eastern side of Noisy Tree; the Ninvellyn cradled its western aspect. South-west of the town, the colossal Ostraad dam interrupted the Ninvellyn with breathtaking abruptness. It had taken eleven thousand men a decade to build from the day Sturmsinger had ordered its construction. He didn't live to see it completed. Numerous silver tributaries veined the forest. The smaller border towns glinted like grey pearls swathed by the Paiva: Appledor to the north-west, Whimsy further west, Tiptoe tucked between them.

The road widened to a plateau at the summit of the hills, offering unbroken views of the east to their left and their first glimpse of the land downriver of the Ostraad.

It was as though the latter pages of a book had been ripped out at the spine.

The hills beyond the dam descended to an expanse of sallow grassland, rolling southward to meet the horizon. Here the Ninvellyn had been slain, its silver entrails gathered in a wide puddle at the southern side of the Ostraad, sending feeble streams and tributaries flailing limply through the grasses.

'Sturmsinger's blade,' Arik breathed.

They'd stopped without meaning to. The rest of the caravan trundled on ahead.

The hair stood on the back of Klaus' neck. A sense of wrongness engulfed him. Later it would torment him in dreams that were as fresh and biting as the heartless snow of the Sterns.

Nearby, Alizarin paused astride his chestnut mare.

His travelling cloak was rust-red, the colour of the earth. On the cusp of the summit, he could have been an extension of the hillside beckoning the skies. A black storm brimmed from his cobalt eyes as he gazed over the land, savagely expressionless.

Their eyes met for a moment, and Klaus heard thunder in the look that passed between them. Then the Derindman rode on, and they steered their wagon forward.

*

By midday, the sun was high and hot in a cloudless sky. Verdi watched his uncle riding ahead, apprehension souring his admiration. Even Ravi seemed awed, keeping to Verdi's shoulder and monitoring the silver-striped tigon Saya with unblinking eyes.

'You'll get a chance to talk to him,' Klaus reassured him.

'I don't know if I want to,' Verdi mumbled, though unable to look away.

His uncle barely glanced in his direction. *Maybe he's disappointed.* But what interest Alizarin lacked, the remaining Derindin happily supplied.

'Ahh, Master Viridian. Welcome, welcome.' Verdi's hand was taken more times than he could count; his cheeks kissed, his shoulders squeezed in strangers' embraces. Derindin hospitality was highly praised, but this surpassed all his expectations. Most humbling of all were the happy tears in the eyes of an old birdkeeper of clan Mantelon, whose wagon of cages and perches left little room for a human nest.

The birdkeeper sought Verdi at their first rest stop. 'When the ruby-breasted perlao journeys east, sometimes it does not return for many summers. But always it does, and only with the brightest plumage, when it is ready.'

Verdi smiled weakly. *Ready for what?* But the birdkeeper was gentle-tempered and welcomed Arik and Klaus warmly, immediately putting Verdi at ease.

'What a handsome creature,' Verdi told him, watching a kestrel circling over their heads.

'She is, is she not?' The birdkeeper smiled at her fondly. 'And yet not so majestic as Fera, the queen of birds, who caught the wisdom of the Simyerin in her wings. But one day you shall discover this for yourself, Master Viridian.' He clasped Verdi's hand again. 'I am sure of it.'

*

'You can't risk going from one village to another without a company of tumblers now.'

Saarem, an Elendran tumbler, struck a chord with the two Invelmari immediately, the common language of soldiers being simple enough when there was no quarrel between them. A dozen – or a fist, as the Derindin called it – of these fist-and-foot Derindin fighters guarded the caravan. They were mostly Elendrans, but a few were soldiers hired in Noisy Tree for the return journey in response to intensifying pirate raids. They carried slender blades slung across their backs and an impressive array of knives. Their silver-haired general, Ayla, welcomed them with clipped courtesy. A short and wiry middle-aged woman with eyes of deep olive, she was dwarfed by her fist of tumblers. But for her forked spear, her weapons were virtually invisible.

'Eight weeks on the road, eh?' Saarem steered his horse expertly, and she in turn seemed to anticipate every small shift of his body.

'A few of the roads were flooded,' replied Arik, a practised liar. 'Took us almost two weeks just getting to Dunraven from Malvern. It's a northern town near the Sterns. We'd been on a campaign in the Far North.'

Saarem's eyes widened. 'You are Isarnanheri.'

Klaus laughed. 'No. We were serving with the Invelmari Guard.'

'What'll you do in the South?'

'Adventure,' said Arik cheerfully, almost sounding sincere.

'Sell our swords, perhaps,' said Klaus. Saarem nodded; this was commonplace enough. 'When did these pirates start raiding?'

'Oh, there've always been bandits in the desert. Especially here along the Saffron Highway to Romel, and during the trading season. Some folk have waited weeks for safe passage.' Saarem lowered his voice. 'There are clanfolk here who might have otherwise spurned our company. Folk from Lebas, Fraivon … clans who aren't enemies of Elendra but aren't friends, either. You never know where you stand with them. But this year … I've never seen such raids. Bandits steal. Now they'll slit the throat afterwards too.'

'What changed?'

'Desperation, maybe? People are nervous that trouble up north might raise the cost of grain. 'Course, bad news travels faster and gets worse along the way. Folk forget good news quickly enough.' Saarem grinned at Verdi. 'Though here's a bit of good news they'll not forget.'

After he moved on, Arik remarked, 'Never seen a general escort a caravan home from the market before.'

The grassland stretched on. It was dotted with silveroaks and cedars, clusters of slender cypresses, swathes of bracken turned fiery gold by autumn. The sun had begun its molten descent when they broke to make camp. Terim, the caravan's larder-keeper, welcomed the donation of their supplies.

'So this is Alizarin's nephew,' Terim beamed. Nearby, his wife Mayda built the campfire with Fibbler's help. 'We thought you'd been lost!'

'I might just keep a bit of this for Ravi … or he'll never forgive me.' Verdi cut a piece of dried sausage, stuffing it into oil-paper. Luckily the oceloe was in their wagon, tormenting the horses.

'Aaah, that is how he has grown so fat and sleek. On soska!' Terim laughed heartily, ensuring the rest was stored well out of the reach of little boys and oceloes.

But Fibbler had set his sights higher than sausage. He trotted after Klaus to help gather brushwood, chattering away, first asking about Invelmar before proceeding to tell him all the stories he'd ever heard about the North.

'And one kid said they build palaces from ice! I en't never slid on ice, but I bet it's fun. Sliding around from room to room!'

'Bit cold and wet though.' Klaus kept a straight face. 'And hard.'

'True.' Fibbler paused thoughtfully. 'And your face must stick to the pillows in the morning…'

Next, Fibbler regaled him with the stories he'd gathered of forest beasts marauding Northerners in their citadels, with all the hallmarks of the Babble in his tale.

'I have to tell you something, Fibbler,' Klaus said gravely as they returned to the camp. 'There are no ice palaces in Invelmar. Can't have people laughing at you for thinking it.'

Fibbler's face fell. 'But the Babblers said –'

'They were pulling your leg. If you're going to repeat a story, you should always first make sure that it's true.' *And I was an Intelligencer,* Klaus thought wryly. But he was free of that burden now. 'Now, I'll tell you what you *can* find in the North…'

He told Fibbler about the Stern mountains, so tall that their highest peaks had never been seen by a human eye from the ground, and so cold that their great waterfalls had remained frozen for thousands of years. He named Invelmari forges, where Northern alchemists tested every ounce of prized ironstone and where the hammering of metal drove men to madness. Fibbler devoured his words with the wide eyes of childhood. He told him of never-ending summer days in northernmost Invelmar, which by winter forgot the sun altogether. He told him of deep fire mines and hot springs amongst the glaciers; of the white wilderness where the Far Northerners lived. Of the treacherous Hvítrmýrr ice-swamp inlets of the Shining Sea, frozen so long its true shape was forgotten, so that it was impossible now to know whether one walked on land or frozen water.

The warm smells of onions and juniper and smoke gathered the Derindin around the fire after sundown, when trailing wisps of night-clouds softened the face of the moon. Amongst them were traders and farmers; youths seeking their fortunes beyond the desert; a few families, the youngest passenger barely three; and the intriguing birdkeeper, whose wagon chirruped and trilled with birdsong. Klaus noted worn and ill-fitting boots, the shabbiness of their clothes. There wasn't a portly belly in sight. Hardship kept them lean, and the desert had made them strong.

'There've been pirates in the Plains for as long as there have been clans,' Meron told them. 'But each year there seem to be more of them, like the windstorms.'

'Who are they?' asked Verdi.

'Unclanned lonemen, exiles. Derindin who found no place for themselves in the clandoms, raiding for a living. They're more active ahead of winter, when folk are taking profits and supplies home from the market towns, but this year's been especially bad.'

'Can't anything be done about them?'

'Each clan deals with them as they see fit. If they're caught, of course. We Elendrans have been fortunate. Ours is the most eastern clandom, not far from the Sourgrass Sea. Elendra raised an arboretum from the sand – the only great green belt left in Derinda. It's well guarded, so pirates steer clear of our clandom.'

Verdi had to clutch Ravi with both fists to stop him from getting into the cookpots. A girl poured a thin soup of citrus-soured yogurt into their bowls, fragrant with dill. The main meal consisted of thick peppery barley porridge, glistening with dark beans.

Meron watched them eat. 'First time you've had lamh'met?' Ravi perched on Verdi's knee, face dipping greedily into his bowl whenever Verdi's spoon wasn't in it. 'Shaved deer's heart and offal. A desert staple. Keeps the wheels going. Ha! Slow down. It'll sit heavy in your bellies.'

Verdi flicked Ravi off his bowl. 'No more. You'll make yourself sick!' The oceloe curled on his side in the grass, tiny belly bulging, leaving Verdi to finally eat in peace.

Fibbler ran over, plonking himself down beside them. 'Tell me more about the mountains.'

He listened, transfixed. Klaus described the haunting howl of wolves and the heavy ambling of bearded forest bears. He told Fibbler of hunting deer in the heartlands; of the mysterious gas-venting swamps in the east of Invelmar, where the forests gave way to the perilous road to Pengaza; of battles he had chronicled between Far Northern barbarians and Dunraven.

Meron pulled out a long pipe and filled it. His smoke was more woody than the prized cigars Invelmar imported from Semra. Around them, the comforting bumble of chatter fused with the crackle of the fire.

'What about further north?' Fibbler asked. 'Beyond the Far North?'

'That's all ice. No one travels or lives there.'

'Why?'

'Well, it's so cold that nothing grows. There's nothing to burn for fuel. And there's a lot of water … but it's all frozen, and some of it is saltwater, so finding a drink is harder than you think. And there's nothing to eat, so animals are especially ferocious.'

Fibbler crossed his legs cosily, very satisfied with this. Knowing a good snuggling place when he saw it, Ravi burrowed into his lap with all the signs of settling down for the night.

'What can you hunt there?'

'Not much. But you can fish. The four rivers that come down from the Sterns bring a lot of fish. Do you know many fish?' Fibbler shook his head, bewitched. Others fell quiet now, listening. 'Rainbow trout and silver trout, giant carp, tiny minnows. Salmon, bream and yellow riverbass…' Fibbler's eyes rounded to saucers. Klaus may as well have been naming jewels. 'They swim south in hundreds of little rivers running through forest –'

'A big forest?'

'Many forests. And yes, some of them very big, with trees thicker than you can imagine. The tallest trees in the Seven Parts are in Eisnach, near Malvern. Some of the best hunting is further south near the Helftads, where it's warmer. That's where the Queen's hunters go.' Klaus told him of how to track the bucks by their deer rubs and droppings; of spotting the dark eyes of rabbits hidden in dense green undergrowth; of the best way to shoot antelope. He told of the four rivers of Invelmar; their confluences; their tangle of silver arms. A painful ache grew in his breast.

'That's an awful lot of water,' said Fibbler wistfully. Verdi looked up from cleaning his knife.

'And you've seen this water already. Those four rivers join to make the Ninvellyn. So the water you've been drinking in Noisy Tree has come all the way down from the Sterns.'

The little boy marvelled at this, looking pleased to have had some encounter with a bit of this alien northern world.

'And then it stops at the dam,' he said, and the spell was broken.

'Everything stops at the dam, child. Everything but the war.'

Klaus followed the voice to a rough-hewn Derindman smoking nearby.

'The war's been over for nine hundred years, Parin,' said Meron mildly.

Parin grunted. 'Lives and battles can be over … but the land never forgets. We of clan Lebas certainly don't. Look around you. Don't tell me the war is over. The Years of Sorrow may as well be time itself.' Parin nodded at Verdi. 'Welcome home, young man, what's left of it.'

Meron smiled at Verdi between puffs of his pipe. 'Home's a long way off yet.'

'We'll be home soon enough, and home's where he belongs.' Parin jerked his head at Arik and Klaus. 'But it'll be a long way for your friends.'

Verdi's back stiffened. 'It's little distance between brothers.'

Keeping his gaze averted from the two Northerners, Parin got up and left.

'Fibbler, why don't you tell our guests about Samsarra?' Meron suggested. 'Viridian left when he was a babe, you know.'

Verdi stiffened; this snagged Fibbler's attention and would have no doubt spawned a train of unwelcome questions. Luckily Terim called, and Fibbler sprang up to collect their empty bowls with the eagerness of one who'd been promised a reward.

A flute hooted softly across the camp.

'You are most welcome here,' Meron insisted, not without a note of apology. 'And Emra our Chieftainess will be anxious to meet you, Master Viridian.'

Verdi's eyes rounded in alarm. 'Me?'

'She is Alizarin's aunt. A moment, friends; I'd better check my horses.'

Arik whistled after Meron left. 'That explains your uncle's escort.'

Klaus' eyes drifted across the fire; Alizarin was in conversation with the general. Verdi was too stunned to reply.

Arik elbowed him, grinning. 'Now you're a Chieftainess' great-nephew. Next thing you know, you'll turn out to be someone important.'

'Don't joke,' Verdi pleaded.

The flute swelled into song, spilling hauntingly into the night. More pipes emerged, mellowing the air. A man threw a patchwork cloak over his shoulders. Klaus knew a bard when he saw one, although when he began to sing it was like no bard he had ever heard. The edge of his voice was pure and sweet, like a knife dipped in honey.

'What's he singing about?' Klaus asked when Meron rejoined them. The words were in a Derindask dialect; familiar yet foreign.

'One of the currents that passes through the fifth chamber of the southern heart.' Meron gazed into the flames. 'In Derindask we call it *namathra*, the prayer for rain ... it dances with its sister, *sehresar*, the soul of the river.'

The rest of his poetry changed into Invelmen, in notes that were lovingly drawn out. He sang a soliloquy to the desert before slipping into a song that rolled and undulated like a river after rain. The caravan picked up his refrain, and night swelled with their chorus. Next he told the story of a maiden lured from her mother into a sorcerer's lair, immortal in her longing for her home. Then his tale changed into a lament for a time when the Plains had been green and alive. After just one night on the shore of the desert, it made Klaus yearn for the thumping heart of Northern forests; for the dewy breath of the Paiva. He sang tenderly of the Ninvellyn as though cut off from her like a lover, longing for the day when she would return to the Plains.

Klaus had been edging towards sleep, but the lament sharpened his mind and threw shivers down his spine. He recalled the Ostraad jutting like an ugly scar across the bottom of the Paiva, robbing these people of the bounties of the river.

Arik stood abruptly. 'I'm going to bed.'

Klaus soon followed. Verdi stayed to supervise Fibbler's torment of Ravi. The wagon was cold. A light snore came from the sheepskin where Arik had settled down on the floorboards. Arik had no trouble sleeping anywhere. But though Klaus was exhausted, turbulence lurked beneath his Form. Fear for Elodie wormed through his heart. The Wintermantels *must* have had reason to fear for her, if they had planted Klaus in their house as a distraction. *Dear Sturmsinger, let her be safe.* He longed for Gerlinde with another sharp pang. He must have fallen asleep, stirred fitfully and fallen asleep again ... he was certain he dreamed but could remember none of it, and was grateful. He finally woke with a great thump in his chest, and the fog of dream was replaced with the fog of the waking world, where the sounds of distant flute-song and fireside laughter were the breeze that filled the lungs of the still desert night.

Verdi crept onto the opposite bunk; this was what had woken him. He jumped when he realised Klaus was awake, hitting his head on a shelf.

'Sorry,' he whispered. 'Didn't mean to wake you.'

'Did you get a chance to speak with your uncle?'

'No.' A short pause. 'He barely says a word to me.'

'Give him time.'

A longer pause.

'I have a great-aunt,' Verdi marvelled. 'Even if only by marriage. She's Alizarin's father's sister. She might have known my mother...'

Klaus smiled. Privately he wondered why a Chieftainess would have permitted her great-nephew to be sent away to hostile territory.

Verdi gently extracted a sleeping oceloe from his pocket. 'What do you think Terim meant, when he said they thought I'd been "lost"?'

'Perhaps Alizarin never told anyone much about you.' Klaus chose his words carefully, still undecided over what to make of the Derindin. 'They're very ... welcoming of you.'

'I wish he would tell me about my parents.'

To this Klaus had no reply, but at least now he understood.

'*Your Form should be the last thing you hold before you sleep, and always the closest.*' Master Arnander had been particularly strict about this. '*Nothing must come between you and Form. Not your heart, not even your lovers. There is no space for distraction. A distracted man is divided.*'

But there was definitely a space growing between Form and repose. A space crammed with the storm sparked by thoughts of Elodie, and faceless parents, and memories he'd had no right to make of a time before the Plains.

Outside the Derindin's song eventually fell silent, but the ghosts they had summoned rustled on through the grasses long after the embers of their fire had faded.

8

Sand

IN HIS FIRST DECADE, YOUNG ANSOVALD TASTED
THE BITTERNESS OF WAR WHEN HIS KIN BURNED IN THEIR BEDS,
BETRAYED DURING TRUCE-TIME. AND SO HE VOWED TO UPROOT
EVERY LAST TRAITOR, TO HURL LITTLE KINGS
FROM THEIR LITTLE THRONES.

SONNONFER: THE RISE OF ANSOVALD STURMSINGER

Alizarin had led many caravans, but this one was different. It wasn't just the lateness of the season and the growing risk of windstorms, or the shadow of pirates. He had never had as precious a cargo as this.

'Shall I send word with Petra to the chieftains?' Suman asked again.

'No. They've waited twenty-four years, they can wait a few weeks more.'

He watched his nephew at every opportunity. The boy was smaller than he'd expected, and his face was an open book. He was quick and observant but unbelievably clumsy when he was anxious, which was too often. He'd learned how to understand his minibeast without any instruction – not as a pet, but an aid, for oceloes were highly sensitive to danger. He had his nose in a manual of medicinal formulations or anatomical dissection whenever he could. And he followed those

Northerners around like an attendant.

Inwardly, Alizarin scowled. However was he going to be cured of that?

They won't stay. The fugitive will keep running, out of the Part altogether. The Ealdorman will be drawn back to the North.

'It ought to be enough to invoke Merensama at the Assembly.'

'It'll take much more to rally the western clans,' Alizarin reminded Suman. Clans Baeron and Hesper were a lost cause, though Suman nursed ardent hope otherwise, like all Mantelonians. 'But the clans will raise other matters first, like the fact we tried to pursue a treaty with Akrinda.'

Merensama. Another Derindin dream that grew more unlikely each year, like the future of the Arboretum. Both their clans had spent years preparing for the long-promised union of clans across the Plains. But for Alizarin, cynicism had set its roots deeply. He could see no such end to the Years of Sorrow. It was a disease to have so much doubt, Emra told him. At what point precisely did an absence of hope become despair?

But something yet anchored him in belief, however tenuously. He could recall the dream as if it had come to him yesterday, though he'd been a boy at the time. It was the only dream he had ever remembered on waking. And the sage's interpretation of what Alizarin had seen haunted him more than the dream itself: '*A man will die twice to awaken in the Plains a light so great that it shall illuminate the entire Part…*'

Alizarin dismissed the rest of the sage's words, for he disliked speculation.

Emra and the Elders were certain it would be Lorendar's blood to restore Merensama. Peacetime across the Plains at last. Had it not been promised, after all, that Lorendar's descendants were fated to finish what he had started? Derindin were obsessed with prophecies and dreams.

Alizarin didn't like to hedge bets on visions. In the tradition of his family, he had studied the layers of the earth; the mineral complexities of its crust, its trove of soils and stones. These were things he could comfortably hold, measure and predict.

Of all people, why had the vision come to him? He was not a holy man. He had asked this of the sage, too. The sage was long dead now, and Alizarin had never sought to ask this question again of another. It was said one should never ask a sage the same question twice, though the sage's answer had underwhelmed him: '*So that you may have certainty.*'

Alizarin looked at the boy curled up with his book again and felt further from certainty than ever.

*

74

'Do you mean to stay in Derinda?'

Ayla commanded the tumblers with a steely eye and a quiet voice. She rode a grey mare as lithe as she. Nothing of the little that she said was idle.

'Perhaps,' said Arik. 'Or else travel to Semra. They pay well for fighters.' He measured carefully what he told her, because he decided she would remember every word.

'Not so well as Invelmari pay, I should think.'

Arik nudged Verdi. 'We couldn't desert our friend here when he decided to discover his homeland.'

'I tried to talk him out of coming,' said Verdi blandly.

Ayla would not be distracted by jokes. 'I imagine you'll want to return to Invelmar, after your work here is done.'

It struck Arik as an odd choice of words. 'What's the fun in planning so far ahead?'

Still, she was courteous, and whatever their personal feelings towards Northerners, her tumblers followed her cue.

'Don't mind the tongues of farmers and the like,' an Elendran tumbler named Broco told Arik. 'I'm sure the Chieftainess will be glad of your services to her nephew.'

Services. Arik itched to confess his ill-defined suspicion to Klaus, but the caravan afforded little true privacy. And ever since they'd crossed the border, Klaus had grown even more withdrawn. Intelligencers gave away nothing that they did not wish revealed, but Arik knew what ailed Klaus – the *cutting away* of Invelmar had begun. After the North had finally broken him in, Klaus had surrendered himself to it with an unhealthy, all-consuming loyalty. Now he had everything to lose.

Not like me. What did Arik have to leave behind? His Warrior mother had been killed on a campaign when he was barely three. His Blacksmith father had been the court's Master of the Forge, commanding Invelmar's great steel-making machine, and had died in a mine before Arik was even born. There was no one to mourn, and no illusions about why his uncles kept him close. Their endless schemes, the bastards – as though he didn't have a string of cousins slavering to indulge his uncles' ambitions. For all Klaus' faults – bookish, behaved, sometimes a little boring – he was more a kinsman to Arik than the Prosperes, and his little Derindin shadow not far off. For his part, Arik saw a clean slate before them.

But something about the Plains made Arik uneasy. Maybe it was the open land, the endless sky, the lack of interruption.

Here, a man was forced to look into himself.

The problem was Klaus looked too deeply.

Arik poked his side. 'Where are you now? Moping over Gerlinde?'

He earned himself a disparaging look from beyond the Intelligencer's mask. 'Good, I'm glad you've regained your senses at last.'

'That was never a problem. She wouldn't have me even when she thought I would be king.'

Arik clapped Klaus' back. 'If it's any consolation, I'd have gambled my sword she would have accepted a proposal of marriage. Whatever she thought of you, she wouldn't have been able to resist being queen.'

'Heaps of consolation, thanks.'

Arik ignored Verdi's appalled look. He wasn't ready for the mask to return. 'She was no good anyway. For a bed-warming, maybe, but no more.'

This time he got a punch. He dodged the next one, chuckling happily to himself. The Derindin gathered for supper around the fire. Klaus retreated back into whatever held him hostage within, though he resurfaced for the Mantelonian birdkeeper's stories. Even Arik found himself drawn into these.

'Little children are sent away into the desert when they are weaned from the breast, sometimes for months at a time, under the tutelage of trackers and nomads to learn the way of sand.' The birdkeeper peered up into the night. 'There is space here for a mind to know itself.'

It sounded terrible. But was it so different to what Klaus had endured training alone in the snow blizzards of Far Northern cliffs, or Arik's own plights in the salt swamps and derelict mines of Eradottr in the Sterns?

Yes. Those were trials intended to force you apart from your self, until you feel nothing but your Form.

This brittle voice was Lisbeta's, his Form Mistress. Though she'd been gone these three years and Arik had all but shut it out, sometimes he heard it still. She too had been steely-eyed, quiet-voiced, lithe-limbed. She'd been the only thing about his training that he had hated.

Arik glanced across the fire at Ayla Taahn. The desert was a clean slate, but already it was scuffed with a little too much of the North.

*

It was the Mantelonian birdkeeper, his face wrinkled as a walnut and his wagon at all times noisy, who interested Klaus the most. The caravaners visited him often, to delight in the songs of his birds and his simple company. While most of the Derindin kept a cold distance from the Northerners, the soft-spoken Mantelonian was rarely without a smile and a story.

'For the feathernuts,' he said, when Klaus found him kneeling in the dry grass at dawn scratching in the dirt, his tin pot full of pale worms. 'Their hatchlings are too young yet to forage for themselves.'

He invited Klaus to his wagon to watch the young birds, each the size of a quail's egg, make short work of the worm meal. Everywhere were perches and baskets for his feathered menagerie; the birdkeeper himself slept in a tiny cabin behind the wagon seat.

Klaus asked him, 'Why do the Derindin have such fondness for birds?'

'Look up.' The birdkeeper craned his neck. The golden flecks in his moss-green eyes snagged the sunrise, eyes as young as he was old. One of his kestrels soared overhead, its wings spread wide and still. 'They are closest to the heavens. In the sky, who knows what they have tasted?'

A dozen tiny suncatchers flitted restlessly near his wagon roof, arguing amongst themselves in full-throated trilling that belied their size. The birdkeeper smiled.

'Watching them, the heart is lifted.' He offered one a crumb; its siblings hurried forward for a peck. 'They force a troubled mind out of its darkness.'

There was some truth to this. Even Klaus was soothed by their darting-chirruping-flickering. But it was their keeper himself who was the greater comfort, embodying what his birds gave him. He had a different way of seeing to the other Derindin. Like his birds, he seemed to view the Plains from a greater distance, unfettered by daily particulars. In his company, Klaus momentarily forgot the dull ache in his side left by the loss of the North.

Klaus had hoped to learn more about the clans from the birdkeeper, but on this count he was disappointed. 'Who controls Romel?'

'A truce has held in that city for centuries. Folk from all the clans live there, as do others who are clanless – a dangerous choice now. Not in all the Plains is there a truce such as Romel's. But it is not wholesome, friend chronicler. Not wholesome.'

'What do you mean?'

'I keep out of the affairs of the shadows of men.' A troubled wrinkle amongst wrinkles appeared on the birdkeeper's brow. 'Long have they been, the Years of Sorrow.'

'The dam has brought great suffering here.'

'No, Master Invelmari. Our sorrow was born long before the dam, born of the endless tug-of-war that thrives even between brothers. The lawlessness that holds us hostage to chaos. And the only will to govern comes from the shadows.'

He would say no more of Romel, so Klaus sought answers from Meron.

'Romel isn't under the clans' control,' Meron explained. 'No fighting is permitted there, on pain of death.'

'The clans enforce this?'

'Not the clans.' Meron's voice dropped to a murmur. 'The Murhesla. The marked guardians of Romel. They do not belong to any clan.'

Not wishing to discomfit him, Klaus saved his questions. Meron and the birdkeeper became a welcome antidote to the tense tolerance of most of the other caravaners. What peace Klaus borrowed from the birdkeeper, however, was short-lived.

'What do you think will happen to Elodie?' Verdi asked.

Klaus kept his eyes on the road ahead, steering the wagon. It was a question that had the tension of one long suppressed. They'd never spoken of Verdi's attachment to his sister, and now it was a chapter better left closed.

'She'll be safe,' he reassured Verdi. Elodie would hate being primed for the throne, but the Blood Pact that made her a prisoner would also keep her from harm. *And from what the Wintermantels had feared might threaten the safety of their heir.* She would be suffocated with safety.

'How can you be so certain?'

Klaus exchanged a look with Arik. Verdi had been beside him so long that it was easy to forget he didn't really understand Sturmsinger's prophecy, no matter how well he could recite it. How did one explain the hold of the Blood Pact over the Northborn? Somewhere in the penumbra of love and fear hovered the Invelmari's bond to land and lord ... and if necessary, more fear than love. The great sacrifice of the dead who had fallen for Invelmar could never be in vain. The Ealdormen would preserve the Chain, for fear of bringing to the North the desolation that Sturmsinger was promised, if ever their alliance should crumble.

'No one will be more closely guarded in all the Seven Parts,' he told Verdi with a painful *thud* in his breast. 'Put it out of your mind. Someone is always listening.'

*

Someone was always *watching*, too. Verdi found that eyes followed him everywhere; searching, even hungry. It was unnerving. The Derindask that Rigo Firefin the palace horsemaster had taught Verdi was broken and limited, and some of the caravaners spoke almost no Invelmen, but one thing was clear: *he*, at least, was welcome.

For now, his audience was much less disconcerting.

Fibbler gaped at the dagger Verdi was cleaning. 'Is that Invelmari steel?'

Verdi had grown accustomed to the blade, but to the uninitiated it was wondrous: its surface was so polished it looked wet, and untold hues of silver danced along its length, splitting light with every fractional movement.

'Yes.' Verdi offered it to him by the handle. 'Be careful, it's terribly sharp.'

The tip was so fine it was difficult to grasp with the naked eye; Verdi had tried many times, giving himself a headache if he looked too long. Fibbler held it reverently, watching the play of light on steel. Several heads turned at the sight of the child holding the dagger.

'It's so light,' Fibbler exclaimed.

'If you think this is special, you ought to see Marcin's longsword, or Tristan's.' Fibbler looked up eagerly, and Verdi sat up in alarm. 'Careful! Never take your eye off the steel, it will bite quicker than you can look back...'

Fibbler returned it and darted to Arik, who shook his head before the question had left Fibbler's lips. Next Fibbler sidled over to Klaus, who sat beside their wagon reviewing a map. Klaus smiled slightly at Fibbler's hopeful face. He rose and drew his sword, laying it on the ground before sitting down again.

'Can I pick –'

'Better not. It's longer than you are and a bit heavier than that dagger.'

So Fibbler sat beside the sword, admiring the expressive steel.

'This was made in Stahlaz, the greatest forge in Invelmar. Only a very fierce fire can destroy it.'

'You mean it's unbreakable?'

'Everything can be broken. But the blacksmiths haven't discovered yet what will break this.'

'How do they make 'em?'

Saarem and Verdi chuckled at his innocence.

'Forging Invelmari steel is a great secret,' Klaus explained solemnly. 'There are several kinds, some only just passable, some very fine. But even the worst Invelmari steel is stronger than any other metal. The very finest is never sold and kept only in Invelmar, reserved for Ealdormen and Isarnanheri.' Klaus resheathed the sword. 'But more important than the weapon is the one who wields it. A good warrior will be more dangerous with a plank of wood than an idiot with this.'

'Then I oughter begin soon,' Fibbler declared.

'We don't put blades in the hands of children in these parts,' a Derindman muttered. 'In the South little boys are better off helping feed the horses and cleaning the wagons. Why does a chronicler need a blade, anyway?'

Catching his eye, Fibbler meekly scuttled off, though whether it was to heed his warning or to avoid the chores he'd threatened remained to be seen. Ravi, decidedly a firm friend of the child, darted after him. Verdi leaned forward to catch his oceloe and missed.

'What's that?'

The talisman Verdi wore on a leather cord around his neck swung into view. It was something Elodie had delicately left rather than gifted him on her fourteenth nameday.

Verdi's fingers closed around it. 'A walrus tooth, for protection.'

A hiss of disapproval rose from several of the Derindin gathered in the sparse shade. Verdi's cheeks warmed. To make matters worse, he realised Alizarin was repairing his saddle nearby.

'Do you really think such a thing brings protection, hanging about your neck like that?'

'No,' Verdi replied hotly. 'But it was a gift from a dear friend.'

This did little to appease the Derindman. 'You, of all people, ought to know better.'

Alizarin glanced up then, and the man fell silent.

Another Derindman shook his head. 'How can anyone believe a bit of dead beast can bring luck?'

Verdi shrank into himself. *I can't get anything right here.* For one wild moment he wished they were back in Dunraven, where no one paid him any attention hiding behind Klaus.

'Hush, Ferinc,' a woman replied. 'It's just a trinket.'

'Not to them,' Ferinc retorted. 'Northerners think wearing a bit of snowlion or a shrivelled bear claw will protect them. How, I'd like to know?'

Klaus folded his map away. 'Not all of us. I don't believe these objects have any power except in the mind.'

Ferinc, a Lebasi cloth merchant, seemed grudgingly placated. But another Derindman leaned forward in the doorway of his wagon, lowering his pipe to speak

'Right you are, Master Invelmari, but some things *do* have great power. Granted not by men or women, mind, but by the Great Sentience. Things that are lost, misused or no longer used at all – like that lodestone device that vanished in the North.'

'The Umari instrument?'

'That's the one. Oh, the things Orenthians once made.' The man sighed through his pipe. 'If ever a thing was to be made well, it was made here in the South. Then it was taken up North or across the Sourgrass Sea and they'd try to make more of its like.'

Derindin nodded around them.

'The Redrawers were good at one thing only: taking what wasn't theirs,' growled Ferinc. 'Looted everything they could get their hands on.'

Verdi's heart sank. Everything fanned the flames of the Derindin's discontent into a fully-fledged furnace.

'I thought no one knew what the instrument does,' Klaus replied mildly.

'Much was known once, now all gone. More secrets than water in the river.'

Verdi braced himself. Any mention of the Ninvellyn was sure to unleash yet more sourness. Fortunately, Ayla signalled their midday rest was over, and they returned to their wagons. To Verdi's surprise, his uncle lingered. Alizarin hardly seemed to notice him most of the time. He nodded at the Invelmari dagger at Verdi's belt.

'May I?'

Verdi handed it to him. Alizarin unsheathed it, looking over it with a far more discerning eye than Fibbler's. It was perfectly measured for Verdi's hand, arm span and height. The rare mammoth bone hilt was plain enough that only close inspection revealed its true value – the only reason Verdi had been able to risk taking it from Dunraven at all. But there was no disguising the calibre of the blade; the finest many-layered steel of Invelmar, forged for Ealdormen and sold to none.

His uncle murmured, 'That is a very fine blade.'

Verdi's cheeks reddened. 'It was a gift from Lady Wintermantel. She had it made for me.'

'Did she, now.' Alizarin raised an eyebrow, returning the dagger. 'A very generous gift to bestow upon the Derindin servant of an imposter.'

'She was very kind to me.'

'Evidently kinder to you than to your friend.'

Alizarin walked away, and Verdi felt dismissed. Another opportunity wasted. *Am I ever going to learn what happened to my parents? Why I was sent North?*

In Dunraven he'd accepted that he would never know. Perhaps that had been better than this torment of *possibility*. Still holding a mouthful of questions he hardly dared spit out, he rejoined his friends on the wagon.

*

Fireside, it was easy to retreat into the shadows. Klaus learned more in these resting hours than by day. In the soft music and pipe smoke, the Derindin became readable.

Arik stretched out beside him, content for now to have escaped the Arm of the Court, a diplomatic marriage and his uncles. He whittled away at a chunk of deadwood. Arik had always had a natural ease. In some ways they were an unlikely pairing; Arik broke every Ealdormen's rule that Klaus kept. He wouldn't feel the absence of the North the way Klaus did now: like a crippling and inescapable ache, always burning at the periphery of consciousness.

A grey shadow erupted silently from the birdkeeper's wagon nearby, disappearing into the deepening night.

Arik watched the bird vanish. 'Do they worship them?'

'Birds?' Klaus considered this. 'I think they envy them.'

'Fibbler! Don't go chasing it, it's gone hunting.' Mayda wagged her finger at the child. 'Not unless you want to be disturbing Elenhem.'

Arik glanced at Meron. 'Who?'

'What we call the lost clans.' Meron smiled. 'A ghost story to frighten children who've not yet learned to respect the desert.'

It certainly helped rein in Fibbler, who finally sat by Terim's wagon fidgeting with his bowl, waiting for stew. The birdkeeper, however, leaned close so his voice wouldn't carry.

'No ghost story.' He gazed beyond the fire to where darkness smudged the boundary between land and sky. 'Elenhem is as real as the wind.'

'What are the lost clans?' Klaus asked.

'All the families and bloodlines that have perished,' the birdkeeper replied in his papery voice. 'Once there were many more than just ten clans. All slain. All restive.'

'Not the Second Redrawing again,' Arik murmured under his breath. He had underestimated the birdkeeper's hearing; a man who lived partly for the sounds of his many birds.

However, the birdkeeper shook his head. 'Far worse than that. Darkness visited this place long before the invasion from the North or the damming of the river. *'The noose or the North,'* my people say now. That is who they curse; Northmen and their dam that killed the river. But some of us remember what came before the dam. And worse will come again.'

'What do you mean?'

But the birdkeeper would say no more. Klaus shivered, and not for the evening chill. Inevitably his mind turned to Elodie. *Dear Sturmsinger, keep her safe from suspicion over her part in our escape.* For the sake of the Sturmsinger Chain and the sanctity of the Blood Pact, Invelmar's five royal houses regarded the safety of all Ealdormen as paramount as their own. And the Wintermantels would risk no harm to their only heiress.

But no matter what reassurances he'd given Verdi, Klaus was still afraid.

Her spirit will be broken. His former place in the Chain had robbed him of something he would never have back: the light-footed freedom of youth. What little reprieve Elodie had had from this would be over now.

*

Every child was told stories of the great forge of Stahlaz. Its location was a guarded secret known only to very few; its steel the finest in the world. The smiths and miners who lost their lives now and then in its great fire pits or maze of tunnels were heroes, immortalised as shards of light amongst the Northern constellations. In the heavens they joined the table of Sturmsinger himself, their triumphant afterlife song said to echo in the blows of every ounce of Invelmari steel produced by the forge, striking fear in the flesh of foes and igniting strength in Invelmari hearts.

At his first visit, Klaus had been seven.

It was a dark beast of a place, alive with the screeching of metal and the hissing of steam. Men worked at great bellows and pushed carts laden with wood and coal and ore. The heavy fall of yellow water in its gullet was the artery that fed its machinery. A mighty place that fumed and spluttered with acrid smoke; mighty and terrible both.

Klaus remembered the Forgemaster well: Fridumar Greydove, a tower of a man with the thickest forearms he had ever seen, who was a quiet-spoken incarnation of his forge. A man of humble roots but the noblest blood, Father said, and greatly honoured by the Ealdormen. Metal danced between his fingers, which were capable of such delicate movement though rough with scars. He seemed to see every fragment of steel, to meld not with his hands but his presence.

Arik, nearly nine and settled into his Form, was enthralled, his eyes as bright as the smelting fires.

'When you return a fully-fledged Warrior, Lord Prospere, I will make you a sword called Thunraz that will be the mightiest in a generation,' Fridumar told Arik. They watched his hammer fall on a battered anvil, effortlessly forming it into part of a breastplate for the new armour Father had commissioned for Lady Wintermantel. He annealed the piece again in his furnace and lifted it carefully with his tongs, dipping it into water with a hiss. The din of countless hammers rang around them, echoing throughout the forge.

'And for Klaus?' asked Arik hopefully.

'And for Prince Ulfriklaus. But he will have no need of it.' The Forgemaster paused then. 'You, Prince Ulfriklaus, will one day wield a weapon bearing three jewels far superior to anything I or this ironstone could make.'

Arik scoffed, 'What on earth could possibly be greater than Invelmari steel?'

Klaus waited eagerly to hear more. But the Forgemaster did not reply, raising his hammer once again in the sacred song of the North.

*

Three days into the grasslands they reached Ilmen, a shanty town that sprung up like a patch of weeds around a large spring where caravans stopped for water.

'This area was famed for its vineyards and cotton farms,' Meron told them. 'They live on charity now.'

The grassland around Ilmen was baked dry as chalk. Its inhabitants fashioned their shacks from whatever they could find – old wagon parts, broken crates, deadwood and skeleton grass, all bound with mud. Shacks huddled together like a tired herd. Ragged screens fluttered across open doorways of dwellings shared by man and beast alike. Emaciation gave the town's inhabitants a false appearance of height, thin arms and legs lost in rags.

Here there was nowhere for two Northerners to hide.

Children played with a skipping rope. A handful of sheep grazed around the spring, as lean as their keepers. The shanty Derindin greeted the caravan with familiarity.

'What news, Alizarin?'

'None worth repeating, Joyen. Except for those blasted pirates.'

Their eyes burrowed into Klaus, utterly empty. Their resignation was more troubling than any measure of hostility.

'Invelmari,' Klaus heard one man tell his fellows in Derindask.

The man had at least seven decades on him, and sat on an upturned bucket braiding rope with a youth. Their faces were dull, as though even the flame of animosity couldn't kindle some display of emotion. Faces so worn, they'd long stopped caring.

'I don't think we're very welcome here,' Arik murmured as they helped unload empty water barrels.

Klaus set down a full barrel. 'Is that what you see?'

The spring formed a small lake thronged with grasses; the most water they'd seen since leaving Noisy Tree. Green growth rimmed the lake, but without an irrigation system to the surrounding land, it was an island of incarcerated life. The horses drank as they refilled the water wagons. They washed their faces gratefully in the sun-warmed lake, though Klaus felt uneasy lingering by the water. *We've no right to share this.*

An old woman knelt amongst the rushes, eyes veiled with the white film of blindness. She gripped a waterskin in one hand and leaned forward, reaching for the surface of the water with the other. Klaus drew closer.

'Here.' He took her waterskin and dipped it into the water, waiting for the air in its belly to bubble out as it filled. 'This shouldn't be your work.'

84

The woman smiled with a serenity those unseeing eyes could only know so long as they were robbed of the yellow desolation of the Plains.

'You are not Derindin.' Her voice was as thin as the whispering of the grasses.

He was glad she couldn't see him. 'No.'

'But you are kind.' She straightened slowly, leaning on his arm. 'It is kindness that's a foreigner in these parts. May ilnurhin brighten your shadow in all the corners of the world.' She touched Klaus' forehead, then the corner of his eye, then his chest. 'These will be your eyes.'

'Come, nonna.' Joyen took the waterskin from him and led her away from the lake.

'Why do they stay out here?' Arik asked Suman when they returned to their wagons. 'Surely the Plains have more to offer than this.'

'Their ancestors were expelled from the Paiva. Even if they had the means, they will not travel further away from their birthright.'

'Then why don't they go to the border towns?' asked Verdi.

'They can buy and sell nothing. They are not wanted there.'

Arik interjected, 'By Akrindans? The border towns aren't theirs to choose who stays.'

Suman's mouth twisted, halfway between grin and grimace. 'The border townsfolk will share the bottom of the valley with no one, least of all with beggars, which is the only work they'll allow these people. Or would you have them take in all those the North cast out?'

'There's plenty of room around the dam,' Arik objected.

'True,' Alizarin agreed blandly. 'Invelmari settlers retreated north long ago, when they missed their drink and tired of our women. They left the valley to traitors and thieves who grabbed it and drove the Paivans out. Now the Paivans are barred from challenging clan Akrinda for their own land – by the banner your Queen flies over the border towns.'

Arik raised an eyebrow. 'There'd be no need for any challenge if the market towners looked after their own kind. They're all Derindin, aren't they?'

'Are they? In the border towns, a sprinkle of intermarrying around the dam is over-remembered. Akrinda forgot long ago where their forebears came from.' Alizarin spared them another humourless smile. 'We have a saying in the South: a drop of Northern blood taints a whole tree of Southern seed.'

'Derindin don't need enemies like us,' Arik muttered when Alizarin and Suman departed. 'They have each other.'

Mildly, Klaus replied, 'We drove them out first. We dammed the river and the river was their lifeblood.'

He stopped Alizarin before he returned to bid Joyen farewell, holding out a wrapped sweetmeat.

'He won't refuse you. Make sure he knows it's for the blind woman.'

Alizarin asked, 'From where shall I say it came?'

'Tell him that for a long time it was lost and has now been returned.'

Buried inside the fig-paste nugget, the twist of paper containing a ruby unpicked from Elodie's trinket box would be unmissable. Klaus rejoined his friends in the wagon, where Ravi lay splayed on Verdi's lap, his tiny belly bloated with fresh water.

He returned to the road gladly, wishing he could as easily leave his shame behind.

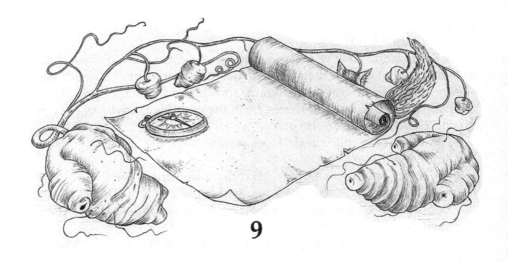

9

The Hallowed Harvest

HE VOWED NO WRONG WOULD GO UNPUNISHED, NO BLOOD DEBT
UNPAID. THUS, IN HIS SECOND DECADE, THE LIFEGIVER REWARDED
STURMSINGER WITH JARNSTIGA: THOSE SACRED STEPS
THAT SAFEGUARD WARRIORS FROM STUMBLE.

SONNONFER: THE RISE OF ANSOVALD STURMSINGER

The desert crept up on them in degrees. Waves of balding yellow grassland faded gradually into gentle dunes tufted with scorched brush. The sun raked the land with searing claws, and the daytime sky emptied of clouds to unmask a perfect and ruthless blue.

'This may be your last chance to fill your water skins for a while,' Alizarin warned when they stopped at a waterhole hidden by thorn bushes. If there was water to be found, the Derindin knew its coordinates, some of which were jealously guarded. They gave the horses a long drink before refilling the kegs in the water wagon.

Verdi recalled the mulberry water seller. 'What are water tokens?'

A couple of the Derindin hissed, scowling darkly.

'Pirates have started bartering water for tokens,' said Suman. 'They stalk waterholes and springs, hoping to take advantage of desperate travellers.'

'On pirate land?'

'Pirate land? They've no land. The only land any Derindin can claim as theirs is what they or their clan can defend. That's our *ghabala* for you – the cursed law of grab-and-defend, and the only law that prevails in the Plains. Some of the waterholes are in the middle of nowhere. They're no one's, and therefore everyone's.'

Arik sealed a full barrel. 'Does no one have the authority to stop the pirates?'

Suman's laugh was brittle. 'The only authority in the Plains is the might of the sword. A few years ago you could cross the desert safely, but bandits have grown commonplace. Now we must take soldiers everywhere we go.'

Mayda frowned. 'Why do you ask about water tokens, Master Viridian?'

Verdi blushed, already regretting his question. 'Someone tried to sell them to us in Noisy Tree.'

Her face darkened. 'Those bloody Akrindans! They've allowed the practice to take hold, peddling tokens like rolls of bread. If only your uncle had had better luck with them.'

They moved on as soon as they'd refilled. Daylight was precious, and there was never time to linger.

'What did she mean about my uncle?' Verdi asked Meron at supper, glancing across the fire to where Alizarin sat with Suman.

'Your uncle is Elendra's envoy. He tried to reach an agreement with the Chieftain of Akrinda. Their talks didn't go as he had hoped.'

Envoy! Why did no one bother tell him anything? *No wonder he's always so tense.* 'What were the talks about?'

'The tax that Akrinda levy on all Derindin trade across the border.'

Arik sat up. 'What, in addition to the taxes paid to the Invelmari crown?'

Meron nodded.

'But they're Derindin!'

Verdi's indignant exclamation was louder than he'd intended, drawing curious glances.

'When it suits them.' Meron puffed on his pipe. 'The distance between Akrinda and the rest of the clans is greater than a desert crossing. Only Akrinda managed to keep a foothold in Invelmar after the Second Redrawing, and they guard their luck jealously. Invelmari may have driven Derindin out of the Paiva first, but after the war it was Akrinda who continued the expulsion of all clans but their own. Hardly out of loyalty to the Invelmari crown, mind. They did the Northerners' work out of greed, and were allowed to keep their foothold around the dam in reward. There are few things the clans agree on, but on Akrinda they're united: south of the dam, there's very little love for the market towners.'

Verdi had met Akrindans in Dunraven; amongst the court jesters were at least two, and they were always mirthful and malleable. *Oily.* Perhaps they had no loyalties at all.

Arik looked unsurprised by this. 'What does Elendra want? A waiver of the levy on trade?'

'Ha! Not a snowball's hope in the desert of that, if you ask me. But clan Akrinda would be valuable trade allies if they could be wooed. Their support of our merchants would have put Elendra and its allies in an enviable position. It was a big gamble, and now there'll be a price to pay for trying. Some believe that even approaching them amounts to treachery.'

Verdi asked warily, 'Does that mean war?'

Meron gave him a curious look. Verdi blushed. War was common currency in Invelmar; the Isarnanheri were loaned to serve campaigns throughout the Parts, sometimes even on both sides of the same battle.

'You will discover there are countless ways for clans to punish each other without throwing a single knife.' Meron smiled sadly. 'Now that you are returned at last, I pray we don't disappoint you.'

'I knew your uncle's been hiding something,' said Arik darkly after Meron bid them goodnight.

'You can see why,' Verdi replied defensively.

'*Taxes.*' Arik scowled. 'If the Queen knew how overreaching they've become, she'd expel them all.'

Klaus hardly looked up from his map. 'She knows. It's the price we pay for ensuring the market towners continue to keep a solid border for us. And a payment they earn for themselves without disturbing the royal coffer. Seamless.'

It was the first time Klaus had spoken all evening. His former master had once again burrowed into his secrets and his maps, his mind veiled. *He will always be an Intelligencer now,* Verdi thought sadly. *No matter how far we run from the North.*

*

'Klaus,' said Arik quietly. 'Why does Ayla seem to think we're guarding Verdi?'

The question hooked Klaus out of a quiet contemplation of what trials Elodie's Jurist Form might be enduring now, wedged as she was between her parents' treason and Adela's blistering justice. He looked up from his map. A cluster of acacias hosted them with the most midday shade they'd encountered for days, and the caravan was resting.

'That's why they tolerate us,' Arik added. 'She thinks we're in his service.'

'Alizarin's been playing with fire by talking with these Akrindans,' said Klaus. 'The consequences may be more dangerous than we realise. Maybe Alizarin's happy to let people believe we're here to bolster their guard.'

'But why would *Verdi* need a guard? No one knew he was coming, either. And you've told them you're a chronicler, not a soldier.'

Verdi was curled up with his formulary in the wagon nearby. *He's certainly received a very warm welcome.* But Verdi was a Chieftainess' great-nephew. Once again the question nagged at Klaus: why had he been sent North, away from a position of privilege?

'Screwhorn!'

The cry came from one of the wagons. A short-legged antelope with long twisted horns stood on the dunes.

A handful of Derindin sprang into their saddles. Too late to overtake the antelope; its pale coat was soon lost in clouds of dust. But as the dust settled, a dark smudge appeared in the brush: the rest of the herd.

Arik grabbed his horse's reins. Notes abandoned, Verdi followed. Riding with two of the Derindin, they separated a buck from the herd. Arik's longsword swung; shouts of excitement rang out. Klaus dropped to a knee in the sand, nocking a bolt to the string of his crossbow. Face to the eyescope, he calculated the moment his target would meet his bolt, and let it loose. His prey buckled in the midst of the fleeing herd.

'Two bucks! Two bucks!'

Fibbler jumped up and down beside him, watching the Derindin carry them back. Klaus retrieved his bolt from the buck's flank. Children hopped from foot to foot as the Derindin set about a masterful butchery. No parts of the animals were wasted.

Verdi patted his mare, face flushed. 'She's like a bolt of lightning!'

'Good work!' Meron clapped Arik's shoulder. 'There's little time to stalk deer, with the winds so close behind us.'

That night, tongues loosened and laughter came easily with the aroma of roasting meat. A few more of the Derindin greeted the Northerners around the fire. Fibbler and the other children ran back and forth as Terim turned the roasting spits. Each time Mayda shooed them away, they darted off making long hyena cries, until exasperated mothers threatened them into some useful task, leaving Fibbler scampering about the camp.

'Where are his parents?' Klaus asked Mayda, watching Fibbler chase Ravi around the fire.

'He's got none.' Mayda's wagon was the hub of the children's play, her little oil-paper parcels of treats often finding their way into grubby hands. 'He was orphaned in one of the villages, and he's stayed with us since. No Derindin child will be finding themselves alone.' She stretched dough into sheet-bread to cook on hot stones over the fire, her hands kneading it with a fierceness that belied her gentle face.

Fibbler finally settled down by the spits with a waiting bowl; a ragged little bird of a boy. *I could just as easily have been him.* Klaus' appetite vanished.

'People are the same wherever you go,' Meron remarked, cleaning his pipe. 'If you fill their bellies, they'll remember you more fondly.'

Klaus asked, 'What's ilnurhin?'

Meron looked up in surprise. 'I believe your people call it *slight matter*. You'd be much better off asking Suman. Elendrans study sciences. Mantelon are the desert's philosophers.'

Suman sat across the fire with Alizarin. Klaus had learned he was envoy to Mantelon.

'We may have a name for it, but in the North talk of slight matter is forbidden,' he said. 'Any study of the Lost Sciences is conducted only by the court's Engineers, and even that is restricted. Perhaps that's how they've become lost.'

Meron inhaled on his refilled pipe. 'In the South there is nothing "lost" about them.'

Good eating mellowed the camp. It was at these firesides that Klaus teased out the spirit behind the Derindin's stony faces. They were passionate, dignified, easily roused by fury or mirth. Their music stirred dark creatures in his heart, unearthing nostalgia for something he'd never realised he had lost, and more – anger, anguish; serpents that slept in his loins. A Derindwoman laughed across the camp. For a moment, she summoned the shape of Gerlinde through the smoke, her golden hair a lick of the flames.

Ferinc leaned across empty bowls. 'Northern blademasters are known the world over. But I've never seen a crossbow used so well, and of all places in the hands of a chronicler.'

Klaus received the compliment with a bow of his head. 'In Involar every boy is given a weapon to master when he begins learning his letters. Most girls, too.'

Someone snorted.

'So that's how you raise a nation of warmongers,' said Osringen, a Fraivonian. Someone elbowed him; Osringen ignored this. 'I'll not pick any battles, but the truth's the truth, whether it's popular or not.'

'Far Northern raiders have raped and plundered many villages since the Queen's peace treaty with Täntainen was broken,' said Arik. More of the Derindin fell quiet to listen. 'Would you have those villagers unable to defend themselves from attack?'

'What right does the Crown have to make of every man a soldier, his mind shaped for war before it is full of understanding? Even a farmer –' Osringen jerked his head at Klaus. 'Even a chronicler!'

'Every boy born to Invelmar belongs to the Crown,' said Arik. 'A sacrifice worth making to protect the kingdom.'

There was muttering around the fire. Klaus glanced at Arik warily, wondering if the Warrior had realised yet what parts of him the desert had polished.

'Sacrifice,' repeated Osringen to his companions. 'That's why war runs in their blood, they're damn well reared on it. They don't stand a chance of knowing any different, and I suppose we can't entirely blame them for their ways. Sacrifice, you call it. I call it heartless.'

'Is it heartless to protect the weak?' Arik challenged.

A Derindwoman interjected, 'You protect the might of Invelmar, not the weak.'

'Might is our reward. And it brings bounty to all. There are no shanty towns in the North.'

'But at any price?' asked another Derindman. 'Take those Prosperes whose heir was found dead with the prince. A soldier, like his mother. She was packed off to the Sterns on a mission when the boy was still at the breast, and captured by Far Northerners. Set ablaze there, they say, after they tore her limb from limb.' A woman shuddered. 'Now, who would sacrifice a young mother of their own blood for glory? And for what – the ice? You say it's barely habitable.'

'As habitable as the bare sand,' murmured Suman.

'Now her son is just as dead. And if he had lived they'd have likely buried him under the mountains too. This is the way of the North.'

Ferinc jibed, 'Arm of the Court doesn't reach so far after all.'

'So you see, Master Invelmari, what we see in the North, we do not envy.'

The firelight thankfully softened the stony silence of Arik's face.

Klaus spared him a reply. 'If Far Northerners are left to their own devices, they'll grow bolder, and skirmishes will become war. As you've just told, the Ealdormen sacrifice their own blood for common folk far from their castles in Dunraven. A noble trade, is it not?'

Ferinc puffed on his pipe.

'Perhaps, Master Invelmari, but blood shouldn't be so cheap.'

'Ealdormen,' a Derindwoman half-whispered. 'They say they're not quite human. Maybe even more than human.'

'Rubbish,' grumbled Osringen. 'The same blood runs in royal veins as in every peasant from here to the Sterns.'

'Nothing to do with the blood ... it's the *Forms*. The creatures they carry.'

'Creatures?'

'Children of the pacts they make with the devil to grow demons of their own. From where else do they draw their power?'

Ferinc waved a hand dismissively. 'Forms are just royal ranks. They're mind games and training, that's all.'

'I tell you, it's uncanny,' a Derindman interjected, shivering. 'Ever seen an Ealdorman up close? I did once, in Pengaza. A Jurist. Her look stripped you to your bones … sure she could see the thoughts in my head.'

Broco smirked. 'Maybe that was your guilty conscience. I'll bet some of those thoughts that go through your head would earn you a good flogging.'

The Derindin laughed.

'They're not half so bad as those Intelligencers,' said Sora, an Elendran horse mistress. 'Shapeless, like water filling a cup. I'm sure they exchange their souls for a bit of shadow to wear. Not even Isarnanheri are so eerie, and everyone knows they're barely human.'

'Oh, everyone does, does they?'

'Northern flesh may be built stronger, but it bleeds and bruises just like any other,' said Ferinc gruffly through his smoke. 'Northmen train hard, there's no mystery to it.'

'What d'you say, Master Marcin?' asked Sora. 'Are they human?'

'Ealdormen?' Arik's smile hovered between amusement and disdain. 'As you say, they're trained from the cradle. The mind has an incredible power over the flesh. There are weak Ealdormen as well as masterful ones. But of course they're human.'

The Derindin argued next about the price of Hesperi lamp oil. Klaus glanced warily at Arik again, but whatever the Warrior hid, it was buried deep beneath the black ice of his Form.

*

'Strike lower,' said Arik. 'You can move faster than that. On your toes!'

Fibbler joined them for sparring sessions almost daily now. Arik found him an old wooden slat and fashioned a handle at one end, around which Verdi had wrapped a rag so he wouldn't get splinters. ('In the beginning, the weapon is the least important thing,' Klaus had reassured him.) He was small, but nimble and attentive. Klaus smiled to himself, glimpsing the excitement of his own first day of training in the child's earnest face. The cavity in his heart throbbed.

'Good swordsmanship begins in the feet. Moving your own, watching those of your opponent,' Arik told the little boy as he plopped onto the ground, panting. He ruffled his hair. 'We'll make a swordsman of you yet.'

Fibbler raised his wooden slat. 'I'm sure I could do better with a real sword.'

Arik smiled. 'Do you think the swords that made the Blood Pact were any finer than a humble soldier's battered blade?' He twirled his own wooden stick with absolute control. 'It's the mind that moves the blade. And nothing can make up for time and practice.'

'What's the Blood Pact?'

'Not heard of it before?'

Fibbler grinned. 'Only in between a lot of cursing. More cursing than anythin' else...'

Arik kept a straight face. 'Everyone tells the version of the world that they know. Sometimes they don't know very much at all.'

'They knew a lot of cursing I en't ever heard before.'

Verdi hid a smile behind his book.

'Let's see,' said Arik. 'Did you ever hear the name Ansovald Sturmsinger between all this cursing?' Fibbler shook his head. 'No? I'm surprised. He was a Far Northerner who allied the five most powerful tribes of the North with his own army and created Invelmar. He led the Second Redrawing.'

Fibbler frowned. 'He fought us Southerners, then.'

'Before that, he and his armies fought both Northern and Far Northern tribes who didn't want to join his alliance.'

'Did he win?'

'Oh yes. That's how Invelmar was born. But a lot of life was lost before the war was won – entire houses forgotten, villages and towns emptied. Now, on the night of Ansovald's victory feast, a spaewife brought him a gift to thank him for saving her life.'

'What's a spaewife?'

'A seer who tells the future. Her gift was a vision. She warned Ansovald and his wife Dagmar that after so much life had been sacrificed to *make* the new kingdom, Invelmar would be destroyed if his allies ever returned to fighting each other.'

'Why?' the child demanded.

'The dead asked the Lifegiver to curse Invelmar with ruin if any more blood was shed to break the kingdom they died to build. They demanded peace as repayment for their lost lives. The Lifegiver granted their wish. And that led to the Blood Pact: a vow Ansovald and his allies took to always keep the peace.'

Fibbler's eyes were as enormous as Ravi's, transfixed. Arik rapped Fibbler's wooden stick with his, disarming him.

'Always be on your guard!'

Fibbler scrambled to retrieve it. 'And then Ansovald became king?'

'He was never crowned. He and his army died while extending their conquest south. Dagmar died, too. Some say she pined away when he never returned. His allies agreed to take turns ruling over Invelmar for three generations each, in the Sturmsinger Chain. They're the five houses of Ealdormen who govern now in Dunraven.'

Too young still for genuine hatred, Fibbler was fascinated. The story was the earliest one Klaus could remember, having heard it countless times at his nurse's knee. Like all good stories it had cast a spell on him then, becoming deeply rooted long before he was old enough for uncomfortable questions to form in the corners of his mind.

'What about Ansovald?' said Fibbler. 'Didn't he have any family?'

'He was from one of the few Far Northern tribes willing to ally with Northerners. Rival Far Northerners burned his village down in revenge for betraying them. None of his children survived.'

'That's not fair! Who's the ruling family now?'

'House Rainard. Queen Adela's the third generation to rule for them.'

'So another family takes over when she dies?'

Arik glanced at Klaus. 'Yes.'

'Who –'

'I reckon that's enough for one day.' Arik stood. 'Keep up your exercises.'

'Can't we do some more?'

'For a little while.'

And so time passed in the dunes. They rode, stopped for meals, and always rested at noon when the sun was at its blistering zenith. Sometimes the Invelmari sparred while the caravan slept, swapping snow for searing sun. Fibbler joined them, eager to practise with his wooden slat. Sometime the tumblers watched, fingering their own blades, occasionally engaging in a duel.

'You should set your sights higher than a child,' Ayla told them one afternoon. 'There are many who could learn from you. Better than wasting your talents on cheap contracts and gamblers' fighting rings.'

Klaus glanced at Arik, who despite his grumbling would be content to put his blade to good use. For a time, at least, until the blood of Prospere awoke in his veins and agitated him to some cause or another.

'I don't think we'd be welcome,' Arik told her, just as Klaus replied, 'We left those ambitions behind in the North.'

Ayla's face was unreadable. 'You may find that in Samsarra, a soldier makes his own welcome.'

*

Days were faceless on the shore of the desert. Waves of dry yellow grass rolled by seemingly without end as the caravan trundled on. The Derindin were patient travellers. They carved through heat and dust and thirst by day, and navigated the stars by night. It was easy to adopt their simple routine: gathering firewood, collecting what meagre edibles they found amongst the scrawny vegetation, feeding the horses, fetching what water they encountered. Measuring the wind. Alizarin regularly sampled the desert sand, and Meron collected specimens for his research – a bit of root, vials of soil, seed pods.

'Sour fennel,' Meron told Klaus triumphantly after one of his prowls. 'A bloat absorbent. It's all but vanished in the South. I'll try to propagate it in Samsarra.'

Meron was especially proud of Elendra's seed bank. It was the largest in the Plains, he said, describing the painstaking development of drought-tolerant species that would thrive in the harshest reaches of the desert and withstand the blight of scorching wind. Klaus would have enjoyed these stories more were they not overshadowed by the ugly memory of the Ostraad that had spawned them.

'Why are the storms getting worse?' Klaus asked.

'No one knows. But all my work suggests it's linked to the decline of what green growth we still have. With so little vegetation to break the wind, I fear it gathers terrible force as it moves across the open desert. That's why the Arboretum is so precious.' Meron glanced heavenward. 'All we can do is have *namathra*, and hope rain arrives.'

Klaus nodded towards Meron's freshly-dug bulbs. 'Will those survive the journey?'

'I hope so. I ought to record an image for our archives in case they don't, but I've no talent for drawing. One of my students does all the illustrations. Her hand is marvellous.'

To Meron's delight, Klaus copied the bulb's likeness well enough. As he drew, Meron happily described Derinda's terrains. The Arboretum was in the east of Elendra's clandom, where the earth was veined with deposits of limestone and gained the groundwater flowing from the Sourgrass Sea east of Derinda. The Plains were as inconstant as the clans. Often, the caravan followed trails that disappeared under dunes at the whim of the wind. Sometimes, they favoured winding detours around suspicious ground where the horses' hooves seemed to sense the approach of deep ruts or sinksand.

It was a land as barren as the North was abundant, but as empty as a clean page in a forgotten book. There'd been no sign yet of the dreaded wind. Klaus had never felt anything like this bleak tranquillity before. But it burnished rather than buried his gnawing ache for the green breath of Invelmar.

So he started a map.

It began with longing for the North. He gazed over the dunes as they rolled by, emptying his mind of thoughts. If he didn't focus on any single spot, the dunes melted into ribbons of dusty gold, and his mind drifted away until the unfettered particles of his consciousness flowed as easily as the innumerable grains of sand. Thus the land imprinted itself first onto his mind, then onto parchment.

While the others duelled or chatted over cards, he sharpened his pencil, drew upon every memory he had of Invelmar, and preserved each passing hour for his parchment. Later, he would immortalise it in ink, but not yet. Onto the page he put the memory of cold northern mountain crags and hidden cave entrances buried in snow; the twists and turns of the four Invelmari rivers; the rich green entrails of the Paiva. Fibbler or the Derindin would sometimes sit beside him, watching his map grow. He drew the gush of the Ninvellyn past the border market towns. At a tangent to Noisy Tree, he marked the Ostraad with a stubborn smudge of lead. Then he began again with the grasses and dunes and the rolling hills of the Plains.

'It is an uncommon eye that can so clearly summon the land,' the birdkeeper told him.

They'd paused to escape the midday sun under a huddle of eucalyptus trees. A sweet-throated grassthrush rested in the branches above them, offering soft interjections.

'Good instruments and many measurements do the work for me.'

'But it seems you do not forget a thing once you have seen it,' said the birdkeeper. 'No doubt the memory of a chronicler serves you well. Is that where you learned cartography?'

Klaus glanced at his parchment. Making maps was something he had always had, like the colour of his eyes.

'No. It was just the next best thing to visiting new places and taking them home. Even if they're beyond all reach.' He paused. 'Foolish, I know.'

'Not foolish.' The little man smiled. 'What is a map, Master Tristan? Is it merely a means by which one man tells another what belongs to him? Or is it a reminder of the sacred duty that binds him to the boundaries entrusted to him?' He glanced up at the dozy grassthrush. 'These birds, would they see this map as you and I, or do they see a truer reality – of the promise of wind or haven, of good foraging, waiting peril... A land drawn not on divisions born of whim, but of necessity. A world built not on our demands of the land, but on *its* demands of *us*.'

Klaus lowered his pencil. 'You know something of the Simyerin, then.'

'The very first mapmakers understood all this. For them, a map was not for measuring kingdoms, but for the striking of symmetry. Without symmetry there can be no justice. Even the great Lorendar himself had to learn this.'

'Was he Simyerin?'

'No. He was the last Custodian in the South,' said the birdkeeper almost lovingly. 'A man who grew wise enough to remake himself before his doorway arrived. Few of us are so fortunate.'

Klaus shivered. For a moment he imagined an unintelligible current that flowed not from his mind onto the page, but washed back into him from the paper and ink. *The sun's getting to my head.* An indignant trill sounded overhead as Ravi displaced the grassthrush, and the tree shook with their ensuing argument. The birdkeeper laughed, but Klaus' finger hovered again over the smudge that was the Ostraad dam, momentarily as heavy-hearted as though he had delivered this grave injustice himself.

*

The dunes rolled on.

It was a wonder how the daytime heat contrasted so starkly with the freezing nights. At midday it found and seared every patch of bared skin. They took to wrapping cotton sand-masks around their faces like the Derindin, leaving just their eyes visible. Verdi's sand-mask caught both perspiration and the sharp sand kicked up by the wind and the horses. It was stifling, but he'd learned to be grateful for it.

'Will the water last?' Verdi asked his uncle. Even with the rationing, it seemed a tall order. His heart shook with sudden pity for these people, so dependent on scavenging trickles of water.

'So long as we stay on course,' Alizarin replied. 'There's a spring on the way in the Nerej oasis. Keep your eyes peeled for derina bush. That'll mark the way to the spring. Saved many a nomad's life, has derina.'

In the heat haze that shimmered over the dunes, it was difficult to imagine how they'd be able to spot the thorny thickets Meron had described.

'I've got a headache,' Arik groused after an hour of squinting at the ground. 'If anyone's going to see this blasted bush, it won't be me.' His waterskin was halfway to his lips before he thumped it down again.

'Stop staring at the sand,' Klaus suggested. 'And you're going to put a hole in that if you're not careful.'

Arik made a face but examined it for leaks.

Verdi pointed east, to their left. 'What's that?'

There wasn't even the slightest breeze. Hot air shivered almost visibly like a swarm of silver flies, blurring the horizon. If he peered hard, Verdi thought he could see the incomplete outlines of a building.

Klaus brightened. 'Ruins.'

A commotion came from the head of the caravan. Riders jumped down, some with shovels. They dismounted and joined the Derindin, who were crowding around a nondescript plant with small fleshy leaves of palest green.

'Well-spotted, Rasan,' Meron told a young tumbler of clan Periam.

Nearby were several more. The Derindin set about digging around the derina bushes until their shallow roots were exposed, careful not to touch the thorny stems. Under the hot sand were chains of leathery tubers the size of small melons.

Arik eyed the derina crop doubtfully. 'This is it?'

Rasan gave him a thin smile. 'Try not to sound *too* impressed.'

'Gather as many as you can,' Alizarin ordered. 'We're losing daylight.'

Rasan sliced her knife along a smaller tuber, releasing a trickle of faintly milky liquid. She offered it to Klaus and Verdi to taste. The nutty fluid inside, cool and fractionally more viscous than water, was refreshing.

'And mine?' Arik pouted as she walked away.

'Let's see,' said Klaus drily. 'It's almost like you just scorned the crop that's so important to these people, they took its name for themselves.'

The Derindin cut the tubers carefully at the stalk, avoiding damage to the long main stem. Meron picked up a section of the heavy ground-vine that sprouted them, trailing thin sheets of sand. It sprouted deeper roots piercing into the ground as well as trusses bearing more tubers, some connected by fibrous tendrils to the next plant. He tugged gently; a nearby patch of sandy ground rippled.

'The tubers must draw water from a source,' he explained. 'If you follow the vine, it'll lead to the spring that feeds it. Healthy vines mean a healthy water source. Even a short stretch of ground-vine can accurately predict the coordinates of nearby water. Take note of its course.'

They harvested as many tubers as they could. Suman and Meron plotted the growth pattern of the derina plants.

Klaus unloaded the last sack of tubers by Terim's wagon. Verdi wiped sweat from his forehead and gazed eastward again. The outline of ruins had grown clearer as the shimmer of heat abated.

'What's over there?' he asked Suman.

But Suman averted his eyes. 'May no step ever fall there again. Do not look.'

There was no time to wonder at this; they rode on, rejuvenated by their derina harvest – a reward for their *namathra*, the birdkeeper jubilantly proclaimed. Alizarin was keen to gain the last few hours of daylight, veering south-west with the derina tuber vines, aiming to intercept their water source.

They had to make camp earlier than usual, however, because by evening several of the Derindin had taken ill.

'Is it the tubers?' asked Verdi, watching Mayda soak dried leaves in boiled water. The concoction smelled awful, but he followed closely, eager to learn.

'No. They've been bitten by a saffbeetle. You find them around waterholes, and it takes a week or more for the sickness to show itself. Must have been bitten when we were in the grasslands.'

Two of the sick were children. One man developed a blotchy red rash beneath which his face and eyes were tinged with yellow. That night the Derindin erected a tent by the fire, for though saffbeetle fever wasn't contagious, it was easier to care for the sick in one place. A new anxiety stifled the caravan's relief.

*

By morning the camp was unnaturally quiet. Mayda prepared a thin salty soup for the sick. A woman whose little girl had fallen ill emerged from the sick tent.

'They're too sick to travel, Alizarin.' Her eyes were red from lack of sleep, her brow taut with worry.

'We'll stay here today, Verna,' he reassured her. 'Perhaps the rest will hasten their recovery.'

He craned his head skywards as she returned into the tent.

'What's he worried about?' Klaus asked Meron.

'The winds. So far we've been lucky, but time's getting on...'

That day the sun was relentless. It was difficult to imagine a storm disturbing the sweltering stillness. Trackers rode ahead and found more derina an hour's ride south-west of the camp, collecting as many tubers as they could carry. There was no surplus liquid; the sickness had increased the caravan's water requirements. Klaus rode out with a second party to harvest more, keen to see more of the land.

'There'll be water if we follow the derina,' Suman said firmly. The Derindin around him nodded.

They sheltered from the midday sun in a second larger tent they'd erected for shade. Leaving Verdi and Arik in the tent over a game of cards, Klaus returned to the quiet of their wagon. He found Ravi curled up beneath his map.

'What are you doing here?' He stroked the oceloe's head, eliciting a feeble meow. The little beast was dazed, his breathing fast and shallow.

Klaus filled a tin cup with derina water from his waterskin, into which
Ravi's face gratefully disappeared.

There was peace in plotting the map. It was the only peace Klaus
found now from thoughts of the Wintermantels. Correcting his scale, he
pencilled in the day's observations and marked the ruins. What did Suman
mean by telling them to look away? He left them unnamed.

Fibbler climbed into the wagon to sit beside him.

'Not sleeping?'

Fibbler shook his head. 'I hate day-sleeps. Fat waste of time. Mayda
told me off, said it was too hot to be hopping around like a rabbit.' He
fidgeted. 'Wish we would get to the oasis soon.'

'How are the sick ones doing?'

Fibbler's face fell. 'I dunno. Verna wouldn't let me go into the tent.
She been cryin' a lot. That can't be good.'

He watched Klaus draw for a few moments.

'That's amazing.' Fibbler pointed to the scale. 'What does this say?'

'Do you not know your letters, Fibbler?'

The little boy shook his head.

'Well, that won't do. I'll teach you.'

So Klaus pulled out fresh parchment and wrote the first three letters
of Invelmen script. Fibbler was clumsy with the pencil, gripping it in his
fist and moving his hand slowly, tongue caught between his teeth. After
a few minutes, however, he had memorised them. Ravi sat on the table
and watched, occasionally nibbling the parchment.

'This,' Klaus told him firmly, 'is better than a hundred swords. I'll
show you a few more every day until you know them all.'

Pleased with himself, the little boy nodded.

A thin sigh hissed through the stiff air.

Klaus' ears pricked immediately, though it was barely audible. He
lay a hand over Fibbler's arm, stilling the scratch of his pencil on the page.

It was too quiet.

A scream came from the tents.

In a heartbeat, Klaus was outside the wagon, crossbow in his hand.
He paused only to stop a pale-faced Fibbler from following him.

'Stay here. *Don't leave.*'

Klaus pulled his sand-mask up over his nose. The camp was huddled
against a great dune, sheltering the two tents and the wagons from the
worst of the sun, and his wagon was at its western periphery. Now there
were shouts. Voices he didn't recognise. He crept towards the tents,
stopping behind a wagon.

Alizarin and Saarem stood backed up against a wagon. A mounted
horseman faced them, masked, his sword drawn. Armed riders surrounded
the two tents. *They must have descended on us from beyond the dune.* Klaus

counted twenty of them. Several more waited further up on the dune, their bows aimed at the tent, where Meron knelt with his arms raised over his head. Riders herded caravaners around him, forcing them to their knees in the sand.

Pirates.

Klaus scanned the desert. Where was the tumbler keeping watch? His eyes fell on a pair of arrows protruding from a dark shape at the foot of the dune.

The mounted pirate gestured with his sword at the tents. 'Order the rest of them out.'

Alizarin drew a knife in reply. Saarem already had a sword in his hand.

The pirate's sand-mask muffled his laugh. An arrow flew through the air into the smaller tent, punctuated by a short scream.

'Disarm, or my men will fire on them all.'

Alizarin lowered his knife, dropping it on the ground and kicking it away. He spread his empty hands. His eyes could have sharpened flint. Reluctantly, Saarem followed.

Klaus had left Arik and Verdi in the tent. *Where are the tumblers?*

At a signal from their leader, one of the pirates lunged forward on his horse and slashed at the sick tent. Cries of alarm rang out as a panel fell away, revealing five makeshift beds, Mayda kneeling amongst them. She tried to hold back a terrified man as he struggled to sit up. One of the children began wailing.

'Please! They have saffbeetle sickness,' she cried.

The leader replied, 'Then you should be thankful if we kill them first.'

A scuffle broke out amongst the Derindin; they restrained Verna.

'What do you want?' said Alizarin. If he were angry, it didn't touch his composure. *He would have been a superb Intelligencer.*

'Your water tokens will buy you their lives,' said the leader. 'And everything else will buy your freedom.'

'There are no water tokens here.'

The pirate's eyes were just visible above the sand-mask; cold chips of shallow blue. 'I've heard about you fools, going where you like and expecting to pay nothing in return. Did you think turning a blind eye to our conditions would protect you? You must be from clan Sisoda or Elendra, or maybe Mantelon. Which is it?'

Alizarin said nothing.

'Fools.' The pirate jerked his head towards the wagons. 'Gather everyone where we can see them. Quickly, or I order my men to wet their blades.'

Klaus mounted a bolt to his crossbow. Beads of perspiration trembled on his brow.

The pirate archers pulled their bowstrings taut as Derindin stepped out of the other tent, hands raised. Verdi emerged with them, but there was still no sign of Arik or the tumblers. Verna started towards the dismantled sick tent with a strangled cry, and a pirate kicked her into the sand.

'Anger is a weapon that will just as easily turn on its source as its target.' Master Arnander had often reminded Klaus of this, perhaps mindful of the infamous Wintermantel rage ... unaware Klaus had nothing to fear from *that*, at least. This anger, though, would release toxic heat into his veins, triggering a racing of his heart and a tremor in his muscles that he couldn't afford. Klaus forced himself to keep Form.

'Check the tent and the wagons,' the leader barked. Three of his men began hacking at the tent's guide-ropes. One raised the curtain over the entrance.

Arik and the tumblers spilled out of the tent.

Klaus released his bolt. He had fit another before it hit, swinging round to shoot down the next archer, and the next.

The caravaners scattered in terror. The pirates recovered quickly, their leader screaming orders in Derindask. They closed around the tumblers, at an advantage on their horses. The tumblers moved around them deftly. Alizarin threw a handful of knives into the air; a pirate toppled from her saddle. Arik's longsword flashed in the sunlight through pirate and beast alike. Horses screamed, unseating riders. The tumblers fell upon them with full-bodied fighting, each moving as a single fist. Klaus downed the last archer and was about to exchange the crossbow for his sword when he spotted several bandits making for the remains of the sick tent.

Aim. Fire. Aim. Fire. Bolts flew home like diving birds.

One was injured but not killed. His horse kicked in fear, galloping towards the wagons.

'Stop him!' Verdi yelled, dragging a fallen Derindman aside.

Ayla and Saarem vanished after him. The tumblers made short work of the remaining raiders. Their ringleader felled a tumbler and broke away, screaming: 'See how far you get now, you bastards!'

The handful of surviving pirates fled through the caravan after him, slashing at the wagons as they galloped out towards open desert. Klaus chased them for a few paces before dropping to one knee in the sand. He fit another bolt into his crossbow. Arik pelted past him on a fallen pirate's horse, disappearing into their dust.

Three more of his bolts found their targets before Arik's horse got too close to the pirates to risk firing a fourth. Riders mingled, consumed by the heat haze and clouds of sand.

Broco stopped beside Klaus, catching his breath. 'What's he doing?'

White outbursts of light flashed as sun and steel met. Man and horse fell, momentarily lost in a great eruption of sand. Arik ran a second pirate down and felled his horse, but the third got away.

Klaus lowered his crossbow. His calf muscles cramped punishingly. Saarem threw the body of a pirate onto a dozen others. Klaus retrieved his bolts from their corpses.

The Derindin regathered to tend to the wounded and inspect the damage. At least two wagons had been smashed open. The sick tent was destroyed. The sick girl, Yenvin, lay quiet and pale, blood blossoming through her dress. Verna tried to shake the child awake. Fibbler had emerged from his hiding place and watched with terrified eyes.

Arik returned, dragging the ringleader beside him in the sand. Blood splattered his sand-mask. 'The last one escaped.'

'He'll be carrion food,' said Broco. 'There's no water and nowhere to go.'

The ringleader was caked in sand and bleeding from a crooked leg. Arik pulled him up onto his knees and unmasked him. His pallid face was clammy with blood loss.

He coughed up blood and teeth, then scraped together a feral grin.

'You'll never make it to the spring,' he managed hoarsely, swaying. Arik threw him back to the ground in disgust.

Suman pushed past the shaken caravaners. His face was pale, but not with anger. 'They hit the water barrels.'

It was the death blow the pirates had not managed to deal. Gasps were followed by an awful silence.

'We'll ride out for more derina in the morning,' said Alizarin.

The pirate laughed. Arik shoved down his own sand-mask. Invelmari steel fell. Pirate blood sprayed the dunes, and the desert drank without reluctance.

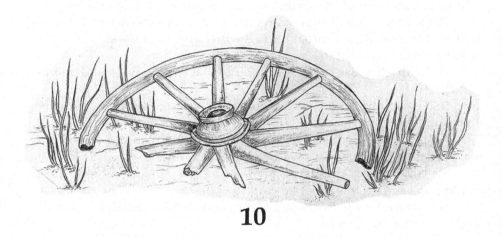

10

The Problem with Pirates

BY HIS THIRD DECADE, THE LIFEGIVER ENDOWED STURMSINGER'S
STEEL WITH SUCH STRENGTH THAT EVEN BARBARIANS WITH THEIR
BLOOD-AND-BONE MAGICK TREMBLED AT THE DIN OF HIS FORGE.

SONNONFER: THE RISE OF ANSOVALD STURMSINGER

There were three caravaners to bury. Klaus was only glad there weren't
more.

Verna curled up around her daughter, crooning comfort and prayer.
Yenvin had lost a lot of blood and was still poorly with saffbeetle fever.
Verdi cleaned and dressed a wound over her abdomen before helping
Mayda see to the rest of the injured.

Suman inspected the water wagon. Half of the few barrels that had
been full that morning were pierced, spilling much of the derina water
they'd painstakingly collected.

'The spring is close,' Alizarin reassured them. 'And it hasn't dried
up or soured.'

Arik looked around. They were in a sea of sand, adrift amongst dunes
that rose and fell as far as the eye could see. 'How can you be certain?'

'The derina plants *must* feed off a water source. The pirates were likely hanging around the spring, waiting to intercept those tracking it.'

All around were dismayed and dry-lipped faces, weary with travel and heat fatigue. Klaus' throat burned with thirst, but he was saving the derina water in his waterskin.

'Why do they use water tokens?' he asked. 'Why not just demand gold?'

'Gold can't be traced,' said Meron. 'Tokens can help them measure their influence.'

'We're losing daylight,' growled Osringen. 'You can yap later. What we need now is water or we won't make it to Romel.'

Rasan kicked a splintered barrel viciously. 'Bloody Elders! *They* could put a stop to this.'

She walked away in disgust. Osringen's face darkened, but Suman laid an arm on his shoulder.

'Then let's scout for more derina,' Klaus suggested.

'There are only a few hours left of daylight,' Ayla objected. 'If you're cut off from the caravan and get lost at night … that would be more treacherous than pirates.'

But Alizarin shook his head. 'We can't afford to wait. We'll ride on ahead. Follow us while there's some light left, it'll make our return journey shorter.'

'What about the sick ones?' Verdi asked.

The Derindin were exhausted, but no one wanted to linger.

'Suman, come with us and navigate,' said Alizarin. 'Ayla, pack up the caravan. Don't make camp until sundown. We'll ride back to meet you.'

'And if you should run into more pirates?'

Klaus slung his crossbow over his back. 'My bolts will find them first.'

No one questioned him. The Derindin watched him and Arik more warily now, as though they had become more Northern. It made Klaus feel more a stranger than ever.

'We'll leave as soon as all the dead are buried,' Ayla told Alizarin.

Verdi scowled. 'Why not leave the pirates to the vultures?'

A hiss of disapproval rose from several Derindin. The colour rose in Verdi's cheeks.

'All life belongs to the Great Sentience,' said Suman sternly. 'The dead belong to him.'

'Surely it'd be quicker to build a pyre,' said Arik.

'Neither do we burn the dead, Master Marcin. The earth has the final claim upon them. Even if they aren't our dead. We don't do this for them. We do this for our own selves.'

Other Derindin looked away, clearly not sharing Suman's conviction. But nobody argued.

Klaus retrieved the last of his bolts, anxious not to lose any more. Would he ever again be able to acquire such Ummandiri war-birds, so far from bowmaster Kelselem? He dulled a stab of pain; another one for Afldalr. They searched the pirates' corpses and saddlebags: waterskins, compasses, pouches of smokeleaf and kahvi bean. There were valuables, too – rings, trinkets and coin.

'Looted from another unfortunate caravan, I'll warrant,' said Saarem. 'Set it aside for their clans, Felid. We'll find out more in Romel.'

'There's water in these skins,' said Felid, an Elendran youth. 'The spring can't be far.'

Arik called, 'Tristan?'

Klaus joined him by a pirate's body. On the dead man's shoulder blade was a curious tattoo, ornate and larger than the span of Arik's hand.

Klaus lowered his voice. 'Did he carry anything interesting?'

Arik shook his head.

'Copy it,' Klaus told him before he left.

They rode out with an extra horse. Suman stopped periodically to check his compass, and Klaus used each opportunity to consult his own. The sun was two hours from setting, and mercifully the heat was abating. Forty minutes later, they spotted the first derina bush.

Klaus' heart leapt in relief. But when they reached it, Alizarin cursed.

'They've stripped this vine already. They must have come this way before us.'

The sand around the bush had been disturbed, and a good part of its many-armed vine lay exposed. The pirates hadn't bothered to bury it again, which the Derindin had done with great care to help it re-sprout.

Klaus helped Suman cover the vine with sand. 'Come on. You said sister plants shouldn't be too far away.'

Over the next hour, they found three more stripped, exposed vines. Worry wormed through Klaus. Alizarin remained silent but tight-lipped. But their patience was rewarded: the fourth bush, hidden behind a dune, nurtured beneath it a great crop of fat tubers.

They drank gratefully. Klaus felt guilty when the cool, slightly milky water touched his lips, thinking of the others. They collected all the tubers they could find before re-burying the vines.

'Almost dusk,' said Alizarin, perpetually scanning the sky. 'We shouldn't go any further. We can pick up the trail of this vine at dawn.'

To Klaus, there was light enough to go on a while longer. But he recalled the rapid fall of darkness here, and the open cage of waiting night. If the Derindin feared anything almost as much as being without water, it was the desert in darkness. Suman whispered to his falcon and threw her up into the air. She flew back, retracing their steps and soon returning to Suman's shoulder. Klaus marvelled at his understanding of her little movements, the array of sounds she made, the click of her beak.

'They're not far behind,' said Suman.

Klaus helped Alizarin collect deadwood, leaving Suman to start a fire.

'Tongues are wagging about the way you shoot your bolts.'

There was a warning in Alizarin's voice, but also a reluctant curiosity.

'I was taught by an oathkeeper from Ummandir,' Klaus told him. 'I picked up my first bow when I was three, and a drop of rain at dusk was my first target to master.'

'Was he a slave?'

'Keeping slaves is forbidden in Invelmar.' *And I'm sure he knows this.*

'Then what else would possess an Ummandiri to stray so far from home?'

Klaus smiled inwardly, the knife twisting in his heart. 'He's one of the only three people I've met who've travelled all the Seven Parts. They say he reached Invelmar last, and made a vow to Lord Wintermantel that he couldn't keep. Rather than dishonour himself by breaking his oath, he offered his lifelong service to the house of Wintermantel.'

Sadness stirred deep beneath his Form. Kelselem, the *Nihtauga* or Eye-of-the-Night as the court named him, had been almost as much a pillar of his training as Master Arnander. Klaus dug the heel of his mind into the memory and crushed it into the sand.

'If you are to remain above suspicion, perhaps you ought to confess to more than scribing battles and poetry.'

Alizarin seemed genuinely keen to guard Klaus' secret. *He hardly cares for my safety.* Which meant his true motive was to protect Verdi from any association with the Wintermantels. Why could it not be known that Verdi had been raised in an Ealdorman's house?

'What's that?' Klaus asked as they walked back, pointing. The sun had almost set, and illuminated against its fiery palette was the outline of something more angular than a dune.

To his surprise Alizarin murmured, 'Don't tell Suman.'

Once the fire was going, Suman plotted the coordinates of the derina vines, checking them against the spring's coordinates. Klaus watched, learning what he could of these Southern constellations. Night waited in the wings of evening, its breath bated and laced with a stinging chill. Klaus scanned the growing dark. The caravan never travelled so late into twilight.

'We should steer slightly south tomorrow,' Suman concluded.

'Are the crop trails more reliable than navigation?'

'No. The most accurate routes are found using the coordinates of both the springs and the derina trail.'

'The springs move,' said Alizarin. Klaus raised an eyebrow.

'Smaller springs can dry out or get buried under sand,' Suman explained. 'That's where the derina is useful. The vines won't grow towards a dried out spring ... and provide us with water on the way.'

'Your instruments are far superior to mine,' Klaus told him. 'My readings would have led us a little more west.'

Suman added kindling to the fire. 'Southerners named the stars and then built the instruments to follow them. Even now we don't make them like they used to.'

He'd grown less distant since their first meeting over the unlading pen, but only a little. Klaus asked him, 'Where was Gelengahal?'

Suman's face remained empty. 'Take a look around you. What do you find?' Klaus held his eyes, unfazed. 'Gelengahal was a great citadel not far from here, and hosted the oldest library in the South. It was ransacked after the First Redrawing, and what remained of the sacred lettervault was made rubble at the Second Redrawing. All its scholars were slain or driven out, all its artefacts destroyed or stolen.'

'Like the Umari instrument.'

'That was made even before Gelengahal's time.'

'Do you think it's somewhere in the South now?'

'Wherever it is, it will be useless. No one knows how to use it now.'

'Let's hope it's not in the desert, waiting to fall into the hands of bandits,' Alizarin murmured.

'When did the pirate raids begin?' asked Klaus.

'How long have we had clans?' Alizarin unrolled a wallet of smokeleaf. 'Pirates are the sewers of the clans. Exiles and lonemen. Unclanned, all of them. So they make do with the roads. And now they haunt the waterholes. Thirst is the biggest peril in the desert. They learned to prey on that fear.'

'They seem to have grown a lot worse, all of a sudden.'

'This summer's been the worst in living memory,' Alizarin conceded. 'Water grows more scarce every year.'

'Fools,' Suman muttered. 'Only a fool would believe a pirate can be trusted to conjure water.'

'Fear drives people to all manner of foolish things,' Klaus said mildly. 'Like spending good gold on tokens for water.'

Alizarin lit his filled pipe. 'An old trick. Gold leaves no footprint. But the pirates pay sellers to track who's buying their tokens. Those who cave to trading with tokens signal their willingness to pay for water. The token sellers will remember who's too afraid to risk travelling without them, and who would not be broken with fear. It's a good way to sniff out weakness and spot resistance.'

Klaus watched the flames. He had never seen wood burn as quickly as it did in the desert. 'Doesn't seem like the work of mere raiders to me. Sounds planned. And purposeful.'

'The pirates are scattered across the desert. Leaderless, homeless. They're pests, nothing more.'

A horse neighed nearby; the caravan was approaching.

It was a sombre reunion. Derina broth was soon simmering over the fire, and many hands got to work milking water from the tubers. The wagons huddled closer together than usual, as though seeking comfort as well as warmth.

'Any sign of more pirates?' Verdi asked. Klaus told him of the stripped derina vines.

'We left too late,' Alizarin told Ayla. 'I shouldn't have waited so long.'

'This isn't your doing,' she replied.

'How is the child?'

'She's lost a lot of blood.'

The Derindin gathered around the fire, wrapped in heavy cloaks and muttering over tin cups of derina tuber tea. Appetites were as low as morale. Even Ravi emerged only to sniff half-heartedly at Verdi's bowl before ducking back into his breast pocket. A full moon bore witness to their quiet mourning song, the prayers for the fallen mingling with their never-ending *namathra*. An older Derindman leaned over Arik's shoulder.

'Tonight we owe you our lives,' he said in heavily accented Invelmen. 'We are not ungrateful.'

Around him, Derindin pressed their hands to their chests. Amongst them were those who had so far ignored the two Invelmari altogether.

'What will the clans do about the pirates?' Verdi asked Broco.

'What *can* they do? They're unsworn Derindin who refuse to pledge allegiance to any clan. Worse than that, some are deserters and outcasts. They can't be brought to heel, so they must be hunted.'

Saarem shook his head. 'Bandits have always pestered travellers, but never dared anything like this.'

'May tesh take them all,' muttered Osringen.

Saarem caught sight of Verdi's blank face. 'Tesh is the fatal thirst. The thirst that kills after weeks of wading through sand for water.'

Klaus suppressed a shudder. He'd faced merciless mountains and harsh terrains across the Parts, but such thirst was an alien notion. He could now imagine the terror of a slow, roasting death in pursuit of relief that would never come.

'Take comfort,' said Osringen's wife. 'They won't last. We'll have Merensama soon enough.'

A sharp look from her husband silenced her.

'Sounds like the pirates aren't going anywhere, then,' said Arik. 'Surely the clans have enough clout to rein them in?'

'What would a Northern swordhand know of our clans?' Ferinc retorted.

Arik raised one eyebrow. 'Enough to bet that maybe if they had contained the pirates, three of your caravan wouldn't be buried back there. We in the North learned to rally together long ago. Even when their *gods* divided them, the Northern tribes put their differences aside to survive.'

'To conquer southward, you mean,' someone sneered.

'To quash Far Northern rebels who ransacked villages and left no man standing but on a stake, and no woman that was not violated. Children mutilated or stolen, taken for sacrifice. Derinda is not the only place in the world to have known suffering.'

Fibbler shrank into Verdi's side, eyes widening.

'And yet one wrong word against the Ealdormen or their precious Blood Pact is as good as a death wish in Invelmar,' Fenric returned.

'Only a fool would speak against the armour that shields him,' replied Arik calmly.

'You fought the pirates bravely,' Osringen said gruffly. 'You're young and strong. But steel doesn't solve everything. All young people think the world is easy to fix.'

'Everything he says is true,' Rasan interrupted. 'The Plains are ruled by rabbles who can't see eye to eye on anything while Elders look the other way. The only law that Elders uphold is ghabala – taking whatever they can and claiming their right to "defend" it. They're as bad as the pirates.'

'Hold your tongue,' snapped Ferinc. 'The Elders deserve better than your insolence – a tumbler who thinks with her fists and hasn't yet seen more than a handful of summers!'

'I will not,' she said coldly. 'If the Elders want respect, they should earn it.'

She got up and stalked away.

'You ought to keep your tumblers in check,' Parin muttered to Ayla.

'I command their bodies,' she said coolly. 'I've no reach over their minds.'

Osringen took his pipe out from his mouth. 'Your precious survival began with the destruction of everything else, Master Northman. There's nothing noble about that.'

'And that should not have been the price paid for peace,' finished Klaus.

He felt rather than saw Arik's scowl. But to this, even the Derindin had nothing to say.

*

The memory was as clear as morning. It was Klaus' first visit to Kankaan, and his last assignment before his expected graduation to fully-fledged Intelligencer.

He ought to have asked himself why Master Arnander had waited until the end of his training to set Klaus an assignment here.

The Kankaanian were obscenely wealthy. A small coastal kingdom in the western Zmerrudi Part, Kankaan was rich in gold and coral. It was the coveted rival of Dorenya and Ungal further south, who would love nothing better than to annex it, to extend their Alabaster Road all the way to the Kankaanian coast. Then they'd no longer have to charter expensive ships through Morregrat's waters to take merchandise across the Zmerrudi Part.

Power had changed hands in Ungal, and its new queen was young and hungry. Fearing invasion, the Kankaanian king had finally called on Invelmar's might. A shipment of steel and a new station of Isarnanheri in Kankaan's port would send a message of iron resistance to any southern Zmerrudi troublemakers.

Of course, these contracts began in smoke-wreathed dalliances between nobles and Intelligencers and needed as much careful tempering as the steel the Kankaanians desired. Isarnanheri were expensive. Klaus had come to soften the asking price. To make it attractive and necessary, even. To politely decline King Tanouk's proposal for a new alliance across the three Parts that shared the Zmerrudi Sea – preposterous, of course – without offending and driving him away. And, evidently, to stomach particular Kanaanian perversions.

'They are inordinately proud,' Florian had cautioned. 'Their pride is outdone only by their profanity.'

Master Arnander was not one for morals, so his words stayed with Klaus.

Problematically, envoys from Zenzabra, Nékke, Pengaza and even Semra had agreed to hear King Tanouk's proposal. Some of them might welcome a new alliance. The Pengazans wouldn't dare; they felt the proximity of thousands of Isarnanheri stationed at Port Ellenheim too keenly to defy Dunraven. The Nékkei were really there to learn the intentions of their neighbours, with no desire to share power or gold. Most of the others couldn't afford the funds for membership of another expensive alliance. But the Semrans were genuine contenders. A handshake across Zmerrudi soil could just overtip the balance of power between the Silfren and Sirghen Parts.

'A very likeable woman, your highness,' Klaus said to King Tanouk of the Zenzabran minister. The seat of honour to the right of the Kankaanian king had been reserved for Klaus, future heir to the Invelmari throne. 'I have had no dishonest exchanges with her.'

The king was a little too susceptible to his many vices and had run to fat bloated further by the extravagance of his gold-embroidered silks. His eyes lit up.

'That is promising, then?' he said, jowls rippling. Thankfully, his Invelmen was fair, because Klaus had learned only just enough Kankaani to flatter his wife.

'It would be, but there's something else to consider…' Tanouk drew closer as Klaus' voice fell to a whisper, wincing in pain as he rustled in his silks. He'd been hobbling on the right foot, probably swollen with gout. 'The Zenzabrans

have been struggling to pay for our Isarnanheri for three years now. I fear any commitment they make to your alliance will be little more than lip service. If the time comes when you should request that they honour your agreement and provide aid, you may find yourself calling on light coffers. A sad obstacle to your great vision, but I would not wish to see your generosity abused. I share this with you in the strictest confidence.'

Klaus let the seed germinate, conjuring up just enough delight over the mediocre juggling skills of the king's young nephew.

Tanouk fell quiet, likely realising his big dream was deflating by the hour. Klaus had already introduced the Morregrati envoy, the handsome nephew of Morregrat's King Lorcuat, to Tanouk's favourite mistress. And earlier he'd re-arranged their seats so that their flirtation had been in full view of the Kankaanian king all evening. The effects of the spiked wine Klaus had sent to their table was going to sour relations with Morregrat for a while. He'd also planned for each of them to be simultaneously called away for just long enough to cement Tanouk's suspicion. With Zenzabra out of the innings and Pengaza and Nékke already dealt with, the only real remaining threat was Semra. A treaty with the smaller Zmerrudi nations would be worthless. But the Semrans were ambitious, and a far more difficult chalice to poison.

He needn't have worried in the end. When they withdrew to the King's private quarters, the serving boys brought not platters of fruit and sweetmeats, but a giant sheet of hammered gold bearing a young man. Buttered and herbed, deeply asleep but still living. Too-handsome-for-his-own-good Morregrati almost fell off his cushions. The Zenzanbran minister paled. Semra's envoy, an old hand, was a shrewd nobleman who Klaus had met once before.

'I forget we have not previously had the pleasure of your company,' Tanouk told the Morregrati, not without a glint of malice. 'Here is an old delicacy we reserve only for our most honoured guests.'

Whatever he felt first, Form clasped Klaus around the throat. Action stifled reaction. He leaned forward for a better look: genuine curiosity seasoned with approval. This was the Intelligencer's true mask.

'Ungali, your highness?' The king looked pleased that Klaus had guessed correctly. 'A fitting choice.' Klaus slipped a slight frown. 'He is a soldier?'

A servant had already lit the roasting spit. Another began sharpening a set of carving knives.

'Ah, yes. Not the young suckling pig my forefathers preferred...'

The Porvayans of the southern Zmerrudi Part were no strangers to manflesh and lounged comfortably. The Zenzabran minister looked as though she might be sick.

'But a fitting choice, after all,' Klaus murmured. He smiled ruefully at Tanouk. 'For the sake of Sturmsinger, however, the warrior is honoured. Alas, it would be sacrilegious to taste of this man's flesh.'

Tanouk was anxious not to offend. The will of Invelmar was iron. For *them both; its cold fist suppressed the heaving of Klaus' stomach. He flogged his Form to obey, channelling his mask. Gracious, observant, charming. There was no place for his revulsion except in Afldalr. Not so for the Semran envoy. He countenanced the carving of morsels from the drugged man's breast, but the smell of roasting meat proved too much for him. He jumped to his feet.*

'There is no place for Semra here.' Anger coloured his gold complexion. 'Heaven forbid that we should share in such depravity as this!'

Tanouk clearly spoke no Semran, for the envoy's parting remark before he stormed out would have been enough to broker war.

The king was already too drunk to separate injured pride from disappointment; that would come tomorrow when he would wake to a headache and his grand plans in tatters.

Klaus accepted another goblet of wine, slipping into it the cotton wick that would slowly drain his cup. For now, Tanouk would eagerly recount his defence plans to his new Invelmari confidante as his eyes greedily followed the dancing girls he could no longer satisfy. The youth slept on through death as he was consumed. The heart was the prized delicacy; it was still beating limply when exposed.

Klaus glanced across the foul smoke to where Master Arnander stretched across his recliner. A contract worth a fortune in gold and coral. A new Invelmari outpost in Kankaan; another faultline for Invelmar to nurture, once the Eye began to gather intelligence about its latest customer. A dangerous alliance derailed in its first flush. This, and not the solemn ceremony awaiting them in Dunraven, was the moment in which Klaus' Form was deemed complete.

His fellow guests feasted and unravelled with wine, and Afldalr reeked.

Acrid sweetness burned his nostrils as he awoke.

Klaus opened his eyes, relieved to find the humble contents of the wagon huddled around him. He'd not been asleep long, for outside the desert was still sonorous with the Derindin's night vigil for the dead.

He lay in silence until the sour dream relinquished its grip on the desert, where flute-song and ancient mourning were the breath of the desert night.

*

Sheer cold drove him to get up too early, leaving Arik and Verdi in the cramped wagon. Klaus envied them their slumber. There wasn't enough water to waste on cleaning his teeth with saltwood. At least while he was cold, he didn't feel quite so dirty. That would come later, when the heat kicked in.

The sun had not yet broken over the dunes. The camp was quiet. Mayda grated a dark block of dried calf's liver into a pot over the fire.

'I can make a bloodchaser for the child, but it works slowly,' she told Alizarin. 'She's lost too much blood.'

Klaus surveyed the horizon through his eyescope. That irregular shadow hovered in the south-east.

'I'd hoped we could leave before anyone else notices,' Alizarin told Klaus when he pointed it out again. 'Some believe ruins bring bad luck. Won't go near them.'

Klaus could well believe this; Suman had refused to even look at the ruins. 'Do they think they're haunted?'

A distasteful smile touched the corner of Alizarin's mouth. 'There's no need for make-belief ghosts when the past still casts its shadow over the present.'

Klaus collapsed his eyescope. 'I want to take a closer look.'

'We can't afford to lose more time. We had a week's grace at most.'

'What's chasing us?'

Alizarin looked up at the skies. 'The winds.'

By mid-morning the sun was blazing and the still air nipped at the skin with heat. Was it his imagination or had the sky grown sallow?

Verdi squinted. 'What's up there?'

Several black dots moved across the cloudless yellowish-blue. The little birdkeeper seemed agitated, as did his birds; he kept murmuring over his shoulder at his wagon in reassurance. Petra flew up towards the dots. She became a speck on the horizon, circling before returning to her master. Suman frowned.

Ayla rode over to them. 'There's something up ahead. Be ready, just in case.'

She continued to the front of the caravan. She'd come to warn them before her tumblers.

'They're buzzards,' said Verdi.

And they were slowly multiplying.

It was another half hour before they discovered what had drawn the buzzards. The wagon train stopped. They dismounted.

The smell hit them first.

Arik reached down to grab Fibbler's wrist as he jumped down from Terim's wagon.

'You're staying here.'

He held the squirming child easily, deaf to his protests.

Mayda led Fibbler away, pale-faced. 'Come, child. There's nothing for you there.'

Through the shimmering heat-haze, dark shapes littered the dunes. Then they made out the broken wagons.

'Oh,' said Verdi, voice folding. 'Oh…'

Most of the Derindin stayed back, holding close children whose eyes were still free to roam.

'Watch the caravan,' Alizarin barked at the tumblers, face cast in iron.

Roaring filled Klaus' ears as they drew close. The remains of a caravan lay scattered across the sand, bodies of every size tossed about like broken leaves. Most of the dead had been felled by sword and axe, but a few had been struck by arrows. A tumbler was violently sick. Klaus glanced at Arik and found the ice of the Isarnanheri in his face.

Ayla lowered her sand-mask. 'They can't have been much further ahead of us. The oasis is nearby…'

'And that's how the pirates ambushed them,' Suman finished. 'All they had to do was wait.'

Verdi sat heavily on the ground. Ravi curled up into a tight ball the size of a peach and took shelter under his collar.

'Go back,' Alizarin told him. Verdi stood again, carefully averting his eyes from the carnage, but stayed.

They searched the wagons; some of them had been set alight. The pirates had left nothing of value behind.

'It's a miracle this hasn't drawn a whole pack of hyenas yet,' Broco muttered.

Ayla froze. 'Something just moved.'

The hiss of blades being drawn greased the air. Arik elbowed Verdi behind him. A rasping sound scratched against the silence.

'There's someone still alive!'

Verdi found him by the remains of a wagon. It was the horsemaster from Noisy Tree who'd sold them their horses. He was bloodstained and battered.

'Search for other survivors,' Alizarin ordered.

Tumblers scattered. The horsemaster's face was ash-grey. Sweat glistened on his face. Verdi tore a strip of cloth from his shirt and tied it above a bleeding wound in his leg. Alizarin crouched down to help him.

'Don't waste your time, old friend.' The horsemaster's voice was a tatter in the wind.

Alizarin raised a waterskin to his lips. 'When did they attack, Kirono?'

His throat rasped as he swallowed. 'Some three days past…'

Three days of lying in the sweltering heat without drink and with one leg rotting, of shivering in the punishing cold of night surrounded by the remains of his companions. Klaus suppressed a shudder with Form. Alizarin clasped Kirono's hand. The poor man gripped it as though clinging to life through him. His breathing was shallow and fast.

'We killed them a day ago,' Arik told him. 'I'm sorry they didn't cross our path sooner.'

Kirono appeared to recognise the Northerner who'd bought his horses in Noisy Tree, his fingers tightening around Alizarin's hand.

'Alizarin!' His voice grew urgent. 'Looking – they were looking for something...'

Alizarin's frown deepened. 'What were they looking for?'

'They came back ... looked several times. There was something else...' Kirono coughed, dark blood staining his lips. He raised his eyes to Arik. 'Movement in the North ... movements in the chain...'

Alizarin drew closer. Kirono coughed again, and Alizarin hushed him instead.

'Let go,' he told Kirono gently. 'The concerns of this world are behind you now.'

Kirono's breaths became desperate, erratic.

'Did you find the boy?' he managed. 'Did you get my message?' Alizarin nodded. 'Let me see him again.'

His eyes reached over Alizarin's shoulder to Verdi. They seemed unfocused, but he smiled very faintly.

'Good.' Kirono closed his eyes. 'Very good.'

He cried out in pain with every step as they carried him on a makeshift stretcher back to the caravan, where Verdi tried to make him comfortable.

'Their caravan's been stripped bare to the last grain of barley,' Saarem reported.

'Then they must have taken it somewhere,' said Alizarin. 'The pirates who attacked us carried little. Or else there are other pirates nearby.'

By dusk they'd buried the dead in the cooling sand. Horsemaster Kirono took his final parched breath with sundown and joined them in the last grave.

Klaus draw an arm around Verdi by the fire. 'Alright?'

Dirty tear-trails streaked Verdi's face, but he nodded.

Their fire blazed that night, well-fed with the remains of the wagons, though it warmed no one.

'We've lost another day,' Ayla murmured over the Derindin's prayers.

Alizarin looked haggard. 'What's done is done. Double the watch tonight.'

The Derindin sang in their own tongue, but no barrier could garble the language of mourning. Rasan sat silent amongst them, arms wrapped around her knees, her eyes dull.

Alizarin joined the two Invelmari standing back from the fire, apart from the Derindin's grief. 'Surely Kirono was speaking of the Sturmsinger Chain?'

Arik and Klaus exchanged an uneasy look.

'I can't imagine what he meant,' said Klaus. The Chain was intact. Klaus' own presumed death was no threat to its next turn. *So long as Elodie was safe.*

'Could the pirates be looking for the Umari instrument?' Verdi suggested.

'What the hell for?' Arik kicked the sand in irritation. 'It's an ornament that sat in a library for hundreds of years, gathering dust. Every so often some Engineer would fiddle with it and come up with a new theory, and then it would go back on display again, like all the other instruments. I don't see how it's of any relevance.'

'"*Movements in the North*",' Alizarin repeated.

'It's no secret that Far Northerners' raids have intensified in the Sterns,' Klaus reminded him.

'But why would pirates care about what's happening in the Far North, or in Dunraven for that matter?' Verdi wondered.

'A good question,' Alizarin replied. 'But you heard Kirono's words for yourselves. Are you certain he wasn't speaking of a threat to the Sturmsinger Chain?'

Arik pursed his lips. 'It's forbidden to even speak of this.'

'You're not in Invelmar. Who'll be your witness, the stars?'

'The Sturmsinger Chain has been unbroken since its inception,' Arik insisted.

Alizarin glanced at Klaus. 'And yet here we are, staring at a link in the Chain that is now missing.'

The knife twisted between Klaus' ribs again. 'Except I was never part of it. The cycle will keep turning. The Chain is intact.'

Mourning song filled the silence.

'Ansovald Sturmsinger,' Alizarin murmured towards the flames. 'Incredible, that he found a way to rule your people so long after he turned to dust.'

Klaus flinched beneath his Form. It felt vile to hear Sturmsinger's name spoken without reverence, let alone with Alizarin's soft disdain.

'Perhaps Kirono misheard,' said Verdi. 'Or overheard empty talk.'

'I've learned never to dismiss a man's last words,' Alizarin replied. 'And pirates may be a pack of rats, but rats frequent the sewers. Their talk is worth listening to.'

'If anything's certain, it's that these aren't just ordinary raiders,' said Arik.

To his credit, Alizarin didn't rebuff this. 'I've never heard of pirates searching for anything other than what they can use to fill their pockets.'

'Could they be mercenaries?' Verdi asked.

'Working for whom? Pirates will take any job if the price is right.

But anyone willing to pay a pirate needs to be too strong for them to rob, because that would be faster. It would take a powerful hand to bargain with pirates.' Alizarin searched the Northerners' faces again. 'If it ever comes to light that the pirates are doing the work of a Northern hand...'

Arik's lips paled with anger. 'The pirates *are* the hand. Your own brothers are the scourge, whichever purse pays them. I know which I think is worse.'

Alizarin raised an eyebrow. 'I was going to say that it will make it harder for you to settle here amongst us.'

'We'll worry about that.' Arik strode away to join the night sentry.

Klaus caught sight of Fibbler, curled up against a wagon by the fire. The bowl beside him was suspiciously half full. He didn't look up when they joined him.

'Not hungry?' Verdi asked.

The little boy shook his head. Ravi scampered down to lick Fibbler's hand with a tiny pink tongue.

Verdi nodded towards his unfinished supper. 'Sure? That's going to be an oceloe treat in a minute if you're not careful.'

Clearly not so devastated that he was ready to make this sacrifice, Fibbler swiftly moved his supper away.

'Come on.' Klaus reached out his hand. 'Arik's taking the first watch. You can stay with us tonight.'

'You can keep Ravi from having bad dreams.'

For the first time, the night sky was overcast. A dusty gauze diluted the crisp light of the stars, as though shrouding them with a film of the Derindin's tears. The blazing fire illuminated the dark figure of Alizarin, his neck craned as he searched above for whatever it was that loaned him comfort.

Fibbler settled in one of the bunks as Klaus spread a hide on the wagon floor for himself.

'Are there pirates in the North?' A pause. 'Will you tell me about when you were a boy?'

He couldn't tell Fibbler how his heart ached for the howling of his huskies in reply to their wilder brethren across the mountains, or for the silence that surrounded the first flake of snow.

'We agreed to sleeping, not jabbering,' Verdi grumbled from the other bunk. But there were cracks in his voice. Later, Klaus could contemplate why a dying horsemaster wished to lay eyes once more on the face of a Derindin orphan. For now, there was a child's fear to soothe.

'There are men and women like the pirates everywhere in the world. But I'll tell you the best part of the North.' No amount of furs softened the wooden boards of the wagon. 'On the darkest nights when there is no rain-crystal in the air and the light-currents in the wind are just right, the first woman of the heavens shakes out her hair across the sky and fills it with colours: green and blue; even violet, red and gold – every colour you can imagine. Her name is *Aurora,* although sometimes she is called *River-in-the-Sky.* She left a child behind somewhere on the earth, and every night that she can, she escapes from her lover, the sun, and raises her lantern high over the world to look for him amongst us...'

11

For a Drink

WARRIORS SEVERED ANCIENT BONDS AND FLOCKED TO THE BANNER
OF STURMSINGER, UNTIL HIS ARMY BOASTED SHIELDS
FROM EVERY CORNER OF THE NORTH.

SONNONFER: THE RISE OF ANSOVALD STURMSINGER

'The first symptom is general malaise, then yellowing of the skin and bilious vomiting. Abdominal pain soon follows. Those with an accompanying fever fare worse – signs of desiccation develop, sometimes with mottling of the flesh. This phase has so far been the peak of the illness.'

Verdi's pen hovered over his entry. How many times had he written by oil lantern just like this, wrapped up in the draughty cabin of a ship or in the dizzyingly thin air of the Sterns? In truth, his mind was otherwise occupied. He set the pen down.

Outside, a third night of prayers for the dead had ended. Ravi was asleep in the crook of Verdi's elbow, having never outgrown his preference for awkward places. Klaus slept in the other bunk, if it could be called that; he tossed often, his breathing never quite deepening to repose.

Arik looked in around the door of the wagon. 'Is he asleep?'

'After a fashion.'

'Then I won't wake him yet.'

The hour was much later than Verdi realised, if it was already time for the Invelmari to switch sentry duty. He closed his book, joining Arik outside.

The embers of the fire smouldered, but an otherwise endless darkness engulfed them. Stars burned holes into the heavens. Night had never seemed so infinite.

'What is it?'

Verdi shivered. 'I keep thinking about what the horsemaster asked my uncle – about whether he'd found me...'

'Me too,' said Arik. 'Has your uncle said anything yet about why you were sent North?'

'Nothing. Absolutely nothing.'

In fact, Alizarin seemed to be avoiding Verdi altogether. The other Derindin had welcomed him; his uncle was the only one who seemed not to want him there. But no one spoke of Verdi's family or of his departure north. And, wary of offending his uncle, Verdi was afraid to ask.

But Kirono's eager face haunted him. *Did you find the boy? Let me see him again.*

Arik blew out a stream of smokeleaf. 'He isn't being entirely honest with you. Which means he can't be trusted.' Miserable though it made Verdi to admit it, he knew Arik was right. 'If he's still said nothing by the time we reach Romel, perhaps we'd be better off making our own way.'

'Perhaps.'

'I'm sorry. I know you'd hoped for more.'

Perhaps the horsemaster was another relation of mine. It did no good to speculate. Now Verdi would never know whether their encounter in Noisy Tree had in fact not been his first meeting with Kirono.

The early hours brought an eerie stillness. Arik took Klaus' sentry duty, he too seemingly disturbed rather than soothed by the quiet. Verdi looked in on Yenvin, who slept feverishly beside her mother, then sat sleeplessly outside the sick tent.

'Why so sorrowful, Master Viridian?'

The birdkeeper, who rose with his birds before sunrise, sat beside him.

Verdi was always glad of his company. 'I'd hoped she would improve like the others...'

'Even if she does not, her suffering will have been eased by your kindness.' The birdkeeper paused. 'But that is not all that troubles you.'

Verdi had not expected to become so inflamed by the Derindin's plight. He wasn't sure when it had happened, but he had acquired their twin burden of desperation and helplessness.

'Coming back is harder than I thought,' he admitted.

'Even the desert begins with a grain of sand,' said the birdkeeper gently. 'They may gather in great numbers, but they are still only grains of sand. Can a man be crushed by a grain of sand?'

Verdi smiled half-heartedly. The birdkeeper's serenity reminded him of Elodie. 'I suppose not.'

The birdkeeper waved his hand. 'It was not always like this here. Just as this place was not always a desert. Custodians once maintained the order between the earth and the heavens. And they will again. Did Lorendar not promise?'

'I've not heard that name before.'

'No matter. I have already said too much. But we Derindin know relief is coming. It must.'

*

By morning, the winds had finally overtaken them.

A chill awoke Klaus towards the end of the second watch of the night, which he should have taken. They had let him sleep.

Movements in the North ... movements in the chain... His last thought falling asleep was now his first as he woke.

In place of dawn, a sickly haze crept over the dunes. Outside, an eldritch breeze rippled the surface of the desert. Little waves of sand tossed restlessly around his feet. The quiet was unnatural.

'Storm!' cried a tumbler. 'Round everything up. Storm!'

The caravan awoke quickly. They'd dealt with this before. Arik and Verdi hurried back to the wagon.

'Saddle your horses,' Suman called. 'We need to pack the wagons together as closely as we can.'

Within fifteen minutes, the wagons had been repositioned into a tight ring around the horses. Sand rose boldly from the ground now, its fine-toothed wavefronts nipping at their legs. The Derindin threw heavy leather hides over the nervous horses, whispering to them until they were more at ease.

'Take cover,' Alizarin shouted over the growing bellow of the wind.

They ducked into their wagon, bolting its wooden shutters. There was a loud *thud* as someone threw leather storm hides over their wagon. At first this muffled the storm, but soon barely dampened its roar. Arik lit the swaying oil lamp. Verdi patted his pockets frantically before Ravi's head poked out from one of the bunks, his grey fur standing on end as he jumped into Verdi's hands. They peered out through one of the tiny windows, seeing little between a gap in the hides cladding the wagon. Now the air was thick and brown with sand that swayed like dancing snakes, lashing at the skies with grainy whips.

A whinny stuttered through the growling storm, or it might have been the wind itself.

'The poor horses,' Verdi said miserably.

'They'll be alright, they were raised in this,' Arik told him, sounding less than certain.

Klaus sank into one of the bunks. This wind was like nothing he'd imagined. If it had a form, it would be a many-armed serpent, each limb flailing riotously in a destructive path of its own. The wagon trembled under the hammering of livid sand, creaking at its tired joints.

'The graves,' said Klaus. 'They're freshly dug.'

After that no one spoke, huddling under their cloaks, the howl of the wind crouching with them in the tiny space like a fourth companion. Verdi fell asleep, Ravi buried under his chin, then Arik. Eventually the lantern went out, and Klaus couldn't check his pocket-clock. Time unwound to waiting, and wondering, and wallowing. In the cramped stale darkness, wounds re-opened and throbbed; he shoved them into Afldalr – *became* Afldalr – burying them again. It felt as though a full day had passed before the wagon stopped shaking in the wind.

Eventually Arik asked, 'Is it just me, or is it quieter?'

Klaus unlatched the door and opened it a crack. A faint howl lingered in the half-dark, but the storm had definitely abated. He opened it further, pushing a hide aside.

Flurries of sand had piled against the wagons like drifts of golden snow, part-burying wagons and horses alike.

'Looks like it's passed.'

'Sure? Could be a lull...'

Others stepped out of their wagons cautiously, as though fearing the sand might cave underneath them like a sinkhole.

The darkness of the storm clouds lifted, but only to reveal a wan yellow-grey sky. The Derindin's measures had protected the horses from the brunt of the wind. They bred horses strong enough to withstand assault from flying sand, Meron said, showing them some of the damage to a hoof-guard that would have stripped away a man's skin.

Klaus shivered. He could have sworn he heard echoes of eerie laughter in the shadow of the wind, swallowed back into its invisible belly. *More pirates?* But how could anything ambush them in this weather?

'Hyenas,' Broco panted, helping Klaus haul an overturned wagon. 'The winds must have thrown them the scent of the dead.'

'It could have been worse,' Meron muttered. The shutters of two wagons had been pulled away, and another had splintered down one wall.

'Could it?'

A panel of the water wagon had shattered, and a stream of derina water leaked from broken barrels.

Having helped painstakingly collect those tubers, Klaus's heart sank. Palpable fear spread through the caravan. The Derindin understood what it was to be waterless in this endless waste.

They made what repairs they could, building a great fire now fed with the debris of their own mishaps. Their water supplies were more exhausted than they'd realised. Arik offered to ride out in search of more derina, but Alizarin shook his head.

'It's too dark, and the winds are not yet spent. If we're fortunate, we can outrun the next storm. We'll pick up the derina trail at first light.' Alizarin paused. 'Even the pair of you may not be able to take on a band of pirates alone.'

'And if there's no more derina to guide the way?' Verdi asked.

'Then we continue as we started. We will follow the stars.'

The word *tesh* kept coming back to Klaus. The bards in Dunraven had told of desert men voyaging for days without a drop to drink. He couldn't see how those tales might have been true.

Silence now reigned in the birdkeeper's wagon, which until the ambush had been a haven of sweet syllables and darting movement.

'How are the birds doing without much water?' Klaus asked.

'No differently to you or I.' The birdkeeper had grown more withdrawn since their grisly discovery a few days before. 'They are quiet but not despairing. They sense suffering better than many other creatures. Don't be disheartened, Master Tristan. This morning I fancied I saw an emperor hoopoe at dawn ... they are so rarely seen now that each year I fear they've deserted this Part altogether. They nest in the Mengorian mountain range and beyond – too far South for the likes of me to pursue them now. A good omen, friend. A good omen.'

'Bit hard to pin hope on an omen.'

'The humble emperor hoopoe was once the messenger of wisdom itself, dear chronicler.' The birdkeeper smiled, in defiance of their empty waterskins and the eternal barren sand. 'A good omen.'

But *tesh* seemed to be the only fate the Derindin saw in the distance, and for all their understanding of the pathology of its slow delirium, there was nothing to do but wait while it unravelled their will and their minds and visited their darkest and most desperate thoughts upon them.

*

Adela had never been given to purposeless torture. But in judgement she was without mercy, and it was the delivery of judgement the Ealdormen had assembled to witness.

Mother and Father took their positions to her left, as the next link in the Chain, and Klaus stood with them. To her right were the closest to her in blood of house Rainard: her brother's children, for her own were dead. Ealdormen of the three remaining houses surrounded them on the platform overlooking the Queen's Basin, the ancient arena of justice beneath her dungeons. The chamber had seen so much blood spilled that more drains had been dug into its stone floor, and a dedicated aqueduct from the Larin brought fresh water to wash away the grisly residue.

Elodie's small hand in his was cold. Flickering lantern-light masked the pallor of her face. She was doing well, her terror mostly confined to the death-grip of her fingers. He couldn't expect more of her at only seven. Klaus smiled at her with his eyes.

The thane who was led into the Basin was from Herenburg in the foothills of the Sterns. He was old enough to have learned to master his terror in the face of death, but young enough to have hope that death was yet far from arriving. Youth was the stronger contender of the two.

'Adalbern Braun of Herenburg, you are guilty of sheltering Far Northern spies in your land.' The Master of Judgements had been elderly at Adela's coronation; now he was the creak in a coffin lid. 'Of feeding and favouring them, allowing messengers to pass between them and our enemies in Kamkalka, and partaking in the highest treason against your Queen and the Chain.' Adalbern listened impassively; he had already confessed his guilt, which had been proven beyond all doubt by the Eye of the Court. Mother herself had caught him. 'Death is the sentence pronounced upon your house.'

Klaus would never forget the second of confusion on Adalbern's face. Perhaps Adela did know mercy, for she had spared him the worst of her sentence until this final moment. And perhaps she didn't, for there was no time now to appeal for clemency for the rest of his house. The executioner's axe fell swiftly, and he would not see the distraught woman brought in after him, or the string of terrified prisoners after her – his wife, his brothers, his half-demented father, every man and woman named Braun of Herenburg, sparing no one –

A small gasp escaped beside him. Klaus squeezed Elodie's hand. Adalbern's youngest son was a late windfall, younger than she. The chamber had never been so cold as the moment in which the child, barely old enough to have memories of his own, was split in half over the executioner's block.

'Is this really necessary?'

Lord Wintermantel was the only Ealdorman who dared question the Queen. Some said it was because her hand was stilled against him, the next heir of the Chain; others whispered that even she feared uncorking the infamous Wintermantel fury. Klaus knew it was more than either of these.

'Have I taught you nothing, Wolfram?' Adela's voice had always set Klaus' teeth on edge: dove-gentle, maturing to gravel. 'How else will we have certainty? He would not confess his collaborators, and no spy can be left behind. Now there will be no breeding ground for vengeance. You will go to Herenburg and install Avery Fearn there as thane, and then we will ensure any distant relations of Braun's are well favoured and harbour no ill will for the crimes of their kin. Only then can there be certainty.'

He visited Elodie at bedtime, knowing how demons tended to reserve their worst for the night, and was glad to find Mother already there. She knelt beside her, trying with little success to console her.

'Hush, my love. Hush.' She embraced the shaking child and kissed her head. 'What will your father think? Hush now.'

'But why the boy?' Elodie muffled sobs. 'And the grey-haired ones who couldn't kneel?'

'It's done, Melodia. They are with the Lifegiver now. The innocent amongst them will sup tonight at Sturmsinger's table. He'll know they died to keep his peace. When you are older you'll know the answer for yourself.' This was no consolation. She squeezed the child again; in the falls of her chestnut hair Elodie was lost altogether, and for a moment Klaus was uncertain whose comfort was sought and whose was given. 'Oh, my little quail. Stay as long as you can in the world you have now. If I could, I would keep the rest of it from you.'

She looked up. Their eyes met then, mother and son, and in hers was the admission she was already too late. Innocence was the impossible virgin in the North, and a child's world had changed, and captivity would follow soon enough.

*

Morning was once again as hot as the night had been cold. They ate the porridge grain dry. It stuck in their teeth and throats. Even the Derindin couldn't conceal their anxiety.

Klaus longed for the smell of rain; of rich, wet earth.

'This is the last barrel,' Terim told them as they refilled their waterskins. Meron said derina water was salt- and sugar-rich and more hydrating than water, so that even the horses didn't need as much to quench their thirst. Maida set a little aside for the sick, who were recovering – except for Yenvin, whose wounds had set her back.

'How far are we from the spring?' Verdi asked his uncle.

'With no delays, three days' ride. The storm's tail may hide a lagging wind. Let's get moving.'

'I've never seen such storms,' Klaus told Meron.

'And they will only worsen the more green growth we lose,' Meron replied tiredly. 'I hope some of what we've lost here still survives further North, at least.'

'You've never been north of the dam?'

'I fear it will break even my spirits.' The Derindman's smile was not without sadness. 'Better to live small where there is welcome than to purchase wonders that kick dirt in your face.'

Nothing Klaus and Arik had encountered compared to the days that followed. They'd been trained for hardship; had seen and dealt death, but this slow drawn-out injury was different – riding endlessly for hours under the pitiless sun; breathing air that stood still, resisting inspiration. Skin paper-dry and dusty, throats persistently parched. Everything was sand. The dunes stretched around them in an endless golden ocean, shimmering in the heat with the promise and threat of shade and shadows. Even the unadorned turquoise sky seemed to expand and gain mass of its own, becoming a crushing blue weight. Klaus at last understood why the Derindin had paused to cry farewell to the Ninvellyn at the edge of the Paiva, and felt the *sehresar* that haunted the Southern heart.

They didn't find any more derina, which puzzled the Derindin.

'Surely there should be more derina plants if we're approaching the spring?' Verdi fretted two nights after the storm over their smallest meal yet. Food made them thirstier, and with so little to drink, thirst dented hunger.

Suman shook his head, scanning the horizon for Petra's return.

'Many caravans have crossed the desert ahead of us, harvesting as they go. And crop patterns change based on the vitality of the springs. That's why we use the derina trail together with navigations.'

'Does the spring move?' Arik said, only half-joking. He'd never been comfortable navigating by 'that blasted tree', as he called the little derina shrubs.

'The oases have been known to vanish and reappear elsewhere,' said Suman, straight-faced.

Verdi looked alarmed. 'Is that why we haven't found it yet?'

For the hundredth time, Alizarin glanced up at the skies for the evening's earliest stars, as though waiting for them to draw a shorter road in the heavens.

'I don't know,' he said.

On the third day, they set off with no more water.

Petra returned to Suman's shoulder at dawn dry-feathered; whatever understanding they shared, he deduced no promise of water. The horses had not had a drink that morning. The Derindin whispered to them words of comfort. Ravi had taken to hiding in the coolest corner of the wagon, sleeping for entire days at a time – their one blessing, Arik remarked, guiding their wagon in stony silence. Even good-natured Verdi was surly, curling up in the wagon out of the heat like his oceloe, his notebook abandoned.

None of Klaus' assignments had taken him anywhere so desolate. In the pages of books, he had imbibed accounts of being marooned in the middle of oceans, cut off from all lifelines. In this dry uncertainty that promised only sand, Klaus thought he had tasted that terrifying isolation.

At noon, he began to feel light-headed. His heart raced on light feet that sometimes stumbled. The horizon flickered; he squinted, struggling to concentrate. Was it a reflection of water? He looked again and it was gone.

'It's a light-jester.' The voice sounded far away. His eyes focused; Meron, passing on his horse. 'They cast illusions in the desert. Are you well enough to ride, Master Tristan? Perhaps you should get into the wagon.'

Klaus shook his head and rode on.

Minutes and hours were replaced with dry heat and thirst and the infinite sand. It was easy for the mind to wander. The naked skies offered an empty slate on which his thoughts wrote themselves, sometimes in strings of gibberish. Dunraven would have now shed the russet robes of autumn, the rains freezing to snow. Klaus thought of his old life and his heart ached, too tired now to restrain itself. The strong arm of the man he had known as his father around his shoulders; the comfort of knowing his future even if he had never desired it … anger for every sacrifice he'd made to earn that future, only to be robbed of it anyway. Even in escape, there was no freedom. How long would it be before his friends regretted coming with him? Afldalr trembled. Under this glaring sun, his heart was laid bare, and there was no energy left in him to suppress its backlash or escape its diatribe, no strength to summon his Form. Pitiless skies stood over him like a magnifying glass.

This must be tesh. If so, it was more malignant than he could have possibly imagined, for it germinated an alien creature within him: it hatched the maggot of bitterness.

*

Yenvin died the following day just before noon. The sun was at its zenith when her mother emerged from her wagon cradling her little body, dazed with heat and thirst and grief.

An hour later they found the oasis.

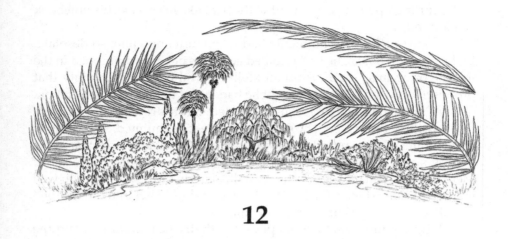

12

The Watchtower of Ilaria

FIVE TRIBES WITNESSED THE VALOUR OF STURMSINGER AND WEPT,
RECOGNISING THE LIFEGIVER'S FAVOUR UPON HIS SERVANT.
WEARY OF WAR, THEY SLEW INNER SERPENTS TO KNEEL
BEFORE THE MIGHT OF ANSOVALD STURMSINGER.

SONNONFER: THE RISE OF ANSOVALD STURMSINGER

Nothing tasted like water after the absence of water. They drank, stopped for breath, drank again.

Klaus lay back in warm sand by the lake under a canopy of gently swaying trees, savouring relief at last from the piercing blue gaze of the sky.

The oasis that erupted around this spring was as startling as a diamond in dirt. Palms towered over an abundance of growth, as plentiful as the desert was bare. The spring itself spilled into a generous pool of blue-green water. It was a place that felt removed from the Plains altogether, at least until wind parted the trees to reveal the naked dunes beyond.

Verdi marvelled, 'How can all this possibly grow out of wasteland?'

The Derindin gathered around Verna's wagon by the lake. They'd washed and wrapped Yenvin's body in white gauze, her taste of the spring arrived at long last. Verna hid her face in the small bundle.

'She must be laid to rest,' Mayda told her gently.

They buried her under the date palms in the last of the daylight. Their voices ribboned in yet another mourning prayer, gathering softly into a lament as light as the breeze rustling the trees. Verna succumbed to that stony emptiness that hardened so many Derindin faces.

'She passed through the doorway unblemished,' soothed the birdkeeper. 'In the next life she will have no stain of regret upon her.'

'Why must the desert take everything?' Verna demanded. 'These sands know nothing but death ... death in every cursed grain.'

*

Waking to the soft lapping of water and the whispering of leaves felt alien now. Klaus wished he didn't have to open his eyes, imagining instead he was on the banks of the Larin. This was when Afldalr was at its weakest: that first moment of waking, when the shroud around his heart thinned to gossamer.

A shower of cold drops hit his face. He bolted upright. Verdi yelped in the other bunk, apparently not spared.

'*You!*'

Ravi, who had disappeared soon after their arrival, was perched on the lamp sconce looking like a drowned rat.

'I suppose it was too much to hope that he'd been eaten by a snake,' grumbled Arik, throwing off his hides. 'Stop it, you arse. *Stop it!*'

The oceloe shook water out of his thick tail. Moments later, the wagon was empty.

'Little git,' Arik said darkly. 'Can't believe you were worried about where he got to. I'd have been grateful.'

'You're an unrefined oaf with no appreciation of beauty,' Verdi replied imperiously, but stayed clear of the wagon.

Pre-dawn had recast the lake in silver. They washed their dirt away. The drought had taken its toll, and most of the caravan still slumbered. Thirst had left a fatigue in Klaus' limbs that would take more than a drink to remedy. They strolled around the lake to where the spring frothed over its rocky mouth. Here the water tasted colder, even sweeter.

'The pirates must have been here not long before us,' said Verdi. 'This is their lure.'

Klaus cupped a hand for another sip. 'You can see what a powerful currency thirst can be.'

Beyond the trees, the misshapen shadow of a tall ruin grew clearer in the daylight. Something in its crooked spine beckoned to Klaus. A movement in the trees broke his gaze; Saya emerged, her master not far behind.

'Wish the runt in our wagon was as well-mannered as your tigon,' Arik told Alizarin.

'Oceloes are not the most docile of minibeasts.'

Verdi rapped the back of Arik's head when Alizarin stooped to offer Saya his palm. She darted up his arm, settling on his shoulder.

'What's that to the west?' Klaus asked Alizarin.

'Ruins. There are more ruins in the Plains than the living. Have you not heard that said before?'

'I'm going to take a look.'

'What about pirates?' said Verdi immediately.

'It's not far,' Klaus reassured him. Drily, he added, 'If any pirates are hiding in the rubble, we're already too close.'

'We leave as soon as the water wagon is refilled,' Alizarin warned. 'The windstorm season has only just begun, and there could be more pirates about. This may prove a dangerous place to linger.'

'I won't be long.'

'Suit yourself.' Arik yawned. 'You're nuts. I'm going to get more rest, if that blasted oceloe has stopped raining.'

'I'd better go and make sure he doesn't kill him,' Verdi whispered, hurrying after him.

To Klaus' surprise, Alizarin joined him when he set off towards the ruins.

'May as well check for signs of pirates,' said Alizarin. 'Go quietly. If Fibbler finds out, we'll never be able to make him stay behind.'

It was a short ride. The only remaining structure on the site was a square tower rising several storeys high, surrounded by rubble. It was now roofless, as though a great hand had torn its scalp away. The open mouth of a crumbling doorway gaped in its eastern wall, allowing a glimpse of a gutted chamber beyond.

'This was once a watchtower.' Alizarin gazed up at the ruin. 'Little remains of its original height. It was destroyed in the Second Redrawing. What was left was looted – even the hinges of the door were picked away. They would have looted the very stones of its walls, if they could.'

They dismounted. The horses were skittish; Alizarin laid his hands on their necks, whispering into their ears until they calmed. There were no signs of recent visitors. The foundation stones of smaller buildings surrounded the watchtower, destroyed. The site spanned some forty paces across. Eastward, the lake sparkled turquoise under the risen sun, cupped jealously in the green fist of the oasis.

'The tower is unsound,' Alizarin warned as Klaus picked through the rubble to the wide step before the empty doorway.

'I'm not going up.' As much as he'd have liked to, the bed of stones looked like an overgrown garden of tombs. Now that he was here, the strange lure of the watchtower had abated; he might have even imagined it. He walked around it. It had narrow windows where archers might have once perched with their bows. The doorway was twice his height. The stale, grey smell of dust and time lurked beyond. He stepped inside.

It opened into a single chamber. A stairway at the back was missing several steps. The ground was thick with rubble. He could see the storey above through gaps in the ceiling.

A sudden urge to climb up came over him.

A moment later he found himself on the stairs, one foot on the third step. He couldn't remember going up.

Something squeezed his forearm. Alizarin was shaking him, returning him to his senses.

'What are you doing?'

'I don't know. I had no intention of going up...' The stone shifted beneath his boot, ready to give way. Curious as he was ... he *hadn't* planned to climb.

Alizarin stared up at him from the foot of the stairs.

His head was spinning. His hand went to his brow; it was slick with cold sweat. Now the tower bore down on him, as heavy as it had once been tall. His heart began hammering. His head spun dizzyingly, blurring the room. Roaring filled his ears. Was it going to fall on them? Every stone, present and missing, was grinding him into the ground – *climb or leave, climb or leave* –

He gasped, 'I have to get out.'

He stumbled out of the watchtower. Alizarin steadied him so that he didn't quite fall but sank heavily to his knees on the step outside.

Eventually, his breathing slowed, and the hot wave of nausea subsided. Alizarin waited for him to regain his composure, perplexed.

'What happened?' Klaus asked. 'I was sure it was going to crush us.'

'Perhaps you panicked. It's a dark enclosed space; you wouldn't be the first to react with a turn.'

Klaus hadn't ever suffered nervous attacks in small spaces. He'd lain in crypts to discipline his Form, and pulled dead men from collapsed mines that had never known light. But he had no other explanation.

Alizarin stood, glancing at the sun. 'Are you well enough to ride back?'

Klaus rose on shaky legs. He was turning away when he noticed faded letters underfoot; they were etched into the step before the door, obscured by dust and loose stones. He brushed aside some of the debris with his boot, revealing a line of flowing script.

'Can you read this?' he called to Alizarin, who was already halfway to the horses.

Alizarin came back to look. 'Read what?'

Klaus swept more debris away with his hand. Alizarin stared down at the step, very still.

'I'm afraid I can't.' It was always hard to read Alizarin's face, but he was definitely taken aback. 'Suman might, but you'll never be able to get him out here.'

Klaus traced a letter with his hand; it spanned the length of his palm. They were engraved deeply, the crevices half-filled with dust and sand.

Alizarin straightened. 'We should go back.'

Klaus hastily copied the inscription onto a bit of parchment. The horses were impatient to be gone. As they rode away, Klaus thought he felt the gaze of all the eyes that had ever looked through those windows boring into his back.

Silence was not awkward with Alizarin. In fact, it felt harder to break than to keep.

'Where are you planning to take Verdi?' Klaus asked, undeterred.

'I had not planned to *take* him anywhere.'

'That was your first lie.'

Alizarin's eyes didn't stray from the road. 'I would be relieved if he accompanied me to Samsarra, but I'm well aware I cannot force him.'

'You want him to stay there?'

'It's the ancestral home of our clan. His birthright, if he accepts it.' Alizarin paused. 'And if you care for his welfare, you would encourage him to.'

'Why should I do that?'

Alizarin said nothing.

'You knew who I was immediately,' said Klaus.

'I knew which house raised my nephew. When news broke about the disappearance of the Wintermantel heir, it wasn't difficult to guess who you were. Or thought you were.'

'You didn't seem surprised by any of it.'

'No treachery out of Dunraven would surprise me.'

'How did you know Verdi had left Dunraven?'

'Do you truly think I wouldn't have kept watch over my sister's child?'

'He was abandoned to become a servant. No neglect would have surprised me.'

Alizarin's knuckles whitened around his reins. 'How was it that you learned the truth about your parents, before they pronounced you dead?'

Klaus flinched behind his Form. 'My sister was the one who found them out.'

'And you trusted her?' Now Alizarin's cobalt-blue eyes were as clear as the ruthless desert skies. 'A princess who has everything to gain from removing you from the Wintermantel household?'

'Elodie would never deceive me.'

'As you wish.'

There were many more questions with which Klaus could have baited him. But they'd reached the caravan.

'Anything interesting?' Arik asked.

'Everything is interesting to a chronicler.'

The caravan was leaving when Alizarin noticed his hunting knife was missing.

'I must have dropped it in the ruins,' he said, scowling.

'Do you want me to go back?' Klaus asked, feeling partially responsible.

'I'll go.' Alizarin nodded to Ayla. 'Don't wait, I'll catch up with you.'

'Only three day's ride to Romel now, if the Great Sentience is willing,' said Meron after Alizarin left for the watchtower. Verdi glanced back wistfully at the shade under the trees.

'Do not mourn the paradise that grows from a mass grave, Master Viridian,' Suman told him, catching his look. 'And now we have added one more grave.'

Klaus glanced at Meron. 'The oasis?'

'There are many stories about the oases. But yes, most are fertilised by the massacres of the Second Redrawing.' He climbed onto his horse. 'Don't let that ruin their bounty. We must be thankful instead for their gift to us after death.'

Verdi pulled a face. 'Is he joking? He must be joking.'

It was easier to leave after that.

*

Alizarin dismounted at the watchtower. He had none of Suman's Mantelonian superstition. Regardless, he didn't care to loiter. His hunting knife was safely inside his pocket where it had been all morning, for he was too seasoned a desert traveller to misplace it. Like all Derindin children, he had visited many ruins throughout the Plains, before either learning the fear of getting caught or catching the fear of some unnamed consequence. And later, he'd ridden through this particular place with a sweetheart in the saddle behind him

He was certain there had been no inscription on the doorstep of the watchtower.

The tower's shadow was a little longer now, but the place was otherwise frozen in time. Saya refused to leave his saddlebag. He walked carefully through the rubble. Where had the writing come from? Pirates or vandals could have added it for some joke, perhaps. This seemed implausible. He could credit them with neither such skill nor sophistication, and besides, no one lingered here, not even pirates. Mystics? True mystics were now few and far between, but they too shunned these shadows of dark history. They had no love for this chapter of the past, only shame.

He stopped outside the watchtower and stiffened, hand immediately going to his sword as though a blade would help. The hair rose on his neck.

The inscription was gone.

The ruins were deserted. No birds flew over such a place. Even the snakes avoided it.

He walked around the watchtower as the Northman had done. It had definitely been there on the doorstep. He kneeled, looked more closely, brushing away dust. There was nothing on the step; no sign a single stroke had ever been etched into its worn surface.

And yet his eyes had not deceived him that morning, with the Invelmari standing where he did now.

Alizarin was not a man of such arrogance as to dismiss unsuitable facts, nor to speculate on matters he did not understand. *Unlikelihood does not disprove reality*, Suman liked to say. Alizarin would have to consult someone more knowledgeable than himself. The question was who to trust in this age, when every charlatan claimed to be a lost sage, and ignorance had blurred the lines between knowledge and superstition.

But of course, he speculated all the same. Was it because of the Northman? He didn't know what had come over Klaus inside the tower; stumbling like one in a trance up those crumbling stairs, not answering to his name. Something about this discarded false prince unsettled him, with his pertinent questions and his impenetrable mask.

Alizarin grew wary of being alone by the watchtower, and of the hand that had written and unwritten its piece. Dissatisfied, he remounted his restless horse and departed.

13

The Sage-Bird

ÁSGEIRR WINTERMANTEL, WARLORD OF THE HEARTLANDS, PROCLAIMED
THE FIRST OATH: 'IN THE NAME OF THE LIFEGIVER, I BIND MY BLOOD AND
THE CHILDREN OF MY BLOOD TO THE SERVICE OF THE HOUSE OF
STURMSINGER, AND TO ANSWER WITHOUT FEAR
THE SUMMONS OF THE HOUSE OF STURMSINGER...'

SONNONFER: THE FORGING OF INVELMAR

'The Great Sentience calls back who He wills, young healer,' the birdkeeper
told Verdi gently. 'We must all pass through the doorway, and our time
is not ours to choose.'

But Yenvin's passing had been *preventable*.

'If only...' Verdi struggled for words. *This is not the North; there
shouldn't be so much bloodshed.* He gripped the bow Klaus was restringing.
'Those bloody pirates!'

'Perhaps tribulation is what will finally waken this land from the
Years of Sorrow.' The birdkeeper threw a handful of seed for a clutch of
warblers to catch; they exploded softly into the sky in a flurry of feathers.

'You'd think a thousand years of drought might have done that,' Arik murmured through a puff of smokeleaf.

'We must nurture hope,' the birdkeeper insisted. 'When Lorendar felled the great sage-bird, did he not finally see his own faults, and his the hardest of hearts?'

Verdi was eager for distraction. 'Tell us.'

The birdkeeper's eyes filmed over, straying into an unfathomable distance.

'He dismantled a great many corrupt kingdoms and returned stolen land to its people, but he was hard and unforgiving.' The birdkeeper scratched Ravi, whose purring became obnoxious. 'It was a wonder he became Custodian of the Plains at all, for the tradition had been abandoned for centuries. On the eve of his succession feast, in a moment of vanity before his challengers, he shot down a great bird from the sky.'

'Now, when he went to collect his trophy, Lorendar was horrified to find his arrow had downed for sport none other than the sage-bird: a noble creature and the queen of all birds. Her wound had turned her back into a woman, unable to escape. A very bad omen – what could be greater than the abuse of innocence?'

'A woman,' Arik repeated. Verdi threw him a warning look.

'Not just a woman … *Simyerin*, and the oldest Custodian of Orenthia come to bear witness to another Custodian reborn.'

Klaus glanced up from his bow.

'Her wisdom had gifted her with her wings, and she had departed for the heavens ever since, concealing her true form. For three moons Lorendar nursed the sage-bird, setting her broken wing. He sought her forgiveness, but she would not grant it because he had brought her down to earth in arrogance. He promised to repent by planting of the only tree from which she ate; she declined, for it only nurtured her flesh. He promised her a protected portion of sky in which she could fly undisturbed and never again be harmed; this too she declined, for her safety was not his to guarantee.'

Verdi was enthralled. Even Arik listened without interruption.

'She taught him many things while he sought her clemency. Finally he offered her all the children of his line to learn from her as he had done, and do the will of the Great Sentience as stewards of the land. This she accepted in return for her forgiveness.'

The birdkeeper stirred the fire.

'One day, he discovered she had disappeared. He ran out and looked into the sky, and saw a great bird whose wing eclipsed the sun. But when she vanished, it was in the place of dawn. A promise of reward to those who keep hope.'

'What did he do after that?' Verdi asked.

'He spent the rest of his life doing as she had taught him in the ninety nine days he tended to her, though he was grey of hair then. He kept his promise, planting the limolan tree on which she could feed. It flourished, though it never flowered nor fruited until after his death, and every so often during his stewardship there were sightings of the sage-bird; a sign of her approval. He taught his children's children to sow the limolan seeds so she would always feast well. But after Lorendar died and his treaties crumbled, and the Second Redrawing broke what remained of the South, the limolan trees died out and there were no more visits from the sage-bird.'

The birdkeeper stopped. Suman had appeared by the fire.

'That's quite enough for one night,' Suman said quietly.

Something about the birdkeeper's bashful fumbling as he gathered his seed-bag made Verdi feel very protective of him. He glanced resentfully at Suman's retreating back. Perhaps he had offended his clansman, but buried in the birdkeeper's stories was a little of the South that Verdi had longed to find.

*

'Was no one in Dunraven concerned about the pirates?'

Klaus returned to the wagon to find Arik already awake, waiting to relieve him for the rest of the night watch.

'The Eye watches everything,' Klaus replied. 'There've always been bandits here.'

'These aren't ordinary bandits. They're looking for something. Even the Derindin are surprised.'

Klaus said nothing. There was little to gain from compounding Arik's unease with his own.

'I don't like any of this,' Arik muttered. 'I don't like the way these people orbit Verdi. They know something about him. They've been told to keep their mouths shut. And I'll wager I know who's put them up to that.'

This much was obvious now, but the caravan was as tightly closed as the desert was wide, and Klaus didn't want to stir Alizarin's suspicions with questions.

'I'll find someone in Romel who'll talk. Alizarin can't hush a whole citadel.'

Arik was still dissatisfied. 'That's hardly the way for you to lie low.'

He was right. But the restless cogs in Klaus' mind were picking up pace. Perhaps it was no coincidence that strange activity in the Far South had secretly mobilised a handful of senior Intelligencers from Dunraven, while an explosion of irregular pirate raids arrived like the storms. What were the pirates looking for, that they needed to conceal their search by killing those they would have previously just robbed and left behind?

*

They reached Romel three days after leaving the oasis.

A wall of rough-hewn stone embraced the citadel like a great arm scooping it jealously to an unseen bosom. It rose gently to a plateau, offering glimpses of glass-paned domes and great bells, ornate bridges and clocktowers and turrets. Cedars towered and golden willows stooped over its ancient stone.

Klaus was glad that Verdi's eyes widened with wonder, fears briefly displaced. He smiled for his friend, then ached for himself. *As one is lost, another is found.*

'I can't force you to choose your path from here,' Alizarin told Verdi impassively. 'But for now, at least, I ask that you remain with me. As my nephew, you'll be as much a target for hostility as any Elendran. Romel is not Noisy Tree. The Babble that works these parts is well-established.'

'Something's up, Verdi,' Klaus warned when Alizarin had moved on. 'Stay close.'

Even half-cloaked in twilight, Romel was magnificent. The gates opened onto a fountain square, though its fountains were dry and its ornate planters of marble and turquoise empty. Towers and edifices of pale stone stood over wide streets, harkening to a time of power and prosperity. But the stonework was chipped and bolt-pitted like worm-eaten carcasses, and many windows stared down empty of glass like blinded eyes, with only rags fluttering across them in the breeze. The market was shutting up for the evening, sellers packing away a bewildering assortment of wares: fruits, smokeleaf, derina root, tools, sacks of grain, cloth, boots, lanterns, kahvi, spices, caged birds and precious stones.

The great iron gate of Romel was unmanned. Here the caravan finally disbanded.

Ferinc's wife sought them. 'A pirate hand you stilled that day would have cut my throat. This I will not forget.' She pressed her hand to her chest, glancing back at her husband. 'Neither will my kin.'

Klaus and Arik bowed.

'I hope you finish your journey in safety,' Arik replied.

Her gaze drifted to Verdi. 'Perhaps there's still hope, if even Lorendar himself can be redeemed.'

Ferinc remained by their wagon, but he nodded at them, pressing his own breast.

Klaus was most sorry to part with the birdkeeper.

'Your name, Master Birdkeeper,' he said, nudging the little man gently yet again.

'Ahhh! In truth I had almost forgotten it. My name is Niremlal, Master Northerner, and my hamlet is not far from Samsarra, especially not for a collector of stories and roads.' The birdkeeper's face broke into his wrinkled smile. 'Farewell, friend chronicler. May *sehresar* keep you company on every road. Look after the young Santarem.' He touched Verdi's forehead before pressing his own chest, making Verdi blush.

They were leaving the square when a grey horse tore through the gates.

'A physician!' bellowed the rider. 'Fetch a physician!'

Alizarin gripped Verdi's arm as he darted forward. 'Wait.'

A bundle slumped across the rider's horse. He jumped down and dragged it from his saddle. Several horses followed. A young man dismounted amongst them, staggering forward. Klaus noticed that Ayla wasn't watching the arrivals; instead, her eyes roved over the closing market, the square, the walls. The tumblers fanned out. *But fighting is not permitted in the citadel.* Klaus resisted the beckon of his sword.

A crowd gathered around where the young man was kneeling and weeping.

The bundle was so small that at first Klaus thought it was a child, but as they drew closer he glimpsed a grey beard and thin, twisted hands.

'Too late,' said the rider.

'They left him for dead,' the young man sobbed. 'He lived a dog's life, my father. And only to pass through the doorway like this –' He was inconsolable.

Alizarin parted the crowd easily. The dead man had been starved so that his eyes sat in grey hollows, and gutters ran deep between the tendons of his fingers. His legs were black and bloated with dehydration, soles rubbed away by hot sand and festering with wounds. His knees were drawn up forever against his thin chest – he had died like this, curled up in despair beyond imagining.

'*Anger must be your servant.*' Master Arnander's voice always rang as clearly in Klaus' mind as though he were standing over his shoulder still. '*Master it, and it will be the true steel in your scabbard.*'

'His family was ambushed by bandits on the Cinnabar Highway,' said his rescuer. 'We found the remains of their wagons some ten miles west of Romel. The old man was abandoned in the desert another few miles away. When we found him he was still alive.'

Alizarin's back was straight as a blade, blazing eyes more bruising than a pair of fists. 'And the others?'

'They took everyone else.'

A frightened murmur rippled through the crowd.

Alizarin raised his voice. 'Who will claim the honour of washing and burying this man?'

They left father and son to their grim parting. The crowd dispersed, their fear lacing the growing dark. One man remained, standing with his back to the sad spectacle in the square.

'Now here's a face I've not seen for a long time.' He spoke to Alizarin, but it was Verdi who had his eyes. 'A kinsman, Alizarin?'

Alizarin's reply could have sharpened their swords. 'Yes.'

The man nodded to himself. 'A terrible business, these raids. But they will pass, and we'll be here to remember the treachery of Elendra.'

'I doubt the bereaved will be so easy to distract from their dead.'

The man's smile was frosty. 'The dead are easily forgotten … although some less so than others.' He thew Verdi another glance before he departed.

Arik frowned, but Ayla stopped any questions in their tracks. 'Let's get to the inn.'

They passed Derindin who had no curiosity to spare for the Northerners, and others who made no secret of their resentment. Klaus blessed the deepening dark. The inn was in the citadel's eastern quarter. The innkeeper and his wife greeted the caravan warmly, calling upon two cheerful daughters for stew and kahvi. The chatter faltered when Arik and Klaus lowered their hoods.

'My guests, Riorga,' Alizarin told the innkeeper loudly. 'And my nephew.'

Riorga found his tongue. 'I'll have some rooms made up.' He squeezed Verdi's shoulder. 'An honour, young man. Welcome back.' His wife stared at Verdi as she cleared a table.

Arik muttered in Klaus' ear, 'I knew we shouldn't have trusted him.'

'Patience. I'm sure this is hard enough for Verdi without us imagining the worst.'

But Klaus was fast growing uneasy.

Arik was far from placated. 'If the pirates left only the old man for dead, what did they do with the rest of his caravan?'

A Derindman came down the stairs, a clean-shaven man of at least sixty. His coat was fine, his clothes clean. The Derindin stood to greet him. His eyes landed immediately on Verdi. A measuring look, holding far more than it ought to have done for a stranger. He glanced at the two Northerners once before disappearing above stairs with Alizarin, Suman and Ayla. Klaus had never been able to teach Verdi how to master his face, and it was furrowed with worry.

'Who was that?' Klaus asked Meron when he joined them with a pot of kahvi.

'That's Elder Tourmali, of Elendra's clan council –'

'Master Meron! We were expecting you a full week ago.' A youth hurried across the room, stopping so abruptly at the sight of Arik and Klaus that he hit his shin against a chair.

Arik winked at Verdi. 'Wonder how long it'll be before that wears off.'

'Storms, Bevro. This is Alizarin's nephew and his friends. Bevro is one of my students at the Arboretum.'

Bevro didn't look too sorry to be elbowed aside by a handful of tumblers.

'Elders better swap yapping for some action soon.' Broco joined them with a pitcher of cider. 'Every other caravan that's passed through Romel has either seen or tasted pirates. That bag of bones they brought into the market – that was just the beginning. May the Great Sentience rest his soul,' he added quickly, catching sight of Rasan's face.

'If Garet hears you talking like that about the Elders, he'll have your hide.'

'Even he'll have to pull his head out of his arse sooner or later. Notice *he* stayed in Samsarra.' Broco ignored Saarem's warning look. 'The Cinnabar Highway is a death wish. There's even talk of Sisoda sending out battalions to round up the pirates.'

Rasan snorted. 'I'll believe it when I see it. Chieftain Zakra's afraid of his own shadow, whatever his Elders think.'

'Bollocks. There must be more to Zakra than soiled pants if he's held onto the S'beyan Strip for a decade.'

They ate: parchment-thin bread as soft as butter, another loaf thick and studded with smoky seeds; a stew slightly sweet with figs and fragrant with wild thyme.

'Will Romel be safe from pirates?' asked Verdi.

Broco laughed. 'Even pirates aren't that stupid.'

'Romel follows the laws of the Murhesla,' said Meron. 'There can be no bloodshed within the citadel.'

'Do they guard the citadel?' asked Arik.

'Day and night,' said Broco. 'Murhesla took Romel from the Chieftains and banished them from it until they agreed to adhere to their terms. Everything from the Custodian's Palace to the gutters is watched. Romel's seen far worse than pirates.'

'There was no one at the gates,' said Verdi doubtfully. Broco smirked at Rasan as though sharing some secret joke, but her face remained blank, and at a look from Saarem his smile vanished into his cider.

'They don't guard the roads, however,' said Rasan.

'That might change if the roads to Romel end up paved with bones.'

'That's enough of that,' growled Saarem.

Tourmali returned, this time making his way to their table with

Alizarin and Suman. The tumblers fell silent.

'Welcome home, Viridian. No, please keep your seat.'

They ignored him, chairs scraping the ground as they stood. Arik and Klaus bowed. Tourmali was polite but closed; a thawed offering of Alizarin.

'Welcome, Masters Invelmari. We have few Northern visitors, and even fewer who wish to remain.'

'I don't know if we're staying,' Verdi said quickly. 'But we travel together.'

'For their services to our caravan, I'm certain Chieftainess Emra would wish to thank them herself. We return to Samsarra after the Assembly tomorrow.'

Verdi swallowed. 'Assembly?'

'The clans meet in Romel every third new moon. To bring news, make treaties, air grievances. And I fear that this moon there will be much of grievance.'

Something plopped on the wooden floor. Ravi had fallen from Verdi's shoulder in his sleep. He tottered on his paws, too dozy to be annoyed.

'Forgive me,' said the Elder. 'It's late, and your journey's been long. I shan't keep you from your rest.'

Riorga's daughter showed them to their room, stealing furtive looks at Arik which restored a semblance of normality at last. A boy brought up water for the washstand and trimmed the wicks in the lanterns.

'We shouldn't have come,' Arik griped again. 'There's something no one is telling us.'

Klaus caught sight of Verdi's face. 'Well, we're here now.'

He listened to Verdi tossing long after Arik had fallen asleep. His own eyes were heavy and his body ached, but he was too troubled to rest.

'Do you think I could sit out this Assembly?' Verdi finally ventured.

'You're free to do whatever you wish. But your uncle will notice.'

'I'm not ready to be noticed,' he said in a small voice.

To this Klaus had little comfort to offer. 'Verdi, why did you suggest we go to Derinda?'

Bed sheets rustled as Verdi turned.

'It seemed the easiest option,' he said slowly. 'It would have been easier to disappear in Semra, but ... you'd have to get there first. Even Elodie thought it was a good plan.'

Klaus was suddenly wide awake. A cold claw closed around his heart. 'You told her we might travel South?'

'It was her idea in the first place.'

Eventually Verdi's breathing slowed, leaving him with his demons.

*

Alizarin paced the adjoining chamber. 'These are not the pirates we've swatted away in the past.'

'Things are worse than you think,' Tourmali replied. 'For a fortnight now, stories have trickled in of captives taken alive.'

'So we discovered tonight at the gate.'

A heavy silence followed. Even the Second Redrawing had not brought a slave trade to the Plains.

'All this will strengthen our petition for Merensama,' said Suman.

Tourmali shook his head. 'Without proof, we'll meet with much resistance. Not all clans have been badly hit by pirates. Besides, Merensama shouldn't be muddied with such matters. No, it's not yet time. We cannot thrust the boy into this rashly.'

Suman pressed his lips together. 'What of Kirono Folma's warning?'

'Was he certain the pirates were looking for something?'

'He died before he could say more. Their caravan had been ransacked.'

'Did they search your caravan too?'

'They never had a chance.'

'Yes … these Northmen, Alizarin.' Tourmali paused. 'It may have served you well, but theirs is not the company anyone had imagined for him.'

'It's the company he has chosen.'

'We should just be glad he's safely returned to us now,' Suman reminded them. 'Pirates or otherwise, the time is ripe.'

Far from it, Alizarin thought, more relieved by this than he dared to admit.

*

Verdi woke with a start, and struggled to get back to sleep.

Ravi was sleeping against the small of Arik's back; being the biggest of the three of them, Arik was also the warmest. The little traitor had done this at every opportunity for at least fifteen years. Arik had no idea.

Smokeleaf fumes wafted in through the window, and the warm spill of lanterns from the street below nudged the great edge of darkness.

Verdi had dreamt of a desert air unfettered by Adela's decree, and lettervaults filled with scholars, and a train of long-lost cousins. Instead, the shadows seemed as deep here as they had been in Dunraven.

Arik was right. We shouldn't have come.

He got up and pulled on his boots.

Out of lifelong habit, he paused to check on Klaus; miraculously he was asleep, turning only once. Faint singing and the clink of cutlery drew him out to the landing. At this hour, the smell of kahvi was comforting but out of place. In Invelmar they took kahvi in the morning. In Derinda, it was a balm the Southerners rubbed into the wounds they sang of at night.

The door of the adjacent room was ajar. He peeked inside; all four beds were undisturbed.

'You shouldn't be out here on your own.'

Verdi jumped so loudly he was sure his clumsy thud against the wall must have been heard at the citadel gate. Alizarin sat almost lost in shadow by the window.

'I didn't see you,' Verdi stammered.

Alizarin's silence was more mocking than any reply. A soft roll of smoke unwound and faded around him.

They had never been so alone together. A lifetime of questions lined up. Verdi would have liked to ask why he was sent away. He should have dared to ask about his mother and father. Forget all sentiment; he ought to have demanded what was being kept from him, that moved strangers to take him into their arms and bid him tearful welcome. Always the words evaded him, sticking in his throat.

'Why are you still awake?' Alizarin said finally. 'Your friends are sound asleep.'

'Klaus hasn't slept soundly for thirteen years. He thinks I don't know. Ever since…' Verdi stopped. His uncle looked irritated now, as though irked by the reminder that his nephew had been an Ealdorman's servant. Oddly, this restored Verdi's defiance. 'Derinda is nothing like I expected.'

'What did you expect?'

'Not this.' Truthfully, he'd had no idea. Oh, how he had dreamed … but children outgrew dreams, and his life in Dunraven had absorbed him. There had been no prospect of any other life. 'I know I never expected so much cruelty.'

'You've come from Dunraven, where only weeks before you left you must have seen Adela execute a thirteen-year-old child for slander,' said his uncle, incredulous. 'And yet the pirates have calibrated your measure of cruelty?'

'These pirates are *Derindin*,' Verdi retorted. 'The men who slaughtered that caravan were Derindin … the people who abandoned that poor man, after taking his family hostage, are Derindin.'

He wondered at his own words. Death was too readily embraced in the North … but such was his disappointment to find it was no stranger here.

'You may despise the Blood Pact, but it works,' Verdi continued. 'In

Invelmar there would be no pirates.'

His uncle exhaled another cloud of smoke. 'You become a man when you're angry.'

Immediately Verdi felt foolish again, and his irritation cooled as quickly as it had come.

Alizarin lit an oil lamp on the table. He was still wearing his travelling cloak.

'You're quick to defend your Northern friends. That's loyalty speaking.' Alizarin jerked his head towards the adjoining chamber. 'Would your master over there have deserted Dunraven for you, had your positions been reversed?'

Verdi glared at his uncle.

'You've been in the North too long,' said Alizarin.

Bluntly, he replied, 'I've been where you put me.'

There was another silence, and he could now see his uncle's face, and it was stone.

'Go to sleep,' Alizarin told him. 'The others will soon return.'

Sure enough, voices rose on the stairs, and Verdi hurried out.

He lay awake for a long time. A faint murmur of conversation scratched softly at the adjoining walls as three Derindmen talked late into the night. He did not know then that they were as lost as he in the new currents tossing about the world they knew, and so morning would find them having had no rest at all.

14

The Romelian Assembly

NEXT, NANTELM PROSPERE CHALLENGED LORD STURMSINGER
TO A DUEL, SURRENDERING BOTH PRIDE AND PLEDGE UPON
NOBLE DEFEAT: 'IN THE NAME OF THE LIFEGIVER, I BIND MY BLOOD AND
THE CHILDREN OF MY BLOOD TO THE SERVICE OF THE HOUSE OF
STURMSINGER...' SELEWYNE ELDRED, ADALBERT HAIMRIC, WILFRID
RAINARD – ALL PLEDGED TO ANSOVALD STURMSINGER.

SONNONFER: THE FORGING OF INVELMAR

The Assembly began at noon.

Klaus looked around the pillared building. 'Are we in a mausoleum?'

'Close. This is the shrine to Kanthra, a Simyerin of Orenthia,' Broco replied. A pleasant shiver grazed Klaus' spine. 'The Elders hold the Assembly here hoping to revive a portion of her wisdom.' Derision crept into his voice. 'Have you been to a theatre, Master Tristan?'

Derindin from every clan but Akrinda crowded around a central dais ringed by stone benches. They spilled out into the street, high- and low-born alike crammed shoulder to shoulder. A great domed roof paned with jade and coral glass directed a pillar of jewelled light onto the needle of a sundial standing in the middle of the dais. The air crackled, bloated with the momentum of the promised storm.

If anything, Verdi had made Arik and Klaus more visible, thanks to the curiosity that followed him everywhere. Klaus merged with the crowd. Even here, Form softened his otherness.

Quiet fell as Elders arrived. They gathered around the dais, shafts of light standing sentry around them. They raised no banners; still, the invisible clan divisions between them were unmistakable.

'There you are!' Fibbler squeezed in between Klaus and Verdi. Klaus raised him up for a better view. He glimpsed Rasan across the dais, flanked by her native Periami clanfolk. His pulse tripped: at least two Invelmari waited in the crowd.

'Derindin!' a silver-bearded Elder called across the dais. His voice was amplified and thrown around by the generous dome, filling every crevice of the chamber. 'If I may speak first: for weeks, Lebasi farmers have been looted by pirates. Two of our caravans have not returned from Invelmar's border towns. A third disappeared a week ago returning from our silver mine on the Kassian Road.'

He looked across the dais at Alizarin.

'Now we've heard accounts of unforgivable cruelty. A fortnight past, just one woman returned from a caravan of fifty. I bring her testimony. Every man, woman and child was slaughtered. Twelve children, one a babe in arms!'

The crowd stirred, echoing his anger throughout the chamber.

Someone bellowed, 'How dare they!'

'They must be stopped,' shouted another to cries of support.

A pale woman stepped forward. 'So pirates are now to blame? Chieftain Mensil initially accused Fraivon of orchestrating that attack on the Kassian Road, to avoid paying for a delivery of silver ore that we never received. Who's to say Lebas didn't strike their own caravan so they can accuse us of stealing their silver?'

More jeering: 'Bollocks to that, thieving's what Fraivon does best!'

'That didn't take long.' Broco shook his head. 'Nothing ever changes.'

'What about the caravan your clan lost three weeks before, Elder Kira, returning from Romel?' Mensil fired back. 'Or the cargo of kahva you sent North that was ambushed near the Chefren oasis – escorted by a fist of Sisodan tumblers, no less? Who robbed Fraivon's caravans then, if not pirates?'

'Perhaps we should ask how you know so much about our losses!'

'For shame, all of you!' The chamber fell silent immediately for the woman beside Suman. 'These pirates are not your game piece. Their shadow falls across *all* our borders. There are hamlets and villages within Mantelon's lands that have woken to find their winter stores stripped and their stables empty.'

'The East has no right to stoke fear in all the Plains just because it can't cope with a nuisance,' an Elder mocked.

'And it's Hesper's way to sneer at everyone else's misfortunes,' Mensil retorted. 'Pirates are far more than a mere nuisance now.'

'What are they, then? An army of warriors?'

Laughter spread through some factions, hissing through others.

Mensil was determined. 'These raiders come daily, and they take far more than a sack of grain.'

'Anyone would think they've got more to fear from each other than pirates,' Verdi whispered, so annoyed he didn't notice Ravi nibbling another hole in his cloak.

'What about the rest of you?' Mensil demanded, looking around the dais. 'Or do you all deny being stung by pirates?'

The Elder who next spoke was dressed as a tumbler. 'Raiders haven't troubled Voista much. We only see them on our northern front, for we're fortunate enough to be fortified to the south by our dear neighbour, Elendra.' She mock-bowed towards Tourmali and Alizarin, eliciting a smattering of laughter.

'Clan Periam deny such flagrant raids,' another Elder announced stiffly.

'Shame!' cried Mensil. 'Didn't Periam lose two full caravans of winter stock? My own clansmen saw them leaving Appledor! Yet they've not returned.'

'Perhaps, like Fraivon, we can't conclude the identity of the culprit.'

'The identity of the culprit is no mystery,' the Mantelonian Elder interrupted. 'For too long, pirates have taken what is not theirs – emboldened by our tolerance. It's time to hold them to account.'

'And how do you propose we do that, Cilastra?'

'By forming an alliance against them, of course.'

Muttering filled the chamber, suspicion and support scuffling in equal measure. Klaus recognised the next speaker: the man who'd threatened Alizarin at the citadel gates.

'Pirates trouble Baeron little, for they know they'll be swiftly dealt with.' He was younger than most of the Elders, and handsome. 'But how can all this be the work of pirates, who are scattered and powerless? Fraivon and Lebas can't even decide who's to blame for their misfortunes. Chieftain Mensil claims he has a single survivor's testimony, and the rest is based upon hearsay. Be reasonable, brothers and sisters.' He spoke as much to the crowd as to the Elders. 'The desert is vast, but we know its roads and waterways. How can the Plains hide such a scourge? Are they not merely still a handful of bandits, sowing fear to ignite a fire amongst us?'

He was sly and persuasive; toxic and charming. To an Intelligencer, his method was all too familiar.

'I'm sorry for your losses, Chieftain,' he told Mensil graciously. 'But what you suggest is preposterous. We've only one account of a raid, and from a woman likely dazed with sun-stroke.'

'Will an entire caravan of survivors be testimony enough for Baeron, Elder Agatin?' Alizarin interjected. '*My* caravan survived the raid. My passengers will tell you of a company of pirates who tried to rob us near the Nerej oasis.'

Alizarin addressed the Elders of both Fraivon and Lebas.

'Last night I had the burden of sending word to Kirono Folma's wife. His caravan was butchered, picked to the bone. Many of you knew Kirono. A good Fraivonian man who kept stable for many of us in Noisy Tree. He was left to die under the sun, breathing in the stench of his rotting clansmen.'

Alizarin paused, gazing over the crowd. He had the better measure of his audience.

'Shall I tell you of corpses barely the size of lambs, dismembered and defiled in the sand?' The air grew torrid with anger. Alizarin knuckled his forehead, then his heart. 'For the bereaved among you, I have submitted to your Elders what personal effects we reclaimed.'

'A purge!' a man burst out. 'Hunt them down like a pack of rats and be done with them!'

Cheers of agreement overwhelmed any dissent.

'Brothers and sisters!' Tourmali called. 'The pest has become a plague. Already the pirates demand tokens for a drink. Do we allow them to demand a tax in return for sparing our villages?' Shouts shook the assembly. 'If they become strong enough, will they be allowed to control our passage through the Plains? Control the roads to the border towns on which we all depend?'

He waited, allowing the anger he'd fanned to flare.

'Derindin! How can we possibly purge our lands without an alliance?'

'A pledge!' someone roared, and the chant was taken up throughout the chamber. *Pledge! Pledge! Pledge!*

Uneasy glances darted like mice between the Elders around the dais.

'I raise a pledge for an alliance against the pirates,' Tourmali cried. 'Together we can crush them once and for all!'

Mensil responded at once. 'Accepted! We will avenge our dead.'

Cilastra nodded. 'Mantelon accepts.'

Cheers rose around the chamber.

'Deferred!' Kira cried. 'Until the slander against Fraivon has been lifted, we may as well all be pirates.'

Baeron and Hesper echoed one another: two rejections. The chamber buzzed with a confusion of cheers and hisses. Common folk wanted safety, vengeance. But Klaus had already gauged Voista's reply: another rejection. Then the Periami Elder abstained, and the bewildered crowd paused to judge which way the scale had tipped. One Elder, armed and powerfully built, hadn't yet spoken; Klaus deduced he had to be Sisodan. Every last whispering street urchin in the chamber fell silent when he stepped forward. Tension stretched taut the air.

'Bandits are as native to the Plains as sand to the desert,' he said. 'You want to root them out without a fight? You may as well strike a bargain with the drought and hope for rain.'

He glanced across the dais.

'But until we know the real culprit behind the attack on the caravan that you contracted our tumblers to escort, Kira of Fraivon, there'll be no commitment from Sisoda. And once we learn the truth, we'll punish the guilty, pirates or otherwise.'

It was a moment before the crowd realised Tourmali's motion against the pirates had failed. Anger swarmed, but there were also cheers. In the dark silence of stony or stricken faces, Klaus saw hope dismayed; fear fuelled rather than mollified. Rasan had vanished.

Agatin tried to speak again, but the chamber was too restive for further business, and the Elders stepped down from the dais.

Klaus spotted Mayda, ready to wrench Fibbler to safety. He jostled his way out, keeping Verdi within his sight. Did Murhesla have eyes even here, where a knife could be slipped quietly between the ribs? Someone squeezed his arm; he looked down into the eyes of a grey-haired woman. She reached up to touch his forehead, then pressed her breast before disappearing into the crowd.

'Yenvin's grandmother,' said Broco into his ear. 'Sisoda won't forget. Our memories are very long here in the South.'

*

'That was worse than I'd feared,' said Tourmali wearily back at the inn.

Arik groaned inwardly. They'd barely been in Romel a day, and already it was beginning to feel like the inside of a war room. Except that, in Dunraven, the yapping bore fruit.

Alizarin replied tartly, 'We got exactly what we expected.'

Arik drummed his fingers on the table where the remains of a meal sat half-eaten. The Derindin were impatient to leave for Samsarra, but repairs on the water wagon weren't yet complete.

'What will you do now?' asked Verdi, dismayed.

'Try to persuade them to pledge against the pirates before the next Assembly.' Tourmali paused. 'It would be wise not to mention that the pirates were looking for something, until we know what they're after.'

Privately Arik agreed, but still found himself irritated. 'Why are Baeron and Hesper so keen to downplay the pirate threat?'

'An alliance against the pirates is more detestable to them than any number of raids,' Alizarin replied. 'They're old allies, and two of the most powerful clans. They'll consider any wider alliance a threat to their power.'

'And unfortunately much of Derinda's wheat comes from their western clandoms,' Tourmali added. 'Were it not for Sisoda, Baeron and Hesper would control the Cinnabar Highway and have a monopoly of the entire market. No clan will cross them lightly.'

They were interrupted by a knock at the door, all rising when Cilastra entered. Arik regarded the Mantelonian Elder with interest, mindful of her sway over the Assembly. She was at least sixty, her grey hair pulled back from a handsome face.

'I couldn't leave without greeting your nephew, Alizarin.'

Verdi's cheeks turned rosy. Even Ravi had the grace to look bashful.

'You do us great honour,' Alizarin replied, as expressionless as ever. Arik ground his teeth. Only for Verdi's sake had he agreed to follow this man to Samsarra.

'I knew your father as a boy.' Cilastra's faint smile at Verdi's startled face was tinged with sadness. 'But it is your mother who I remember most often.'

'You knew them both?'

She nodded. Verdi's face fell when she offered no more.

'Rumours are already spreading on the Babble that we've declared war against the pirates,' she said, with a healthy garnish of Arik's own scorn for the Babble. 'If the pirates should retaliate, I must warn my clan.' Her eyes fell on him and Klaus. 'Are you here to raise your steel for us, Masters Invelmari?'

Klaus bowed deeply. 'That was not why we came, my lady.'

She nodded. 'They are few who exchange the North for our Plains, but I hope you shall find nothing to deter you.'

With that, she departed. Verdi picked up their packs, old habits being difficult to break. Arik stifled annoyance. *If old habits end up giving us away, I'm going to kill him.*

'I need some air,' Verdi mumbled.

'The wagons are almost ready,' Alizarin warned.

'I'll just check the horses, then.'

Arik rose to follow him, but Verdi shook his head. He looked so despondent that Arik didn't have the heart to argue. Ravi parked himself by the remains of a bowl of soup, shamelessly making up for the dent in all their appetites.

'Is that what you mean to do in Derinda, Masters Invelmari?' Tourmali asked once Verdi had gone. 'Put your swords to use for coin?'

'Seems a healthy trade,' Arik replied blandly.

'Many Northmen come to put their steel to work here. Some even stay. Mostly mercenaries, but others too. Exiles, eccentrics. Spies.' Tourmali remained unabashed. 'I have seen your land, and in your place I would not leave it.'

Arik forced a smile. 'As you say, sir, we're mostly mercenaries.' At least Tourmali spoke plainly. *Wish everyone else did.* 'Perhaps even friendship makes the crossing.'

A small *plop* came from the table; Ravi had rolled sideways in contentment, led – or possibly weighed down – by a very full belly. Broco announced the repairs were finished, and Arik and Klaus gathered their belongings and a very sleepy oceloe. They loaded their wagons in the yard and headed for the stables.

The horses were still in their bays, and there was no sign of Verdi.

15

Starblossom

WITH HIS VASSALS FIVE AND THE LIFEGIVER'S BLESSING, STURMSINGER
VANQUISHED DISSENT AND UNITED THE NORTH'S MANY TRIBES.
ALL BUT THE MOST DEPRAVED, WHO FLED INTO THE WHITE WASTES
AND COWERED BEHIND THEIR IDOLS. THEY COULD NOT PERCEIVE
THE LIGHT OF ANSOVALD STURMSINGER.

SONNONFER: THE FORGING OF INVELMAR

'He asked to take kahva,' said the flustered innkeeper. 'I was attending to a traveller enquiring after rooms… My daughter saw him walking towards the stables after that –'

'A traveller?' Klaus interrupted.

'Not one I knew. A slight fellow. He didn't uncover his face. I told him we'd have rooms later but he left without reserving any.'

Arik cursed colourfully. 'Of course he did.'

Verdi had vanished before his kahvi had even arrived. Increasingly frantic, they searched the stalls again, finding no sign of a struggle. Alizarin stormed through the inn; no one had seen anything untoward.

Ayla ordered the tumblers to search the surrounding streets.

'Are you certain he might not have just wandered off?' said Tourmali.

'What do you think he is, a child?' Arik snapped.

'He knew we were leaving soon, he wouldn't have gone.' Klaus checked Verdi's horse; it wasn't saddled. 'I doubt he even made it as far as the stables.'

The inn overlooked the marina, now busy with boatmen. To the front, its yard led onto a main road. Worry cemented in Klaus' stomach. Verdi was quick and an excellent knifehand, but he was no soldier. He'd only been gone ten minutes, but irrationally Klaus' mind kept creeping back to the man delivered to the fountain square, desiccated alive ... fear gripped his heart. He caught sight of Ravi, wide awake and trembling pitifully on their wagon seat, and knew then that Verdi was no longer nearby. He ran back to the stables.

'Where are you going?'

'Fighting isn't permitted in the citadel.' Klaus swung into his saddle. 'Only a fool would keep someone captive here after the gate's shut and wait to be found, which means he's not going to be in Romel long.'

He galloped out of the yard, Arik on his tail, dimly aware of angry insults hurled at the two Invelmari scum tearing through Romel's streets. He kept his eyes peeled, but it was the gate they needed to reach. Moments later, they burst into the fountain square.

Arik panted, 'Where now?'

Surely a kidnapper couldn't have already carried Verdi to the gate unseen – *unless he's bundled up in the back of a wagon*. It was a chilling possibility. The square bustled: merchants loading carts and closing up stalls, children playing, caravans entering the citadel.

'Watch the gate for anyone leaving,' he told Arik. 'It's nearly dusk. No one travels in the dark.'

'What if they're keeping him here?'

But Klaus was certain. The citadel would be a cage once the gate was closed. His only comfort was that Verdi's kidnappers wouldn't make it far before night forced them to stop. But it would be difficult to search for a camp by night, even one near the citadel.

He insisted, 'If he's alive, they won't keep him here and wait to be found.'

Perhaps we were too slow. Klaus' heart lurched; perhaps Verdi had passed through the gate under their very noses, stashed between sacks of derina tubers. Then Klaus saw two things at once. A dun mare crossed the square, followed by a larger stallion that stepped more heavily than it should. And when Alizarin and Ayla appeared, the mare broke into a gallop towards the gate, the stallion close behind.

Klaus tore after them even before he spotted the bundle slumped across the back of the stallion.

A great commotion of upturned barrels and curses erupted as six horses stormed through the square and out of the citadel. The kidnappers galloped west, not caring what they hit. Klaus dug his knees into his mare's flanks. As soon as he'd passed through Romel's gates, he pulled his crossbow into his arms.

But the mare ahead was fast. Arik's heavier stallion was a few paces behind him, Alizarin and Ayla lagging further still.

'Bring the stallion down,' Arik bellowed into the wind.

I'll have to slow down to shoot. But Klaus' lighter horse was their best chance of catching up to the kidnappers. *If I miss, the race is lost.*

There was no time to reason. Another moment, and the stallion would be out of range.

Klaus slowed down to fit a bolt as Arik raced past.

A fine tremor shook his fingers. He summoned Form, stilling his hands. Either side of him, horses pelted past like shadows as Alizarin and tumblers overtook him. He raised his arms, gripping his horse with his thighs. A white wave filled his mind, the world shrinking into his target. Holding his breath, he released his bolt.

The stallion let out a long ragged neigh and fell to the ground.

The mare's rider glanced back, losing the advantage.

The second bolt was easier. Klaus didn't wait to see where it landed, galloping forward.

Arik reached the mare and slashed her flank. She rolled in the sand, her rider flung from the saddle.

Klaus dismounted, pushing past the tumblers surrounding the stallion. The kidnapper was dead, neck broken. Verdi lay beside him, eyes closed. Nothing was at an odd angle; nothing open or wounded. Alizarin knelt beside him, tight-lipped. He sniffed Verdi's breath.

'He's been drugged.'

Relief washed through Klaus. He followed Ayla to the dead mare. Arik hauled up the second kidnapper, ripping the sand-mask away.

It was a woman, not much older than Verdi. Her jaw was bloodied, one shoulder very square under her torn sleeve. Klaus' second bolt protruded from her belly.

Others were arriving now: more tumblers, Tourmali, spectators.

'Who are you?' asked Alizarin harshly.

She squirmed once, twisting her dislocated shoulder and stifling a gasp of pain. Her breathing was fast and ragged, her face pale.

'Are you Murhesla?' Saarem demanded.

'No,' said Ayla. 'She's a pirate.'

The woman remained silent.

'Listen to me.' Alizarin's voice grew deadly cold. 'There is no one here who will save you. No one will avenge you. Tell me who you do this for and you might secure your life.'

Still she said nothing, skin now clammy.

Alizarin tried again. 'The clans will cull your kind. Your loyalty will be entirely wasted.'

Saarem spat into the sand. 'She won't tell you anything.'

Arik drew his longsword. 'Then she doesn't believe her life depends on it.'

'You have already killed me,' said the kidnapper, her voice thick with secretions. Blood frothed at her mouth; Klaus must have pierced her gullet. She looked down at the bolt in her stomach, bubbling as much as breathing now. 'At least I die at the strike of Ummandiri lightning –'

Steel swung before she could finish the sentence. She crumpled to the sand.

Gasps came from behind them. Arik wiped his blade clean. Shock stole Klaus' breath, her final words flash-freezing through his veins.

'She could have spared herself,' said Alizarin heavily.

'She chose death the moment she came to the inn,' Arik retorted. 'And now the citadel will remember what happened to the one who tried to abduct your nephew.'

Ears still ringing with the pirate's words, Klaus crouched beside Verdi. 'He's unrousable.'

'Send for a physician,' Tourmali ordered a tumbler. 'We'll not leave Romel until he is recovered.'

A search of the kidnappers yielded nothing useful. But Klaus lingered over the dead woman who had recognised his Ummandiri bolts.

Her knife was Derindin. She'd carried a forked spear and a curved blade in the style of the tumblers. She had been prepared for death; she kept no personal effects, her pockets empty. Something caught his eye through her torn tunic; a strikingly ornate tattoo covering the back of her shoulder. He pulled aside the cloth, committing it to memory. Under the pretence of retrieving his bolt, he inspected the man. He had no tattoo.

Klaus wiped his bolts clean. No trumpeting Babbler could have been as loud as the silence that greeted them beyond the gates of Romel on their return.

*

Verdi slept heavily. Ravi twitched on the pillow by his head. The physician, a Mantelonian, gave them a draught to administer once he was awake and told them to wait.

Klaus left him to sleep, a tumbler stationed outside his door. He followed the voices rising heatedly in the adjoining chamber.

'You knew he was in danger.' Arik's face was white with anger. 'You even warned him to be careful. From the moment we joined your caravan, he became visible.'

Alizarin was almost as angry. '*This* is hardly what I meant.'

'Why did this Agatin recognise him?' Klaus interrupted. 'Could Baeron have a hand in this?'

'Perhaps for now we should just be grateful he's safely returned,' Tourmali suggested.

Arik wasn't about to be dismissed. 'Yes, in spite of what you've been hiding. What are you hiding? Why was he snatched?'

'Enough,' snapped Alizarin. 'You'll not make demands here, Master Northman.'

'Perhaps you don't think you owe us any explanation,' Arik fired back. 'But at least tell your nephew.'

'Tell me what?'

Verdi swayed in the doorway, face flushed and hair tousled.

'I could kill you,' Arik snapped. 'How do you feel? Are you alright?'

Verdi stared at his uncle. 'The woman who drugged me said "*the bolt must not be raised*". What was she talking about?'

A commotion broke outside. Tourmali glanced through the window.

'A Babble.' He rose, frowning. 'It's better if I see them off myself.'

Alizarin waited until the door closed behind him.

'You were sent to Invelmar for your own safety,' he told Verdi quietly. 'And you weren't expected back so ... yet.'

'What the hell does that mean?' said Verdi, beginning to get angry. 'And you should never have expected me to return. I'm not in a cradle still. What on earth would make you think that one day you could summon me back?'

'The fact that hundreds have died so you could live,' snapped his uncle. He caught himself, reining in anger. 'Through your mother – my half-sister – your forbears were guardians of the Old Kingdom.'

Hair spiked on Klaus' neck.

Verdi spluttered around his frustration. 'There hasn't been a kingdom in the Plains since the Second Redrawing.'

'Even earlier than that.' Late afternoon cast shadows across Alizarin's face, aging his tired brow. 'Yours is the bloodline of the last Custodian of Orenthia.'

Verdi gaped. Even Arik was too angry to speak.

'You've had sworn enemies and followers both since the day you were born.' Alizarin got up to close the window. 'Obsidian Lorendar was your forefather. He witnessed the death throes of Orenthia as it tore itself apart. He vowed to restore the Old Kingdom, but came to that task too late.'

'I thought that was just a story,' Verdi managed.

'His was true. He did become Custodian near the end of his life. He vowed to reunite Orenthia and restore its ways, but what lands he consolidated were carved up again after he died. The rabble rousers of the day fought for crowns of their own even if only to rule over a mountain of corpses, and it is their like that has endured.'

Klaus glanced at Verdi. 'Is that why you sent Verdi away?'

Alizarin's face tightened. 'Lorendar may have died, but the Derindin haven't given up on finishing his work.' He looked at Verdi. 'Now they believe his efforts fall on you.'

'But why Verdi? This man died before the Second Redrawing... has he no other heirs?'

'Why, indeed? Obsidian's blood runs in the veins of many Derindin now, why not one of them? Why not your mother?' Alizarin stared at his nephew. 'In the final year of his life, Lorendar saw the last sacred limolan tree die. He promised its seed would sleep until his successor arrived to rekindle his oath. A limolan seed finally sprouted right here in Romel when you were conceived. And now most of Derinda believes you will be his successor.'

There was no mistaking Verdi's horror. He looked rather ridiculous thanks to Ravi's oversized tail swinging over Verdi's chest, his furry rump abutting Verdi's ear.

'So you've just been saving him for this?' said Arik, incredulous. 'His entire return is a coincidence.'

'I did everything I could to keep him far from the fanatics waiting for him here.' Alizarin smiled at Klaus coldly. 'And you brought him back.'

Verdi sank into a chair.

'A dead man's dream,' Arik breathed. 'He could have died, and for nothing more than a children's tale!'

Alizarin's restraint in the face of Arik's contempt was worthy of an Intelligencer.

'There's no hiding your lineage here,' he told Verdi flatly. 'You must take precautions now.'

Klaus pulled in the trajectory of his reeling mind. 'Against whom?'

'Everyone. Lorendar has a great following, but do you suppose that every clan is eager to relinquish power? To abolish ghabala? There's no prosperity in peace. You Northerners of all people should know this. There are as many who have feared Lorendar's return as those who pray for it.'

Arik shook his head in disgust. 'Meanwhile, you've done a fine job of crippling him with ignorance.'

Alizarin paled. 'I'm the only living blood relation he has, and I sent him away. You brought him back – and you'll keep him from returning

North to save your own skins. You accuse *me* of crippling him?'

'We could have taken measures to protect him, *if* we had known –'

'You?' snapped Alizarin. 'Two fugitives running from the North with your tails between your legs?'

Klaus stifled his own anger. 'I didn't come here seeking refuge for myself in order to endanger the life of a brother.'

Footsteps sounded on the stairs. Tourmali returned, glancing at Alizarin. 'I'm afraid the Babble's already hard at work. I sent word to Emra.'

Verdi swayed in his chair, face flushed.

Arik steadied his arm. 'Maybe you ought to rest.'

'The physician said the drug would wear you out for a day or two,' Tourmali told him kindly. 'Take some water, child.'

Verdi's chin rose. 'I'm not a child.'

Wobbling slightly, he returned to their room. This time, Arik went with him.

'Master Invelmari –' Tourmali appealed to Klaus. 'Yes, you've kept him safe. But he'll be safer in Samsarra. And there he will find answers to his questions. We'll leave at first light.'

Klaus bowed. 'That's for him to decide.'

He rejoined his friends. Verdi lay on the bed. Ravi had settled on his chest.

Verdi rubbed his forehead. 'Everything's spinning…'

'The physician said the hypnotic will linger a while in your blood,' Arik told him.

Klaus perched on the edge of the bed. 'I'm sorry, Verdi. You'd never have come back here if it weren't for me.'

Verdi closed his eyes. 'Staying in Dunraven would have been far worse.'

Arik and Klaus shared a look and a loaded silence.

'What your uncle said…'

'I don't want to think about that now.'

It was no good talking at Verdi when he wasn't minded to reply. *Stubborn as a mule.* Klaus squeezed his arm. 'Whatever you wish to do, I won't leave you to it. You have my word.'

'And you're more likely to be rid of that oceloe before you see the back of me,' Arik added. 'Now that Klaus is safe, we can worry instead about who's after you.'

Verdi groaned. 'Don't joke.'

'He's not joking,' Klaus told him. 'Your uncle's suggestion might be best.'

'What, go on to Samsarra with Alizarin?' Arik grimaced. 'He's insufferable. Do you really think it'll be safer?'

'It has to be better than staying here, where we can't even raise a weapon.'

Verdi pressed a wet cloth to his head, batting away Ravi, who began licking at the drip of water. 'I shouldn't have dragged you both here.'

Arik snorted. 'Maybe when you're better we can consider where to go next. I hear the women of Gelgayel in the Koral Part are particularly beautiful.'

Verdi managed a laugh.

'You can't ignore this,' Klaus told Verdi quietly. 'There's a birthright for you here to claim… if you want it.'

'I don't know what they could possibly expect from me.'

'You ought to at least find out.'

'What about the pirates?'

'What *about* the pirates?'

'Don't you think we should…?'

'What, help?' finished Arik. 'A minute ago you wished we'd never come. The pirates are none of our business.'

Klaus said nothing. He didn't think he'd forget the devastated caravan near the oasis, nor the ravaged old man in the fountain square.

Verdi sat up. 'The tumblers are not Isarnanheri.'

'We're just two foreign mercenaries now,' Arik reminded him. 'Even if the Derindin wanted our help, what difference can we make?'

'That Mantelonian Elder invited you to fight.'

'And her offer wasn't particularly well received by the others. Put the pirates out of your mind for now.'

They left him to rest, withdrawing to a pot of kahvi by the window. Romel twinkled with night lanterns. The citadel was as sleepless as they.

'You should have left the pirate to the tumblers,' Klaus told Arik. 'Now we're two Northerners executing Derindin.'

'You know why I didn't.'

Fear roiled Klaus' stomach again.

Arik lowered his voice. 'She recognised your bolt. You don't think she was spying for the Eye, do you?'

Klaus fingered one of his bolts. They'd been made for him especially, once Kelselem was satisfied he had finally earned them. Only Lord Wintermantel's cunning bargain had secured his training with the Ummandiri bowmaster; it would have otherwise been unheard of for an Ummandiri to pass on their sacred skill to a foreigner. Klaus took care to retrieve every bolt he fired, and if that wasn't likely, he used an ordinary arrow. The Ummandiri believed that losing one of their war-birds was a bad omen. How many other Invelmari possessed Ummandiri bolts? *I was foolish to use them here.* They were rarely seen; not just in Derinda, but throughout the Parts. So how had a Derindin pirate recognised them at all?

'Do you think anyone caught what she said?' Klaus asked.

Arik shook his head. 'More important is whether anyone understood. Or whether she wasn't the first person to recognise them.' He lit a cigar, releasing heady smoke. 'What a bunch of bunglers.'

'The five families would have been just like their clans if it weren't for Sturmsinger and his Blood Pact.'

Arik snorted. 'What do you make of this … tree story?'

'I don't know.' He didn't share Arik's scepticism, but Klaus' questions were multiplying by the minute. 'But whatever Verdi's walked into, the Derindin still have to deal with the pirates.'

Arik pulled a face. 'You were at the Assembly. Those fools wouldn't be able to coordinate a caravan, let alone a defensive operation. The pirate scum's scattered everywhere. Where would the Derindin even begin?'

'South. Sounds like the clans there have been hit hardest.'

'Assuming they're telling the truth,' said Arik. 'The rest might not want to admit they've been as badly hit.'

But Klaus' thoughts were already fanning out. Perhaps it was just coincidence that the Mengorian mountains, where a party of senior Intelligencers feared a mine had been discovered, were also in the Far South, beyond the clandoms of Fraivon and Lebas. In his ear, Master Arnander's voice warned: '*Nothing is coincidence until it is.*'

'The pirates can't be this successful without a base.' Klaus rummaged through his pack, retrieving the scrap of parchment onto which he'd copied the inscription outside the watchtower of Ilaria. He began drawing the kidnapper's tattoo.

'The Derindin say they just roam the Plains.' Arik poured another kahvi. 'Why would pirates send those two kidnappers?'

Klaus finished the drawing. 'Do you have the other one?'

Arik produced something which did not look like parchment. A piece of skin, dried and leathery, bearing the now-shrivelled tattoo. He shrugged at Klaus' raised eyebrow.

'You know I was never much good at drawing.'

Klaus copied the pattern and held the two images side by side. 'Look.'

Each tattoo was made up of an intricate collection of interlocking motifs. The first tattoo was shaped like a knot. The kidnapper's larger tattoo consisted of a series of rings.

Arik shrugged. 'There's not much resemblance between them. Except for the middle.'

'Yes. I couldn't put my finger on it at first… What does the centre of these look like to you?'

Arik stared so long that Ravi ambled onto the parchment to join the inspection. He stiffened. 'That's Sturmsinger's starblossom…'

Klaus traced the six-petalled flower at the heart of both tattoos with his finger. It was their only shared feature. Though it closely resembled the starblossom of Invelmar, it came from an older banner of the five houses; from the Far Northern crest of Sturmsinger himself. So old, it was almost forgotten by the commonfolk. Now it was only seen in the earliest copy of the Sonnonfer in the royal archives at Dunraven.

Arik brushed Ravi away, looking more closely. Once Klaus had recognised it, the flower with its interlinked marquise petals was unmistakable. The five-petalled starblossom of the Invelmari banner conceived after Sturmsinger's death was more simple, its petals tear-shaped and unlinked, the sixth petal removed after his death.

'You think this is the pirates' mark?'

'No. I've found this on only two of the pirates we've killed. I think this is the mark of the Murhesla.'

'What? Why?'

'Because of the woman who kidnapped Verdi.'

'Ayla thought she was a pirate.'

'Perhaps that's what she became, but she was something else first. She was far too disciplined for a mere bandit. Maybe that's why she recognised my bolt. Even Saarem asked her if she was Murhesla. Do you remember what Niremlal the birdkeeper said of the Murhesla? He called them the *marked guardians of Romel*.'

'Why on earth would a Derindin guild of guardians borrow the oldest sigil of Invelmar?' said Arik reluctantly.

'An excellent question,' Klaus replied, reaching for his cloak.

Ayla was downstairs with a few of the tumblers. The cantina was mellow with smoke and the quiet strumming of a lute. A cheer rose when he appeared, a handful of Derindin rapping on their tables.

Saarem winked. 'I think they might approve of you now. Care for a drink?'

It was better than being hissed at. Klaus pulled up a chair across from Ayla. 'How did you know that pirate wasn't Murhesla?'

He knew at once he'd asked the right question. At a look, her tumblers left the table.

Ayla rose. 'Let's walk.'

He followed her out of the inn. The day's events had unsettled the citadel, and conversations huddled in doorways and street corners. With their hoods raised in the torch-softened dark, it was easy to keep to the shadows, sampling talk as they went: kidnappings, pirates, and a whisper of Lorendar's heir.

She stopped outside a quiet square lined with willows. It was overlooked by a row of fine houses, a sanctuary, and a long pillared building gated with solid iron.

Ayla pointed to the latter. 'The guild house of the Murhesla.'

The dark blue banner hanging above its iron doors depicted a white vine bearing little fruits. Klaus had seen this banner elsewhere in Romel, not realising then to whom it belonged.

'Don't go into the square,' said Ayla. 'We will have already been seen.'

'Should we not have come?'

Her face remained closed. 'Some of their customs are questionable, but Murhesla observe an honourable code of conduct.'

A flicker of light at one of the windows was the only sign of life. Even the trees didn't stir.

'Tumblers present themselves to Murhesla for the final phase of their training,' she said. 'Some of them are kept, becoming initiates of the guild. Most are discharged to serve the clans as tumblers. But once they pass back out through those gates, there's no return to the guild. Murhesla require allegiance. Pirates have no loyalties. They can't serve Murhesla.'

'Kept'. They returned to the inn. Klaus paused outside, unfolding his sketch of the tattoos. 'Do either of these mean anything to you?'

Ayla glanced at the parchment. 'When an initiate joins the guild, they're branded with a mark containing their name. The Murhesla's names are not spoken. They're shown.' She paused. 'Where did you find these?'

'On two of the pirates.'

Her silence confirmed his suspicions about Verdi's kidnapper, who'd recognised his Ummandiri bolts. She *had* been Murhesla.

'Then they must have deserted the guild.'

'Is that permitted?'

'That depends on the nature of their oath to the guild. Those who are fully initiated can't leave. But the bond of Murhesla to the guild is … variable.'

'Odd place for a name, where its bearer can't see it for themselves.'

'They're not meant to see it. The initiate's first trial is never to look upon the mark they're given until they're awarded permission to do so. If they're retained by the guild, the mark grows. At each stage of training, they're probed about their name. If they lie, they're cast out.' She glanced at his drawing again. 'And they always know who's lying.'

What else does she know? She had a poise that most of her tumblers lacked. She didn't have an Intelligencer's mask, but she had mastered that emptiness that shrouded the faces of the Derindin.

'The Murhesla serve Romel, Master Tristan. They've kept the feuding out of the citadel. And they safeguard Romel from ghabala.' Her voice was just audible beneath music drifting out from the inn. 'Now I have told you all a stranger ought to know of the Murhesla. It would be wise not to ask more questions. There's a saying here: a question asked about Murhesla is a question heard.'

'Will Verdi be in danger in Samsarra?'

She was quiet for longer than he liked.

'Sometimes an idea is so dangerous that some may wish to drive it out of living memory altogether,' she said finally. 'Elendra have spent generations rekindling Lorendar's prophecies. Others have sought the opposite. But the desert is changing, and so must we. Perhaps people haven't had as much need of such change as they do now.'

Inside, they ran into Suman.

'I thought you'd left already,' said Ayla.

'I was delayed, then heard what happened. My caravan leaves for Yesmehen at dawn.'

Klaus seized his moment. He showed Suman the other side of his sketch, bearing the inscription from the ruined watchtower.

'I found this in a passage that I couldn't decipher. Can you read it?'

Suman stared at it for a full minute. His face gave nothing away, but he returned the parchment gently.

'No, but near Samsarra there'll be someone who can,' he said. 'Ask for the olive keeper. If there's an answer for you, Master Chronicler, you'll find it there.'

Upstairs, Verdi was asleep again. Ayla ensured more tumblers watched over the inn that night.

'The limolan tree is in the citadel,' Tourmali told Verdi the following morning. 'Would you like to see it before we leave?'

'No.'

The Elder didn't ask him twice.

Klaus raised his eyescope as they left Romel, seeking one of the dark blue banners hanging in the market square. As he'd guessed, the white vine bore not little fruits, but the same six-petalled blossoms which adorned the heart of the Murhesla's mark.

*

After weeks on the road, a couple of nights in a bed made the short remainder of their journey feel far longer. Samsarra greeted them late the following evening, when the sun had flooded the sky with rose gold. Verdi thought his heart might as well announce their arrival, drumming as loudly as it did with as much fear as excitement.

Samsarra was smaller than Romel. Farmhouses and homesteads were scattered around its walls, as though it had spread tentative fingers out into the desert. The citadel boasted a collar of welcome greenery, thanks to the three springs on its eastern side. Olive trees, sandwillow and stately cedars dotted its streets. Autumn-crowned fruit trees clustered around houses of white and honey-tinted stone. It was a quieter creature than Romel, smoother of brow and more gentle of pace.

The caravan disbanded for the final time. Verdi and his friends followed Alizarin into a courtyard where the doorway of a handsome house was already wide open.

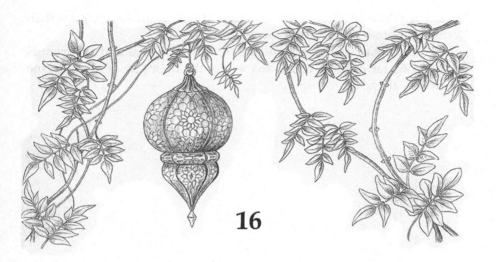

16

The House of Emra Selamanden

THUS VICTORY RANG FROM THE STERNS TO THE LOWER NORTH,
AND LORD STURMSINGER NAMED HIS NEW KINGDOM INVELMAR.
TO HIS FAITHFUL VASSALS HE AWARDED LANDS AND DUTIES, AND
APPOINTED THEM HIS EALDORMEN. IN HIS GENEROSITY, HE SHARED
WITH THEM THE SECRETS OF HIS STEELCRAFT AND HIS JARNSTIGA.

SONNONFER: THE FORGING OF INVELMAR

'You have been brought before the council, Eresk Laminhad, on charges
of treason against this clan.'

Alizarin led them into a white hall dazzling with mosaics. Across one
wall stretched a great map depicting trading roads and waterways and
clandoms, their boundaries drawn with jewel-headed pins; a testament
to the shifting borders between clans.

Tourmali joined three Derindin seated behind a table, attended by
a clerk and several tumblers. Verdi's stomach clenched. *Elendra's Elders.*
The accused, a middle-aged man, stood in the middle of the hall, leaning
on a crutch.

A chill crept into Verdi's bones. *This is not Dunraven*, he reminded
himself.

His uncle stopped in the wings of the hall. Amongst the Elders was a woman whose eyes were the same piercing cobalt blue as Alizarin's. Verdi's heart fluttered. His great-aunt Emra, Chieftainess of Elendra.

Her eyes fell on Verdi immediately. The stern-faced younger woman beside her read out the charges, and the Chieftainess looked away.

'Divulging to pirates the route and departure day chosen by the caravan of Gerin Taslisem – a man with whom you have been bitterly at odds for years. Consorting with suspected pirates. And bringing about the theft of six wagons of grain and a dozen horses, and the death of the four men and two women in his caravan.' The woman looked up from her notes. 'How do you answer?'

'Seems like it doesn't matter how I answer, Elder Fenral,' Eresk replied. 'My guilt has already been decided.'

'Very well.' She set down a sheaf of parchments. 'Then we'll close this hearing and proceed tomorrow to a trial for treason, for which the penalty is death. You may leave.'

'Wait –' A wrinkle appeared in his confidence. 'Yes, Gerin and I have hardly shared the best of relations. But to pay pirates to strike at him – to betray my clan – that is depravity beyond imagining.'

'What evidence does Gerin Taslisem bring in support of his accusation?' asked Tourmali.

The clerk read out each article. 'Gerin Taslisem alleges that Master Laminhad brought back no profits on his return from Romel, despite reporting the sale of his goods, and claims Master Laminhad used the gold to pay the pirates to attack Gerin's caravan. He deferred his workers' wages. Gerin also alleges that Master Laminhad was in ill condition when he arrived home –' He paused, scanning his notes. '"Bloodied and bruised, his clothes torn and dishevelled"'. These were the words uttered in the market the following day by Master Laminhad's wife.'

'I did sell my stock, but was robbed of my earnings in Romel,' said Eresk evenly. 'I stayed at Chaarim's inn. He'll attest to a break-in that night. And on my return, I took a fall from my horse – she was put down, and my leg had to be seen to by a surgeon.'

'Was it broken?'

'Badly sprained.'

Eresk withstood the Elders' scrutiny well.

The clerk raised his scroll again. 'Gerin Taslisem claims only three people knew when he was leaving for Romel. One of them, Gerin's wife, is dead. One was Gerin. The final person was yourself, Master Laminhad.'

Eresk was resolute. 'I knew when he would leave because Gerin told me himself.'

Fenral's eyebrows rose. 'Why would he have disclosed that to you? You can't stand each other.'

'He gave it away while boasting that his caravan would be back from Romel before mine had even assembled.'

The Elders' silence dissected Eresk more loudly than any amount of interrogation. Verdi realised he was fidgeting and made himself stop. Waiting beside him, Alizarin would notice his every shortcoming, and the Derindin didn't fidget. Ravi shifted uncomfortably in his pocket on his behalf.

Fenral didn't bother hiding her disbelief. 'You travelled alone, from Romel to Samsarra, when even tumblers now only make the journey in groups. And you arrived unscathed but for a fall from your horse.'

'Hardly unscathed.'

'To have escaped two misfortunes with your life was very fortunate,' remarked the fourth Elder, who looked as old as the other three combined.

'Then I should have died to seal my innocence? As you say, Elder Maragrin, I was fortunate.' But a drop of perspiration glinted on Eresk's brow. 'What exactly does Gerin accuse me of doing?'

Goosebumps rose on Verdi's skin when the Chieftainess spoke for the first time.

'Travelling to Romel to hire the services of bandits, to end the feud between you over your neighbouring farms,' she said. 'Paying them with your goods and your gold.'

Eresk knuckled his brow, then his breast. 'You've known me from my mother's knee, Ahena. You know I couldn't have done this.'

The Chieftainess stood. She was almost as tall as an Invelmari woman. To Verdi's alarm, she walked around the table towards him.

'Do you know who this is, Eresk?' She stopped before Verdi. 'This is my great-nephew. Lorendar's heir, finally returned amongst us.'

Verdi's face burned. She kissed him on each cheek. Her hair smelled faintly of sandalwood.

She turned back to Eresk, who was now plainly startled. 'Did you sell your clansman to the pirates?'

His guard was down. Only for an instant, but his confidence stumbled. He recovered just as quickly. 'I did not.'

Verdi noticed Saya's claws digging deeply into Alizarin's arm.

Emra returned to her seat. 'Masters Invelmari, welcome to Samsarra. You've heard the charges against this man. What is the measure of his conduct?'

Verdi stole a look at Klaus. His former master bowed as deeply as though before Adela herself.

'Whatever your heart tells you, my lady, the testimony of this man's accuser cannot demonstrate his guilt beyond all uncertainty.'

'Uncertainty?' repeated Elder Fenral. 'He can't prove any of his claims to innocence.'

'But that is not certainty. And anything less is insufficient to cost a man his life.'

A dizzying memory of Dunraven engulfed Verdi, as powerful as it was fleeting. Every eye now latched onto the Intelligencer, sparing Verdi from scrutiny. The Elders conferred, and the Chieftainess rose.

'Mercy comes from the strangest of places, Eresk Laminhad. Today it comes from the North.' She signalled to the clerk. 'This hearing is adjourned for lack of evidence. There will be no trial until your accuser can justify his claims. He will be given three moons to answer.'

No one's surprise was greater than Eresk's, who glanced back over his shoulder at Verdi as he limped out of the hall. Verdi's head began to spin again. Now Alizarin was leading him to the Elders. There had to be some remnant of the hypnotic in his circulation... How foolish he must have looked, nodding stupidly as Elders rose to greet him... He followed Alizarin to a courtyard in the heart of the house.

Outside, Verdi's senses slowly sharpened: a verdant thunderclap of a garden; ornate lanterns hanging from bare branches. A jasmine-laden pavilion sweetly scenting the night.

Arik gripped his arm, steadying him. 'You alright?'

He inhaled fresh air. 'Yes.'

The room spun again; nausea threatened. Arik steered him towards a cushioned chair.

'The skies rained arrows and the squares were filled with our shackled women and children, the last time an Invelmari set foot into this house.'

Verdi's eyes refocused; the declaration came from Maragrin, the snowy-haired Elder.

Arik bowed deeply in Invelmari fashion. 'Then it must be a very old house.'

Maragrin's cheeks were wrinkled and his neck sunken between his shoulders, but his bright blue eyes were as sharp as a falcon's, and his gaze held the snap of its beak.

'How many moons have you seen so far in this land, sir warrior, and how many Derindin lives have you taken from it already?'

Arik didn't flinch. 'As many as was necessary to protect your clanfolk.'

The Elder bobbed his head. 'And very brave of you it was.'

'Careful, Maragrin,' said Tourmali drily. 'Our guests don't yet know the keen edge of your wit.'

'I'm told we are greatly indebted to you, Masters Invelmari,' said the Chieftainess. Verdi cringed; there was nothing to draw her attention from him now. 'You've returned one who is more precious to us than you know. Please, share our table.'

Verdi's cheeks warmed. Again, the cloud in his head thickened. Arik sat on his left side, Klaus to his right; there was nothing to fear.

Servants brought warm papery bread and herbed cheeses, and a sweet spicy tea that smelled of oranges and cinnamon. The Elders listened to Alizarin's accounts of the raids. The sun slipped below the horizon; lanterns became night-fruits shining throughout the darkening courtyard, and the sweet breath of evenrose and jasmine grew with the balmy twilight. Unseen birds filled the air with nightsong. Ravi disappeared to explore the softly chirruping darkness. Nothing felt more discordant with this perfumed tranquillity than Verdi's unease.

He wasn't wrong to worry. Once the meal was cleared away, the Elders' eyes gathered upon him.

'Have you heard the term *Merensama*, Viridian?'

Verdi shifted uncomfortably at his great-aunt's question. Until he'd arrived in Derinda, the only person who'd called him by his full name had been Lady Wintermantel.

'Once or twice,' said Verdi. 'I don't know what it means.'

'Perhaps your friend chronicler, then?'

'I believe it means *the opened sky*, my lady,' Klaus replied. 'Or so our bards described it. Beyond that, I couldn't tell you.'

'A fitting translation. Merensama was the first peacetime Orenthians forged across the South. It was a treaty that reigned between the Paiva and the Zmerrudi Sea, before this land was broken up into countless kingdoms that cannibalised each other. Now it is legend.'

Verdi found himself listening in spite of his trepidation. Ravi crawled into his lap, resting his paws on the table.

'Restoring Merensama was the great ambition of Obsidian Lorendar, your mother's forebear: an end at last to the Years of Sorrow. A union of the clans, beholden to laws that end territorial grabs and decree fairer distribution of the Plains. An end to ghabala. It was too much to achieve in Lorendar's lifetime. But though his flesh has passed, his will is immortal. And when he took his Custodian's vows, he took them not just for himself, but for all his descendants. He called upon the Great Sentience to choose one of his line to finish his work.'

Verdi's dry throat made swallowing horribly loud. 'But what does that have to do with me?'

'After the last limolan tree died, Lorendar promised the land would produce another fruiting tree once a worthy successor appeared in his line.' The lanterns ignited embers in Emra's eyes. 'A limolan seed is still planted each time a Derindin child is conceived. For fifteen hundred years, not one seed has given life – until your mother sowed one when she became with child.'

Verdi stared at the Elders. 'You must be mistaken. I came here by – by accident.'

'The Great Sentience makes no accidents. You were drawn back to embrace your legacy. There would be no limolan tree thriving now in Romel if you were not intended for this path.'

'But what do you expect *me* to do?'

At a nod from Maragrin, Tourmali extracted a flat leather pouch from his cloak. Inside was a curious object: a giant arrow-head mounted on a stick. Or so Verdi first thought; in fact it was a triangular metal device twice the length of his palm, with two straight edges and an ornately curved hypotenuse, and a tapering skewer protruding from its base.

'Do you know what this is?' Tourmali held it by the skewer. Feeling stupid, Verdi shook his head. His pleading glance at Klaus was involuntary.

'It's a gnomon,' said Klaus, coming to his rescue.

Of course it was; the slanting triangle, once placed perpendicular to the ground, would cast the shadow of a sundial. The skewer was probably meant to anchor it in the ground, holding it upright. Verdi felt daft for not spotting this sooner.

Tourmali nodded. 'It is. But this device is not intended for tracking the movements of the sun. Merensama is no ordinary treaty; it's a pact with the heavens. If it is to succeed, it must be invoked in a precise moment: during a hidden phase of the moon – which, in the hands of Lorendar's successor, can be revealed using the moondial cast by this gnomon.'

Tourmali passed the gnomon to the Chieftainess.

'There are three conditions for Merensama, Viridian,' she said. 'The first is the regrowth of the limolan once Lorendar's successor emerges, which you have already guaranteed.' Her smile of encouragement did little to reassure him. 'The second is the oath taken by the restorer of the limolan, to uphold Lorendar's bargain with the Great Sentience. And the third –' She traced the skewer. 'The third is the most difficult: finding the hidden phase of the moon that signals a successful bid for Merensama.'

Verdi's jaw fell. He looked at his friends, but they were each unreadable behind their Forms. Shadows hid his uncle's face. The silence in the garden was growing more expectant by the second.

'I don't think I'm the right sort of person for any of this,' he said finally. 'I wouldn't know where to start.' He hadn't even arrived yet at the matter of whether he *wanted* to.

'We will help you.' The Elders nodded around Emra. 'You may be unprepared, but we've spent our lives preparing for you. Since Orenthia fractured, more blood has been shed here than all the Ninvellyn's waters. Merensama is a bridge back to what we were before. Don't answer now, when you are tired and overwhelmed. There's time yet for questions. You are barely arrived here, while we have spent years rekindling hope throughout the Plains for your return.'

And yet, Alizarin had not seemed keen for his return at all.

'What about these pirate raids?' Arik asked. 'It was a pirate who abducted your nephew.'

'And we are greatly indebted to you for his safe return,' Emra replied. 'Do you mean to stay, Masters Invelmari?'

'With your permission, Chieftainess, we would remain here with him,' said Klaus.

'Invelmari mercenaries have passed this way before you. The only thing they sought was gold, and they had no scruples where it came from. There are clans who have a taste for the services of such mercenaries, and this clan has never been one of them.'

Indignation finally loosened Verdi's tongue. 'They're only here because of me. We stay together or not at all.'

Klaus bowed again, a master of courtesy. 'We've no need of gold to keep your nephew safe.'

Fenral looked far from pleased. 'How will this look to those we want to call to our cause, Ahena? Isn't it difficult enough without a deterrent?'

Verdi thought the Chieftainess threw her a warning look before she replied.

'You've my permission to stay, Masters Invelmari, because General Ayla holds you in high regard. But it goes against the grain.'

Alizarin leaned forward to pour another kahvi. He might have as well remained in the shadows; his face betrayed nothing.

'This is not Invelmar, and here we do not own our menfolk,' Emra told Verdi. 'I can't command you to stay, Viridian, but I implore you to choose carefully. For those who remember Lorendar, you will be a beacon of hope.'

'There seemed to be little hope for an alliance against the pirates at the Romelian Assembly,' said Klaus.

Coldly, Fenral told him, 'You know nothing of this country or our clans.'

'What if I believe I know where the pirates may be gathering?'

Verdi gaped at Klaus.

Klaus targeted the Chieftainess, ignoring everyone else. 'There is a mine near the Mengorian range being sought by the North. A mine, and a spring. I scribed for a party of nobles who feared it had already been discovered. An odd thing to coincide with the surge of pirates, who've been busiest at work in the clandoms nearest to those mountains.'

Only the rustle of the trees overhead disturbed the silence that fell over the courtyard. Arik was rock-still. Even here, many miles from Dunraven and Adela's Spyglass, Verdi grew suddenly afraid.

Alizarin's voice could have cut stone. 'When did you learn this?'

Klaus spread his hands. 'I'm a chronicler. I've scribed for plenty of nobles, though *that* wasn't something I was ever meant to hear.'

Emra stood.

'Viridian, Masters Invelmari; we've kept you long enough from your rest. Stay in this house for as long as you require. But I would request your presence at a council with our allies tomorrow.'

Clearly dismissed, they returned into the house.

*

'What in hell possessed you to tell them about the mine?'

Arik was as furious as Klaus had expected. Verdi glanced nervously between them.

Klaus shut the windows of their rooms. 'We need them to trust us. And you saw what pirates did to Kirono's caravan. Don't you think they deserve all the help they can get?'

Arik looked away, angrily shrugging off his coat. Ravi darted out of his way, sensing a foul undercurrent that would prove inhospitable even to oceloes.

Now that it was done, Klaus felt numb. He was no longer an Ealdorman, but this made his first act of treason no easier. For a wild moment, he wondered whether he hadn't been reckless. *Perhaps I deserve exile from the North.*

Arik raked his hair. 'Have you turned your back on *everything* because of what the Wintermantels did?'

'I'd sooner stop breathing.'

Arik exhaled slowly. It might have been relief, or it might have been Form retaking the reins. 'Do you really think the pirates might have taken possession of this mine?'

Klaus lowered his voice. 'Anselm Rainard was as close to the last Spyglass – Spyglass Adelheim Haimric – as an Intelligencer could be. If he's afraid this mine has been found, then so am I. Whether this spring is discovered by pirates or the likes of Agatin, in the wrong hands it would be dangerous to Dunraven *and* Derinda.'

Arik raised his eyebrows. 'Is that what we're going to do, then? Run back to Dunraven with intelligence?' He closed his eyes. 'I'm sorry, I didn't mean to salt the wound.'

Klaus let Form close around the sting of his words. 'No one wins if either water or native iron fall into the pirates' clutches.'

'Well,' Arik said more evenly. 'Now we know why someone tried to kidnap Verdi.'

They both looked at Verdi, who quailed under their gaze.

'We came here to help Klaus escape.' Verdi hugged himself. 'We have enough problems without looking for new ones.'

'Aren't you even a little bit curious?' Klaus asked. 'There might be a future for you here.'

'I wouldn't know where to begin,' said Verdi, wide-eyed. 'I just want to finish my training. This is the sort of thing *you* should be doing, not me – I'm sorry, I didn't mean…'

Klaus waited for him to untangle his tongue. Form absorbed everything.

Verdi gave up. He suggested hopefully instead, 'Let's leave Derinda, go somewhere else.'

'We only just got here,' Arik told him irritably. 'Look, no one can force you to do anything. If we stay, you can find another apprenticeship. And tomorrow we're going to find lodgings elsewhere.'

'We'll see things more clearly in the morning.'

But Klaus couldn't wait until morning. He tossed in bed with his thoughts. The very notion of the gnomon was thrilling: *the hidden phase of the moon.* He wished he could see the gnomon again, test its dial under the light for himself. Again, that exhilarating prod of *possibility* pulled him taut.

None of it mattered, however, while Verdi's safety was at risk, from pirates or anyone else. *It can't be coincidence that this plague of pirates has arrived just as the likes of Anselm Rainard are poking around the South.* Klaus lit a lamp after his friends fell asleep and unrolled his map. He added: *Samsarra. Abode of clan Elendra.*

Despite everything, he couldn't help a thrill of excitement looking over the unmarked southern expanse covering the parchment. This land was built on faultlines, its fate unresolved. Verdi's fortune might be buried in its sands. *I can help him unearth it.* His former servant deserved no less. Tomorrow, he would enquire after the olive keeper, as Suman had advised. Tomorrow, he would take another step towards leaving the Wintermantels behind him.

*

Alizarin had to wait until the Elders had gone.

'Forgive me the hour,' he told his aunt. 'But I must speak with you.'

'Sit down, Alizarin.'

His eyes darted to the windows, anxious not to be overheard.

'I know you're worried,' she said. 'But this is where he belongs. It's good that he's home at last.'

'Yes, I'm worried.' He rubbed tired eyes. 'We couldn't have hoped to keep his return quiet, even if we tried – one night in Romel and he was abducted. Who put the pirates up to it? Agatin spotted him by the gate, he looks just like… Lorendar's enemies haven't gone away. Word will spread soon enough.'

'That was inevitable, Alizarin. You can't hide from the past forever.'

Even Emra didn't know where Viridian had grown up, or the world he had imbibed there. Alizarin had guarded that knowledge. 'I was wrong to send him to Dunraven. I was wrong to think our enemies would not become part of him.'

'You sent him to a place of safety, where he has grown into a fine young man,' she corrected. 'You sent him to a place without clans, where he could witness the unity between those who were once themselves no more than warring tribes. And that's a lesson he would never have learned in the Plains.'

'And at what cost?' Alizarin was in no humour to listen to any praise of the North. 'What if he's just learned disdain for his own people? Even now, he'll put those friends of his first.' He stopped himself, inhaling. 'But that's not why I came. I came about the chronicler.'

He told her about the visit to the ruins at Ilaria with Klaus, and the transient Orenthian inscription.

'You've been to the watchtower,' he said. 'You know there's nothing there.'

'Are you certain of what you saw?'

'Absolutely.'

'Did you write down the words?'

Alizarin shook his head. 'But he did. He records everything – he keeps his own maps.'

Emra listened to her nephew closely. Perhaps it was because he was so rarely shaken, or perhaps it was because this stranger seemed to preoccupy him even more than all his fears about his own nephew, but something about his words, about his grudging wonder, made her take notice. Alizarin was a sensible man, and not a particularly romantic or imaginative one. Like him, she had been hardened by the many trials of the desert. But unlike him, she still had longing.

Her heart shivered in excitement. 'Tell me more of him.'

Alizarin frowned. 'What do you wish to know? He's a Northerner, stubborn and set in Northern ways.'

'Set your prejudices aside. Ilnurhin favours neither creed nor blood. Tell me what you have *seen*.'

He rose, prowling the room. He began with their first meeting in Noisy Tree, and the more he spoke, the more he realised he'd noticed. She listened without interruption. He told her everything he could remember.

He did not speak of Klaus' escape from the Wintermantels. He was a man who kept his word.

Finally, she nodded, tired but bright-eyed. Outside, the ghost of the newborn moon faded in the sky as false dawn unveiled the morning.

'Rest,' she told him.

'What do we do?'

'I am certain that this Northman has awoken ilnurhin in places that have been long asleep, Alizarin. We must guide him to wherever that leads.'

Alizarin was a sensible man, and not a particularly romantic or imaginative one, and unlike his aunt, the trials of the desert had hardened his heart. But for the first time since his youth, he tasted hope.

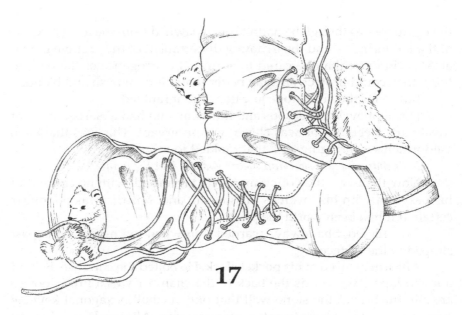

17

The Memory of Oceloes

YET NO MALICE DID TARNISH HIS MIGHT. IN THE BATTLE OF HVÍTRESTEPPE, HE CHANCED UPON A WOMAN CRIPPLED AND SURELY IN HER FINAL YEARS. HE TOILED TO FREE HER FROM FLAME. AND RICHLY DID THAT GRAIN OF MERCY REWARD HIM, FOR SHE BESTOWED UPON HIM A GIFT...

SONNONFER: THE HARVEST OF MERCY

Alizarin paced the council chamber where the Elders would soon convene. Irritated with his restlessness, Saya jumped down from his shoulder.

Why had he confided in his aunt about the Northman? He wished he hadn't.

And yet he couldn't ignore what he'd seen.

The truth was, Alizarin didn't *know* how to look at the past except through his own torment, and that was something he had no wish to resurrect.

The boy was inseparable from the two Invelmari. There was little opportunity to speak to him alone. The insufferable self-righteousness of the Prospere – as though he hadn't been spawned from the most noxious of the Ealdormen – and the irritating discernment of the fugitive grated at Alizarin more than he cared to admit. The arrogance of the pair, to think they could protect Viridian better than his own flesh and blood.

But so far they had done just that, and it rankled.

His nephew was nervous and diffident, and had absorbed none of Invelmar's steel. But he was clever and observant. This was thanks to Ealdormen's upbringing, and that rankled too.

Isn't that why you sent him there? Wasn't that the point?

Now the boy – the young man – had returned, with no concept of his past and with his loyalties misshapen, and Alizarin was no longer certain if it had been worth the price.

Saya hissed. She always warned him when too much of the past slipped to the surface.

Alizarin glanced at his pocket clock. He bolted the entrance. Behind a faded tapestry towards the back of the chamber was a little door so artfully flush with the stone wall that only a small hexagonal keyhole gave it away. It had been twenty-four years since Alizarin had fashioned it. He locked the bezel of the ring on his index finger into the keyhole and turned his wrist clockwise. The door sunk into the wall, rose on the pulleys arranged behind it, and exposed a small niche containing a slim leather bundle. He removed it and pressed a lever inside the niche. The stone door reappeared, sliding closed.

Saya stalked over, sniffing it cautiously rather than curiously.

'Yes,' he told her. 'You remember.'

They left, hoping rather than believing the time was ripe.

*

For once, Klaus had slept dreamlessly. Early morning bathed Samsarra. Even in this moment of Afldalr's daily weakness, the ache that nipped constantly at the edge of his awareness like a starved beast was briefly numbed.

A horse neighed outside. Klaus opened his eyes, and the hollowness that had usurped the middle of him was restored.

'I learned something terrible...'

The thunderclap of horror had been replaced by resentment now, but he didn't think he would ever forget Elodie's stricken face, or find anything to thaw the cold that had since replaced the marrow in his bones.

The doors opened. Through the ornate panel screening their sleeping quarters from the rest of the chamber, Klaus glimpsed Verdi enter with a covered tray. He got up.

'You can't do that anymore. Not here.' Klaus took the tray and set it down. Beneath the cloth were bread, figs and honey. 'Not anywhere.'

The torment twisting Verdi's face only loosened the shackles on Klaus' resentment.

Klaus softened his voice. 'After the council meeting, we'll look for lodgings of our own.'

Verdi nodded.

The Chieftainess' house stood in a square lined with junipers and bougainvillea bushes, flanked by two small watch houses. It was simple; the Derindin shunned opulence for the detail they lovingly invested instead into the delicate complexities of the things they made: rich weaves of silks and rugs; the impossible mechanisms of their poetry; the clever innards of clocks.

It was a citadel of cobbled alleyways, courtyard-roofed houses and rambling jasmine. They passed through a market square filled with a smell of baking bread that set Ravi's nostrils twitching furiously. Fibbler ran towards them in excitement.

'There you are!' he exclaimed through a mouthful of crusty roll. 'Been hopin' I'd see you if I hung around.'

Klaus ruffled his head. 'Good thing you did, too. Where does Terim live?'

'On the other side of Samsarra, near the wool market.'

Arik squinted at the sharpening sun, edging into the shade of a citron tree. 'Does the day ever get cooler here, Fibbler?'

'Oh yes. In a couple of months it'll be freezin'. The winds are worse than the cold, though.' Fibbler took another chunky bite. 'Can we do more sword practice?'

'Maybe later. Any news about the pirates?'

Fibbler shook his head. 'Babble says we might be ambushed any minute.' He looked far too excited at this prospect, which meant he didn't believe it. 'Queen Adela's sick, and a dozen Derindin were hanged so she could get better. A sac-ro-fist. One of 'em was only nine!'

'Who are you talking to, Fibbler?' A man stepped out of the nearby bakery to load a cart with bread, his forearms white with flour; most likely the source of Fibbler's breakfast. Ravi scuttled towards the cart, sniffing at the baskets. Verdi scooped him up before he could pounce on the bread.

Arik glared at the oceloe. 'He's only just had breakfast!'

Fibbler puffed his chest. 'Guests of the Chieftainess.'

But the man's face had grown wooden. He went back inside without a word. Klaus waited until he was out of earshot.

'Fibbler ... where did you hear that?'

The little boy looked a little less sure of himself.

'The Babble,' he stammered, reddening at the look on Arik's face. 'Every month they bring news of a Derindin sac-ro-fist...'

'We do not sacrifice humans in Invelmar, Fibbler.'

Fibbler's face fell, the rest of his roll hanging limply from his hand.

Klaus patted his shoulder. 'It's not your fault, it's only what you've heard. These lies do nothing but encourage Derindin to hate us.'

'I'm sorry,' the little boy said miserably. He perked up. 'Next I see 'em, I'll tell 'em it ain't true –'

'No,' said Klaus quickly. 'Don't do that. If you start arguing, it might draw too much attention. But d'you reckon you can keep your ears open? You can tell us what you hear.'

Fibbler nodded eagerly.

'Better hurry up if you still want that ride, Fibbler,' the baker called.

'Goin' to market.' Fibbler jumped onto the cart only just in time. 'Got jobs there all day. I'll keep all my ears open!'

Arik nodded at the departing cart. 'No wonder the Derindin can't stand the sight of us, if they're regularly being fed horseshit like that.'

'The Derindin already have reason enough to despise the North,' Klaus replied drily.

'Could it be true the Queen's fallen ill?' Verdi wondered.

Arik frowned. 'She's tough. But at her age ... still, this is the Babble talking.'

How many years had Klaus longed for an end to Adela's reign? An end to the cycle of Rainard, after a bloody dusk. Even the remote possibility shook his heart in its iron cradle.

'Whether we like it or not, there's a kernel of truth in most of the Babblers' stories,' Klaus reminded them. 'I've never heard a Babble invent a story from nothing.'

And if it's true, and Adela dies, and Wolfram Wintermantel becomes king? The possibilities gave him no relief, his mind always turning, always churning. Would the Wintermantels wait until they were crowned to risk hunting him, or would they consider themselves finally free to bury their treasonous past and let him disappear?

Lord Wintermantel was an Intelligencer. Klaus knew what Intelligencers thought of stray secrets. He was no admirer of Adela, but Klaus offered a silent prayer for her health.

*

Emra rode east, past the pastures nurtured by the aqueducts of her fathers' design, past the Arboretum, beyond the cattle-breeders' fields.

It had been years since she had dared seek this road, for it remained hidden to the uninvited. She'd left early; one never knew how long this journey might take. Two hours later, she dismounted by a cluster of ancient olive trees east of Samsarra. Dawn still streaked the sky. She hadn't been certain whether she would find the way, and how she would be received if she did.

But this time she did find the way, and took heart.

The olive trees stood watch over a small house whose master was older than even their gnarled and twisted trunks. She hesitated at the door. It had been twenty-four years since she had come here last, when a young woman heavy with child had sought her help in desperation. She had failed that woman then; she would not fail her child now. But she waited, and remembered, and cowered from herself. Just as her resolve began to waver, the door opened.

'You've returned,' said the man at the door.

'I need your help, if you'll give it.'

'Help has always been given but rarely taken. That is the way of the Derindin, who ask but do not heed.'

But he remained in his doorway, in spite of her heedlessness. She chided herself. It wasn't the time to dwell on errors past.

'I want to enquire about someone,' she began. 'A man –'

'I know who you mean.'

Her heart leapt in excitement. 'Then am I right? Does he –'

'You have your own work, neglected these many years, and it must be done. Why do you look for more that does not concern you?'

Protestations jumped to Emra's mouth; she swallowed them back. 'My great-nephew –'

'Must seek the moondial in his own way. Let him be.'

Her heart beat wildly. 'The Northerner claims many things. Is he lying?'

'No.'

Many other questions rose in its place, but she knew there would be no more answers.

'I hope you will help him,' she breathed.

'If he is in need of me, he'll find his own way here.'

He paused.

'The doubt that wearies away at you is born of your own prejudice.' His voice plunged into her heart. 'Ilnurhin favours neither creed nor blood. This you know.'

Then he closed his door, and the morning dimmed around her. A breeze through the olive trees whispered her own words back at her; the taunting echo of a splintered self. *But I found the road.* She had been given another chance. And this time she wouldn't squander it.

She swung into her saddle and rode back to Samsarra.

*

'So it is true. Lorendar's blood has mingled with the sons of the Forge.'

The Chieftain of Mantelon latched hungrily onto Verdi in a way that troubled Klaus. Three other Mantelonians were gathered in Elendra's council chamber: their envoy Suman, Cilastra, and another Elder with a scarred face.

'An honour, sir.' Arik embellished this with a deep Invelmari bow.

If anything, the scarred Elder was affronted, rising from his chair in protest. 'How far have we fallen, that Northerners can join this table now?'

Cilastra clicked her teeth in irritation. 'Sit down, Halmir. The Great Sentience knows we've trodden this road long enough – by now your wheels must be worn to the spoke. This is not your house to decide who may enter it.'

Fenral made no secret of her disapproval of the Northerners' presence at the council meeting. But Navein barely noticed, pulling Verdi into an embrace.

'You will not know yet what you have rekindled, son of Lorendar.'

Verdi seemed to have lost his tongue. Ravi had disappeared in a fit of stage fright.

They joined the Derindin around a wide, oval table. The woody smell of kahvi rose from a handsome samovar standing over the fire. Alizarin poured it into tiny brass cups. Ravi, who wasn't allowed to drink it, nonetheless enjoyed the smell and was lured out from behind Verdi's lapel, whiskers hard at work.

'Master Tristan, I must impose on you.' Emra unrolled empty parchment. 'Will you show our friends what you told us last night? I hear you have a good grasp of the road.'

Klaus had already chosen his guise for the Derindin; here he would be courteous, witty, charming. 'As you wish, Chieftainess. But I know only a little of the Plains.'

'That's quite alright.'

It was difficult to refuse her. What he knew of Derinda he'd learned piecemeal, or teased out of Meron and the tumblers. But he relaxed the instant the pen touched the page, yielding to the tranquillity he always found when he summoned the spirit of *place*.

He began at the Ostraad. The grassland rim of the desert approaching Romel; the pastures around Samsarra. Voista, to the north-east of Romel. To the south-east he outlined the territories of Mantelon, then Fraivon further south. Periam's clandom stretched north-west of Romel, sheltered by a mountain range Klaus recalled from a study of Periam's salt mines. He added the western clandoms last – Sisoda, Hesper, and, northwest of Fraivon, Baeron. His own memories demanded their presence on the page: Ilmen; Ilaria; nameless ruins; and the dunes, springs, rocky outcrops and clusters of trees where they'd rested – every day of tearing himself from Invelmar.

'Brothers and sisters, I'm as worried about the pirates as you are,' said the Chieftainess as his pen moved across the parchment. 'The scale of their attacks betrays a far greater number of bandits than we've seen before. We can't ride aimlessly across the desert and eliminate them one by one. But every vermin has a nest. We should begin by finding it.'

Navein frowned. 'They're scorpions, passing from under one rock to another. They have no nest.'

'Then where do they keep the captives?'

Emra paused until Klaus reached the Far South, as though waiting for him to arrive here.

'Master Tristan believes there's a mine in the Mengorian range.' As she spoke, Klaus outlined these mountains, wishing he could better depict their heights and faces. 'Possibly an iron mine, discovered by someone in Derinda.'

'Impossible,' said Navein at once. 'There's nothing in that wasteland. It's a burial ground.'

'And yet, Invelmari spies fear it has been captured. They even believe there's an untapped spring nearby.'

'If that were true, Fraivon would have long found it,' Cilastra reasoned. 'I mean you no offence, Master Invelmari –'

'The Keeper of the Branches believes Tristan speaks the truth.'

Klaus looked up. The Derindin had fallen very quiet.

'And it's not only Fraivon who neighbour this treasure, but Baeron,' Emra continued. Klaus glanced at his map; the Mengorian range was long, spanning both clandoms. 'Fraivon might bleat their fortune to the whole world, but would we know if Baeron found it? *They* can afford to bide their time. All we know is this: pirates have troubled the southernmost clans the most, and they take many prisoners alive. They must be holding those prisoners somewhere our roads don't reach.'

'Are you suggesting *pirates* might have found this mine?' interrupted Halmir. 'Preposterous!'

'No more preposterous than an Invelmari advising a council of clans,' said Maragrin mildly. 'No one in living memory has *sought* water there. Why would they, if they've been told it's futile?'

'Why does this Northman see fit to reveal any of this to us?' Halmir demanded.

'You may as well ask what Master Tristan has to gain from misleading us,' Maragrin countered, though he scoured Klaus with the beaks of his eyes. '*I'm* more interested in how it drew the attention of Invelmari spies.'

Halmir struggled with his reservations. 'Fear of an ore that might rival Invelmari steel?'

Klaus forced serpents' heads back under the dark waters of his own fears. 'I doubt that very much. But any kind of iron – and a spring – is treasure indeed.'

'One spring will hardly break the drought, Master Invelmari. Your dam is the slavemaster there.'

'No, it won't. But what if it could open a road to the North Zmerrudi Sea?'

Stunned silence followed Klaus' suggestion.

'Well, sister,' said Navein. 'What do you propose?'

'That we discover their nest, if it's there,' Emra replied. 'They tried to kidnap Viridian. If they'd succeeded, it would have destroyed any hope for Merensama. Can we really afford to ignore another enemy of Lorendar, quietly multiplying and perhaps building a base?'

'An armed search party from either of our clans would be unwelcome in Fraivon or Lebas' territories. They barely tolerate our merchants taking their lesser roads as it is.'

'Then we must warn them of a pirate gathering in the Far South, and ask them to help us investigate.'

Halmir's nostrils flared. 'And draw their attention to the mine?'

'A moment ago you didn't believe it was there,' Maragrin remarked.

'Is there any other way to gather intelligence so far south without stirring suspicion, General?' Emra asked Ayla.

'Not openly. Lebas *are* best placed to scout the land. Their clandom neighbours Baeron's to the south-west; they're the least likely to be suspected if they stray across the border.'

'Then let's ask Lebas,' Emra suggested. 'Offer them reinforcements against the pirates.'

'I agree with Emra-hena,' Cilastra declared. 'If there *is* such a place, we should invest all our efforts in finding it. No one will want the pirates to raise their own clandom.'

'Now we're leaping to pirate clandoms!' Fenral set her cup down loudly. 'We should be teaching Lorendar's heir how to use the gnomon, not speculating about some Northern rumour! Pirates aren't going to abduct him from Samsarra. The time has never been more ripe than now to turn the tide in favour of Merensama.'

'You're wrong. You weren't at the assembly.' Alizarin ignored her scowl. 'People are too afraid of the pirates to think about anything else. The clans want to protect themselves, not sign a new treaty that may very well lead to open war with the dissenters.'

Navein stared at Klaus' parchment again. 'A mine will bring riches, and iron will raise an armoury. And riches are a magnet for every leech south of the Ostraad. The pirates' ranks would swell. *If* it's there, and in their clutches.'

Fenral's jaw tightened. 'Wealth will be no use to them if they can't survive so far south. They can't buy water.'

'And what if this spring is real?' Cilastra demanded.

'So we're to trust this intelligence, then?' said Halmir icily. 'Are these men sellswords or are they spies?'

'Tristan's signed his own death warrant just telling you any of this,' Verdi said heatedly, speaking for the first time. '*I* trust him entirely.'

Halmir moderated his scorn a fraction. 'I would by no means disparage your judgement, Master Viridian. But we're talking about a perilous journey through unfriendly territory to a desolate place. Storms, sinksand and drought have felled many of those who've tried to tame that waste. That's what we would be asking Lebas to risk for the sake of suspicion.'

'A risk worth taking.' Cilastra looked around the table. 'We *cannot* allow anyone to take control of the corridor to the Zmerrudi Sea.'

It struck Klaus as an uncanny echo of Eohric Ealdwhine's fears, so many weeks before. The Derindin exchanged uneasy glances.

'Then we'll draft our proposal to Lebas,' said Emra, when no more objections came.

Halmir wasn't ready to mute his displeasure. 'I'm surprised the news from the Far North hasn't turned your horses homeward already, Masters Invelmari. Or is it true that only failed Invelmari warriors seek work in the Plains?'

Arik bowed low. 'I'd not been told that we have failed anyone on this side of the Ostraad. Besides, it's not the North that pirates are looting and burning.'

Emra rose, diffusing the moment. 'Thank you, Viridian, Masters Invelmari.'

Dismissed, they left the council chamber feeling even more unwelcome.

*

'And now your aunt is using us,' said Arik irritably outside, all civility cast aside. 'Berengar was right. These two clans are allies and even they can barely see eye to eye. No wonder bandits are running rampant.'

It was difficult not to catch his pessimism. Klaus wondered what the Elders were arguing about now.

Ravi darted out of Verdi's pocket and vanished down the street.

'Hey!'

Verdi shot after him.

Arik swore thunderously. They hurried after Verdi past several houses and through an open door, where they were greeted by a chorus of chirruping, meowing and high-pitched barking.

Arik stopped in his tracks. 'I hope – I really hope that's *not* what I think it is.'

There was an unmistakable smell of feathers, fur and straw-smothered droppings.

Klaus grinned. 'Sorry.'

The shop was filled with large cages and cribs of every shape, containing an assortment of minibeasts: tiny newborn oceloe kitterlats, bearling cubs, exotic species he couldn't name and others he'd only seen in books – fox-ferrets and wolveri and hatchling dart-hares. The beasts grew excited as Ravi jumped from cage to cage, peering inside.

'Hello, hello!' A round-bellied man with a balding head and a generous beard strolled out from the back of the shop, balancing a tray of wriggling worms. He stopped short. 'Ahh!'

He took in the two Invelmari and Verdi. Then he leaned down and peered at Ravi.

'Well now, it's been a long time, little one.'

Ravi's whiskers trembled furiously. Then he rose on his hind paws and rubbed his head against the stranger's cheek. The man's laugh was rich, bubbling up from his belly.

'It's like he knows you!' Verdi exclaimed, astonished.

'Knows? I gave him to you, twenty-four-and-a-half years ago. You hadn't yet seen four moons, but you chose him and he chose you.' The man scratched Ravi's grey head. 'Coaren never forgets a creature that he's handled, does he?'

Klaus looked around. 'Do you raise these creatures, sir?'

'I breed them, yes. But alas, the skill of raising new creatures – minibeasts, greatbeasts – that vanished long ago. Now we just preserve what remains and pray we don't lose another species to disease.' Ravi clambered onto Coaren's forearm, now interested in the worms; Coaren plucked him off and returned him to Verdi's shoulder.

'Greatbeasts,' Arik repeated, clearly enthused at the thought of Ravi in any other proportion. 'It's bad enough having a terror like him in miniature.'

'Bred for war, Master Invelmari. Fought alongside soldiers, and more faithful than some of them too. All gone now.'

Arik edged towards a cage of tiny cooing kitterlats in spite of himself. Verdi cleared his throat. 'Do you mean to say we've met before?'

'You were a babe in arms,' said Coaren. 'Then your ma got sick, and I was told you were bundled off. They said it wouldn't be forever, but once a boy disappears up north there's no telling if he'll come home. Most never do. Didn't expect to see this little face again, at any rate. One of the handsomest breeds I ever did see.' He smiled fondly at Ravi.

Verdi's eyes glistened. Sparing him, Klaus asked, 'How long do oceloes live?'

'Ha! I've seen them outlive a man, and he was the sort of man who hardly stayed out of trouble. Cats may have nine lives, but oceloes live on past all nine of them.' He lowered the tray of worms into a cage of egg-sized fox-ferrets, missing the horrified look on Arik's face.

A crash came from a corner of the shop as a large cage toppled to its side. Four or five coal-black bearlings scuttled out across the floor.

Coaren roared, hurrying first to shut the door, then grabbing a leather sack. 'Blasted fruitnoses! A lively lot. Mind you close that door when you leave, they're too young to fend for themselves.' Then he went after them, for unlike their ambling full-sized animal brethren, the bearlings were cat-like in speed and just as agile.

Outside, Klaus drew an arm around Verdi. 'Alright?'

Verdi nodded.

'Courage.' Arik slapped Verdi's back, propelling him several feet forward. 'We can return to ask more questions if you like. Just don't leave with another oceloe.'

'Can't promise I won't, though,' Klaus murmured, relishing Arik's murderous scowl. He winked at Verdi, managing to stir a watery smile. It was short-lived. A horse had appeared down the street, its hoof-falls weary, carrying a slumped rider barely clinging to the saddle. The rider half slipped, half fell to the ground.

It was Rasan.

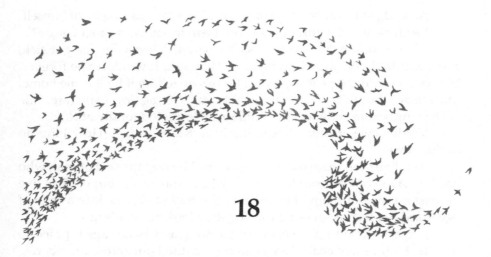

18

A Murmuration of Starlings

LORD STURMSINGER ASKED OF HER,
'WHAT GIFT COULD A CRONE BESTOW UPON A WARRIOR?'
'A CRONE?' SAYETH SHE. 'LOOK AGAIN, O STURMSINGER.'
HE LOOKED AND SAW A SPAEWIFE, AND THROUGH HER
A WINDOW UNTO THE WORLD YET TO COME.

SONNONFER: THE HARVEST OF MERCY

They carried her into Coaren's shop. The creature handler hurried out and drew water from a street pump.

'It's just a scratch,' Rasan protested as Verdi cut away her trouser leg. 'It looks worse than it is.' But her face was pale beneath her desert tan.

'Lie still,' said Coaren gruffly. She clenched her teeth as Verdi examined the remains of an arrowhead from a flesh wound in her thigh. The wound around it had begun to ripen.

'Luckily it's not too deep. It's safe to remove. But if this isn't cleaned, it will fester and you'll lose that leg. Lie still, girl.'

And that was how they ended up huddled by a roaring fire at the height of midday heat, searing the wound with a hot iron. Ravi scuttled away at her first scream, and briefly the entire menagerie of minibeasts fell silent.

Once Verdi was done, he dabbed a wet cloth at Rasan's face. Coaren raised a cup of her water to her lips. She moved gingerly. Welts and bruises bloomed through her torn clothes.

There would be time for anger later. For now, Klaus knew this might be their only chance to speak.

He crouched beside her. 'What happened? Who did this?'

'I went home to Bel Betras after the assembly.' Her voice remained hoarse after a drink. 'Periam had refused to pledge tumblers against the pirates, but I'd hoped our Chieftain would reconsider if I told him what I'd seen on the crossing home.'

Arik raised an eyebrow. 'And did he?'

She gave a caustic laugh. 'Chieftain Eskandan? If Kirono had been his own flesh and blood, Eskandan would have ignored what happened to his caravan. Anything to pander to that Baeronian scum, Voldane.' She coughed on her next sip.

'Slow down,' Verdi warned. 'You'll choke.'

She fell back into the fur, exhausted.

'I left Periam,' she whispered. 'I couldn't bear them any longer. Taunting us with promises to stop currying Baeron's favour ... the Elders say Periam won't survive without Baeron, but really they just line their pockets with Baeron's bribes while the rest of us give up rights to our pastures and wells. Eskandan's an old man, he'll be gone soon. I thought I could wait him out. My father was loyal to Periam, he died fighting for Bel Betras ... I became a tumbler for Periam. But the Elders – half of them are no better than Eskandan, and the rest are too cowardly. Their clerks are corrupt. Nothing will change.'

Klaus asked her, 'But how did you end up here?'

'I left to join another clan. Yes,' she said, catching the surprise on Verdi's face. 'You can switch clans. You didn't know that? How little you know.'

'Were you attacked on your way to join Elendra?' Arik pressed.

'No. I was on my way to Yesmehen, to pledge allegiance to Mantelon. My grandmother's mother was Mantelonian... Pirates tracked me from Romel on the Cinnabar Highway. I don't know where they took me. I thought they would kill me. Eventually they let me go.'

She looked away. Klaus quelled the dark creatures of his imagination. Cold rage burned in the pit of his stomach. She struggled to sit up, gasping when this jolted her leg. Arik pulled her up the fur.

'Did you recognise any of them?'

'I never saw their faces. I wasn't the only one. They joined with other pirates holding a whole caravan captive – men, women, even kids. They interrogated anyone old enough to talk. About their clans, their tumblers, everything. They killed anyone too weak or too old to travel.'

Pain coated her face with a light sheen of perspiration. 'These aren't just pirates. Pirates don't ask questions.'

Klaus met Arik's eyes over her head. 'No, they're not just pirates.'

'They let me go so I could give you this.' She fumbled inside her tunic, then held out a black pouch to Arik.

Inside was a small, clean bone. Arik stared at it. 'What's this?'

'It's a jemesh,' said Coaren, taking it. He held it up in the light, frowning. 'From a broken spine. And it feels as though it's not been long since it was turning someone's neck, either. A death-promise to the recipient.'

Klaus examined the death-promise. It was a little thing, chillingly inert for such a purpose. 'You've seen one before?'

'Feuding tribes would exchange them,' said Coaren. 'Not so much now. You could guess the price on a man's head by what kind of jemesh he was sent. This one sat at the hangman's angle, behind the windpipe...' He looked up at Arik, troubled. 'These are old customs, Master Invelmari. Things I'd hoped not to see revived.'

'They'd heard of the pirates you caught in Romel.' Rasan looked away, ashamed. 'I couldn't ... they asked about a pair of Northern soldiers.'

Arik looked from the bone to the pale young woman lying on the floor. His shoulders shook with anger. 'And you – *you* are their message.'

Her voice grew weary. 'Someone wants to avenge the woman you killed. And it's a warning to anyone who gets in their way.'

'In the way of what?'

For the first time since they'd met, Klaus found fear in her eyes.

'There were many of them.' She looked away again, as if voicing the darkness gave it the shadow of solid substance. Klaus could imagine too well what those eyes saw when they were closed.

'Verdi,' said Arik with great restraint. 'I think you should get your uncle now.'

*

When Verdi arrived at the council chamber, only Suman and Alizarin remained. Suman was at the door before Verdi had finished explaining.

'Where is she now?'

'Coaren's, the creature handler's –'

'Fetch a surgeon and take her to my aunt,' Alizarin told Suman. 'Wait a moment, Viridian.'

Verdi paused, impatient to return. 'Rasan's badly wounded. I need to go back –'

'Coaren's as good a carer for men as for beasts, and there'll be more help soon enough.'

Reluctantly, Verdi obliged. He realised he'd left Ravi behind and wished he hadn't. The little menace would have been a welcome presence. Being alone with his uncle ignited as much dread as desire. *It's as though we don't share a common tongue.* Saya watched from a sconce on the wall.

'There's something I was entrusted to give to you, should you – when you returned.'

'From my parents?'

'No.'

Disappointment gave way to anger. How long was Alizarin going to bait him? But anger was hobbled by years of a servant's silence in Dunraven. His uncle didn't seem to notice, unwrapping a faded leather wallet. The last thing Verdi expected to see inside it was a pen.

'This is *Zarroq'ullim*,' said Alizarin. 'Have you heard the name before?'

Verdi shook his head.

'It is the pen-that-never-runs-dry. This was left by Obsidian Lorendar for his successor.' Alizarin fingered the pen almost tenderly. 'The keepers of the Custodian's Sanctuary entrusted it to your mother when she fell pregnant with you. She only had it for a few months.'

Verdi looked again at the pen, his anger arrested by the exhilaration aroused by any scrap of discovery about his past. But only briefly.

'What do you expect me to do with this?'

'This is the pen which invokes the oath of Obsidian Lorendar.'

Verdi's mouth fell open. '*This* will bring about Merensama?'

His uncle folded the leather over it again. 'My forbears were geologicians and engineers, not alchemists. They studied the rocks and built the aqueducts that saw this citadel through every drought. I don't see how a pen can fix a yard, let alone the desert.'

'Then why are you giving it to me?'

'I do as I promise.'

Verdi stared at the pen mutinously. 'Why bother, if you're not even sure the stories are real?'

'The stories keep belief alive.'

'Belief in myths?'

'Belief in a better world. One without clans forever defending their borders. No more embargos and monopolies on grain and metal and water. No more ghabala.'

'What if the clans don't agree?'

'Then we fight.'

Verdi gaped, aghast. 'And you think *I* could lead them?'

'No,' said his uncle bluntly. It stung, even though Verdi had no such expectation of himself. 'But that's not the point. Lorendar was a great leader with a sacred vision, and his name has the power to bring the clans together. This pen is rightfully yours now.'

'So that I might be seen to have it,' Verdi finished.

He stared at his uncle. Alizarin stared back, unfazed.

'Do you even believe?' said Verdi at last. 'That any of that might be true?'

Alizarin held out the wallet. 'What we each believe is our own business. Our duties remain what they are.'

Verdi imagined what he really wanted to say, as he'd often done in Dunraven when Klaus wasn't around to shield him from casual Invelmari contempt. *Keep it! I'm not taking this until you tell me everything.* But he did take it. He wanted to be alone with the pen that his mother had once held, as he did now.

'This is just bait to convince me to stay in Samsarra,' he spat. The words tumbled over each other recklessly; he knew he was being childish, but he couldn't stop. That was the problem with keeping quiet: the deluge that followed. 'I don't think you believe any of what you just said. I don't think you even care if I stay at all! *Emra* probably put you up to this – she hasn't realised yet that I'm not going to be of any use to you. I'm not a bloody warrior and I never will be.'

Alizarin waited for him to finish.

'I know you're angry.' His uncle stood. 'Try not to let that cloud your better judgement. You will only spite yourself.'

Faced with his calm, Verdi felt rather foolish. Then he panicked; *I might not get this chance again.*

'Tell me about my parents,' he blurted. Weeks of failing to muster the courage finally gave way to yearning. 'I have a right to know.'

Alizarin strode to the door, stopping to fasten his cloak.

'You were a babe in arms when your mother died.'

Verdi was so surprised that for a moment his tongue stuck to the roof of his mouth.

'How did she die?'

'There was a drought not long after you were born. There's constant drought, but that year ... it was a particularly bad season. The winds had all but destroyed the harvest, and even derina crops had been ravaged. Our aqueducts were damaged. People were desperate ... many were driven to drink from sick wells. Too desperate to fear disease. I was away hunting for derina. She was dead when I returned, along with many others who risked drinking from a stagnant well.'

Verdi's pulse raced, hoarding his uncle's words. 'What about my father?'

Alizarin's face hardened. 'The less you know of him the better.'

'Did he leave her?'

'No.'

'Is he alive? Where is he now?'

'He became a tumbler. He doesn't know you survived the drought, and if he's still alive it's best that he doesn't.'

Questions scrambled over each other as they finally took hold of Verdi's tongue.

'Why did you send me away?'

'We thought it would be safer. There are some who would like nothing better than to see Lorendar's line finally ended, to destroy his vision for the clans once and for all. People who will do anything to safeguard ghabala. But you're no longer a child. Besides, it turned out for the best. Haven't you had a fine education? With a few important gaps,' Alizarin added sardonically. 'You've obtained scholarship, skills, knowledge. In short, training worthy of an heir of Obsidian Lorendar.'

Verdi was numb. Dazed with information; famished for more. A hundred protests clamoured to be hurled back at his uncle. He *had* been raised with a twisted sort of privilege. The few friends he'd made may have as well shared his mother's womb. But stripped of those friends, what did that leave him?

'Be mindful, Viridian.' Alizarin seemed to measure his words. 'There will be many people eager to mould you. The danger to your mind is perhaps greater than any to your flesh. Take care.'

'What people? Why?' Frustration spilled over. 'We had a whole desert crossing to talk about this, and now – now you give me nothing but hints and warnings!'

Alizarin turned away. 'I need to inform the Chieftainess of Rasan's report before our allies leave the citadel.'

'What was her name?' Verdi called.

Alizarin looked over his shoulder. 'Yirma.'

With that, Verdi heard an invisible key turning, as though his uncle had closed a chamber of his memory again for good.

*

Whatever they chose to call it, a sacrifice was a sacrifice. The feast they held in honour of the widowed queen-consort was nothing but more of the fanfare that paved the path to her death.

'That's twice,' Master Arnander told Klaus under his breath, raising his wine glass to feign another sip. Intelligencers drank sparingly, if at all. 'If you look at her one more time, you're either sympathetic or lustful. Both will be terribly inconvenient.'

Klaus ground his teeth, certain that Master Arnander would spot the slightest tensing of his jaw. But he busied himself with his plate and the courtiers of the Morregrati palace. The ascending king, Lorcuat, the third-born child of the dead king's first wife, was barely fourteen; only a year older than Klaus. A peacock of a boy, covered in jewels and gold, grinning foolishly at his own fortune. His older brother had died in infancy, and the second-born had been a girl and could not be crowned in this court. Unlike Lady Wintermantel, Invelmar's queen-in-waiting, and thus given a seat of honour at the king's table. Here she reigned already, charming them with silken words and dazzling them with pitiless beauty.

'How do you find our feather-dancers, my lord?'

The soft-spokenness of the king's lovely sister, Klaus decided, hid a keen eye that would remember and relate everything. He lowered his lashes to half-mast, raising her hand just shy of his lips. She was not Invelmari, and besides he was wearing gloves.

'If you really want me to notice them, princess, you'll have to first find yourself a seat elsewhere.'

Behind her blush she was pleased, and Master Arnander was happy.

'The Queen wishes to continue securing Morregrati contracts,' Arnander had warned him, when Klaus had protested their presence at this abominable ritual. 'This boy-king Lorcuat is impressionable. His advisors may undo his father's policies. Do not offend them.'

Across the table, bowmaster Kelselem was noble in the solid silence he was never without. Klaus glanced enviously at Arik sitting with his soldiers; Warriors were permitted to wear masks, like the Isarnanheri they led. Arik's golden mask was raised above his head, his drink and his laughter. Intelligencers had no masks. Their faces were the thickest mask of all.

After hours of feasting, they gathered outside the royal mausoleum for the solemn ceremony that had assembled queens and princes and warlords from across the Parts. Master Arnander hovered over Klaus' shoulder; a guiding and deadly hand.

The first to enter the opened tomb was the elder first wife of the dead king, attended by two slaves. She walked like one who had long accepted this path awaiting her.

After her came the young queen-consort, who the last king had married only six moons before his death. Her face was pale behind the glorious Morregrati ripened-wheatsheaf complexion, but her chin rose stubbornly as she entered the tomb where she would be sealed alive. There would be no food there; no light, no air, no comfort. Morregrati mothers whispered tales in the night to rowdy children of thin screams that escaped the tombs each time a new king was declared; of the snarls of women-turned-wild as they ate each other alive.

Klaus might have forgotten the queen-consort's face, but he couldn't so easily dismiss that of the last of her young maids: faltering behind her, turning back, scrambling to get away from the stair into bottomless darkness. She pleaded *piteously when guards caught her by the arm and was thrown roughly down the steps. Her stricken cries were snuffed out as the great stone door of the tomb was closed.*

Klaus hoped the fall had broken her neck; a quick and painless death. He tasted blood where he'd bitten his tongue to enforce its silence. It would spew its rant into Afldalr instead. The blacksmiths began the work of sealing the metal bolts across the door and the dead king's wives. His pity for the young queen-consort vanished. What would the woman need three maids for, anyway? She was already as good as dead.

Watching, the boy-king was a little green around the gills. Only his mother had been spared. The eulogy for the two royal widows would be followed by his coronation celebrations. Tomorrow, he would bed a girl who would, should she outlive him without producing his heir, walk the same gruesome path. Such was the savagery of the world. But an Intelligencer's task was to bottle and unleash the world, not to pass judgement upon it.

'They knew this day would come when they married the king,' Master Arnander reminded Klaus. 'How much pity can you have for them?'

It wasn't much comfort. How many more such terrible silences would he have to keep? He was glad when they departed for the port and the sea crossing home. He'd never liked Morregrat anyway.

'There is a place we all go to when we gaze into flame,' murmured Kelselem over their camp fire on the shore. 'But I cannot tell you where it is.'

Out of sheer loyalty to Father, Kelselem rarely worded his silent disapproval of Invelmar's methods. His eyes were far away, in his beloved Ummandir perhaps. Klaus knew exactly and yet not even remotely where it was the bowmaster meant; it was the coordinate of every salvaged soul, and one that had so far evaded him. *Sturmsinger forgive me.* His Intelligencer's soul was surely buried by now in a place as dark as that tomb, hopelessly irretrievable.

The click of the closing door woke Klaus; he'd drifted off to a suffocating sleep in the noon sun over his map. Verdi entered alone. Arik hadn't yet returned from the tavern.

'How is Rasan?'

'Resting. They won't let anyone but the physician see her.'

Klaus found his shirt folded neatly at the foot of the bed. Seeing Verdi's forlorn face, he deferred his rebuke. He pulled it on and joined Verdi at the window. Ravi sat quietly on his knee, watching his master. No matter how hard Klaus had tried, he'd never been able to teach the little Derindman how to hide his emotions.

'Don't be disheartened,' Klaus told him.

'I was much better off being nobody,' Verdi mumbled. 'Coming here was a mistake.'

'But you've always wanted to discover your home.'

'I didn't think it would mean any of *this*.'

Verdi gently nudged Ravi away and removed a wallet from his coat. Klaus examined the pen tucked inside it. It was nothing like the unlading pen in Noisy Tree, and was made from a lacquered metal patterned with golden leaves. *The-pen-that-never-runs-dry...* Even its name summoned a thrilling sense of infinity.

'I'm sorry,' Verdi told him.

'For what?'

'If I'd had any idea I would draw so much attention to us, I would never have suggested coming here. I'd have rather risked the slog to Semra.' Verdi paused. 'And for ... well. For my uncle. And the Elders.'

'And all the Derindin?' Klaus smiled slightly. 'What you really mean is you're sorry for turning out to be someone important just as I discover I've been a nobody all this time.'

Verdi turned beet red.

Klaus folded the leather around the pen, gently returning the wallet.

'If you choose it, here is an honourable cause and a prosperous future – and much more. A chance to make a difference. And it couldn't have been bequeathed to a more deserving person.'

'I'm not a soldier,' Verdi protested. 'What could they possibly expect me to do?'

'This is not the North. Not everything begins and ends with war.' Klaus rose. 'It's early yet. Let's find Arik.'

'Assuming he's not found prettier company.'

'Far too early for that, even for Arik. And I'm fairly sure he doesn't have any surrwyrte.'

But outside the tumblers' favoured tavern they found an angry crowd gathering around a dishevelled man. The noise drew diners out from the tavern, Arik and Broco amongst them.

'What's the matter?' Arik asked one of the Derindin.

'He's confessed to using water tokens.'

'Scum!' a man spat. 'Have you no shame? And now you'll bring the sickness here!'

Verdi looked around in confusion. 'What sickness?'

Klaus looked more closely at the man; his cheeks and eyes were sallow.

'Look at him, yellow as a lemon!' an accuser replied. 'He's drunk pirate's water. And now he pays the price!'

A pebble flew through the air. Verdi pushed through the Derindin to peer at the man's face. The man shrank away but had nowhere to go. Klaus eyed the growing crowd. The only reason the mob hadn't made a grab for him already was fear of his supposed contagion.

There was an audible gasp as Verdi raised his hands to feel his neck.

Verdi stepped back, annoyed. 'This man isn't contagious, he's got collier's bile from ore poisoning. It's no more catching than bad breath!'

The man looked rather worried at the prospect of being declared non-infectious to this mob.

'And you know that, do you?' shouted one of the onlookers. 'Just like your friend knew that scum Laminhad was innocent?'

Verdi's back stiffened. 'I do, and I'll vouch for the state of this man's health. I'll share table and cup with him, too.'

'This clan's prohibited the use of water tokens,' someone interjected. 'A punishable crime, to line the pockets of murderers with gold. Wouldn't you say, son of Lorendar?'

There was a sharp intake of breath followed by a hush as the Derindin identified Verdi. He glanced at Klaus, not without a hint of panic.

'I was desperate!' the accused man protested. 'There were no escorted caravans left for safe passage ... pirates at every well and waterhole. We couldn't afford to hire tumblers. Tokens were the only way, we would have thirsted to death –'

'The coin that saved your neck will have bought a noose around another's,' roared a man in reply. 'Now you bring back sickness –'

This was enough for Verdi. 'This man's fear is what needs treating, nothing else.'

'You heard what Master Santarem said,' said Broco loudly. 'Be off home, all of you.'

The rabble rousers knew better than to cross three warriors. As they drifted away, Klaus blocked the path of the accused man. 'A full explanation in return for your safety, I think.'

The man had little other choice but to accompany them into the tavern. No one was keen to serve the table they now shared with him, as promised.

'What's your name?' Verdi asked more kindly.

He looked wary. 'Saepe, son of Kirkaar.'

Klaus asked him, 'Where did you barter tokens with the pirates?'

'At the Nerej oasis.' Saepe looked warily from Klaus to Arik. 'I returned with a small caravan of Voistans. Pirates tracked us there. I wouldn't have bought the tokens, but...' He grew defensive again. 'If you've lost a wife to *tesh*, sir, you would understand.'

'I ask without judgement.' Klaus kept his voice calm, even sympathetic. 'You may yet be of more help than you have been of harm.'

Saepe relaxed a little, then paled; Ayla and several tumblers entered the tavern. Arik pinned him to his seat.

'Master Viridian,' Ayla called out. 'I'm told you've a report for me.

Thank you.'

'Don't challenge her,' Klaus said quietly in Verdi's ear. 'She's trying not to undermine you.'

'This man's sickness is not catching,' Verdi said stubbornly when Ayla reached their table.

'Glad I am to know it,' she replied. 'You may intercede for him if you wish, but he must still answer to the law.'

'The noose!' someone shouted behind her. 'Might as well invite the pirates under your roof next!'

'Calm down –'

But the Derindin were angry. 'The baker's son's been missing a week long. Those bastards wouldn't have the gall to snatch folk if not for traitors like this!'

'Get used to it,' a man retorted. 'I don't see any clans calling their warriors to arms.'

'Who said we'll wait for that? The time of Elders is past. We'll not be waiting to round up pirates!'

The tavern erupted into a row, anger growing thicker than smoke and kahvi. Ayla's voice carried easily, grinding shouts down to a grumble.

'Mutiny against our Elders is as bad as piracy itself.' She singled out no one in particular with her warning. 'And have a care; vigilantes will be no match for these pirates. But pirates are still flesh and blood. We'll cut them down, like any other renegade. Are we not the only clan to have punished bandits when they attacked us?'

Someone cheered; it caught quickly.

Ayla turned to Arik and Klaus. 'Will you train my tumblers, Masters Invelmari?'

The cheering jarred to a halt. Every ear stretched around them.

Klaus chose his words carefully. 'What services a chronicler can offer are yours, General.'

She glanced at Arik. The two warriors appraised one other.

'You assume I'm in need of the work,' said Arik.

Ayla shrugged. 'We're in need of each other, I believe.'

When Arik finally nodded, Ayla slipped him the ghost of a smile. Chatter flooded the room, as she had no doubt intended.

Ayla leaned down to speak in Verdi's ear, lowering her voice. 'The citadel is restive. I can't now arrest a man who you have shown clemency. But your aunt will want an explanation.'

She straightened, waiting expectantly. Verdi cast Klaus a worried look before following her out of the tavern.

'She waited until we couldn't say no,' Arik grumbled, grudging approval glinting in his eye. 'She knew we wouldn't refuse and embarrass Verdi.'

Ayla had played her hand well. Klaus was certain that Ayla's endorsement of them would be quick to spore throughout the citadel.

Briefly off the hook, Saepe darted out of the tavern. A moment later, Klaus followed him without a word.

*

Verdi's stomach churned. It was only his second day in this beautiful citadel, and he had already been summoned to his aunt's house in disgrace. She was disarmingly charming. It made matters worse.

'How do you like Samsarra, Viridian?'

'I've not yet seen much of it.'

'We must remedy that. Have you given any thought to what you'll do here?'

Too many questions crouched behind her question. Ravi hadn't yet emerged from his breast pocket, dipping his nose out periodically for a sniff of the honeysuckle climbing past the window, making Verdi more cautious still.

'I don't know yet,' he admitted. 'In Invelmar I'd been seeking tutelage under a physician…' Feeling rather exposed, he changed course. 'My lady – Ahena – that man has no catching illness. People mustn't be allowed to think the pirates have that kind of power.'

The charm lost some of its warmth. But she was listening.

'He has collier's bile, not an uncommon condition in Northern blacksmiths and their suppliers. There's a toxin in some ore stones that can overwhelm the liver. I've seen it many times…'

'That is wise,' she said. 'It will do no good to allow the pirates any more of a hold over people than they already have. But there are other ways to undermine them, such as prohibiting any trade that strengthens and legitimises their attempts to usurp travellers' water. And punishing collusion accordingly.'

Verdi shifted nervously. But he thought of the many, far more precarious, interrogations he'd watched Klaus endure, and found his tongue.

'This man's fear is what needs to be treated, in order to gain the trust of those like him,' he insisted. 'People motivated by desperation and necessity. Rather than punishing disloyalty, which only spreads fear – fear of those who ought to be protectors.'

He spent the next moment squirming under her gaze.

'Well. At least the North has not touched every part of you yet.' She smiled. 'It's no wonder you're so lost. You've been left to navigate a whole new world alone. Don't worry, you'll have a teacher. Why do you look so reluctant?'

'I'd hoped to find an apprenticeship...'

'As you wish. But a wise man seeks knowledge in all places.' She paused. 'Before all else, Lorendar was a man who fell hard, and spent the rest of his life trying to get up. Do not forget this.'

'I don't know that I can help you, aunt.' Verdi floundered for words. 'However am I to find this moon phase?'

'You've already helped, Viridian. You have stirred hope.'

She beckoned him to the open window.

'Look up,' she said. His gaze climbed above the honeysuckle vines to a late afternoon sky, clear as glass. 'Wisdoms of every rank have sought to summon the heavens to the earth, to strike justice. Obsidian was not wise until the very end of his life, but he understood quickly that Merensama could not be achieved while our people divided themselves into kingdoms pitted against each other. We must restore their hope in something more than clans.'

He realised this was as good an answer as he would get for now.

'As for Saepe, Viridian, he will be tried fairly for aiding pirates. Justice is owed, even if its claimants are absent. His circumstances will be taken into account.'

'I understand.'

'A word of caution, nephew. In the South, clanship is as valuable as a dagger at one's belt. Elendra is your ancestral clan. Join us, and we can better protect you. Think carefully but not too long.'

*

Arik lingered in the tavern, surrounded now by tumblers, stew and cider.

'They should have sent the envoy to Fraivon first,' said Broco. 'Fraivon's clandom stretches further south than Lebas'. And if they refuse, we should just go south ourselves. It'll be worth the risk.'

'It is?' muttered Tesnan, a captain who had been much slower to warm to the Northerners. 'It'll be a hefty price to pay if none come back.'

'Keep your voices down,' Saarem warned.

Ayla had informed a few tumblers of Klaus' suspicions about a pirate stronghold, though not the mine itself. Arik wasn't sure if this was a mistake or a boon.

'Any news of Rasan?' he asked.

Broco shook his head. 'She'll be more or less a prisoner now until the questions dry up.'

'How do you think Lebas will answer?'

'Difficult to say. They've been bit hard by pirates, and they'd love the advantage over Fraivon. But to really get far, you need water and your luck with the wind. The storms are worse southward. And they'll want to avoid Baeron's questions, if they're caught sneaking along Baeron's western border.'

'It's a fool's errand.' Tesnan avoided Arik's eye. 'And on shaky grounds, too.'

'I prefer being called a liar to my face,' said Arik calmly.

'So you've accepted a contract with General Ayla, Master Marcin.' Broco wagged his eyebrows provocatively at Tesnan, who looked away. 'Elendrans have never paid a Northern mercenary, and now here's one training up Isarnanheri…'

'Hardly,' said Arik. 'Even if I were Isarnanheri, instructing anyone but the Northborn in the way of Isarnanheri is treason.' He winked at his companions, beckoned over the serving girl and raised his cup. 'And it's much more fun staying alive.'

They cheered to this and refilled their flagons. *No soldier is too small to notice,* Mistress Lisbeta had once scolded. Quietly, Arik tipped a little more drink out of his cup and set to noticing them all.

*

Klaus followed Saepe into another tavern, where he promptly disappeared behind a counter. Klaus stayed for kahvi and a few questions for the pretty tavern maid, but Saepe didn't re-emerge.

'Master Invelmari!' Eresk, the man on whose behalf Klaus had intervened at the hearing, spotted him across the room. He was finely dressed, his belt embellished with gold. Rising from his table, he announced loudly, 'This is the man who convinced the council of my innocence. He saw reason when even those who know me couldn't. A noble guest, friends!'

A cheer rose around the tavern. Eresk was amongst allies, his table crowded with admirers. He left them to join Klaus.

'To whom do I owe my gratitude, Master Invelmari?'

Klaus bowed his head. 'Only a chronicler. My name's Tristan. How's your leg?'

'Recovering well, by the grace of the Great Sentience. Stay and have supper on me.'

'Very kind of you, sir. But I've duties to get back to.'

'But of course – a guard of Lorendar's heir, friends!'

Another cheer, this one more hearty and accompanied by several raised glasses; Eresk wooed his audience well.

'To the Northman!'

Eresk escorted Klaus to the door, greeting everyone they passed.

'My heartfelt gratitude,' he said quietly before they parted. He had lost the limp he'd had at the hearing. His smile was brilliant.

Klaus returned to the first tavern. He stopped outside and barked twice. Arik stepped out a moment later.

'Anything?'

'Not yet.'

In the early twilight, trees cast sinewy shadows across the paving stones, and a cool breeze swept the day's warmth away. They relieved a pastry seller of two large pies and walked slowly towards the Chieftainess' house.

'This mine...' Arik hesitated. 'You don't think the ore...?'

'Could rival the ironstone used for Invelmari steel?' This had been Klaus' first consideration, and one he hardly dared revisit. 'No. And as you well know, it's as much the smithy as the ore. But any iron would be a game-changer here.'

Arik looked slightly reassured, but Klaus felt uneasy even as he dismissed the Warrior's fears. They intercepted Verdi hurrying away from the Chieftainess' square.

'Aren't you going in the wrong direction?' Arik asked.

Verdi was in no humour for jokes. 'Let's stay away from the house a bit longer.'

So they sat in a square high in the citadel, from where they could see the desert ocean stretching beyond the wall. The hot pies were delicious. Ravi took residence in Verdi's lap and stole the first bite of everything Verdi lifted to his mouth.

'What are you going to do about the jemesh?' asked Verdi.

Arik shrugged. 'Think about it tomorrow?' He winked at the look on Verdi's face. 'Why are you worrying about me? You're a wanted man, Verdi. I'm just keeping up.'

Verdi slapped his arm. 'What about Saepe?'

Other than confirming Saepe hadn't lied about losing his wife to drought, Klaus hadn't learned much more about the man they'd rescued from the mob.

'I wonder where he contracted collier's bile,' Verdi mused. 'His caravan disbanded only recently, in Voista's land... We ought to watch out for more cases.'

'Maybe it was from the water, not the rock,' Klaus replied. 'He bought water from the pirates. Could have been contaminated.' He paused. *Contaminated, with water the pirates had carried from a mine?*

Someone hurried up the street, panting. It was the creature handler, Coaren.

'Evening! Glad I am not to have to go all the way up to the Chieftainess' house.' He paused to catch his breath. 'Master Marcin, you left this.'

He held out the pouch containing the jemesh. His face was solemn.

'I wouldn't take this lightly, Master Marcin,' Coaren cautioned. Next he pulled out a pipe and a tin of smokeleaf. 'Mind if I join you?'

He puffed away as he talked. 'Need *some* peace and quiet from the little blighters,' he chuckled, absent-mindedly scratching at a grubby bandage over one wrist. 'The Chieftainess won't let anyone question that tumbler until she's rested, but that Navein – he's a hard one. Good man, but hard.'

'Will you tell me about Lorendar, Master Coaren?' said Verdi timidly.

The beast master sucked long at his pipe. 'You're better off asking a lettered man. Maybe a Mantelonian, they follow him the closest.'

'I'd much rather ask you.'

Coaren blew a smoke ring. 'Lorendar had larger dreams than a simple man like me. Mind you, they were praiseworthy.'

'Then why do so many people fear them?'

'People fear change. Even good change, and especially when it comes at a price. If we're being honest, the only road I can see to Merensama is war. And who wants that?'

The sinking sun lit a great hearth in the heavens, ribboned with wisp-thin clouds. For all the green majesty of the North, Klaus had never seen such splendid skies as over the Derindin Plains.

Ravi ditched Verdi and even the pie crumbs to curl into the crook of Coaren's elbow. Coaren chuckled and scratched his head fondly, skilfully puffing at his pipe without setting the oceloe's enormous tail aflame. Ravi's whiskers twitched in delight at the leafsmoke.

'Little traitor,' Verdi muttered.

'Do you know where we might find good lodgings?' Klaus asked.

Coaren cast a sidelong glance at him and Arik. 'Not many far-flung travellers around these parts. I would try at the house of old widow Thillaina. Takes in just a couple o' lodgers, mostly for the company. She's a decent sort and she doesn't mind strangers. She'll put you up if she's got room to spare. Ahh!' He pointed. 'Look yonder. Starlings, clouds of 'em.'

Hundreds of birds appeared together in the golden-pink dusk, rising and falling in wave-like formation. The flock grew, swelling to fill the sky with a dance that shimmered like a shoal of fish bending water. Something mirrored their movement in Klaus' breast; a bright chasm splicing the darkness.

'My word,' said Coaren, open-mouthed. 'I've not seen a murmuration like that in my lifetime.'

'What are they doing?' Verdi asked, admiring.

'No one knows. It's a rare sight. Something's afoot.'

Arik raised a dubious eyebrow. 'Another bad omen?'

'Nay. Good tidings. The land feels change before we do ... and birds are the first to know, and tell each other once they do.' Coaren smiled at Verdi. 'Perhaps they've seen hope.'

The birds gathered into one great wing, saluting them with swarming grace. They watched the murmuration until it dissolved into the twilight.

*

A much wider gaze than they knew witnessed the starlings over Samsarra. Some, like Coaren, remembered the lore and wondered. Others simply watched and marvelled.

The Chieftainess of the Elendra paused at her window. The tumbler's story filled her with foreboding. More reports of disappearances trickled into the citadel each day; too many to ignore. And the Wisdom had stirred memories of a shame she had suppressed for so long it was now a greater burden than ever.

But, for a moment, she stood and watched the birds, and when tears came they were not for hurting.

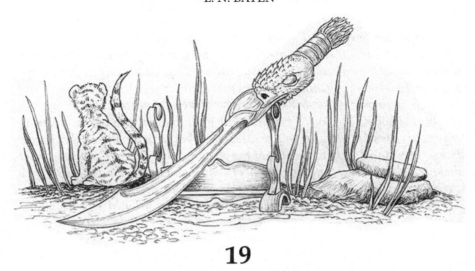

19

The Bed of Ashes

'AN OCEAN OF BLOOD YOU HAVE SPILT FOR YOUR TRIUMPH,
O STURMSINGER, AND AN OCEAN OF BLOOD MUST NOW BIND YOU.
IF ONE MORE DROP SHOULD YOUR PEOPLE SHED AGAINST EACH OTHER,
O STURMSINGER, YOUR KINGDOM SHALL CRUMBLE, YOUR THRONE
RETURN TO DUST. THIS WARNING IS MY GIFT TO YOU,
WHO HAVE TRIUMPHED WITH BLOOD.'

SONNONFER: THE HARVEST OF MERCY

A soft bed that always waited faithfully; a warm hearth burned down to glowing embers. Every one of his muscles ached after the trials of another campaign. But for now, there was only the burrowing comfort of his chambers in Dunraven.

There was no watch to take over tonight, but that internal clock still woke him in the small hours. Or perhaps it was the howling of a wolf in nearby Longtooth, or the silent music of the stars.

In fact, it was the feeling of being watched. He opened his eyes to look up into the face of a hazel-eyed woman, the familiar scent of mahonia drifting from the chestnut coils of her hair. Drowsiness muffled his surprise.

'Mother.'

So tender, her smile. 'I'm sorry I missed the banquet.'

A great curtain of sleep hovered over him, forcing his eyes closed. Her presence made the pillows softer; the fire warmer. He felt her fingers in his hair, a kiss on his brow; the gentlest of slopes into slumber –

– a searing pain erupted in his breast. His eyes flew open. Now clouds of chestnut shadows swallowed her face, but those eyes burned on the faltering edge of his consciousness, as cold and remote as unmarked paths in the Sterns. His fingers closed around the hilt of the dagger in his chest … then the hand that had delivered it was no longer that of Lady Wintermantel but Elodie, Elodie gazing at him with horror in the stables: 'Klaus – I learned something terrible…

Alizarin's derision, echoing in his ears: 'And you trusted her?'

Klaus awoke with a ragged breath.

It was still dark. Arik and Verdi were asleep.

His fingers fumbled to his chest, to his rioting heart. The sweat coating his neck was cold. There was a distant stirring in the house below. He fancied he heard Mayda's voice. Then everything became quiet.

He lay back; too troubled to sleep, too disquieted to stay awake. Eventually, the pounding of his heart settled, but his thoughts did not.

*

'The most important thing, Viridian, is the dial.'

Of all the Elders, Verdi decided it was Navein who made him most uncomfortable. Confusingly, Ravi had remained on Verdi's shoulder, unperturbed.

He tried to set jittery nerves aside to focus on the gnomon instead, which the Mantelonian Chieftain had wished to personally explain before his departure.

'This probe attached to the gnomon is an anchor. It must be plunged into the ground.' Navein leaned down and slipped the probe into a patch of earth beneath the citron trees in the Chieftainess' courtyard. 'There's a whole science concerning the probe, but the dial is your main concern. The dial of this instrument is twofold. Do you see where it falls now?'

Now secured upright in the morning sun, the gnomon's shadow fell just shy of eight o'clock, forming a sharp shadow-dial.

Verdi nodded, feeling stupid. 'Yes … but I only see one dial.'

'Correct. This first shadow is the sundial. This gnomon produces a *second* shadow, a moondial that follows the movements of the moon –

which only appears at night. *That* dial is much harder to grasp.'

'I thought a moondial is only accurate when the moon is full...'

'Ordinarily, yes. But the probe that anchors the gnomon allows this dial to reveal far more than an ordinary horological device. It has properties allowing it to converse with both phases of the heavens, day and night. To us they appear as phases; in truth the heavens are constant, and it is only our perception of a permanent truth that changes. Thus this probe is sensitive enough that it will work by any amount of lunar light. And *this* moondial is only visible to the one of Lorendar's line for whom the limolan has regrown.'

In spite of his wary awe of the Chieftain, Verdi found himself intrigued. Something about the gnomon was pleasantly unsettling; enticing. 'Why must Merensama be invoked in a certain phase of the moon?'

'Because of the bolt that was placed on the passage between this world and the next, as punishment for burying truth so deep in our hearts that we lost sight of it altogether.' Navein straightened. 'Merensama is a taste of the peace that reigns in the Unseen World. We strive to emulate the perfect symmetry of that realm. But how can we borrow from the Unseen World while this passage remains closed? The bolt can only be lifted in that precise moon phase. Lorendar committed his line to the service of the Great Sentience, but his successor had to be sound of heart. Finding the hidden phase of the moon is as much a trial of his successor as it is a condition for establishing Merensama.'

'That's what the pirate meant!' Verdi exclaimed. 'The one who abducted me in Romel. She said *'the bolt mustn't be lifted'*...' He gaped. 'Do the pirates hate Lorendar as well?'

'We don't know who employed her. Pay attention, Master Viridian.' Navein's blue gaze became steely. 'We can negotiate, make alliances ... wage war when words fail. What we can't yet do is unlock the Merensaman moon phase to gain the peace of the heavens. It is imperative that you apply yourself to making the moondial appear.'

How do you know that I want to? But Verdi nodded meekly. 'I will.'

The Chieftain smiled, neither benevolent nor malicious. 'It is a great burden, to learn that generations of faithful invoke your name with Lorendar's in their prayers every night. You will hear many lies about your forebear, but don't be misled. Were it not for him, Derinda would have decayed long before Northern warbringers ever dreamed of a dam. But Lorendar fought for something greater.'

'He was a warrior, then?'

'Eventually. But before that he was a farmer, his first army raised from the fields to take back the land bit by bit.'

'There you are.' Alizarin strode into the courtyard. 'I've been looking for you high and low. Are you ready to leave?' He nodded apologetically at Navein. 'Forgive me, Chieftain. I'd promised my nephew his first glimpse of the Arboretum.'

'Of course.'

Verdi found himself swept out to the stables. He wasn't altogether ungrateful for the interruption, though he was confused.

'And now that I've said that, you'll have to come with me,' Alizarin muttered. 'For once, just do as I say.'

'I don't understand...' Verdi hurried to keep up. 'I thought Mantelon were Elendra's allies.'

'And they have been since the dawn of clans. But if you wish to be free to make your own choices...' Alizarin's jaw tightened. 'I told you once before, the danger to your mind is perhaps greater than any other.'

After that, it was difficult to speak over the horses' hooves pummelling the dirt. Alizarin led him east through pastures, and then woods that grew thicker as they went. *I wish they would all leave me alone to explore – the citadel, the woods.* Oh to be Fibbler, free to discover this world he'd so longed for. Within the hour, they dismounted in a forest that might have been plucked from southern Invelmar.

'Surprised?'

'Well, yes...' Verdi gazed around. 'What am I doing here?'

'It won't do to have the Chieftain of our oldest ally think I was lying.' His uncle was already walking away. 'In any case, you may as well take a look around the Arboretum. One of Elendra's great achievements. You ought to show an interest.'

Disgruntled, Verdi followed. The path led to a long building he first mistook for a temple, but which in fact was a laboratorium. Inside, Verdi was greeted by rows of specimens, storage cylinders, instruments, and many more tools of a natural philosopher. A distilling apparatus hissed from a nearby workbench. His uncle had already forgotten him, walking out into the courtyard. Verdi drifted towards the bench, where a youth was adjusting the fire under a glass cylinder. He noticed Verdi with a start.

'Sorry, I didn't mean to startle you. My name's Verdi...' The young man's eyes widened just as Verdi recognised him. 'You're Bevro, from the inn in Romel!'

This time, there was nowhere for Bevro to excuse himself. Verdi felt oddly at ease with someone even more nervous than himself.

'This is the first time I've been to the Arboretum,' he told Bevro. 'It's like a little of the North hidden away in the desert.'

Gradually relaxing, Bevro showed him around the experimental houses surrounding the courtyard, pointing out the underground seed bank. A bell was ringing on his workbench on their return, and he hurried towards it.

'What are you doing?'

'Distilling this solution of derina root. Will you pass me those tongs?'

Happy to oblige, Verdi rolled up the sleeves of his shirt.

*

Klaus had disappeared at dawn. Arik was accustomed to his brooding spells and unannounced departures; it was an Intelligencer's nature to be obscure. But Arik also remembered a playmate who was riddled with mischief. The severing of Klaus' ties to the Eye of the Court had done little to restore any of that. When Klaus wasn't disarming the Derindin with calibrated charm, he was increasingly wooden and withdrawn.

It was enough to dampen even Arik's spirits. He'd hoped Klaus would eventually remember life before the Eye had taken him. But the Forms of Intelligencers cut deeply, Mistress Lisbeta had said. Not like those of Warriors, who couldn't afford to catch too close a sight of their own reflections. Warriors kept a safe distance from the dreaded *self*.

Leaving Verdi to fend off Navein in the safety of Emra's house, Arik rode out with Ayla into the pastures around Samsarra, to the tumblers' training ground beyond. The land around Samsarra was dotted with homes and the camps of nomadic Elendrans, who came to graze their herds and fetch water from Samsarra's springs.

Arik counted more tumblers guarding the north-eastern clandom. 'Patrols?'

'The watercourses that bring water to Samsarra are buried here,' Ayla replied. 'We must safeguard the lifeline of the citadel as much as the land itself.'

The sun was high when they reached the training ground, where Ayla was keen for him to begin.

'If you can earn the respect of these tumblers, Master Marcin, they're yours to command. But I warn you, they're set in their ways.'

A challenge, then. Arik had run with too many battle-hardened dogs to be daunted. With the exception of Isarnanheri, soldiers were the same everywhere. And if Derindin tumblers were particularly proud, Arik probably thought better of them for it.

Let's make this harder. The tumblers he'd supped with in the cantinas were the good-natured sort who could stomach a drink with a Northerner. These were not the tumblers who interested Arik most.

'A dozen warriors,' he told Ayla. 'No more.'

'Are you sure? Only one fist?'

'A dozen.'

He chose them himself; half of them men and women with whom he'd shared a tavern table, and the remainder who'd never met his eye.

All Isarnanheri could recall their earliest lesson. Ealdormen Warriors were yet more than Isarnanheri. In the making of a Warrior's Form, that first moment of study was a pearl that was deliberately chosen for each Warrior, never to lose its nacre. Arik's had not yet dulled.

'Death is the true opponent. The steel will only become fully yours once you have shed your fear of falling.'

He walked slowly along the line of his chosen dozen, stifling errant thoughts. He wasn't raising Isarnanheri, and now he never would do so again – that would be treason second only to sharing the secrets of making Invelmari steel. But Lisbeta's voice seemed to grow louder the further he was from the North.

'Do you think the steel is a servant in your hands? No. It is the master.'

He asked their names one by one. The unwilling made their dissatisfaction known in every portion of their presence.

'And your name, sir?'

The last tumbler, a man perhaps just shy of forty, stared over Arik's shoulder.

'Very well,' Arik told him. 'Perhaps your good general can instruct a soldier without a name, but he's useless to me without a pair of ears.'

At the mention of Ayla, the man's eyes flickered. *Good. He has honour enough not to want to disgrace his general.*

'Sendar,' he said, breaking his silence woodenly.

'Thank you, Sendar.' Arik turned back to his fist of tumblers. 'Leave your weapons. Today we ride.'

They obeyed reluctantly, the curious and the sullen alike. No one questioned why he began with an exercise in which the Derindin excelled over Northerners. They rode east along the aqueducts and back north around the citadel, through small woods where the ground was rocky and twisted with roots. The sun reached its zenith, growing unpleasantly warm. Arik stopped them for water once and continued almost as soon as the horses had had their drink. It was after some hours of this, as they re-approached a grassy dune they'd crossed once already, when a surly tumbler named Marsulo finally aired his frustration.

'What's the point of this?' Marsulo brought his horse to a halt. 'We know this terrain.'

A few of the tumblers also stopped. Arik noted them all, his voice as sharp as the blades they'd left behind. 'The point is not to have asked.'

This earned Arik a few baleful glares. They continued for another two meandering hours, returning to the training ground in the early afternoon. Several tumblers dismounted in disgust to retrieve their swords and spears. Again, Arik noted those who hesitated in their saddles, awaiting his orders.

'Why are you hurrying back to your weapons, Sendar?' he called. 'After all, you didn't leave them all behind.'

The stony-faced tumbler looked both surprised and angry that the subtle tug of the knives hidden in his sleeve had given him away. 'What kind of madman rides out unarmed with bandits about?'

'And what kind of warrior thinks he can be trusted though he does as he pleases?'

Arik stared around the dusty riders, meeting the eyes of each tumbler in turn. *These are men and women who've passed through the guild of Murhesla.*

'Any of you who are prepared to depart from the command of Ayla Taahn may choose now to depart from mine.'

No one moved. Arik turned away and rode back to the barracks.

Verdi sat waiting for him outside, looking the happiest he'd seen him in weeks.

Arik eyed him suspiciously. 'What's got into you?'

He only half listened to Verdi's chatter about the research station and the Arboretum. Klaus would make him retell it all again, and Arik's mind was otherwise preoccupied. *They're only soldiers.* The common training he had planned was a far cry from the shaping of Isarnanheri, or the journey Arik had himself taken so long ago under a merciless Form Mistress.

He was just tightening these soldiers' shortcomings. There was no treachery in that.

*

Klaus stood in the open doorway of the Samsarran lettervault and felt immediately at home. It was a shallow-domed building of honey stone, smothered with jasmine vines and late autumn wallrose. It wasn't far from the main market square, but as soon as he turned into the street, the cries of stall sellers and barterers vanished, replaced by the familiar tranquillity of books.

He stepped inside. A soothing hush; the musty breath of yellowed pages. And, beyond the entrance hall, an inviting glimpse of shelves stacked with manuscripts and scrolls.

A bell tinkled; he must have trod on a trigger concealed beneath the flagstones. He stopped and waited. A little man appeared, his spectacles slightly askew and his robe trimmed with dust.

'Who's that?' he said irritably. He straightened his spectacles. 'Ah.'

'Are you the librarian, sir?' said Klaus, who recognised this species all over the Parts.

'I am.'

The librarian was well-ripened, slightly balding and appropriately creased, commanding order over his work rather than his person. His blue eyes appraised Klaus critically.

'I've not much time for the Babblers and the chatterers, but I heard there was a Northern chronicler about. Would that be you?'

'Yes. I would be very grateful if you would admit me.'

The librarian appraised him dubiously. 'Northern visitors tend not to knock on this door.'

Disappointed, Klaus bowed. He could persuade him with Form or else obtain Emra's permission to enter, but this would earn him no favours with the librarian. His was a heart Klaus preferred to win.

'I shan't force my company upon you, sir. Would you be willing to recommend a teacher? My Derindask has grown rusty, and I'd like to remedy that if I'm to pursue my work.'

The librarian's eyes twinkled; some approval, at least. 'I shall think on it. Come back another day.'

Slightly buoyed by this small victory, Klaus departed.

At least I can learn the streets. He passed through a couple of taverns, stopping to sample the kahvi and the talk. There were rumours about the nature of Rasan's arrival, and of more abductions across Derinda. He was definitely more welcome in some places than others. The association with Verdi had somewhat lent him and Arik a shield, but it was brittle. In the tavern where he'd run into Eresk Laminhad, the innkeeper escorted him to a table and wouldn't take coin for his drink. In the next, a few Derindin refused to look his way at all. The handful of girls who stole glances at him kept their tongues in their head. *A good arena for a student Intelligencer,* he thought wryly to himself.

He was about to head to the training ground when a refrain lured him into another tavern.

It was quiet but far from empty. The youth attending to his table was none other than Felid, the pleasant youth from Alizarin's caravan. He greeted Klaus with a smile, though it was furtive.

Ignoring curious looks, Klaus studied the singer whose song had drawn him in. He sang in a tongue that flowed gently, holding the room captive. A cheer rose around his final notes, and when his next song began in Low Invelmen, tavern chatter replaced the quiet he had hitherto commanded.

Felid returned with his kahvi. 'You look well, Master Tristan. You've decided to stay in Samsarra, then?'

'As long as Master Viridian is here, yes.' Klaus juggled an idea, raising his voice. 'I don't suppose you know where I can find a speaker of Orenthian?'

'Bit beyond my learning, I'm afraid. You could try the lettervault.'

'That's a good idea.'

A nearby Derindman twisted in his chair. 'What need does a Northman have of Orenthian?'

Around them, ears pricked and tongues fell still.

Klaus poured himself a kahvi. 'A chronicler collects whatever treasure he finds.'

Someone jeered. 'Warbringers wouldn't know a treasure unless it fits into a scabbard!'

Laughter followed. Klaus downed his kahvi. He rose and crossed the tavern to where the bard was now playing a jig by the empty hearth.

The bard's fingers faltered on his strings. He was grey-haired, his dancing days likely behind him. Klaus picked up the poker. Scraping the ground loudly, he drew in the layer of ash on the hearth: the inscription from the watchtower in Ilaria.

The bard's eyes rounded, but his face held surprise rather than comprehension. The tavern had fallen quiet, heads craning for a closer look. But, like the singer, the Derindin registered the words with solemn recognition rather than understanding. *They can't read it, either.* Klaus gazed questioningly around the room. This time, no one spoke.

There was no more jeering after that, though a tension stifled the air, and they left Klaus to himself. He departed feeling lonelier and more disheartened than ever.

*

In the afternoon, Klaus found Arik in the tumblers' favourite tavern with Verdi.

'Hungry?'

Klaus shook his head. 'I'm going to see Mayda. She was at the Chieftainess' house last night.'

Arik sighed. 'The problem with you is you're no *fun*, even now.'

It was easy to find Fibbler in the market square. They located the busiest stalls and then kept their eyes out for the fastest little rascal darting through them.

Sure enough, a shout soon erupted; a man dropped an armful of shirts to chase someone from his stall, where a contraption now released a cacophony of discordant chimes.

The man soon gave up, cursing. A few moments later, Fibbler strolled blithely out of an alley back into the square. He spotted them immediately and dashed over.

'Hurrah!' Proudly, he tapped his hip, where he'd tied the wooden sword to his belt. 'I've been carryin' this around, hoping we can get back to practice!'

'Soon, Fibbler,' said Klaus. 'Where can we find Mistress Mayda?'

Fibbler chattered loudly as he led the way to her stall.

'Do you know farmer Taslisem, Fibbler?' Klaus interrupted.

'Tight Taslisem?' Fibbler blushed. 'Master Gerin, yes.' His eyes grew wistful. 'He keeps a good watch over his apricot trees.'

Mayda greeted them warmly. 'And there's Terim saying you'd forget the likes of us. Stay a while, stay a while.'

She insisted on serving them cool sweet-milk. Fibbler disappeared once he'd inhaled his portion. For Ravi, she filled a thimble, which he promptly emptied before nosing her hand for more. 'Milk's bad for your stomach,' she told him sternly. 'Gives oceloe innards the watery runs.'

'Something to look forward to later,' Arik told Verdi darkly. 'Hopefully, Thillaina will wait a full night before she throws us out.'

There was something comforting in her warm and uncomplicated company. A baby's cry drifted from a basket behind her, much to Ravi's alarm; he dropped his thimble and darted under Verdi's coat. Mayda lifted an infant from the blankets.

'Left behind when his parents went up to the border towns on account of him being so little, and their caravan didn't return. Now he's alone. His grandparents can barely feed themselves as it is.' She clucked over him until the crying stopped, sadness watering down her smile. 'Poor mite. We take one in every so often, Terim and me. Get them started in the world or see them set up somewhere.'

'There must be many more like him now,' said Verdi. Ravi extended a cautious head past his lapel, whiskers twitching.

'That there are. Fibbler was one such. But he never found anywhere else to go.' Mayda's face darkened. 'You don't know where he's been this morning, do you? Only he's beginning to spend an awful lot of time with the Babble. One in particular … a quiet mouse, but a clever one. Never liked the look of him.' Her frown deepened. 'They're saying you've been marked, Master Marcin. Why did you have to go and put steel in that pirate? Bounty hunters won't give you any peace now.'

Arik slipped her an easy smile. 'Speaking of pirates, we thought you might have visited Rasan at the Chieftainess' house. How's she faring?'

Motherly and gentle, with her generous bosom and hearty laughter, Maida was no fool.

'Don't go harassing that girl,' she said sharply. 'It's bad enough the Elders wouldn't let her be. They'd have hauled her before the council for interrogation if the Chieftainess hadn't forbidden it.'

'Fortunately, you'll be there to nurse her,' Klaus soothed, guessing correctly. She nodded, mellowing.

'However she managed to get away alive...' Mayda rocked the bundle in her arms. 'They took her all the way down the Cinnabar Highway, you know.'

'I thought she didn't see where she was taken.'

'She didn't. But her nails ... underneath them was a good bit of red dirt, and I'd know that colour anywhere – I only ever saw the like of it once. We called it red gold when we were little ones ... if we were ever little ones once. Sometimes I think that's another dream I had.'

'Oh? Where's it from?'

'An old quarry where we were never allowed to play, so naturally there were prizes for who brought back the biggest skeleton without getting caught... I'll never forget the colour of the dirt, Master Tristan, because it looked like old blood. Her fingernails were full of it, scratching and scratching the dirt...' She shuddered.

Verdi gently touched her shoulder. 'Did you mention this to anyone?'

'What, and have them upset her with prying? No, let her sleep. There'll be time enough for questions.' Maida blinked back tears. 'Took forever to wash away.'

Klaus changed the subject. 'Do you know much about Eresk Laminhad?'

'Of course. Everyone knows Laminhad. Well-liked, even if he's extravagant. He's generous, though, and has a smile for everyone. Good stock.' She hesitated.

'Yes?'

'I don't like to give much weight to my imaginings, Master Tristan. But I never did like how bitter his feud got with Taslisem. A truly generous man wouldn't hold onto such grudges.'

'What's their grievance?'

'Taslisem's land neighbours his but gets less of the wind and more run-off from the aqueducts. Laminhad's wanted it for years, but Taslisem won't be bought out. And Laminhad's not used to being refused.' She shook her head. 'A sad business. Taslisem's a sour one, but he had to make himself from nothing while Laminhad inherited his lot. This raid ... can't be easy, losing one's wife and workers and harvest and all at once. Wouldn't wish it on my enemy. They said in the market you saved Laminhad's skin, Master Tristan.'

'I suppose I did.'

'What will you do in Samsarra? Do you mean to stay?' Her eyes finished on Verdi.

Arik came to Verdi's rescue. 'For now. Though enough of your fellows would be happier seeing the backs of us.'

'Oh, don't you pay any mind to them,' Maida said scornfully. 'It's because you carry the steel, even though you've raised it in their defence. Northern merchants have an easier time of it than you. But steel – steel reminds them of the past. We're stuck in our own misery, us Derindin, like wheels jammed in mud. They'll be lucky for every night you sleep in this city, and one day they'll even thank you for it.' Her eyes drifted to Verdi again. 'And perhaps better times are closer than they seem.'

Verdi shifted uncomfortably, so Klaus bowed. 'Do you need anything, mistress?'

'No, sir. Just a good wind and the favour of the Great Sentience. Only he knows what'll come of us if another twelvemonth passes with so much wind.'

Her eyes widened at the weight of the silver Klaus slipped into her hand.

He silenced her protests. 'Save it for the child.'

Fibbler peeled away from a gaggle of playmates when they left, skipping along.

'They're saying you'll be training Elendra's tumblers!' He punched the air and kicked three or four invisible foes, spinning until he came to a groggy stop.

Arik steadied him. 'And what are people saying about that?'

Fibbler looked uncomfortable.

Arik muted a smile. 'Fibbler, are you still running errands for the Babble?'

The little boy puffed out his chest. This was clearly a great honour. 'Yep. I'm a word runner now. Sometimes they ask me to check things, or even chase a story…'

'There's something I want you to let slip to the Babblers.' Arik lowered his voice, ignoring Klaus' warning look. 'Let them hear that the pirates are taking slaves.'

Fibbler's mouth fell open.

'*Slaves?*' A tremor shook his voice. 'Really?'

'And lots of them. Remember, don't tell anyone who told you.'

Wide-eyed, the little boy nodded and dashed off.

'We don't even know for certain if it's true,' Verdi protested. 'It'll be all over the clandom by sundown.'

'I hope so.' Arik smiled humourlessly. 'Fear will make these people angry. And anger might move their hand at last.'

Loathe as he was to burden the child with their worries, Klaus couldn't help but agree.

*

The small boy who answered Mistress Thillaina's door froze at the sight of two armed Northerners. Eventually, Thillaina herself appeared, waving him aside with her walking stick.

'Well now,' she told him sharply. 'Shall I fetch a stool while you keep them standing there? Is gawking at strangers what your mother taught you? *Tsssk!* Take the blue to Master Branto's and come back for the next one in a week. Now run along. Give my regards to your mother.'

He blushed, leaving with a roll of brocade twice his size. Thillaina shook her head.

'All this talk of pirates … it's got him rattled at every door-creak. I don't know what this Part's come to. Master Coaren told me you might come. Let me have a look at you.'

Klaus hid a smile as the little bird of a woman inspected them. They might as well have been cattle at the market.

'I have a soft spot for oceloes,' she remarked – a weakness Ravi must have sensed, for he rose on his hind paws to cling to her skirt, mewling for attention. 'Luckily I can only take three lodgers. I'll not have any smokeleaf in the house. We'd go up like a bonfire. But you may come and go as you please, and there'll be fresh bread and milk every morning.'

Thillaina was a cloth weaver and lacemaker. The large house was packed with shelves stacking skeins of yarn, and rolls of fabric stood propped up in every corner. The guest rooms were the only two which her stock hadn't yet invaded. She made no mention of Lorendar or Merensama.

'Did we actually agree to taking those rooms?' Arik wondered as they left.

Klaus told him wryly, 'I think she's decided she's taking us.'

Rumours of the pirates taking slaves were indeed all over the citadel by sundown, and would soon fly further afield: Samsarra's inns drew travellers from Romel as well as locals. They supped at a quiet cantina where the proprietor welcomed them heartily ('Any friend of Lorendar's heir is a friend of ours!'). They weren't left alone for it.

'They say you made short work of the pirates, Masters Invelmari.' A little meat-smoker named Maki invited himself to join them, chattering around a pipe that never left his mouth. 'The tumblers are strong, but I reckon some of 'em leave the guild before they're ready.' He lowered his voice. 'They say the Murhesla guard the art of the blade-and-snake closely, after all.'

'An unpopular topic, Murhesla,' commented Klaus, preparing to reel him in.

He didn't have to try hard; Maki seemed more eager to please than to heed taboo.

'Do you know how the Murhesla came to be?' A happy glint lit up his eyes when they shook their heads. 'It was after the Second Redrawing.'

'Not as far back as the First Redrawing, then?' Klaus asked. The North hadn't been responsible for *that* war, at least; the First Redrawing had been triggered by Southerners' destruction of Orenthia.

'Oh, no. It was after Sturmsinger's invasion – begging your pardons – that the Murhesla appeared.' Maki puffed on his pipe. 'Every patch of land was contested. There weren't yet any clans, and it was each man to his own. Well, a young upstart named Yelariz was fed up of the feuding. He formed a band of vigilantes to protect Romel, and they became the Murhesla.'

'Why don't they claim Romel for themselves?' asked Verdi. 'It's already in their grip.'

'A good question, and rather you ask it than me,' Maki remarked. His voice dropped conspiratorially. 'There are some who say the Murhesla might yet form their own clan. There are enough of them for one, too! But don't let talk like that cross your lips where ye can be heard.'

Verdi raised his eyebrows doubtfully. 'We didn't see a single one when we were in Romel.'

'What, Murhesla? 'Course not. They say if shadow had a claw, it would be Murhesla.' Maki leaned across the table. 'If you've seen one, it might already be too late.'

'Will they do anything about the pirates?' Verdi asked inoffensively. Klaus was content to listen. That knack Verdi had for wide-eyed inadvertent burrowing was as furtive as his hand with a knife.

'If Romel were threatened, maybe. Not a day passes now without more news of murders and abductions. There's even talk of the pirates taking slaves,' Maki muttered. 'But ye'll be safe inside these walls, Master Santarem. Samsarra is a mighty giant.'

'Thank the Lifegiver for that,' Arik murmured drily.

'And soon we'll have something that will put jelly in pirates' knees – Merensama!' Maki slapped Verdi's shoulder. 'Merensama will set things right. Isn't that so?'

Verdi shrank away.

'Ahhh, is that General Ayla I see? A fine tumbler.' Maki ducked, smoothly making himself and his kahvi pot scarce.

Ayla threaded her way through the crowd to join them. 'You seem to prefer the tavern over your aunt's table, Master Viridian.'

Arik pulled out a chair. 'It's as good a spot as any to pick up the word on the Babble.'

'So long as it's not actual news you're after.' Ayla raised her voice. 'Every sort of rabble comes through these doors.'

A hat that might have been on the head of one sheepish meat-smoker shuffled towards the door.

Ayla lowered her voice. 'Elder Tourmali's returned. Lebas retracted the pledge they raised against the pirates at the Assembly.'

'But they suffered some of the biggest casualties,' Verdi exclaimed. 'They led the protest!'

It *was* a blow. *We need the support of a well-placed clan to search around the Mengorian range for the mine or a spring.* Klaus asked, 'Did they at least agree to send a scout?'

'They did at first, but by morning they'd retracted that offer too.' Her eyes roved the cantina. 'They may be afraid of losing favour with Baeron and Hesper by colluding with us. And if there's a threat growing in the south, Lebas' clandom could be the first to come under attack. Perhaps they're afraid of alerting the pirates to our suspicions.'

Arik grimaced. 'They might not have that luxury. The pirates could come to them first, unprovoked.'

'Lebas won't stir the hornet's nest if they can help it.'

Verdi scowled. 'You mean they'll bury their heads in the sand.'

'What about Fraivon?' asked Klaus.

'They're our biggest hope now. There'll be a wedding between our clans soon, though it was forged on a different understanding well before this plague of pirates.' Ayla paused. 'The Chieftainess means to invite you to accompany our envoy to Ahravel to seek Fraivon's assistance against the pirates, Master Tristan.'

Klaus suppressed a jolt of surprise with Form. 'I can't imagine the Elders approve.'

'Some of them have advised her to distance herself from you.'

Arik rolled his eyes. 'That's no shocker. Half the citadel can't stand the sight of us.'

Ayla smiled mirthlessly. 'Why do you think I'm sitting here with you?'

They drew every eye as they quit the tavern in the general's company, having entered Samsarra hoping to become invisible.

*

Emra closed the door of the chamber where the young tumbler was now asleep. *If only the mind could convalesce as easily as the flesh.*

She joined Navein on the veranda. 'I don't believe she'll have much more to tell us.'

They watched the housekeeper scold a servant in the garden below. The evening whispered sweetly with honeysuckle, but the air stretched taut between them, torrid with the sleeping tumbler's statement.

'"*Hordes*" … is she sure of what she saw?'

'She's sound of mind. After her ordeal, I'll not do her the discourtesy of doubting her word.'

'If only she had seen where they took her.' Navein frowned. 'Why didn't they kill her?'

'They wish to be feared,' Emra replied. 'That's why they sent their token to the Invelmari warrior who executed Viridian's pirate abductor at Romel's gates.'

'No tyrant is satisfied until he can revel before all in his own tyranny.'

'If we share what she's seen with the other clans, would they be more willing to help?'

'Even "hordes" of captives might not be enough to secure their support.' Navein shook his head. 'And now Lebas has reneged their pledge to punish the pirates. Too costly, Mensil claims. The appetite for retaliation is cooling by the hour.'

They fell silent, neither wanting to give their fears more magnitude.

'What of your great-nephew?' said Navein. 'I see he's now taken leave of your house.'

'He's not my prisoner. He's taken no oath of allegiance to this clan and I cannot force his hand. All we can do is wait for him to choose his path.'

'Not too long, I hope,' Navein warned. 'Hesper and Baeron have sought to strengthen their hold in the west almost as long as we've waited for a limolan to grow back. People are afraid, and they'll seek strength wherever they can find it. We can't afford for them to flock to the West for protection.'

'They've not fooled people yet.'

'*Yet.* We need him if we are to present a worthy rival, Emra. Otherwise, we'll have to fight for Merensama with blades rather than words. And that battle's been lost dozens of times over.'

She repeated, 'All we can do is wait.'

A calculating edge sharpened his gaze. 'The pirates could be a blessing in disguise. Even the heathens won't resist Lorendar's banner if it means we'll rid them of pirates.'

'You sound like Maragrin.'

'He's fought this battle the longest.'

'And without success,' Emra reminded him. She weighed out her words; Mantelon were Lorendar's most fervent champions, sometimes to a fault. 'Lorendar's banner shouldn't be raised in deception. Either we invite people to Merensama, or call for war against the pirates.'

'Why not do both at once?'

'What will rally the clans to us after the pirates are defeated? There are still those who haven't forgiven Lorendar. No, we mustn't disguise our intentions. For now, it's better if we try and discover if these pirates have a stronghold, and raise support armed with the truth.'

Navein was quiet for a long moment. 'You should not have allowed the Invelmari to attend the council meeting.'

'And yet we've learned more from them than the entire Assembly,' she replied.

'Are you sure they can be trusted?'

'Do you think they're lying?'

Emra knew he wouldn't dare refute the Wisdom. It was partly for this reason she had braved seeking that unmarked road again.

'No,' he said at last. 'But the chronicler could be mistaken. Our Elders deserved more of our regard in this matter. People will question why we sought the counsel of two strangers from the North, of all places.'

'Perhaps guidance comes from unlikely places.'

Another silence followed.

'I know you've taken an interest in the chronicler. But a clever head can be fed by an empty heart. Take care, Emra. Don't seek to remedy the errors of the past with errors new.'

Something in her faltered. But she thought of Alizarin's account of Tristan at the ruined watchtower, and of her own vision ahead of Viridian's return before Alizarin's letter had even arrived.

'I'm surprised at you, Navein. You've always had more faith than I.'

'Yes, but I have less guilt.'

They stared at each other. Belief and reason walked a familiar tightrope between them.

'Don't lose sight,' he warned. 'Viridian needs guidance. He *must* find the Merensaman phase of the moon. He is our vessel to fill.'

Emra watched her old ally ride away. Perhaps Navein was right, and she was looking for answers in the wrong places.

But she was certain the Northerner had found his way into the service of her great-nephew for a purpose. And the Wisdom had not refuted her.

*

Thillaina's rooms were comfortable enough, but Klaus couldn't settle. He left his sleeping companions for a familiar prowl of unfamiliar streets.

A web of memoranda jostled for his attention: the dirt he'd mistaken for blood under Rasan's nails; the Murhesla; the pirate mark. The fascinating gnomon awaiting Verdi. The Intelligencers' musings about the mine, filling him by turns with doubt and conviction.

He passed through a couple of cantinas, listening to poets over a quiet kahvi as he had often done in Dunraven. *'You know a soul by the threads it spins,'* bowmaster Kelselem had said. Everywhere he went, the souls and their stories were the same: love, loss and longing. Hope and betrayal. Only the players were different. Here, they recited soliloquies on clan bonds forged and broken, on battles of the Second Redrawing. Love songs to the Ninvellyn, to *sehresar.* He did not know the Derindin until he listened to their songs, and then he did not know himself.

Klaus drifted towards Coaren's shop, glad to find the beastmaster's door still open.

'She's going to lay her litter soon.' Coaren stroked the head of a very bloated oceloot, the blue of a peafowl. 'Beauties, they'll be. What brings you here at this hour, Master Tristan?'

'I threatened Marcin that I might find a little furry friend of my own.' Klaus watched the beastmaster fondly tend to the distressed oceloot. 'How did they become so small?'

'Years of clever breeding at the hands of handlers more masterful than I.' Coaren gave her water through a pipette. *'Whisperers,* we called them. They could see the very elements of things, even ask particles to reveal themselves to better understand their behaviour. That's how they bred great warbeasts, before they lost the knack. All gone now.'

Klaus recalled the way Ristowin the metalsmith had examined Elodie's weight. 'What kinds of elements?'

'All sorts,' said Coaren. 'Often the knack ran in families. Alizarin Selamanden's people – now, they were able to see the gem at the heart of a lump of rock and predict its worth before carving it out. But it's been hundreds of years since Whisperers walked the earth.'

Klaus left him cooing over the oceloot's walnut-sized kitterlats, returning to the darkened streets. Next, his feet took him to the Chieftainess' house. Oil lamps lit the quiet square outside, and the frivolous shadows of rustling eucalyptus trees flirted with the lamplight. He glanced up at the windows. Was Rasan still somewhere in there?

A horse's hooves clattered against the cobbles. A moment later, Alizarin dismounted.

'You have to find a way to scout that mountain range,' Klaus told him.

Weariness hardened Alizarin further still. 'It's more difficult than you think.'

'The woman who abducted your nephew in Romel was no mere bandit. She recognised my Ummandiri bolts. Wherever she learned of such things, I do not envy her enemy. If there are others like her amongst the pirates, they should be feared.'

Klaus left Alizarin to his worries, descending into the citadel again. Still restless, still far from sleep. It wasn't too late to find the tumblers haunting their favoured inn. He conjured a broad grin and joined them, accepting a drink he never tasted. The shapes of women in the smoke and lantern light cut a longing through him for Gerlinde. There was still no useful news. It was after midnight when he finally grew tired and left the tavern.

He'd barely stepped outside when the tavern door opened behind him. Klaus turned, hand cupping his sword hilt. A slight figure followed him out, face obscured by a deep hood but for the hint of a short beard.

'The words you wrote in the ashes,' said the man. '"*Surest is the way of the healer, the wanderer and the hermit.*"' That is their meaning.'

Klaus was now wide awake. 'I was looking for an Orenthian speaker, not a translation –'

'But you did not know, and here is the answer. Goodnight.'

Klaus didn't stop him, for his step held the hurry of one who didn't wish to linger.

Back in their rooms, Arik had also risen from his bed. He sat charting pirate raids by the light of an oil lamp.

'Where've you been?'

Klaus shrugged off his cloak. 'Listening.'

Again, it was as if they were still in Dunraven: one planning, one spying. *Such creatures of habits we are. No matter our coordinates.*

Arik raised the jemesh to the light. 'I don't know how we're going to find out much about this quarry Rasan was taken to without drawing suspicion.'

Worn and weary, Klaus made no reply. He wished for the sound of a servant drawing a hot bath, and the roaring hearth in his sprawling quarters at Sunnanfrost, and the quiet kinship of his huskies, and the knowledge that Gerlinde lay sleeping somewhere in the citadel.

Arik leaned back in his chair. 'What are we going to do, Klaus?'

Klaus unfastened his sword belt, tracing the Invelmari starblossom on the strap. 'I don't think anyone at court will object if you return. You're too valuable.'

Arik looked confused for a moment, then threw a scroll at his head. 'I don't mean to go back, you dolt. What are we going to do about the pirates?'

'There's not much we *can* do. Though it looks like we've signed up to help. It's the least we can offer.'

Arik's voice sharpened. 'We don't owe anyone anything for the crimes of the past.'

But Klaus heard the Warrior tossing in his bed well into the early morning.

He put a fresh log on the fire. *The healer, the wanderer, the hermit.* He fingered the words in his thoughts like jewels. The truest of voices spoke from the heart of darkness, where distractions slumbered and the mind was at its clearest. But even here, his mind was murk.

20

Ahravel

LORD STURMSINGER HEEDED THE SPAEWIFE'S GIFT, FOR HIS OWN
HEART WAS HEAVY WITH THE PRICE OF HIS VICTORY. AND SO
HE SUMMONED HIS EALDORMEN TO WITNESS HIS DECREE.

SONNONFER: THE BLESSED BLOOD PACT

Thillaina was true to her word. She didn't mind when they returned late in
the night after frequenting taverns to keep an ear on what kept Samsarran
tongues wagging, or when Klaus stirred in the early hours to pace the
quiet house or slip out into the darkened streets. His friends' early trips
to the tumblers' barracks cast an all-too-familiar shadow of the life Verdi
had left in Dunraven. But Verdi preferred shivering over their duels at
dawn to the summons that soon arrived to the Chieftainess' House.

'I'll go with you,' Klaus reassured him. 'There's nothing to fear.'

The tower room cemented Verdi's fears: a small library with a solitary
desk, perhaps added just for him. But his reluctance vanished when he
saw what waited on the desk: the gnomon, lying quietly on its side.

'Yes, it's high time you took this back.' Maragrin half-glared at him
from beneath the shelves of shaggy eyebrows, which did little to moderate

his disapproval. 'You've been in Samsarra for three days. That's three days of not searching for the moondial.'

It wasn't mine to begin with. But the gnomon beckoned to Verdi, and curiosity quelled his reflexive irritation at the Elder. He took a chair at the desk, staring at it.

'The first thing you must understand is that no one besides Obsidian Lorendar has been able to use this device for anything other than telling the time.' Maragrin's glower softened. 'Anything we know about its true function comes from Lorendar's own teachings, not experience of our own. You must supplement your studies with experimentation.'

'Then how do you know it works?'

'With belief.' Maragrin jabbed Verdi with the beaks of his eyes. 'But now we have a chance to find out.'

Discomfort diluted Verdi's intrigue; he was much less keen on inheriting any great expectations.

'How is it *supposed* to work?' Klaus seemed just as fascinated by the gnomon, and it wasn't long before the Elder warmed to the Invelmari's earnest curiosity.

'The first dial is dictated by the sun. The second dial – the moondial – is moved by *intention*.' Maragrin prodded the slant of the triangular gnomon. 'Intentions of the user towards the land, the laws that govern it. That is the dial that will reveal the moon phase signalling our readiness for Merensama. If we attempt to force unity on the clans before that moment, we will fail.'

Verdi realised his mouth had fallen open. '*Intentions?*'

Crows landed in Maragrin's gaze again. 'Physician Fresmo has an excellent wax-clearing device for the ears, if you're in need of it.' He cleared his throat. 'The second dial moves anticlockwise, mirroring the moon's orbit. An adept user will form a bond with this instrument – an understanding. This understanding is mediated not by the gnomon, but the *anchor* –' Maragrin ran one finger along the anchoring skewer protruding from the gnomon. 'You see, the anchor reaches into the earth, and possesses properties that translate the will of the land to one who can be trusted. You must gain the trust of the land before you can hope to serve it.'

The notion was so wild, so fantastic, that Verdi was at a loss for words.

'And once – *if* – the moondial appears, and points to this … perfect moon phase, how is it supposed to help? What's so special about a phase of the moon?'

Despite his badly veiled scepticism, Maragrin was solemn rather than reproving.

'It is a celestial moment, Viridian. One that will unlock the bolt placed on the passage between this world and the Unseen World. The world we can only dream of, while we reside on this side of the doorway.'

The bolt that must not be raised, his kidnapper had said. Verdi knew nothing of the Derindin's beliefs, but even he felt the thrill of something *sacred*.

Klaus kneeled beside Verdi. 'May I?'

The Elder nodded.

Klaus picked it up. He turned it, examining its edges and the long metal anchor. 'This anchor is really a sensor, then, is it not?' Maragrin nodded again, an appraising glint appearing in his eyes. 'Was Obsidian unable to find the moon phase himself?'

'He discovered *how* to use the gnomon – even made the moondial appear. But he died before it fell upon the right phase. Perhaps the time was never right, in his age. The world is much changed since Lorendar first dug this anchor into the ground.'

'You mean the Second Redrawing?'

'The dam. When he first devised it, the moondial responded to the river tides of the Ninvellyn. The river made the dial appear, though not meaningfully. After his death, sages were even able to make the second dial appear – but only in pursuit of the moon's movements; they couldn't reveal the phase for Merensama either. When the river was dammed, that dial disappeared.'

'Then how do you know it can work again?' Verdi realised he feared the possibility it might not. 'Maybe Lorendar *needed* the river for the dial to appear.'

'I believe those movements were just reactions to its tides. It is intention alone that can incite action.' Half-smothered sadness blunted the sharpness of Maragrin's eyes. 'Take this with you, it's yours by right. Study it, come to know it. The river may have dried up, but the tides of the heart have never been dammed.'

It was bewildering; another storm-current whipping up this dizzying new world. But it was the most exciting thing Verdi had ever discovered, stirring a vertigo in his heart.

*

Samsarra welcomed the two Invelmari reluctantly.

Klaus had hoped to join Verdi for his next visit to the Arboretum, where Verdi had begun to study Meron's collection of medicinal plants – a subject more familiar to him than moondials. But Klaus' plans were curtailed by the Chieftainess' invitation to accompany Elendra's envoy to Ahravel, just as Ayla had warned.

'The Elders don't want you to go,' Arik told him. 'They've given you an hour's notice.'

'Don't go, then,' said Verdi immediately. 'Or let's go together.'

Klaus squeezed his arm. 'Your time is better spent here. See if you can speak to Rasan again.'

'Mantelon are our closest allies, and even they didn't take kindly to Invelmari advising our council,' Alizarin had warned Klaus. 'Keep that in mind before you speak in Chieftain Ferenjen's hall.'

'I'm just a mercenary now.'

'Mercenaries speak with their swords. That's what we're used to here. If nothing else, a Northerner's sword can be trusted, because his life depends on it.' Alizarin's smile was sardonic. 'The same can't be said for a Northerner's counsel.'

Tourmali seemed none too pleased when Klaus arrived in time to join the half-dozen tumblers preparing to leave, though he remained courteous. 'Fraivon's territory extends farthest south of all the clandoms, Master Tristan. Luckily, Ahravel is in the north of their clandom. Five days' ride in fair weather, a week or more in wind.'

At least Saarem greeted Klaus with a broad grin. 'I was hoping to find you here. Ready?'

The growing map of clandoms hovered invitingly in Klaus' mind. He followed the Derindin out of Samsarra, hungry to cover the peripheries of his pages.

*

Winter had crept up slyly on the desert.

South of Samsarra, small woods transformed to barren plains and back to sparse woods again; nut trees and mustard trees the Derindin harvested for salt-bark. They stopped once at an oasis that erupted like emerald fire from the desert. Pockets of wind broke out restlessly, churning up little whirling puddles of sand. Klaus took regular readings with his compass. Ahravel was only four windless days from Romel. He gazed into the heat-haze that still blurred the horizon at midday. Somewhere to the south-west, in a place so thirsty the Derindin had forgotten it altogether, Intelligencers had sent spies like the tendrils of derina running under the sand to unearth surely the greatest discovery of this age. And if Invelmari could do it, why not the Derindin?

But the Derindin were doubtful.

'No council will risk soldiers with those stakes,' said a tumbler named Porva over their evening fire. 'A pirate stronghold in the south? It's another two weeks from Ahravel just to their southern border. Without water that's a death sentence.'

Saarem grunted. 'I didn't know they'd trained you up at the Guild to think as well as fight. No? Then that's enough of your postulating.'

But Porva wasn't alone in his doubts, and Klaus found himself ignoring some dark looks.

Raela, a more agreeable tumbler, watched him add to his map before the light failed. 'Sure you've not been to the Plains before, Tristan?'

'He's hardly likely to forget,' said Saarem wryly. 'The skirts at Romel will melt even Invelmari steel.'

This drew hearty laughter. For all their suspicions, they gradually warmed to his homage to their desert; even Porva, the surly veteran, admired his growing map. There was much more than coordinates to capture. He marked their stories of skirmishes, their assorted treasures: the joy of forgotten wells and rare sightings of an emperor hoopoe; the peril of wind-traps and sinksand. Elder Tourmali listened in silence, keeping his own counsel. The tumblers provided a relief from Klaus' old life, and yet cast a shadow of it. When he closed his eyes at night, he could almost imagine that the cold of the desert was the cold of the Sterns, and the eddies of wind became the howling of wolves haunting its lonely peaks…

'They were maybe two hundred men,' the tracker told Klaus' father. 'Another dozen Isarnanheri would have dispatched them.'

It was freezing, and what was not snow was steel. And it was dark, for light deserted the heavens in the heart of Far Northern winter. So these were to be the shades of his future: cold and dark.

Isarnanheri gathered in the cave and along the pass. Their faces were mostly concealed behind their visors, but Lord Wintermantel had a way of knowing every one by the smallest of details.

'Where is Barrett?' he asked.

'He took a fall…'

Heavy-hearted, Klaus peered into the gullet of the valley below, which had claimed several other Isarnanheri. He too knew them all, for he had taken the trouble to learn the importance of this from Father: a world existed behind every name. A plume of smoke rose from the Far Northerners' camp across the valley. He thought he heard a scream rip through the howling of wolves, and tried to untwist the sound into that of a wolf again.

'We'll wait until they've drunk to their victory,' Father decided. 'Then we strike.'

It would be a bloodbath: their reinforcement from Malvern was two hundred-

strong. But they couldn't take chances. This enclave of barbarians had been moving south through the Sterns for two months now, raiding villages as they went.

It was only Klaus' third campaign into the Far North. Duty made this path bearable, if not palatable. But it was still purpose without passion. This was not what he had dreamed of for himself.

Father's gaze pierced through him, as if he'd heard Klaus' thoughts.

'Take the third company down on my command, Ulfriklaus,' Lord Wintermantel ordered. 'And no sooner, no matter how the first two attacks go. They must be fooled into thinking we're still only two companies. These are Bear Skarnstaahin's soldiers. They're dirty fighters, and they know the valley better than we do. Give them time enough to call all their soldiers out of hiding. Hold your nerve.' A dark warning lurked in his eyes. 'If I am killed, Arnander will take command. Do not falter.'

Klaus nodded, Form quelling the flutter of his heart at the thought of Father falling in this black snow. Kelselem, who still rode with Lord Wintermantel everywhere, was at Klaus' shoulder. He measured his words as tightly as he did the bolts he had taught Klaus to fire.

'To look away even for a second is too much.' His voice was molasses. 'This is your target now.'

Inexplicably, the hot sting of tears pricked the back of Klaus' eyes. Form kept them at bay.

The Isarnanheri took their positions along the pass, waiting. Father was ahead with the first company, Master Arnander with the second, and Kelselem shadowed Klaus at the helm of the third. Kelselem always seemed to radiate with the warmth of the land to which he had vowed never to return, even here in the most desolate of the Parts. His words echoed in Klaus' ears throughout the first battle, and the second, and the screams of men and steel: 'This is your target now...'

His sword had to swing with his heart in its blade, or else even Invelmari steel would falter.

'This is your target now...'

The biting cold, the jolting pain of hitting ice, the hiss of hot blood on the snow, the weight of armour, the stink of dying men's bile and excrement, the mournful wailing of their dogs, the song of wolves drawn to the scent of death on the wind... the executions of survivors, a sour dawn. This was his target now.

But Kelselem's voice was changing, perhaps garbled by the incessant howl of the wind. 'The healer, the wanderer, the hermit...' Or perhaps it was the dizzying air of the Sterns, distorting Klaus' mind. 'This is your target now. The healer, the wanderer, the hermit...'

*

Verdi was grateful for any distraction. Several times now he had picked up the gnomon, hoping his inexplicable attraction to it would lead *somewhere*. The moon was a waning crescent; an ordinary moondial wouldn't work for a half-lunar month yet, when the moon would be full. After several hours of staring at its three sides and poking its polished anchor, he gave up and sought something more comprehensible. In the morning, he fled to the Arboretum, where he helped Bevro tweak dials of mechanical filters and adjust the light over germinating seedlings. Bevro's company was easy, and there was nothing mercenary about his curiosity.

'You'd not been to Derinda before, then?'

'No.' Verdi snatched a seedling out of Ravi's reach. 'I'd not heard of Merensama until I came, either.'

Bevro paused, astonished. 'You really didn't know?'

Verdi shook his head. And what little he'd been told concerned his supposed future, not his past. He listened to Bevro's retelling of Lorendar's life as they weighed experimental varieties of derina tubers, stumbling into a story even older than the Blood Pact: a young farmer whose first victory was to restore ownership of a valley to its true deed-keepers, and whose ingenuity tore down crooked kings. Through Bevro's eyes, it was a tale stripped of the ambition of Elders, adorned instead with hope.

The only problem was, Verdi had no idea how to find his own place within it.

'Have you seen the limolan tree?' Bevro asked. Verdi shook his head. 'It's a wonder. It's hard enough to coax back to life a seed from a few seasons ago, let alone fifteen hundred years.'

'Lorendar's not popular with everyone, though,' said Verdi.

'Not everyone tells the same story. If you go west then Lorendar's a conqueror, as bad as the kings he ripped down. Merensama will prove them wrong. We'll all be better off for it.'

But Verdi wanted more. He wanted more of *everything*. There were no longer chores, and war campaigns, and the criticisms of Ackley the palace butler. No dismissive glances in Dunraven's markets. Eyes lingered, but not with scorn. He knew the Derindin's curiosity chafed his friends … but for Verdi, Elders' schemes aside, Samsarra felt impossibly *right*.

Careful. Klaus was still a fugitive; the Wintermantels were only a few weeks of road away. *We might not be here for long.*

If only he could enjoy Derinda without the baggage of his lineage. He longed to speak to someone whose eyes didn't mist over fondly at the mention of Lorendar or Merensama. Alizarin's certainly didn't. His uncle ought to have been a trove of knowledge, but instead remained as distant as ever.

Verdi decided to try his luck again on their return to the citadel.

'Why have half the clans denounced Lorendar?'

Alizarin glanced around the tavern where they'd stopped for food. Wryly, Verdi added, 'I won't tell the Elders what you really think...' This almost earned him a smile.

'Even a legend has his flaws.' Saya sat primly on Alizarin's forearm. 'Lorendar may have died a good man, but he was not forgiven by some of those he conquered.'

'But all that was a long time ago.'

'And his opponents keep the hate alive. As long as we're divided, we remain weak. And that suits clans like Baeron. People need to be reminded of a time when that was not so.'

And I am that reminder. It was Verdi's turn to fall quiet.

'An unclanned Derindin is anyone's target,' Alizarin told him. 'It's dangerous for anyone to remain Unsworn, but especially so for you. You ought to have considered carefully before removing yourself from the safest house in Samsarra.'

Verdi scowled. 'My safety is no more important than anyone else's.' He lowered his voice. 'And in any case, there's a Prospere at my door.'

They glared at one another. Verdi didn't look away this time, though Ravi sniffing behind his ear made him feel a little ridiculous.

'Have a care,' said Alizarin at last. 'Whether you embrace this path or not, the past has already marked you.'

*

Five days' ride from Samsarra, the desert was laid bare. Dunes rose and fell like rivers of golden stillness, casting lithe shadows that hid craggy rocks in their involutions. Klaus scanned the horizon with his eyescope again.

'What's wrong?' Raela asked.

'Just keep an eye out.'

She raised an eyebrow. 'Surely not this close to Romel. Why, we're still in Mantelonian territory. The pirates would be stupid to try their luck here.'

Saarem shook his head. 'The pirates rely on travellers' dependence on the springs and waterholes, and the Chefren oasis is only a day's ride away.'

Porva shot Klaus a sour look. 'Based on the word of someone who's barely set foot into the desert?'

'Based on the word of someone who's downed a few pirates,' Saarem growled. 'Until that's you, I'd keep that tongue resting in your head.'

And it was indeed near the oasis that trouble arrived.

They had barely crossed into Fraivon's clandom. The heat had a sound, Klaus decided. It was the dry hiss of a blade being sharpened, and scathing steam, and despair. The air felt strained, blunting bird calls as they hit the dunes.

So when cries came, they sounded like bleats, swallowed up by the sand.

They stopped abruptly, reaching for weapons. Tourmali raised his eyescope.

Great dunes hulked ahead. A yellow wall of trees stretched south-east. To the south-west, rocky mounds formed islands in the sand.

A cloud of dust caught Klaus' eye above the rocks. 'There!'

They broke into a full gallop, soon ascending a dune. From the top, they saw the ambush raging on its other side. Several Derindin already lay lifeless on the sand.

'Stay on the high ground,' Saarem roared to Tourmali, as Klaus raised a steel-braced forearm in time to deflect an arrow.

They charged down the dune. Tumblers' curved blades flashed wildly in the eruptions of sand and grit thrown up by horses' hooves. Even counting their dead, the victims had been easily outnumbered. Saarem and Porva ran to the aid of two tumblers shielding an older Derindman from several pirates.

Longsword in one hand and halberd held high, Klaus remained mounted as he helped cut through the remaining pirates. Soon none were left alive.

Tourmali hurried down to their survivors: the older man and just three tumblers. 'Elder Melad … what happened?'

'They came out of nowhere.' The Elder looked over the bodies, dazed. 'There were ten of us returning from Romel…' His face paled. 'My grandson, where's my grandson?'

But there wasn't a child amongst the corpses.

Klaus raised his eyescope. The wind warned of dark momentum gathering in its bosom, so much so that it was an effort to hold the eyescope steady. *There*: a grey smudge on the dunes, drifting east.

He pointed. 'There are more of them.'

'They must have escaped when we attacked,' said Tourmali. The Elder covered his face with shaking hands.

Klaus sheathed his sword. He pulled on his reins, breaking into a full gallop towards the moving smudge. The wind quickly swallowed the shouts that burst out behind him.

The wind went with him. Gradually, the smudge took the shape of a horse. Then it disappeared into yellow woods.

Klaus followed it into the trees.

He slowed down, picking up the sound of hooves ahead. Within a few moments, he glimpsed the dun flank of horse, a red saddle –

– and broke into a small clearing where his quarry had joined half a dozen pirates.

The crossbow was in Klaus' hands before his next thought had formed.

A pirate began to laugh. 'You even lured one back –'

A few bolts later, half of them were dead.

The rider he'd been chasing threw his captive from his saddle. The boy landed with a cry of pain. Klaus used the moment to throw a dagger, steel hissing as softly as the wind that shook the dead leaves crowning the trees.

Here in the woods, there was no need to mute his Form. He lowered the veil around it, towering over the clearing with dark presence and deadened gaze. The remaining four pirates darted around him like mice, but they didn't stand a chance against his Form and his steel.

Moments later, he stopped and waited, but the woods had finally fallen quiet but for the wind.

The boy backed away, huddling against a tree. Klaus dismounted, stroking his mare's head.

'Good girl,' he said, breathing easily at last. 'Good girl.'

He retrieved his bolts and daggers, giving the boy time to recover. He was barely sixteen, shrinking away in terror when Klaus dropped to one knee beside him.

Klaus held up his hands. 'Don't be afraid. I'm with Elendra's envoy to Ahravel.' The boy was clutching one of his legs. 'Are you hurt?'

The boy nodded, nostrils flared with fear. The wind blew harder now, sending leaves scuttling even here under the thick canopy of the trees.

'Are you Elder Melad's grandson?'

The boy nodded again, eyes rounding when Klaus pulled his sand-mask down.

'That's a nasty gash.' Klaus stayed back; he could see it had bled a fair bit already. 'Let's go, there may be more pirates around. Can you ride?'

The Elder's grandson finally found his voice. 'I don't think so.'

'What's your name?'

'Hedar.'

Klaus looked around. 'Well, Hedar, there are no horses left anyway. We'll have to ride together.'

He tore a strip from a dead pirate's cloak and tied Hedar's leg above the wound, then hastily looked over the pirates' corpses. *No more tattoos.* He helped Hedar onto the mare.

'Did – did my grandfather –'

'He's alive.' Klaus didn't mention the rest of his companions, but Hedar's eyes brimmed with tears. Klaus swung into his saddle. 'Let's rejoin him.'

If any of the tumblers had followed him, they would have surely reached them by now. There was no use waiting. The woods might be sheltering more pirates, or attract others. The hoarse whisper of air through the trees warped Klaus' hearing. His sense of direction disrupted, he lingered only to consult his compass.

When they reached the edge of the woods, he saw why no tumblers had arrived. The trees had sheltered them from the brunt of a brewing windstorm that now tore the sand upwards from the ground so that he couldn't see his two hands before him.

*

Hours later, the wind still howled. They'd retreated into the woods, away from the sand-toothed edge of the storm. Klaus leaned back against a tree, senses whetted. He didn't dare let his eyelids close, keeping a bolt to the string of the crossbow cradled in his arms. If there *were* more pirates lingering between the trees, the woods would be a cage.

Hedar dosed fitfully. He came to with a groan of pain.

Klaus peered up into the growing dark. The woods' rusting crown of leaves blotted out the sky.

'How long can the storms last?'

Genuine fear filled Hedar's reply. 'Sometimes days.'

Under the frost of his Form, Klaus' heart sank. He passed Hedar his water skin. He drank like all Derindin, with calculating care.

'You're Invelmari.' Awe laced Hedar's words.

'I am.'

'What are you doing in Derinda?'

'Putting my sword to work.'

Hedar's eyes fell on the blade, widening in a way that reminded him of Fibbler.

'Are you Isarnanheri?'

'No.'

Hedar stiffened. 'There's a snakeskin over there!'

He pointed across the clearing. Sure enough, the pale husk of a moulted snakeskin hung from a low-hanging branch.

'Well spotted. Don't worry about snakes.'

'The Plains viper's poison will kill a man in under a minute. And we're sitting on the ground...'

'Then we'll have to be faster than the Plains viper.' Klaus rose. 'There's a stick of smoked meat somewhere in my saddlebag. You need to keep your strength up.'

'What about you?'

'I don't have a hole in my leg.'

Klaus passed him the strip of meat. Hedar looked even younger as he ate, child-like with apprehension. At sixteen, Klaus had already returned from dozens of campaigns and spying assignments across five of the Seven Parts. At sixteen, he'd put treacherous men to death by his own hand or else by virtue of his intelligence reports. Again, a bilious bitterness gurgled in the gullet of his consciousness, but only for a moment. Such distractions would threaten his Form, and Form was what was going to get them through the sandstorm.

Soon it was difficult to separate the darkness of the woods from nightfall. Hedar fell asleep again. Eventually, even the howling of the storm subsided.

Klaus woke the boy gently, startling him anyway. 'The wind's stopped. Let's take a look.'

They rode back to the fringe of the woods. The sandstorm *had* ended, but so had the day.

'Then we're stuck here for the night.' Hedar shivered, pulling his cloak closer.

'We can't stay here. More pirates may be sheltering in these woods, or more may arrive at first light when we'll be exhausted. Besides, you've lost a lot of blood.' Klaus helped Hedar up onto his mare; the mention of more pirates boosted him up as much as Klaus' shoulder. 'Ahravel's not far now. Come on.'

'But how will we find the way in the dark?'

Klaus looked out across the dunes. They had shifted; great drifts of sand and fine grit rehomed by the storm. The wind had distorted everything he remembered of the lay of the land. Twilight was fast darkening to an indigo that would swallow the very moon if it could. And, unlike the lighter northern skies, here in the South the heart of night was truly black.

'I can navigate.' Klaus paused to read his compass one more time in the dredges of the light. Before long, he would have nothing left but the cryptic coordinates of the stars. He waited for the needle of his compass to still. 'We just need to stay warm.'

'Not even the astronomers travel by night,' said Hedar doubtfully, though exhaustion made his resistance feeble. 'It's too easy to get lost. There are snakes and scorpions, and you won't be able to see sinksand coming.'

'Then we'd better hurry up before it's really pitch black.'

Something scuttled across the sand, its shape bloated by shadows. Hedar yelped.

'It's just a sand fish.' Klaus scanned the trees behind them; any pirates lurking in the woods would have heard them now. He drew his pelts around them both, grateful for Northern seal-furs. 'My mare's too clever to let her legs get nibbled.'

'What about the pirates?'

'No one in their right mind will be travelling now.' *Except us.* But he kept that to himself. He steered his horse south-west. 'When we get to Ahravel, tell them there were only a couple of pirates.'

Terrified, Hedar nodded.

They stepped out into the dark waters of deepening dusk. The desert came alive with the whispering-scampering-scuttling of countless unseen creatures. Klaus didn't possess the Derindin's bond to their horses, but he leaned forward to whisper to his mare, hoping to soothe her. Half a moon offered little comfort. He craned his neck to check constellations he still barely understood, willing his senses to pick out small dangers in the darkness throttling the desert – the whites of a wildcat's eyes, perhaps, or the drift of hyenas' cackles mingling with the death rattle of the windstorm, or the splintering of starlight by bared steel. They saw nothing. Then they became engulfed in nothing – a nothing made of heavy anthracite darkness broken only by the star-littered heavens. Soon it swallowed his sight entirely, until Klaus felt their next step could have plunged them from a precipice without warning. He put his trust in his horse's footing, and in the half-deciphered instructions of the stars.

Hedar's breathing became shallow. Klaus urged his mare onward, trying not to imagine her stumbling into sinksand. Panic almost broke through the surface of his Form more than once, clutching at his throat; he stamped it down.

'Hedar?'

The boy was too quiet. His head bobbed limply. He had passed out.

Klaus broke into a run. His heart cried out first desperately, then angrily. Once summoned, anger swelled … anger for the storm, the butchered caravans; for Rasan, the pirates, the Wintermantels, the parting of a baby boy from unknown parents, the false promise of the future that had finally ensnared him, the loss of long years beyond clawing back – years marked by sins upon sins… *This isn't justice*, anger screamed through the shackles of his Form. *There must be justice!* Eddies of sand rose around the mare's hooves, as though the very ground was rising up to meet her footfalls. A protest cried out from the depths of his being. *Where's the justice?*

For one wild moment, he imagined he felt a reply in the sand – a thrill underfoot, a shock that jolted his horse. He glared at the skies, correcting his course with his broken understanding of these stars, and hurtled through the desert, wearing a blindfold of night.

The desert heard him and carried him forward.

Though he knew they couldn't be far from Ahravel, he felt they'd been riding for hours, his fingers frozen around his reins. He lost track of how long Hedar had been unconscious.

Eventually, the flicker of torches on Ahravel's gates hovered like fireflies in the distance. Torchlight diluted the darkness around the citadel. He felt for a whistling arrow in his quiver and fired it high over the gates to announce their arrival. It arced over the citadel walls with a long thin screech as they approached.

The watchman who admitted them at the gatehouse was flanked by a fist of tumblers, their weapons drawn. He fell back at the sight of Hedar.

'Alert the Elders!' he cried.

'Send for a physician,' said Klaus. 'He's bled quite a bit.'

Their lamps dazzled his eyes. His head began to spin.

The startled face of the watchman was the last thing he remembered.

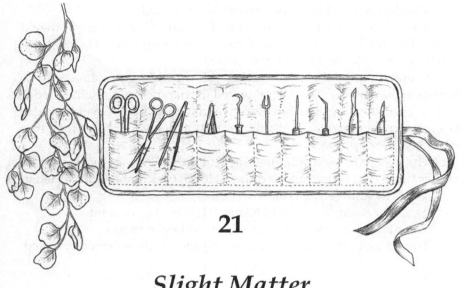

21

Slight Matter

LORD STURMSINGER SPOKE: 'AS I HAVE FOUNDED YOU, SO I BIND YOU
NOW WITH THIS VOW TO THE LIFEGIVER: A TERRIBLE RECKONING SHALL
BEFALL INVELMAR SHOULD ANY OF YOU MOVE AGAINST EACH OTHER.
THE HEAVIEST SANCTION I SHALL IMPOSE UPON THOSE WHO BREAK MY
PACT, AND THEY SHALL BE EXILED FROM MY COMPANY HERE
AND IN ALL THE WORLDS.'

SONNONFER: THE BLESSED BLOOD PACT

When he came to, he was in a long room lit with many lanterns. A fire
spoke softly in the hearth. The scent of eucalyptus sharpened the air. A
kettle whistled.

Klaus became aware of two things at once: the weight of his sword
and the tug of his crossbow strap were missing, and a bandage was
wrapped around his upper left arm. As soon as he acknowledged the
latter, it began to hurt.

He sat up slowly, only partially mitigating the rush of blood to
his head. He was on a small bed in the corner of a room crammed with
bookcases and instruments and cluttered countertops. Outside, footsteps

approached. He lay back and closed his eyes.

Someone entered, pausing at Klaus' side before walking away. The kettle stopped whistling as it was moved off the fire.

'I know you are awake,' a woman said. 'Ilnurhin moves differently through the veins of one who is asleep.'

Klaus opened his eyes. A grey-haired woman poured hot water into a basin.

'How's Hedar?' he asked.

'Asleep. He did come round briefly. But as you surmised, he's lost a lot of blood. May I see your wound?'

Klaus raised his left arm. She unwrapped the bloodstained bandage, exposing a long gash. She added tincture of iodine to the water and began cleaning the wound. She said nothing of his assorted scars.

'Hedar said you rode from Ghorsom's Thicket to Ahravel in the dead of night.'

Klaus winced at the sting of the iodine. 'A war chronicler must navigate every kind of terrain in the North or else find himself quickly replaced.'

'You don't have the hands of a scholar.'

Klaus rubbed his fingers together, feeling the calluses. 'In Invelmar, even scholars must master steel as well as scrolls.'

'Sounds terrible.' There was no derision in her words. She squeezed water from a wad of gauze. 'We remember many things here in the South. An awakened man can signal his need even as he sleeps in the dark.'

'What do you mean, an *awakened* man?'

She smiled slightly, dabbing his wound.

Klaus glanced at a cabinet of medicinal vials. 'You're a physician?'

'For the most part. Hence, I'm far more interested in the remarkable intuition of a navigator blinded by night than the fact that he slew half a dozen pirates unaided.' Her eyes glinted when he didn't reply. 'Ah, young Hedar knows better than to hide anything from old Sonru. He is young. Forgive him.'

Klaus stared at the ceiling. Would he venture now into the Plains night unaided? Probably not. *'Desperation can be the maker of masters,'* Master Florian would say in the ice-plains beyond the Sterns. Klaus had never looked at a coordinate that he hadn't been able to recall, nor forgotten a poem or star chart if he'd seen it once. A wayfarer's eye, Kelselem called it. But for all this, he knew now something had happened out there in the dark, as though the very heart of the earth had heard his desperation and replied. The thought seemed akin to madness.

'I've never been lost anywhere,' he said finally.

'Such was the sight of the Simyerin.'

His heart shivered. 'I don't know about that.'

'Nor should you. Much of what was known about them has been forgotten. I believe your Engineers even named those sciences *"Lost"*.'

'In Invelmar those sciences are forbidden knowledge.'

'How can knowledge be forbidden?' She applied a light poultice of honey to his cleaned wound. 'The very notion is absurd.'

Klaus had been so long accustomed to quelling his own dissent that it felt sacrilegious now to agree, even this far from home. 'Did Elder Tourmali make it safely to the citadel?'

'Yes.'

'Did your Elders agree to Elendra's proposal to search for the pirates' base?'

'They did not.'

Sonru seared a tiny needle in candle flame, then cooled it with a short *hiss* in the boiled water and threaded it with silk.

Klaus slumped back into the sheets. 'The pirates will only grow stronger.'

'They will. And this clan will realise that only too late. Scattered as the clans are, pirates will do them more harm than a conquering army. An insidious disease.'

'I'm told another future is possible, if the clans choose it.'

'Ahh, yes. Lorendar's seedling has returned a sapling.' Sonru nodded. 'Spoken like a true friend.'

'Will Fraivon resist Merensama, then?'

'Fraivon is divided.' Sonru patted his wound dry. 'Let me tell you something about Obsidian Lorendar that you won't hear in Samsarra. He died a great man. But he came after a time of kings, and had a king's hand. Many people hated the tyrants who lorded over them in their little kingdoms. And now there are too many who fear a new alliance that may give rise to another tyrant.'

Klaus clenched his teeth as Sonru began to stitch his wound with small bites of the needle. 'And what do you believe?'

She tied off the sutures deftly. 'I believe a great deal more ilnurhin must be stirred in our hearts to dispel those particular demons.'

'I still don't really know what "ilnurhin" means. Each time I ask, the answer is different.'

Sonru's face broke into another smile. 'That's because it slumbers deeply, now more than ever, and few are left who understand it, even if they host it in their hearts. And when it wakes, it speaks differently to each of its hosts.'

'What does it feel like for you?'

'To me it is the mind of flesh and bone. I can tell you this wound will heal well without infection, though it will scar. Or that Hedar's blood loss amounted to a quarter-portion of his circulation, and will need three moons to reconstitute before he will regain his full strength.'

If he concentrated on anything other than the needle, the pain faded to the edges of his awareness. 'So it's an acquired sense, then.'

'It is not a sense.' Sonru tied off another suture. 'It is a substance with quantity, though its particles are immaterial. That's why your Engineers call it *slight matter*. One of the few things they got right. Its particles are generated by the fifth chamber of the heart, and sensed by all other organs. These qualities are universal. Only the manner in which its particles are perceived or used varies from one creature to another.'

'Then it has no fixed form?'

'Ilnurhin has as little or as much form as light itself.'

'How does it have substance, then?'

'How does light?' Delicately, the physician snipped another suture. 'How does anger, or love, for that matter?'

'These aren't substances.'

'Ah, but they are – in the fifth chamber of the heart. There, the rules are different.'

'The fifth chamber...' Meron had only briefly described this nebulous host of *namathra* and *sehresar*.

'The seat of human consciousness. Stationed in the thinking heart – not the mind.'

This was contrary to everything Klaus had been taught, but oddly not jarring. 'Is there less ilnurhin in the world now?'

'Perhaps there isn't. But what good is that if it remains latent? Most people are still asleep, and sense the world only with their minds. For them, the fifth chamber is closed.'

His body was exhausted, but Klaus couldn't remember the last time he felt so awake. Slightly self-conscious, he asked, 'How did ilnurhin feel to your mapmakers?'

'I thought you would never ask,' said the physician blithely. 'Though I suppose one cannot enquire about what he doesn't know.'

'I heard of Orenthia's mapmakers in Invelmar.' There was little to be learned about the Lost Sciences in the lettervaults or royal smoking rooms of Dunraven. 'Only the bards had anything to say. And most of it speculation.'

'And what did your bards say?'

'That the Simyerin drew powers from the earth. Some claimed they were sorcerers.'

Sonru chuckled. 'They're a clever lot, bards and poets. They can find a way to say whatever they wish without fear of reprisal, for what is more harmless than poetry? Artists learned long ago to speak the truth unnoticed, dodging the penalties that befall common folk. To bury a pinch of honesty in a ballad or song without risking blasphemy.'

'So they *were* sorcerers?'

'No. But in saying they were sorcerers, the bards protected themselves. You yourself told me the Lost Sciences are forbidden. Nobody can accuse them of telling a dangerous truth if they mix truth with such far-fetched notions.'

Thank the Lifegiver for that. Klaus had little regard for claims of magic.

'As for your question: the Simyerin spoke to the land as this wound speaks to me,' said the physician. 'Through slight matter, they sensed the land's needs and what it could offer in return – its layers, its cycles, its ailments. They governed people with this knowledge.'

'Were they mapmakers or were they rulers?'

'Theirs were not the maps we keep now, which are made so that each person knows what belongs to his neighbour. They made maps with ilnurhin, with slight matter. Their maps were pacts with the land that struck an equilibrium between duty and reward. Those maps founded Orenthia's laws. But laws must come with reckoning.'

Klaus barely felt the sting of her needle now. 'When did the Simyerin disappear?'

'When the hearts of men changed. They stopped listening to the earth, and the earth stopped listening back. Their sight was corrupted, and they could no longer remember as they did before.'

Klaus' head throbbed. Questions were tangling together. Sonru snipped the last stitch and dressed the closed wound.

'I have something to return to you.' She produced Klaus' whistling shaft from her robe. 'This landed in my door.'

Unlike his Ummandiri bolts, it was plain, but he'd made it himself and was grateful not to lose it. He touched the whistling tip. She watched him searchingly. The question he'd been resisting finally broke loose.

'Are you the healer?'

But the physician replied, 'I am not.'

Disappointed, Klaus lowered his head back onto the bed.

'Where can I find Elder Tourmali?'

'His party left the citadel before you arrived. They hoped to find some sign of you on their return.'

The last of his energy ebbed away. 'Thank you.'

'Your weapons are over there by the fire. Now sleep. No one will disturb you tonight. They know better than to cross Sonru.' The physician extinguished the lamps, pausing in the dark. 'The stars burned brighter last night. It was ilnurhin that guided your whistling shaft to me.'

A moment later the door clicked shut behind her.

He couldn't sleep until he had Invelmari steel back at his side and his bow and halberd within reach. Only then did his Form settle. Stirred as deeply as it had been, however, it took longer for his mind to fold.

*

'*A soldier is not a horse to be broken,*' Mistress Lisbeta had told him. But break him she did.

Each meeting with Arik's fist of tumblers seemed to cement them more deeply in their ways. Arik knew he had to be patient. Derindin were stubborn.

For several days they continued to ride, weaving around the hills and woods and dunes until Arik could have done so blindfolded. On the fourth day, there were finally no complaints; no questions. For hours they rode without a word, watching every turn of Arik's body to anticipate his intended course. The tumblers sensed what they'd created now: a sinewy creature that moved through them as one, supple and unhesitating.

'*Silence is the sharpest of commanders.*'

Lisbeta ensured he became her greatest student. How he had loathed her.

After a water break, they gathered under a cluster of cedars where the ground was even for an area spanning only the length of three horses.

Arik told them, 'Here we will spar.'

'With what?' Starra was a stony-faced woman whose silences still declared volumes of dissent. 'We left our weapons at the barracks.'

'With your flesh. Isn't that what tumblers learn first?' Arik removed his coat; the disciplined amongst them followed suit. 'I've seen tumblers fight. There's nothing wrong with your weapons. Now you'll make a study of how you carry yourselves.'

'Not much space, is it?' said Pebr cautiously as he stepped forward.

Too many questions.

'Exactly enough space. Does the terrain of battle send word to solicit your preference? Today we begin in the shade. Tomorrow we won't have that luxury.'

Lisbeta was not an Ealdorman. She had been unequalled amongst his mother's Isarnanheri, retiring to become Arik's Form Mistress when his mother died. '*This is hallowed Form. None but Isarnanheri can know the way of Jarnstiga.*'

Not if his life's blood depended on it would Arik share that sacred teaching - the footsteps of Sturmsinger himself; a deadly wardance written on merciless mountainsides, with the blinding snow overhead and the slide of ice underfoot. But what he needed now wasn't the guarded discipline of Jarnstiga but a new method, fashioned for the sinksands and treacherous stone-littered footholds of the dunes.

'Now. Pebr and Marsulo, stay within the perimeter of this even patch. Begin.'

The Derindin were strong and resilient, but they had more agility yet to coax out of their limbs. Isarnanheri were raised from seedlings. Mistress Lisbeta would have thrilled in the challenge of reshaping this flint, rather than the clay that came from the cradle. Her tutelage was a cold poetry. She'd been ridiculed at court, her appointment by the Prosperes questioned; some said the steel had driven her mad. Never to her face, of course. Arik was not given to fancies and had spent his early years listening through the absurd musings that underpinned her instruction, much to her chagrin. Perhaps it was because the North was denied to him now, but Arik found his mind wandering to those musings now.

Everything has a lining, even steel. It was nonsense, of course. But she had been without rival, so he had given her everything.

He barked again at Pebr; his footing was far too insecure. Reeling in his mind, he turned it back to his students.

*

If he were honest, Verdi had actually been looking forward to the next sitting with Elder Maragrin. He'd brought the gnomon with him, hoping for more instruction on how to use it. Maragrin raised one overgrown eyebrow.

'And what are you expecting to do with that?'

Verdi looked down at the gnomon blankly. 'I thought ... you're not going to teach me how to find the moondial?'

'*Teach*?' Maragrin's second eyebrow joined the first. 'Did you listen to anything I told you? If no one's been able to use it, how do you expect anyone to show you? This is a skill you must discover for yourself.'

'But –'

'But nothing. There is, however, a great deal to teach you about the man who left it to you.'

And so Verdi found himself in a classroom of another kind altogether. The glint never quite left the Elder's eyes, even as he recounted pedestrian details of Lorendar's early life: farming a valley contested by two neighbouring kingdoms; Lorendar's first rebellion against their usurpation of ancient land rights. A popularity built on the loyalty of smallfolk. It was the sort of teaching Klaus would have relished, and which Verdi observed dutifully and without satisfaction.

Maragrin was not impervious to this, despite Verdi's patience.

'Utterly blank,' he remarked. 'Nothing to interest you, Master

Santarem?' Verdi's back straightened. 'Half asleep, I'll warrant. What was I just telling you?'

'About the Battle of Heskenet,' Verdi replied, indignant. 'When Lorendar was not yet thirty. Two thousand soldiers offered themselves to his army and rode with him west to tear down the castle of Tabir. They only succeeded because he was able to bribe the watchtower keeper with only a crumb of copper to say nothing of their approach. "Such was the price of people's loyalty."' He glared at the Elder.

'You are clever enough, I see. Then where did you master the art of looking so empty-headed?'

The hint of a smile never seemed entirely removed from his wrinkled mouth, either. Verdi smouldered, stubbornly holding his tongue.

'Well, Master Santarem?' Maragrin pressed. 'What should I be telling you instead, eh? Enlighten me.'

How is Klaus so much better at this? Some of the steam escaped his latches.

'All this is about the past,' Verdi muttered. 'What about now? Merensama, the pirates?'

'How do you hope to understand the Plains if you are ignorant of their making?'

'I didn't say it was irrelevant. But –' Verdi struggled for words. 'We're just wasting time. Pirates are picking off people at their whim and no one does anything –'

'Answers will come in time.'

'Well, at this rate it'll be a long time before I get to the present.'

'None of that time will have been wasted.'

'I *should* be learning how "intentions" could possibly help conjure this moondial –'

'You would do very well to listen,' Maragrin scolded, irritation finally breaking free. 'A boy who knows nothing of his heritage and who's less than eager to claim it – yes, still a boy.'

This was too much for Verdi. 'Claim it? I've no idea how I can help!'

Maragrin pursed his lips. 'Begin by learning the land that was once here, so you can understand how it has become what it is now. Lorendar's life; the clans' histories. Our laws, so that you appreciate why a man who barters with water tokens had to be banished.'

Verdi's mouth fell open. 'I didn't know he'd already been tried. Why did no one tell me?'

'Of course you were not told. Do you think you could have defended a man's crime without yourself sharing in his disgrace?' Maragrin frowned. 'You would have tainted your name. Your aunt did you a favour, protecting you from your own haste.'

'He shouldn't have been banished. Now people will believe he was punished for a *sickness* –'

'The charge against him was clear. To have overlooked his crime would have been the greater danger; it would have rendered the law meaningless. Clan vows are sacred, Master Viridian. Loyalty cannot be secured when disloyalty goes unpunished.'

Verdi sagged sullenly in his seat. 'People are already afraid. You can't let people believe the pirates have more power than they do. It will be blown all out of proportion.'

'A pertinent observation.'

Taken aback by his praise, Verdi floundered.

'And now you have formed a desire that can be channelled into intention, Viridian – a desire to protect your kin.'

Verdi ran out of replies. *He's right.* Perhaps the pirates were the catalyst, but already he felt closer to the Derindin than he'd expected to. At quiet firesides or in moments of smoke-wreathed evensong, he could even feel the starry-eyed tug of Merensama. But how could he entangle himself in any useful way if he had no idea how?

He slid the gnomon back into its sleeve, relieved to be dismissed. He was surprised to find Arik hurrying up the hill to the Chieftainess' house.

A cold snake writhed in Verdi's belly. 'I thought we were meeting at the barracks...'

Arik's face was leaden. 'Klaus didn't come back with them.'

*

Chieftain Ferenjen was almost as old as Maragrin. His back was rounded, and the asymmetry of his face betrayed a frailty that belied the ferocity of his pale blue eyes. But there was also kindness in them.

'Your companions left yesterday, soon after they arrived,' he told Klaus the following morning in Fraivon's council chamber. 'They hoped to meet you on their return.'

Elder Melad grasped Klaus' hands. 'I'm indebted to you, Master Invelmari. Not only for myself, but for my grandson.'

Klaus bowed, glancing back at the Chieftain. 'What word did you send back to Elendra?'

Ferenjen didn't waver. 'This clan can't promise aid against the pirates. Not yet.'

'Then don't thank me.'

'You are new to these sands, Master Invelmari.' Klaus recognised Kira, the Elder who'd spoken for Fraivon at the Romelian Assembly. 'Don't be fooled. If Elendra so badly need our help, they would have sought it sooner.'

Klaus raised an eyebrow. 'Like they did at the Assembly?'

'Or before first consulting Lebas.' Her voice hardened. 'Elder Tourmali perhaps didn't expect us to know about that.'

'You may wonder at us,' said Chieftain Ferenjen. 'But storms have buried this citadel in sand several times, for here we bear the brunt of the winds. Our main water supply is in the path of the fouler storms, and a few days of ill winds are all that's needed to cut it off and cripple the citadel. This is a small clandom, and there are those who would salivate over the chance to take Ahravel at the first sign of weakness. We need our tumblers always ready to defend us against power poachers.'

Klaus listened expressionlessly.

'I'm only a Northern scribe,' he said slowly. 'But I helped bury the remains of your caravan near the Nerej oasis. It wasn't a windstorm that killed your clansman, Kirono Folma. And his final words were not of defending Ahravel.' Several Elders looked away. 'This is only the beginning. If the pirates are as strong as Elendra fear, there won't be anything left of your territory to take.'

Hedar burst into the hall, sparing Ferenjen a reply. He was still pale and limping.

'Hedar! You should be resting,' his grandfather scolded.

Hedar's face broke into a grin on spotting Klaus. 'I was worried you'd already left!'

'I'm about to.'

'Here I can be frank with you, Master Invelmari. There are raids on the outskirts of our land every few days,' Ferenjen warned. 'How are you going to return to Samsarra?'

'As I came. How else?'

'My tumblers will accompany you at least as far as Romel.'

Hedar's face fell. 'Won't you stay a few days?'

'Let him be, Hedar. If his mind is made up, it's best he goes in the light.'

'He didn't need the light!'

Klaus smiled at the young Derindman. 'Please thank the physician for her attentions.'

He left at once. Ferenjen's tumblers rode with him past Ghorsom's Thicket before turning back to Ahravel. He rode hard, Form and a prayer in his wing. He didn't risk riding after dusk again. Samsarra's gates were still open when he arrived with the full moon five days later, late enough in the evening that he found Arik supping in the tumblers' favoured tavern.

Saarem greeted him with a bear hug.

'Saw you like to get these out of your pirates,' he said, returning Klaus' three cleaned bolts. A cheer rose around the tavern.

'Verdi's a wreck,' said Arik cheerfully. 'He thinks your disappearance is all his fault since he dragged us here. Which it is.' He lowered his voice. 'D'you reckon you can lie low for another night?'

He dodged Klaus' punch. A weary relief strained Arik's humour. They had been blessed with many reunions, but the uncertainty never waned.

'Where's Verdi now?'

'Pining in the Arboretum. Told him you'd be back in your own time.' Seeing Klaus' face, Arik added hastily, 'He's with Alizarin, and Alizarin might actually kick me out of Samsarra if I suggest he can't be trusted escorting his own nephew.'

'Has he made any progress using the moondial?'

'Not likely.' Arik was predictably sceptical over the gnomon. 'He's found another distraction in the Arboretum, though – thank the Lifegiver. He hasn't slept for six nights. And all for a waste of time. I knew Fraivon would refuse their help.'

But Klaus would have travelled twice as far for the company of Sonru the physician. He had still not grasped the nature of slight matter, but the weight of the Wintermantels dragged a little less at his heart. He put the bolts back in the quiver with their brothers, the whistling arrow sleeping somewhere between them.

*

'Ferenjen knows we tried to seek a treaty with Akrinda. Baeron will have made sure of it.' Alizarin rubbed tired eyes. 'They'll hold it against us, wedding or no wedding.'

'Perhaps they might have given our proposal more consideration if we had sought their help before that of Lebas,' said Maragrin lightly.

Curtly, Tourmali replied, 'It's no good lamenting that now.'

'I suspect that was just an excuse to decline,' Alizarin added. 'They've no appetite for stirring Baeron's suspicions by getting caught spying along their border.'

'We'll have a stronger case if we tell them the pirates are looking for something.'

'Too late,' said Tourmali. 'Their pride's too wounded now. And I wouldn't trust them with that information yet.'

Emra hadn't been surprised by Fraivon's refusal. 'We've no option now but to turn to Sisoda.'

'Chieftain Navein thinks they're heathens,' Tourmali reminded her. 'You may as well hope for rain.'

'Cilastra will make Navein see reason.'

'And who'll make Sisoda see reason? They've little regard for Lorendar, and now you're promoting his heir – an heir who's as far from finding the Merensaman moon phase as we are. Hardly an incentive.'

'Sisoda are wild horses. A few of them still honour Lorendar.'

'If you ask them for warriors, they may listen. If you want to seduce them with rumours about a pirate stronghold...' Tourmali shook his head. 'Abandon this search of the south-west, Ahena. Or else risk sending a spy of our own.'

'We can't afford to be caught spying in any of those clandoms,' Maragrin objected. He rose, leaning on his stick. Sarcasm buttered his words. 'So much for diplomacy. The chances of a peaceful Merensama are looking better than ever, don't you think?'

He shuffled back into the house. Emra gazed over Samsarra from the veranda. Torches bloomed like golden night-flowers on the south-eastern wall of the citadel.

'How did he find the way to Ahravel at night?' she murmured.

Tourmali's face was lost in shadows. 'I don't know.'

A cold wind stirred, seasoned with the taste of sand.

22

A Shade of Green

HE TOOK HEARTH-MAIDEN DAGMAR FOR HIS WIFE, FAIR OF FACE AND
FIERCE OF HEART, PLUCKED FROM THE CONSTELLATIONS OF THE FAR
NORTHERN HEAVENS OF HIS FIRST HOME. TWO BAIRNS SHE BORE HIM...

SONNONFER: THE RISE OF ANSOVALD STURMSINGER

Healer, wanderer, hermit ... the words from the watchtower danced through
Klaus' dreams.

He wished he had stayed the stranger who had gifted him this
portion of their meaning.

'Only half of Elendra's clanfolk live in Samsarra,' Arik confided
over breakfast in Thillaina's kitchen. 'The remainder maintain smaller
settlements around the citadel, and at least a third are pastoral nomads.
They have some six thousand tumblers to call on. Most are stationed
here in Samsarra, the rest across the clandom. There are a few thousand
more in reserves.'

'And the other clans?'

'Elendra's army is larger than most, though no one can match
Sisoda's. Mantelon keep fewer tumblers. Without knowing how many

pirates there are, we can't know how many soldiers are enough. But how many pirates can the desert hide?'

'If Lebas and Fraivon refuse to lend support, I don't see much hope of convincing the other clans.'

'You'd think a summer of raids would have convinced them,' Verdi grumbled. 'But most Elders still think the pirates are just pests.'

Arik pushed his empty plate away. 'Every plague begins with a handful of pests.'

'Good morning.' Thillaina arrived for the kahvi she insisted on making herself every morning. 'Kahva? I'm going to need a steady stream to stomach these preparations.'

Ravi's head appeared in her apron pocket.

Verdi sat up. '*That's* where you've been all morning!'

Thillaina laughed. 'He probably remembers being carried around as a kitterlat. I caught him sleeping in my robe the other day.' She scratched the oceloe's head. 'Better take care you don't find yourself in the washergirl's laundry load, young man.' The rumble of his purr had never been louder. Verdi looked slightly put out.

Arik rolled his eyes. 'Preparations for what?'

'The wedding of Elder Maragrin's great-grandson,' she said. Arik's eyes lit up. 'A dozen yards of silk to embroider. Of course, there must be a fuss made of it. She's a wellborn Fraivonian girl. Got to court the whole clan, don't we? Whole clan has to be disturbed and dragged out of their beds to cheer. Not to mention Winterfall feastday is barely a week from now.' She bustled about filling the pot as she grumbled. 'Big market, tournaments. I'm already stretched for time. Why they would hold a wedding right before the feastday is beyond me. Probably did it to kill me finishing that gown. Got tired of my scolding, I expect. Who needs an embroidered train that could trail from here to the Paiva? Pass me those cups on that shelf, Viridian.'

Verdi reached up, knocking over a glass decanter that fell and smashed on the floor. Ravi leapt in fright from Thillaina's apron, prompting a roar of laughter from Arik.

'I'm so sorry!' Verdi dropped the tiny copper cups next, scrambling after them as they rolled about.

'Not to worry, not to worry.' Thillaina stirred her pot of kahvi unperturbed. 'No harm done. Though it was a rather nice decanter. Picked it up from Rainsthwen. But don't trouble yourself. It was only irreplaceable.'

'Fortunately you're not this clumsy in the Arboretum, Master Viridian.'

They looked up. A young woman stood in the open kitchen doorway, holding a basket.

'Ah, Nerisen,' said Thillaina briskly. 'Thought you'd never come. What were you doing, growing the cotton for that yarn? Set it down here, thank you.'

'My horse threw a shoe.' She stepped inside, putting the basket on the table. 'I'll clean that up.'

Klaus recognised her voice immediately: she was the woman who'd been so offended by his interest in the unlading pen in Noisy Tree. Her hood was lowered now. Her hair was the fold of a raven's wing and fell richly around a face that saw much of the desert sun, and the green of her eyes was the first leaves of spring. She picked up a broom, and a black panfarthing as dark-haired as his mistress jumped out of her pocket and onto her shoulder. Ravi's head immediately re-appeared around a chair leg. Arik had stopped laughing.

'Sorry,' Verdi mumbled, meekly stepping aside.

'Nerisen brings me the finest dyes for my yarns and lace.' Thillaina poured the steaming kahvi into the tiny cups. 'And then robs me of my scraps in the name of charity.'

Klaus accepted a cup, conscious of Nerisen kneeling nearby, gathering the broken glass.

'Don't cut yourself,' Thillaina warned.

'Too late.'

Thillaina tutted, passing her a clean rag. He risked a glance; Nerisen pressed the cloth to her finger. Their eyes met briefly. She had recognised him, too.

'Some kahva, Nerisen?'

'No. Master Meron is waiting at the Arboretum.' Nerisen swept up the remaining shards and left as quietly as she had arrived.

Arik leaned forward slightly towards Klaus. 'You can breathe now.'

Klaus kicked his shin under the table, earning a broad grin in return.

'Sorry about your decanter,' Verdi mumbled, cheeks still aflame.

Thillaina patted his shoulder. 'You should never mourn the breaking of glass; it came from the earth and has a life and a death like the rest of us. And the Great Sentience takes back what's his and we can't begrudge him that.'

Arik downed his cup. 'This kahvi is delicious.'

'Isn't it? Nerisen gets it for me. The folk in Cora grow the best crop and roast it using an ancient recipe that foolish men fought over once. And still do.'

Verdi shielded his cup protectively from Ravi's twitching whiskers. 'I didn't know you've been to Invelmar, Mistress Thillaina.'

'Oh, many times.' She looked bemused by his surprise. 'I'd go every season with my father's caravan as a girl. For a few years I even stayed. Not many Derindwomen in Invelmar. That's how I built my business, along the border towns and upriver. Northerners like to trade with Southerners without having to see them, but I wasn't having any of that. Even in Dunraven I made sure they sought my work. I made lace for the queen herself, when she was marrying. There's not a better bit of brocade to be found in all the Part than Thillaina's. Then I settled here when my bones couldn't take the bumps of the road any longer.' She looked wistful. 'It's a good life if you've got the strength for it.'

'You didn't want to stay in the border towns?'

'Ha! They should be so lucky. Settling anywhere wasn't easy. But an old woman like me can't manage without a clan's protection. Clanship is a shield in the Plains, remember that. Without it, you're anyone's meat. And I needed younger hands, and more of them. With all this?' She waved her arm. 'I need an awful lot of help to get through the work now.'

'Nerisen?' asked Arik innocently.

'Nerisen's no lacemaker. She's a Plainswalker.'

'A what?'

'A desert ranger. Keeps an eye on the folk beyond the citadels, takes them supplies. She's one of Meron's students up at the Arboretum, extracts pigments for my dyes.' Thillaina finished her kahvi. 'Better go see what those girls are getting up to. Can't take your eye off them for a moment.'

*

This time when Klaus arrived at the lettervault, its doors were locked.

Like so many Derindin doorways, the brass overlaying the wooden doors told a story. It was divided into thirds, each containing an item: a quill, a wheatsheaf, a sextant. From the corner of his eye, he caught a movement in the window. When he looked up, it was empty.

He left feeling thoroughly disheartened.

Hoping for a better welcome at the Arboretum, he rode east, marvelling at the Elendrans' irrigation system and the woodlands they had nurtured in spite of the drought.

'At last!' Verdi beamed at him over a workbench in the laboratorium, sleeves rolled up. 'You remember Bevro?'

Bevro gawked at Klaus. An alarm clock sounded, and they both hurried off to a mechanicontraption clamped over a fire.

Klaus had hoped to probe Verdi about the gnomon, but Verdi seemed the happiest he'd seen him since their arrival in Samsarra. He barely noticed when Klaus wandered away to explore the research station. Klaus glimpsed Nerisen disappearing down a stairwell, and was glad to stumble upon Meron in another laboratorium.

But the scholar's welcome was strained, barely looking up from his work. 'I was glad to hear you'd safely returned from Ahravel, Master Tristan.'

There were few Derindin from whom Klaus had come to expect a warm greeting, but Meron had certainly been amongst them.

'I wondered if you kept a record of the old riverways, Master Meron?'

'Sadly, no. Most of them dried out soon after the dam was built, though some of them are still marked by waystations or watchtowers.' Meron's reply was definitely lukewarm.

'Shame the abandoned quarries can't be turned into reservoirs.'

'Can't fill a quarry without rain.'

Klaus nodded. 'I imagine there aren't many left, either.'

'Voista has one. Hesper's got several, all sitting empty – they used to mine marble. There's not enough water for the digging now. But those quarries made Hesper rich.'

'Pity. Are you acquainted at all with one Gerin Taslisem?'

His aim was true. Meron stiffened; fingers coiling, face becoming unreadable.

'He's grown many of our saplings for the Arboretum on his land, when we needed plots more sheltered from the wind.'

Klaus searched his empty face. 'What sort of man is he?'

'He is the sort of man who does not raise the price of grain when it is much in demand.'

With this, Meron excused himself back to his work.

'What's wrong?' asked Verdi as they rode back to Samsarra. 'You were in fine spirits this morning. Now you've wandered off again.'

'Journey's catching up with me,' Klaus lied. He felt Verdi peer at him sideways.

'You must be very low.' Verdi's neck reddened. 'I mean, I suppose after what happened – well –'

'Would you like to stay in Samsarra, Verdi?'

Verdi looked as though he'd much rather untangle his words than answer this.

'I don't know.' Now he avoided Klaus' eye. 'Elder Maragrin...'

'I don't think you'll find the answer to that in a classroom,' Klaus told him. 'And I wasn't suggesting you invoke this oath. But have you considered joining the clan?'

Verdi's eyes widened. 'Why would I join Elendra?'

'Because clanship gives you a protection that Arik and I can't. Unclanned folk are fair game.'

Klaus waited.

'Maybe,' Verdi conceded, unconvinced.

'Think about it. Clan bonds aren't irreversible.'

'What if you have to leave suddenly?'

'That should never be a consideration in your decisions now. How are you getting on with the gnomon?'

Verdi looked away. 'I'm not.'

'You seem interested in learning how to use it.'

'I've no idea what I'm supposed to do with it.' Verdi scowled. 'And no one can tell me!'

Admittedly, Maragrin's instructions *had* been scant. They arrived at the Chieftainess' house where Maragrin was expecting Verdi for the evening.

'I'll try to help you.' Klaus nudged him forward. 'Use this time with him well.'

'It's hardly helping.'

'Be patient.'

*

'Put your knucklers away, Tarit. You must be the most dangerous thing here.'

Tarit, an overly eager tumbler not long out of the Murhesla's guild, raised the wooden pole Arik had given him. 'This is a child's tool.'

'When you become the weapon, you may adorn yourself with more teeth.'

Arik watched the tumblers' sprints of combat within the narrow perimeter he had set. '*The sword is not your servant.*' Mistress Lisbeta had been particularly fond of this. '*It is an extension of yourself. So what must you become in order to bear this deadly fruit?*'

In the afternoon, Arik reduced their sparring space to the shade of a cedar tree, tightening their movements further. Even his most enthusiastic students, Tarit and Gerlana, grew frustrated. To their credit, they gave no voice to their discontent, though their sour faces did the talking well enough.

'Wouldn't you prefer to be on the Far Northern front, Master Marcin?' Marsulo asked less-than-innocently over their noon break. 'Last night, Babblers were saying that two hundred Invelmari soldiers were felled in Loggrwald.'

'I would not.'

Only a Derindin could goad you with the face of a cold poker iron, Arik thought darkly. *A Derindin or an Intelligencer.* Arik had been closely following the rumours of intensified fighting on Invelmar's northern border. Bloody Babble. Hardly a reliable source. But if the reports *were* accurate, how had they dented Invelmari's stubborn defences?

Klaus joined them late in the afternoon. His face just then was truly an Intelligencer's: as empty as virgin clay, ready to be moulded into whatever was next required of it.

'Everything alright?' Arik asked.

A single nod. Always in complete control.

'Good. Take a pole.'

Arik paired the tumblers against him, watching Klaus move within the tight sphere of the cedar's shade like a lifeless machine. Arik barked at the tumblers' every error – low hanging arms, slow legs, premature lunges.

'Think you're tired?' Arik ignored the sun's slow descent. 'What happens when you've been riding for days before your battle has even begun? Will your enemy wait for you to rest then?'

Arik didn't let them go until the sun finally set, returning alone with Klaus to the citadel. The Intelligencer was still buried behind his Form.

'What's wrong?'

Klaus steered his horse through Samsarra's gates. 'There are several places where that quarry could be, but Rasan was probably taken to Hesper's clandom. Maybe Hesper are friendlier with the pirates than we think.'

This was no answer, but Arik knew there was no point in pressing an Intelligencer. Besides, they had work to do.

*

The bookshelves rising from the tower room hid a discrete mezzanine. Emra stood in their dusty shadows and watched her great-nephew below.

He was attentive enough. He made notes, recalled things well. If anything, he was to be commended for the patience with which he listened to Maragrin's monologues. The Elder was certainly a test of the young man's character. And he of Maragrin's, it seemed.

'No questions, Master Viridian?'

'Of course I have. Questions, I mean.'

Maragrin paused. 'Are they going to ask themselves, then?'

'I didn't want to interrupt.' Viridian blushed. 'I wanted to know more about the kingdoms that came right after Orenthia.'

'Too many to count. Orenthia crumbled into factions led by warlords who fought like dogs. The sway of power shifted so often, historians struggled to keep up. But perhaps next time.'

No sooner than Viridian had left, Maragrin glanced up directly at her. 'I may be old but I'm not yet blind.'

Emra descended the stairwell concealed behind the bookshelves. 'Will he be able to find it?'

Maragrin pursed his lips. 'Let us hope our efforts towards Merensama don't stoke war before he has time enough.'

She offered him the letter. 'A response from Periam.'

'"*Vanished*",' Maragrin muttered, scanning it. '"The pirates have all but vanished." Is Periam so naïve?'

'They're eager to downplay a risk that their puppet-masters in the west want to belittle. But you've heard the reports from Romel. There *has* been less pirate activity this past fortnight.'

Maragrin pursed his lips to prunes. 'For now. The market season's over; fewer caravans are out. This lull is temporary. Do we wait, then, until another summer of attacks?'

'No, but it makes it more difficult to gather support.'

'If they're stupid enough to mistake a lull for an end to their misery, let their clandoms burn.'

'Maragrin!'

His eyes glinted, unrepentant. 'This is the dangerous moment. Even our allies will be tempted to sit back. And then there's the boy to think of. Too many are praying for either his rise or his demise. Including pirates, apparently.'

And it would be far more difficult to protect Viridian while he remained resistant to the reality that he had more real freedom while pledged to Elendra than not.

*

There *had* to be some truth to the troubling reports from the North, for in the coming days sibling rumours drifted downriver from the border towns. There had never been as much activity as this on the Far Northern front in Arik's lifetime, thanks to Adela's pact with the now murdered Täntainen. In the taverns, talk of a Far Northern uprising even overtook grumbling about pirates and speculation over the council's plans to root them out that winter.

'They heard the Queen was sick and struck hard, one attack after another. How long before Invelmari villagers along the border abandon their land to the Far Northerners?'

'But how? Far Northerners are a mound of worms strangling each other for the same dirt.'

'Not any more. This warlord has united them.'

Arik rolled a small crust of bread under his finger on the table. He took another mouthful of stew. He had little appetite, but he didn't have to talk if his mouth was full.

'What, united *all* the Far Northern tribes?'

'Don't be daft. That lot? They still sacrifice each other to heathen gods!'

'Not all the tribes, but enough to gather a sizeable army. And who knows how many more will join them?' This was from a Romelian horse breeder who frequented the border towns. 'Banasár, that's his name. Every now and then, someone comes along who can turn the tide.'

Banasár ... "the mortal wound". Arik was no expert in Far Northern speech, but this much he understood.

'Did they say anything else about him?'

'Little, and who knows what's to be believed of it. A grey-haired man without a soul to find in his face, apparently. They say he's waited a long time for his reckoning with Dunraven.'

The horse breeder groused on, mostly worried about the impact of trouble on his trade.

'Have no fear, sir,' Arik reassured him. 'It'll take a lot more than Far Northern skirmishes to cool Invelmari demand for your horses. No pirates bothered your journey home, I hope?'

'Fortunately, a caravan of fifty Romelian tumblers doesn't get bothered much, Master Northman, on account that there may be Murhesla amongst them.'

Talk turned again to the approaching wedding, and at this hour became increasingly more crude than useful. Klaus sat near the fire with Verdi, imbibing another grizzly-bearded tale of Lorendar. It wasn't until they finally left the tavern that they could speak.

Arik asked in a low voice, 'Were you listening?'

'Yes.'

Yet Klaus had nothing to say about the prospect of an organised Far Northern uprising. Three moons ago, he would have been scouring for details; he'd worshipped devoutly at the altar of Sturmsinger's Blood Pact. Now there was no way to know if Klaus even cared. *Perhaps it's just his Form at work.* That was the uncanny skill of the Intelligencers, turning them outwardly to stone.

But when Arik went to bed, Klaus was still hunched over his map, face haggard with strain even darkness did little to mask.

*

Drums boomed with full-bellied resonance that tunnelled into the night; a summons to the Northern heart that was born entrained to the march of soldiers. It was not for war these drums sounded, but Feldrday, the mid-winter festival marking the four noble Forms of Invelmar – Warrior, Intelligencer, Jurist, Blacksmith.

Klaus watched the crowds spilling into the forest: men and women and children; fire-eaters, pie-sellers, jugglers, magicians, fortune tellers. The air smelled of smoke and roasting meat. Beneath that, of pine needles and snow. And beneath that: bloodlust and brutal triumph. Ealdormen gathered according to Form, not house. Nearby, Lord Wintermantel was deep in conversation with Cenric Eldred. Mother's face shone in the torchlight, her eyes not once straying to Elodie, who was newly initiated to the Jurists and now buried in their ranks. Klaus stole another glance at his sister.

'It's not so dull an affair,' Master Arnander remarked drily under his breath. 'If you look at her one more time, you may as well snub the Queen's protection directly to her face.'

Klaus ground his teeth. Feldrday wasn't dull; it was loathsome. Of course, the four glorious Forms warranted celebration. But every execution decreed during the whole month leading up to Feldrday had been deferred until this night, anointing glory with blood. Mostly, they were men and women who deserved death: traitors, murderers. But all death was deplorable. Why the two events must be entangled, Klaus had no idea. That was the way it had always been for Feldrday: a feast and a bloodbath.

He thought darkly: this will be the first thing I will prohibit when I am king.

There was a hint of warning in Florian's voice now. 'Ulfriklaus.'

Klaus looked away from the Jurists, willing the liquid guile of his Form to possess his face. A mould; that was all he was now. A chalice to be filled with fairest poison.

Queen Adela, a Jurist, arrived. Klaus forced himself not to look at his sister again. She was brave, but six was young to embark on a study of the sway of justice. Especially the justice of this iron Queen.

'Why do we imitate Far Northerners?' he muttered. Feldrday was almost as bad as the human sacrifices the barbarians made to their false gods, as though the Lifegiver would appreciate this brutal return of his gift.

'Perhaps you'd like to be overheard and be offered up on the scaffold yourself,' Master Arnander suggested.

It was a charade Klaus endured unwillingly, hiding behind this soulless mask; a liar's face, a deceiver's face. Was this to be his life? A journey of burrowing for dark truths, only to bury or bend them further? At least Arik had the golden mask of the Warriors to raise to his face. But Klaus was an Intelligencer, not a Warrior, and there was nowhere to hide.

Much later, after the executions and the ice-swimming races, Master Arnander would skewer him with that inescapable gaze that seemed to find

Klaus' every thought. Even Lord Wintermantel, a master Intelligencer, did not pierce through him so searchingly.

'It is like a hidden root in the forest, Ulfriklaus. It will trip you when you least expect it.'

At fourteen, he ought to have been too old for sullenness. 'What is?'

'The dissidence.'

Something woke him, or almost woke him; the hooting of an owl in the night, perhaps. Starlight tinged the darkness silver. He was drowsy, but the words that had begun tormenting his first waking moments nudged insistently now at his half-consciousness: *the healer, the wanderer, the hermit.* Master Laminhad swam in and out of his mind, clad with the shapelessness of an Intelligencer's face.

'It is a maggot that will become a serpent. Your Form will never be complete until you root it out.'

'What if I can't?'

Klaus turned again, unbearably tired. *The healer, the wanderer, the hermit...* Elodie's eyes, wide and white-rimmed with terror, filled the world behind his closed eyelids: *'I learned something terrible...'* How was he ever to know what had really happened to him? War drums shuddered in his breast, in place of his heart.

'You must. One day you will. But until then, you have Afldalr.'

Master Arnander was right. Not long after this Feldrday, he would take that last step to truly gaining his Form. But for now, there were the dying throes of dissidence. The smell of the roasting spits melted into the acrid smell of Far Northern pyres. Smoke distorted Gerlinde's rising arms as she danced, and when it cleared, her wrists were bound at a stake and the spill of her dress was melting into flames, and his ears were filled with a thin and desperate scream.

In the morning, his nostrils were filled with the sickly-sweet smell of acrid smoke, and Afldalr trembled again beneath its bonds.

23

Andaera

BUT HE COULD NOT IDLE ON A LAVISH THRONE, DESIRING
DOMINION OVER EVIL. HE COULD NOT REST WHILE OUTLAWS YET
THREATENED HIS KINGDOM, THE TRUE JEWEL IN HIS CROWN.

SONNONFER: THE VICTORIES OF ANSOVALD STURMSINGER

Gerin Taslisem's farm was quiet. The gate of a pen swung in the early
morning breeze. His stables were empty.

Klaus dismounted after the short ride from Samsarra. Hills to the
west sheltered Gerin's orchards from wind, and the slight incline in
the land probably encouraged the downflow of water from Samsarra's

aqueducts. It was clearly an enviable plot.

He followed the sound of light hammering to an outbuilding behind the house. A man looked up as Klaus approached.

'Excuse me my trespass, sir. You must be Master Taslisem.'

Gerin looked like a man who had aged over days rather than years. The loose skin over his jaw and the gaunt circles around his eyes mirrored Klaus' own torments. Klaus reprimanded himself. *This man's lost something far greater than I have.*

Gerin resumed hammering the links of a chain. 'There's no milk or grain to sell here.'

Klaus knew from the taverns that Taslisem had sold his animals ahead of a winter through which he couldn't afford to feed them.

'I was told your nut crop is the finest in the clandom.'

It was the only crop he would have kept in reserve, destined for Invelmar where pistachios were a prized delicacy.

'Makes no difference. Haven't got the horses to take it up to the border towns now.'

'No need to bother with all that, if you'll take my gold for your stock.'

Gerin stopped hammering. 'What's a man going to do with a dozen bushels of pistachios? I'm not in need of charity.'

'That's not for me to judge,' Klaus replied briskly. 'But Master Santarem needs a worthy wedding gift for Fraivon's bride.'

The Derindman considered him. Klaus had done his research; Gerin was a staunch supporter of Merensama.

'I'm sure you know a good deal when you see one, sir, and, if you'll excuse me for saying so, you're in need of a return on your harvest.' Klaus looked pointedly at the broken chain. 'You're not an ironmonger, after all.'

Gerin, who must have heard by now of Klaus' hand in his fortunes, didn't accuse him of meddling. 'You should see what you're buying first.'

'As you wish.'

The nuts still smelled of summer. A late crop; their red-pink-purple-green skins were yet fresh, splitting to release a smell that reminded Klaus of geranium and pine sap. Inside, their flesh was an astonishing green and almost sweet. Klaus paused over a bushel, exerting the excoriating scrutiny of his Form on the farmer.

'Where did you bury your wife and workers, Master Taslisem?'

The farmer was quiet for a long moment.

'On the Qardamom Road,' he said finally. 'I had to go back to do it. Couldn't bring them home without a wagon and couldn't leave them behind.'

'I'll send a wagon for the nuts.'

Klaus insisted on paying higher Noisy Tree prices. The gold was likely several times the value of the stock and horses stolen from Gerin, such was the crop's value so late in the season. But Klaus knew no amount of gold would provide much comfort now.

*

Arik poured his tavern conquest another drink. He was a scrawny farrier, pot-bellied thanks to his fondness for derina wine, and a little too carelessly interested in Arik's steel.

'You'd better watch your back, Master Marcin. There are enough fools who'll throw a knife into it for that blade.' The drink that dulled the farrier's sensibilities unmasked a greedy gleam in his eyes.

'They'd have to be damned stupid,' Broco guffawed. 'Might as well mark their own graves while they're at it.'

'I'm just sayin', Broco, I'm just sayin'. Even a great warrior is made of flesh and blood.'

'Well spoken.' Arik smiled indulgently at the farrier, who was also too easily flattered for his own good. 'You must know a thing or two about metals yourself, sir.'

'A thing or two,' the farrier agreed. 'Not much mining these days here now, though. Can't spare the water. Most ore is buried westward, and those bastards demand more than it's worth too. Almost what we pay for imports from your own patch.'

'Is it worth that much gold?'

'Hardly, but beggars can't be choosers.'

'I'm sure there have been fine ores to boast of here,' Arik said graciously. 'A blacksmith once told me of a cinnabar that was superior even to Semran stock. Red gold, he called it.'

'*Red*?' The farrier laughed. The tumblers had lost interest, turning their attention to teasing the tavern's pretty pair of maids. 'No such thing.'

'That's what he said.'

'Maybe he meant the dirt it's dug from. There's a mine with earth an odd rusty sort of colour. Good ore, while it lasted. Hardly gold, though.'

'All mined out?'

'Hesper are a greedy lot.'

'Are they the only ones who had that ore?'

'There were other deposits, but only one bell pit was big enough to be worth anything. *Red gold!*' The farrier laughed again.

Arik glanced at Klaus. After weeks of avoiding news from home, he was now scrounging for it. He was still artfully relieving some nearby tumblers of news picked up from a caravan recently returned from Whimsy. More guests had arrived in anticipation of the wedding, and with them a variety of reports.

'A karrionhjord,' a cotton trader said. 'Sighted near Malvern.'

Arik's heart dropped a beat. He poured another drink and tasted it this time.

'Aren't you from thereabouts, Tristan?'

'I am.' Klaus sipped kahvi. 'When was the karrionhjord spotted?'

'Must have been at least a month past now. Messenger-birds are slower flying down from so far North; their reports always lag behind the river traffic. Can't be good news, can it?'

But some of the listeners made no secret of their dark satisfaction at the prospect of this Far Northern threat.

'A karrionhjord was never good news for anyone in this Part, sir,' Klaus replied. 'The kind of soldiers who've forgotten their humanity altogether. Before the First Redrawing, they gutted towns as far south as the Paiva.'

This cooled some of the glee considerably. The Derindin cider was too tart for Arik's liking, but he took another swig. He couldn't add that karrionhjords contained the only soldiers feared by Isarnanheri; that the Eye of the Court sacrificed dozens of Intelligencers in the Far North to keep the Arm of the Court abreast of even a whisper of any new hatchlings. That the Isarnanheri themselves had roots in the ice-blooded soullessness of those infamous hordes bred in the desolate fringes of the Far North.

'There's no chance,' Arik insisted when they returned to their lodgings. 'There's not been a karrionhjord sighting in ninety years. No one's had the brains to raise any.'

But Klaus was quiet for longer than he liked.

'More and more insurgencies, this new warlord ... even Adela's sickness. The tide's turned since Täntainen's death, Arik.'

Arik remained dubious. 'Täntainen was assassinated only twelve months ago. It takes a generation to raise a karrionhjord.'

'There've been enough irregularities that I wouldn't scoff even at the Babble.'

'You must have heard about this warlord calling himself the "*mortal wound*".'

'Yes ... Banasár. All we can do now is wait and listen.'

It wasn't the reassurance Arik had sought. But Verdi had joined them and was wound up enough without the addition of their worries.

'What's wrong with Klaus?' he asked, after Klaus first went to bed and then got up again for another of his night prowls of the citadel.

'Tired, I expect,' Arik lied. 'He's been training like a mechanicon.'

Arik knew, however, that it wasn't fatigue now perpetually shrouding Klaus in his chilling veil, his mask pleasant and attentive and wholly discordant with whatever festered beyond.

*

In her offhand way, Thillaina proved to be as great a resource to Klaus as half the taverns of Samsarra combined.

The wedding of Maragrin's great-grandson was far more than a marriage and had necessitated a suitable amount of pomp. It fell on a clear-eyed night that briefly forgot the sting of winter. The fine garments they'd requisitioned for the occasion were too warm and constricting for Klaus. Or perhaps that was his mind, twisting thoughts together until they choked.

'Fraivon are the most ill-disposed to Akrinda,' Thillaina confided. 'They led the last revolt against Akrinda over their tax on kahva beans when I was still peeking around my mother's knee.' She looked Arik and Klaus up and down critically. 'Double the cloth and the work, Northerners always take. Though those girls didn't mind measuring you up for it, I'm sure. Master Tristan, you ought to have chosen something finer.'

Klaus mollified her with a winning smile. 'Are the Elders hoping the marriage will thaw Fraivon's resistance to a treaty with the border towns?'

'If they are, they'll be sorely disappointed. Even Panthica knows her daughter's not so precious as *that*, and she's the richest merchant in Ahravel.'

She jerked her head towards the bride's mother, sitting proudly with the Elders. In Invelmar, a common woman earned the liberties of men if she became a shieldmaiden. Not so these candid Derindwomen, whose clans forbade them from one thing only – migration north, for fear they would sediment in Invelmari brothels for their jewel-cave eyes.

'I'll bet the Elders had their work cut out wooing the mother,' Klaus murmured.

'Elendra agreed to let the bride keep her clan ties to Fraivon or else she'd have likely refused the match.'

Verdi straightened. 'She didn't have to join Elendra?'

'No, and I've never heard of such nonsense. Most clans require a highborn bride to renounce her clan ties when she comes to the marriage bed. Grooms, too. But Elendra allowed her to keep hers and waived the taxes on some of our trade with Fraivon besides. They're hoping it will give them sway. But it'll come to nothing.' Thillaina sniffed. 'Fraivon are a pig-headed lot. As guilty of hiding behind ghabala as the rest.'

The handfastening ceremony was held in the Chieftainess' square under the cedars. Lanterns hung from half-dressed trees and the twisted tendons of the bare wisteria, and rosewood incense suffused the evening with sultry sweetness. The citadel swelled with well-wishers.

'Thanks for the wedding gift,' Verdi whispered, unhappily stationed beside Elendra's Elders.

Klaus murmured, 'You're welcome.'

Derindin brides wore blue. In homage to the Ninvellyn, Thillaina said, and in the hope of capturing some of the blessing it no longer delivered to the Plains. Almost-strangers, bride and groom stumbled dutifully through their vows. The sage who blessed their union spoke in Derindask that Klaus followed easily, but his prayers changed to something else, causing every head to bow in deference. Klaus jolted: *probably Orenthian.* The sage joined the couples' hands, engulfing them in cheers.

'Careful,' Arik warned Verdi. 'There are more strangers than tumblers about tonight.'

And not all of them looked pleased to spot the rumoured heir of Lorendar, watching Verdi hawkishly. Klaus grew uneasy behind his Form.

The wedding feast filled Emra's garden with music and dancing that spilled into the streets. Her courtyard was soon crowded: Elders, highborn Elendrans, Mantelonians, wealthy merchants like Thillaina, envoys, senior tumblers. Talk of pirates was inevitable.

'A bad season, that's all it was,' the bride's father declared dismissively. 'There are fewer raids now.'

Cilastra would have none of this. 'Only because the market season's over.'

'It's a chance to gather our wits, and look instead to the future,' Tourmali interrupted, raising his glass to the newlyweds, his eyes straying to Verdi as he drank.

Hedar's rescue had earned the two Northerners a lofty place in Fraivon's regard, and the feast ought to have been pleasant. But Klaus grew restless.

Verdi almost panicked when Klaus rose from their table. 'Where are you going?'

'Stay with Arik.'

Klaus slipped out into the square, now merry with food-laden tables and entertainment. He spotted Suman amongst the revellers, listening to a poet singing alongside a flutist.

Klaus joined him. 'A rather melancholy melody for the occasion, I'd say.'

'They're few and far apart, those who remember the old ballads of the South.'

The elderly poet sang in a rural Derindask that Klaus only partially understood. The Plains seemed to have as many tongues as clans.

'One day it'll be their loss,' Klaus replied. 'The best record of history is what people remember, not what their kings inscribe on their own tombs.'

Suman glanced at him almost appreciatively. 'A chronicler would know.'

'What's he singing about?'

Suman listened for a moment. '*Betrothed of the silenced daughter, what do you say to the Mountain King who stole your fair maiden away? Snatched as she fled to southern skies, bewitched by sorceress Andaera's lies... Forever trapped in the bosom of her forebears blue... Forever forbidden to bear her fruit to you.*'

Something stirred in Klaus' memory. 'The silenced daughter...'

'A very old ballad.'

'*The greatest of debts shall hold prisoner the lord and slave of the Silenced Daughter.*' Klaus felt as though a lifetime had passed since they'd stumbled upon that riddle upon the doorway in the Paiva. Understanding dawned: *of course – the daughter is the Ninvellyn, rushing south to her grave.*

But it wasn't this that raised goosebumps on Klaus' arms. He had heard the name *Andaera* before, and she was no sorceress, but a constellation in the Far North that he had seen just once – from a lonely summit in the Sterns, during a terrible campaign in the eastern Northlands. A discovery Klaus wasn't likely to forget, for he'd learned of this constellation Andaera from a singular source: the only fragment of the Septentrional Scrolls of the Far Northern tribes permitted in Invelmar. *Andaera* ... a Far Northern name found, to his knowledge, in neither Invelmen nor common Derindask.

Why would Southerners sing of Far Northern stars they had never seen?

The young flutist picked up a lively jig, and the poet's song changed. Suman rejoined the Elders. Klaus would have liked to ask the poet about his ballad, but he was surrounded by dancers now.

The curious mention of Andaera gifted him a sudden thought. *What if Cenric Ulverston's knowledge of the mine had come not from the scrolls of the Sonnonfer, but from the Septentrional Scrolls?*

The notion hadn't crossed Klaus' mind; so forbidden were the Scrolls in Invelmar that possession of them carried a death sentence. Only that short astronomical excerpt was permitted, and only to Intelligencers. Even now, so far beyond Dunraven's reach, the thought of looking upon any other part of the Far Northerners' Scrolls raised the hair on Klaus' skin.

The idea was unthinkable. But how many unthinkable things had lately come to pass?

'Master Tristan!' Laminhad hurried towards him, accompanied by a well-dressed woman. 'My wife, Kema. My dear, it's to this fine man I owe my freedom.'

Klaus bowed. Laminhad's wife, a good deal younger than he and very pretty, avoided Klaus' eye. 'Far more credit than I deserve, sir. How's your leg?'

There was a split-second of confusion; then Laminhad's smile broadened. 'Very good of you to ask. Yes, much better. If you'll excuse my saying it, I'd say the festivities suit you.'

'Only thanks to the skill of a fine needlewoman. I'll pass on your compliments.'

Klaus drifted across the square. Girls spun as they danced, wearing necklaces of the crimson trumpet-flowers the Derindin swore would bring steadfast lovers. His pulse jolted; Nerisen sat alone under a nearby tree. A faded shawl was wrapped around her shoulders, her panfarthing curled at her throat.

'Definitely the right idea,' came Arik's voice over his shoulder, eyeing the dancers. 'Far more fun out here than the banquet.'

Klaus raised an eyebrow. 'Where's Verdi?'

'Wedged between Ayla and his uncle. Probably regretting that wedding gift, what with the fuss Fraivon's making over him for it.' Arik winked at a girl, who missed her step in response. He spotted Nerisen. 'Oh good, you've set your sights on a girl as morose as you are.'

'Watch your voice.'

'She's beautiful, sure. Probably the best looking girl I've seen the length of the Plai–' His words trailed off into a smirk at Klaus' face. 'But pick one who dances. No … you stopped dancing years ago. Well, it's about time you did. Pick one who sings. Or smiles.'

Klaus held his tongue.

'Come on, Klaus. Lighten up. Can't carry all that baggage forever. If you ask me, leaving Dunraven is the best thing that's ever happened to you.'

It was a ridiculous enough thought that it was impossible not to be mildly amused.

Arik lowered his voice. 'I remember what things were like before the Eye took you. What's an Intelligencer allowed to *do* besides work? You couldn't drink, you couldn't even swear. You couldn't put your friend into the milkmaid or the tavern girls, though one or two of them were sweet on you –'

'Technically those laws are for all Ealdormen, not just Intelligencers,' Klaus reminded him drily. Arik made no effort to moderate a guiltless grin.

'It's a good thing Gerlinde wasn't hot for you or it would have been a prime waste of a perfectly good pair of hips.' He dodged Klaus' elbow. 'Start again. What would help you do that? Shaving your head? No, don't do that, it's one of your better features –'

He stepped out of Klaus' reach again and this time had the sense to hurry back towards the house, his laughter trailing behind him. Klaus smiled in spite of himself.

It faded quickly. *Start again.* Years of making serial sacrifices had left a cavity in his heart, but filled Afldalr. *So what now? What's stopping you now from starting again?*

He waded through dancers to Nerisen, producing an easy smile. 'Not celebrating?'

Now her eyes were as green as the hearts of those pistachios. 'I promised Thillaina I'd help her get home tonight.'

'Then why not join her at the banquet?'

She stood up. She couldn't have looked more out of place, with her faded shawl and wisps of hair escaping the braid hanging over her shoulder.

'Will you see her home instead? I have to call on Master Taslisem in the morning.'

Klaus bowed deeply. 'Of course.'

He returned to the banquet, where a lute strummed more sedately now. Leafsmoke and kahvi filled the air. Arik was in the thick of the laughter under the pavilion. Verdi had resigned himself to the scrutiny of Emra's guests, which Klaus supposed was exactly what the Elendrans had wanted for their precious trophy. Klaus joined Thillaina, who sat drinking with Saarem, of all people. He nodded towards the bride, now looking tired and a little bored.

'It's a beautiful piece of threadwork, Mistress Thillaina.'

'Of course it is.' She sniffed. 'Doesn't make her look any better though, does it.'

Klaus hid a smile. 'Ready to go home?'

'A Northern escort, eh? You'll set tongues wagging. But Nerisen –'

'Left early so she can call on Master Taslisem tomorrow.'

'Of course she did. He's barely eating. Yes, an old woman like me should have been in her bed hours past. I'll pay my respects.' She batted away Saarem's proffered hand, creaking as she rose, and shuffled to the Elders' table.

Arik took her place, mirth giving way to disgust. 'Are these Fraivonians so stupid that they believe the pirates have just vanished? You'd think they would at least want to avenge their losses.'

Saarem downed the rest of his drink. 'No one has an appetite for war, Master Marcin. Given half a chance, Elders everywhere will be all too happy to look away.'

Klaus only half-listened, thoughts pulled away to a pair of pistachio eyes and a poet's ode to the Silenced Daughter.

*

'What do you expect to find, Master Tristan?'

'I'm not sure,' Klaus told Ayla honestly. 'But one man is free despite the accusation of another who's too ruined to challenge him.'

Ayla was none too pleased at his request to inspect the place where Gerin Taslisem claimed to have buried his wife and workers. At first Klaus thought she would refuse, and was relieved when she relented. Her tumblers were sour-faced at being summoned so early after the previous nights' festivities; at least, until they arrived.

The carcasses of two upturned wagons were already half-buried in wind-borne sand. Scavengers had picked over the remains of several dead horses. There was no sign of Gerin's other wagons. Not far off, marked with a ring of stones, were the graves he'd gone back to dig. Something had begun to scratch at the dirt heaped over them.

One of the tumblers knelt over the mounds in silent prayer.

'We should make sure those graves are properly covered,' a tumbler murmured.

'Before we do that, can we ride on a little further?' Klaus asked Ayla.

Because, it was the road itself that had drawn Klaus here. Grassland soon surrounded them, thick enough to force wagons to keep to the road. But horsemen could certainly take a detour through the tall grasses. A couple of hours ahead was the unexpected finding of another, much smaller, wreckage: two wagons, stripped of metal parts and abandoned.

Raela shook her head. 'Never used to have so many raids on any road.'

Ayla looked around the wreckage. 'Do you think...?'

'That this was part of Laminhad's caravan?' Klaus finished. 'Yes. Not much of a fight here, though. Just looted.'

Everything he'd seen so far conformed to his theory. Eresk had arrived in Romel late at night, without his wagons; Gerin had been attacked the following morning. *Not by chance.* Klaus ran his hand over the side of one wrecked wagon; someone had burned away the name of its owner. The same was true of the second wagon. The tumblers watched his inspection in uneasy silence.

'What does Master Laminhad sell in Romel?' asked Klaus, having already verified this.

'Grain, green produce and jewellery,' said the other tumbler. 'He inherited his family's farms, but he's a goldsmith by trade.'

Klaus picked up a ring-shaping mandrel from the wreckage that looters had missed. 'A singular combination of wares.'

Ayla's eyes were as quiet as caves. 'If you've no more to inspect, Master Tristan, perhaps we should continue to Romel.'

When they arrived, Ayla stopped at the door of every surgeon, this time leading the enquiries herself. No one had offered services to Eresk Laminhad for an injured leg. Their last stop was at the inn where

Laminhad had stayed.

'Wait out here,' she told Klaus. 'And you, Raela. I'll speak to innkeeper Chaarim alone.'

When she returned, her mouth was set in a grim line. 'It'll be a slower ride back against this wind. Let's not hang about.'

The innkeeper had attested to giving Laminhad a room for the night, but denied there'd been a robbery at the inn. Laminhad had arrived dishevelled, claiming he'd walked to Romel after his horse had thrown a shoe.

'And the horse?' Klaus asked.

'Oddly enough, he didn't think Laminhad used the stables at all.'

Klaus was certain there had been no horse, nor a fall from one. His fears were now confirmed: Laminhad had encountered pirates on the road to Romel the night before Gerin was ambushed. They had relieved Laminhad of his gold, horses and wagons, leaving him unable to pay his workers on his return to Samsarra. How did one man escape pirates while another paid for it as dearly as Gerin had done?

'Do you think Laminhad bribed the pirates to ambush Gerin?' Ayla asked him quietly.

'No, I think he was ambushed by pirates first, when he tried to get to Romel to sell his stock before Gerin brought his. Then, to escape with his life, he tipped them off about Gerin's caravan, knowing it would pass that way the next day. All they had to do was wait for Gerin in the grasses.' Klaus paused. 'When you inform the Chieftainess, tell her to speak to his wife.'

*

In the morning, Klaus made straight for the lettervault, this time with as much trepidation as determination.

He found the door open. The bell tinkled as he entered, and the librarian appeared.

'Good morning, Master Chronicler.' The librarian removed his spectacles. 'Come in.'

The weariness of another dreamless night vanished. Wondering at this change of heart, Klaus bowed low and stepped inside.

'Come and go as you require,' said the librarian. 'As to your other enquiry: you are in search of a teacher, but it is not I. You could try the observatory. You'll find better scholars in residence there.'

It was old and orderly, hung with tapestries depicting greatbeasts and blueprints of the citadel's precious aqueducts. The librarian briefly orientated Klaus, who had a much different purpose now.

'Master librarian, do you keep any transcription of the Septentrional Scrolls?'

The librarian's eyes were a particularly piercing shade of crystal blue. 'Have you the courage, then, Master Invelmari, to break free from the bonds of your kin?'

Blessedly, he didn't wait for Klaus' answer. He led Klaus to a dusty bookcase, muttering to himself about the state of it. Then he left Klaus on his own.

Klaus carried over an oil lamp and turned up the flame.

This collection of Far Northern works comprised a small but broad assortment: handbooks on flora and fauna; expedition letters and explorers' journals; the sagas of barbarian tribes. And nestled amongst them was a fur-bound sheath marked: *'Invelmen Translations of the Most Holy Septentrional Scrolls'*.

The translation made little difference to Klaus. Intelligencers were taught as many Far Northern dialects as they could muster.

Klaus' hand shook as he reached for the volume. *This is treason.* He glanced around the deserted corner of the lettervault and pulled it down.

He set it on a lectern and gingerly flicked through the pages. Bizarre relief washed over him; it wasn't the full collection but a handful of excerpts, inexpertly sewn together as though hastily compiled.

Stop. A hot wave of nausea welled up in his throat. The march of black ink blurred across his vision. He couldn't bear to look at these pages. Perspiration beaded on his skin. Revulsion almost forced a gasp from his lungs. *Stop!*

Klaus shut the volume, returning it to the shelf. His skin burned where the fur touched his palms. Hungry for air, he hurried out of the lettervault.

That night he would dream again of a burning pyre atop the Sterns, lit by a pale-faced sorceress. He would look down from the pyre upon Queen Adela and rows of masked Isarnanheri, and feel his oath torn forcibly from his purging flesh: *Cometh the fall of the kingdom of destruction made if its fate is bartered for blood! To the dead we are bound and by our grace are the dead repaid... Cometh the fall...*

*

As though stirred by Klaus' torrid dreams, night also brought a windstorm that damaged an aqueduct.

Klaus spent most of his days duelling Arik's tumblers now. In combat, the Derindin had to wrestle with the desert as much as with foes, sometimes denying themselves water. He and Arik learned to drink when the tumblers did; here there would be no ice to melt. Daytime had grown cooler, but midday still sometimes seared the skin. Klaus knew the cold burn of joint-stiffening ice. He relied on that tolerance now to maintain focus through the stark heat and the dust-laden gales.

'In Invelmar, a warrior learns the sword in the mountains.' Arik drew his blade, Thunraz, for the first time in the tumblers' training. He faced Klaus on a rocky dune. 'It's easier to keep your footing on flat earth. In the mountains, it's another matter entirely...'

The citadel remained tense throughout repairs to the damaged aqueduct. Nowhere in the Plains was secure without water. Broco brought a great jug of derina sourbeer to their table in the tavern that evening.

'These days there's trouble stirring everywhere you look.' He lit his pipe. 'Babble says the Far Northerners are putting the hamlets around Malvern and Eisnach to waste.'

Hair rose on Klaus' skin. Ravi squeaked in indignation as Arik accidentally lowered a cup rather too quickly onto his tail, nearly spilling beer on the map Klaus was updating.

Arik's voice betrayed none of this. 'Unless they're bringing down the Sterns, "waste" is a bit far-fetched.'

'They've broken through Loggrwald's defences for the first time in centuries.'

'For the first time ever,' Arik corrected. '*If* it's true.'

'Whoever he is, this warlord's wasting no time on treaties like the last one.'

Arik took a swig of the sourbeer. 'He sounds like all the other barbarians. Those savages have given us plenty of practice.'

'Well, they've got Adela worried this time,' said Broco. 'Babble says both Wintermantels have left Dunraven for the Sterns.'

Klaus felt Verdi shoot him a nervous look.

'Wintermantels are next in line to the throne, aren't they?' said Saarem. 'You can tell if a battle's going to get ugly if a woman keeps to her man's side.'

'Or else she's keeping an eye on who else might take her place there,' Broco joked, to a round of bawdy laughter.

Klaus rolled up his map, rising. 'Think I'll get an early night.'

'What, now?' Broco looked at the clock. 'The sun's barely set.'

'Is this the secret to your steady hand?' Saarem waggled his eyebrows. 'Secrets don't keep long in the Plains, so whoever's father you're trying to hide from...'

Klaus winked to more laughter. He leaned over Arik's shoulder, murmuring, 'I'm going to the observatory.'

He stepped out into the cold air and fetched his horse from the tavern stable. He had no desire to hear of the Wintermantels, but more than this … the pang of not riding with them to the Northern border cut deeper than he could afford, even now. The Blood Pact had rescued him from selfishness once before, and the Blood Pact bound him still. And now he had deserted that sacred oath.

'*Your home is your heart,*' Master Arnander had instructed. '*This is the thing that must never be silenced.*' But all Klaus held dear was buried in Afldalr. What did that mean, then, for the condition of his heart?

Home is nowhere now, a bitter voice reminded him. *You are no one now.* And the only clue he had to help find his parents was a lump of iron. He couldn't imagine a more useless token.

A group of children scuffled outside the stable, cutting into this sinkhole of thoughts. Klaus spotted Fibbler in the tangle of grubby arms and legs.

Cheering onlookers scattered out of Klaus' way, though the culprits remained oblivious. Klaus reached down and prised Fibbler and another boy apart. They glared at each other, red-faced and panting like pups.

'What's going on, eh?'

The boy wriggled; Klaus let him go.

Fibbler wiped a bloody nose. 'I told them about the ice-plains, and they said I was lying. No one calls me a liar!'

'Only if you're telling the truth,' said Klaus mildly, swallowing a smile. Fibbler glowered at him, and their audience stood back in awe. 'Come on. You can help me on my quest.'

He swung Fibbler up in front of him, and they set off – with slightly too much flourish, to Fibbler's delight – out of Samsarra and into the dusk. The observatory was a short ride, though far enough that the citadel's lights did not pollute the night.

'It's a bit dark to go out riding,' said Fibbler uncertainly. Even he looked worried at the prospect of venturing outside the citadel at night.

'How else will we see the heavens? Don't worry. It's not far.'

'What will we do there, Tristan?'

'Speak to the scholars.' Klaus raised his voice over a playful wind. 'Chase stories of the stars!'

He was glad of Fibbler's company. Truthfully, Klaus would have felt foolish admitting to his friends the way the desert made him feel now. He couldn't explain to Arik or Verdi the lure of its open horizon, or of the splendour that coloured its past. He certainly couldn't confess the way he felt the gaping wound left by the desiccated riverbank, or the bards' haunting songs, or the scratch against his heart of the Derindin sorrow sunk so deeply into the sand. Fibbler still possessed all the raw and untempered wonder of a child. This itself was a comfort.

The round astronomers' tower soon appeared. Lanterns shone in its lower windows.

Klaus helped Fibbler dismount. 'Have you been here before?'

'Kids en't allowed up in the tower.'

'That's not what I asked.'

Fibbler looked shifty.

Klaus hid another smile. 'I won't be telling anyone.'

'I snuck inside Terim's wagon once, when he was here deliverin',' Fibbler admitted. 'I planned to get to the top, where everyone said there was a treasure … lost that dare *and* got my ears boxed.' He scowled. 'Still got nearer than them other kids, though!'

The doors boasted a chart of stars with alien names. There was no reply when Klaus rang the bell. Fibbler shivered.

'P'raps they've gone back to the citadel already,' he suggested hopefully.

'Do you know what an astronomer is, Fibbler?' The little boy shook his head. 'It's a scholar who studies the stars and everything else in the sky. They are the owls of the scholars, and to do their great work they need night.'

Klaus tried the door; it was unbolted. They stepped inside.

It was a splendid sight. A brass astrolabe adorned the wall, overlooking numerous quadrants and a lovingly enamelled orrery. Stellarscopes perched in sconces. Oil lamps lent soft company to a low fire. Most alluring was the winding staircase at the back of the room.

'Don't touch anything,' Klaus warned his young protégé, who immediately looked slightly guilty. 'If anything goes missing, you and I will have a very steep falling out.'

Fibbler nodded, wide eyed; this was hopefully too terrible a punishment to risk.

Klaus peered up the staircase. 'Anyone there?'

His voice echoed up and down the steps. A gust of wind was the only reply. He picked up a lamp and began to climb.

Niches in the stairwell housed more marvels: models of planets and cuneiform charts; clay tablets and celestial rocks. The staircase tapered into another smaller stairwell hewn into the tower itself.

'What if there's someone dead at the top?' asked Fibbler tremulously. 'That might be why they didn't answer the door.'

Klaus winked at him. 'Only one way to find out. Watch your step.'

But there were no corpses at the top. Instead, there was a figure gazing through the eyepiece of a magnificent mounted stellarscope. She straightened when they appeared.

'Ahhh. We have been waiting for you, Master Invelmari.' Her eyes twinkled. 'One librarian warned me a Northern chronicler might come calling.'

Fibbler drew closer to Klaus.

The astronomer stepped down from the telescope. Her bespectacled eyes were as bright as the stars that kept her company. If someone had asked Klaus twenty years earlier to describe a scholar of astronomy, it would have been this woman: white hair fell gently to her shoulders, and time had twisted her hands even as the turning of countless dials and charts had smoothed her fingertips.

Klaus bowed. 'I'm Tristan, and this is Fibbler. Forgive our intrusion...'

'How may I assist you?'

He glanced at Fibbler, whose fears had vanished at the sight of the stellarscope.

'A metalsmith told me of a place named Ettsrakka in the Silfren Part where an ancient starfall left a deposit of iron ore with unique properties.' Sudden hope swelled, gripping Klaus by the throat, and he resented its irresistible hold. 'In the Sonnonfer we know this place as a bloodland, rather than a starfall, and its whereabouts are unknown. At least, they're unknown in the North. I want to know where the star fell so that I might find the bloodland.'

'If Ristowin had no idea where it fell, I'm afraid that neither will I,' said the astronomer. 'Oh, do not wonder that I recognised his mind at work. Only one or two metalsmiths still reach such ilnurhin through their craft.'

Klaus' hopes contracted just as cruelly. 'Is this account true? Does such a place exist?'

The scholar looked up at the sky. 'It's true that from time to time the heavens walk upon the earth. My brothers and sisters have long recorded the wandering of celestial bodies that sometimes lingered as visitors amongst us. If the only mention of this starfall were found in your Sonnonfer and nowhere else, one might doubt its veracity. Fortunately, there are others who have written of it. Yes, it struck the earth. But what need does a son of the Forge in possession of Invelmari steel have of humble iron?'

'Not iron.' It was mortifying that she might mistake the reason driving his interest. 'I am a chronicler. I'm trying to trace a story rumoured to have originated from this place, Estrakka.'

The scholar peered at him through her spectacles. 'No one's recorded the exact location of where that star struck the earth.'

'How long ago was the starfall, do you know?'

'Go back to your Sonnonfer, Master Invelmari, and I will consult my charts. I'm no expert in the verses of the North, but they may help you trace this bloodland better than the journey of a star.'

Klaus couldn't tell her that he already knew every word of the

Sonnonfer by heart. Hope quashed, he risked one more question.

'Have you heard of Andaera?'

'Indeed, though alas I'm no poet and couldn't tell you more of her.'

So she doesn't recognise it as a constellation, either. And why should a Derindin astronomer know Andaera was in fact a family of Far Northern stars, if Ealdormen alone had been permitted to learn this fact from a guarded fragment of Septentrional Scrolls? But they were in the South now, and no knowledge was forbidden in the South.

Klaus bowed, waving Fibbler over from the stellarscope. 'Thank you for your help.'

'I fear I've served you little, but the teacher you seek is not I,' she said. 'It's the olive keeper you need.'

'Where might I find –'

'That I could not tell you.'

Form closed around Klaus' frustration. Fibbler was asleep in his saddle by the time they reached Mayda's door, as was Verdi when Klaus returned to their lodgings. But Arik lingered by the window, rigid with invisible strain. No Ealdorman was spared from the bondage of Form.

Klaus knew what was preying on the Warrior's mind. 'Do you want to go back?'

Arik didn't turn from the window. 'Even if barbarians *have* breached our northern defences, they'll be stamped out. There are as many soldiers in Invelmar as blades of grass.'

'That's not what I asked.'

Arik looked at him then. 'Can you really just forget?'

The question was reluctant, as if he didn't want to know the answer.

'No. But if I'm a corpse on the Wintermantels' battlements, I'll not be any use to anyone.'

Arik looked relieved, though he seemed unwilling to scratch any deeper. 'I took an Ealdorman's oath. We both did, but I wasn't forced to break mine. I chose to.'

'I know.' Fear knocked at Klaus' heart, and he wondered if the moment he'd dreaded since their escape had finally arrived. 'We also made a promise to Verdi, and he's not got anyone to trust but you and me.'

Eventually, Arik's shoulders relaxed. Klaus wasn't sure this would be enough to fully stifle the much deeper calling they had both known first. But for now it was, and he was glad.

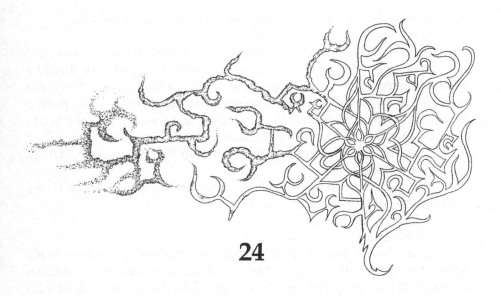

24

Sfarsgour Sickness

WHAT OF IVAR NÓTTSHIELD, WHO THOUGHT HIS
MOUNTAIN-IDOLS WOULD SHATTER THE ROCKS BENEATH
STURMSINGER'S SOLDIERS? HIS PRAYERS WERE NO MATCH FOR
THE SACRED STEPS OF JARNSTIGA.

SONNONFER: THE VICTORIES OF ANSOVALD STURMSINGER

Verdi stared at the gnomon lying on the ground. Four weeks, it had been in his possession. Four weeks of wondering how on earth he could possibly make the moondial appear.

Maybe if I find the moondial, someone else can use it in my place. A life in Samsarra, if he dared set root here, beckoned sweetly – if he could slip out of Lorendar's shadow. *If the three of us can stay here together.*

He'd been up long before dawn to try his luck with the gnomon either side of moonrise. Once again, he'd stuck the anchor into the patch of earth behind Thillaina's kitchen, where trees shielded her yard from the bedroom windows above. Once again, nothing happened.

A full lunar month had passed since he'd started fiddling with the gnomon. *What* must he intend in order to make the moondial appear?

How could an intention possibly accomplish this? He was a scientist; he believed in forces that he could see and test and measure. Or so he had been in Dunraven. Perhaps being in Samsarra had warped his formerly solid grounding in the rational world. Perhaps, had he been given the gnomon in Invelmar, he would have dismissed it as a charlatan's ruse.

But he couldn't ignore the unsettling desire the gnomon stirred in him even as he puzzled over it. He *wanted* to make it work.

Now he was tired and had nothing to show for another wasted morning. Frustrated, he hurried back into the house.

When he found Klaus still asleep, he knew something wasn't right. Arik had long left for the training ground. Ravi had taken up residence in the centre of Klaus' chest, though Klaus looked well enough. But an unexpected visitor intruded on Verdi's worries: the maid knocked on the door to announce that Alizarin was waiting downstairs.

'Good morning,' Verdi greeted him, conscious of his missing oceloe.

'Have a seat, Viridian.'

He obeyed, forcing himself to stop fidgeting.

'In a few days I'll take an envoy to meet Zakra, Chieftain of Sisoda,' Alizarin announced. 'What do you know about Sisoda?'

'They have strong warriors and the largest armoury in Derinda,' Verdi replied dutifully. 'And they're not on good terms with Hesper and Baeron in the west.'

'Paying some attention to Elder Maragrin, I see. You may find his teachings dull, but here's one instance where his lecturing will serve you well. Sisoda are all that's left of the last kingdom to fall before the Second Redrawing. It was Sturmsinger who defeated Sisoda's ancestors, not Lorendar. So Sisodans aren't entirely opposed to Merensama, although some of them won't be led by anyone but their own. The Chieftainess will ask you to travel with us. It would be far more convincing if you came not as our guest, but as an Elendran.'

Verdi was jerked fully awake. 'What? Why?'

'We need strong allies if we're going to root out the pirates. This will be the first time we have tried to bargain with Sisoda in generations, and we have something that may sway them: you.'

'Isn't it enough if I go with you?'

'We can't claim to be ready to restore Merensama if you've not even pledged to our clan, let alone taken Lorendar's oath or mastered the gnomon. You shouldn't need this explained to you like a child.'

It was always Alizarin; Alizarin who made him snap. The words came easily now.

'So that's all you really need me to be. A tool – to bring sheep to your fold and then be put away again until you need me to herd them. Well, I've no intention of doing that.'

Alizarin wasn't riled, but his eyes blazed. He stood. 'You ought to consider that the longer you remain here unclanned, the longer you make a mockery of your aunt and all our efforts. And I suggest you spend less time cutting up tubers and more learning to use the gnomon.'

Yet again, they parted in anger. Whenever Verdi felt closer to the Derindin, his uncle pushed him away again. But Verdi had more pressing concerns. He hurried back upstairs and found Klaus tossing in his bedsheets, perspiring heavily, a frown creasing his brow. Ravi jumped into Verdi's arms, frightened.

'Wake up.' Verdi shook Klaus by the shoulder. 'Wake up!'

Klaus' eyes opened but seemed unfocused, filled with whatever tormented him. He gripped a fistful of sheets, his voice a harsh whisper.

'I must find the healer.'

Verdi stared at him anxiously. 'Shall I send for a physician?'

The storm cloud across Klaus' face cleared, as though that invisible lever of his Form had been pulled. He replied more evenly, 'No.'

Within moments he was preparing to join Arik at the training ground as though nothing had passed.

*

Petra spread her wings and took off from Suman's arm.

'She'll be in Yesmehen within hours,' he told Emra. 'Your reply won't be intercepted.'

Alizarin was glad Suman had come to Samsarra alone. 'When will the Sisodans arrive?'

'Three days from now. But not at Yesmehen. They want to meet at Hawkswing Summit, no doubt to avoid spawning rumours.' Suman watched Petra until she disappeared. 'What will Elendra be prepared to give Sisoda in return for a pledge?'

'Give?' repeated Tourmali. 'Is it not enough that we're trying to root out the pirates, to everyone's benefit?'

'They're fighting to keep their S'beyan Strip out of the clutches of Baeron and Hesper. It would be naïve to think they'll be easily persuaded.'

Tourmali shook his head. 'We're surrounded by fools who can't see the greater danger.'

'It's in all our interests that Sisoda win that struggle,' Alizarin reminded him. 'If Sisoda lose control of the S'beyan Strip, Baeron and Hesper will finally share a boundary and we'll lose the west altogether. We must factor that into our negotiations.'

'We'll be splitting our resources even more if we pledge to help

Zakra defend Sisoda's territory *and* pursue the pirates,' Suman warned.

'The alternative is we fend for ourselves,' Emra replied. 'We *have* to consider offering them tumblers to help defend their S'beyan Strip.'

'We've helped Sisoda before, three hundred years ago when they pleaded for aid to take back their valley from Periam,' Fenral grumbled, who still favoured ignoring the pirates altogether. 'Their bloodlust overpowered their regard for the terms of our agreement. Do I need to remind you how they killed every man and boy in the valley even after it was won, and sullied our name? Periam have never forgiven us for that massacre. Sisoda's blood is too hot.'

'Three *hundred* years ago,' Maragrin repeated.

Alizarin's heart sank; this was an argument they had rehearsed many times.

But this time, Emra was resolved. 'There's no one left. We've appealed to those who've suffered most and failed. Now we look to those who are only just nearer to us in friendship than enmity. If we fail again, our only remaining option is to ask the allies of our enemies.'

Tourmali nodded. 'We must convince Sisoda: their real enemies now are the pirates.'

'Easier said than done,' said Suman. 'Baeron and Hesper have the strength to protect themselves, and the patience to wait while the rest of us tear each other apart.'

Emra looked around the Elders. 'Well?'

Willingly or unwillingly, they agreed: if Sisoda pledged swords against the pirates, Elendra would promise them tumblers should their defences against Baeron and Hesper falter. It would have been a momentous agreement had it not been forced by sheer desperation. Alizarin wondered how many more such battles they would have to fight with words before the first arrow was fired, and the answer left no room for even a feeble triumph.

*

It was difficult to escape the preparations for Winterfall feastday. They filled the taverns with the buzz of bargains and the streets with sweepers getting in the way of sellers decorating jaunty stalls and spilled into the workrooms of Thillaina's house. Apprentices and errand runners came and went. Nerisen brought Thillaina dyes, taking off-cuts or imperfect weaves of fabric for donation in return. She helped keep Thillaina's accounts when the work finally knocked the wind out of the elderly woman – though Thillaina was too stubborn to admit it – but otherwise kept to herself.

Klaus didn't want to study her by degrees from the peripheries of his vision, or through the inflections of her voice. But there wasn't much opportunity yet to claim his share of her green gaze.

'Who thought it would be clever to have a wedding two nights before a feastday?' Thillaina grumbled as the maid cleared away supper. 'One night of fanning and wining is enough for a girl, surely. Wouldn't they be better off left to their bed?' She raised one of Nerisen's bottles to the light. 'And I know you'd much rather be cooking up potions at that Arboretum than keeping an old woman's stall, Nerisen, but try not to be late tomorrow.'

Nerisen didn't look up from Thillaina's ledger. 'I won't.'

There was a clatter of cups as the maid overbalanced a tray. Klaus glanced up from his map and caught her blushing. Arik looked far too innocently into his kahvi cup.

'What's gotten into you, girl? Set that down. Yes yes, I know you're excited. Run along, you'll be pressing a dress and tying curls in your hair all night, I'm sure.'

Arik kept a straight face. 'Don't be too hard on her, mistress. At least she'll know a jig when she hears one, which is more than I can say for one chronicler.'

Thillaina raised her eyebrows. 'Not fond of a good tune, Master Tristan?'

Arik met Klaus' leaden stare with a grin.

'He's not to blame. Still pining, you see.' Arik winked at the errand boy. 'Spoilt princess of a girl, but yellow-haired and doe-eyed … skin like milk.'

Thillaina shooed the gawping boy away. 'Be off home too now, Nerisen. Long day ahead, though I'll warrant you'll be doing no dancing. Against every bit of advice I ever gave you.'

Nerisen shrugged on her coat. 'There's no time to waste.'

'However are you going to get settled, gadding around the desert?' Thillaina tutted disapprovingly. 'A girl's waist needs to be *seen*. Her ankles should jiggle their way with silver into a husband's ear.'

A hint of pink faintly coloured Nerisen's expressionlessness. 'Please set aside anything else you can spare. I'm making another trip to Cora before the storm season hits.'

Thillaina's prickly humour vanished. 'I wish you wouldn't go, dear.'

'The people there will be cut off all winter.'

'They choose to stay there and starve, and inconvenience those compelled to help them. At least wait until a caravan's passing that way and take your supplies then.'

'It'll be too late by then. Good night.'

Verdi waited until the door had closed after her. 'Where's Cora?'

'A valley hamlet on the northern edge of Fraivon's clandom, east of Lebas' land. Lebas have whittled away at it for years, but Fraivon won't let it go. The pair of them finally agreed not to take it by force in exchange for equal shares in its kahva harvests, but Lebas have spent the last few decades driving its people out, hoping to make it worthless enough for Fraivon to concede.'

'How?'

'Dirty tricks,' said Thillaina distastefully. 'Frightening away their cattle. Diverting the water supply until it was but a trickle. There are ways to destroy a place without a single soldier setting foot in it. And it worked; there's only a handful of people left – the others either starved or scattered. And they'll die there.' She nodded at Verdi's dismayed face. 'That's the soul of the desert, young man. A mountain of little injustices, all biding their time.'

By Klaus' reckoning, this put Cora to the south-west of Samsarra. Likely still quite east of the mine, but deep enough into the South that the idea of Nerisen travelling there made him uneasy.

'She shouldn't go south.' Klaus thought of Rasan, and *she* was a tumbler. 'Even if the raids have let up a bit.'

'You try telling her that,' Thillaina retorted as she left, genuine worry hiding behind her sharpness.

Arik yawned. 'Think I'll get an early night too.'

Klaus raised an eyebrow. 'You should. All that idle talk must be really wearying you out.'

'Oh, come on.' Arik looked back innocently but wisely kept a safe distance. 'Nerisen's hardly going to go snitching on you to the Spyglass for sneaking under Gerlinde's skirts. Wait, I forget – you never lifted a single petticoat, you just spent all your time pining.' He ducked, dodging a ball of wool. 'Besides, it does no harm for a girl to know of the rivals her admirer once courted…'

The feastday market began the following day at noon. Garlands of ribbons and sprays of eucalyptus decorated the streets and the market squares. Children darted about like brightly coloured mice; girls wore dresses of buttercup-yellow that floated teasingly about their calves, with broad sashes pinching their waists.

'Keep your wits about you,' Ayla had warned. She had doubled the guards throughout Samsarra. 'Winterfall feastday draws visitors for miles.'

They joined the festivities before dusk, when the market was winding down. Music spilled into the streets. Fibbler ran up to them in the market square, joined by a gaggle of children holding paper animals and hot nuts in twists of paper.

'Here they are! Here they are!' Fibbler whooped in excitement, echoed immediately by several others. Proudly, he declared, 'I tried to rob Master Tristan once, and he caught me the fastest you've ever seen. I reckon he *heard* me thinking about his pocket before I even got close!'

He spun in circles with his playmates until they were dizzy, running through imaginary tunnels within the crowd. Arik chased them away with a feint.

Verdi looked around nervously. 'I didn't think there'd be so many people.'

The three of them were a familiar enough sight in Samsarra by now, but a hush and stares greeted them each time someone pointed out the harbinger of Merensama. Klaus was glad when twilight fell, smudging faces in the torch-studded dusk. Hood raised, he wandered through the square, spotting Nerisen closing up Thillaina's stall. She wasn't wearing yellow.

He drifted towards her, mouth dry and pulse quickening.

'You shouldn't make that trip to Cora alone. It's too dangerous now.'

Nerisen looked up from rolling up a ball of ribbon. 'What would a Northman know about the Plains?'

'I know enough about pirates. If you must go, at least wait for a caravan.'

In the low light, her green eyes were olives and silver. 'I'll have words with Thillaina about spreading my business around.'

'I mean it,' he said quietly.

Her voice became less scathing at what she found in his face then. 'What I do is none of your concern.'

Now anger lent a gold glow to the impossible green of her eyes. Her hair was dusty and her apron stained, but she was the loveliest girl in the square.

Klaus bowed and walked on.

He wandered past acrobats and fire-eaters, and youths twirling yellow-skirted girls. He found a stall selling mulberry water and took a cup, reflexively glancing around to check Ravi was nowhere in sight. To his surprise, he wasn't the only Invelmari at the stall.

'Eisen's blade!' A sun-beaten Invelmari froze, his cup halfway to his mouth. He was as tall as Klaus and still had a smattering of red-gold in his beard, though his head was mostly grey. He grinned. 'A Northman, as the Derindin say, right here in Samsarra!'

He paid for both their drinks, batting away Klaus' coin. He was dressed like a Derindman, and even the contours of his Invelmen had softened, as though he'd spent many years in the South.

'The name's Adilmar.' He beamed at Klaus. 'I did hear a rumour of new sellswords in Romel, but that's not uncommon. Never thought I'd find one in Samsarra, though. Elendra's battles are few, and they're choosy about who they keep.'

'I'm Tristan.' Klaus clasped his hand, contented with being remembered as a mercenary. 'Have you been long in the South?'

Adilmar nodded. 'These thirty years past, and not once looked back in regret. Oh, the droughts and the winds are hard. But they toughen your hide.'

'What took you away from the North?'

Adilmar's dark eyes twinkled. 'A woman. What else? But she's long gone now. You'd do better to ask me why I stayed.'

Nearby a flute-player trilled, and a woman began to sing.

Klaus replied, 'I wouldn't wish to pry.'

But Adilmar was loose-tongued and all too happy to meet a countryman. The oil lanterns lent a gentle glow to the deepening dusk, melting away some of the years on his face, but his dark eyes betrayed his age.

'I was too lazy to return north, and that's the truth. Had a forge up in Herenburg, but after I met Herma in Romel I sold up and became a smithy here. Southerners love our work. By the time I lost her, the work was too good to leave. Then I met another woman.' Adilmar chuckled. 'Might sound odd to a young man like yourself, but there's much to gain here. Oh, the clans clash and clang, and the desert's a tough bird to chew. But there's no court, no blasphemy, no Blood Pact.' His eyes flashed. 'I joined a clan, and that kept someone at my back. So long as you're not Unsworn, there's naught to fear. My sons don't belong to the Crown and the air here is easier to breathe.'

Klaus feigned surprise. 'A clan took you in? An Invelmari?'

'Most of the clans don't care so much about who you are as what you're worth. And that the other clans aren't going to be better off for taking you in instead!'

'Which clan did you join?'

'Sisoda. They've a handful of Invelmari clansmen. They hate Sturmsinger, but can you blame them? If you mean to stay, Master Tristan, you ought to consider joining a clan yourself. Gives troublemakers some pause before they cross you. I only ever met one settler who remained Unsworn, and he's dead now.'

'Oh?'

Adilmar raised his cup to the seller for a refill. 'A sugar merchant who came south from Rainsthwen to trade Pengazan stock. How he managed to secure lodgings in Romel, I'll never know. It was exactly fifteen years ago, when my youngest was born. He used to come and go, even brought his son from the North to stay with him ... I remember his boy well – quiet redhead with only one ear.' He paused for a gulp of mulberry water. 'Anyway, he was a rich man but never joined a clan. Vanished one day in the middle of a big trade deal ... made himself an easy target. Unsworn are dog's meat. Do you mean to stay?'

Klaus' heart was racing. He kept his voice as even as his face. 'We don't know yet. Do you think he was murdered, this Unsworn merchant?'

'There was no proof if he were. That deal he never closed would have raked in his weight in gold. Why would he walk away? The son said his father had contracted sfarsgour sickness. Unlucky, because there'd not been a breakout of sfarsgour sickness in two hundred years.'

'Very unlucky. When did he die?'

'Thirteen years ago now. The rumour was someone finished him off to stop the disease spreading. His son went back north after that.' Adilmar tapped his nose. 'But if you ask me, I reckon he more'n likely got on the wrong side of a Baeronian and was poisoned … someone who wanted that deal for themselves, maybe. He'd probably still be alive, if he'd had a clan to avenge him.'

Klaus opted for the arrogance of youth. 'I'll try my chances for now.'

'Have a care, that's all I'm saying. What brought you south anyway?'

Klaus produced a care-free smile. 'Adventure.'

'A dangerous mistress. Not in trouble, were you?' Adilmar winked. 'Only half of the Invelmari around here are usually running from something.'

'Well, perhaps the angry father of a girl or two,' said Klaus lightly, thinking of Arik. He nodded at the singer. 'What's she warbling about?'

'The Ninvellyn,' said Adilmar. 'Everything here comes back to the Ninvellyn. She's the Derindin's open wound, festering for all time. You'll learn that the Derindin live yesterday.'

But Klaus' mind raced in another direction. *A redhead with only one ear.* He had no doubt that the sugar merchant's "son" was Clevenger Eldred – squire to Spyglass Adelheim – who they'd spied upon in the Paiva. Adilmar downed the last of his drink.

'Very well met, Tristan. Better get back to my caravan before it gets darker.' Adilmar grasped his shoulder warmly. 'If you ever find yourself in Pir Sehem, ask for Adilmar. We'll show the Sisodans the cheer in a good mountain tune!'

Klaus was finally free to chase the tireless cogwheel of his thoughts.

There was nothing noxious about Adilmar himself, though he was likely watching his own back. The secrets of Invelmari steel-forging were highly guarded, and the Eye scrutinised any Northern smiths leaving Invelmar. But the forging process was known to a select few smiths, and Adilmar would never have been allowed to leave had he been privy to such knowledge.

What was Spyglass Adelheim's squire doing in the South? Could his "father", this alleged sugar cane merchant, have been none other than Adelheim himself? Adelheim, who'd briefly been Adela's Spyglass following Master Arnander's retirement, had certainly died in suspicious circumstances. But he had died four years after the sugar merchant of Adilmar's tale, in his bed in Dunraven. Adela had appointed an undisclosed Spyglass after that whose identity was known only to her – the first secret Spyglass to be appointed in decades.

Fear gripped Klaus' heart. However long ago, a Spyglass might have been at work here in the heart of Derinda.

*

Verdi had never been to a fair where he hadn't been in attendance to Klaus. It was still strange to walk around as he pleased. This newfound freedom, at least, he cherished.

But Klaus had been gone a while. Mindful of his increasingly withdrawn behaviour, Verdi was troubled. Hood raised, he left Arik talking to the tumblers and slipped into the crowd.

Years of watching Klaus had taught Verdi how to disappear. A dancing girl briefly caught his hands, spinning him; he passed her to the next dancer. At every turn, there was something at which to marvel: snake trainers, contortionists, jugglers. No one noticed the heir of Lorendar. Briefly, blessedly, he was once again invisible.

A bard sang on a dais in the market square, verses punctuated by the strumming of strings. *Here we go,* he thought. *This is where he'll be.*

But there was no sign of Klaus' head towering over the Derindin.

Verdi couldn't make out the bard's words, but they undulated like the wind, snaring him.

'He sings of the fear in a mother's heart each time her children set out across the desert,' said a voice quietly over Verdi's left shoulder. 'He sings of the pain of parting with the river upon returning from the Paiva to the Plains.'

Verdi's pulse jumped. He glanced over his shoulder, the hilt of his knife already slipping into his cupped hand. A man stood just behind him, face hidden in the shadow of his hood.

Fear pricked Verdi's heart. 'That seems to be a common theme.'

A soft laugh. 'How do you like the South, remnant of Lorendar?'

Verdi scanned the crowd. Where was Klaus? Where was Arik? 'It's not what I expected.'

'And what did you expect?'

The bard's song changed into a festive chorus; his audience cheered, singing along. Now Verdi's cry for help would be drowned out.

'I don't know. I didn't expect to be known everywhere I go.'

'But you are not yet known,' the stranger replied. 'Certainly not by yourself.'

He turned slightly, and Verdi glimpsed a man in his middle years a little taller than himself, blue-eyed and handsome. His smile was clean, like the skin of steel. He nodded towards the bard.

'Now they sing of the joy of loved ones returned, delivered from wind and thirst.' Contempt darkened the man's voice. 'But alas, look at what awaits them on their return: misplaced faith in foolish Elders who let pirates run riot. They say you've been kidnapped by pirates, and that Northern mercenaries protect you.'

The hair on Verdi's neck stood on end. Something about this stranger felt deadly. *Where's Klaus? Where's Arik?*

A shout came to his right, then gasps. Verdi spun around, knife raised. Arik stood in the midst of the commotion. Heart galloping, Verdi pushed through the crowd and found one of the knife throwers skewered on Arik's sword, dead. Arik looked unharmed.

Breathlessly, Verdi asked, 'What happened?'

'He followed you when you snuck off.' Arik withdrew his blade from the dead knife thrower, holding his corpse upright. 'He stuck out. Wasn't as good as the rest of his troupe.'

Several tumblers materialised, shielding the body.

'Don't ruin your evening,' Saarem told the revellers. 'Trouble's already been dealt with.'

Only a dozen or so people had noticed the deadly exchange, swallowed up by the music. But it was enough to start the unmistakable smoke of a wildfire: *'An assassin, in Samsarra…' 'He was making for Lorendar's heir!'*

'Who were you talking to?' Arik asked.

Verdi looked around. The hooded man was gone.

The tumblers removed the knife-thrower's body. Trembling, this time Verdi kept close.

*

Verdi watched Klaus check the body in the barracks. He'd been far more armed than a performer had any reason to be. There was no mark on his shoulder.

Alizarin's anger at Arik finally broke, barely allowing his aunt a word in edgewise. 'You've been marked by that jemesh. How do we know he wasn't an assassin sent for you?'

Arik matched him for rage. 'He was sent for your nephew, not me.

That's who he was following. *Here*, in Samsarra, where you vowed he would be safe!'

'Half the desert's here for feastday –'

'Which means you should be trying to track down the pirates' ringleader to find out why they abducted him, if you really want to protect him –'

'Master Santarem is Unsworn,' Ayla interrupted. 'He's not under our protection if he hasn't sworn fealty to this clan. There is no deterrent to any attack upon him.'

Verdi shrank into his cloak as all eyes turned to him.

Remnant of Lorendar. The stranger's words echoed in his ears, rekindling anger. *Why should I be a shadow of the past?*

'I'll join your clan, aunt,' he said.

Silence fell over the barracks. Verdi's heart crammed into it.

'But I'll not take Lorendar's oath yet,' he added. 'And I'm keeping my guards.'

His great-aunt and uncle looked as stunned as he felt. Even Ayla seemed surprised.

Emra folded Verdi into a relieved embrace. 'It is done. The Northerners may stay as long as you choose.'

She swept out of the barracks with Ayla, and the tumblers removed the assassin's corpse.

Verdi sat heavily on a bench. Ravi perched on his knee, sniffing his hand. Perhaps this moment had been inevitable. He risked a look at Klaus, heart full of apology. But his former master smiled, and it made him feel worse. Arik squeezed his shoulder.

Alizarin was stony. 'I hope you know what you've promised.'

Verdi scowled. 'Anyone would think you weren't pleased.'

'Do you understand the risk?' Alizarin lowered his voice to a rough whisper. 'Sooner or later, the North will hear of mercenaries guarding a Derindman... How about you, son of the Forge? Will the mighty of Invelmar be satisfied with this simple station?'

Arik's eyes flared with the spark of Far Northern lightning. 'There's nothing lowly about protecting a friend.'

'You've been marked. Bounty hunters will seek you until the bid for your life expires. You'll become a danger to the very thing you protect.'

Arik pulled the jemesh from his pocket, now swinging from a leather cord.

'Then I'll draw them out like a poison,' he said, and hung it around his neck.

*

The feastday celebrations continued until dawn. Alizarin stood on the fringes of the night vigil and seethed. What were they celebrating, really? The inexorable grind of time without growth? Another year of drought? And now, a plague of pirates?

'He was here,' he told Emra tersely. 'He was seen leaving the citadel right after the assassin was intercepted. He *wanted* to be seen.'

Songs flickered softly in the darkness like the light of the street lanterns.

'We knew this moment would come,' she said.

'What do we do?'

'We must trust Viridian to choose his own way.'

A multitude of rebuttals were ready on Alizarin's tongue. That the man had no right to seek the child he had abandoned. That his sister would not wish it. That Viridian was better off without the influence of this man.

'The boy's not ready.'

'He came to us,' the Chieftainess objected. 'He sought us out at last. Of course he's ready.'

Alizarin rubbed his temples. There was no way he could admit Viridian's return was an accident. If he hadn't followed that blasted Northman, Viridian would have likely never left the Wintermantels.

'At least he will be protected,' Emra added lightly.

'By Invelmari steel.' The words sounded bitter even to Alizarin's ears.

'They've proven their loyalty, and these are troubled times. If Lorendar's heir must be preserved by the strength of Invelmari steel, so be it.'

Alizarin had never broken a vow in his life. He'd promised Klaus his secret was safe. But his mind strayed to the fears cowering in its darkest corners ... the hand of Invelmar, finally reaching for its missing Ealdormen, endangering them all by association – would keeping his oath seem so noble then?

He took a deep breath. 'Their assistance won't come without a price.'

But his aunt interrupted him. 'I had not slept easy enough to dream for twenty-four years, Alizarin, until the eve of your return. And then I found repose. I dreamed of a star with two moons in its orbit. And I knew tranquillity such as I'd never thought possible.'

That tranquillity softened her voice, and he was envious.

'Let them be, Alizarin. Let the pieces fall.'

25

The Selvaran Cradle

WHAT OF FREJVÖLVA? SHE SOUGHT TO DRIVE A WEDGE
BETWEEN STURMSINGER'S EALDORMEN, BUT THEIR FAITH
WAS MORE POWERFUL THAN A WARWITCH'S LIES.

SONNONFER: THE VICTORIES OF ANSOVALD STURMSINGER

The blueprints for the citadel's expansion were as old as Alizarin, for his father had drawn them. They also contained the most accurate record of Elendra's aqueducts. He and Meron surveyed the repaired water shafts serving the Arboretum. An experimental wheat field had dried out after the storm broke its irrigation system, but that was the brunt of the damage. With pirate thefts compounding Northern rations on grain, arable land was dear.

'They should hold up to another storm season,' Meron reassured him.

'With the cost of steel and fewer caravans importing it, they'll have to.' Alizarin returned the blueprints to Nerisen. 'I'm sorry the storm's ruined one of your trials.'

She gazed at the yellow field. 'I have more seeds.'

He spared her a smile; she was as determined as the relentless drought. 'We might as well archive these plans. As long as we're forced to hoard wheat and water and pay more tumblers to guard all this, not one foundation stone will be laid in our lifetimes.'

Nerisen rolled the scrolls. 'Maybe things will change soon.'

Alizarin noticed then the pendant hanging around her neck: a limolan seed cast in a resin, popular with many Derindin. *And I took you for a sensible creature.* But Merensama shone a flame for even the most sceptical of Elendrans, and Alizarin's misgivings were better left contained. Besides, Meron would disapprove. Theirs was a clan of believers.

Better to keep to facts instead. Alizarin cautioned, 'I wouldn't make too many assumptions about my nephew's long term plans.'

'He seems to like it here. Hasn't he just pledged to Elendra?'

Alizarin looked away; his relief over Viridian's clanship was laced with dread. 'He ought to be spending more time in council chambers and less on rooting derina shoots.'

Nerisen stiffened. 'He is kind. There are politicians enough.'

She rejoined the workers clearing her field.

Meron shook his head. 'Don't turn all my students as sour as you, Alizarin.'

'She has sense enough without any help from me.'

Like many of the Plainswalkers, Nerisen was what Alizarin had been twenty years before; hope that still dared, but only just. In another twenty years, she would be the mirror of his own despair.

But you've not quite despaired. A sage's words still whispered in his heart. *A man will die twice … a light so great, it shall illuminate the entire Part.* Alizarin glanced over his shoulder, half-expecting to find the sage, but nothing spoke to him now except the worrying of the wind.

*

There was no reprieve for Verdi. News of his pledge spread throughout the citadel like wildfire, almost dwarfing news of the attempt on his life.

Klaus' shadow had been an honour; Lorendar's was a foreign place. And then there was the added burden of an instrument he couldn't understand.

There would be a ceremony, Maragrin told him, to mark his pledge to the clan. He spent the rest of their lesson in a daze and was scolded mercilessly for retaining none of what the Elder tried to teach him.

At the training ground, at least, Arik kept the tumblers too busy for gossip. Verdi sat in the shadows, watching Klaus alternate between sparring like a mechanicontraption and waiting lifelessly until he was required. Verdi had lost count of how often he'd wished he could read the Intelligencer's thoughts, but had never wanted to more so than now. And in the evening, Klaus vanished.

'He's probably gone to the observatory again,' Arik reassured him, but even he seemed perturbed.

They returned from supper to find Klaus in Thillaina's house, standing by a window in the dark; the spirit of solitude.

'If this is how you plan to court that green-eyed girl, you're better off leaving it to me,' Arik joked.

'Do you remember how Spyglass Adelheim died?'

Neither Verdi nor Arik had expected this.

Arik frowned. 'You always said nobody knows what he took ill with. Why?'

A chill marched down Verdi's spine as Klaus related his encounter with the blacksmith at Winterfall feastday. *So this is what's been chewing at him.*

'How contagious is sfarsgour sickness, Verdi?'

'Highly ... so much fear muddied fact that whole villages starved during forced quarantines.'

Klaus nodded in confirmation of what Verdi was sure he already knew. 'That story Adilmar told me at Winterfall feastday ... this "sugar merchant" was likely Spyglass Adelheim, if Eldred was his "son".'

Verdi shivered. Suddenly the might of Invelmar and the tyranny of the Wintermantels breathed down his neck again. It was enough to disperse all Verdi's own anxieties about the gnomon and the impending ceremony.

'Adelheim may be dead, but his squire's still watching the South.' Klaus's voice was as colourless as the night. 'That's how they've been leeching information about this mine.'

'Clevenger Eldred? We saw him return to Dunraven with Ealdwine and the others,' Arik said stubbornly. 'And if Adelheim *had* been spying in Romel posing as this sugar merchant, it was long ago, and now he's dead. Put it out of your mind, we've enough to worry about.'

Verdi had feared this moment from their arrival. 'Maybe Samsarra isn't the wisest place to stay.'

Klaus picked up his coat.

'Where are you going?'

'To the observatory.'

Verdi shook his head as the door closed after him. 'The Eye's far behind us, but he's never been more an Intelligencer than he is now.'

Even Arik couldn't joke this away. 'He's going to drive himself insane,' he said.

*

Klaus sifted through the tumblers' tattle: Sisoda were considered Derinda's finest warriors, favoured blades before words, and were indeed the most accepting of Invelmari into their fold. But Mantelon were still none too pleased with Emra's plan to negotiate with the western warrior-clan.

Hoping to smooth any lingering friction, the Chieftainess' party first rode for two days to Yesmehen; a city that greeted them with the tinkling of hundreds of tiny bells. There was no applause for Verdi from the Mantelonians filling its streets, only hungry eyes.

'Lorendar is remembered even more fervently here,' Alizarin reminded them as they rode past hushed crowds to the Chieftain's palace.

Navein and his wife welcomed them with a banquet, gifting Emra with prized honey harvested from Mantelon's hills.

'Welcome, Elendrans, allies since the dawn of clans.' Navein's words were echoed throughout the hall. 'Welcome, Lorendar's heir, Elendran at last. May he know the best of health and serve his people well, and never be without *sehresar*. May he deliver us the sacred Merensaman phase of the moon.'

A passionate cheer erupted. Klaus felt Verdi contract beside him, his face burning.

'This could be so much worse,' Klaus murmured. 'Alfred Haimric could be dribbling into his drink in the corner, with Arnander skulking over us to make sure we're not secretly laughing at him.'

Verdi choked back laughter. He relaxed a little, but Klaus remained restless. He'd already solicited permission from Cilastra to visit Yesmehen's famed lettervault. He excused himself after the meal, pleading an ache in his wounded arm.

Verdi lowered his cup at once. 'I can take a look –'

Discreetly, Arik stayed Verdi in his seat. 'You're not deserting a feast in your honour.'

Klaus slipped out into the cold, fresh night. In Dunraven, Verdi had been his shadow. *Well, it's my turn now.*

It was a city of glass-windowed spires and garden sanctuaries; a warren of winding streets smoothed by pilgrims' circumambulations. The streets had emptied, but Klaus fancied he could still hear the silver ghosts of Yesmehen's bells. A quadrangle of wisdom enclosed the Chieftain's palace: lettervault, apothecary, startower, mechanicolodge. He thought of the four Forms of Invelmar and felt hollow.

He found the lettervault easily enough. Its open doors were lovingly polished and bare, the mystery of knots and knuckles of walnut wood surpassing the mastery of any artisan. He walked into its lantern-lit entrance hall and stopped.

It was marvellous: a honeycomb of reading rooms; staircases that dipped underground and spiralled up to reading platforms; a glass dome at its heart vaulting into the heavens. A handful of visitors kept to their perches like owls. Oil lamps burned brightly. A shallow stone basin of water stood in the central round reading room, and blown glass ornaments hung from the ceiling. Incense burned, doing little to mask the timeless smell of books.

Silence yawned around him; an invitation into pages beyond counting. Immediately, he felt at home.

'Who the hell are you? And what do you mean by frightening me near to death?'

A round woman appeared in the hall. She juggled an armful of parchments, her spectacles slightly crooked. She coughed, batting away as though at invisible cobwebs.

'My sincerest apologies.' Klaus bowed. 'I came with the envoy from Samsarra.'

She straightened her spectacles, eyes steely. 'We never had a guard at our door before Northern armies burned Yesmehen to the ground. But here in the South there are no barriers to the search for knowledge.'

Turning on her heel, she left him in the maze of books.

Now the silence stood over him sternly, pushing back at him rather than coaxing his curiosity; or perhaps that was his conscience. The lamps that had moments ago shone brightly now beamed their light accusingly on the crimes of every Invelmari to have trod in his steps. He had no right to go further –

'Don't mind Menal.' A wispy shadow of a girl emerged from behind a bookcase, holding a sweep as slender as she. 'She doesn't like strangers coming here, but she knows she can't stop them.'

She was probably sixteen or so, around Elodie's age, her pale blue eyes large and luminous. Unusually for a Derindin, a mahogany sheen warmed her dark hair. But her speech reminded Klaus of Niremlal's, the birdkeeper, as though she too spoke Invelmen rarely.

She cocked her head to one side. 'What would you like to see?'

'Everything.' A sick feeling wrung Klaus' stomach again. 'Although I was looking for some Northern manuscripts...'

'This way.'

She led him past row after row of books. Tomes and scrolls covered every surface; clay tablets and yellowing parchments sat protected under glass. He had never seen such organised disorder, and yet everything seemed to have a nook or cranny to call home.

She stopped in the north wing of the ground floor. 'Here.'

'Do you know if there's a copy of the Sonnonfer?'

'What's that?' She shrugged. 'I can't read.'

Klaus thanked her, waiting until she'd disappeared before he began his search.

It was an impressive curation. Despite appearances, everything was meticulously filed. He looked over his shoulder again; there were no other visitors in sight. He found the Sonnonfer, and then with shaking hands sought his real target. Sickening revulsion grew in the pit of his belly as he searched. His heart started hammering. *Wrong,* it screamed. This was treason. *Wrong! Wrong! Wrong!* Waves of nausea threatened; he grappled with his Form. *This* was its true toll; a dutiful Ealdorman would never know this consequence of defying such well-honed Form. *This is the free will I gave up for the Wintermantels.* But he had to know more; he had to help Verdi, the Derindin. Swallowing back bile, he searched on.

The next aisle housed Far Northern texts, and it wasn't long before he spotted it: a modest book of mongrel parchments, it pages mismatched as though painstakingly collected over time. The Septentrional Scrolls. Written in Far Northern, it was unreadable to most Invelmari and likely all of Derinda.

His hands shook as he picked it up from the shelf.

Selecting a volume of Invelmari bard lore, he sat down with both books and removed his coat. The script was small, but he was hungry. More hungry than afraid.

He slammed down on fear, forcing the might of his Form to serve rather than defy him. The hair rose on his skin as he stared at the humble little book his kinsmen had been denied.

Before fear overcame reason, he opened it and began to read.

*

Verdi sat back, forlorn. Arik was still talking to Ayla. *So this is what is means to be an heir. An ornament, to be kept in the dark until it needs to be displayed.*

Alizarin sank into Klaus' empty chair. Verdi straightened. Ravi's head darted out from under his lapel for a reverent glimpse of Saya, curled primly on Alizarin's shoulder.

'You need to remember you're no longer a servant.'

Verdi glowered. 'That's what you sent me to become in Dunraven, isn't it?'

'I sent you to the North to acquire a good education, which you have achieved, and some manners, which is up for debate. Not to go running off to patch up wounds.' Alizarin's voice was low and brusque. 'It's high time you carve out a future for yourself. You can't rely forever on two Northern guards. What if your friends are captured? Have you thought of what will happen to you?'

'Before I came here, I had a purpose –'

'You were a servant.'

'– I had a physician's apprenticeship!'

'Keep your voice down,' Alizarin warned. 'Your *friends* are trained survivors. That's the legacy of the North – to survive, like the mould on a tombstone. The day will come when one will realise he's not near far enough from Dunraven and be forced to flee this Part. The other one will be pulled back by his sword to their Blood Pact like iron to a lodestone. They'll not risk themselves for you.'

Before Verdi could find a civil reply, Navein called the two councils to attention.

'Tomorrow we meet with Chieftain Zakra of Sisoda.' His face was impassive. 'This is not the will of Mantelon. But you keep your promises to us, and we will honour ours to you.' He glanced at Emra. 'We've agreed: Mantelon will offer horses and weapons to bolster Sisoda's defences in the S'beyan Strip, but we can spare no tumblers yet.'

'Not quite perfect partners, are they?' Arik remarked when they finally retired to their guest quarters.

But Verdi's mind was elsewhere. 'Do you really think Klaus can stay here unnoticed?'

Arik inspected the lock on their door. 'He's an Intelligencer. I'll worry about that when he does.'

'You know, I always thought he wasn't like the other Wintermantels,' said Verdi after a moment. 'The stories they used to tell about the rage sleeping in Wintermantel blood ... he's far too mild for a Wintermantel. Even Elodie has fire. I never saw Lord Wintermantel angry, but I heard about it. And you knew he had it in him, even if he never let it loose.'

'Why d'you think most Wintermantels become Intelligencers?' Arik replied drily, shuttering the windows. 'As to Lord Wintermantel, everyone knows his wife's where he lets off all *his* steam –'

'Arik!'

The Warrior shrugged. 'Anyway, I just always assumed Klaus never showed anger because he's such a skilled Intelligencer. Form is all that helps the Wintermantels master the disease.'

Disease. No one but an Ealdorman could call it that and escape a sound hiding; perhaps worse. Verdi thought again of Elodie, anxiety mangling his stomach. He stroked Ravi's head restively. Ravi nipped his finger.

Timidly, he asked, 'Are you sure you don't want to go back?'

Arik straightened. 'Yes, you dolt. What's gotten into you?'

Verdi had planned to wait up for Klaus but, weary after their journey, fell asleep with the tinkle of bells in his ears.

*

Hours darted past like birds. Klaus only looked up when soft footsteps approached. Quickly, he replaced the Scrolls on their shelf and returned to the desk.

'Still here?'

The letterkeeper Menal raised a lantern. Klaus stood, closing the book of bard lore.

'I was just leaving.'

Outside, Yesmehen was bathed in dawn. He would have marvelled at its golden palette, but his heart was too heavy. He returned to the palace to find Arik and Verdi preparing to leave for the summit.

Arik raised an eyebrow. 'Were you at the lettervault all night?'

Klaus took off his coat. 'Cenric Eldred and Berengar Prospere were talking about the Septentrional Scrolls, not the Sonnonfer. That's where Invelmar learned of the mine.'

Arik's face paled. Even Verdi looked shaken, his protest hushed: 'But it's forbidden!'

'Yes, they drilled us to blindly obey. Like sheep, and kept us just as dumb.' Klaus met Arik's eyes. 'And we were stupid enough to follow.'

Arik stiffened. 'Loyalty to the Chain doesn't make you a sheep –'

'*Loyalty?*'

Verdi's eyes darted to the door.

Klaus forced his voice down to a furious whisper through clenched teeth. 'What good was loyalty when the Wintermantels decided they had no more use for me?'

His friends stared at him. Klaus inhaled deeply, summoned Form. What had come over him? Grown up and burnished between the iron cloak of his Form and the formidable lock of Afldalr, he wasn't given to outbursts. He herded wildling thoughts into calm, coherent words.

'I ought to have known better than to blindly obey.' He used to wonder about the Far Northern Scrolls, before the veil of loyalty fell over his eyes. *It was my own fault for not looking sooner.*

Verdi's eyes darted warily to Arik. 'Do they mention the location of the mine, then?'

'Indirectly. It was Sturmsinger who found it. The Scrolls are full of Sturmsinger.'

And what must not be known about Sturmsinger.

300

'Of course they are.' Arik had recovered his colour, defensive now. 'The barbarians never forgave him for driving them back into the Far North and deserting them to merge his army with our warlords.'

'Then the Scrolls should curse him, but they don't. They worship him.' Klaus looked around for parchment. There would be time later to interrogate his horror. 'The Scrolls tell a story about a strange rock Sturmsinger found in the South in a place called "the Selvaran Cradle". He ordered his men to set up camp there, because there was a water trough nearby big enough to provide for his army and all their horses.'

'A *water trough*?'

'Each night, the rock cast a spell over the camp, luring them to stay. Sturmsinger forgot himself – even forgot Dagmar, his own wife – until he realised the rock had bewitched them. He threw the rock away and broke the spell so they could finally leave.'

Arik tapped his temple. 'And now we know why there's no value in reading that rubbish.'

'The Spyglass' men found this mine *based* on that rubbish,' Verdi pointed out.

Faithful Verdi, always ready to defend me.

'I checked the Derindin's maps,' Klaus continued, dispassionate now. 'The Selvaran Cradle is a valley between two southern mountain ranges – standing *"a wolf howl's call apart"*, according to Sturmsinger. A place where there used to be a black rice grove – a thirsty wetland crop, so it had to have been near the Ninvellyn.' Klaus drafted outlines on the parchment. 'There's only one place where two mountains stand that close to each other along the old riverbank. It's past Fraivon's clandom, even further south than I'd imagined.'

Verdi's eyes widened. 'Where you thought the mine might be?'

'I think the rock *is* the mine.' Klaus circled the imagined valley. 'And the water trough is the spring – and a great one, to have provided for his whole army. Sturmsinger must have known it was a dangerous discovery and disguised the truth. No one would identify the rock as a mine unless they knew one was there. How many Derindin do you imagine can read the language of Far Northerners? And barely anyone does in Invelmar – by design. That's why no one's gone looking for it, despite it being described in the Scrolls for all to see.'

But Arik was resistant to anything to do with the forbidden Scrolls. 'Or spies could have found it themselves.'

'In a place so remote that even the Derindin consider it dangerous? Not likely. Even Baeron haven't tried to annex it, though it's near their territory. If you don't know about the spring, the place is useless.'

Klaus got up, pacing the room. Fragments of the *other* passages fluttered through his mind, like invisible bats, their unruly wings jarring practical thoughts.

'...*a cloak cut from darkness itself, that he purchased from shadow and donned to blot out light...*'

He throttled miscreant slivers of memory, bolting Afldalr shut around them.

Verdi stole another look at Arik. 'Isn't this a good thing? Narrowing down the location of the mine, rather than stabbing in the dark?'

Arik looked away.

'The Scrolls also describe how Sturmsinger died.' Klaus rubbed tired eyes, crushing the words still swimming before his eyes. 'Once the spell was broken, the further away Sturmsinger's army got from the Selvaran Cradle, the more they forgot where it was – except for Sturmsinger. He became obsessed with it and finally went back, and died trying to find it.'

'Oh, come on!' This was too much for Arik. 'Sturmsinger commanded whole armies. He died fighting – that's all we know from the Sonnonfer. When would he have gone off chasing fairy tales? If he *did* discover this mine, why's there no mention of it in the Sonnonfer, the record kept by his own allies?'

'Maybe he didn't trust them enough to tell them,' Klaus suggested. 'Maybe he was tired of war. Tell them there was more water in the Plains, after he started damming the Ninvellyn? Can you imagine his allies leaving it undisturbed?'

A struggle raged on Arik's face. Arik wore his loyalty like his armour. It would take a great deal to dent it.

'You're still only *assuming* the pirates have based themselves around this mine,' Verdi reminded Klaus. 'It would be impossible to build a stronghold without water.'

'Then the pirates must have found the spring that Cenric Eldred said was sealed.'

Arik wouldn't meet his eye. They quit the palace, the citadel once again chiming with bells as they departed. Arik finally broke his silence under the stuttering echo of prayers outside Yesmehen's gates.

'Why would he go back for a rock?' Desperation crouched behind his whisper. Klaus recognised it; desperation for the foundations upon which they were both built to remain unchallenged.

'For a mine,' Klaus corrected. 'He was a son of the Forge. Maybe it contained something as precious as Invelmari steel. Something worth hiding.'

Arik's face become foreign. 'Impossible.'

Klaus' mouth soured with unexpected bitterness. *What prisoners we are.* Arik hadn't batted an eyelid at fleeing Dunraven with him, but a glance into the forbidden Scrolls had shaken him beyond reason. To Klaus it mattered little where or how truth was sourced, but *he* had an

Intelligencer's agility. Loyalty had tried to get in the way and failed. But Warriors' Forms were grounded, like the rock. Fear tightened its noose again around Klaus' heart.

And if he had any idea of what else is hidden in the Scrolls?

But they were riding to meet Sisoda; these suspicions were better stored in Afldalr for now. Klaus hoped Arik would grow less angry with him for this betrayal, and more so with the Ealdormen for the truths they had imprisoned. He hoped.

*

The plateau of Hawkswing Summit afforded far-reaching views of Mantelon's clandom to the east and rocky yellowgrass plains to the west. The Sisodan Chieftain sat astride a grey stallion surrounded by his tumblers; a well-built man, younger than Klaus had expected. A great tawny eagle circled overhead.

Cilastra frowned. 'Where's Chieftain Zakra?'

'Zakra Raille is dead,' replied the tumbler nearest to the Chieftain. 'We've appointed Yodez Senned in his place.'

Derindin from all three clans bowed their heads.

'Forgive me,' said the young Chieftain. 'Chieftain Zakra fell ill two weeks ago after taking a poisoned pirate arrow. There was no time to send word.'

Emra pressed her hand to her breast. 'I am truly sorry for this news. Thank you for honouring his appointment with us.'

'Your clan has chosen well,' Navein rumbled. 'Yodez-hen, you've seen the blight of pirates. Our clans have had their differences, though we've not been enemies. We've no intention of living in terror. Will you bolster our alliance to root out the pirates?'

'Those differences are long in the past,' Yodez replied. Klaus watched his companions; the Elders and warriors who had elected him. 'But our situation remains what it's always been. We defend two borders from Hesper and Baeron, and we can't afford to look away even for a moment from either.'

Emra wasted no time. 'You have two other borders to consider, Chieftain, and we fear the pirates may be building a stronghold in the Far South.'

The Sisodans froze. Yodez exchanged looks with his companions. 'Impossible. Seasoned travellers can cross that terrain, but an enclave? The wind, the drought...'

Tourmali grimaced, still as unconvinced as these Sisodans.

'We've met these pirates, and they're an empty-headed lot,' added another Sisodan. 'Maybe they're too great a challenge for you Easterners.'

An Elendran tumbler hissed. Ayla quelled this with a half-turn of her head.

Yodez shook his head at his tumbler. 'For shame, Sarit. Many good people have lost their lives to pirates. But we've seen nothing to suggest that they're capable of anything more than raiding as they go.'

'What about those they've kidnapped?' Cilastra demanded. 'Or the havoc they've caused – paralysing trade routes, emptying winter stores?'

Yodez didn't budge. 'We're already stretched guarding the S'beyan Strip. I'll not dilute our strength and expose my clan to ruin.'

'And yet two weeks ago they killed your Chieftain!' Cilastra exclaimed. 'Was it in Pir Sehem they got him?'

Yodez's eyes flashed. 'Have no fear, we'll waste no time in avenging Chieftain Zakra.'

Emra tried again. 'We can offer you horses and arms to defend your borders, even if it risks Baeron's wrath. You needn't stand alone.'

A soft hiss rose around Yodez. He raised an eyebrow. 'Elendra promised us this once before. And when the time came for swords to uphold words, Elendra stayed back, safe in your eastern haven.'

'Shame!' Navein reproached. 'Many Elendrans and Mantelonians died protecting your lands. We honoured our bargain. And now's not the moment to dwell on a time before time. We look to the future.'

'Yes, the future.' Yodez's gaze ferreted past him to Verdi. 'I heard Lorendar's heir walks amongst you again. Have all the terms of succession been fulfilled? Have you found the Merensaman phase of the moon?'

Verdi's back straightened, ears reddening.

Yodez rode to Verdi and pressed his hand to his breast.

'Sisoda once honoured Lorendar before he faltered.' Klaus couldn't decide whether Yodez's murmur held more of hope or regret. 'You're young yet. If you can master what he could not, I wish you well.'

The other Sisodans remained impassive. Yodez raised his voice, picking up his reins.

'Do not let them know your fear. The pirates want to frighten us, but at their heart they're still a rabble. Sisoda won't be cowed. A monster's shadow can greatly dwarf its true nature in the dead of night.'

Navein's face was grave. 'Your father was a wiser man than Zakra. Think, Chieftain. What can you do, standing alone in the west?'

'We'll not wait for pirates to come to us.' Yodez's voice hardened. 'We'll root them out of our lands. But we'll do so on our own terms.'

He turned and his party followed, leaving the two Eastern clans alone on the plateau.

Sadness crept into Emra's voice. 'And now the beacon of hope in the West is extinguished.'

'How easily are the fates of men fashioned by folly,' Suman murmured.

'Do you really think you'll find the pirates gathering in the most unlikely corner of the desert?' Navein muttered to Emra. She made no reply.

Cilastra bristled. 'Can they really be stupid enough to think they can cull the pirates alone?'

Ayla shook her head. 'No, but Sisoda won't let anyone get a whiff of their weakness.'

'Our timing couldn't be worse,' added Tourmali. 'This new Chieftain has to please the Elders who elected him, and they have their old Chieftain's pride.' His eyes slid to Verdi. 'Though they may well notice one who's mastered the moondial.'

Verdi shrank away from their collective scrutiny. Klaus drew closer. *How he must hate this.*

Navein cushioned Tourmali's rebuke with a squeeze of Verdi's shoulder. 'I had hoped, Master Viridian, that you would have made some progress since our last meeting.'

'Even the sages struggled to move the moondial, and they had the best of teachers,' Alizarin reminded him. 'He needs time.'

'Time that we can scarce afford.' Navein raised his eyes heavenward. 'You've given us hope, young man, but I've not sensed such darkness as I do now.'

Klaus watched Sisoda's dust trail dwindle on the horizon. However clear stretched the sky, an invisible cloud seemed to always hover in its outskirts, and it was indeed dark.

*

Verdi stared at the gnomon, hands idle in his lap.

'You're still in your travelling cloak.' Klaus tugged it from his shoulders. 'We've only just returned. At least wait until tomorrow, when your mind will be clear.'

But Verdi's mind was a bit *too* clear. Every time he'd tried to use the gnomon, all he found was the sharp edge of the sundial by day and utter darkness by night – and the yawning cavern of his own ignorance.

'What am I supposed to *feel*?' Ravi squeaked as Verdi's fingers tightened absently around his paws. 'I've stuck it into the ground every other day for weeks – through every phase of the moon. It's just a bloody sundial!'

'Perhaps you're trying too hard.' Klaus picked up Verdi's formulary. 'It's not like a book to be studied, with answers spelled out. Where are intentions made, after all? Look *within*.'

'I don't have any intentions…' Verdi trailed off. *He mustn't know how much I do like it here … oaths and moondials aside.*

'Isn't that the problem?' The full weight of Klaus' attention always felt a little too exposing. 'You're not even sure you want any part in Merensama. Maybe the gnomon senses that –'

'The *gnomon*?'

Klaus tried again. 'You've been trying to coax an answer out of it. Everyone's told you it responds to your intentions. Maybe *it* needs to coax an answer out of *you*.'

The idea was ridiculous. It was the first time Verdi found himself doubting his former master, whose instincts were usually impeccable. *That's why I'm not getting anywhere.* Perhaps Verdi was more like his uncle than he cared to admit. *I don't* believe *in any of this at all.*

So he focused instead on things he *could* grasp: solid, rational facts. At his next meeting with Maragrin the following day, he felt no qualms leaving the gnomon behind.

'Why did Sisodans turn away from Lorendar?'

Maragrin didn't rebuke him for the interruption. 'That account will differ greatly depending on who you ask.'

Verdi wasn't satisfied. He recalled the parting words of Fenric's wife: '*If even Lorendar himself can be redeemed…*'

'Lorendar was clearly no saint. What about the time he shot the sage-bird down from the sky?'

Maragrin's scowl was dark enough to dim the room. 'Elendrans are people of method and reason, Master Viridian, unlike those led by hearsay and hope.'

'Hope is not a product of reason.'

Once again, master and student scowled at one another. But Maragrin's feathers soon settled.

'More useful is the story of why Sisoda grew distant from Elendra.' Although Maragrin had swept aside his scepticism, Verdi was eager to hear this. 'Sisoda are all that remains of the last Southern kingdom, and for many years a few of them have wanted nothing more than to rebuild it. Those dissidents became separatists and colluded to fracture Sisoda, almost destroying the clandom. Sisoda's Chieftainess called on Elendra's aid to fight their civil war. The separatists were defeated and their survivors defected to Baeron and Voista, but Sisoda's Chieftainess wasn't satisfied. She wanted them destroyed. Elendra helped root out the dissidents, but refused to lend arms to a revenge hunt that would have led to open war with the West.'

'Even I could see they've not fully forgiven Elendra for not backing their revenge.'

'It was more than three hundred years ago, and most Sisodans now will tell you it was folly. But enough of them still remember the day Elendra recalled its army back to the East on the eve of battle, once they discovered Sisoda's intentions had turned dark...' Maragrin pushed his spectacles up his nose. 'So you see, Master Viridian, there's an explanation for everything, if only you would stop interrupting and listen long enough to hear it.'

It was a tug of war at times, but in the end Verdi found himself burrowing under those stones he hadn't been keen to turn. He lingered longer in the tower room and regaled Klaus with Maragrin's lectures unprompted. Or perhaps it was all distraction from worrying about when his friends would have to move on, and from the dust now gathering on the gnomon.

Still the darkness grew in the air like a brewing storm.

It was inexplicable, because yet fewer reports trickled in now of pirate raids. A weary disinterest began to take hold even in Samsarra. Disheartened by Sisoda's refusal, the council's appetite to launch a challenge against the bandits abated. News of pirates was increasingly replaced by whispers of more unrest in the Far North. The name *Banasár* peppered more of these stories. Tumblers grew restive in their barracks; Arik reprimanded his tumblers harshly when they erred. Klaus barely slept and spent every free moment deep in his maps. And a week after their return from Hawkswing, Mayda knocked on Thillaina's door, eyes raw with weeping.

Cold dread flashed through Verdi. 'What's wrong?'

'Fibbler's gone missing.' She wiped one eye on her shawl. 'Nobody's seen him since yesterday morning ... it's not like him to spend a night out.'

'*What?* Where was he last seen?'

Nerisen abandoned Thillaina's ledger to bring her a glass of water.

'At Terek the baker's. He left earlier than usual ... he took a coat, he never does that.' Guilt wrangled with her brow. 'It's been getting colder ... I didn't think anything more of it.'

Verdi laid a hand on her arm. 'I'm sure he can't have got far.'

But she didn't look so certain. 'He's been running a lot more errands for that blasted Babbler. I told you I never liked him. A few times he mentioned leaving the citadel with the Babble, but he knows it's absolutely out of the question...' She trailed off. Discomfort writhed in Verdi's stomach, and Arik's brow tightened.

Klaus was fully present now. 'Did he ever mention wanting to go anywhere in particular?'

'North-west, towards Periami land.' She covered her face with one hand at the thought.

Arik squeezed her shoulder. 'Come, at least rest. If he's with a Babbler, he might be safe. They know the desert.'

'I can't. Terim's gone out looking for him, and I'm going to keep asking around. Maybe he'll turn up...'

Klaus stood. 'You go home. We'll look.'

But she shook her head. 'I can't bear sitting at home, waiting.'

She hurried off into the dusk. Verdi scooped up Ravi. 'Why would he run away with a Babbler?'

'Probably to prove himself,' Klaus replied heavily. 'I imagine he thought he was being useful.'

Verdi glared at Arik. 'Did you put him up to this?'

Arik raised both hands. 'I would *never* send him into the Plains with an ass like a Babbler.'

Verdi jumped up. 'Let's ride out after him –'

Arik grabbed Verdi's arm. 'It's almost night. He could be anywhere by now, and we don't even know whether he went for sure. We can't expose you to more danger.'

Instead they stalked the citadel on foot, asking after any sign of a small scruffy boy. Fibbler was as well-known as the citadel gates and rather talented at keeping both visible and invisible; he was either nowhere or everywhere. But Maida had been the last to see him, leaving home. Night was as perilous for grown men as it was for errant boys, and Alizarin instructed a group of tumblers to begin a wider search at first light.

When they returned to Thillaina's house, Nerisen was preparing to leave. 'Anything?'

Klaus shook his head. 'Can I go with you to Cora, Nerisen?'

Her startlement was quickly replaced with annoyance. 'I told you once already, I don't need help –'

'No, but I do. I need to scout the land, and you know the roads well.'

She considered him, her eyes lingering briefly on his open maps on the kitchen table.

'I'll think about it.' Her voice sharpened. 'I don't need a guard.'

Verdi waited until she'd gone. 'What did you do that for? It's not even in the same direction as the mine – if it's there.' He turned to Arik. 'Talk some sense into him.'

But Arik was smirking. 'I think he's being very gallant.'

Klaus ignored Arik. 'Cora is too north-east of the Selvaran Cradle, but it's still further south, along Lebas' eastern border. I may learn something useful.'

'Why don't we all go, then?' Verdi suggested.

Arik's smirk vanished. 'You're not at liberty to gad around casually, Verdi. You joined this clan, and you're no ordinary Elendran. Lebas spurned your great-aunt's envoy. As her nephew, you need to consider how your movements may be interpreted in their clandom.'

Verdi folded his arms. Anger seemed always just beneath his surface now.

Soberingly, Klaus' mask shuttered his eyes again. 'I'll see what I can find out.'

'You're not still serving the Eye,' Verdi told him irritably. 'You don't need to do this.'

'I'm a spy.' Klaus' brusqueness stung. He lowered his voice. 'If there's useful intelligence here, I'll chase it. At least I can still do that.'

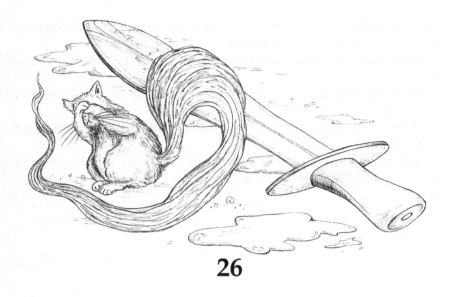

26

A Purchase from Shadow

WHETHER BY STEEL OR PRAYER OR DEAR SACRIFICE, WHOLE-HEARTEDLY
DID LORD STURMSINGER TOIL FOR INVELMAR. HAD HE NOT SWORN TO
SOOTHE EVERY ACHING BELLY AND SHELTER EVERY WAIF?

SONNONFER: THE VICTORIES OF ANSOVALD STURMSINGER

The night in Yesmehen's lettervault haunted Klaus like a ghost.

'*...a cloak cut from darkness itself, that he purchased from shadow and donned to blot out light. For the light came from within, and deciphered what his mind could not, but yet tore a hole in his heart that ripped his armour asunder.*'

By all rights he had no license to claim certain understanding of these words. But the first thing they summoned to Klaus' mind, as reflexively as breathing, was Form.

A cloak cut from darkness...

Form was a noble discipline; a programme of rigorous training that elevated Ealdormen in talent above the commonfolk, based upon the teachings of Sturmsinger himself. It was hard-earned through years of training both body and mind, and achieved to varying degrees of success. Form was an Ealdorman's inner skin; studied until it fused with one's being, never to be discussed openly with another. Even Form Masters – nobles chosen by the Ealdormen for their skill – did not know the nature of an Ealdorman's final Form. But Klaus recognised what he found in this passage from the Septentrional Scrolls at once: *Form.*

It felt wrong, *intrusive*, to read about another's Form, but Klaus couldn't resist his questions: had Ansovald Sturmsinger acquired Form through ignoble means? His hold over the strongest of the Northern tribes had been legendary. From what 'shadow' had he purchased this strength?

Perhaps if he'd never set foot into Derinda, Klaus might have been less troubled by this question. There had been no place for *demons* in Invelmari thought. Now he wondered what shadows Sturmsinger had borrowed and what light he had sought to smother – and recoiled.

I have no right to it now. He was not an Ealdorman; Form should be forbidden to him now. But he could no more dissociate from his Form than he could shed his skin. Guilt whittled away at him in dreams where he was banished to the light-forsaken Northlands beyond the Sterns; abandoned to the toxic fumes of lavafields. Guilt for having Form, and for seeking the Septentrional Scrolls. *You should not have looked.* The voice scolded him; scalded him. A voice that had been nurtured within him and was not his own, but scald it did.

Certainly, Arik's distance was scalding. Klaus no longer knew what kept his oldest friend at bay: Klaus' betrayal, or his discovery.

'I think he feels guilty about Fibbler,' Verdi confided. 'He practically directed him to messing around with the Babble…'

It had been two days now since the little boy had last been seen. Dark thoughts of Fibbler being snatched by pirates lurked in the recesses of Klaus' mind. But there'd been no pirate sightings around Samsarra. Neither was there any word of Rasan.

After another restless night, Arik and Verdi had again left for the training grounds without him. Nerisen's arrival at Thillaina's house, cloaked with a sand-mask loose about her neck, jerked Klaus out of his thoughts.

'If you still want to go to Cora, we're leaving now.'

She hoped I'd reconsider, with such short notice. But he needed little preparation.

'I'll saddle my horse.'

Nerisen followed Klaus' gaze to a second rider waiting outside. 'Pulgo's returning home. His village is on the way.'

Klaus readied his pack and left a note for his friends, hoping they would forgive him.

*

Pulgo was a dumpling of a youth who, swaddled in a heavy coat, looked rather like a roosting bird perched on his horse. He spoke broken Invelmen and was fascinated by the Northerner.

He watched Klaus note readings from his compass. 'What are you doing?'

'Mapping,' said Nerisen. Pulgo gaped. 'Will you be long? We're losing daylight.'

Klaus kept his recordings to a minimum after that. It was difficult to resist watching her. She was a natural rider and had planned her route expertly to avoid wind-damaged roads and shingle fields that tired the horses. Her knowledge of the desert was expansive, sourcing with ease the most abundantly cropping derina bushes or astringent herbs for her pack. She read her wind-gauge swiftly. But she said as little as she could and was as unreadable as the yawning sky. Fortunately, Pulgo kept up a cheerful monologue that teased out the odd laugh, goading Nerisen's panfarthing Onax until he sulked into her saddlebags and re-inventing Derindin ballads.

They rode south, then veered east. So deep into winter, the desert was now cold even by day. Dust shimmered over the ground, darting fitfully like packs of wind-rats, and a watery-eyed sun diluted the blue of the sky. Dry shrub and cottonwood trees dotted the dunes. They stopped to gather derina when they found it, for the desert here was too untrustworthy, Nerisen warned. They passed two dead wells, their chain pumps looted. None of it escaped Klaus' map.

The Plains became hilly as they passed through the northern tip of Mantelon's clandom; both a blessing and a worry, for the rocks and dunes provided as much cover for them as it would for bandits. Klaus' unwavering caution dented even Pulgo's cheer.

'If I didn't know any better, I'd say you were worried about pirates,' Pulgo jested.

Klaus didn't reply, scanning the desert.

Pulgo's smile faltered. 'We've not seen much of pirates down here.'

'Then you've been fortunate.'

Pulgo's face fell. 'They're saying Elendra will round up the pirates soon, and that'll be the end of them.'

'I wouldn't listen too much to what they say in the taverns.'

This put paid to Pulgo's light-heartedness, and they lapsed into uneasy silence.

As dusk approached, Nerisen took a detour east. 'There's a ruin here where we can make camp.'

Pulgo looked worried. 'The old temple? But it's – the villagers say it's...'

'Possessed?' Nerisen raised an eyebrow. 'What's worse, camping out in the open wind with raiders waking you up in the morning, or in a shelter where we can have a fire? Come on, it gets dark quickly now.'

It was refreshing not to be told to shun a ruin, and Klaus had no appetite for a long night watch in the cold. The temple was an elongated structure built into the hillside like a half-exposed burrowing worm, its windows shuttered. Their tired horses, nimble as goats in Mantelon's hills, now picked their way gingerly through rubble. Nerisen led them into the back of the ruined temple where their fire wouldn't glow through cracks in the shutters. She had clearly used the place before; there was a pot, a lantern and a bottle of lamp-oil hidden behind a pillar, and a handful of used candles.

Klaus noticed she checked the dust coating these before touching them herself. 'Sure the pirates won't have the same idea?'

Pulgo stumbled in alarm.

Nerisen was unperturbed. 'Even pirates are superstitious, like everyone else.'

But not you. Klaus unsaddled his horse. 'What's a temple doing here, in the middle of nowhere?'

Nerisen lit the lamp. 'There used to be a river here, and a watermill. The temple was abandoned when the river dried up.'

Klaus helped Pulgo rub down and feed the horses, then familiarised himself with the site before darkness fell.

'Why did you leave the North?' Pulgo asked over their lamh'met, short legs crossed around his bowl; a reminder of Fibbler that brought a pang to Klaus' chest.

'To help a friend.'

'Lorendar's heir...' Awe crept into Pulgo's voice. 'My village has been waiting for Merensama for an awful long time.'

'They may be waiting forever,' murmured Nerisen.

Klaus glanced up at her from his map. 'You don't believe it's possible?'

That Derindin shutter in her eyes remained closed. 'It'll take a lot more than an ancient banner to bring the clans together.'

'Invelmar was nothing more than a handful of warring tribes once,' he pointed out. 'They were no different to what the clans are now.'

'And it took a bloodbath to unite them.'

Pulgo chewed another mouthful. 'What's the North like?'

'Beautiful.' Unexpected pain shook the confines of Afldalr, and momentarily Klaus' Form faltered. He willed it quiet.

'Even with the Blood Pact hanging over your head?' Pulgo wondered.

'It keeps people safe.'

'They don't mind living in an open cage?' Disdain coloured Nerisen's question.

Klaus met her eyes over the fire. 'They're safe. And for that they're grateful.'

Pulgo looked between them, fidgeting with his bowl. 'How do you like the lamh'met? My village makes this one.'

Klaus softened his tone. 'It's excellent. Kept us going on the caravan.'

This cheered Pulgo. 'When will you go back to the North?'

'I don't know that I will.'

He forced himself to avoid looking at her after that. In the warm firelight she was beautiful in a visceral way that made his pulse jump and his stomach tighten. He focused on updating his map. He'd found places on the parchment for the estimations he'd derived from the Septentrional Scrolls: the Mengorian mountains in the south-west; the smaller Ilmaz range to the east; the Selvaran Cradle burying Sturmsinger's rock lying *'a wolf's howl'* somewhere between the two, along the carcass of the slaughtered river. Palms itching, he brushed the empty expanse waiting further south. Nerisen looked in on the horses, and Pulgo's head began to nod. She drew a cloak over him when he started snoring.

Klaus picked up his sword. 'I'll keep watch.'

'When will you rest?'

'In Cora.'

Klaus settled behind the remains of a low wall outside the temple, affording views over the desert. The cold was clean; biting. He'd kept countless night watches before, but none had been so lonely – not even in the Sterns. An overcast sky dimmed the stars, and the smothering curtain of darkness upon darkness threatened to grind him into the sand with its weight. Silence engulfed him, but was soon scuffed with dozens of little noises: the scuttle of little reptiles; the scratchy shuffle of sandfish; the sudden ruffle of feathers as nightbirds pounced on unsuspecting prey. He leaned back against the wall and closed his eyes, and thought of the men and women who must have once tended the temple, imagining every solemn step and secret prayer that had visited this place when the hillside was still green and the river had babbled through the rocks.

His eyes flew open.

Something had pushed back against his thoughts.

There it was: a distant yet visceral nudge, as though the desert had stirred from slumber with a long shuddering breath and turned its colossal attention towards him.

He was suddenly certain he was no longer alone. The skin of his palms thrilled where they rested on the ground. Sensations that were not his rose gently amongst his thoughts – sensations of the sky, the sand, the stones.

Klaus closed his eyes. Opened them again. The ground was hard, his hands freezing. *I am definitely awake.*

Transfixed, he lay back and spread his fingers over the sand.

The feeling returned more slowly, unravelling into as many sensations as the innumerable roots he could now sense in the ground below – their meandering paths; the vibrations in the earth generated by the unseen beasts creeping through them.

He *felt* rather than thought these things, molecules of foreign emotion dissolving into his bloodstream. The land remembered itself to him, and he listened with an impossible inner ear.

He felt the dead roots of trees that had once sheltered the river. He felt cavities and crevices in the rock encrusting fossilised skeletons. He felt the overwhelming thirst permeating every grain of sand. And sorrow – a deep and aching sorrow that clawed into the belly of the earth itself.

He had not knowingly asked any questions, but he was sure this little patch of land had replied: *Here I am. This is what I have been.*

Klaus' heart pounded. This was no dream. He had never been more awake in his life.

He would, however, soon fall asleep, his native mind mingling with that of the desert. The biting pre-dawn cold would wake him to a crisp sky and a clear morning strained of the murk of that starless night. Later, he would remember the strange connection he'd made with the land at the ruined temple, not unlike the one he'd briefly grasped racing towards Ahravel with a wounded boy. All this he would remember, but not just yet.

*

Arik loathed the Babble. But even he recognised the hallmarks of truth in the tattered remains of this story that had trundled from one end of the Part to the other.

He listened through the adornments to the Babblers' patchwork tale in the tavern: rumours of an army amassing in Samaragdtal, a particularly vulnerable valley near Invelmar's fortress at Eisnach. If he had to answer the unthinkable question of where Invelmari defences would crack first, this would have been his guess. Again, there was the whisper of this so-called overlord Banasár, who had tamed enough barbarians that his name now travelled from the Sterns to the South.

This whisper troubled Arik most. Anyone who could unite some of the fiercest Far Northern tribes was a force to be reckoned with. Wasn't that how Sturmsinger forged Invelmar? Bloody barbarians. Again he pushed away thoughts of their Septentrional Scrolls – the Scrolls that apparently dared to speak more of Sturmsinger than the Sonnonfer itself.

Intelligencers sacrifice all manner of things for triumph. Even knowing this, Arik was still smarting over Klaus' readiness to trust those cursed pages.

When they thought he wasn't listening, the Derindin recounted the rumoured battle in Samaragdtal with derision, celebrating any thorn in the side of their oldest enemy.

'What do they hope will happen?' Arik threw his coat off furiously back in their lodgings. 'That Invelmar will be crushed and vengeance will be served? Who do they think the Far Northerners will come for next?'

'They're just ordinary folk,' Verdi soothed. 'They speak before they think. Every man is the same when you put him in company with a drink in his hand.'

This did nothing to diffuse Arik's anger. If anything, he felt more alone. Verdi was spending more time in the Arboretum, oblivious to the fact this was as much an effort to bury his growing attachment to Derinda as to escape waiting for Klaus' return from Cora.

Klaus' note was still lying on the table. *'Going to Cora. Keep him close.'* Worry twisted Arik's gut.

I should be glad at least one of us has the right Form for trickling into places I swore to shun. Wasn't that the difference between a Warrior and an Intelligencer? A Warrior's code of honour was no measuring stick for a spy. Mistress Lisbeta's warning whispered in his mind again: *'Souls flayed away so cleanly, they might as well have been born without them.'*

Arik realised there was another note on the table, sealed with wax and simply marked *'Marcin'*. Verdi was too distracted keeping Ravi off his book to notice Arik pick it up and break the seal.

It was brief. Arik read it twice. There was no signature, only: *'It would be best that none know from whom you learned this.'*

Even his formulary could only hold Verdi for so long. 'What if Klaus runs into more pirates?'

Arik slipped the note into his pocket.

'Don't worry.' His reassurance was as much for himself as it was for Verdi. 'I feel more sorry for whoever crosses his path. He'll be safe.'

*

On the fourth noon, not far from Pulgo's village, a horrible discovery awaited them.

Onax had darted under Nerisen's cloak, setting off alarm bells in Klaus' head.

He pulled on his reins and looked around. They were in a rugged region of Fraivon, scattered with bare trees and rocky mounds that raised misshapen heads out of the ground, providing many a hiding place. Nothing looked out of sorts except for the body splayed over a large boulder ahead.

'Oh...' Pulgo heaved, throwing up by the road.

Pale-faced, Nerisen dismounted and approached the boulder. It swarmed with flies. Klaus held back, sword drawn, eyes combing the surrounding hills. 'How long's it been there?'

Her voice quivered. 'At least a day.'

Satisfied they were alone, he dismounted. The victim had been only a youth, and his clothes had an unmistakable look.

Klaus fingered the tassel fringing his coat. 'A Babble?'

The smell was getting the better of her. She stepped back, taking deep breaths. The desert was hard, but even she wasn't used to this.

Klaus helped Pulgo dismount. 'Don't look.'

Pulgo nodded, risking a sip from his waterskin. The helpless slump of the amiable villager's shoulders beneath his patched and worn-out coat tugged at Klaus' heart.

Nerisen wrapped her arms around herself. 'What shall we do?'

Her lower lip trembled, but she refused to look away from the youth. Klaus turned his body over; his colourful tunic was stiff with dried blood and his face and trunk had taken the brunt of his injuries. But an arrowhead was also embedded in one of his shoulders. His purse and smokeleaf tin had not been looted. His legs were swollen and purple, and his boots were far more worn than the rest of his clothes. His waterskin was dry.

'He might have just fallen from those hills after he was hit.' Klaus looked up; a half-dazed wounded wanderer could have stumbled. 'Pirates would have robbed him. Looks like he'd been walking for a while. Heading north-east, I should think.'

'Why do you say that?'

'His legs. No pack, no water, no horse ... That wound's had time to fester but it probably wasn't enough to kill him.' Klaus stood up. 'And the right of his face caught more of the sun. He may have been running away from whoever shot him.'

Nerisen looked up at the hills, shielding her eyes. 'Pirates?'

'Who knows? Babblers win themselves no favours with their talk.'

'I suppose. Nasty lot of trouble-makers, mostly.' But she touched his dead hand with tenderness. 'I'm sure I've seen him in Samsarra...'

Klaus saw the same unpleasant thought surface in her eyes: what if this was the Babbler who'd lured Fibbler out of Samsarra?

He pulled the body down off the boulder.

'What are you doing?'

'Burying him. I'm not leaving him here for the flies.'

Baked by summer, the ground was now hardened by the dry cold of the Derindin winter. It took the better part of an hour to dig deeply enough. Nerisen didn't comment when Klaus murmured an Invelmen prayer.

Pulgo finally broke his queasy silence. 'Nothing like this has ever happened around here.'

Klaus mounted his mare. 'This is just the beginning.'

Pulgo gaped, returning to his horse without another word.

'Why did you tell him that?' Angry tears were trapped in Nerisen's eyelashes. 'Can't you see he's terrified?'

'Because he needs to be afraid,' Klaus told her bluntly. 'They all do. Only then will they begin to protect themselves.'

Pulgo's village was only a few hours away. Pulgo brightened at the sight of the small stone houses enclosed by pomegranate trees. Camel-goats and cows grazed in small fields, and a grizzled man sat on a stool keeping watch over their well. He jumped up at the sight of Pulgo and tipped his hat to Nerisen, now ringed by a flock of excited children. His eyes bulged as Klaus lowered his hood.

Soon, half the village had gathered around them. Pulgo's parents spent winter making the lamh'met Pulgo sold in the citadels all summer. Their warm greetings turned to horrified dismay upon hearing about the dead Babbler. They watched Klaus with wary fascination. Some of their Derindask was too regional for him to make out.

Nerisen was keen to leave, but Pulgo's parents insisted on serving them food. 'He's told them you guard Lorendar's heir.'

'Please don't trouble yourself,' Klaus urged Pulgo's mother in Romelian Derindask. 'We still have a long ride before nightfall.'

She wrapped a loaf of bread for them to take instead. Her chatter needed no translating; he was the Northerner who'd escorted her son home through a danger that had killed a Babble.

Klaus glanced around the little village square. Several buildings were dedicated to making the villagers' famed lamh'met. 'Do they keep carrier birds here? If there's anything else untoward, tell them to send word to Samsarra.'

'This isn't Elendran land,' she reminded him.

'I know. And tell them to watch over the hills, not just the water.'

One of the older men muttered, and Pulgo turned a little pink.

'He says they've little enough for the raiders to take.' Nerisen didn't translate her sharp Derindask reply. There was clearly disagreement about the pirates even here.

Klaus slipped a little of his Form into his face for the villagers to feel. 'Then tell them the pirates are taking slaves. If they value nothing else, at least they have their freedom.'

Her eyes widened a fraction; so far this had only been a rumour. The villagers looked aghast at the possibility. Now he was the Northerner who had brought fear to their meagre lot.

Pulgo looked shyly at Klaus. 'Father asks if you'll at least drink from our well before you go?'

It was the dearest gift the village could have offered. The water was cool and fresh; a jolting reminder of home. Klaus bowed before remounting his horse. The villagers gathered to see them off.

'How many settlements are there like this one?'

Nerisen picked up a south-westerly road. 'There are as many Derindin in the hamlets as in Samsarra. As many again roam the desert, following the derina trail for water.'

Keeping the Derindin safe seemed almost impossible.

'Caravans have halved since the raids intensified, and it's caravans that buy the most lamh'met from villages like this one.' Nerisen expertly guided both her own horse and the pack horse carrying the donations she'd brought. 'Many people are too scared to travel now. Pulgo's folk will discover soon that it's going to be a lean winter.'

Klaus didn't reply. Inside his pocket, Elodie's trinket box was missing another tiny stone, this one the coveted blue of a twilit sky, of a variety that had been mined to extinction in the Plains. Pulgo would find it safely wrapped in his saddlebag. But all the gold it would bring wouldn't protect these people from what Klaus feared most.

*

Arik wasn't expecting the Chieftainess' summons.

It was the first time they'd been alone together. It felt wrong. In Invelmar, a chaperone would have been present.

Emra received him under the fig tree in her courtyard. 'I wasn't sure you would come.'

Arik bowed, glancing at an open letter in her hand.

'No good news,' she said, following his eyes. 'Raids in the west of Lebas' clandom. Several granaries emptied. Pirates even took a retired Elder's widow.' She folded the letter. 'Periam are missing two caravans intended to restock their winter grain stores. *That* I only learned from Lebas, because the Lebasi tumblers Periam hired to escort those caravans were killed.'

A *'bad season'*, Arik thought scornfully. *They're all fools to imagine the lull in raids was anything more than a brief respite.*

'Send reinforcements to Lebas, Ahena. Go to their aid. If you do so now when they need it most, you'll win yourself an ally, and the rest of the clans will reconsider whether their loyalties to your enemies are not misplaced.'

She remained silent. Twilight smudged her face.

'Forgive me,' he said. 'I have no right to counsel you. But –'

'No, you haven't. But it's not stopped you before.'

Arik bowed.

'Go on, Master Swordsman.'

He straightened, towering over her. 'Don't wait for pledges or impose conditions. Give them the help they need. The pledges will come.'

'Charity?' She raised her eyebrows. 'And if they offer nothing in return?'

'It's a risk worth taking when nothing else has worked and you've no one left to ask.'

'You surprise me, Master Marcin. Taking nothing is hardly the Northern way.'

'You would gain intelligence about both the pirates and Lebas' weaknesses, and the loyalty of folk beyond your borders – some of whom are unsworn and as free as the wind to follow whomever they choose. They'll remember the kindness of the clan of Lorendar's heir.'

Something about the way she looked at him reminded him of a Form tutor. It was a look that saw everything, or at least intended him to feel as much.

He withstood her scrutiny. 'It will be to nobody's advantage if the pirates capture a whole clandom.'

'I don't think Lebas are in such danger as that.'

Arik shook his head. 'The greatest victory is the battle that is avoided. In the North, we don't wait for a trickle of barbarians to gain momentum. Even the smallest win emboldens them. The moment you look away, the trickle becomes a flood.'

Emra tightened her shawl around her. 'Had they not already refused an alliance, we could have helped bolster their defences. But I must honour their wishes. Perhaps now they'll think more favourably of an alliance with us in the future.'

'So you'll punish the whole clan for their Elders' pride?'

'The only way they'll realise their own weakness is if we allow them to feel it. That will save more lives in time to come.'

She flicked the air, as though closing an invisible door on the matter.

'I invited you here to ask a favour of you. My nephew is angry and strong-willed. Pledging to this clan is only the first step. It was always our hope to restore Merensama through treaties. Until Viridian invokes Lorendar's oath, we can't call the clans to Merensama. I wanted to give him time ... but the pirates have diverted us enough.'

Arik kept a straight face. 'I thought he still needs to find the right timing for Merensama using that ... moondial.'

'He does.' Her reply was too hasty. *She's not sure he will, either.* It didn't help Arik's reservations about the gnomon upon which so many Derindin hopes rested.

'And you want me to speak to him.'

'He looks up to you and Tristan.' She paused. 'There are some who would rather distance him from you, but the North has saved his life several times.'

'You can speak plainly, I'm well aware that not all the Elders want us here. If your diplomacy fails, do you plan to enforce Merensama with war?'

'We've a long way to go before we must come to violence, Master Invelmari.'

Ealdorman and Chieftainess appraised one another.

'There's no good asking me to change Verdi's mind about anything,' said Arik. 'It needs to come from within. But I'll try.'

'You are very honourable.'

He bowed again and turned to leave.

'Master Marcin, where is Tristan?'

Arik paused outside the sphere of lantern light. 'He's a chronicler, Ahena. He'll spend the rest of his life coming and going, gathering his stories.'

Hopefully none that will erase what he knew first.

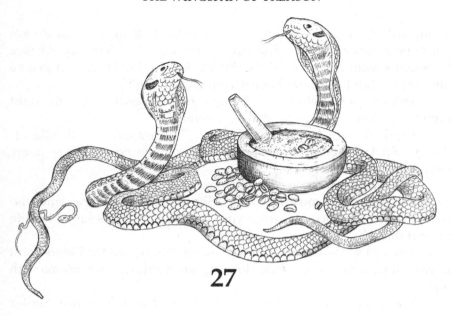

27

Kahvi

TO THE SOUTH HE SAW SAVAGES PLUNDERING THE LANDS
ALONG THE GREAT RIVER, AND SET OUT TO CLAIM THE RICHES
THEY HAD SPURNED IN FAVOUR OF THEIR WARS.

SONNONFER: THE SECOND REDRAWING

She was a delight to watch. As agile in her saddle as her mare and as graceful as the grasses. Her thoughts, when she shared them, betrayed a keen mind. She stopped to consult her wind-gauge or take cuttings the way he paused to collect coordinates or make notes for his maps. It made for a peaceable road.

Klaus was content enough to ride beside her and suspend fear for a time; surely Dunraven couldn't reach him in the middle of this winding wilderness. Only night tested him, when Pulgo's absence magnified keenly her unchaperoned presence.

The last leg of the road was the hardest, ribboning through rocky dunes, sometimes disappearing altogether. They reached Cora at sundown just over a week after leaving Samsarra. The hamlet more resembled a shanty town than Pulgo's tidy village. But it was buried in an oasis erupting from the earth so vividly that the weary traveller could be forgiven for mistaking it for an illusion in the sand.

A spring fed the valley nestled in the bosom of the green-carpeted hills, and fruit trees and swaying date-palms shaded the settlement from sun and wind. It was this climate prism, coupled with the spring's mineral-rich run-off, that nurtured Cora's famous kahvi beans, Nerisen told him.

She paused on a hill overlooking the valley. 'Do you see that peak?'

Klaus could just make out the thumb of a mountain jutting into the early dusk.

'That's the Ghizim range marking the eastern border of Lebas' clandom. All the land up to that range is contested. Fraivonians have always lived here in Cora, but it's not officially Fraivon's because they don't have the manpower to defend it. The only reason Lebas haven't taken it already is because Fraivon agreed to share with them the takings from the kahva bean crops growing in the valley, which both clans need these locals to grow.'

'What's stopping Lebas from taking the valley anyway?'

'Fraivon would burn it down out of spite to destroy the kahva crop if so much as a single Lebasi arrow fell here. So Lebas decided it was more profitable to let the natives work and receive a share of the harvest. Now these farmers grow the beans and give up most of the harvest in return for being allowed to stay on their own land. Their share of the crop is only just enough to live on.' The desert's trials animated her most, her green eyes igniting. 'Meanwhile, Fraivon and Lebas sell their shares to Northerners for a fortune.'

They began the descent down the hill.

'With the marriage of Maragrin's grandson to Fraivon, Alizarin hopes to renegotiate that agreement. But Fraivon's council won't care. They'll say they need the gold to strengthen their western defences against Baeron, because if they fall to Baeron, our eastern clandoms will be next.' Her voice thickened with contempt. At least her scorn wasn't reserved for the North. 'That's the anthem of the Plains. We choose to live by ghabala, and weep when we are the ones wronged.'

The shacks scattered along the edge of the valley were built on the stone ruins of better houses. Klaus doubted they would afford much protection from the storms he'd now sampled for himself.

'I suppose they can't spare the gold to rebuild?'

'They did rebuild. Mercenaries destroyed it all.'

'More bandits?'

Nerisen's derision could have polished flint. 'Hired swords working for Lebas. Not that anyone can prove it. Their Elders claim to know nothing of it. Who knows – the Lebasi farmers coveting this land might have taken matters into their own hands. Who'll these people complain to, anyway? Fraivon don't care how they live, provided they get their bushels of beans.'

She rapped the open door of a shack and went in. Klaus waited. A moment later she ducked her head back out.

'Well? Are you coming?'

The woman kneading bread inside was older than he'd expected, or else had spent too long doing the work of a much younger woman. Her name was Worganeg, and she didn't seem to notice he was Invelmari. Her haunted gaze made her seem perpetually distracted, and her Invelmen was heavy.

'I'm glad to see you, child.' She brushed Nerisen's cheek. 'All friends of yours are welcome here.'

He helped Nerisen distribute supplies around the dozen or so dwellings: sacks of grain, lamp oil and candle wax, tonics and medicines, Thillaina's donated cloth and yarn. Cora's kahvi farmers were delighted to see Nerisen and showed no animosity towards Klaus. *Perhaps their loathing for their Derindin tormenters has merely eclipsed anything they might have felt for a Northerner.* Weariness coloured their eyes as though it lived in their marrow.

Something wasn't right about the hamlet, though Klaus couldn't initially place it. Then he realised what it was: there wasn't a child in sight.

'Last month a pack of starved dogs came.' Worganeg cooked thin bread on heated stones, made from a flour of the kernels of the valley's abundant apricots. The hut's single room was bare but for woven mats on the floor, clay pots in one corner and bedding in another. 'We barricaded ourselves in Colkat's house for three days. It's the strongest. Old Uncle finally killed a goat and threw it to them, and at last they left – but they got his leg and he caught fever. He was dead within the fortnight.' She stared out of the window, eyes latching to nothing that Klaus could see. 'Fifty-five years he'd been here, waiting for them to let off. He's buried under the pomegranates. But now he'll never have to leave.'

'Farmers from beyond the valley release dogs nearby from time to time, hoping to drive these people out,' Nerisen explained. She squeezed Worganeg's arm. 'Old Uncle wanted to be laid to rest here.'

Klaus watched Worganeg flip the bread. 'Have there been raiders here?'

'Pirates? No.' Her voice shrank with fear, and he was glad. 'Not for years. I've heard the stories, young man. But here we have more pressing concerns than pirates.'

This startled Nerisen. 'Pirates came *here*?'

'Long before you became Worganeg's saviour. Before you were even born, I should think.' Worganeg patted Nerisen's hand. 'Yes, they came here. But they didn't raid.'

'What did they come for, then?'

'They came digging.' Worganeg stirred herbs into a pot of derina stew. 'Hacking at the hills. They weren't the only ones.'

The invisible bowstring in Klaus' mind grew taut. 'Who else came here?'

Worganeg peered at him. 'A tall man, just like you. Not so many years ago, him. Fair-haired, ginger-haired. Not a Derindman.'

'A Northerner?'

'Perhaps. Hard to say. Not met many Northerners.'

'Do you know what they were after?'

Worganeg shook her head. 'Whatever it was, they never found it, because they left us alone.'

'You must be tired, Worganeg,' Nerisen interrupted, frowning at Klaus. 'Let me take care of that pot.'

They talked of windstorms and repairs as they ate stew from hollowed-out bittergourds. Although the hamlet produced some of the finest kahvi in the Seven Parts, the farmers drank little of it themselves, reserving the precious beans for sale. Instead, Worganeg prepared an earthy tea the colour of reddish honey, sweetened with heartnut sap.

Klaus rose after supper. 'I'll sleep outside.' When Worganeg protested, he added, 'I've never seen the stars so far south.'

This she understood. He drew his cloak around him and settled against a tree nearby. A chill wind plucked at him. An owl hooted. Night spared him no stars, however; the sky was overcast again, like his thoughts.

Alone, he could ponder the ginger-haired intruder to Cora. Klaus was sure he was on the trail of Spyglass Adelheim's squire again; Clevenger Eldred. Had the Spyglass *employed* pirates to dig here in search of the mine, before realising Cora was not near south enough? This seemed implausible. The Eye of the Court wouldn't share such intelligence with the Derindin.

Exhaustion finally caught up with him. The last thought he had was of Nerisen's green eyes growing golden in the firelight. Worganeg's quiet Derindask sing-song voice drifted through his dreams.

When he woke, it was still not light. Nerisen slept in the house alone, her back to the door, her loosened black braid spilling dark rivers over her shoulder. He resisted the temptation to steal a closer look. He retrieved his eyescope from his pack and walked up the hill overlooking the valley.

Cora's hills stood over a large spring. Its remoteness deterred most travellers, Nerisen said, and the uneasy truce between Fraivon and Lebas kept others away. Klaus paused on the hillside, taking in the lay of the land. Even with its fruit trees stripped naked by winter, much of it was evergreen. Worganeg appeared on his path.

He bowed. 'Good morning.'

She looked at him as though seeing him properly for the first time, her eyes much more focused today.

'You're a Northerner,' she said sharply.

'The one and the same who shared your supper last night.'

'So was *he*.' The long knife in her hand was drawn. 'He had another Northerner with him. Of course I remember. I just didn't want her to worry, else she won't come back.'

Maybe she's slightly unhinged. 'Forgive me, mistress, if I've offended you, but I've not come looking for anything. I've come to –'

'To meet the land.' Her eyes, a thorny heather green, mellowed. 'I know it speaks to you.'

Klaus stilled. The memory of the night outside the ruined temple rushed back, filling him to the fingertips. However Worganeg had known what he'd experienced that night, he'd had no clear memory of it until now.

How could I have possibly forgotten?

'Do you … can you hear it as well?'

'I'm no reader.' Now her voice was hushed with deference. 'But I know the land's been calling, waiting, though I can't make out the words. I've tended it long enough.'

'Waiting for what?'

But Worganeg continued past him, as though they'd merely exchanged pleasantries, her interrogation over as quickly as it had begun.

He didn't know what to make of her; she had been at least three different women. But the thrill of possibility raised gooseflesh on his arms. He returned to find Nerisen helping a farmer mend a roof.

'Have you seen Worganeg?'

'She begins her work early.' Her eyes flashed. 'Let her be, she has sorrow enough to remember without you stirring it with questions. Have you finished exploring? We should leave after breakfast.'

He helped finish repairing the roof. Worganeg returned with meaty chestnuts and a clutch of eggs, and made kahvi in honour of her guests. She brewed the ground beans carefully, foaming them on and off the fire in a mystery of chemistry and smoke. She smiled at Klaus as she poured it, and he was almost uneasy taking a sip. But Onax liked her well enough, and Nerisen drank happily.

'Welcome, far-traveller, welcome,' Worganeg told him at least a dozen times, as though he'd just arrived. 'This winter will be a long one, Nerisen. Must you go, dear Nerisen?'

'I must. But I'll take whatever you need me to sell.'

'But you won't be back, not for a while.' The older woman's eyes grew sad. 'Not this time.'

'Worganeg, why don't you come back with us to Samsarra?'

Nerisen's mouth fell open at Klaus' suggestion. Worganeg shook her head.

'Cora used to stretch to that mountain.' Worganeg pointed west. 'The first land they stole, they snatched from under our very noses – tumblers in the night. Cleared out every house. Resettled our land with their own folk before our beds were cold, and called it theirs. This is all that's left now, and it's ours. My people can't have died for nothing.'

'There's no one here to protect you,' Klaus reasoned. 'Or to help through winter.'

'Why should I leave?' she demanded. 'So they can steal what's left? They're just waiting for us to do that, you know. To finally give up and go.' The haunted resignation returned to her eyes. 'I will never leave.'

'Hush, now.' Nerisen threw him a dark look. 'I'll come back as soon as I can. When have I ever not?'

Klaus had anticipated this response; it would be easier to move the hills than to remove Worganeg from them. 'Your kahva is truly superior. If I may, I'll buy all Cora can spare. I'll pay you now, so you needn't wait for Nerisen to return with your gold.'

Worganeg cocked her head, bird-like, and quoted the Romelian market price.

Klaus shook his head. 'That's not what Fraivon sell it for when they take their share up to Noisy Tree.' Now she was spry as a cat; he took the opportunity to suggest a substantially larger measure of gold. He reverted to an Ealdorman's voice. 'Invelmari market prices. For an Invelmari, after all.'

It was not a voice to be refused. He went out for a last look at the valley while the farmers weighed and packaged the beans. There wasn't much to spare after deducting the harvest they owed to Fraivon, but their share was almost more than the pack horse could carry. When he returned, Nerisen was taking her leave of the farmers. Klaus grabbed his chance.

'Worganeg, what else do you remember about the Northerner who came here digging?'

Her face became vacant again. 'They left us alone when they were done.'

She went on to instruct him on how best to store the beans. He swallowed back frustration. Here was perhaps the only Derindin who'd crossed paths with the Eye of the Court so far south, and her memory was broken. Before he mounted his horse, however, she gripped his arm, clarity crystallising again in her heathery eyes.

'Will you save us?' she demanded. 'You'll answer the land?'

She released him just as quickly, patting his mare's head as Nerisen rejoined them.

'A lovely horse. A very good girl, Nerisen. A good horse. Be off with you, girl, and your friend.'

Bereft of the company of children, the kahvi farmers saw them off with stirring fondness.

'Don't pay any mind to what Worganeg says,' Nerisen told him. 'Sometimes she's away with the birds.'

'Is that the Derindin way for saying she's not all there?'

Her eyes snapped. 'It's a way of saying she's an innocent who the Plains have wrongly punished. Her fate could strike any one of us.' But after a moment, she conceded, 'Hardship has unwound her mind a little.'

'You know it would be more merciful if Lebas took the land. It would force those farmers to seek safety, instead of this slow extinction.'

'They've been managing for a long time.'

'Come off it, Nerisen. They're a handful of ageing farmers with no means of defending themselves and no young blood to help. If it weren't for charity like yours, they'd have died out years ago.'

Sparks flew from her eyes again. 'Maybe there's only room for the mighty in Invelmar. *These* people may be weak, but they'll never surrender.'

He waited until the green fire had settled. 'In Invelmar, even a farmer must learn how to wield a blade so that he won't need to surrender what's his.'

Her chin rose. 'I didn't expect my pack horse to have quite such a load to carry back.'

It was his turn not to reply.

Nerisen wasn't ready to let him off the hook. 'That gold will see them through at least two winters.'

'Assuming the pirates don't get to them first.'

They fell into an uneven silence. He was conscious of her every move; the way her body rose and fell expertly with her horse, the tendrils of dark hair that escaped at the nape of her neck. In Dunraven, every minute of her company would have been chaperoned.

He broke the silence first. 'When will you go back to Cora?'

'I normally go two or three times a year. But the bandits...' She trailed off, perhaps recalling the dead Babbler. 'Not many Plainswalkers come here. A peddler visits the area every three moons, sells basic supplies and takes some of their beans to Romel. But I don't know what will happen to these people and their trade now.'

'You do them a great service. However do you find time for your studies?'

Now it was irritation that ignited her eyes.

'My apologies.' He looked back to the road. 'I meant no offence.'

Something had soured their simple companionship. Nerisen spoke little, lighting fires and digging up derina with clever fingers and no complaints. In the evenings, she curled under her cloak as soon as she ate. Around her it was more difficult to untangle the web of his thoughts, and a distance stretched further between them the more time they spent together. *Together* was the wrong word – they were about as together as a vessel of oil and water.

Yet she had all the lure of a lodestone to iron, reliably throwing him off course.

The desert grew hilly again as they crossed back into Mantelonian and then Elendran land, where grasses softened the Plains.

'Look out for brush-snakes.' Nerisen pointed to a clump of grass; a white-bellied yellow snake lay in its shade. 'Their bite is more poisonous the further south you go.'

He resisted questions, lest he have to contend with more bite than the snake's. *Perhaps she can't see past my Northern blood.* She was so difficult to read, beyond her love for her homeland.

She dismounted one afternoon, carefully digging out a flower growing between crags. 'The powdered tuber of this orchid is an antiseptic.' She moistened its pearly tubers with water and placed it into a small glass cylinder. '*Mestika.* They've grown more scarce each year.'

'You're fortunate to have grown up with the Arboretum.'

Her silence was better than her sting. After a moment, she said, 'I joined Elendra to study at the Arboretum, but I was born to Akrinda.'

'Did you live in the border towns?'

Her face darkened. 'No, and I never will. Not while Akrinda are too ashamed to admit they came from the South.'

He didn't press her when she offered no more. There was little sun to temper the chill, and a wind had begun to whip up flurries of sand over the ground. Nerisen sampled the air with her wind-gauge.

'A storm's brewing.' A frown creased her brow. 'I hope we get to the temple in time.'

He was about to suggest waiting out the storm in the ruins when a blinding stab of pain seared the side of his chest.

When he came to, he was lying on the ground. His mare was neighing in distress and Nerisen was kneeling beside him.

'What –'

'Lie still.'

There was no one else in sight. His first thought was he'd been struck by an arrow, but there was nothing in his side. Then he became aware of his shirt and steelsilk rolled up over his left side and the shock of her hands on his chest. A milder pain blossomed underneath her fingers.

'You've been bitten.' There was a knife in her hand, and a dead brush-snake nearby. 'It must have been hiding in your saddlebags...'

'I have some woundwort in my pack,' he managed, dazed.

She tore some cloth from the hem of her cloak and pressed woundwort to his chest wall until it stopped bleeding. The back of his head ached where he'd hit it against the hard ground. He opened his eyes again at a howl of wind. It was definitely louder.

'Come on.' He sat up carefully. 'We need to make camp.'

'This wound needs cleaning, their fangs puncture deeply –'

'Later.' He found he felt much better upright, aside from a sting in the side of his chest. How had he not felt the snake slip under his shirt? 'I feel fine. Let's keep moving.'

She was unconvinced, but the wind was blowing their cloaks about them now. They picked up as much pace as they could over the rocks. Within a couple of hours, they reached the ruined temple, where the ancient walls shut out most of the wind. Horses safely inside, Nerisen started a fire.

'Let me see that bite.'

She lit the oil lamp as he shrugged off his steelsilk chainmail, wincing with another stab of pain. His shirt stuck to his skin where the blood had dried.

'Stop.' Nerisen pushed his arm aside and pressed wet cloth to his shirt until the fabric peeled away. She stared at the wound.

'How does it look?'

'You should have let me clean it earlier.'

'It's only been a few hours.'

'Brush-snake venom is nasty. Now be still.'

He lay on his right as she cleaned it until it felt raw. Then she bandaged it with a roll of gauze from her saddlebag, wrapping it tightly around his chest.

Her fingers touched his fine chainmail on the floor. 'Is this Invelmari steel?'

'Yes.'

Her eyes were unreadable: a summary of the great chasm that yawned between them. 'Didn't help against the snake bite.'

She made a quiet meal of lamh'met, after which Klaus felt surprisingly refreshed. She avoided his eyes. Unlike the nights they'd shared under the desert sky, in Pulgo's absence the walls of the soft lamp-lit chamber closed more intimately around them. Onax ignored Klaus, curling up on Nerisen's pack and falling asleep as soon as his belly was full. Klaus had already seen to the horses, but Nerisen went to check them anyway.

He rose as soon as she returned. 'I'm going to keep watch.'

'It's storming outside,' she said flatly. 'And you've been bitten.'

'I can barely feel a thing now.'

It was too windy to stay by the half-fallen wall again. He settled beside the broken door, where it was cold but at least out of the cutting gale, and afforded them a little separation.

At least here she was out of his sight, if not his thoughts.

But his mind was a flooded maze where thoughts choked for attention. What else might Worganeg have revealed, had they stayed longer? How long had the Spyglass' spies been combing the desert for this mine? Twenty years? Thirty? Did its ore possess properties that could rival Invelmar's steel? Had pirates independently pieced the story from the Septentrional Scrolls, as he had done? It seemed unlikely that pirates could read Far Northern script, but even scoundrels could have leaders with learning. Or was there some other record that described the mine and the spring? Klaus stifled one errant thought; it only compounded his resentment. *Why was I never told? Wasn't I an Intelligencer of the Eye of the Court?*

'*They left us alone after that.*' To Worganeg, that was all that mattered. Klaus wondered where else the Northerners had gone, and whether they would be remembered by villagers further west.

'*I know it speaks to you.*'

Would it visit him again here by the temple, that nameless bottomless voice?

Wind howled like a Northern wolf. That had been one of his favourite sounds. The storm caged a pack of wild animals at its heart, calling out to each other across the desert … except the sound seemed to come from the ground rather than the sky – he *felt* rather than heard it. How could that be? He strained his ears; his mind. The land beneath the temple seemed as disturbed as the howling wind, as if it too had a troubled heart.

He shivered; it was growing colder. The shivering persisted despite his heavy cloak. His skin broke out in a cold sweat. Strange; there seemed to be laughter in the wind. He was shivering violently now. *I ought to investigate the sound.* But he rested his head against the door instead. That was stupid, he might as well be asleep if he couldn't keep watch. Something blurred his vision. His head grew light.

*

She wasn't sure what had disturbed her, but Nerisen was suddenly awake.

For a moment all was quiet and very still. The fire had gone out. Onax was still lying on her pack, but his golden eyes glowed wide open.

There was no sign of the Northman. He was mad to stay out in the wind, but she was secretly grateful that he did. She sat up. The faint murmur in the air didn't sound like the storm. More a moan ... she pulled her cloak tighter and lit the lantern. Onax jumped onto her wrist. Knife drawn, she crept towards the entrance of the temple.

The storm hammered against the shuttered windows. Something slumped in the doorway, groaning softly; it was Tristan.

She hurried forward. His face was pale and clammy, his breathing shallow. His eyes were closed.

'Tristan.' She shook his arm. 'Tristan!'

He mumbled something unintelligible. His body was limp. A cold panic took hold of her. What could she do here? She ran back inside for her water skin, holding it to his lips; he was too drowsy to drink. She dabbed at his face with a rag but it was soon slick with perspiration again. She pulled up his shirt. The bandage was clean. But his pulse was running for dear life, his skin scalding.

Nerisen sat back on her heels. *The snake venom must have spread in his blood.* His breathing frightened her. He needed a physician. But he was a lot bigger than she was, and she couldn't even drag him out of the wind. So she tried to keep him cool, waiting for the fever to break.

It was the longest night. His body began to burn. Every so often he writhed, his hands reaching out for things she couldn't see. Several times he sat up with a start, murmuring broken nonsense she didn't understand or otherwise dismissed as a product of the delirium. He opened his eyes once, gripping her wrists with a wildness in his face. She hushed him back onto a pillow of her rolled-up cloak. A grey dawn crept up over the hillside. Finally, he stopped perspiring, and his chest rose and fell deeply in a heavy sleep.

Exhausted, she sat back and looked at him. Perspiration darkened the golden-brown hair gathering at the root of his neck. His features were distinctly Northern; high cheeks, straight nose, strong jaw. Without that irritating pleasant-but-unreadable look he always had when he was awake, he looked almost peaceful. Perhaps not as fine as the other Northman, but it was an undeniably handsome face. If she were honest, he was altogether too well-made. Her cheeks warmed.

'Get it together,' she snapped at herself, startling Onax. Tristan rolled over and opened his eyes.

'Nerisen?'

Her name sounded strange in his crisp Invelmen. He tried to sit up.

'Steady ... have a drink.' She raised her waterskin to his mouth; this time he gulped it down. It was the last of their water. 'We need to get to Samsarra. The venom's spread.'

She loaded the horses. He managed to stand but swooned getting into his saddle, and she feared they would have to wait. Morning had brought some reprieve from the storm, but it hadn't yet passed. Samsarra was almost two days' ride away, longer in the wind. *I'll have to find derina.*

Within an hour of returning to the road, she regretted leaving the temple. The wind had picked up again, and they were riding against the storm. At times, Tristan seemed barely awake, clinging to his horse, head jerking up at sudden noises. Even poisoned, his senses fought to stay alert and his hand strayed to his sword, and she couldn't help but admire his reserve. It was no wonder that Invelmari soldiers were so highly sought across the Seven Parts. No wonder they dealt so much death in so many places.

She had to shout to be heard over the wind. 'Focus on the road!'

But the sky grew sickly yellow, and the storm only worsened. Several times the horses stopped, whinnying restlessly; she urged them on. Onax wouldn't stop growling. She had never heard the wind howl so: with a guttural tone that seemed to come from the very earth rather than the sky, stopping and starting with all the cadence of a stuttering conversation. Her mind was playing tricks on her. Sand thickened the air, and soon she was no longer sure where they were heading. Then a shadow appeared through the sand-wind-wall ahead and took the outline of a horse...

'Tristan,' she urged. 'Tristan!'

But the wind swallowed her voice, and he was slumped forward in his saddle.

Nerisen reached across to grab his reins, praying he wouldn't topple from his horse. She brought their horses side by side, keeping the pack horse behind them. Throat constricted with fear, she peered through the flying sand and braced herself.

But the approaching rider was anything but a pirate. A sand-mask hid his face and a hood covered his head, but the hands that took Tristan's reins from hers were slight, with fingers that twisted like roots.

'Where are you taking him?'

The stranger made no reply. Despite his frailty, he steered Tristan's mare with ease. Nerisen followed, nervous that she couldn't see the ground at all now. She stayed close to them; if she fell only a few paces behind, clouds of dust would swallow up the horses in front of her and separate them entirely. She lost track of time, focusing only on keeping them within her sight, praying they wouldn't step into sinksand or stumble on rocks.

The wind wailed on. She didn't know how long it was before the air cleared a little, and the horses ahead finally stopped. The old man dismounted and led both his horse and Tristan's to a small shelter. She followed on foot, pausing beside Tristan's unconscious form.

'Tristan? Tristan!'

They pulled him from his saddle. The old man threw one of Tristan's arms around his shoulders; she took the other, but he was a dead weight.

Impossibly, the old man carried him forward. Tristan's skin was horribly hot again. The old man steered them back out through freezing sand-toothed wind and into a stone house beside the shelter, where shuttered windows dampened the screeching of the storm. They lowered him onto a mat before a roaring fire.

'See to the horses,' the old man told her.

'But –'

'Do as I say.'

She went back out to the shelter, finding water and feed and blankets. When she returned, the old man had lowered his sand-mask and removed his cloak. The white hair hanging to his thin shoulders belied the deftness of his movements. He'd stripped Tristan to the waist and found the wound, which looked no different. He cleaned it again with a tincture, and dabbed Tristan's face and neck with a wet cloth.

'You must drink.' The man gestured to a jug of water on the table.

She took the wet cloth instead and held it to the Northman's face. 'Will he recover?'

'He is poisoned. The wound is not infected, but the venom is doing its work from within. We can only see what tomorrow brings.'

He's an Invelmari soldier, for all his mapping and chronicling; a warbringer. What should she care if he lived or died? But she had watched him bury the Babble in a grave dug with his own hands, and counted the surplus gold he'd paid for Cora's kahva. She had seen the way Alizarin's nephew looked at him with absolute trust.

'Who are you?' she asked. It was difficult to believe that this aged man had guided them out of the storm and carried Tristan into the house. 'Where is this place?'

His eyes were terribly intense. She grew self-conscious of her thoughts.

'Safety. Go and rest. There is nothing more you can do for him tonight.'

How could he expect her to rest? She didn't know how to explain to him that there was something wrong with the desert that night, with the very wind. Even as she spoke she cringed at what she heard herself saying.

'It was like it was alive…' Her words stumbled over each other. 'Talking – the storm –'

'The desert has a soul too, child, though almost none can sense it now,' he interrupted. 'The bones of the fallen, the living dust … the desert knows when those it remembers are returned.' He pushed a cup into her hands. 'There is bread and milk over there. Go and rest.'

I'm not a child. But at the mention of rest, a floodgate of exhaustion opened. She didn't recall eating or undressing, but she remembered falling into a most comfortable slumber even the storm couldn't disturb.

*

When she woke, the winds were gone.

It was absolutely quiet. She pulled aside the curtain across the window in the small bedchamber where she'd slept. Night reigned, studded with stars.

Onax opened a sleepy eye, watched her get up, and went back to sleep.

She padded into the other room, half-afraid of what she would find.

The Northman was still lying by the fire, now on a thick sheepskin and covered with a blanket, breathing deeply. Nerisen was taken aback by the *thump* of her relief.

She drew closer. The sheen of fever had gone. His skin no longer burned to touch. She realised he was unclothed under the blanket and self-consciously pulled her fingers back.

She wasn't sure of the day, or the time, or their location. Tristan would have kept track of all these things. He chronicled the land as intuitively as a long-lost wanderer returned. *But he is still Invelmari.* So why should he have such an affinity with the desert?

The door opened behind her and the old man entered, carrying a pail of water.

'Awake already?' He set it down. 'It's too soon.'

'Do you need help?'

'Go and sleep. He will still be here in the morning.'

All kinds of irritated retorts reared in her head, but he looked at her as though he already knew them all. Meekly, she returned to bed, falling back to sleep immediately.

*

He did not wake in the morning.

'Oh, *come* on.' She glared at his sleeping form. 'Haven't you held us up enough?'

There was fresh wood on the fire, but the little house was empty. A bowl of fruit and a covered jug of fresh milk stood on the table. Nerisen began to feel afraid. She knew of no sanctuaries or hamlets in this part of Elendra's clandom. How far could they have strayed in the middle of a storm? She knew all the stories of spirits that inhabited desert ruins and tried to borrow the souls of the living, and many such other tales, and scoffed at them all.

In stark contrast, Onax was the happiest she had seen him, content to curl up in every corner as though he had always known this house.

She stepped outside into the clarity of morning. Ancient olive trees clustered around the house, with more olive groves beyond. To the west were grassy dunes and yellowish pastureland. Sudden realisation dawned. Amazed, she wondered how she hadn't understood sooner.

The old man emerged from the animal shelter. 'Are you rested now?'

'We're not far from Samsarra,' she exclaimed. 'How did we get here so quickly? We were a full two days' ride away from the citadel when the storm hit.'

'The road brought you,' replied the Wisdom, for surely he couldn't be anyone else. Nerisen had roamed the clandom all her life and never crossed the fabled olive keeper's grove, including the single time she had tried to find it. And so she hadn't believed the stories were real.

I could go on without him. There was nothing stopping her and Onax from continuing alone, leaving the Northman to recover. He would find his way back easily, and she had experiments to tend and more supplies to distribute. But she didn't want to. *I'm going to stay and show him. He thought he would be protecting me, and instead I'm going to deliver him home.*

'When will he awaken?'

'When he is ready.'

So she set about finding some useful occupation, and waited.

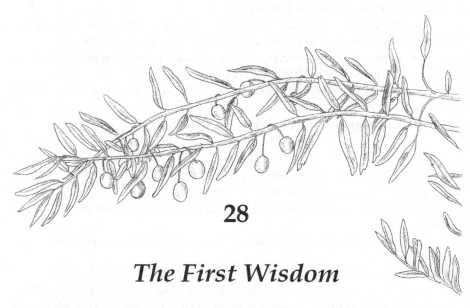

28

The First Wisdom

HE STIFLED EVERY NORTHWARD THREAT, AS PROTECTIVE OF
HIS YOUNG KINGDOM AS A MOTHER OF HER NEWBORN.
GREEDY SOUTHERN KINGS, MISERLY PAIVAN FARMERS –
NONE WERE SPARED FROM ANSOVALD STURMSINGER.

SONNONFER: THE SECOND REDRAWING

The windstorm raging across Samsarra came in from the east.

Every day that passed without any sign of Klaus cast a longer
shadow over Thillaina's house. It had been over two weeks. Arik kept
busy training his tumblers until the wind lashed with sand-whips, but
Verdi struggled to distract himself. The storm forced them each into a
surly solitude in the house.

When the winds finally abated, Samsarrans emerged cautiously
from behind bolted doors and barricaded windows. Alizarin asked Verdi
to join him for a survey of the damage to the citadel, keen for Verdi to
take a more visible role. It was here that beastmaster Coaren found him.

'Begging your pardon, Master Viridian.' Coaren had grown too
deferential for Verdi's liking since Verdi's pledge to Elendra. 'This letter
came to Terim, only it was addressed to you. I've been taking care of their

affairs while they look for Fibbler...'

Verdi tried to contain a flurry of butterflies. The plain seal on the note was unbroken, and it was addressed: *Viridian Wanderer.*

He endured a full morning of inspections before he was able to steal a moment of privacy in Thillaina's house.

He broke the seal with shaking hands. Even holding it, he didn't dare believe it was real.

It was short, in a neat hand he knew well.

'This house is still in mourning, though we've buried no one else. Mother and Father visit the graves daily, overcome with sorrow. They await more ill news. Though our loss has passed, it has not yet departed. I fear we shall never know reprieve.

Wherever you are now, you are always remembered, and not alone.'

His heart raced, excitement disintegrating to fear. He longed for any brush with Elodie, however remote – but this reply wasn't what he'd expected. He read her letter a second time, and a third.

Arik returned that evening, visibly more irritable. He always became cranky when worried.

'Wherever Klaus and that ranger have got to, they've probably been forced to take shelter and wait for the storm to blow over. Hope he makes good use of it. About time, if you ask me.'

Wordlessly, Verdi held out the letter.

'What's this?'

Arik's face became leaden as he glanced over it.

Verdi watched him reading between the lines, as he had done. To his shame, his fear begot more selfish fears. *I can't settle here. They'll be forced to leave, and I'll be left here alone.*

Arik lowered the note. 'They know Klaus isn't dead.'

'Worse than that.' *'You are always remembered, and not alone.'* Arik may have always teased Verdi about Elodie, but she was a princess and never addressed Verdi with endearments. 'There is, or has been, a spy on our trail.'

*

The first thing Klaus noticed was the silence.

It was warm, and every so often broken by the distinct and very comforting rustle of a page turning. An owl hooted outside. A fire hissed and crackled. It was a silence that waited patiently behind all these things, wholesome and absolute.

Eventually he opened his eyes, and felt no instinctive need to reach for his sword for the first time since he had held one.

The elderly man sitting by the fire looked familiar, though Klaus was certain he'd never seen him before. His hands were folded atop a book that lay closed on his lap.

'You have been recovering from brush-snake blood poisoning,' he said. 'You may remember very little of it. It has been three days since you arrived.'

Klaus jerked upright. 'Nerisen –'

'– is asleep next door.'

Slowly he lay back down, head spinning. He was wrapped in a blanket, and there was a bandage around his chest. He stretched; nothing hurt.

'Thank you,' he said. 'To whom am I indebted?'

'There is no debt to the olive keeper.'

Klaus sat up again.

'You're the Healer! I've been trying to find you for weeks.' Maps jolted into his mind. 'Then we must be near Samsarra…'

'You are indeed, and it was not yet time for our paths to cross.'

He'd only ever heard a smattering of them, but Klaus knew without doubt that this healer was a Wisdom.

Apprehension replaced his excitement. *What if he thinks I'm lying?* So much had happened since he'd first been directed to the olive keeper's door. *What if he knows I'm lying?*

'There is water in the jug,' said the Wisdom, and Klaus became aware of his parched throat.

He got up on shaking legs and downed a cup of cool water. It was pitch black behind the curtain over the window. Something drew him to the door. He was hardly aware of himself unlatching it and stepping outside.

The constellations of the southern sky were dazzlingly bright, written across the heavens in white fire that spliced an indigo infinity. The absolute absence of wind was deafening. He thought he could feel every crumb of earth beneath him, and a sense of east and west suggested itself to his mind so that he knew where the road to Samsarra lay even in the utter darkness. He had an immediate urge to reach for a compass to confirm this, but for the first time in his life he knew he needn't bother.

Klaus glanced back. The Wisdom stood watching him in the doorway. For a moment, he felt sure the Wisdom's eyes saw everything, right to the thoughts that bewildered him now. Klaus swallowed, throat parched again; this time not with thirst.

'What is this feeling?' He had no descriptors for it; at least, none he dared speak aloud.

'I think you already know,' said the Wisdom.

The chill bit him, and Klaus shivered. He retreated from the cold and from his mind, afraid to look more closely at where it ventured, and fell back to sleep in the safety of the house.

*

The chair was empty when late morning woke him. His clothes were clean and lay folded beside his weapons and steelsilk chainmail tunic. Behind the house, he found a noisy stream that disappeared into the olive groves, where he washed away the road and the sickness.

When he returned, a pair of bright eyes stared down at him from a shelf: Onax. Klaus hurried into his clothes, irrationally self-conscious under the watch of Nerisen's panfarthing.

The little house was sparsely furnished. A handsome bird perch stood empty by the window. There were few books on the shelves. What learning the Wisdom had, he carried it within.

A whinny drew him back outside; he found the Wisdom leading their horses into the shelter.

He nodded at Klaus approvingly. 'I hope you're rested now.'

'I am. I'm sure I couldn't have been better looked after.'

'Very good. Now, tell me why you were seeking me.'

Now that the moment had finally arrived, Klaus didn't know where to begin. He looked around.

'She is gathering derina tubers,' the Wisdom reassured him. 'She must always be doing something.'

That sounded very much like Nerisen.

Feeling foolish again, Klaus tried to give words to the inexplicable connection he had first made with the desert at the temple. 'Was it ilnurhin I felt last night?'

'No, that was not ilnurhin.' The Wisdom led him back into the house. 'But you feel these things *because* you have ilnurhin. We are all of us vessels for slight matter.'

'Then what do I feel?' The word 'ghost' kept visiting Klaus' mind, and he kept pushing it away.

'The earth. Its heart, its memories.' The Wisdom stoked the fire. 'Whisperers once heard the minds of elements, and learned to reply. With slight matter they commanded the behaviour of those elements – water, rock, plant, cloth. Many elements served their bidding – even spirit.'

He set a pot of water over the fire.

'They used that bond to achieve equilibrium throughout the Parts. But sooner or later the touch of men and women is polluted. All elements are the servants of the Great Sentience. One day, the Great Sentience called his elements back, and they've not listened to the summons of men and women since. We may converse with the elements of our world now, but not subvert their will as we once did.' The Wisdom added dried leaves to the pot. 'All but two elements, that is – earth and iron. Earth, our most material substance, and iron, the symbol of justice. And you know already who commanded these two.'

'The Simyerin?'

'Indeed. At the dawn of Orenthia, they were the only Whisperers left.'

'I was told they vanished with Orenthia.'

The Wisdom smiled, offering no reply.

'Why do *I* feel the earth? Here, of all places, where I've never been before?' Klaus grappled with half-formed ideas. 'What's slight matter got to do with it?'

'To understand that, you need to know the essence of slight matter itself.'

The Wisdom gave Klaus a wooden spoon to stir the brew. He sat and stared into the fire, speaking as tenderly as though calling upon fragments of an unseen beloved.

'Slight matter is a misnomer. It is not ordinary matter, but the purest parts of humanity – the goodness of people, their kindness, their compassion, mercy, purposefulness; all the things that make consciousness great, though it is not consciousness itself. Consciousness is made of thoughts, of awareness. Slight matter is more than our mere thought. Slight matter is our *greatness*.'

Despite the cosy warmth, gooseflesh rose on Klaus' arms.

'That is why the particles of slight matter are generated by the fifth chamber of a wholesome heart, not the mind. A rotten mind can create a dark thought. A poisoned heart cannot produce slight matter.'

'No wonder our Engineers have never grasped it.'

'It is a force so intense that the mind, which is familiar with experiencing physical things and tries to measure everything in material units, tries to turn it into a solid substance – something recognisable. So that we can make sense of it. So that we can *use* it. That is what your Engineers have spent hundreds of years doing, though they'll never succeed: a false alchemy. In truth, slight matter has no more solid substance than the thoughts that pass through your head.'

The Wisdom tested the liquid. Now his voice became filled with sadness.

'Slight matter is what you are missing when you have everything you thought you wanted and still feel hollow. The machine of this life – of work, of war, profit, worry, ambition – all these grease its wheels. But these things cloud the fifth chamber from producing ilnurhin – from sensing it at all. Slight matter is what wakes you up at night with the sudden realisation that all day you have done nothing to elevate yourself above the beasts.'

Klaus shifted uneasily. He knew *this* feeling well.

Satisfied, the Wisdom poured the brew into a cup. 'Drink this for eight days more while the toxin lingers in your blood. These herbs will neutralise it and rest your liver.'

Klaus accepted the cup. 'I've met people who have ilnurhin.' He thought of Sonru the physician, and Ristowin the blacksmith. Even Kelselem Ousur'had, with his absolute command of arrows through the wind.

'Of course you have, it is everywhere. But none of those people can truly command the element with which they have a kinship. They can only listen to its voice, and hope it does their bidding. Remember: only two elements were not summoned back to the Unseen World.' The Wisdom took the chair by the fire. 'And theirs is a rare language now.'

'I met a man in the Paiva who told me of a language I would come to understand.'

The Wisdom seemed perturbed as Klaus described the lonely doorway in the Paiva. 'Did you pass under the arch?'

'No.'

'Tell me exactly what happened.'

'He offered us a drink. A tea; he it made before us...'

'Did you drink of it?'

The Wisdom looked relieved when Klaus shook his head.

Klaus risked the most foolish question yet. 'Was he living?'

'As living as you or I. The Paiva has buried souls beyond counting, but they are not rested. How can they be? They have tasted the gravest injustice of all.'

The inscription on the doorway hovered in Klaus' mind as clearly as though it were before him. 'Who is "the lord and slave of the Silenced Daughter"?'

The Wisdom's eyes, the soft green of rock-mosses, glinted. 'Have you not guessed, Master Northman?'

Klaus' thoughts raced. 'Ansovald Sturmsinger became the lord of the river with his dam...'

'But not its slave?' Infinite sorrow mellowed the Wisdom's smile. 'Justice has turned her back on this Part.'

Something about this left Klaus terribly disheartened, opening a window onto yet more despair. He retrieved Elodie's trinket box from his coat and took out the iron weight.

'Can you tell me anything about this?'

The Wisdom looked at the weight. 'What do you wish to know?'

Klaus' heart raced. 'I want to know if it can help me find my parents. I don't know who they are, but they left this with me. I've discovered the name of the place it came from, but no one knows *where* that is...'

Sudden desperation shook the very frame of his Form. If the Wisdom couldn't guide him, surely no one could.

'Stop trying to trace this thing. Look instead at *what* you were given.'

Klaus stared at the weight.

'Iron is the symbol of justice, and justice begins in the marketplace, where buying and selling reveal the true nature of men's hearts,' said the Wisdom. 'There is a justice you must seek.'

The prospect of admitting his mishaps at the hands of the Wintermantels was too much, even to this Wisdom.

Fortunately, the Wisdom didn't solicit a reply. 'In any case, you have set yourself on another course.'

It was a moment before Klaus understood his meaning. 'I do want to help Lorendar's heir find his way. Though I never intended...'

The Wisdom waited. Klaus stroked the weight. He *had* chosen another path; his own would have to wait. An ache throbbed in his breast nonetheless.

'What about the pirates?' he asked. 'There's little appetite for Merensama while they ravage the Plains, perhaps building a stronghold of their own.'

The Wisdom settled back in his chair, now only half-listening. 'For the pirates, you already have all the tools you need.'

Then he quite unexpectedly fell asleep, leaving Klaus with the weight in his hand.

It was late afternoon. Klaus ventured out, hoping to map the Healer's grove but, finding himself weary, collected kindling instead. Nerisen emerged from the trees, a basket of firewood against her hip.

He bowed. 'I'm sorry I've delayed you so long.'

Her face was as unreadable as ever. 'Are you well enough now?'

'If you like, we can leave at first light.'

She nodded and returned to the house before he could thank her.

They had to hunt for Onax before they could leave the following morning. Nerisen found him curled up in a coil of rope. He became very grumpy when she moved him to her pack and ordered him sternly to stay there.

'Whatever's the matter with you?' she scolded him. 'Anyone would think you don't want to go home.'

Klaus knew just how the panfarthing felt. He, too, was loathe to leave the Healer's grove, where the world and all its worries stood still.

He lingered at the Wisdom's door while Nerisen saddled her mare. 'Will I see you again?'

The Wisdom smiled. 'The road brought you here once you found the right questions.'

It was certainly no promise. As they rode away, Klaus kept looking back until the house disappeared. When he tried to measure their position, the needle of his compass wouldn't fall still, as though the grove's coordinates were too slippery to grasp.

Nerisen stole sidelong glances at him when she thought he wasn't looking. Perhaps she didn't trust him to stay upright on his horse.

'Have you been to the Wisdom's grove before?' Klaus asked.

'No. I've not been able to find it until now.'

No one crosses paths with a Wisdom uninvited, Suman had said. Nerisen seemed unwilling to speak more of the Wisdom. He could only guess her thoughts.

So this time he filled the silence. Gradually, she was drawn into conversation. They spoke of the grove's ancient olives, from which the Wisdom had gifted her a flask of rich green oil, and of Cora, and wind-gauges. The westward trail to Samsarra ribboned through nut trees undressed by winter and sleeping mulberry orchards that eventually gave way to Elendra's planted forests, where Klaus briefly imagined he was home. If he had known last summer that his gaze upon Lingon Wood in Rainsthwen or the Emerald Vale of Eisnach would be his last, he would never have looked away.

Songbirds chattered high in the trees. Nerisen couldn't help smiling at the flurry of little wings. Her pleasure betrayed itself in the deepening of the greens of her eyes under the verdant shade of the holm oaks and in her long intake of breath to catch the scent of wild winter jasmines; in the tenderness of her fingers trailing through the grasses. She was wondrous then, like a glimpse through a door that had opened onto a secret garden.

'That's our fairywren!' She froze as a mellifluous song rose from the treetops, in her delight becoming briefly unguarded. 'It's a drab little thing the colour of the sand, so plain it's near invisible. But have you ever heard anything so beautiful?'

He listened. 'At home we have jewel-nightingales. The size of a peach with a voice just as sweet, and the most magnificent blue plumage you've ever seen.' Her braid was dishevelled and her cloak now torn in several places, and she was beautiful beyond words. 'But no, we have nothing so bewitching.'

She probably saved my life.

But all too quickly they reached the tired pastureland around the citadel, and Nerisen became a closed book again.

'Home at last,' he murmured. However he had yearned to roam, he always savoured the last leg of the homeward road.

She glanced at him through heavy lashes. 'Do you mean to stay, then?'

'Yes.' He ought to have qualified this: *I'll stay while there's any danger to Verdi ... I'll stay while there's work for a sellsword ...* but recklessly he didn't want there to be any doubt in her mind.

And then they were finally at the citadel gate.

'Keep the kahva,' Klaus told her. 'Sell it in Romel and set the gold aside for when you next visit Cora. Worganeg never needs to know.'

She vanished into the citadel. He would see her under Thillaina's roof soon enough, but it wouldn't be the same. He wished they were still on that lonely road that had, for a little while, forced them together.

A distraction I can't afford. He locked those thoughts away in Afldalr and rode into Samsarra.

*

Verdi watched anxiously as Klaus read Elodie's letter.

Worry replaced his relief at Klaus' return. It had been reckless, writing to her. *Elodie will always be his sister.* Verdi was sure Klaus felt the same, whether or not he had any right to.

'Well?' Arik stopped pacing. 'What do you think?'

Klaus sat terribly still. The Wintermantels' cipher was known only to them and Master Arnander.

'*...though we've buried no one else,*' he repeated. 'I think the Wintermantels have received information about us, but only once. When and via whom – who knows. But they're expecting more news. At some point or other, we've been watched.'

Another wave of nausea churned Verdi's stomach. Hearing Klaus confirm his fears made them more dreadful. But there was no ripple upon the still waters of his former master.

Klaus returned the note. 'What did you tell her?'

The absence of judgement made Verdi feel even worse. 'Nothing about us.'

Arik raked a hand through his hair, turning to Klaus. 'What do you want to do?'

A look passed between his friends, crammed with things Verdi had never shared – duty, Northern loyalty; the burden of being woven into the fabric of Invelmar, the burden of being cut from it.

Klaus was invisible behind his mask. 'We should consider what we *both* want.'

'I'm not the one being hunted.'

'You will be – only alive rather than dead. Your house is next in the Chain after Wintermantel.'

'My safety is assured, then. Besides, I promised to guard Lorendar's heir.'

Verdi's ears burned. He was beginning to cringe at the slightest mention of Lorendar.

'Then we stay here,' said Klaus. 'And keep our eyes open.'

Relief was a lightning bolt. Verdi's voice shook. 'But you might not be safe here now.'

'We've no idea *when* we were spotted. Chances are it was in the border towns, not here.' Klaus was a lot calmer than Verdi felt. 'Safety is a luxury we should enjoy while we have it. Besides, the Wintermantels aren't the only ones spying.'

Fear twisted Verdi's stomach again as Klaus told them about the kahvi farmer.

'It was quite likely Clevenger Eldred she saw in Cora,' Klaus concluded. 'Spyglass Adelheim would have been alive then. And years before Invelmari began poking around the South, the first to dig there were pirates.'

'For the mine?'

'Possibly.'

Verdi shivered. 'Maybe the Eye *is* afraid the ore could compete with Invelmari steel…'

'Don't forget the water,' Arik added, toying with the jemesh around his neck.

Klaus nodded. 'If the Derindin suspected a spring lay hidden in their desert, they would have raided Derinda looking for it. Besides, those Intelligencers we overheard thought some sort of seal still concealed the spring.'

'Maybe that's what the pirates have been looking for,' Verdi suggested, fear still wrangling with his guts. 'Something to help them locate the spring.'

'If they are, the Elders are burning time. They should be combing the desert just as hard.' In no time, Klaus was restless again. 'Those Intelligencers were afraid. The Eye has spent decades searching the desert for this mine. The Derindin should be paying attention.'

Verdi scratched Ravi's head. 'Well, no one's going to risk sending a scout now. Lebas has been badly ambushed…'

'And Emra refused to send them help,' Arik growled. 'Just to hammer the last nail in the coffin of any hope of a future alliance.'

Klaus stopped pacing. 'Any news of Fibbler?'

Arik looked away. Verdi shook his head.

They talked quietly late into the night of the unrest in the Far North. Ravi remained glued to Verdi's side, which he only did when Verdi was miserable. *Am I miserable?* For now, Verdi was just grateful for Klaus' safe return. Even the feeble contact with Elodie was a temporary relief from the gnawing ulcer inflamed by her absence. But beyond these things, a drowning awaited him in the ocean of the Derindin's expectations – for he knew now he couldn't desert the Derindin's hopes. Yet the thought of his friends leaving was too much to bear.

'Please don't be angry with me,' he told Klaus after Arik had gone to bed. 'I couldn't resist writing to her…'

It wasn't just the risk. Over years of playful torment, Arik had always quietly reminded Verdi that he was a Derindin enamoured with an Invelmari princess. Klaus had never spoken of Verdi's obvious affliction.

Still, Klaus wouldn't rebuke him, though the letter may have laid a trail to Samsarra. 'If you hadn't, we wouldn't know we've been spied on. We wouldn't know that she is well.'

But Verdi slept uneasily, feeling more helpless now than ever.

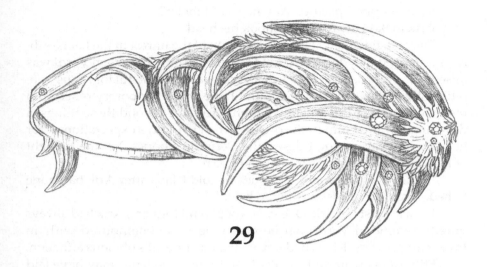

29

Form

IN HIS WISDOM HE GATHERED THE GREAT RIVER
TO THE BOSOM OF INVELMAR, DAMMING ITS WATERS TO QUELL
THE TIDE OF SOUTHERN CHALLENGERS.

SONNONFER: THE OSTRAAD

*He rose from his knees to a triumphant burst of trumpets. Cheers changed into
the shuddering victory chant of the Isarnanheri.*

*Queen Adela smiled at Klaus almost fondly; she'd always had a soft spot
for him. She placed the grímaláta, the ceremonial circlet of the Intelligencers, on
his head. His was a wreath of wolves' claws wrought of Invelmari steel studded
with sapphires. It curved down to cover his left eye: one veiled eye that secretly
saw everything, the other bared to the world but just as unreadable behind the
shroud of an Intelligencer's Form.*

*Next to acknowledge Klaus' graduation would be Adela's heir – his father.
Today, Lord Wintermantel needn't have bothered donning his own grímaláta –
pangolin scales studded with rubies, in homage to services in the Utter East that
no other Intelligencer had managed. His face shone with fierce pride and perhaps
secret relief; this moment had never been certain. Years of struggling against*

Father's orders and his own desires ... Klaus had crushed those now, of course. Lord Wintermantel had been right. Klaus was not free to choose the manner in which he served the Blood Pact.

Disquiet trimmed his elation. How many terrible things had he done to earn this Form, and how many more would follow?

But doubt faltered when Father's hands rested on Klaus' shoulders. It was said the hands of an Invelmari king were as callused and roughened as any worker's, such was his toil for his kingdom. In this respect, Wolfram Wintermantel was a king from Klaus' earliest memories.

It was a day of many colours. Victory bells tolling; Ealdormen's congratulations; Elodie glowing with pride; Arik teasing him relentlessly, his own Form already complete. Mother, grown more distant the older Klaus became, perhaps due to the layers of Form that enveloped her too. One hazel eye remained exposed through her grímaláta – a wreath of tiny pearlberry leaves flowering with emeralds. She was an invisible lodestone, navigating well-wishers with the dark ease of a nightmoth.

'You will surpass them all.' Her voice held the quiet of a breeze softly stripping autumn branches. 'They applaud you now, but in their hearts they know it, and none are immune from envy. A wonder, that you should be of us.'

She squeezed his hand so tightly her nails left painful ridges in Klaus' palm.

'Mother?'

Her visible eye unshuttered once; a mystery of love and guilt and something else.

'We have each poisoned you, your father and I. But you will surpass them all.'

Klaus could almost see her Form grappling with invisible demons. Around him, the ceremony fractured into figments: the weight of the steel grímaláta framing his left eye at last; a rare smile from Master Arnander; Father's hands on his shoulders; Mother's half-translated eyes...

*

Song spilled into the streets. Crowds tinkled with bells, parting around Lorendar's heir.

Samsarra heaved; caravans had drawn Elendrans from across the clandom for the ceremony marking Verdi's pledge to the clan. Klaus' eyes roved the streets, on edge after the thwarted attack at Winterfall feastday. He couldn't see Verdi's face, but Klaus could imagine his dread.

Their procession crawled through the citadel to the Chieftainess' square as the sun set in a golden riot of salmon plumes. A sage led prayers in the lantern-lit dusk, then a Derindask pledge that Verdi carefully repeated, pronouncing him as an Elendran. Tomorrow would be a holiday to mark the addition of Lorendar's successor to the clan. Alizarin's face had never looked so empty.

Klaus squeezed Verdi's arm discreetly. It should have been a joyous occasion, but trepidation stretched the air taut. Reports from Lebas' western hamlets had ended the short-lived reprieve from raids, quashing illusions that the pirates had fallen into dormancy. Rumours of slave-taking had been cemented by the discovery of an ambushed caravan on Lebasi land, with not a single body found amongst the wreckage.

'I am glad you have returned,' Emra murmured under the cover of prayer songs, as though this had been in doubt.

Klaus kept his voice low. 'You should be scouting the Selvaran Cradle, Ahena.'

Her eyes widened a fraction. 'It's a barren waste.'

'But is the prospect of a stronghold there impossible?'

'Truly improbable. After the First Redrawing, an outbreak of water-rat plague killed hundreds of nomads there. The pest vanished when the river dried up, but the area's been shunned since.' Her brow furrowed. 'You can't possibly think this is where the pirates have based themselves.'

'You didn't think it was impossible for pirates to be hiding in the south-west before.'

'South-west, perhaps. But the desert surrounding the Selvaran Cradle is so remote you can't even steal water from Baeron's or Fraivon's wells.' Her face closed off; a shadow of Alizarin. 'You make my task impossible, Master Invelmari.'

She waited for a lull in the chanting to pass.

'I have taken Eresk Laminhad prisoner, Tristan. His wife had too much remorse to deny the truth.' Emra glanced at him. 'If you suspected Laminhad's guilt, why did you speak up for him?'

'I hadn't known then that the burden of proving his guilt would fall to a broken man.'

A falcon circled overhead, soaring west. Klaus didn't miss the small bundle tied to its leg.

*

Arik shook his head at the next offer of more cider. Word of Lebas' misfortunes had soured the citadel's celebrations.

'Of course Lebas deny the raids,' Broco told Arik. 'No clan will want everyone to know they've taken a bashing. Can you imagine Ferenjen's face if he hears Lebas' western defences broke down?' He panted, tongue lolling out. Laughter broke out in the barracks' cantina.

'Watch that old Maragrin doesn't get wind of you doing that,' Saarem warned, a smile playing at his lips.

'It's all talk anyway,' scoffed Faarl, a younger tumbler emboldened by a little too much derina cider. 'They'll spread as many lies as it takes to keep us cowering in fear.'

'And who's *they*, then?' another tumbler challenged. 'Funny how often you hear that thrown around the taverns, though no one's got an answer.'

Faarl scowled. 'I don't see Hesper or Baeron hiding in their houses. Their roads are busy with trade, and they've not put embargos on caravans.'

'So you think Elders just want to scare us? What for?'

Arik glanced around the smoke-filled cantina. More tumblers were listening now.

Faarl swigged more cider. 'I heard Akrinda had a hand in rigging the price of everything from oil to grain after the first raids –'

'*Akrinda!*' There was a round of laughter. 'They may be scumbags, but they've just as much to lose if the pirates block goods from reaching the border towns.'

'Next you'll be saying Northerners put the pirates up to it!'

Faarl's cheeks coloured. He shot Arik and Klaus a dirty look.

'So where do you think people are disappearing to, Faarl?' Broco pressed.

'I don't believe they're taking slaves, if that's what you mean,' Faarl snapped. 'Ever met a bandit? Bunch of imbeciles without a brain to share between them. You really think they could have taken so many captives alive?'

'You don't need a brain to put a knife in a man's back. And there've been many more pirates around, even you can't deny that.'

'In the summer, maybe. Not now.'

'Tristan saw a murdered man a couple weeks back on Fraivonian land. Ask him.'

Klaus didn't look up from cleaning his sword.

Faarl twisted his chair to face Klaus. 'Well, mountain man? What did you see?'

Laughter faltered awkwardly.

Klaus sheathed his sword and wiped his hands. 'A dead Babble.'

A tumbler waved her hand. 'Ehh, Babblers are pissing off folk everywhere you go.'

'Can't prove it was a pirate who did it.'

'Whoever did it, a kill's a kill.'

But Faarl wasn't listening. 'So a lying Northman's all you've got to go by.'

'That's enough of the cider for one night, Faarl,' Saarem cautioned.

Arik eyed Eclen, Faarl's captain. *Pipe up, you fool.* If anything, the idiot was enjoying the bickering, also too full of cider.

Klaus rose from the table. 'Good night.'

Faarl stood, chair tumbling as he swayed. 'Off to collect more lies for your fearmongering?'

Arik leaned towards Eclen. 'Maybe you should rein in your tumbler, captain.'

Faarl shook off Royo's arm and followed Klaus out of the cantina, yelling drunkenly. 'What are the pair of you bastards hanging around for, anyway?' Tumblers laughed as he stumbled, springing up after him with their drinks to watch the sorry spectacle. 'Northern scum! *Northern scum!*'

'Hold your tongue,' Saarem growled. Groaning inwardly, Arik followed them. 'You've made enough of a fool of yourself. And put that knife away.'

Faarl drew his sword instead, staggering after Klaus as he walked to the gate.

'Go home,' Klaus told him, narrowly escaping a mouthful of spittle in reply.

It happened quickly. Faarl lunged forward with his sword; Royo shouted in warning. Arik pushed forward through tumblers. Klaus hadn't drawn his blade. He dodged frenzied swings of Faarl's sword, ordering him far more evenly than he deserved: 'Stop. *Stop –*'

Klaus finally drew his sword. The first clash of their blades threw Faarl to the ground, his sword splintering against Invelmari steel. Eclen cackled with drunken laughter.

Saarem roared furiously, but Faarl scrambled up, flailing with his longknife. He threw himself at Klaus, snarling – 'Fight, you bastard!' – and stumbling back each time Klaus flung him away. Eclen pranced about, jeering – 'He picked his fight, let him make a fool of himself! Finish it, fool! Finish it!'

Finally Faarl lowered his longknife, swaying as he retreated. Saarem cuffed his head. But Klaus turned to the gate and Faarl twisted back, lunging –

Silence fell as Faarl crumpled to the ground, shirt blossoming with blood.

Klaus stared down at his body. For a second, all was still. Then all of an Intelligencer's calm collapsed in a terrible avalanche.

'*Fool!*' Klaus charged at Eclen, lifting him clear of the ground, throwing him down. 'You're meant to discipline him, not goad him – what good is the sword swinging you taught him now? *What good is it? What good is it?*'

Arik fancied his thunder shook the citadel. He grabbed Klaus' arms, and Klaus shoved him back with bruising strength, seizing the hapless captain again, throwing him down violently. Picking him up; flinging him down, again and again as he roared.

The tumblers backed away. They didn't know what they were witnessing. The ice-mountain of the Intelligencer erupted, Form shattered. His rage was terrifying. It was more than a rage – a fury that made him alien. In that moment, Klaus was a stranger.

Arik grappled to contain him. Then the avalanche succumbed to stillness, and Klaus fell still in Arik's arms. The cold contempt in his face for the broken captain was enough to crush a man's spirit.

'Away, all of you. Haven't you got anywhere to be?'

Ayla stood before the gate, stony-faced, Verdi frozen with horror beside her.

Silently, the tumblers obeyed. Eclen staggered to his feet, spitting out blood.

'You've said enough for one night,' she interrupted when he opened his mouth. 'At least he only bruised your pride. I'd have cut out your tongue.'

Whatever she might have said to Klaus, his eyes took her words away: empty and endless, the sole of an abyss. Lisbeta whispered in Arik's ear: '*Behold the true face of an Intelligencer.*'

Arik's hand tightened around Klaus' arm, steering him to the gate. 'Let's go.'

'He was a stingy son of a bitch,' Broco muttered as they passed. 'No loss.'

Back in their rooms, Klaus staggered into a chair and held his head in his hands.

Arik glanced over his slumped shoulders at Verdi. 'Get some water.'

Verdi went at once. Arik pulled up a chair beside Klaus. There were cavities where his eyes ought to have been. He gripped Arik's arm, as though hanging on – to what, Arik was afraid to imagine.

Quietly, Arik told him, 'It will pass.'

Klaus' whisper was threadbare. 'I gave them everything.'

Intelligencers were burrowing creatures; dark tombs erected amongst the living. Where did an Intelligencer's grief go? Perhaps the wound he should have felt that first night fleeing Dunraven had only now appeared.

Arik tried again. 'You're free of them now –'

'I'll never be free of this.'

Arik knew he was right, of course. Form was not so easily shed as an Ealdorman's name. And now there would be a reckoning for this lapse; a severe restoration of Form in which a mind might lose itself altogether.

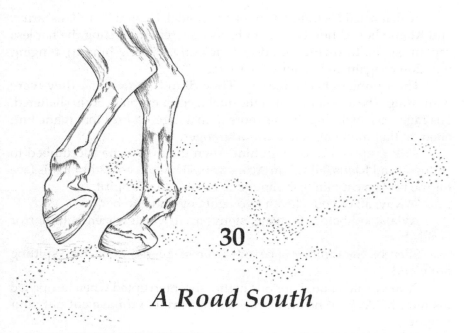

30

A Road South

ELEVEN THOUSAND MEN TOILED TO RAISE HIS GREAT DAM, TO CUT
THE ARTERY OF SOUTHERN SAVAGERY AND HARNESS
THE NINVELLYN'S BOUNTY FOR INVELMAR.

SONNONFER: THE OSTRAAD

Petra had delivered Suman's news ahead of his arrival, but Emra still hadn't absorbed it.

'Perhaps the most recent spate of attacks on Periam's caravans was the last straw,' Suman told Elendra's council. 'Or the prospect of a hungry winter. But Baeron and Hesper have declared suzerainty over Periam, and Periam agreed. They're all but conquered.'

The jewel-pins marking the clandoms on her father's map glittered. How many times had Emra seen them rearranged? Yet this was the worst shift in centuries; Periam had surrendered clanhood in all but name. To become a vassal – surely that was worse than disappearing altogether?

It was a disaster far greater than pirates.

Fenral scowled. 'Baeron and Hesper have ground Periam down; they've wanted their land for years. And while they've been cooking up this conquest, we've been fiddling over pirates!'

'There was no way we could have foreseen this.' Tourmali didn't bother hiding his irritation. The rift between the two Elders had only grown since Viridian's return. 'And we shouldn't despair. Baeron and Hesper are old bedfellows but even they won't share control over Periam equally. And Periam's clanfolk may yet revolt. This consolidation of power might be more brittle than you think.'

'Not if they're afraid of starving in a few months' time,' said Suman.

'Their timing is impeccable,' Maragrin mused. 'What with the raids, Baeron can present themselves as protectors of the very clan they devour.'

'Then we've not much time to spare,' Fenral insisted. 'A new power in the West will push Merensama even further out of reach. Your nephew's joined our clan, Ahena. We should raise Lorendar's banner before it's too late.'

Maragrin raised an eyebrow. 'Before he's found the Merensaman moon phase? What good will that do?'

Fenral's face darkened. 'And how hard is he trying? We can't afford to wait.'

'Whether or not he succeeds, our call will fall on deaf ears,' Alizarin interrupted. 'It's pirates that people are worried about now.'

Emra looked up again at the jewel-pin map that she had so long hoped to one day disassemble altogether. Those dreams seemed further than ever.

*

Klaus awoke empty. He was empty all the time now. It was the most desirable climate for the cold machinery of an Intelligencer. Master Arnander would have been proud.

Verdi brought tea brewed from the Wisdom's herbs. 'Today's the last day you have to drink it.'

The Healer's grove, the haven that had sheltered the precious stirring of something *more* for those few dreamless days, seemed like a lifetime ago. Verdi fussed about, changing Klaus' dressing.

Klaus pulled away. 'It's almost healed.'

'Yes, yes,' said Verdi crossly. 'You shouldn't strain it. The tumblers can do without you.'

'There's nothing to strain. See you after training.'

In the citadel, conversation halted and eyes burned holes into Klaus' back as he passed. Faarl had been thoroughly unpopular, but he had died on an Invelmari sword. And Klaus' hand in the arrest of Laminhad's wife had trickled down into the very gutters in the streets. But by evening, the citadel found better reasons to mutter.

'Suzerain!' Broco slammed his cup down. 'Those bastards will have their eye on Lebas next, you mark my words.'

'Told you all along,' grumbled Porva. 'The pirates have been hired by Baeron – to scare the rest of us into joining their new empire. And so long as these turds drag their feet getting anything done –' Porva eyed Verdi darkly '– we'll all be slaves to the West soon. Periam's just the beginning.'

Saarem waved a dismissive hand. 'They'll have to deal with Sisoda first.'

'Even Sisoda will struggle, resisting an army three-clan strong. Now, if we could offer the other clans Merensama…'

Verdi shrivelled in his coat.

You have set yourself on another course. The Wisdom's words nudged gently through the void that now bloated Klaus' Form. He waited until Arik was sound asleep before he cornered Verdi.

'Any progress with the moondial, Verdi?'

Klaus knew at once that something had changed. Verdi's eyes darted down, scrambling for somewhere to hide. Klaus let silence loosen Verdi's tongue.

'The whole *idea*…' Verdi trailed off, tried again. 'I'd be lying if I said any of it makes any sense to me, Klaus.'

'You couldn't stop trying to make it work, before. Lost interest?'

If at all possible, Verdi shrank further into himself. But there had been no denying his eagerness when he'd first seen the gnomon, once it had been placed into his safekeeping. Or the hours he'd spent sneaking outside the house to place it in the ground when he thought no one would see.

Klaus wasn't ready to verbalise the connection to the land that he had discovered in the Healer's grove. He had no idea how it would help decipher the gnomon's dials, but he felt sure that Verdi needed to search for such a bridge of his own.

If only I knew how I found that bridge myself.

'You don't really know if you want to be part of this, Verdi. That's the first problem.'

Verdi's fingers closed around Ravi's body. 'The first?'

'Could you leave Samsarra if I had to take off tomorrow?'

Panic crystallised in Verdi's face, but it had far more layers now, just as Klaus had hoped. 'Why? Did you hear something? Are you leaving?'

'That's your second problem. You're so worried about whether or not you'll be able to stay here that you're too busy to realise how much you want to.'

'I don't *know* what I want –'

'You have an affinity for this place, these people. Begin there.'

Verdi flailed for a rebuttal before lapsing into a sulky silence, Klaus' words perhaps truer than he cared to admit. Later, Klaus could examine the fresh wound that would be dealt by another parting. For now, he scrabbled past the void, grasping at the sense of purpose he'd affirmed in the Healer's grove – the only purpose that felt wholesome now.

'I just want to continue my studies.' Verdi spread his hands. 'I didn't ask for this. I was quite happy being your servant.'

'I hope you were more than just that.'

Verdi's face fell. 'I didn't mean that –'

'Sometimes, even drunkards in the tavern are worth listening to,' Klaus interrupted before he could start apologising. 'If Lorendar's banner doesn't fly while there are no strong contenders, there may come a time when it'll be too late.'

For a moment, Verdi was quiet. 'What if I want nothing to do with Merensama?'

'Then tell your aunt. Don't bait them with false hope.' Klaus paused. 'Deep down, though, I think you want to help.'

Something clattered downstairs. Ravi stopped cleaning himself to listen.

Verdi's pupils almost disappeared. 'What was that?'

They were alone; Thillaina was visiting a niece in Mantelon, and the maid was asleep.

'Wherever you are now, you are always remembered, and not alone.'

Fear clapped gleeful hands in Klaus' heart.

He nudged Arik awake. He was alert at once. They crept downstairs in the dark. Arik made for the front door while Klaus slipped to the back door in the kitchen, a knife naked in his hand.

It was closed but unlatched. The key lay on the floor, pushed out of the lock from outside. Several clicks later, the handle twisted. Klaus stepped aside as the door swung open.

A cloaked figure stood outside in the dark.

*

At the end of an ancient road an hour west of Samsarra, a small tussock-clad hill crouched over a well where caravans often sheltered from the wind. A family of Elendran nomads always came this way to sell their goods and restock over winter. Like many derina-gatherers, they followed the tubers throughout the Plains, chasing water.

Nerisen reached their camp on the softer side of dusk.

The sight of their wagons filled her with relief; she had feared raiders may have disrupted the roads. Or else that the caravan had disappeared altogether, like so many little people of no importance to anyone but their loved ones; a growing list of the silently missing. But Plainswalkers combed the desert and heard everything.

'Nerisen! Nerisen!' The children always spotted her first. Two butterflies, growing a little older and bolder each season, burst out of the camp and fell upon her with small arms and unruly curls as she dismounted. Tilma, their mother, hurried out of a caravan.

'Ah, Nerisen, it's you.' She scooped up Fraola, the youngest, embracing Nerisen with her free arm. 'These days everyone is always on edge.'

'There've been no raids on Elendran soil,' Nerisen reassured her, but punctuated this with a silent 'yet'.

Their caravan had been spared, but they'd changed course three times after spotting signs of raids. Nerisen left the supplies she'd brought with Tilma and went to find Tilmara, the oldest grandmother and unofficial mistress of the caravan. Tilmara was ninety-eight and had lost most of her sight in one eye since she was widowed. Each year she was a little less steady on her stick, but she had the memory of an emperor hoopoe and was always pleased to see her.

'Where are your little ones?' Tilmara demanded by way of greeting, exactly as she had done for several years.

'You look well, nonna,' Nerisen replied, ignoring the question as she always did.

Tilmara still kept her own wagon, though everyone sneakily helped maintain it. Nerisen unwrapped the orchid she'd carefully transplanted.

'Master Meron sent you this.'

'There used to be scores of this here when I was a girl.' Tilmara rubbed the fragrant leaves wistfully. 'Now you'd be lucky to stumble onto one even as far east as the marshlands.'

Nerisen made quince tea before finally lifting the latch on her thoughts.

'Tell me about the heir of Lorendar.'

'So that's what's been eating at you.' Tilmara chuckled. 'I can always tell when you're impatient for something. It's true, then? The one who finally wakened the limolan has returned?'

'So it seems.'

'Have you seen him?'

'Not enough.'

Every child grew up with stories of Lorendar, seasoned differently by each clan; Plainswalkers sampled them all. Most nomads celebrated the day the limolan sapling had appeared in Romel, twenty-four years ago. The sapling lived on even after the babe vanished when his mother died, and hope decayed to tired but tenacious faith. Nerisen wasn't yet decided if Viridian Santarem would reward that hope.

Tilmara tested the tea; it was still too hot. 'You're better off asking the poets for stories.'

'I've heard all their stories. I want to know more. What was he like?'

'I'm not *that* old, girl.'

Nerisen rolled her eyes. 'What did they tell *you* when you were a girl?'

Tilmara stared out through the window, where falling darkness brightened early stars.

'When I was a girl… Yes, I suppose I was closer to his time than you. And *you* will be closer to it than your little ones, when they come.'

Weariness misted Tilmara's eyes as she looked backwards.

'The land remembers everything. Lorendar's ancestors made promises they then broke, and took what wasn't theirs. He spilled blood, too – all men spill blood, while we women bleed to make more.'

Nerisen waited. Tilmara had many years to remember and countless sorrows to relinquish.

'But by the time Lorendar tasted death he was richer with ilnurhin than anyone alive in this Part. When I was at my great-grandmother's knee, derina grew thick far from the springs, and she had only seen a handful of windstorms in all her days in the Plains. She said a magnificent Derindwoman came to Lorendar on his deathbed to pay her respects before he passed through the doorway, calling herself the Spirit of the Plains. Magnificent, but maimed – no one remembers she was maimed.'

Tilmara had strayed far now, into that gossamer place where memories went to breathe.

'She told him she would enter a deep sleep once he passed, and he despaired. She reassured him then that, for the right price, she would wake again to greet another of his blood – one with greater ilnurhin than even his own – and find peace. And so he foresaw that his blood would yet one day unite the clans. As to the price to be paid – well, the Great Sentience knows, but there will be a price.'

Nerisen combed through these fronds of memory. 'How does Lorendar's heir awaken her?'

'Her?' Tilmara blinked, reverie broken. 'The spirit of the Plains, a woman? It's all poetry, girl. Why do you think men never tell these stories?' She snorted. 'The spirit was the land itself.'

Nerisen had understood, of course, but she held her tongue. 'Yes, but *how* will the land be awoken?'

'Who knows? The sages swear it will stir during that hidden moon phase only Lorendar's heir will find. But so little ilnurhin is left in people, it all seems impossible. Perhaps it's just a tale we pass down for comfort, when there's nought else for the young ones to inherit.'

It might have grown colder, or else it was despair that made Nerisen draw her cloak tighter.

Tilmara sipped her tea. 'I heard my Yannao tell a story, before the Great Sentience took him … a dream told to him by a child. It was from a place of innocence, and so it was worth remembering. My Yannao never shared the dream itself, but I never forgot what he said it meant: "a man would die twice to summon a light so great that it would shine on all the Part."'

'Did he say anything else about this man?'

'Perhaps it'll be this heir of Lorendar. Not since the Simyerin has so much ilnurhin awoken in the Part.'

Nerisen frowned. It always boiled down to this; precarious half-conviction, as close as a word teasing the tip of her tongue. 'How do you *know* that?'

Tilmara smiled. It was the only question she would never answer.

Nerisen listened to the rest of her stories with half an ear and much less appetite. Her mind strayed to the eldritch storm which had led her and Tristan to the Wisdom, and the Wisdom's words. '*The desert too has a soul … the desert knows when those it remembers are returned.*'

*

'Where in the Part have you been?'

Rasan accepted the kahvi from Verdi. 'The Elders released me a fortnight ago once they ran out of questions. They told me to leave the citadel.'

Verdi's eyes narrowed. 'They banished you from Samsarra?'

'They thought I'd make people more afraid.'

Klaus could well believe this. 'Why did you risk coming?'

'To tell you the rest of what I saw.'

Arik caught her eyes darting to the kitchen door. 'No one else is here.'

'After four nights, the pirates made camp.' Her voice was toneless, gliding over trapdoors better left closed. 'I was blindfolded in the back of a wagon most of the time, but I'm sure it was somewhere west, because of the wind.'

'Storms?'

'No, a lull in bad weather. Where they took me, there was barely a whisper of wind. Nowhere else in the Plains was spared that month. I went to Romel to check. There were dozens and dozens of prisoners. Their wagons went on for as far as you could see – perhaps hundreds.'

Arik frowned. 'How many pirates?'

'I couldn't tell you. Each time raiders arrived with new captives, others were taken away. They sorted through them like cattle. They always took them south-east of the camp.'

Verdi hardly noticed Ravi escaping his grip. 'That accounts for the missing...'

'They're clever,' she said. 'When they raid, they kill a few people to leave behind so no one suspects just how many people they steal. They boasted they'd done this for months before anyone even noticed.'

Verdi's face was ashen with anger.

For his, Klaus had Afldalr. 'What else?'

She stared directly ahead, sifting through memories. 'They interrogated everyone. They found out I'd travelled with Alizarin's caravan. That's why they sent me back with the jemesh to give to you.' She glanced at the little bone hanging around Arik's neck.

Klaus' mind raced upon an invisible map. *Somewhere west, because of the wind* ... West, where Hesper's derelict cinnabar quarry lay, caking Rasan's nails with rust-red dirt.

Arik began pacing. 'Where in the Plains could a camp of this size crop up unnoticed?'

'Allegedly unnoticed,' Klaus reminded him.

'What about one of the western clandoms?' Verdi asked.

'I saw no open collusion with Baeron or Hesper, if that's what you mean,' said Rasan. 'Doesn't mean they've not been turning a blind eye to what happens on their land.'

Arik didn't moderate his scepticism. 'You had a chance to tell us all this before.'

'I wasn't sure you wouldn't go blabbing to the council.' Her defiance hid no apology. 'But none of you seem keen to bow to their whims, either.'

Verdi folded his arms. 'Tomorrow I'm going to demand that you be allowed to remain in Samsarra.'

'I don't think your aunt will overrule the council.' Her eyes flashed. 'Especially when I didn't have much to tell them.'

'Why didn't you tell them any of this?'

'I didn't trust them. Elders don't seem to care. All those pledges at the Assembly are dust. And other clan Elders are far worse – taking bribes from rich farmers, terrifying people into stockpiling grain at eye-watering prices ... even half-decent clans like Sisoda are too stubborn to change. At best, they'll just put little fires out. No one takes the pirates seriously. But the council listens to you.'

Arik laughed. 'You came back because you thought *we* could get the Elders to listen?'

Rasan's lower lip jutted stubbornly. 'Can't you speak with the Chieftainess?'

Klaus shrugged. 'I already told her my suspicions about the pirates building a stronghold near the Mengorian range, and she won't risk an investigation.'

'I know what the pirates are looking for.'

Verdi's mouth fell open. Rasan's cheeks coloured faintly, but she didn't flinch under their collective stare.

She lowered her voice. 'I heard two of them talking, full of drink. They laughed about a *skydisc*. One said they were chasing the wind, but the other disagreed. He said this time they won't give up looking...'

A thrill blazed down the back of Klaus' neck, like flame catching.

Arik's eyes slid to Klaus. 'What's a skydisc?'

'It's an astronomical map. A very ancient way of charting constellations.'

'What would pirates want with a scholar's instrument?'

'Skydiscs can be used to code locations.' Klaus leaned back in his chair. Excitement disturbed the void for the first time in days. 'What better way to safeguard a place than to write it in stars, rather than coordinates? Places, treasures...'

Verdi pulled his hand away from Ravi, who was nipping his fingers for attention. 'And you didn't tell my aunt?'

Rasan shifted. 'I didn't trust the Elders.'

Arik raised an eyebrow. 'But you trusted *us*?'

'You don't care about clan feuds or pledges when you save or take a man's skin.'

'Rather naïve of you, isn't it? Trusting two Northern sellswords.'

Her eyes flashed again. 'Prove me wrong, then.' She stood. 'I have to go, before the stablemaster who gave me a bed locks his gate for the night.'

'Where will you go next?' asked Verdi. 'Your clan...'

Her laugh was brittle. 'Periam got what they deserved. They chose the dark, and now it's rewarded them.'

She slipped out of the kitchen door, a light-footed shadow. It was a clear night, but the stars did not burn so brightly here as they had done over the Wisdom's grove. *There is a justice you must seek*, the Wisdom had told him. Excitement shivered in Klaus' blood again.

'Let's go south,' he told Arik. 'Find this camp and sell our swords when we get there.'

It took Arik all of a few seconds of consideration. 'When?'

Verdi froze. 'What – can you hear yourself? Do you seriously think you can infiltrate a pirate camp?'

Klaus nodded. 'That's exactly what we'll do.'

'And assuming they don't kill you on sight, what about leaving? How do you know they'll let you?'

'We won't know until we get there.'

'That's ridiculous,' Verdi spluttered. He glared at Arik. 'And *you* promised Ayla to train those tumblers.'

Arik shrugged. 'I can find out who snatched you in Romel and tried to slip you a knife at the feastday. I'd be doing you and your clan a bigger service.'

'It's not worth it!'

'Intelligence will give your aunt the leverage she needs over the clans,' Klaus told him patiently. 'The pirates' numbers, their plans ... why they're so keen to get you out of the way.'

'Might be a well-timed disappearance, too, if Elodie's letter is anything to go by,' Arik added.

Verdi's mouth opened and closed furiously. 'I can't pull off a sellsword's disguise!'

Arik clapped his back. 'You'll be staying here with your clan.'

If it were at all possible, Verdi's anger swelled further. Ravi shrank away in alarm.

'You can't leave me here!' He rounded on Klaus in explosive fury. 'What are you hoping to achieve? Find something to buy your freedom if you go back to Dunraven?'

Klaus' voice hardened. 'I've no interest in appeasing the Wintermantels. They can burn for all I care.'

Verdi flinched, and Klaus knew he was thinking of Elodie. But callused as he was now, the cold confines of Form safely shielded him from sentiment.

'You can't be serious.' Verdi's voice quaked. 'You might not come back.'

'How's that different to the life we left?' Klaus softened his voice. 'It's always been this way, Verdi. You pledged to this clan, to something better, and deep down you want to stay in Derinda. And I promised you my help.'

'Not like this.'

He stomped out.

'Go after him,' Klaus told Arik, who was already halfway out the door.

Klaus turned his attention to his map, fashioning a new road in his mind. *For the pirates, you already have all the tools you need.* In the olive grove, the Wisdom's words had been a balm. Now that comfort was smothered by the enormity of the challenge he had chosen.

*

Verdi refused to speak of their plan, even when Arik excused himself from training the following day to arrange their supplies. Klaus took his horse to the blacksmith for reshoeing. Suddenly there was no time to lose.

He met Mayda in the market. There'd been no news of Fibbler. Her face was pale and pinched, and in the absence of a smile the many wrinkles framing her mouth only aged her.

'I'm sorry, mistress.'

'He may be out running errands yet. He'll get ever such a smacking when he's finished.'

Her hollow-eyed hope dispelled any doubts Klaus might have had about the waiting road.

'Ayla's doubled the watch around the citadel while the granary's being restocked,' Arik confided over their noon meal in the tavern, ahead of Verdi's return from the Arboretum. 'Let's wait until evening, get as far as we can before dark. The fewer eyes, the better.'

Blessedly, Thillaina was still in Yesmehen. Klaus returned in the afternoon to find Nerisen in the kitchen, collecting off-cuts from Thillaina's looms. Onax guarded her shoulder.

She spared Klaus a cursory greeting, but paused at the door before she left. 'Where are you going?'

'What do you mean?'

Tonight her eyes were the green glades of secret woods. 'I saw you at the smithy's. That horse was in no need of another shoe, unless you're planning to put her through her paces.'

'Marcin and I are running an errand for the council.'

'You only took the one horse to the smithy.'

Though inconvenient, it was pleasing how much she noticed. *I'll have to watch myself around her if I make it back.*

Klaus conjured a virtuous smile. 'I've been meaning to ask you something, Nerisen, seeing as you get everywhere. Have you met any other Unsworn Invelmari settlers lately?'

As he'd hoped, the question took her by surprise.

'Most Invelmari around here remain Unsworn. Sellswords come and go, but they don't settle.' Her gaze was very direct. 'So few Northerners acquire clanship, they're easy to remember. The last time I heard of an Invelmari pledging to a clan was a year or two ago.'

'Which clan?'

'Hesper.' She stacked the last fold of cloth into her basket. 'He married into the clan. I rarely travel west, but Thillaina does. She laughed at the woman who took him. Said she hoped his one ear didn't mean he'd hear his wife half as much.'

Shock jolted through him as the door clicked quietly shut behind her.

'Nothing is coincidence until it is.'

Klaus' ears roared in the empty kitchen. A one-eared Northerner, pledging to Hesper ... surely the merchant's son of Adilmar's tale, and none other than Clevenger Eldred.

The front door slammed. Still reeling, Klaus followed voices to the hallway.

'You shouldn't have risked coming back,' Arik rebuked.

Rasan lowered her hood. 'I don't plan to continue sneaking around the citadel like a thief for long.'

Verdi had returned with Arik. 'Tomorrow, the council will hear petitions. I've told my aunt that unless they charge you with a crime, you're to be allowed to remain in Samsarra.'

Rasan didn't seem encouraged by this. 'I wanted to speak with you before the Elders arrest me.'

'They're going to try and find the pirates' base,' Verdi interrupted, jerking his head at Klaus. But if he'd hoped she would share his reservations, he would be sorely disappointed.

At once she demanded, 'Let me come with you.'

'Not a chance.' Arik led them into the kitchen. 'You'll be recognised; you're a woman and you'll make us more vulnerable.'

Klaus thought she would strike him.

Arik didn't care. 'You're a first-rate soldier, but I saw that limp when you left last night. Your leg needs to heal.'

Klaus unrolled fresh parchment. 'I'm sorry to salt a wound, Rasan. But I need you to think back to where they took you...'

He combed through her memory, extracting every detail of terrain she could recall. Verdi listened in prickly silence. Arik prowled, impatient to leave. Thillaina was expected home from Yesmehen, so no one was surprised when a horse whinnied outside. The maid was still up, but Verdi went to open the door. Moments later, he returned not with Thillaina, but Alizarin.

Arik stared from nephew to uncle.

'You –' His glare settled on Verdi, who had the grace to look guilty.

'I'm sorry,' Verdi mumbled, beet red through his defiance. 'Someone needed to reason with you.'

Klaus' heart sank. There was no point in being angry. *If he orders Ayla to detain us, we'll be prisoners in the citadel.*

'Well?' Alizarin didn't seem surprised to see Rasan. Klaus had to admire his granite. 'What are you hoping to achieve?'

'The donkey work you've been avoiding,' Arik snapped. 'Aren't you tired of stabbing in the dark? Invelmari mercenaries can just as easily find work with pirates as anywhere else.'

'It's madness.' Desperation pleaded behind Verdi's anger. 'Uncle, you told me yourself how difficult it'll be, with the storms and the drought.

It's not worth the risk.'

But Alizarin wasn't listening to his nephew. The long look he shared with Klaus was not friendly, but at last it was one of understanding.

'Take the western trail,' Alizarin said finally. 'It's longer, but you'll avoid Mantelon's patrols. Though you'll have to dodge the battalion Lebas have mobilised to their western border.'

Verdi was momentarily speechless, first with shock and then furious betrayal.

'But you said – you *know* they'll never make it back!'

'We've not failed quite yet, Verdi,' Arik half-joked. 'You won't be rid of us so easily.'

Klaus shook his head at Arik, bracing himself. 'Not you.'

'What are you talking about?'

'One of us needs to stay here with Verdi.'

'*What?*'

'You promised to act as Verdi's guard.' Klaus knew Arik would be much harder to appease. 'Your word will be worthless here if you abandon it now. We don't both need to go, and you'll never forgive yourself if the third attempt on his life is successful.'

Arik stared back at him murderously.

Alizarin watched them with the keenness of one of Suman's falcons. 'Perhaps the warrior chooses glory and bloodlust over his promises.'

Rasan cleared her throat. 'You're marked with that jemesh, Master Marcin. There's a hefty price on your head. Blind men will be able to describe you by now…'

Arik rubbed his temples. Klaus could see him calling on every ounce of his Form.

'If you wish to leave this house unseen, don't delay,' Alizarin told Rasan. 'The last delivery to the granary will arrive any minute, escorted by extra patrols.'

'Wait.' Klaus unbelted his sword when she rose. He held it out to her, his middle contracting. 'This is in your safekeeping now. It is more dear to me than you know.'

She accepted it warily as though the steel might scald. 'But what will you use?'

'Give me your sword.'

There was no disobeying the Form folded into his order.

'This is a poor replacement.' Rasan's hands faltered unbuckling the sheath from her belt. 'That steel might secure your safe passage … why would you leave it behind?'

Klaus took her blade. 'I'm in trouble if a weapon is my only advantage.'

Her eyes shone, raw. 'I'll take the greatest care of them both.'

She left by the kitchen door, leaving an awful silence in her wake.

Alizarin wasted no time. 'The same goes for you, chronicler. No one will stop you if I accompany you through the gate.'

Arik struggled to curb anger with reason. 'What about Dunraven's spies? If you find the mine, there's a good chance you'll be discovered.'

Klaus picked up his pack. 'I know.'

He stifled a shiver. How many times had they shared this moment? The promise of death laced every Form and buttressed Northern devotion to the Blood Pact. But Verdi had never learned to live in this shadow that waited over the passageway to Sturmsinger's table.

'Don't go, Klaus.' His voice was thick with tears.

Klaus embraced him. 'I'll come back. Have faith.'

The house was still quiet. Alizarin opened the door, waiting.

Arik squeezed Klaus' shoulder. 'Bottoms up.'

Klaus rode beside Alizarin through the quiet citadel, now cloaked in twilight. Alizarin's cooperation was a cold relief. *He doesn't believe I'll return, but he's got no qualms letting me go.* After all, Verdi needed only one Invelmari guard. Klaus knew Alizarin wouldn't be sorry to see the back of a man his nephew had once served.

The grain wagons reached the citadel as they slipped out. Alizarin rode past them unquestioned. Klaus stopped outside the gate. His heart raced in livid rebellion, but there was no Spyglass commanding his loyalty any longer.

He asked, 'What do you know about sfarsgour sickness?'

Alizarin's pause betrayed rare surprise. 'It's fatal and highly contagious. There's not been a breakout in the South for a few hundred years. Why?'

That sugar merchant's death was surely a fabrication, then. Most likely he went back home – to die under mysterious circumstances in Dunraven once his uses were up. The lifespans of Spyglasses were notoriously short.

'The squire to Invelmar's last Spyglass joined Hesper in the past two years.' Klaus struggled against the foulness of betrayal. 'He's an Intelligencer, a quiet one. When we left, he was returning to Dunraven – probably from Derinda. He knows about the mine. He's been spying here for years – it *must* be about the mine. I can't think what else has stirred the Eye's interest here.'

Even Alizarin couldn't mask his dismay. 'Could he have been monitoring the pirates?'

'Mere pirates will be of no concern to Dunraven. The North would happily watch pirates terrorise the Plains if it weakens the clans.'

'Then what –'

'Gather your alliance. Make Elders listen by any means necessary. Lie, if you have to. Remind Emra the Blood Pact doesn't prohibit another invasion of the South. If pirates have found this spring … Adela won't let you have the sea. She'll take it, but she'll let the pirates tear you apart first.' Klaus let all masks fall away, determined to impart his fear. 'And if there's something valuable in that mine, pirate raids will be nothing to what will follow.'

'Whose side will you stand by then?'

Klaus gazed into waiting dusk. Alizarin always seemed to coax out the parts of him he tried to bury the deepest. 'Tell Arik to look out for the one-eared man. He may have already returned to Derinda.'

Darkness veiled Alizarin's eyes. 'Seems your hours here were always numbered.'

Klaus picked up his reins. 'Arik understands the pirates. I'd use him well.'

'I have yet to thank you.'

'For what?'

'Viridian would never have returned if you had not been forced to leave the North.'

Invelmari and Derindman appraised one another, both in short supply of words. Then they parted, divided at last by a common path.

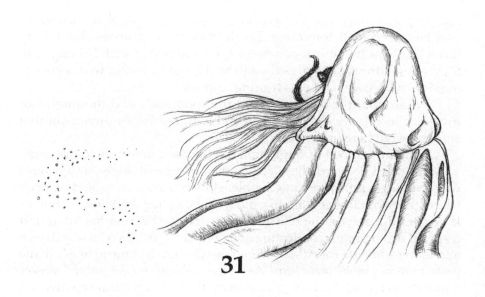

31

Dear Company

He rode west in the dredges of dusk as Alizarin had advised, finding shelter for the night under a clump of cat-willows a few miles from Samsarra. Winter did not spare the desert, and he was glad of his seal-pelt coat.

'I'm sorry, sister.' He filled his mare's nosebag. 'There won't be much fresh grass soon.'

Night birds and beastlings softly scratched the silence. The knot building in Klaus' breast eased once he was outside the citadel, sharpening his awareness of the desert. It hovered beside his other senses now, like a shadow across the periphery of his vision, or the ghost of a smell in his nostrils. He could feel with certainty where Samsarra sprawled behind him, and was dimly aware of a rocky change to come in the terrain ahead once he veered south tomorrow. The desert was an unsurpassable infinity no longer. Now he could touch its enormity rather than merely imagine it. It was a wondrous feeling, as though he'd forged a bridge with a greater mind than his own, and was waiting to cross.

What would it be like, to feel the riverlands and mountains of Invelmar in this way? Would he be able to reach this understanding anywhere but here in the desert?

Longing stabbed through him, fraying the connection to the land.

He gazed skyward; the alien language of these strange constellations was growing a little more intelligible. How much study would he need before they would greet him like old friends, as they had done at home? If he closed his eyes, the Northern sky stretched across his mind and carpeted his thoughts, comforting and familiar ... but then he was drawn into matters fit only for Afldalr, and now was not the time to linger in the past, for it only embittered him. *'And bitterness is the Form's poison,'* Master Arnander rebuked. Klaus was certain of this now: each time he dwelled on his past life and his abrupt departure from it, his heart hardened and the desert turned away from him, so that once again he felt alone in the middle of its sea of sand and stone.

Blessedly, the wind hadn't yet returned. But the cold crept into their bones, so by morning his mare was grumpy and his limbs were wooden. He was grateful to get moving despite the tiredness that followed a broken sleep. He checked his coordinates and set off, wondering what he would do with his dear instruments when he finally met with pirates.

*

Very deep down, Verdi knew it could prove to be a stroke of genius. If Klaus returned with intimate knowledge of the pirates, the Derindin could strike them at their heart.

But Klaus might not return.

How he longed to be a prince's shadow again in Dunraven, avoiding the baleful eye of Ackley the butler and hoping for a brush with Elodie. Dreams of discovering Derinda seemed naïve and laughable now.

Have faith, Klaus had said. He didn't.

Derinda *had* stolen into his heart. Samsarra had enveloped him with open arms. It made Verdi's grievance all the greater. He hated his uncle for not stopping Klaus from leaving. He hated his aunt for not risking a spy. He hated the clans for the pettiness that kept them weak.

'Your friend's risked his life to help you,' Alizarin muttered under his breath at the council's petition hearings the following day. 'You can start thanking him by making a man of yourself. Grown men don't sulk.'

But Verdi was angry, despite one triumph: Fenral alone had barred Rasan's return to Samsarra, making it easier to overturn Rasan's banishment. Anger distilled his thoughts. He'd been floundering through a haze since the first mention of Lorendar. With anger, the cloud finally cleared.

'Most of the damage was to western Lebasi hamlets,' an Elendran scout reported after the last petition was heard. 'There were no raids east towards their citadel –'

The doors flew open. A man strode into the chamber, followed by the tumblers stationed outside. Arik's fingers closed around the hilt of his sword.

'Chieftainess.' The man stopped before Emra. Ayla rose from her chair, scowling at the tumblers lagging uncertainly behind him.

One of the hapless tumblers mumbled, 'Ahena, I didn't know what to do –'

'Chieftainess, I bring news,' the man interrupted. 'Chieftain Yodez deployed sixteen battalions against pirates across Sisoda's clandom, and nearly all of them have been defeated.'

Silence stunned the chamber.

'How is this possible?' Tourmali demanded.

The messenger was a stocky man, dark hair silver-streaked, sand-mask still tied around his face. Verdi thought he looked familiar, but after a lifetime filled with dark-eyed Northerners, every pair of brilliant blue eyes still summoned a ghost.

'Sisoda were overwhelmed, Emra-hena.' The man was still catching his breath. 'Now the pirates are holding hamlets and villages all over the clandom. Chieftain Yodez has called his troops back to Pir Sehem.'

Emra grew ashen. 'Who sent you?'

'Innkeeper Riorga in Romel.' He held out a letter; Emra broke the seal, glancing over it. 'A few Sisodan survivors sought refuge there. I spoke to them myself.'

'See this man's expenses are paid,' Emra ordered the tumblers, who led him out.

An ugly tension stifled the chamber.

'If there was any doubt about the pirates' numbers...' Tourmali leaned back heavily in his chair. 'We should prepare for worse to come.'

'You're assuming they can continue this plunder,' Fenral objected. 'If they had such strength, they would have taken Pir Sehem, not a handful of hamlets. They may have just spent the sting in their tail.'

Ugh. Fenral was the summary of everything Rasan hated about the Elders, Verdi decided: proud, dismissive, arrogant. *And obsessed with*

Merensama.

Ayla's jaw tightened with worry. 'It takes a great many swords to overwhelm a Sisodan Chieftain, Elder Fenral.'

Emra passed the note to Maragrin. 'Hesper and Baeron will be waiting for an opportunity to move their troops into the S'beyan Strip. It's the trophy that's been missing from their troves for centuries. If they take it now, opposition to Merensama will grow. People will flock to strength.'

To strength, not fantasy.

Maragrin's frown multiplied his wrinkles. 'Take heart. Voldane's just declared himself suzerain over a little empire … he's never had as many enemies as he does now.'

'Chieftain Yodez won't leave the Strip unprotected,' said Ayla mulishly.

'Not even to defend the rest of the clandom?' Emra questioned. 'I don't believe he'll sacrifice all of Sisoda for the S'beyan Strip, General. And when he mobilises the reserves stationed there, the Strip will be Voldane's for the taking.'

Fenral sighed. 'Listen to reason. If the pirates had numbers enough –'

'*If!*' Verdi couldn't contain himself any longer. '*If* they're strong enough! *If* they're taking hostages! Is this what you're worried about? The advantage Sisoda's downfall might give to your rivals?' He glared around the chamber, no longer caring what they thought of him. 'What about Sisoda's clanfolk, who may be captives now?'

'You'd do well to think before you speak,' snapped Fenral. 'If Baeron and Hesper take the S'beyan Strip, they'll finally share a border. They would gain control of half of the trading highways between Romel and the border towns - highways Sisoda currently control. Derinda will be at their mercy. You don't think that'll harm far more people?'

Verdi scowled. 'Then stop wasting time second guessing what the pirates *might* do next. Do something about them!'

'I favour your nephew's view, Emra-hena,' Tourmali cut in. 'We need to fortify this clandom lest we sleepwalk into a similar fate. Let's not nurture a false sense of security.'

'Elendrans won't support a call to arms mid-winter,' Fenral retorted.

Emra pinched the bridge of her nose. 'How many more tumblers can you spare to station along our western and southern borders, General?'

'Three hundred. It'll take a fortnight to recall our reserves.' Ayla read the innkeeper's note. 'Yodez underestimated the pirates' numbers. We can't make the same mistake.'

Alizarin broke his gloomy silence. 'So we station soldiers along our borders all winter?'

'*Our* clandom has suffered no raids,' Fenral repeated. 'The west is a long way away. The pirates won't have numbers enough to stretch their hand so far east as well.'

'Forgive me, Ahena, but the pirates will come,' said Arik, speaking for the first time. 'They will come when your tumblers' grain and water has run out.'

Fenral scowled, still sore that Verdi had insisted on Arik's presence. 'Remarkable, how much a riverlander seems to know about sand pirates.'

Verdi restrained venomous thoughts. 'The pirates aren't so different to Far Northern raiders.'

Arik ignored her, addressing the Chieftainess. 'When Far Northerners have no hope of capturing a stronghold, they whittle away at its defences with little skirmishes until they can take what's left in fragments. But they also learned to use that approach to disguise their strength and mislead us. Many Invelmari have fallen for that trap, led by captains who lost their nerve and grew impatient waiting them out.'

Tourmali threw up his hands. 'Are you suggesting we just *wait*?'

'Not idly. Don't abandon the search for new allies. Elendra has only petitioned Lebas, Fraivon and Sisoda. Why not look to the others?'

Fenral looked at Arik as though he'd grown another head. '"*Others*?"'

'If the rumours are true, Voista's lost tumblers all summer intercepting raiders preying on caravans returning from the border towns,' Arik continued. 'They're your northern neighbour. If you gain their cooperation, you would secure eyes to watch your northern front from afar.'

Verdi watched his aunt anxiously; Arik had gathered every shred of news he could find concerning the pirates' movements.

At least Emra heard him out. 'Voistans are amongst the most corrupt of our clans, Master Marcin. Once they stole so much water from our northern aqueducts, drought hit the Arboretum. How do you expect this clan to trust such a neighbour?'

Verdi curbed discouragement. *Klaus is wading through the desert while they jabber.* 'Why not rebuild bridges? Isn't that what Merensama's about?'

'You're still new to this land,' Tourmali told him, not unkindly. 'You've not the memory of the past to focus your vision.'

Maragrin jabbed the air with his stick. 'Perhaps his vision is true, without the past to cloud it.'

Arik appealed to the Chieftainess again. 'Speak with your neighbours, Ahena. As their need grows, you may find them open to new bedfellows.'

'Ah, that famous tactic of Invelmari warbringers,' Feral sneered. '*Speaking.*'

Arik's reply was far more civil than she deserved. 'A thousand words pass between Invelmar and her enemies now before any steel is raised against them.'

But Emra folded the note. 'There will be no bargaining with clan

Voista.'

Verdi hated how quickly hope was crushed here. 'Aunt, if you just try –'

'You joined this clan to continue great work, nephew, not gamble. I'll not risk our people's safety –'

'Their safety, or their pride?'

'That's enough, Viridian.' Emra's patience vanished. 'I've given you my answer. If you can't serve this clan, then perhaps you're not ready to.'

Something snapped inside him.

'If I can't be just like all of you, you mean,' Verdi shot back. 'A sheep, only kept at the front of the flock with a good loud bell on my collar.' He stood, now barely feeling the slice of her eyes, and stalked out of the council chamber.

Anger buzzed in Verdi's ears. *They'll think even less of me now.* But if Klaus could brave Ealdormen and pirates, he could put up with Elders.

'What a waste of time,' Verdi spluttered to Arik. 'I'd happily leave this place tomorrow.'

But that was anger speaking, and they both knew it. Later, he would think of the Fibblers and Coarens, and Meron tending the seed bank; the prisoners the pirates had taken; the shallow graves they'd dug in the sand. There would be no going back to not knowing Derinda.

'Let's get some rest,' said Arik. 'We've plenty of work to do while Klaus is away.'

Verdi grunted. 'We're not going to run out of time waiting.'

'Come on, Verdi. It's not as though we've lost him already.'

But Verdi couldn't imagine how Klaus could possibly find his way back. Anger faltered, and in its ashes he felt foolish and helpless.

*

By noon, Klaus was sure he was being followed.

He'd been riding since dawn. The road took him through a rolling landscape dotted with trees and derina shrubs, becoming more rocky as he veered westward. A small cloud of dust behind him had been growing closer all morning. He stopped behind a thicket and waited.

Eventually, a rider appeared on the road.

He stepped out of the trees, startling Nerisen. She tugged at her reins, her mare almost stumbling.

Klaus shook his head. 'If I had been a pirate, you would be at my mercy now.'

She pulled her sand-mask down.

'What are you doing here, Nerisen?'

'Rasan told me where you were going.' She dismounted. 'I want to go south too.'

'Do you know what the pirates would do to a woman prisoner?'

The look she gave him in reply was withering. 'You shouldn't go alone.'

Their horses tossed their heads and flicked their tails as they wrangled.

'I refused to take Rasan and *she's* a tumbler, never mind a … you.'

Her eyes narrowed, daring him to go on.

He tried to be reasonable. 'What use is it if we both get captured? I'm relying on that –'

'You're going to let yourself get captured? I thought you were going to look for work.'

'Which will probably involve letting pirates take me captive. I doubt they'll let a soldier stroll into their camp, even one willing to swing a sword for them.'

'They were right. You *are* insane.'

'And you came anyway?' Klaus folded his arms. 'Why are you really here?'

Green fire glowered in her eyes. 'Why should a warbringer make this discovery for us?'

He wasn't sure whether she was more angry with him for claiming this honour, or with the Elders who had abandoned it to him.

'I've more right to do this than you,' she said. 'And you've no right to stop me. Unless what they say about Invelmari is true – that you Northerners only strive for gold and glory.'

'The struggle for justice has no proprietor. Does it matter who delivers it?' He crossed the space between them and grasped both her shoulders before she could reply. 'You struggle more sincerely for your people than anyone I've met in all the Part, and I have known Isarnanheri. You would put champion warriors to shame. I swear I seek neither gold nor glory here – if I'd wanted that, I would have left this Part altogether. Don't put those who depend on you at risk for a service a much lesser person could accomplish.'

He watched words shrink in her mouth. Reluctantly, he lowered his hands. Even through his gloves, his palms felt scalded. It was as much a taboo to touch a Derindwoman uninvited as it was to be alone in an Invelmari woman's company. But she didn't berate him. Instead, he could see the cogwheels of her thoughts spinning.

'I'll go with you a bit further,' she said. 'Then I can take a report back to Alizarin.'

'The further you stray from Elendran territory, the more likely you'll run into trouble.'

'I'll take the longer route through Fraivon's clandom. They're deploying tumblers to their borders, it'll be safer.'

There was no use arguing with her. 'I can't stop you.'

'No, you can't.'

Selfishly, he was glad. Nerisen was the passion and the serenity of the desert at once. Pyres of kindness burned beneath her rind, and he had felt their fire. *Have a care.* Her presence was magnetising, like the brightest constellation in an alien sky, nameless but dazzling.

If something happens to her, it will be all the harder.

He shackled this feeling in Afldalr where, for better or worse, the pyres in his own heart were sent to cool.

*

Arik didn't know whether it was born of hardship or the torment of the desert sun, but the tumblers' resilience impressed him. *They may not have Form or Invelmari steel, but they learn fast.*

'Again.' He threw the metal rod to Starra; she caught it with a grimace but didn't stop to rub another bruise to her palm. Wooden switch for agility, heavy iron to build strength. Darkness for mastering absolute control. And he was learning to make use of the wind. Warriors and Isarnanheri perfected the Jarnstiga on rocky hillsides amongst goats and mountain wolves. Many a sprained ankle later, even steel became nimble.

Arik circled the sparring ring again. Form cleared his mind of everything but the duel. When he raised Thunraz, his sword, all other thoughts vanished. And so he'd passed almost every waking moment since Klaus had left: in the present, with what he knew best.

Unlike Verdi, who had initially been nothing short of inconsolable. Now he was like someone coming out of mourning – and not as the little servant Arik knew. Something had happened to Verdi, as though a metal bullied by the forge hammer had finally snapped out of its pliable state in the furnace into something much harder.

Arik felt eyes on his back. He disarmed Starra and turned; Alizarin stood outside the ring.

Efero took Starra's place; a lanky youth who made knives dance between his fingers, but whose arms still lacked the powerful swing a decent blade demanded. He drew his sword.

'Not today,' Arik told him, passing him the heavy metal rod instead.

The tumblers began sparring. Arik left the ring and joined Alizarin, bellowing corrections when their footing slipped.

'I wonder,' Alizarin murmured. 'What would they say if they knew you were training Southern savages in Jarnstiga?'

Arik was in no humour for Alizarin's contempt. *Besides, I'm hardly teaching them Jarnstiga.* 'Verdi's at the Arboretum, if you're looking for him.'

'He ought to spend more time here with you.'

'He's not a soldier.' Arik was blunt. Life was easier like that. 'He's good with his head, and that's what he should be left to use.'

'Actually I came to speak with you.'

Arik raised an eyebrow. Alizarin lowered his voice, though the clash of metal was cover enough.

'I leave for the Romelian Assembly tomorrow. Chieftain Ilgarz of Voista will be there.'

Arik's thoughts moved quickly. 'And?'

'We could seek a private audience with him before the Assembly.'

'What for?'

'To petition Voista for an alliance with our clan.'

'And what will you tell your aunt if he agrees?'

Alizarin watched the tumblers lazily, betraying no sign of conspiring to negotiate with a clan with whom his council wanted no association.

'That it would be foolish to refuse a well-positioned ally.' Alizarin paused. 'Pride is at least partly to blame for this impasse, whatever past grievances my clan may call upon for an excuse.'

'Elendra will be in a very awkward position if your council rejects an offer from Voista.'

'An unappetising prospect, but the truth is none of the Elders believe Voista would consider it, so they won't try. They may feel differently if Voista's cooperation is already secured.'

'But can Voista be trusted?'

Alizarin's smile had never been so humourless. 'Corruption is the air we breathe in the Plains, Master Marcin. But even Voista know they've not coffers deep enough to bribe away this species of pirate.'

'And I suppose you want me to ask Verdi to come.'

'He seems to respond better to you.'

Arik grunted. 'These days I'm not sure he'll listen to anyone.'

'Except for the chronicler.'

So he's noticed the change in Verdi as well. 'And if this Chieftain laughs in our faces?'

'Let's hope he doesn't.'

'Verdi is *not* going to take the blame for this if it backfires.'

Alizarin stiffened, probably deeply offended. Arik couldn't care less.

'Your friend asked me to tell you something.' Alizarin lowered his arm for Saya, face closing off. 'He said to look out for the one-eared man.'

Arik froze. What had Klaus been thinking, telling this man anything? This time when he rejoined the tumblers, his mind was much harder to clear.

*

It had been weeks since Verdi had last removed the gnomon from its sleeve.

He waited until the thick of night, when Arik was asleep with Ravi burrowing into his side. Arik thought the whole business was a waste of time. Verdi was inclined to agree – were it not for the pull the gnomon exerted on him, even now through the cocoon of his anger.

'*Look within.*' Klaus had certainly thought it was worth trying to restore the moondial. '*Maybe it needs to coax an answer out of you.*' But Klaus was gone.

Verdi's throat tightened. *However am I supposed to help these people now?*

Outside, a new moon was quietly born. *How could a gnomon possibly work with no moonlight at all in the sky?* The metal anchor warmed in his grip. His resolve to try again dissipated, and he slipped it back into its sleeve. He brushed away angry tears, falling asleep before the salt mask dried on his cheeks like the crust carpeting the bed of a dried-out river.

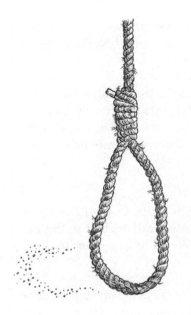

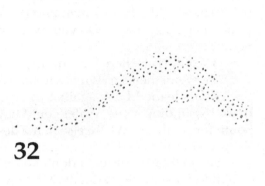

32

Treason

EVERYWHERE HE SAW DEPRAVITY AND AVARICE.
'CONTAIN THIS POISON,' HE ORDERED HIS WARRIORS,
AND EXTINGUISHED ALL THOSE HE ENCOUNTERED SOUTHWARD.

SONNONFER: THE SECOND REDRAWING

They had been riding for five days, occasionally slowed by wind. Klaus read his compass in the dwindling daylight. 'We'll cross into Fraivon's clandom tomorrow.'

Nerisen replied, 'I know.'

He was thirsty. Derina water restored his strength but never seemed to quite quench his thirst. They'd had a good drink at a waterhole yesterday, but Nerisen didn't expect another for some time.

They found a rocky shelf amongst the dunes to rest for the night.

'Be careful,' Nerisen warned. 'Snakes nest wherever they can. The storms force more of them overground.'

There wasn't enough brushwood for a fire. They fed and rubbed down the horses and ate quickly while they could still see.

'South of Fraivon, even derina grows scarce,' said Nerisen. 'Save your water for then.'

'Have you ever been as far south as that?'

'Not quite, but close. There's a village in the outskirts of Fraivon's land that I try to visit if a caravan's passing. But caravans rarely go there now. There's little fresh water, and the storms have grown worse.' She pulled her cloak closer. 'Do you really think there's a pirate base in the South?'

'I wouldn't be here if I didn't.'

'How are they surviving without water?'

Klaus leaned back against the rock. Shy stars braved the early dusk. 'By finding some. Water could have gone undisturbed in the Far South for centuries. Where else in the desert could so many pirates base themselves unnoticed?'

She looked doubtful. 'I don't know.'

Blindness came gradually. Starlight here was generous but did not penetrate to the ground, and the moon had regressed to a sliver of itself. It was a darkness different to anything he had felt in the North; blunt and intelligent and bottomless, without airglow to soften its winding blow.

Nerisen's breathing quickened, sounding shallow.

'Are you alright?'

'Yes.'

But fear laced her voice. He stopped himself from reaching for her hand.

'Those snakes apparently have a taste for Northern blood,' he reminded her. 'As for everything else, I can probably swing a sword in the dark without taking your head off.'

There was an unexpected burst of laughter. It was the first time he'd heard her laugh.

She replied in her own voice. 'I've been out in the open Plains all my life, but I'm rarely without a fire. I don't know what's come over me.'

Her honesty was startling, as though night had stripped away her guard. For this, he would gladly suffer such sightlessness.

'Sometimes big open spaces feel suffocating in the dark,' he said. 'Like lying awake in a grave.'

She shuddered. 'Don't.'

'Isn't there a kind of freedom in not being able to see though your eyes are wide open?'

'Now you sound like a mad man.'

'Quite the opposite. This is when you can see most clearly. You see the things that matter.'

He paused, reaching out tentatively with his mind, listening to the desert.

'What if I tell you,' he said, 'that Cora lies just north-east of where we are now, behind your left shoulder?' He wasn't sure what was more exhilarating; the awareness itself, or sharing it with her. 'And a little to your right, Ahravel ... directly south-west to it, a great ridge will grow into a small mountain that stretches across Fraivon's land. A cluster of big dunes will crop up to the south-west tomorrow and likely slow us down, but there'll be a deep crack in the hill just beyond them where we can shelter tomorrow night.'

For a long moment she was silent, until he thought she might have vanished in the darkness; a lovely figment of his imagination.

'How do you know?' she asked at last.

Truthfully, he admitted, 'I don't know.'

Eventually, her breathing deepened, and he too fell asleep.

In the morning, she took his compass and made three measurements. She returned it without a word, her green eyes unfathomable.

The Plains here rose and fell around islands of dunes that sometimes slid, forcing them to dismount and continue on foot. In many of the reports Klaus had collected, pirates roamed this patch between Fraivonian and Lebasi land. At one point he saw dark lines of movement on the horizon through his eyescope.

'They might be Fraivonian tumblers moving to their western border,' he said, and steered them east. Thus it was late afternoon when they reached the hill he'd predicted the night before, and growing dark when they descended to the long crevice in its flank to make camp. It was almost as he'd imagined it.

Nerisen ducked under the overhanging rock. 'This should be sheltered enough for a fire.'

She was quiet feeding the horses. He warmed some lamh'met with derina water.

'Do you think the clans will agree to move against the pirates if you find their stronghold?' she asked.

'Rasan would say no.'

She rolled her eyes. 'I know what Rasan thinks.'

'Some won't budge, no matter what we find. Seems there are Derindin who would be happy to let the pirates dismantle their rivals for them.' Klaus paused to chew; the porridge was thick and pasty, but they couldn't spare the water to improve it. 'At home, all I heard of the South was of the clans' feuding. They've certainly earned that reputation.'

Nerisen looked put out. 'It's not all petty. Some clans have done terrible things that can't just be forgotten. Grievances make people twisted and vengeful – even good people.'

'But then nothing changes. The Elders make a theatre of their grievances at the Romelian Assemblies and keep fuelling the hatred.'

She frowned. 'Surely the Ealdormen have their differences.'

'Dissidence flouts the Blood Pact. Any challenge to the Blood Pact is treason punishable by death. Differences are set aside.'

'Only by force.'

'Absolutely. Then the living remain safe. A fair trade.'

'Dissidents should have a voice.'

'And what happens if they go too far, and chaos reigns? That's how Derinda crumbled into clandoms. Imagine, Nerisen,' he said. 'Imagine a life without poverty or bribes.'

Her two particular grievances, he knew. But Nerisen's disdain for the North was well-versed.

'I heard Adela once hanged a man and all his family for the "crime" of questioning whether an Ealdorman was fit to be a link in the Chain.' Defiance kindled golden sparks in her eyes. 'At least I think that was the charge – wish I could remember. You can't possibly think that's right.'

Klaus stirred the fire. He didn't need her to remember, for he'd been forced to watch. He had been only nine.

'Queen Adela is … heavy-handed.' Even here, so far from Dunraven, he chose words carefully. 'She had a hard life and lost all her children, and the next heir to the House of Rainard comes from the union of a nephew and a wife whom she hates.'

'Are you *defending* her?'

'No. But it's important to understand the root of a wrong. Only then can you hope to right it.'

'How's she any different to Baeron? Or the pirates?'

'She isn't. Except she protects the kingdom at whatever cost.'

'I bet you would have been punished just for saying that in the North,' she said scornfully. 'Don't you enjoy being able to speak freely?'

Not just punished. He'd been amongst Adela's favourites. His fall from grace would be a very long way down indeed.

'I suppose.'

'Is it House Wintermantel that'll inherit the throne from her?'

Klaus nodded at her full bowl. 'Eat, before it freezes. Yes, that's the next turn of the cycle.'

'Without *any* challenge from the other Ealdormen?' Nerisen tasted the porridge and grimaced. 'You're a terrible cook if you can't make lamh'met.'

'Sorry. I was afraid of using too much water.' He paused, but she was waiting for his reply. 'To challenge the cycle would undermine the Blood Pact.' Speaking of these things to Nerisen was easier than he'd expected. 'When Queen Adela dies, Wolfram Wintermantel will begin the thirty-ninth cycle of the Sturmsinger Chain. The Wintermantels were the first to support Ansovald Sturmsinger when he set out to unite the North and the Far North. Their claim is the oldest and the most undisputed.'

'Astonishing, how long a cycle of kings has been unbroken.' Grudging admiration hid behind her disdain.

He buttoned his coat, cold despite the small fire. 'Thanks to the Blood Pact. Every Ealdorman house has a chance to rule. Dissenters are weeded out. Invelmar won't risk the Pact. If it breaks, we fall.'

'And that's how they're rewarded with tyrants like Adela.'

'She's not a bad queen. Invelmar's coffers have swollen under her reign, and her treaty with Täntainen brokered the closest thing to peace we've ever had with the Far Northerners. Until he was assassinated, Invelmar was the safest she's ever been from their raids.'

'What will Adela do about the raids?'

'I don't know.' He stared into the fire. 'They're saying northern Invelmar has been ravaged these past two moons.'

Nerisen was incredulous. 'How can *Invelmar* be ravaged by mere raiders? At least here I can understand why *we* fall to pirates.'

'Because much like the pirates, Far Northerners hide in the ice, scattered over a terrain harder than you can imagine. But unlike the pirates, they answer to warlords who are clever and cruel. A handful of pests becomes a deadly plague.' Klaus sought her eyes; held them with a glimpse into dark possibility. 'Entire villages torched, families locked in their houses and burned to the ground, children stolen and returned skewered on Far Northern banners raised in the mountains ... raiders without honour fighting to win by any means necessary. And if they can't win, they punish. And that is what I fear for Derinda.'

She looked away, not wanting to see that future. 'Yet Invelmar still stands mighty.'

'Is that all that matters? What about those villagers? *Little people?*' Lord Wintermantel's voice rumbled through his heart again. *'The little people are the bonds that weld our steel and keep it from shattering.'* That voice still bruised him. 'No crime is too small to avenge.'

She shivered, and he didn't think it was from the cold. 'Would you be fighting there now if you weren't here?'

'Yes.'

She finished the lamh'met and cleaned the bowl with a handful of sand. 'Freedom is still not a fair trade for peace. And good kings can be replaced by tyrants. Then the Blood Pact becomes a curse.'

'A curse that's kept many lives safe. The Blood Pact is the true armour of Invelmar.'

'Honestly, Tristan,' she said, exasperated. 'Can you not admit the danger of allowing so much power to go unchallenged?'

'It's better than what you have here, where power has more parts than a pomegranate.' He shrugged. 'Everywhere in the Plains there is turmoil and hardship. Peace depends on the whims of clans. But the Blood Pact –' He leaned towards the fire. 'The more time that passes, the more powerful it becomes. Where else in the Seven Parts has there ever been such a wonder as the unity of Invelmar? The bonds between Invelmari are greater than any fortress or weapon their hands can build – bonds that outlive us when we pass. That's why men will die on the battlefield for the Blood Pact, and why women will leave their children behind to ride with them.' It was her turn to stare into the fire. *Imagining, I hope.* 'You asked if I think the clans might move against the pirates. I don't know, but I know what's possible.'

The fire flickered quietly between them. However tired he was, sleep never came easily. It didn't help that she was lying close. Eyes shut, he knew exactly where she was, felt her little movements.

'Will Lord Wintermantel be any better as king?' Sleep muffled her words.

He gazed up at the stars. 'I used to think so.'

Ironic, that he should serenade a girl with praise of the Sturmsinger Chain even as he ran from its turn.

Shame Arik's not here. He would have been pleased. If he saw him again, he'd be sure to tell him.

*

Verdi had put up with a lot of idle talk in taverns and barracks and servants' quarters, but *this* he couldn't tolerate.

'What right's a Northman got, anyway, poking into Derindin business?' The disgruntled farmhand had been dismissed by Laminhad's wife, for there was no need of his service while his former master was imprisoned, awaiting trial. 'Elders were happy enough to let Laminhad walk free. Would have left him alone, were it not for that chronicler's meddling.'

'It's in their blood.' A grizzly-bearded labourer belched loudly on too much drink and nodded to Verdi. 'Where's your other keeper, anyway? Deserted you already, has he?'

Face warming, Verdi stared back. This particular tavern counted enough well-to-do merchants amongst its regulars that the disgraced Laminhad had some supporters here.

'Bit too much to drink again, Relfi.' Broco poked the labourer's belly. 'Or is that belt of yours not yet snug enough around your guts?' A smattering of laughter followed.

'Traitors, all of them,' grumbled another Derindman. 'Nothing they know better than –'

Verdi's chair scraped the ground loudly as he stood.

'If the Chieftainess has seen fit to arrest Master Laminhad for treason, perhaps you should consider she has good reason to do so. Or is there no code of conduct in the South except for the favour of tavern drunks?'

The Derindin were taken aback by this, but recovered quickly.

'This ain't the North, young man,' Relfi slurred. 'The Elders aren't judge and executioner. We're a thinking people. We don't follow no Elder blindly.'

'No, you just lap up the rubbish of Babbles and shift loyalties from clan to clan instead when it suits, so that a paltry bandit can break one of your legs and snag the other,' Verdi snapped. 'That's why you have no compassion for a man who's been robbed of everything, though he's your own clansman. What kind of people are you if you're happy to let a guilty man walk free unchallenged?'

The tavern fell silent. His voice had carried over the tables. The disgust lacing this anger was heady. *Klaus is somewhere in the middle of the desert for this rabble.*

'Master Laminhad will be tried by the evidence of his actions, not by what favours he's secured from the lot of you.' Verdi turned to the farmhand. 'As for you, sir, if it's work you need, Laminhad is not the only master in the clandom. I'll help you find work elsewhere.'

He glared around the room, daring anyone else to throw in their silver. He'd been dreading Laminhad's sentencing, knowing his wife's confession had sealed his fate. But Klaus' departure gave Verdi bigger things to worry about. Arik came in from the stable, and slowly the chatter and clatter resumed.

*

Laminhad had nowhere to hide after his wife divulged the payment he'd made to the pirates for sparing his life.

'What is your verdict?'

Elendrans liked to think they were clean, but Alizarin would wager that bribes had softened the hearts of at least two of the jury. Far better odds than most of the other clans, Tourmali would say, as though this were something to be proud of.

The woman who rose to reply, a schoolmistress, glanced at Laminhad.

'Guilty by a majority, Ahena.'

The chamber rumbled. Emra had made the trial public, because only a good airing of Laminhad's dirty linen was going to mitigate the anticipated fallout in the merchants' quarter. Wealthy merchants too often considered themselves untouchable.

Emra rose. 'We shall adjourn.'

Ordinarily, a unanimous decision was required for a verdict of guilt where execution would be sought. Except in the case of treason, when the council was permitted to pass sentence. The Elders gathered wearily in the anteroom of the council chamber.

'We could argue that the jury has not fulfilled the law of unanimity...' Tourmali began.

'And lessen the weight of his crime?' Maragrin shook his. 'No. He is guilty of treason.'

Alizarin suspected his aunt's mind had already been made up, whatever the jury decided.

'How can even one of them still have doubt?' Tourmali rubbed his temples, exasperated. 'The sheer amount of evidence we have now – a detailed *confession* –'

Alizarin grunted. 'Gold, that's how. Not that anyone will be able to prove a juror's been bribed.'

'Viridian,' said the Chieftainess. 'Have you anything to say? You've been very quiet.'

Alizarin's heart sank. *All we need now is an outburst of well-meaning doe-eyed naivety.*

'I'm not a jurist.' Viridian actually *looked* sullen today. 'In the North, loyalty is well rewarded. If this man walks free, what incentive do your clanfolk have to remain loyal to Elendra?'

Tourmali pursed his lips. 'He wouldn't be walking free, he'd be a lifelong prisoner. The question is whether he *intended* to harm Gerin, or whether he was acting in desperation in the heat of the moment.'

Alizarin couldn't help but recall the splendid knife Laminhad had left behind at home before setting off on his fateful race to Romel. *Perhaps he's even more guilty than we think.*

'Did Laminhad know beyond all doubt what would happen to Gerin's caravan once the pirates took it?' An uncanny shadow of Klaus hovered over Viridian's shoulder. 'Of course he did, they've been snatching and murdering people for months. Worse, he knew Gerin's wife and workers would be with the caravan. So yes, he had intent. He can't worm out of that now.'

And that was how Laminhad ended up hanging the following dawn, to the shock and chagrin of those moneybags in the citadel. A handful would pack up their warehouses and sever their clan ties, making a great show of taking their fortunes and patronage elsewhere.

Good riddance. Viridian stomached it well. *Maybe he's made of sterner stuff after all.*

Alizarin ought to have been pleased at this glimpse of grit. But it was tainted with a prevailing waft of the North.

*

Saya's claws dug into Alizarin's forearm. He'd never been less pleased to see Romel's gates. Verdi rode ahead, flanked by Arik. Ayla had arranged a sizeable escort of tumblers, but Alizarin was still uneasy. The Murhesla curbed chaos within the citadel but had no qualms with kidnap.

It's necessary. Viridian would never gain experience kept under glass in Samsarra. That was how Alizarin had convinced Emra to let him attend the Assembly in an Elder's place.

There were a few hours yet until the Assembly. Chieftain Ilgarz should be awaiting them. Tenken, the captain escorting Alizarin's party, was a grizzled veteran more devoted to Lorendar and Merensama than to Emra or Elendra, which was exactly why Alizarin had chosen him.

Ayla wouldn't miss his selection, especially in light of what might follow. He would deal with Ayla later.

'Go to our safehouse and find out who's lodging nearby,' Tenken ordered a few of the tumblers. 'We'll regroup after the Assembly. The rest of you – come with me.'

Alizarin led them to a house with a tumbler at the door. Inside, a small party waited.

One of the tumblers clapped. 'I should have raised the wager!'

Chieftain Ilgarz wasn't there, but sitting by the window was Elder Grahza. He was a rotund man, bloated not with fat but water, his legs swollen and sometimes seeping through his trousers. Those who called him Watershin never did so to his face. What he lacked in physical advantage he made up for with callously sharp wit. He was the shrewdest and least malleable of Voista's Elders.

So Alizarin wasn't entirely pleased to see him.

Saya gripped Alizarin's shoulder. 'Thank you for coming, Elder Grahza.'

'Don't thank me yet.' Watershin's voice was much bigger than he was. His perpetual wheeze sounded worse. 'You'll forgive me if I don't stand...'

There were six other Voistans; one was Croso, their envoy. The rest were tumblers.

Croso's face broke into a sardonic smile. 'So it's true. You've hired Northern mercenaries.'

To Alizarin's surprise, Viridian replied for himself. 'The Northerners came with me.'

'What are we here for, Alizarin? It's almost time for the Assembly.' Croso had the swagger of a tumbler with ambitions beyond her station. 'I hope you've not brought us here to jabber about Lorendar. Our reply would be a bad introduction to your nephew.'

'We've not,' Viridian said tartly, before Alizarin could reply.

So this is what he is when he's out of Klaus' shadow.

Croso was as tiresome as Alizarin remembered. She jerked her head at Arik. 'Invelmari swords can be bought and sold. How can we trust him?'

Watershin was also tired. 'Be quiet, Croso.' He looked at Alizarin. 'Well?'

Alizarin had rehearsed from Samsarra to Romel's gates.

'I came to propose an alliance between our clans in the East. To safeguard the north-eastern caravan routes from the border towns to Romel, and protect the water springs supplying both our clandoms.' There wasn't a sneer left in the room. 'Both our citadels have been safe from raids, but you've suffered heavy losses on your northern roads. Together, we can put up a better shield against the pirates.'

Watershin laughed.

Laughter fell from him in a dirty spillage. Alizarin braced himself, having also rehearsed some persuasion. The other Voistans waited in stone-faced silence, even Croso.

'Accepted.'

Viridian's eyes widened. Even Alizarin had to check his own astonishment.

'Surprised, Alizarin?' Laughter had left an unhealthy glaze over Watershin's eyes. 'Why? All of what you say is true. We've taken the brunt of caravan raids in the north, and our losses *have* been great. And now those bastards in the West have bandied together. They'll be the death of us all.'

Why, he had asked. Alizarin hoped the question was rhetorical, because so far this was going better than he'd expected. 'I ask only that you allow me to inform Elendra's council of your reply before our agreement is announced.'

If he refuses, I'll have to risk the council's wrath on my return. Or else renege the offer and inflict a mortal insult on Voista, from which it would take another hundred years to recover.

Croso asked monotonously, 'What conditions does Chieftainess Emra set?'

'No conditions,' Alizarin replied. 'We help defend each other's borders, provide aid and share supplies when needed. No bonds beyond loyalty.'

'No conditions?' Watershin repeated. 'After my clan thieved your water twenty-five years ago? I took you for a serious man, Alizarin.'

'As you say, the West is growing too strong to ignore while we stoke our differences.'

'Well said, Alizarin. Well said.' Watershin's eyes slid to Viridian. 'What about you, Lorendar's sprig? What conditions do *you* have? What glory do you envision for us all on the momentous occasion of your long-awaited return?'

Mocking laughter trailed Watershin's jibe. Surprising him for a third time, Viridian remained expressionless. *Almost like a Derindin.*

'I'm just a physician's apprentice,' his nephew replied quietly. 'I wish you only soundness in mind and flesh. A good night's sleep. A plentiful harvest.'

The laughter faded. Something drew all derision out of Watershin's eye. He stood with an effort that left him breathless, leaning heavily on his stick.

'Accepted, Alizarin Selamanden, and Voista won't speak of our agreement until your signal.'

The two men shook hands. And just like that, treachery against his clan was done.

*

'How are you going to tell her?'

Verdi kept his voice low; the streets were full of spectators heading to the Assembly.

'Hopefully not on the Babble.' Alizarin's face was hardly that of a victor. 'First, let's get through this. There should be enough anger about Baeron and Hesper's union to dominate the Assembly.'

Alizarin froze. Verdi followed his gaze, but only saw the moving crowd.

Tenken drew closer. 'What is it?'

'Go on to the Assembly,' Alizarin replied tersely. Tenken didn't question him, taking the tumblers with him.

Alizarin turned into an empty alley between two houses. A man followed them from the crowd. The hood of his cloak was raised.

'Who's this, Alizarin?' Arik drew his sword. It was only Verdi's second visit to Romel, but the hissing of steel here made him nervous. Ravi, who'd learned to anticipate trouble at that sound, disappeared under his collar.

'Put that away, Master Invelmari,' said the man calmly. 'I'm glad you still recognise me, Alizarin. None of your council did two days ago when I delivered news of Sisoda's misfortunes to Samsarra. Will you answer the warrior's question, or shall I?'

The man lowered his hood. Surprise jolted through Verdi; he was the stranger who'd struck up conversation with him at Winterfell feastday, moments before the assassin struck. A slow smile spread across the man's face as recognition sparked in Verdi's eyes.

Alizarin's voice was frosty. 'Viridian, this man is your father.'

Nothing could have prepared him for the shock. Arik said something, taking his arm. Verdi's legs shook. He couldn't tear his eyes away from this man.

He pushed Arik's hand away. 'Why didn't you tell me about him?'

Alizarin peeled his own eyes away from the stranger.

'I did not trust him with my sister, and I would not trust him with you.' Alizarin had never been more cold or unapologetic. 'I must join the Assembly. Are you coming?'

Verdi hesitated. The thought of staying hadn't even occurred to him.

The stranger smiled. 'If you come with me, Viridian, I will answer your questions.'

Verdi looked between the two waiting men, reeling. He'd promised to stand beside Alizarin as an Elendran at the Assembly. But here was his *father* ... and Alizarin – and all of Elendra – had concealed his existence.

Verdi looked up at Arik.

'I'll stay with you,' said Arik quietly.

Breathlessly, Verdi told his uncle, 'I'll send word after the Assembly.'

Alizarin turned and vanished into the street.

Arik resheathed his sword. The man closed the distance between them to grasp Verdi's shoulders, and Verdi gazed up into a face he had dreamed of all of his life. Ravi emerged cautiously from under his jacket, probably driven out of hiding by the beating of his heart.

'My name is Sassan Santarem,' said his father. 'And I am Murhesla.'

33

Sassan

FAITHFUL TO DAGMAR HE REMAINED, LABOURING FOR THE BLOOD PACT
HE HAD DECREED. FOR THE SPAEWIFE'S GIFT YET HAUNTED HIS DREAMS,
AND HIS HEART FEARED FOR HIS FLEDGLING PEACE.

SONNONFER: THE SECOND REDRAWING

He led them to a quiet part of the citadel, where the streets were tree-lined and swept clean. He stopped outside a heavy gate. Arik held back, so Verdi hesitated, his mind turning somersaults.

'Your laws prohibit bloodshed within Romel's walls,' Arik told the Derindman. 'But I've discovered that those laws hold no power over anyone under the shadow of a jemesh.'

Sassan Santarem smiled. Verdi could barely take his eyes off him, and was grateful Arik was there to think for them both.

'Few people know this,' said Sassan. 'But of course you've unearthed it. I have watched you guard my son from the moment you entered Romel, and I expect nothing less. But you have my word, swordsmaster, that no harm will come to either him or his protectors here.'

Sassan knocked thrice, and the gates opened onto a garden turned russet ahead of its wintry sleep. They tied their horses to a post and followed him, not to the house but down a stairwell hidden by ferns. He lit a lantern from a brazier burning in a sconce at the bottom, and a row of lanterns sprung into flame, illuminating a long passageway stretching ahead.

He's Murhesla! Verdi was hungry for this, but Klaus had been wary of the secretive guild and its strange emblem. Surely Alizarin wouldn't have left them with this man if he were a real danger?

'What is this place?' Verdi asked.

'This is where Derinda comes to bury itself.'

Verdi glanced at Arik; he didn't try to dissuade him. He followed Sassan into the passage.

It bisected into a network of tunnels. There was no chance Verdi would remember the way back. *If only Klaus were here.* They went up a flight of steps and down several smaller passages that opened into a great cavern, flooded with the light of hundreds of oil lamps.

Awestruck, Verdi stepped into the chamber. All around them, hewn into the stone itself, was a great vault hung with tablets and tapestries and relics of every kind. Stairs spiralled up or scaled across the walls to platforms and niches and shelves bearing books and jars. Animal skeletons, mounted weapons, fragments of armour. Nearby stood an alabaster statue of a man twice as tall as Arik, smooth and perfectly fashioned except for the eyes, which had been gouged out.

Sassan nodded towards the statue. 'You wished to learn more about the man they call Obsidian Lorendar.'

There were many things Verdi wanted to know, but he was ready to consume whatever this man wanted to tell him. 'If I am to cast his shadow behind me, I ought to know him.'

'That is as it should be,' Sassan replied approvingly. 'And what have you learned?'

Verdi thought of Elendrans' stories, poets' songs in taverns, Maragrin's musings. After a moment, he admitted, 'Nothing.'

Sassan smiled, and Verdi's heart skipped. 'Very good. You've not been fooled. At least, not yet.'

He stopped before the statue.

'People remember the end of a story, and sometimes the beginning. But rarely the middle … and that is where men and women are made and burnished.'

The vaulted roof of the chamber lifted his voice, teasing from it many hues. Arik's eyes roved the walls. Verdi abandoned caution to him entirely.

'They said my mother planted a limolan seed when she was carrying me, and that it grew the first limolan since Obsidian's death.' Verdi watched Sassan's face hopefully.

'This is the likeness of Lorendar.' Sassan ran a hand over the statue's hip. 'Very fine, is it not? Worth six bushels of gold in materials and labour. He would never have permitted such extravagance in his name. Here is where followers and fanatics smoothed away the stone as they bowed at his feet. And here is where his enemies chiselled out his eyes and his heart.'

Verdi hadn't noticed the rough cavity in the statue's chest. It made him shiver, though it was nothing but stone.

'Murhesla know everything that passed through these Plains. We will not let truth be forgotten. I will tell you a story few will remember, and fewer still will repeat.' Sassan gazed up at the disfigured eyes. 'In his youth, Obsidian's wife was stolen from him, and he amassed an army to retrieve her – his first army. When he discovered she had already been killed, he destroyed her captors' village to the last man. That was not the only time he took more than he was owed.'

Were it not for the hours spent in the tower room with Maragrin, or Elendra's mothering welcome at his return, Verdi might have been less dismayed. 'What do you mean?'

'You truly know nothing yet,' Sassan remarked. 'Of course you don't. Their script is well-rehearsed.'

'You're not taken with the legendary Lorendar, then,' said Arik.

Sassan turned away from the statue. His scorn was palpable. 'Everyone has a script. Behind me there are stories greater still, of a time before Lorendar – the time of Orenthia. If you want to learn what Lorendar envisioned for this land, look not at his lifetime but at what came before – at what he aspired to emulate. Orenthia was the golden age of this Part, when the North was still the battleground of squabbling tribes. Even Orenthia's dying breath was better than what there is now in Derinda.'

Arik looked around the vault. 'Is that what the Murhesla are? Safekeepers of the past?'

'The Murhesla are many things, Master Swordsman. We guard far more of this city than its walls.'

'Sounds like you've a script of your own, sir.'

Sassan spread his hands. 'Everyone you meet will show you the world as they know it, or as they wish you to know it. Here you can discover for yourself, Viridian, the little folk who lived and died in Obsidian's time – not just the odes and monuments made by nobles to immortalise the memories they curated. This timevault will be open to you should you wish to return.'

There were too many things Verdi wanted to say. 'Why are you showing me this?'

'Because no one else will,' Sassan replied. 'I know what they've asked of you – and you should know the unadorned truth that waits beyond the praises sung by the zealots who worship at Lorendar's altar; beyond the lies spread by those who hated him and feared his power.'

'And you'll be somewhere in the middle,' said Arik mildly.

Sassan took Verdi's shoulders again, and a rush of emotion stung Verdi's eyes and tightened his throat.

'I was never told that you were born, let alone that you survived the drought and the sickness that took your mother. I learned of you only when you returned, when you were paraded for all to see. Your very name was a discovery for me. They hid you well.' Sassan's eyes glistened, like his own. 'I do not yet know you, my son, and I cannot guide you if I do not know your heart or what it desires. But if you let me, I will spend the rest of my days trying to learn.'

Verdi swallowed. He wanted to ask why Alizarin hated Sassan so much; how Sassan had become Murhesla and what that meant. Most of all, he wanted to ask about his mother. But for a moment, he glimpsed a father's love, and feared whatever else he learned might taint it.

'I will release you now.' Sassan stepped back. 'There's much more to talk of. But your uncle will be anxious to know you are safe.'

'But –'

'You have many questions, I know. There'll be time for them,' said his father. 'But did you not swear allegiance to your clan? We both have vows to keep.'

Reluctantly, Verdi followed Sassan back overground. The route was circuitous; Ravi grew dizzy and covered his eyes with his tail. Verdi realised then that he hadn't noticed what Ravi had been doing at all. They emerged onto a quiet street, where another gate hid the entrance to the Murheslan timevault. Their horses were waiting outside.

Verdi hesitated. 'How will I find you again?'

His father's smile reached all the way to his eyes in a way Alizarin's never did.

'I will find you now, wherever you tread.' He squeezed Verdi's hand. 'My son.'

Then he stepped back, and the gate swung shut.

Verdi blinked as though waking from a reverie. 'I can't believe this is happening.'

'Neither can I.'

Something in Arik's voice sharpened his senses.

'What is it?' Verdi searched Arik's guarded eyes. 'Do you think he's lying?'

'I doubt he's telling you the whole truth.'

It was Arik's nature to be suspicious. And protective. But Verdi was certain what he had shared with his father – *his father!* – was genuine. Already, he felt a greater connection with this man than he had ever done with his uncle.

'It's better than being told nothing at all,' Verdi said defensively.

'We barely know him yet. Take care, that's all.'

'You don't even like Alizarin.'

'I have a better measure of him.'

'If you had misgivings about my father, why would you let him lead us into the tomb of the citadel?'

'Because anything your uncle doesn't want you to know is worth finding out.' Arik glanced up and down the quiet street. 'Now let's find Alizarin.'

But Verdi was no longer uneasy. The Murhesla guarded Romel from within the shadows, and his father was of those shadows. He was certain that, at least here, the shadows would keep him safe.

*

Alizarin paced his room in Riorga's inn. There'd been neither surprises nor answers at Assembly. There never were.

It had always been a matter of time before Sassan discovered his son. Alizarin wondered whether he would be returning alone with the tumblers to Samsarra.

Viridian would be safe from abduction in Romel now. The Murhesla would see to that as long as he was within the citadel's walls, and perhaps beyond. Now he would be in a very different kind of danger.

Alizarin knew how persuasive Sassan could be. After all, had he not won over his sister? Viridian was an empty vessel. An empty, impressionable vessel.

He tried to distract himself. There was plenty to worry about; the Assembly had been nothing short of a contained riot. But what rage the clans had for the new suzerainty in the West was toothless. By their own decree – their cursed ghabala – the desert was there for any who could defend what they took of it. That was the law by which the clans insisted on living still – each dreaming of the power to take more. To whom had they hoped to hold Baeron and Hesper accountable?

A Sisodan Elder's attendance had done little to reassure Alizarin. Though scorched by pirates not days before and now defending their clandom from attack, Sisoda was keen to downplay signs of weakness in the eyes of their western neighbours. Voista was too proud to admit that raiders had ravaged the roads connecting its northern territory with the Saffron Highway to the border market towns, casually restocking their granary at a premium from Romel instead. Periam in the north couldn't reveal *its* suffering without the blessing of its puppet-masters in the West, and now knelt collared at their feet. And Fraivon and Lebas, rich but small, were as keen to hide their losses as a wounded beast anxious to conceal its injuries from scavengers seeking easy prey.

So once again that left Elendra and Mantelon to uphold claims of attacks and destruction; the naysayers, the fearmongers in the East.

And yet none of this was distraction enough. Alizarin glanced for the hundredth time through the window down at the street.

I may have far worse news to take home than an illicit agreement with Voista.

To his credit, Watershin had kept his word, saying nothing of their agreement at the Assembly. And Tenken and his tumblers wouldn't betray Lorendar's successor.

A horse whinnied; Alizarin hurried to the window. Viridian and the Northerner dismounted outside.

Relief washed over him, but it was ephemeral. Everything was going to be more complicated now.

*

Soon. Klaus felt as though he were taking a slow walk to the gallows. Which, reason chided, he could well be.

They'd crossed Fraivon's clandom now. *Two more days, perhaps.* After they ate, he offered Nerisen a dagger while there was still light in the sky.

'Could you?'

She balked when she realised he wanted his hair cut off. 'What difference does it make?'

The Spyglass may have eyes even amongst pirates. Though Klaus wasn't even sure the guise would help.

'Fine, I'll do it myself.'

She batted his arm away, drawing her own dagger. She was deft, cutting close without once touching her blade to his scalp. 'They're just as likely to kill you as give you work, you know.'

He collected the hair. 'I know. But at least you didn't scalp me.'

The further south they went, the more restless he became. He had been ready to die a thousand times before. Invelmari were raised to serve, and there was no greater service than death. He just hadn't expected to serve here, in the desert among strangers; to die in the sand.

On their nineteenth night, they camped under a clump of glowgum trees. Their tree sap summoned the scents of pine and juniper. Nerisen had already collected a small vial of the sap for its medicinal properties. They doused their fire early – it was growing too risky to let it burn beyond dusk. She lay across the small clearing; too far and not close enough.

'Did you tell anyone where you were going?' he asked.

Her voice already dragged with sleep. 'Only Rasan.'

'Have you known Rasan long?'

'We met first a few years ago in Whimsy. She punched an Akrindan's face after he short-changed me for a bottle of ink.'

Klaus smiled to himself. It was just the sort of thing Rasan would do. 'That day in Noisy Tree ... what were you doing for Ristowin the metalsmith?'

He heard her shift, and she sounded more awake. 'I didn't think you recognised me. Or remembered.'

As if he would forget. 'What were you doing?'

'I've known Ristowin all my life. He did a lot of work for my father before he set up his forge in Noisy Tree when he got weary of the road.'

She had never spoken of her family. He moderated his interest. 'What kind of work?'

'Ristowin made parts for him.' Her words became clipped. 'Father is a clockmaker.'

'Is he any good?'

'At what? Keeping time?' She glanced at him over the embers, shivering. 'You look ridiculous.'

Klaus ran a hand over his cropped hair. 'Thanks.'

'Father constructed a timepiece that loses only half a second every three hundred days. Only Ristowin's parts would do.'

Klaus whistled. 'If I didn't know better, I'd say you were lying. That would reduce navigation error to...'

'He spent his life perfecting the mechanism.' She looked away, pulling her coat tighter. 'The mechanism is his real kin.'

'My time pieces are made by a master Engineer, and each second they drop amounts to a navigation error of barely half an ocean-mile ... but they're still inferior to that.'

'Do you know what it's time for?' she said irritably through chattering teeth. 'It's time to sleep.'

She turned away and curled up into a ball, the smoking remains of the fire at her back.

Rising quietly, he unfastened his cloak and drew it over her.

She was cold enough that she didn't protest much. 'You'll need it for yourself.'

'I've slept in snow. I'll manage.'

But even the ice-clad Sterns were not as cold as the prospect of being alone in the Plains once she left him to take his chances with the pirates.

Victory and valour and certain death: that was the warsong of Isarnanheri. It spilled into the ice-valley and the narrow corridor between the two faces of the mountain, and rumbled through the snow underfoot until Klaus feared the mountain may reply with an avalanche. The first time he'd heard it, it had curdled his blood. Now it poured from him too, from the very belly of his soul.

Commander Prospere raised his arm. As one, the Isarnanheri fell silent.

Klaus could just see Father mounted ahead. A great wolf's fur stretched over his armour, its open jaw resting on his head. Today, Father was more warrior than spy, as Klaus must also be. Today was his first taste of the unrehearsed swing of steel.

Fear flooded his arteries. He grappled for Form, and it slipped from his mind like a thrashing fish. The more he tried, the more it flailed.

Beside him, Arik's horse impatiently pawed the ground. Arik had been riding to battle these two years past, and had almost mastered his Form. He offered Klaus a crooked grin as lazy as the one that disarmed so many admirers. Absurdly, Klaus wanted to burst out with laughter. The distraction loosened the knot in his stomach as they waited.

There, in the distance, the glow of lanterns on black snow; dozens of them, then hundreds. A horn gusted into the night. The Isarnanheri's warsong crashed down the valley again, echoing the growl of giants.

'At last.' Arik lowered his golden visor over his face, pausing for one sly wink. 'Bottoms up.'

And then all was blood, and flesh, and darkness.

When he awoke, the smell of opened bowels and burning pyres singed his nostrils.

The moon had vanished. Clouds swallowed the stars. Night was utter and pitiless.

Klaus forced himself to lie still, clutching for Form as he had done over that valley at the foot of the Sterns. It came meekly.

Nearby, Nerisen's breathing was slow and deep with slumber. His heart stopped racing.

Slowly he sat up, listening: eddies of distant wind, rippling the surface of an abyss of silence beyond. Was it still there, that secret voice? He rose onto one knee, pressed his hands into the hard ground, driving grit and stones into his palms as though it would bring him closer to it. He knew it was only his imagination that this physical touch helped, but it was human nature to attempt to grasp something so otherworldly with the senses it already knew.

Just there, on the periphery of his mind: a whisper of shifting dunes and parched earth. He'd wondered whether he could sense water as well as earth. He'd tried to at the last waterhole, unsuccessfully, but though he couldn't feel the water itself, he *had* felt where the earth lapped greedily at the *presence* of water. Klaus cast his mind forward: there were knots in the earth where rocks and roots were buried, and soft gullies of sinksand, and the ebb and flow of the land's irregular topography.

The Isarnanheri's warsong flitted through his memory, summoning that fear that had gripped him at the bottom of the valley, and the awareness of the land shattered, brittle as his dream.

In its absence, a different sort of quiet filled the desert; a flat, dampened silence. If he sought it, somewhere in this starless darkness would be a doorway to despair.

In the morning, he remained hollow. They broke the monotony of trudging over rock-strewn sand only for his measurements, and her sampling of specimens. Even here, growth found its way to Nerisen. Klaus had lost count of the rare findings that had crossed their path. *The land blessed their unrewarded kindness,* Derindin poets said of the Plainswalkers. He could well believe it now.

Nerisen noticed something was amiss.

'My father chose his work over us.' Her rekindling of the story hauled him out of his abyss. 'He married my mother in secret. Her Akrindan family refused to acknowledge him. He left her; it was too much for his pride. They cast her out of Akrinda when I was born.'

'What happened to her?'

'She took farm work to feed us, and died of wasting fever in a shanty town when I was eight.' She was riding just ahead of him, so he couldn't see her face. 'A goat-herder took me to Romel to my father. But he was obsessed with mastering his craft. Fortunately, you can shed your people the way a snake sheds its skin.'

I wonder if I'll ever be able to remember the Wintermantels with as much grace. Or shed the Ealdorman's bond to the Blood Pact, woven as it was into his soul.

Nerisen stole a sideways glance at him. 'What about your family?'

'Don't know them.' At least this was truthful. 'Even if the truth is ugly, it's better to know it than to wonder.'

'Perhaps it's better to wonder. At least then you don't carry certain disappointment all your life.'

Is that what comes next? Intractable disappointment? Some days he feared even Afldalr wouldn't contain the bitterness fermenting within him.

'Have you been further north than the border towns?' Klaus asked her.

'What for? To grieve for what the dam has stolen from us?'

'You would deny yourself such wonder because of the past?'

'You may call it the past. Here it is renewed in every moment of the present.' She steered them around a rocky mound. 'I'll not go north.'

'The only one you punish is yourself. The world's there to be discovered.'

'And that's what they teach in Invelmar, is it?' Scorn returned to her voice. 'Derindin still aren't permitted to settle in Invelmar without an Invelmari's offer of work.'

Silence. Silence, and sand. It seemed difficult to find anything on which they didn't eventually disagree.

No point trying to avoid provoking her further, then. 'Do you believe Merensama is possible?'

She was quiet for so long, Klaus thought she might not answer. 'The clans are what they are, and … I can't imagine them changing.'

'You've lost hope?'

'No.' Green fire flared. 'Would the North tolerate a united Derinda, after all Invelmar's efforts to keep it fractured?'

'The North has other matters to occupy it.' But there was an untruth in that, too.

'Will Viridian find the Merensaman moon phase?' Her voice was loaded with doubt.

'In time.' If Klaus hadn't discovered this bond with the land, he would have just as much doubt. But so much *more* seemed possible now. 'I don't know much about moondials or Merensama, but I know the one they call the heir of Lorendar. I wouldn't lose hope.'

It wasn't hope but rather the tremulous *torment* of hope that hovered in her face, and he wished he could pull her close.

*

They arrived in Samsarra after a blessedly uneventful crossing from Romel, though Alizarin's mind was in so many places he barely worried about a pirate ambush.

Two suns had now set on the deal he'd struck with Voista. He hoped he would reach Emra in time.

And then there was the boy.

Since Klaus' departure, Viridian was hardly recognisable as the shy pup who'd arrived in Samsarra not three months past. Whether this pluck would last was another matter. And whether he would resist his father's charm – well. Yirma couldn't, and Viridian was every bit his mother's son.

'The only regret I have is going behind your back,' Alizarin told his aunt that evening. 'I took no pleasure in betraying my clan. But it was the right thing to do, though no one had the humility to do it.'

She listened in silence. Saya sat very still on his shoulder. Servants lit the lanterns in the garden. A parliament of rooks passed overhead. Were rooks not the heralds of storms?

'We *can't* stand alone against pirates who've hobbled Sisoda, Aunt. It's madness to think Mantelon's forces will be enough –'

'Be quiet, Alizarin.'

Emra rubbed her temples.

'I'm sorry,' he said quietly. 'We've so few alternatives … I didn't know what else to do.'

'It wasn't the wrong thing to do,' she snapped. 'But you leave me no choice now but to impose my will on the council.'

'You are Chieftainess. You don't need their blessing.'

'That's beside the point, nephew,' she said more gently. 'That wasn't the kind of Chieftainess I set out to be.'

Alizarin *was* sorry then, for his aunt was fair and well regarded across the Plains. He had no wish to compromise her good name.

'There's more.'

Emra hardly flinched as he told her about Sassan, though he wished she would. She had never been as wary of Viridian's father as he. But she hadn't lost a sister to the man.

'As you said yourself, Alizarin, their meeting was inevitable.'

'Aren't you worried? That man's poison…'

'Did Viridian not choose to return with you? He was bitten by the serpent and was unscathed. He honoured his promise.'

'What if Sassan fills his head with lies and turns him against us?' Worse than lies … he could fill his head with the truth – the truth as Sassan saw it, as the Murhesla painted it.

'Then it will be our failing for not having shown him the beauty of our vision.' She shook her head. 'Viridian will make the right choice. He may be inexperienced, but he has a good heart. He's not grown up with our vision of Merensama, but a just cause appeals to him. All the more so for having tasted the greatest peacetime the Seven Parts have ever known. That's why he will stay and restore the moondial. Sassan Santarem cannot compete with that.'

Alizarin didn't know what grated his nerves more – her praise of the North, her underestimation of Santarem, or her complete faith that Merensama would fix everything. Viridian was right about one thing;

Alizarin was just as much a fraud as his accidentally-returned nephew. And with each passing moon, it was growing more difficult to reach deeper and claw out some shred of conviction from himself.

*

This far South, the desert was definitely different.

Samsarra and the Arboretum were a distant dream. In the heart of the Plains there had at least been pastures and oases and swathes of dry sand-willow trees that whispered with parched voices. As they neared the southern edge of Fraivon's land twenty days after leaving Samsarra, the ridge that Klaus had predicted gave way to a more rugged and rocky landscape, where the hard ground gleamed ivory under the sun and the derina tubers were shrivelled and small. It was the heart of desolation. When he had imagined the Plains from his lush Northern home, this was what his mind had conjured. Klaus shuddered to think what waited beyond.

'Nerisen…' He stared across the desert. 'You have to go back. I don't even know how you're going to manage alone from here as it is.'

It was the wrong thing to say.

'Do you think I've needed some soldier to hold my hand all these years? Until the pirates, I moved between clandoms alone. Caravans were a privilege, not a necessity.' Her eyes blazed with untempered contempt. 'I know where to drink and how to feed my horse, and I can navigate the bloody desert. I don't need a *riverlander* to guide me.'

'I'm sorry,' he said when she stopped to breathe. 'I didn't mean that you're incapable. The thought just frightens me. Call that my weakness if you like, not yours. But this –' He gestured at the horizon. He let her see his fear. 'This is definitely too far. There is going to be no derina here.'

They stared at the expanse together. *She's just as afraid as I am.* He understood now why clans abandoned prisoners here by way of slow execution.

'Do you still think pirates can make their home out there?' She was calmer now. 'Because if you have any doubt, you should turn back here as well.'

Klaus tried to absorb the white waste before them.

He had not felt so daunted for a long time. Perhaps not since his maiden campaign into the Sterns, seeing for the first time the sheer mountain drops and ice-desert of the Far North.

What if the Septentrional Scrolls were wrong? What if they'd been banned in Invelmar because they really were full of lies and blasphemy?

Or if the Eye of the Court had been mistaken about the very existence of this mine?

'*You already have all the tools you need.*' He could doubt the Spyglass and the Septentrional Scrolls, but he didn't doubt the Wisdom, and the Wisdom hadn't refuted his suspicions.

'Now you understand.' Shutters fell over Nerisen's eyes again, and he realised her fragile hope had been built on the scaffold of his conviction. 'This is why no Elders, why no reasonable Derindin, believe anyone could hide an army out here in the death pit of the desert.'

'Then why did you come with me?'

'Because I wanted to find the snake's nest.' Even her anger was extinguished now. 'I was ashamed that I didn't have the courage to go myself.'

'And you didn't want it be a Northman who found it.'

Of course she'd had her own reasons for following him, and they were nothing to do with him.

Form raised walls around the bit of him that was crushed. 'Yes. I do still think this trail will lead to the pirates' lair.'

She shook her head and climbed onto her horse. 'We're losing daylight.'

'Nerisen…'

'I'll cross Fraivon's border with you.'

'There's no sense in delaying –'

'There's a summit called Kastava's Point just beyond from where the poets say you can see as far as the North Zmerrudi Sea. Not literally, of course,' she added quickly. 'Through the eyes of a little lark, who can only just manage such a big journey to taste the fish. I should like to look from that summit. You can see far out, and if we spot anything important, at least I can tell the others when I get back.'

He doubted very much that a pirate base would be visible from a summit at the edge of Fraivon's territory, because Fraivon would have already seen it. But she was in earnest, and stubborn as the rock besides.

A few hours' ride along Fraivon's border saw his fears confirmed.

The rocky terrain hid the devastation at first. Klaus checked his eyescope often, acutely wary of being ambushed before Nerisen turned back. Their horses crossed another ridge, and the shallow gutter in the ground behind it was littered with corpses.

Rasan's sword was in his hand with the next thud of his heart.

'Get behind me.'

But there nothing for a sword to bite. There wasn't even a breath of wind to rattle the rags clinging to the grisly remains. Flies punctuated the air. Carrion and hyenas had come and gone, leaving stripped bones behind.

Spear in his other hand, Klaus edged forward. They were days dead. Nerisen remained in her saddle, Onax nuzzling her neck.

'Will you be alright?'

She nodded, pale-faced. He offered her a flask of precious derina water. She sipped, closing her eyes and inhaling a few times before opening them to look straight at the dead.

'A caravan?'

'Unlikely. They look like tumblers. One of Fraivon's patrol parties, maybe … remember the reports of pirate raids in retaliation for increased patrols?'

There were forty, perhaps fifty dead. A few were probably pirates, but not many. *This is more than a skirmish.* How many pirates had it taken to decimate this battalion? A silver ring dangled from the cord still hanging around the stalk of a tumbler's neck. Someone's love-token, once. A black sash was tied around one arm of the nearest corpse. *Pirate.* A heavy breastplate had protected this pirate's thorax from carrion. Klaus turned his body over and cut away his tunic; an extensive tattoo sprawled over his left shoulder blade.

Nerisen joined him. 'Can we go?'

Her fingers were white with gripping his flask, but she refused to look away.

'Yes … always keep your hands free.' He took his flask from her and kneeled for a closer look. In the middle of the tattoo, he found it: the six-petalled starblossom of Sturmsinger.

'What are you looking for?' Her eyes fell on the tattoo, and she was unguarded enough that he glimpsed her confusion.

'Have you seen this before?' he asked.

She looked around, shivering. 'Let's put some distance between us and this place.'

He took the silver ring on its cord. Then he murmured a prayer, calling upon the company of Sturmsinger for the fallen tumblers, and offered a silent apology for leaving them unburied.

They rode away in silence. He watched the road for any waft of dust; any glint of steel.

'What do you know about that Murheslan tattoo?' Klaus asked.

Nerisen's lips tightened together.

'No one can hear us,' he pointed out. 'And if they could, we have bigger problems than getting caught talking about Murhesla.'

'I don't know what you want to hear.' Curiosity overwhelmed her reluctance, however. 'What are Murhesla doing amongst the pirates?'

'I don't believe those pirates are still serving Murhesla. Ayla said they were probably initiates who'd left the guild, or else had been cast out of it.'

'I'm surprised she told you anything.'

'Why?'

'Ayla left the guild after serving the Murhesla longer than anyone else who managed to get out of it alive.'

I was in Samsarra for months and missed this. 'No one ever mentioned that.'

'Very few people know. And if you make it back alive, you'd better remember that, or I'll kill you myself.'

Klaus suppressed a smile. 'You managed to know.'

She ignored his bait. 'Nobody speaks of the Murhesla because they've forbidden it. You don't know whether they might be listening – often you don't know who they are. And we don't defy them. They purged the rebels who tried to besiege Romel and returned it to us, and we don't forget the debt we owe them. They keep Romel safe from wars waged under the pretext of accursed ghabala. So we look the other way.'

It was late afternoon when they finally reached Kastava's Point. The gentle ascent to the summit hid a sheer drop on its southern side to a rocky valley below. From this eyrie, the land looked horribly barren – naked, raw. They hadn't seen derina all day, resorting to their water. How long would this last? Klaus looked through his eyescope and suppressed a shiver of excitement; to the west was the hazy outline of the Mengorian range, and the smaller bulk of the Ilmaz mountains reclined in the east.

Somewhere between those two ranges was the spot where Sturmsinger and his armies had been bewitched by a rock.

The sun was worryingly low in the sky, and Nerisen was still not northbound.

'Nerisen?'

She was transfixed, gazing across the dry ocean of sand crowned by a broken-toothed horizon. Her lashes trapped unshed tears.

'What must it have been like,' she said quietly, 'when it ran down all the way through the Part? When there was no need to fear *tesh* every step of the way? Can you imagine?'

He pictured the ghost of the Ninvellyn as she saw it: through the eyes of a desert wanderer whose world had been shaped by the root system of a succulent tuber and the fickle promise of water. Constantly pacing the precipice of hope, *namathra* lacing her every breath. In his ears rang the Derindin's farewell song to the great river at Invelmar's border; their haunting homage to *sehresar*. He had not understood then what it meant.

'Yes,' he said, for he didn't need to imagine. 'These hills would have been so green that at a distance they would have looked black. So wet, the earth would have had no chance to dry. There would have been no space for silence … crickets and cicadas, little rivers that never sleep.' The memory of cold valleys and the timeless thick of trees squeezed his heart.

'I'm sorry for it, Nerisen. I would give all of the North to see it restored.'

As soon as he'd said the words, he realised with a shock how much he meant them.

He wanted to touch her and resisted, leaving her standing on the plateau of rock. He surveyed the terrain. There was a westward path from Kastava's Point that would get him down from the summit before dusk if he set off soon. He gathered his instruments and maps and added them to Nerisen's pack, keeping nothing but one Derindin compass. He rejoined her, certain it was only a matter of time before their luck would run out.

'Come on,' he said at last, increasingly uneasy. 'Go back. Use my eyescope. Watch out for any sign of raiders. Hopefully you'll run into Fraivon's forces on the way back.'

She stepped down from the summit. He waited impatiently as she mounted her horse. *I shouldn't have lingered over the fallen tumblers.* It would be dark in just a few hours; she would have to stop soon to make camp, and would remain close to Kastava's Point until dawn. *I should never have let her come so far.* A slight wind toyed with the lightest particles on the surface of the ground, whispering slyly of a coming storm.

She looked back at the summit and stiffened. 'Tristan –'

He had seen it too.

Klaus grabbed his eyescope again. A dark shimmer drifted towards them from the west like a puff of smoke, gaining speed as it grew, and it was not the wind.

He pushed the eyescope back into her pack. 'Go. They're riding uphill; they won't have seen you yet. Ride hard and stop at that cave we passed, it's a good hiding place. Don't light a fire tonight. And Nerisen – tell them about the dead tumblers, and how many they were. *Go!*'

Her fear was naked for one wild moment. Then she was gone, riding away with his instruments, a ribbon of dust in the north. The last glimpse he caught was of those startling eyes that caged the green-blue blood of a stolen river.

Klaus released a ragged breath. There was no need to hurry now. He remounted his horse and set off down the path for a meeting with pirates.

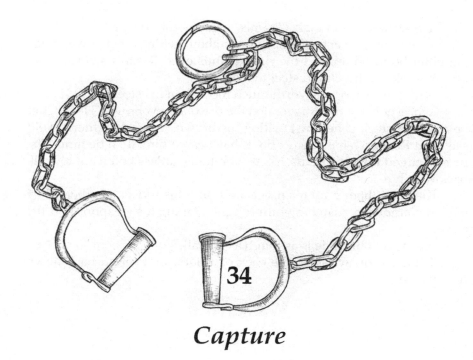

Capture

AND STURMSINGER PRAYED TO THE LIFEGIVER TO FORTIFY
HIS CHILDREN'S HEARTS, AND GRANT THEM THE WISDOM
TO COMMAND THE EALDORMEN IN HIS WAKE.

SONNONFER: THE SECOND REDRAWING

'It's a Northman!'

Masked riders surrounded him. There were thirteen of them. One wore another of those black sashes tied around his arm.

'What's a Northerner doing in this arse of the Part?'

'What all Northerners do outside Invelmar,' Klaus replied. 'Selling my sword.'

'That's a long way to go for a steel-whore.' The pirate wearing the black armband, presumably their leader, pulled his sand-mask down. His beard was grey, his face lashed by the desert sun. 'Unless he means to disappear, of course.'

Klaus met his pale blue gaze with silence.

'Looks like it won't talk, Tramis,' said another pirate.

'Good thing we know a thing or two about getting tongues wagging.' Laughter bounced around the ring. Tramis eyed Rasan's sword. 'That doesn't look like Invelmari steel to me.'

'A decent warrior is worth much more than his steel.'

'Oh, is he?' Tramis exaggerated the rise of his eyebrows. 'He'd better be made of steel, if he's just selling his brawn.' More laughter. 'We'll see what Renegash has to say about that. Search him, then tie him.' The pirates edged towards Klaus. 'Now, you fools, unless you want to walk back with him.'

Klaus let them grab his hands and bind his wrists together. They gained confidence, searching him roughly, taking his weapons and the compass.

'Let's see if his hide is as tough as his talk.'

They tied his wrists to the back of a horse and set off back down the hillside.

*

Formal announcement of the alliance with Voista broke the morning after their return. Verdi burrowed himself into his notes on older-age ailments. The tavern was abuzz with the news, but that wasn't why he couldn't retain a word.

He couldn't stop kicking himself. *So many questions I could have asked!* About his mother; her death, his father's absence. Instead of answers, he had Sassan's uncomfortable words about Lorendar, words that may have as well been lifted right out of the Sonnonfer.

'What did you expect?' Arik had told him when Verdi confessed his doubts. 'Did you hope to find a hero in all those stories about Lorendar? *I'm* not the least bit surprised. The world's the same, wherever you go.'

But Verdi *had* hoped to find a hero. *After all, this is not the North.* These people *had* to be better than Adela and the Ealdormen. Deep down, though, he feared his father had told the truth about Lorendar, while everyone chose to look the other way. If it were true, not only were they no better than the Ealdormen, but they were trying to pull him into the same darkness he longed to escape.

Elodie would have told him to go riding and leave his thoughts in the stables; return to them once clarity was restored. Perhaps that cool wisdom had been a glimpse of her budding Form.

'Isn't Maragrin expecting you for your studies today?'

Alizarin had finally stopped nagging Verdi about taking up more respectable residence in the Chieftainess' house, but he had plenty of other critical opinions yet.

Verdi shut his notebook. 'Not today.'

And that gnomon can stay in its wallet. Stuff their nonsense.

*

'Your battalion will march to Manfrell tomorrow,' Ayla told the assembled tumblers. 'Voista will instruct you from there. Gerit, as my second in command, you'll lead negotiations with General Rahdib.'

A week had been ample time for Arik to sample the response to this new alliance in the streets and the taverns.

Too many Elendrans mistrusted Voista and grumbled. An equal number celebrated any response to the self-proclaimed suzerains in the West. Word would soon spread of the unlikely alliance and perhaps force other clans to reconsider their positions, but at what cost? Tomorrow, a sizeable number of Elendran tumblers would be redeployed to bolster Voista's northern defences, leaving Elendra with fewer soldiers. It was too early to tell whether this had been a terrible idea.

Ayla paused by Arik as the tumblers dispersed. 'It was a good suggestion, Master Marcin.'

Arik made no reply. Alizarin arrived as she left the barracks.

'I hope you have the general on your side,' Arik told him.

'Makes no difference now.'

'How did the Elders take the news?'

'Sourly. It was your suggestion, after all.'

'As far as they know, it was Verdi's.'

'They're not stupid. You may find yourself becoming less popular, Master Marcin, once rumours spread that the Chieftainess is taking advice from an Invelmari.'

'I just serve the heir of Lorendar.'

Alizarin's eyes slid to Verdi, brooding over a book across the yard. 'If that's true, you'll understand my concern about the influence of Sassan Santarem.'

'Then you won't like it that he's already decided to return to Romel to see Sassan again.'

A dark cloud passed over Alizarin's face. 'Viridian is impressionable and knows nothing about his father. He'll be easily manipulated. And once a seed is sown –'

'You've kept him at bay too long,' Arik interrupted. 'Did you not think he'll want to know his father, given half the chance?'

The Derindman's eyes were sharp as flint. 'I suppose you ought to know.'

Arik flinched. Alizarin knew enough about the Ealdormen that his blow was likely no accident.

A little steel slipped into Arik's reply. 'Motherless as he is, I would have thought his own uncle might have anticipated his reaction to finding his father.'

A stony silence reared between them as each gingerly touched upon scars long faded but never erased.

'Tell him to get his head out of that book,' Alizarin said tonelessly, and left.

Laughter came from the training ring. Arik returned to find Gerlana struggling to swing Thunraz, his Invelmari sword. She blushed, dropping her arm quickly and with too little control over the weapon for his liking.

'What d'you expect of a sword not made for a woman?' Marsulo scoffed as she hurried to resheath it.

'Wait.' Arik jerked his head towards Thunraz. 'Pick it up, Marsulo. Gerlana, get your own blade.'

Her blush deepened as laughter broke out again. Recovering quickly from his initial surprise, Marsulo took Arik's sword. From the way he moved, he didn't look all that comfortable either.

Arik slipped Gerlana a wink. 'Go easy on him.'

She stepped as he'd taught them without fault. *Amazing, what reward a small token of faith can reap.* Marsulo moved clumsily, unlike himself, Arik's sword proving more a hindrance to him than an advantage.

'Keep going,' Arik warned when Marsulo paused. 'Do you want to be bitten by a woman's steel? Keep going!'

The tumblers watching grew quiet. The more frustrated Marsulo became, the more mistakes he made. He used Arik's sword to block Gerlana's blows, which came fast and light as birds. He may as well have carried only a shield. Finally, she struck flesh. He tripped over Arik's sword to the ground.

Not intent on compounding his humiliation, Arik swung him up and clapped his back. 'Think twice before you judge the warrior by their weapon.'

But Marsulo eyed Thunraz with confusion, perhaps even fear. It was the first time someone had looked at his blade in such a way. Arik would remember that look well.

*

Where's Klaus now?

Finding Sassan in Romel had provided a welcome distraction. Verdi longed to return.

He set down the callipers he'd cleaned for Meron. The laboratorium was where he felt most at ease. It wasn't the work he wanted to pursue, but it kept him busy. Nobody badgered him about Merensama here, or asked him if he'd fixed the moondial, or, worse still, asked for his blessing.

'Finished already?' Meron was kind. 'We'll run out of polish at the rate you're going.'

He unwrapped a parcel of bread and cheese and dried figs, offering them to Verdi.

'I'm not hungry, thank you.'

'It occurs to me that such an eager pair of hands that work so hard despite a distinct lack of appetite may very well belong to a rather troubled mind.' Meron bit into a fig. 'What do you say?'

Ravi, who'd been asleep, popped out of Verdi's jacket. Meron chuckled, breaking off a crumb of cheese.

Verdi didn't have the heart to stop him. 'I say he's eaten three times already today, and it's only noon.'

'How is it a young man with such a promising future can be so dejected?'

Verdi flinched. But Meron was neither intrusive nor bloated with expectation.

'I've no idea why anyone is so sure of that.' Words tumbled out as though a latch had been lifted. 'Half the Elders want me to be a diplomat, the other half wish I were a warrior. They must be so disappointed. I still don't know what to do with the gnomon. And I don't see how they'll *talk* the clans into Merensama. They'll be forced to fight for it in *my* name – and can you see me leading tumblers?' Meron made no interruption, feeding Ravi crumbs of cheese. 'Successor? I'll be Lorendar's joke. All these people praying and dreaming, for *this*.' He pointed at himself. 'I'll be like one of your seedlings, wilting after too much sun.'

Meron laughed, and Verdi couldn't help but join him. Ravi tried to sneak another piece of cheese and Meron tapped his tiny wet nose. 'You'll be sickening tonight. Stop!'

Once they'd prised Ravi from the cheese, Meron told him, 'Lorendar left you only one thing, Master Viridian: a destination. Not a route. Nor a method. No one knows much more than that, even Elders. No one can teach you how to find the moondial, but that means you're free to discover it for yourself. Perhaps the way forward is to pay less mind to others and shape your own path.'

It was the most refreshing thing Verdi had heard.

'I don't know what I believe about visions and signs. And Lorendar...'

411

How much could he trust Meron? 'Apparently he was everything, from a man who couldn't sleep until every belly under his watch was filled, to a warlord blinded by bloodlust.'

'Remember he was a mere mortal, just like you and I,' said Meron. 'Not a Wisdom, or even a sage. He had faults, but more important is how he overcame them.'

'Yes...' The larvae that had hatched in Verdi's heart since visiting the Murheslan timevault had grown fat on his fears. 'I can't help but feel there's more to him than anyone's prepared to say.'

He searched the scholar's face, unsure what he hoped to find.

'Even the best of us may carry darkness,' Meron admitted. 'Sometimes it's extinguished. Too quickly forgiven, perhaps. But Obsidian provided a constant in a very fragmented world. We have few enough constants that we can't afford to lose the imperfect ones we do have.'

Verdi wasn't sure what to make of this. 'Derindin sneer at the North, but it's whole. Everything was so much easier in the North. I used to dream of coming here, but now I think perhaps I belonged there.' He sighed. 'I would have finished my studies.'

'You wished to become a physician?'

'I still do.' Verdi brightened. 'I don't suppose you can help me find an apprenticeship?'

A frown creased Meron's brow. 'Have you dismissed taking Lorendar's oath, then?' Catching sight of Verdi's face, he added gently, 'It's a tall order to chase two destinies, Master Viridian.'

Verdi's shoulders slumped. Clearly, this was not what Meron had meant by suggesting Verdi choose his own path.

'Through Merensama you could help so many more people. Build a whole new world.'

'That's different.' Verdi tried to explain. 'Most people don't want to be helped, even when they need it. But sickness forces them to think. Weakness makes them *equal*. Disease strips away their differences. And then they see what matters most.'

The Derindman considered him for a long moment.

'I'll see what I can do,' he promised.

This, at least, was cheering. They talked of the alliance with Voista, and the rumours still circulating about pirates spreading collier's bile. North, South ... wherever it took hold, fear was fear, far more catching than any ailment, and infinitely more difficult to treat.

*

Klaus walked for hours before his captors stopped, making camp after the last of the day had drained from the sky. They bound his feet and tied him upright against a boulder. Then he was left in the dark.

Somewhere behind him, they lit a fire. The smells of food came and went. Gradually, their voices fell, save for the sentry who visited him with taunts and kicks.

When they untied him in the morning, he fell like a tree, stiff and wind-chapped. They laughed and dragged him to his feet.

Their leader had little time to waste. 'If he falls again or doesn't keep up, kill him.'

They tied him to the pack horse again and set off across the Plains.

For three more days and nights Klaus walked, jogged and ran behind them, twice passing other groups of pirates. Only his seal pelts saved him from cold, and the mesh of Invelmari steel woven into the leather of his boots spared his soles from being rubbed raw. At night someone left dried derina nearby that he couldn't always reach, and he was given water twice each day. The land became undulating, strewn with loose stones and lashed with crevices that tripped tired legs. His feet knew mountains well, but his eyes disliked the glare of sun on naked rock. Sleep-deprived and aching as he was, the barren Plains and the enormous sky spelled a kind of madness. Bodily ache turned to something different – pain that was angry and ugly and scarring. If he gave himself to it, his precious awareness of the land disappeared.

He shoved his whole mind into Afldalr, funnelling Form into a cage around himself ... the pain was yet consuming, the bitterness irresistible. Walking by day, standing by night, memories of Dunraven mocked him. Even good memories; of Elodie, of his *mother* and *father* – but these were so incongruent with the Wintermantels' betrayal that they pulled him apart in a hundred directions, until anger and confusion left nothing but a shrieking din in his mind –

'*Make a box*,' Master Arnander commanded him again. '*Here you will banish all things...*'

He had never called upon on Afldalr so much as he did in the days spent following the pirates through the desert.

Verdi waited in Samsarra; a morsel for the picking. The Elders needed to be shaken, to release the coiled spring of their fears into motion. He couldn't afford to lose focus, to stop mapping the terrain in his mind, or – now that the awareness of the land was a regular visitor – to cut off the spirit of the desert guiding his inner compass. Hills, great dunes, little caves, rock piles – he strained every shred of consciousness he could spare to noticing and remembering everything. While he focused on this, he maintained a sort of numbness...

A meeting with another pirate caravan changed his fortune a little

'Who do you have there?'

Their leader, whose caravan included many horses and two sealed carriages, spotted Klaus immediately.

'A mercenary.' Tramis smirked, pleased with himself. 'Offering services, he says. Renegash needs men, he might fancy a Northern sellsword.'

'So you'll take him a sellsword you've worn down, will you? Clever. I'm sure a blunt blade is exactly what he'd want.'

After that, Klaus still had to walk behind the horses, but at night he was tied on his side and there was plenty of preserved derina tuber to eat.

Six days south of Kastava's Point, when the land had become a mosaic of dunes, dry grasses and rocks, and the blue shoulders of distant mountains rose more clearly in the distance both to east and west, they finally arrived at the place Klaus had suspected, and the Derindin had doubted.

A sea of tents and wagons, stretching as far as he could see: the lair where the pirates had taken root in the desert.

*

Klaus strangled apprehension as a pirate led him through the tents. He looked straight ahead, but what he saw on the peripheries of his vision chilled his blood.

All around were tents full of both pirates and Derindin prisoners – gaunt prisoners with dirt-darkened faces, moving as though they carried the mountains on their backs. It was dusk, and pirates were herding captives into their tents. Prisoners' tents were erected in groups, surrounded by armed pirate guards. *Probably to avoid gatherings and mutiny.* Klaus saw cages, shackles, chains. Occasionally, a pirate pulled a prisoner aside.

'This one's spent,' Klaus heard a pirate say. He didn't see where he took the unfortunate man hanging limply from his grip. But others struggled, fear igniting strength they didn't have enough left of to satisfy the pirates.

Tramis strode through the camp with an arrogance Klaus had encountered in overconfident and rusty-bladed soldiers whose station had got the better of them; the kind who couldn't be trusted to guard anything other than their own hides. He led Klaus to a great tent. The guards outside were tall and attired differently to the pirates. Black-painted helmets hid their faces, and they didn't carry the curved blades favoured by the Derindin. Tramis stepped past them into the tent.

'Lord Renegash –' He stopped. 'What are you doing here, Sharlo?'

A pirate sat in a chair draped with striped furs. A gloating smile split his face. The rugs on the ground and a painted amphora suggested this was the tent of a leader; the overly smug and nervous discomfort of the man sprawled in the chair hinted it was not his natural place.

'He's not here.' Sharlo wore a black sash around his arm. 'Gone to receive another company. He's left me in charge.'

Tramis spluttered. Klaus didn't miss Tramis' hand inching towards his knife.

Neither did Sharlo. 'Careful, now. One word, and the guards will have you confined.'

Klaus' captor seethed, but lowered his hand.

Sharlo's gaze fell on Klaus. 'Who's that?' He straightened, narrowing his eyes. 'Not...'

'Unless you're going to tell me this one's a yellow-haired giant, no, he's not the bounty.'

Sharlo stood and walked around the table to Klaus, wrinkling his nose and stepping back.

'Filthy, aren't you?' He looked Klaus up and down. 'Know anything about a jemesh, riverlander?'

So this is who sent it to Arik. Klaus shook his head. 'I stopped looking for it when I decided to come here.'

'You were hunting another riverlander?'

Klaus shrugged. He willed his pulse to slow with Form. 'Gold's gold to a sellsword.'

'He's for Renegash,' Tramis cut in. 'He wanted good soldiers.'

Sharlo scowled. 'Is he Isarnanheri?'

'What, here? What would one of them want in the desert? And letting us capture him like a bitch? No, he's just a soldier. But even a Northern toy soldier is better than the lot you're putting up.'

Sharlo considered Klaus. He was younger than Tramis. A scar ran up one cheek to his scalp, distorting his hairline. *Is he renegade Murhesla, too?* But Sharlo already smacked of a lesser calibre than that of the kidnapper Arik had killed outside Romel's gates.

'No,' Sharlo decided. 'He'll work the mines with the rest.'

'But –'

'I'm not having a riverlander rub shoulders with my men after what that bastard Northman did!'

Klaus' thoughts raced. As a prisoner, his movements would be much more limited. 'Am I to pay for another Northerner's crime? I'm offering a good trade.'

Sharlo was a full head shorter than Klaus, but he grabbed him by his coat and boxed the side of his head. Klaus waited for the ringing in his ear to stop.

The look Sharlo gave him was one of undiluted loathing. 'No Northern scum in my ranks.'

Tramis shook his head. 'Don't get carried away. Renegash will be back, and I'll make sure he knows you turned a decent sword away because you're still crying about a dead whore.'

The two pirates glared daggers at each other. *So it's pirates who've been targeting Verdi.* But for what purpose? *They must have a brain hidden somewhere, to have kept track of what goes on in the Plains.*

'He won't last long enough for Renegash to know,' Sharlo said scornfully. 'Now get out.'

Outside, Tramis took one last look at Klaus and spat at the ground in disgust. He stopped a passing pirate. 'Put this one to work in the morning.'

'What work?' Klaus began. There was little point persuading these foot soldiers, but Tramis seemed eager to curry favour with his superiors. 'I could offer –'

'You shut it, or they'll shut you up for good.' Tramis turned on his heel, and once again Klaus found himself being herded by a pirate.

The camp was a maze of tents, and it was fast growing dark. He was led to a dimly lit tent enclosure where chained prisoners crowded on straw mats, under the watch of several pirate sentries. The Derindin looked up as he entered, with eyes as empty as the desert.

Sentries clamped irons over his wrists and ankles but didn't bother freeing his hands, so when a tray of stew came round he couldn't pick up a bowl. Prisoners talked quietly, eating cooked derina with their fingers. A grunt sounded from across the enclosure as a sentry cuffed someone's ears.

Klaus lay back on a mat and stared at the roof of the enclosure.

What had he got himself into?

'Here.'

A young man shuffled closer and untied the rope around his wrists. Without a knife, he had to pick knots slowly.

'Thank you.' Klaus flexed and unflexed his wrists; they were stiff and cold.

The Derindman offered Klaus his bowl of derina.

Klaus shook his head. 'I had something not long ago,' he lied.

They fell silent as a sentry walked past.

'Sometimes they don't mind if we have a bit of jabber,' whispered his rescuer. 'Other times, it'll get you confined.'

'What's your name?'

'Merik.' Blood stained his tunic. 'You look like you're far from home.'

'Only one kind of Northerner comes this way,' muttered an older Derindman behind him. 'Didn't expect to get caught, did you, riverlander?'

Merik frowned. 'We're all in the same mess here.'

The other Derindman snorted, turning away.

'How long have you been here?' Klaus whispered.

But the sentry passed again. The prisoners returned their empty bowls and the torches were put out. The enclosure fell silent.

There was one blessing in sleeping in such a cramped space; their collective body heat warmed the night, though it thickened the rankness of the air and did nothing to soften the hard ground. Klaus lay on his side, arms folded against the cold. Every bit of him ached. Hunger became a nagging cramp in his belly. Outside, the nocturnal sounds of a barracks filtered through the quiet. And something else – an occasional muffled cry; dampened screams. He told himself it was a bird, and tried not to dwell on the observation that there were no women in the tent.

How many other enclosures were there?

'Sleep,' Merik whispered. 'You'll need it.'

Klaus tried lying on his back. The full scale of his situation slowly crystallised in the dark. Horror turned to anger. Nobody escaped his wrath – pirates; Elders; the Murhesla; the petty, infighting Derindin comfortable in their clandoms. A new rage began simmering in his blood. He gave himself to it happily, for it was stronger and more acute than raw feet and aching flesh and the blistering cold; more acute than the pain of being wrenched from Invelmar.

And then anger cooled to a darker creature: fear; of being at the mercy of these monsters, of never being able to get out.

He had no compass. In the tent, he couldn't see the Southern stars. Even if he could, he still barely understood them. And disquieted as he was, he could no longer sense the land when he reached for it. First his identity had been torn away from him; now he was placeless.

If he'd had any lingering idea of remaining who he had once been, here it was finally extinguished.

I'm never going back. Doubt became despair. *This is my own doing.*

Later he would slay those demons, but it would be this first night as a slave in the pirate camp that would bury at last the ghost of Ulfriklaus Wintermantel.

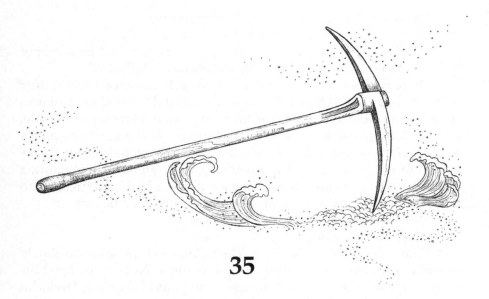

35

Eh Menishian

AND ALL MANNER OF PEOPLES STURMSINGER ENCOUNTERED
SOUTHWARD, YET NO VICTORY NOR RICHES COULD QUENCH HIS
LONGING TO RETURN HOME TO CLAIM HIS WAITING CROWN.

SONNONFER: THE SECOND REDRAWING

'Decided you're ready to resume your studies, have you?' Maragrin arrived late to the tower room, where Verdi was already waiting. 'I expect you think three months of being here was education enough.'

'How many more people did Lorendar execute after his first wife was murdered?'

The Elder stopped in his tracks. Even the slight tremor in his left hand disappeared.

'*Perspective,*' said Maragrin finally. 'Lorendar faced a great deal of tyranny –'

'Excuses!' *Klaus would have probably told me off for giving in so easily to anger.* 'Really he was no different to an Ealdorman, winning by any means necessary. What makes you think I want to walk in his footsteps?'

'How is it that you can be so gullible? Your forefather was –'

'A tyrant, even if you choose to look the other way –'

'– a man who redeemed himself. Or is there no provision for redemption in your grand portrait of us, Master Viridian?'

Verdi paused to catch his breath, but he would have hesitated then anyway.

Maragrin removed his cloak. 'A man's sacrifices can be as great as the crimes that shaped the beginning of his journey. The Great Sentience alone knows whether one can eclipse the other. We began at the end, where your own story begins. But I have told you: there is a great deal yet you must learn.'

How easily doubt upended him. Verdi chewed his lip, stumbling back into the thick of its clouds.

*

Arik was finally growing more bored than frustrated.

Cilastra tapped her notes. 'Fraivon may be the keenest of the other clans for Merensama, but they're in no position to share their soldiers or armoury until the raids stop.'

'At least they agreed to lift the toll on our caravans through their Carnelian Wells country,' Tourmali replied. 'But not the levy on kahva trade in their eastern valleys.'

The two councils had been debating proposals for hours. Most of it was trivial next to the raiders, but Arik kept his own counsel now. *No one wants to know what I think.*

Verdi fidgeted in his seat. 'How can negotiations for Merensama or anything else begin while pirates are ravaging the clandoms?'

'Merensama existed long before pirates,' Cilastra replied. 'And we can't delay these talks indefinitely. The real power in Derinda lies along the desert's trade routes, Viridian.'

'All the more reason why we should propose Merensama as a *means* to crush the pirates,' said Tourmali again. 'If we offer a military incentive…'

'And dupe clans into joining our alliance?' Maragrin jabbed the air with his stick. 'They'll desert any agreements we make as soon as the bandits are snuffed out.'

'You're all forgetting something,' Navein added. 'We can't promise to deliver Merensama before Lorendar's heir has signed the Book of Oaths, let alone unlocked the Merensaman moon phase.'

This united the Elders in sombre disapproval. Arik felt Verdi contract beside him. *For Sturmsinger's sake! They swapped the blasted Umari instrument with this imaginary moondial to wind me up.*

'Until those terms are met, hope is about as good as rumour. What do you say, Master Invelmari?'

Ha! Fat chance I'll be feeding the fantasy. Arik manicured a smile for Navein. 'I say a promise given willingly is more valuable than one pulled through the teeth, Ahen.'

Fortunately the arrival of supper concluded their discussions. Arik barely tasted the food. Verdi couldn't get away fast enough, clamming up on their walk back to their lodgings. He was starting to resemble Klaus – brooding silences, sleepless nights hounded by the shadow of Lorendar that he still kept at bay. To what end? *We've been here nearly five months.*

'You know…' Arik began.

A shadow *wooshed* overhead, and a familiar figure hurried across the street towards them.

Verdi's face broke into a delighted smile. 'Master Niremlal! What are you doing here?'

The little birdkeeper wore a well-worn leather armguard upon which his eagle had stood moments before. A broad smile splintered his wrinkled cheeks further.

'I came with the Chieftain's caravan for supplies. With the roads so hostile, I can't choose my own comings and goings any longer. And now I must let Feranzia out to hunt.' Ravi's head shot out of Verdi's breast pocket at the birdkeeper's voice; Verdi caught him before he pounced.

'It's so good to see you,' Verdi told Niremlal earnestly. 'I've longed so many times to ask you about the sage-bird…'

But the birdkeeper's eyes had strayed to the jemesh hanging around Arik's neck. He shrank back. 'Ah! Master Marcin, I was sorry to hear you had been touched by this foul omen. A foul omen, Master Marcin.'

Arik brushed the offending death-token. 'Unless you're about to tell me it has magical properties that will harm me, sir, I'd put it out of your mind.'

'Magic?' A frown multiplied Niremlal's wrinkles. 'No, Master Invelmari. The only magic that remains in the world now is illusion.'

'Is that how Lorendar's gnomon works, then?' Arik asked, only partly joking.

'The world is rife with forces we don't understand, Master Marcin. The Great Sentience can rearrange the particles of things so that they can speak to us, even respond to our command. All things speak, if we know how to listen. Even your steel has a spirit that knows its master.'

Arik had never been spiritual; that was Klaus, who followed the

Blood Pact and the Ealdormen's decrees religiously, praying each night for a seat at Sturmsinger's table. But an uncomfortable shadow of his Form Mistress darkened his thoughts. Lisbeta had sung to the sword, swearing by the secret language it returned. Only her prowess had enabled Arik to see past her unravelling. Now she was a recluse, ridiculed behind her back.

Arik suppressed a shiver. 'If it comforts you, I'll bury the jemesh in the desert where it belongs.'

But Niremlal shook his head. 'It does not belong here, dear Invelmari. It is one of many innovations that wormed their way into the Plains after the fall of Orenthia.' He glanced at Verdi. 'Why do you think the sage-bird deserted us? We became lost.'

Verdi's eyes lit up. 'Yes, tell me more about her.'

'Some say she will never darken our land until the limolan tree bears fruit once again.' His eye twinkled. 'After all, what would she have to eat?'

Verdi couldn't help but laugh. 'I wish you could stay and tell me more, Master Niremlal. I'd much rather hear about Lorendar from you.'

'Ahh, I know less than nothing, Master Viridian.' There was nothing insincere about the birdkeeper's modesty. 'Perhaps there is only one lesson you must learn. After Lorendar nursed the sage-bird back to health, she gave him two precious gifts: a panacea secreted from her lacrimal ducts, and a poisoned talon. How can poison be precious, you might ask? She showed him that the one exists to balance the other. Nothing thrives without balance. And Lorendar had lived a life without equilibrium. That is wisdom beyond price. Everything else will find its own way into your understanding, like the moss on a tree.'

Nothing thrives without balance. That evening, Lisbeta pestered Arik's thoughts again. She had been obsessed with equilibrium; with the 'awakening' of a mastered blade in a 'warrior-at-balance' and other delusions, like the *will* of steel. He wondered whether she was still alive, and whether the solitude she'd finally chosen had driven her deeper into madness.

Arik set down his smokeleaf cigar and unsheathed Thunraz, careful not to wake Verdi, who was sleeping easily for the first time since Klaus' departure. Since it had come to him from Stahlaz, Arik had not exchanged this astutely calibrated blade for any other. They had grown together. He recalled how it had seemed so heavy, once. Now it was neither too light so that he overbalanced, nor too heavy so as to tire him. *The reward for years of practice, obviously; for perfected Form.* And yet...

He dismissed the thought. There was no room in his Form for such fancies. Even Meron thought Niremlal was a little eccentric. And Lisbeta was probably dead, the madness gone with her.

*

By daylight, the camp was even larger than Klaus had first thought. After a breakfast of dried derina, he and the prisoners in his enclosure were blindfolded before being herded out of the camp at first light.

Luckily, he was behind Merik for the long walk that followed. 'Where are they taking us?'

Merik waited for a sentry to pass before he whispered back, 'The shafts.'

So they've seized the mine. Klaus found little triumph in this confirmation. He tried to clear his mind, casting it forward to feel the earth. But he hadn't regained his awareness of the land, and had no idea in which direction they were being led.

'What –'

A whip lashed at his legs. He hadn't heard the guard hovering behind him.

'Shut it!'

It was perhaps an hour later before their blindfolds were removed. They were at the foot of a long cavern that opened into a low hill. Surrounding them were pits and carts piled with lumps of rock. Several tunnels vanished into the hill. Pulleys and ladders criss-crossed every tunnel entrance like overgrown thick-limbed webs.

How long had the pirates been digging here? Where did they get the tools, the timber? Klaus' Form tightened around growing unease. *This is not the work of a rabble.* This was not the work of a single season. He had feared this from the start.

A pirate took him to a small quarry nearby and gave him a pickaxe. 'You'll start here.'

Another prisoner showed Klaus the ore they sought: reddish deposits embedded into the rock. The foreman was a swarthy pirate with a keen eye for slackers and weaklings, and his men needed no encouragement to liven up the slaves with their whips. They stopped digging twice, at noon for a meal of dry derina bread, and water in the late afternoon. *Fresh water, not derina water.* Klaus learned to strike his pickaxe softly to save his strength, but by the early evening every bit of him felt tender. Then they were blindfolded again for the long walk back to their enclosure.

Klaus' mind raced, storing every observation. There'd been at least a hundred Derindin working in the quarry. More slaves marched passed them, so there were other sites nearby. At the base, he counted at least as many pirates as slaves. The pirates were well-armed. His blindfold came on before he could see where they stored pickaxes and chisels. Even such basic tools were expensive, with Northern restrictions on metal trade and limited native ore in Derinda. Who'd supplied them? What were they mining?

How long would a man last at this work?

That evening there was finally a chance to talk. The sentries guarding their enclosure became jovial enough with wine that they were more interested in riling each other than keeping the slaves' silence. Klaus sat with Merik in a corner of the tent. Grey hollows cupped Merik's eyes, and his smile was weary.

'How long have you been here?' Klaus asked over their frugal supper.

'Three months. My caravan was raided on the Qinnamon Road. Everyone was taken.'

Not long after I arrived in Derinda. 'Are they all here?'

'The ones who are left.' Merik's fingers tightened around his bowl. 'They split you up. Then you might be lucky to catch a glimpse of someone in passing.'

'I'm sorry.' It was cruelly effective. Many of the prisoners wouldn't try to leave without their loved ones. *If escape were even possible.*

'Some have been here much longer.' Merik picked at the derina. 'What about you?'

'I got captured too,' Klaus replied. 'Do you know how long this camp has been here?'

'Feels like it's always been here. It hasn't changed much since I arrived.'

Another prisoner leaned into their exchange; an older man with grey whiskers long unshaved and heavily accented Invelmen. 'You'll find folks here who've almost forgotten their names, let alone how they arrived.'

Merik's soft voice melted easily into the murmur of the prisoners' talk. 'No one knows how long slaves have been working the mines.'

'I thought the raids only got worse last summer,' said Klaus.

'Is that what they told you?' The older prisoner looked too beaten down to summon any real anger. 'Unclanned men and women have been brought here for years ... no one cares when they disappear. Only a little weed of a place it was, in the beginning. An experiment. Now the clans are hit, they begin to notice.'

Klaus looked around the enclosure. 'How many slaves are here?'

'Hundreds,' said Merik. 'They bring more every week...'

'...and replace the ones they wear out, like a pair of boots.'

There were innumerable stories of violent raids; of hamlets gutted and villages torched. Often the raids began with a search, but no one mentioned a skydisc and Klaus dared not ask. He squirreled away every place and name he heard. He was indeed a chronicler now.

Another pirate entered and barked at their guards, one of whom lashed immediately with his whip at the nearest prisoner. After some cursing, the guards were replaced with a sober pair. The enclosure once again fell silent.

In the morning, Klaus witnessed for himself what his fellow prisoners had described; a horse-drawn cart bearing several bodies, bruised and broken.

It would be the first of many such days in the camp. Klaus clung to the purpose he salvaged for himself in recording observations, making the brutality and monotony bearable. He glimpsed again the strange soldiers who'd guarded the tent of the one called Renegash; they were few, and never removed their black-painted helmets. They moved with an oiled precision Klaus recognised instantly: they were elite soldiers. They didn't mingle with the pirates. He asked Merik about them. The Derindman looked too frightened to reply, and Klaus didn't press him.

After a few days, he began to form a mental blueprint of the enclosure. The base was the size of a small citadel. Smoke often rose over the east of the camp. *From a forge, perhaps?* The pirates regularly patrolled the camp with dogs. Klaus spotted human remains in their kennels more than once: a bone that was too long and thick, or clumps of hair. After the clean empty air of the desert, the camp had a curious stench; of smoke, and excrement, and fear. The women were kept elsewhere. Some had young children, and many of them were with child.

'What do they do with the children?'

No one wanted to answer this. Later, Klaus would see children sent to test newly dug tunnels ahead of the prisoners. Some of these tunnels proved sound. Other times, the children never returned.

Then there was the matter of sustenance for hundreds of prisoners, horses and pirates. Klaus discovered what the pirates did with the loot from their raids: in the south of the camp was a guarded area stocking food and supplies, regularly replenished. The pirates were resourceful. The timber, wheels and parts of looted wagons were stripped and repurposed; nothing was wasted. But still this was not enough – the base was too large and well-established to be sustained by the pickings of bandits. They were getting goods from somewhere, he was sure of it – a black market, or traders with no scruples over whom they supplied. And, of course, there was the most important question of all: water.

The prisoners received enough fresh water rations that there *had* to be a nearby source. This more than anything made Klaus fear the spring had been found and the alleged seal on it broken. But this didn't make sense: the Septentrional Scrolls, the veracity of which he no longer doubted, suggested the spring was west of the Selvaran Cradle – the strip of desert lying between the Mengorian and Ilmaz mountains. The Scrolls had stopped short of naming the mountains: '*...a stone brother in the west that gazed upon his little sister in the east, each reaching out to embrace the other*

*but always denied, though there was scarcely a wolf's howl between them …
and in their arms rocked the Selvaran Cradle…'* Both mountain ranges were
visible on the horizon, but were yet south of the camp.

Which means this isn't the whole mine. This place wasn't the site of the
'rock' that had bewitched Ansovald Sturmsinger. *Perhaps the camp is just
north of it.* But if they continued digging, the pirates would surely soon
unearth the promised treasure Sturmsinger had 'reburied'.

And the ore they were collecting? Klaus had held the rock that
yielded Invelmari steel, and it was nothing special to look at. Was there
anything singular about this ore, or was it the sheer profitability of any
metal that had drawn the pirates here?

His questions were endless, but opportunities to ask them were
sparse. Slaves kept to their enclosures. In addition to Merik, Klaus
befriended Gonsar, the grey-whiskered prisoner he'd met on his first
night, and two merchants who were likely hiding the fact that they were
brothers. Sometimes the only chance to speak freely was deep in the
tunnels where the pirates didn't venture, guarding their exit instead.

Merik had been a carpet weaver, his fingers dye-stained and callused
with pulling threads. On better days, he spoke of his Lebasi village; of his
family's small business, sometimes even rekindling an artisan's longing
for the beauty of his craft as he spoke. His family's ancestral pattern was
eshreyara; an ornate template of interknitted decagons which he drew
for Klaus in the sand. It might have been his timid nature, or his detours
into the stories behind his beloved tapestries, but he reminded Klaus of
Verdi, and through him Klaus felt more keenly the absence of his friends.
Merik was kind, but imprisonment and the labour had taken a toll on
him. Each day before their blindfolds came on for their walk to the mine,
he sought his scattered family. Most days, he withdrew into depression
when he found no sign of his kin, fearing the worst. It was difficult to
pry conversation out of him after that.

'Take heart,' Gonsar would say. 'Maybe they're not always working
in the mines.'

For not all the slaves were sent down the shafts or ordered to hew
at the rock. Others were assigned to see to the slaves' diet of derina stew
and tuber-bread, or to digging latrines, or serving the pirates. One day,
Klaus glimpsed a train of slaves unloading great barrels from a cart
arriving from the south-east. Gonsar was convinced they brought water
from a well the pirates had dug to the east.

'They separate us from the prisoners who bring the water,' Gonsar
murmured as they walked to the mine. 'To keep its location secret. A
boy told me he heard them say it was found long ago, under a temple
that kept it hidden.'

This was troubling, but neither this description nor its south-eastern location fit with Klaus' estimations about the sealed spring. 'Did he say how long ago they found it?'

Gonsar shook his head. He muttered darkly, '*They* found it.'

At first Klaus thought he meant the pirates. But then he finally got a better look at the black-helmeted guards.

He had only been at the base for a week, but already Samsarra was a distant dream; Dunraven seemed another life altogether. His attempts to commune with the land still fell flat, isolating him further. The prisoners' digging routine became the clock by which time was set, so when they were assembled one morning before the day's work began, Klaus knew something was untoward. The pirates herded prisoners to the southern fringe of the camp where four shackled prisoners had been stripped naked.

Full of foreboding, he stood with the rest.

Five black-helmeted guards were present, this time holding the leashes to what Klaus could only describe as great dogs. They were spotted like hyenas but larger. A guard stepped forward, removing his helmet.

He was not Derindin.

His dark hair was pulled back in many braids before falling loose in a straight sheet to his shoulders, and his elongated sharp-cheeked face was very fair. His thin nose curved sharply. It was unlike any face Klaus had seen across the Seven Parts.

He spoke in common Invelmen, but with an accent Klaus couldn't place.

'I am told there are those here who wish to leave.' He addressed the naked men; mostly terrified youths. 'Who have remarked that this camp does not have walls.'

The crowd's silence was now absolute. A familiar warning buzzed in Klaus' ears, but more horrible was the powerlessness that accompanied it.

'Unchain them.'

Pirates unbound the prisoners, keeping their distance from the dogs, who began to prowl the ground restlessly beside their keepers.

The man gestured towards the open desert.

'Go.' The freed prisoners eyed each other with a mixture of confusion and dreadful realisation. 'You were planning to leave, here is your wish.'

A dog punctuated a deep growl by lunging towards them, held back only by his leash. One of the naked prisoners broke into a run. Nerves crumbling, the others followed.

The man watched for a few moments as they grew smaller. Then he crouched down and whispered something to the beasts as each was uncollared, and they tore away after them.

The freed prisoners were not so far that Klaus couldn't hear their screams. Someone vomited behind him. The smell of excrement filled his nostrils. The man replaced his black-painted helmet. He paused over the assembled prisoners.

'Perhaps now you will see the walls around here better.'

He and his companions walked away, and the pirates dispersed the crowd.

Klaus relaxed his fists. His Form had withstood far worse, but here he had to feign *less* discipline rather than more – lest someone more perceptive than pirates were watching.

Later, he would hear that the hapless youths had been overheard planning their escape. He had no idea how they'd hoped to achieve it.

'What were their names?' he asked. They were known to a few prisoners from shared travels along the Kassian Road; Lebasi who took cotton and kahvi north to sell in the border towns.

'I wonder how the pirates found out,' Gonsar worried.

'Snitchers, how else? Keep your mouths shut, that's what I say.' A prisoner shot Klaus a dirty look. 'Can't be too careful.'

Form kept Klaus' anger cold, but cold fire still burned. The angrier he became, the less clearly he was able to think. Master Arnander insisted anger was a servant to be commanded, but even Master Arnander's tenants didn't seem to help him now. He mowed savagely through the rock with his pickaxe that day until even the guard hesitated to collect it from him, waiting instead for him to throw it to the ground.

Even under the half-watch of another lax night sentry, heads didn't dare huddle together that night, lest they too were suspected of troublemaking. But eventually tongues wagged into bowls.

'It was a Fraivonian who snitched on them,' a Derindman muttered. 'A long time they've had it in for those Lebasi.'

'Didn't do him much good,' replied another. 'I heard he was given more work for disturbing the guard he went ratting to.'

'How were they hoping to get out, anyway?'

'Cold scum, them metal-faced folk...'

'Who are they?' asked Klaus.

His fellow prisoners fell quiet. Some of them simply mistrusted him, but there was also a palpable fear at any mention of the alien guards.

'When I first came, a fellow heard the pirates talking,' a man whispered eventually. 'Said they were *Eh Menishian*. Not from this Part. They've got the pirates under their thumb.'

'Where did they come from?'

But this was a question to which Klaus found no sensible answer. Some said they were from the Black Lava Plains, which was impossible. Others said they arrived from the east beyond the great Sourgrass Sea. Klaus had travelled as far east as Semra and had never seen their like. One prisoner was convinced they had come from the belly of the earth, born of men and snakes.

Merik was particularly shaken and had sustained several lashes that day for stumbling as he worked. He hadn't spotted any of his relatives for three weeks and couldn't eat for fretting. Klaus used his water ration to clean the Derindman's wounded shoulder.

'Eat,' Klaus urged, as Merik had told him a fortnight earlier. 'You'll need it.'

Yet he struggled to take his own advice. *Eh Menishian.* Klaus had never heard the name before. Where could they have come from? He knew what lay to the north, the west and the east. Southward there was only desert. They were not from the Zmerrudi Part, further south beyond the sea. And how had they come to control the pirates?

The Plains were full of mediocre mercenaries. But the pirates Klaus had fought during the attack on Alizarin's caravan had been willing to die for their cause, whatever it was, and that was not the way of a mercenary. He heard again the screams of the butchered youths, and again the hot beast within him howled.

'It will do you more harm than good.'

Klaus didn't recognise the middle-aged prisoner who interrupted his thoughts, though there had been no new arrivals to the enclosure for a week. The man sat against a tent post, watching him with half-closed eyes.

Klaus glanced at his full bowl of derina.

The stranger shook his head. 'The anger. The malignant anger that stifles higher things.'

His gaze was far too meaningful for a stranger's face. *As though he knows about …* but no, that wasn't possible. *My imagination's getting the better of me.*

Klaus studied him. He was likely in his fifties, his stubble full of silver. Unusually for a Derindin, his eyes were dark. Klaus was certain he hadn't seen him before; he would have singled him out for the impossible tranquillity that smoothed his brow.

The guard changed, extinguishing the lamps, and prisoners curled up on the ground. Klaus lay back and closed his eyes for another night without stars.

*

A hearty cheer greeted Rasan's arrival at the training ground following her pledge to Elendra.

Verdi's eyes narrowed. 'Did my aunt –'

'No, joining the clan wasn't a condition for being allowed to stay. It just makes sense. I promised Tristan I would guard you and I will.'

Her face grew serious. 'If this is the road to Merensama, this is where I will serve.'

Verdi's cheeks grew pink.

Arik clapped her shoulder. 'It's good to have you back.'

She lowered her voice. 'Is there any word...?'

Arik shook his head, and Verdi looked away.

'At least he won't be alone,' Rasan reassured them. 'Nerisen went after him. She was determined to go when I told her.'

Arik froze. 'And you thought that was a good idea?'

'She's a Plainswalker. If anyone's going to find food and water there...' Rasan became defensive. 'You don't know Nerisen. If she'd had any idea of your suspicions about a spring, she'd have gone herself long ago.'

Rasan took to Samsarra as though she'd been born there. Verdi soon realised that her regard for Lorendar was as fervent as her contempt for Elders. She was matter-of-fact and forthcoming. This would have been refreshing, had her favourite topic been anything other than himself.

'Are you undecided?' she asked.

'About what?'

'Taking Lorendar's oath, of course. What else?'

Rasan flopped down beside him between chores in the barracks, ignoring the volume of anatomical notes open across his lap.

'No...' Verdi almost wanted a challenge so that he could vent his frustration. 'Well, yes.'

'Why?'

He longed to verbalise his confusion, his fear of being left behind by his friends in exchange for a prize he hadn't sought.

He couldn't, of course. 'I don't think I'm quite the right person for all this.'

'Is that all?' Rasan flicked the air as though swatting an invisible fly. 'You will bring the clans together. You're meant to.'

Verdi closed his book. Her conviction was as warming as it was frightening. 'You can't know that.'

'I knew it the instant you spoke.' There wasn't any mockery in her words. 'You see the things the Elders don't want to notice. And that's what we need to restore Merensama – another way. Otherwise why bother? Everything else has been tried before.' Rasan rarely smiled; she almost did then. She began polishing a boot as though they were merely complaining about the work and the weather. 'Sometimes kindness is a much harder edge than all the might of the world.'

Ravi nibbled his shirt, as he often did when Verdi grew idle. 'Do you think it'll take war to restore Merensama?'

'Definitely.' Her voice hardened. 'These clans need to be broken before they can be re-made. A purge is long overdue.'

Arik bellowed across the ground, and Rasan got up to investigate. Verdi should have been dismayed by her faith, but in truth his heart felt a little lighter for it.

*

Nerisen had fled from Kastava's Point as hard as her horse could ride. She was angry, ashamed, then angry again. She'd set out hoping to follow Rasan's trail. Instead, she had abandoned it to a Northman.

'You're supposed to warn me about bad decisions,' she told Onax accusingly.

Tristan was right, of course. It would be no place for a woman. Rasan's ordeal was all too fresh in Nerisen's mind. She was resentful all the same.

Nerisen examined the instruments he'd left her. They were very fine, but they were tools: metal and needles and dials. She rummaged in her saddlebag again for the snippet of his hair; a pinch of golden brown strands. *Why did I keep it?* Onax watched.

'We may need it as proof.'

He stared back at her with bright golden eyes, uncannily human.

She couldn't help but admire the Northman. Beyond all reason, he had prescient understanding of the Plains. How was this possible? Or *fair*? It was probably Tristan's need that had led them to the Wisdom's door, and she at toil all her life for the sake of the desert! She wondered if he was still alive ... *he's a warbringer*, she reminded herself. *A warbringer!*

It was better not to think of him now.

After three days, she came across signs of a camp, this time thankfully with no grisly remains, and spotted unmarked wagons through Tristan's eyescope. Tumblers of pirates? Vagrant fireside laughter strayed so close that evening, she almost risked travelling on in the dark. Madness, to even consider it – sinksands, poisonous snakes, her horse falling and leaving her without a mount and, worst of all, surrender to *tesh*. The desert had never felt so hostile to her. She spent night praying for protection from windstorms and pirates, and day praying her water wouldn't run out. For days there was almost no derina, even for her.

Even for one for whom loneliness was an old companion, it was her loneliest journey yet. At least the arrival of spring had thawed the desert cold a little, though it also sharpened the sun's rays. It was a fortnight before Nerisen encountered a Mantelonian hamlet where she restocked her supplies, and another week before she reached Elendra's southern border. She rode not to Samsarra but Tilmara's camp, hoping her caravan hadn't yet moved on.

It hadn't. She was too exhausted to notice how the sight of her frightened the children.

'I need to speak to your nonna,' she demanded. Then she swooned out of her saddle.

When she awoke she was finally warm, wrapped up in a bunk in Tilmara's wagon.

It was night. Tilmara sat crocheting. The glow of oil lamps flickered playfully on the walls.

'Gently now,' Tilmara warned as Nerisen sat up. 'You took quite a blow when you fell.'

Nerisen became aware of a throbbing in the side of her head. She touched it gingerly, finding an impressive egg.

Tilmara shook her head. 'What have you been doing, that you've grown so thin?'

'Tell me again that child's dream.'

Tilmara peered at Nerisen with her one good eye. Nerisen braced for a sharp word for impertinence, but she couldn't see the pallor of her own face, or her feverish eyes.

'What's the matter with you, child? Where have you been?'

'*Please.*' Nerisen levelled her voice. 'I need to understand.'

Tilmara leaned back in her rocking chair. She sat close, so that whenever Nerisen would recall this night in time to come, it would be laced with Tilmara's essence of violet.

'I can't. Yannao never repeated the dream itself.' Tilmara rocked her chair. 'Sages derive the *gist* of things. That's the part they tell you. "*A man will die twice to awaken in the Plains a light so great that it shall illuminate the entire Part, from the frozen northern voids to the parched southern wastes ... until milk flows from the South to the Sterns and iron marches from the North to the sea.*"'

Nerisen's head hurt all the more for the cacophony of her thoughts. 'What do *you* think it meant?'

Tilmara was quiet for so long that Nerisen thought she'd fallen asleep.

'Sorcery is not Southern,' she said at last. 'So I don't know about anyone "dying twice". Or being reborn. Necromancy is foul ... not even Invelmari dabble in it. Unlike their Far Northern mountain brethren.'

'But what about the rest? What's the North got to do with us now?'

'I don't know anything about the North.'

It struck Nerisen as the wisest answer Tilmara could have supplied.

Her mind steered her in an impossible direction. Nerisen resisted. It was unthinkable. 'Perhaps the boy made a mistake about what he saw. Aren't the meanings of dreams altered if even the smallest detail is misremembered?'

For the first time since Nerisen had known her, Tilmara was severe in her reply.

'You can't change the truth just because it doesn't please you.' Her rebuke was sharper than a rap on the knuckles. 'Do you think truth is here to serve us? No. The lowest sort of person is one who turns away from truth because of her own idea of what it should be. Or worse still, casts aspersions on a truthful messenger.' A bout of coughing diffused Tilmara's steam. 'Foreshadowings of the future are revealed only to the purest, for foresight is a portion of divinity itself. That's what my Yannao used to say.'

A little ashamed, Nerisen paused before she dared continue. 'It just doesn't make sense...'

'You should ask the boy himself.' Tilmara swept her anger aside easily – she had chided many a foolish person. 'You know him well. Ask what he told my Yannao. Ask Alizarin Selamanden.'

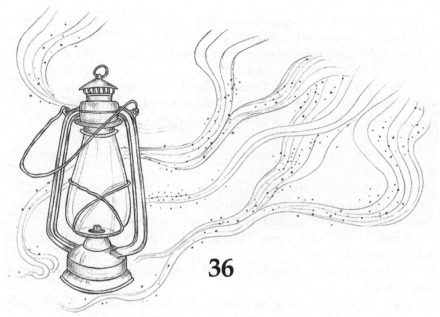

36

The Second Wisdom

BUT THE LIFEGIVER REACHES FOR US ALL, O INVELMARI.
IN THE SOUTHERN REACHES, THE DARKEST DAY DAWNED
UPON THE SILFREN PART: A BATTLE WOUND THAT FINALLY STILLED
THE HEART OF ANSOVALD STURMSINGER.

SONNONFER: THE PASSING OF ANSOVALD STURMSINGER

Arik tried not to think again of where Klaus had got to now.

He had plenty else to worry about. *'Look out for the one-eared man …
he may have already returned.'* Could Clevenger himself have been the spy
to whom Elodie had alluded in her letter?

There was no respite.

Each evening, reports of raids from freshly spawned Babbles filled
the taverns and bathhouses, mixed with ragamuffin news. A sweet-faced
Derindin girl had taken to lingering near Arik's usual table. The distraction
would have been welcome, but Saarem had already warned him about
Derindin women.

'Surely Invelmar's preparing for war,' said a farmer recently returned from Romel. 'Voista have sold more barrels of dry-fruit to the North this past fortnight than over the whole summer. And there's not a bit of kahva to be found in the market towns.'

Even Verdi looked up from his book, his little monster using the opportunity to steal a piece of bread from his plate. Arik knew Verdi's concern was really for Arik's sake. Verdi didn't have the Blood Pact in his veins.

'Let's have a game.' Broco pulled out his knife, heading for the throwing board.

Arik was in no mood for play. 'I'm going to get some fresh air.'

A man appeared at their table as he stood. Arik froze. Sassan Santarem's blue eyes were unmistakable under his raised hood.

Verdi's mouth fell open. He glanced furtively around the tavern. 'But are you safe here?'

Sassan Santarem laughed. 'Safe? Yes. Whether I am welcome is another matter.'

As if to prove a point, he lowered his hood. Arik sat down again, and Sassan took the seat beside his son. He inclined his head at Arik. 'Good evening, Master Swordsman.'

Ravi had disappeared. Most of the tumblers had retired, and the rest were engrossed in their game, so they were almost alone.

'Good evening,' Arik murmured.

'How do you pass your days, Viridian?' Sassan transformed into a regular patron before their eyes; he relaxed back into his seat, angling his face so that none could glimpse it. There was no hint of the weapons he certainly carried. In a dozen little ways, he became part of the evening, as though he'd always been there.

In fact, he reminded Arik a little too much of Klaus.

'I help at the Arboretum. And I train.' Verdi blushed, hurrying on. 'But I'm not a soldier. I was apprentice to a physician in Invelmar before I came here.'

Arik curbed irritation. *Our deaths will be in the little details.*

Sassan asked, 'Why did you leave?'

Sometimes Verdi was a terrible liar, and his father unsettled him. *Hopefully he's practised enough for this.*

'I wanted to discover my home...'

'And have you?'

'A little.'

Sassan smiled. 'So you wished to become a physician. A noble calling. If you like, I can find a scholar of great skill to train you.'

Verdi's delight outshone the lanterns. 'Really?'

'Or, if it is the medicines you prefer, the science of potion-making and alchemy – poisons and their remedies. Everything from sleeping draughts to surrwyrte. That, I can teach you myself.'

Breathless with possibilities, Verdi grinned at his father. Rasan had noticed him now, stealing looks at them across the tavern between throws of her knife.

Arik changed the subject. 'What brought you to Samsarra?'

Sassan's eyes never left Verdi's face. 'My son. What else?'

They might as well have been words of magic.

They talked of the properties of healing herbs, the worsening windstorms, and the calibre of Derindin apothecaries. Sassan was courteous to Arik but lavished his attention on his son. Nothing he said either answered Verdi's real questions or revealed anything of importance.

When he rose to leave, Verdi stood too. Sassan laid a hand on his shoulder.

'Stay. We are merely testing the waters. It will be better if I go as quietly as I came.'

'But the citadel gates are locked now. Someone's bound to see you – won't you stay?'

'I will go as quietly as I came,' Sassan repeated, winking. 'All this I can teach you – if you wish.'

Verdi's struggle was naked now. 'I *will* visit you in Romel.'

Already, there seemed to be an understanding between them. Sassan slipped out into the night.

Verdi watched him go. 'Do you think he'll be safe?'

Arik breathed easily at last. 'I don't think you need to worry about that.'

All the same, he wondered what *was* the official position on the Murheslan's presence in Samsarra. Each time Sassan had entered the citadel, he had been cloaked in secrecy; hardly the trappings of a welcome visitor.

Or perhaps he was proving a point to the son he hoped to woo in a sly courtship.

Ravi's nose appeared above Verdi's collar, sniffing suspiciously. *For once, we're on the same page.*

Verdi's shoulders slumped. 'I wonder why he would risk coming all the way.'

To pry you open and yet tell you very little. Aloud, Arik pointed out, 'He's still not said much about himself.'

Rasan abandoned Broco's game, rejoining them. 'Who was that?'

'My father,' Verdi replied proudly.

By the time they'd returned to their rooms, Arik was certain of Sassan Santarem's mission: to seduce his son away from his promise to Elendra.

*

'No one speaks of the Murhesla,' Arik complained to Rasan. 'Keep your arms high.'

She looked sharply around the training ground. 'There's a reason for that.'

She stumbled; his final blow with the wooden pole was heavier than the others.

Arik growled, 'It's getting really tiresome.'

She followed him out of the sparring ring, rubbing her shoulder. 'Not here.'

Verdi, as usual, was sitting with a book on the bench in the yard. Arik sat against a wall from where he could see him.

'They're the armour of Romel.' Rasan dropped to sit beside him. 'They took Romel from warlords and returned it to the people. No one dares ban them from a citadel – they wouldn't wish to risk the anger of their own clanfolk, let alone the Murhesla's. So long as they don't take what's not theirs, they can come and go as they please.'

Arik said drily, 'So there *is* something that unites the Derindin after all.'

Verdi sat up indignantly; Ravi had pinched the pencil tucked into his breast pocket and was trying to make off with it. Verdi caught the oceloe by the tail, earning himself a nip on the wrist.

'Do all tumblers train with Murhesla?'

'Yes, but our vows –'

'– bind you not to speak of it. I know.' Arik paused. 'But you can tell me whether I should be afraid that Lorendar's heir is growing close to Murhesla.'

She didn't seem as worried as Arik had hoped. 'Perhaps.'

'What if Merensama pushes the clans into a wider war? Where will the Murhesla stand then?'

'In Romel.'

'They wouldn't interfere?'

'Only if Romel is endangered.'

'And if Merensama becomes the new order of the South? They'll just tolerate the revival of the Custodianship in Romel, will they?'

'Romel doesn't belong to Murhesla, they only safeguard it.'

Too reflexive. Her replies had the rigidity of an Invelmari reciting the Blood Pact. Arik's fingers drifted again towards the jemesh around his neck. *What is it about a little bone that allows me to shed blood, even in Romel?* Arik had destroyed that helpful message now, but he wished he knew who'd sent it.

He sat up in alarm; the bench across the yard was empty.

Verdi crashed breathlessly into his side. 'Nerisen's returned.'

She was dismounting outside the barracks. Dark circles ringed her eyes and dirt dusted her braid, but even the worse for wear she was beautiful.

And she was alone.

'Where is he?' asked Arik immediately.

'He gave himself up to the pirates,' she said. 'We got as far as Kastava's Point before we saw them … they came from the south. I turned back, I don't know if he managed to bargain with them for work. When I looked back…' Exhaustion softened her voice. *Just exhaustion, not compassion.* 'They had bound him. I'm sorry.'

Verdi had been morbidly convinced that Klaus' plan would fail, but he was still distraught. Arik laid a hand on his shoulder, his own ears roaring. *Maybe Verdi was right. Maybe Klaus knew it would be suicide.*

Verdi shrugged his hand away. 'He was alive when you last saw him, he might be still. He'll have talked them into giving him work.'

But they both knew the odds were too far stacked against him this time. Arik preferred to mourn than torment himself with false hope.

'Verdi…'

Verdi stomped back to his bench.

'I'm sorry,' Nerisen said again. 'I'd meant to stay, but he insisted I go back –'

'Staying would have been stupid, and he was right,' said Arik, more abruptly than he'd intended. 'The pirates have only one use for women like you.'

'Invelmari mercenaries are valuable. His plan might work.'

He knew she was trying to soften the blow, but it didn't help much. 'Thank you for coming here first. I'm sure you need to rest.'

She left the barracks with Rasan. Moments later, Alizarin rode into the barracks.

'Where's Kastava's Point?' Verdi asked his uncle, repeating Nerisen's account.

'Beyond Fraivon's clandom. It looks over no man's land.' Alizarin paused. 'If that's where he's gone … even if he hadn't been captured, he is more than likely dead.'

'But –'

'He is one against many, Viridian, no matter what he's capable of. He's likely been long dead – if for no other reason than revenge for that jemesh.'

Arik didn't want to hear any more. He picked up Thunraz and went back into the training ring where every kind of anguish went to be stunned, if not slain, by the clash of swords.

*

It was some four weeks after Klaus arrived when he saw the first cave-in.

The others had told of shaft collapses, but he'd spent most of his time in the open pits and witnessed none for himself. Children sent down into the newer extensions of the mine had been returning with promising reports, and the yield pleased the foremen. More prisoners were sent into the expanding tunnels. Some were terrified of the dry darkness and pleaded to remain overground in the pits. The pirates made sure they were sent down first.

Klaus' turn to join them in the tunnels arrived. Oil lamps did little to dilute the darkness, and the stifled air in the shafts was more a stranglehold than a lifeline. Merik had been jumpy all day, his pickaxe sliding in slick palms as he hewed. His fingers were meant for much lighter work, and his demons seemed to swell in the darkness.

'It's not so far to the surface,' Klaus reassured him. 'No more than a cellar. Focus on that.'

This wasn't strictly true; the tunnel, although not deep, was a quarter-mile long. The pirates measured their takings by weight and punished whatever fell short of their standard. Klaus had taken to working twice as hard to ensure their carts were full enough for both Merik and himself. The bell rang to signal the end of the day's work, and the hewers stopped hacking at a new tunnel. At the end of the tunnel was a narrow passage they'd been struggling to widen. Merik and Klaus were awaiting their turn to crawl back to the main tunnel when the lamps went out.

'Oh God!' Merik's breathing erupted into a ragged seesaw of panic in the darkness. 'Oh Great Sentience … oh God oh God oh God…'

'Stop.' Klaus grabbed his arm, shook him. '*Stop*. Breathe … slowly.' Merik swallowed loudly and eventually obeyed. 'I'll guide you through the passage. Can you lie on your belly?'

Merik's breathing became ragged again.

Klaus squeezed his arm. 'Do as I say.' Klaus half-pushed, half-lowered him to the ground. Merik was whimpering now. 'Now crawl … go on, I'm right behind. I've got your ankle, I won't let go.'

It was slow and painful. Rocks dug into his knees and shins and his thighs burned, but eventually they emerged from the passage. A lantern warmed the main tunnel with light. Klaus stood and rubbed his knees as Merik sat by the lantern, breathing deeply.

'See? It's not so bad –'

The ground rumbled. Klaus jumped forward into the tunnel while Merik froze in fear –

'No!'

A series of crashes came from the newly dug passage behind them. An explosion of dust thickened the air. Once again, the light went out.

Klaus waited until the silence rang true. He edged back towards the passage. He could now sense the way out because of the faint breeze kissing his right cheek.

'Merik?' He listened. 'Merik?'

Noises came from the entrance. A lantern's glow announced two pirate guards.

'What the hell are you playing at?'

Their lanterns illuminated the ruined passage he and Merik had exited not moments before. Loose rocks now blocked its entrance. Klaus began throwing them aside.

'What's he doing?'

Klaus scrabbled through the mound. 'Someone's trapped in there.'

'Leave him.'

A pirate yanked at the back of his shirt; Klaus threw him against the wall with enough force that the pirate shouted for more guards. He continued searching. He felt a leg between the rocks; then an arm, and another arm. Blessedly, Merik's head had escaped the rockfall, and the rest of him had been showered by smaller debris. Klaus pulled him free.

'Merik!'

He opened dazed eyes. Klaus hauled him upright just as more guards arrived. A whip cracked against his legs a few times, but so long as they both got out, he didn't care. He half-dragged Merik out into the open air.

'What happened?'

The foreman was furious over the collapse of the new tunnel. He barked orders at his men before bearing on Klaus.

'If you're told to get out,' he thundered, 'then you get out. I've lost a valuable tunnel thanks to your loitering.'

Klaus tossed his pickaxe to the ground. 'That tunnel was dug under your instruction. You should have ensured it was secure before sending anyone in. Every man you leave behind is worth many bushels of ironstone. What will your superiors think of your shoddy planning?'

The prisoners assembling to leave watched in uneasy silence. The foreman's small blue eyes bulged with disbelief at his insolence, but fury was threatening to seep through Klaus' Form. One of the black-helmeted guards arrived, however, and the foreman dropped the matter. Klaus prayed silently as Merik stumbled into line; if he fell, they would discard him. But Merik managed the walk back to the enclosure despite the wound bleeding through his trouser leg. By the time they reached the enclosure, he was horribly pale.

'That looks bad,' said Gonsar gravely. He wasn't wrong; Merik's wounded thigh was still seeping blood. A bright red blood that worried Klaus.

'Wrap it tight.' Klaus tore away a strip of cloth from his shirt; a couple of other prisoners followed suit. The pressure eventually stopped the bleeding, but Merik looked dreadful.

'Thank you,' he whispered over supper. 'You didn't have to help.'

His breathing was too rapid. Klaus gave him his water. 'I wasn't going to leave you behind.'

'Not that,' Merik said. 'For always filling the carts.'

Klaus couldn't hold his gaze; anger threatened to break his Form as it had done once already in Samsarra.

He tightened Merik's bandage. 'Sleep, you've lost a lot of blood.'

Merik ate some derina and quickly fell asleep.

'You'd better watch that foreman,' Gonsar warned. 'He's a piece of work. I saw him beat a boy to death for dropping his lamp.'

'He's afraid of their masters,' Klaus replied. He knew where to strike the pirates now.

The following morning, Merik was missing from the tent. It was the first thing Klaus noticed.

'Wound started bleeding again,' said one of the prisoners. 'A guard took him in the night. Said he needed a physician.'

Klaus looked at him blankly. There were no physicians for prisoners here.

They were led back to work, this time to the pits. They'd been following the deposits with their pickaxes, fashioning a cave that ate into the quarry like an ulcer. Klaus waited for his wrist cuffs to be released so he could begin, but the guard shook his head.

'Not you. You're carrying on with yesterday's work.'

Klaus forced his fingers to remain loose. If they curled into fists, he was sure they would swing. 'Work on what? The tunnel's caved in.'

A whip cracked against his side in reply.

The new tunnel was a short walk from the quarry. Several guards loitered by its entrance, already crude with drink.

One of them told Klaus cheerfully, 'You're going to clean up your mess.'

Two of them followed him into the tunnel. The collapsed passage was a quarter mile into it. The guards sat nearby with a lamp, drinking as Klaus began clearing loose rocks. There was more rubble than he remembered. Had there been another collapse? Klaus eyed the walls warily. He was certain there'd been another fracture in the ceiling here. Perhaps it had been his imagination. After a while, all rock began to look the same.

The guards were unusually jovial for this hour. *Probably happy to be out of their masters' sight.* The rubble loosened too easily beneath Klaus' blows. He struck again, and this time his pickaxe thudded without a *crack*, and rocks shifted readily. The foreman joined the guards. The little smile playing at his lips told Klaus something was wrong.

He raised a bottle and swigged. 'Don't let me distract you.'

Instead of hacking, Klaus forked through loose rubble with the handle of his pickaxe. There was an arm, and another arm. A leg. Roaring filled his ears. The guards talked and laughed in Derindask they didn't know he understood. He didn't stop until he'd teased away the rocks from Merik's smashed face, now barely recognisable.

'Good work,' said the foreman softly over his shoulder. 'I think they'll see now the tunnel's not worth salvaging.'

More laughter. Klaus' eyes latched onto the limp hands, bent at odd angles, white with death and dust. The fingertips were ripped and raw. He had been alive when they left him there, scratching at the dark.

Klaus glanced up at the ceiling. He *hadn't* imagined the crack running through it, just above the mouth of the tunnel.

He threw his pickaxe into the fracture with full force.

It didn't immediately collapse, but the tunnel ceiling crumbled. Then a huge crash sounded on the other side of the rubble that had made Merik's grave.

Chunks of the roof showered them. Swearing, the pirates ran out in terror without looking back.

Klaus waited until there was once again silence. He kneeled down and closed Merik's unseeing eyes, leaving a piece of rock on each. He removed the frayed cord Merik wore around his neck. Then he walked out with the oil lamp.

When he emerged, the pirates at the entrance were no longer laughing, and their drink had disappeared. The foreman was still panting. None of them came towards him.

'Take him back to the quarry,' snarled the foreman once he'd caught his breath.

A horse neighed; a black-helmeted guard dismounted behind Klaus as he walked away. Eyes bored into his back. The pirates dared no misbehaviour in the presence of the Eh Menishian.

His rage roiled, unsatiated. In the quarry, they were stupid enough to put another pickaxe in his hands. He paused inside the cave his fellow prisoners were expanding, his ears still ringing with fury. He could have killed all three of the pirates in the tunnel. It would have served no purpose and ended his mission, but his blood roared for blood.

'And now they have cut you off at last.'

It was the dark-eyed Derindman who'd warned Klaus about his

anger after the execution. Klaus realised why he hadn't seen him digging; he was a light bearer, slight of stature, and was likely sent in to test new tunnels like the children. The man raised a lantern, illuminating the cave.

Klaus swung his pickaxe at the rock.

'Strike,' said the Derindman quietly. 'But strike purposefully.'

Klaus struck. Again and again, he struck.

'An anger that is caged ferments to poison. An anger that is released unguided has a handle sharper than its blade. But an anger that is *bridled*...' With each blow, Klaus felt the entire rockface respond to the trembling tip of his pickaxe. '*That* is the tamed wild stallion that leaps longest.'

Something snapped. Later, he would realise it was his Form. Like a starving beast falling on its prey, rage ripped through his body and thrust him at the rock, hammering and shredding until he *was* the axe, savaging the face of the wall.

Eventually, the storm passed. The axe rose and fell more evenly, like his breast. A wide berth had formed around him, both prisoners and guards keeping their distance. And all the while the light bearer stood over him, waiting for the fire to burn out.

Klaus' breath finally became level. 'Who are you?'

'One who knows that a voice you once heard has fallen silent.'

Klaus' hand shook holding the axe. He had told no one but the Healer of his ability to sense the desert. A prisoner dragged away Klaus' cart, spilling over with chunks of ironstone.

Klaus waited until he'd gone. 'How do you know that?'

The distant crack of a whip announced an approaching guard. Klaus resumed hewing at the rock, more lightly so he could hear the light bearer's reply.

'Because the earth will not bend to a will that has been corrupted.'

Klaus' hands faltered, throwing off his aim, and the misdirected force sent a painful jolt through his arm. He *wasn't* imagining things. There was no chance he would forget where he'd heard these words before, but more striking was the utter conviction with which the light bearer repeated them. *What I wouldn't give to have such certainty about anything.* He stared at the light bearer.

'You're a Wisdom.' Then, with a little shock, he breathed, 'You're the Wanderer...'

He struck the rock again as another guard passed.

'And who are you?' said the Wisdom, watching him with eyes that were lit from within.

Klaus stared at the pockmarked rockface.

'I don't know,' he said.

*

'A thimble's worth,' a prisoner named Spaero confided. 'That's all you need of brush-snake venom to kill a hundred grown men. It's powerful stuff.'

The prisoners conferred quietly over supper, their heads huddled together. The guards were laughing riotously, spilling drink.

'And how are you going to get it?'

'I was a tanner,' said Spaero. 'We got good silver for their skins. After we caught them, we took 'em to the apothecary to extract the venom. Worth a decent bit of silver, especially if it's fresh, so I'd take them there regular. Seen it done a hundred times.'

'So we're going to serve the pirates a lick of brush-snake venom, and none of the hundreds of other pirates are goin' to notice when the first hundred start foaming at the mouth,' whispered Gonsar scornfully. 'What a stupid idea. You need something that'll get them all.'

Spaero leaned closer. 'That's why you put it in the water...'

The others listened earnestly now, but Gonsar was unconvinced. 'And where are you going to store it until then, back of your throat?'

Every so often the guards were so drunk that even such talk was allowed to ferment in the cracks and crevices of the camp. Klaus listened in silence. He saw no merit in anything he'd heard, only obstacles and certain death.

But he knew the power of hope, and he wasn't about to snuff out its flicker.

Following his second meeting with the Wisdom, Klaus sought him constantly. At first it seemed as though he'd vanished as quietly as he'd appeared. *But he is the Wanderer,* Klaus reminded himself, and felt lonelier than ever for his disappearance. For days, the story of Merik's murder had travelled around the camp with the water carriers, and all but the most mistrusting of the Derindin hailed him as a hero, buoyed by his stand against the pirates. It only made him feel worse. Merik might have lived had he not intervened at all.

So by the time Klaus next saw the Wisdom, his rage had mutated to guilt, and three days of near-solitude with his thoughts had ripened his resentment. After another long day in the pits – where the guards now preferred to keep him, out in the open – Klaus looked up to find the Wisdom delivering his evening water ration. The other prisoners lounged about the enclosure talking, for the guards were too busy playing cards to care.

'They won't hear you,' said the Wisdom. His tranquillity spilled into his voice, mellow as milk. 'You've not been sleeping well.'

'I've never been one to sleep well.'

'Never?'

Klaus shrugged. Perhaps there had been a time when he hadn't been plagued with nightmares. How old had he been then – eight? Nine?

'How did you end up in this place?' he asked the Wisdom.

'More important is *why* I am in this place.' He was dressed in the humble shirt and tunic of a peasant, and like all the prisoners these were dirty and worn.

Klaus lowered his voice. 'Who are the black-masked men?'

'Have you seen their like before?' asked the Wisdom. Klaus shook his head. 'What do you make of them?'

Klaus glanced at the drunken guards. 'They've made the pirates dangerous.'

'True. Without the pirates, the Eh Menishian would have no foot soldiers, and a commander is worthless without foot soldiers.' The Wisdom's voice hardly changed as he spoke, gentle as a fledgling wind.

Klaus shook his head. 'Too bad most of the clans still believe the pirates are just a rabble.'

'They *were* a rabble, once, but now they have a master. Some will be quick to blame the master for all the horrors you have seen and any horrors yet to come, but the pirates are just as much to blame. Derindin men and women with no sense of duty or honour, willing to capture and kill their own brethren and turn them into slaves ... to cull those not fit to serve them, and raise another generation of slaves bred on hate for the purpose of hate...' The hair stood on Klaus's arms. 'Derindin men and women, many of them cast out of clans and driven away to the harshest corners of the Plains, to settle feuds so old and senseless that none remember how they began ... exiles whose children can have no home to remember, and with whom even Unsworn nomads will exchange neither greeting nor merchandise ... *untouchables.*'

'You're *defending* them?'

'The truth has many parts. Choices must be examined in light of the conditions and intentions that spawned them. Only then can their consequences be fairly comprehended.'

Calm but not extinguished, Klaus' anger growled beneath his battered Form. 'How can I hear the voice of the desert again?'

'With ilnurhin. How else? Its voice is one of truth. Only a heart polished of its blemishes to the brightness of a mirror will have ilnurhin enough to reflect truth, which is a portion of the Unseen.'

'Then I will be blind for some time yet.'

The Wisdom smiled. 'If you should find yourself a free man again, there is a mirror you should seek in these Plains that will show you a path to that end.'

'Will it show me how I can regain the connection I lost with the land?'

'You already know why the connection was severed,' said the Wisdom. 'Anger and resentment only harden your heart and cloud your mind, burying ilnurhin under their grime. Your slight matter has been stifled. How can you gain the gifts of the Unseen world if you cannot even reach your own self?'

Something inside him lashed; frustration, chased with more anger. *Why must everything be difficult?* Had he not earned the right to a share of anger, deserved to feel it? Why should even this be taken from him? But he knew this was impatience speaking and rebuked himself. He had no right to demand anything for nothing, least of all something as great as the bond he had forged with the desert, and he not even a native of this land.

The Wisdom was right; he had severed the connection himself. It was buried somewhere beyond the rage against pirates and traitors and Wintermantels, and in order to find it...

'I don't know where to begin,' Klaus confessed, weary.

'I can teach you a way,' said the Wisdom, moving away to distribute more water. 'But the bitterness that cocoons your heart – it is yours to banish.'

Klaus didn't think that could be true. Nothing about this disquiet felt like it was under his control. The sentry changed and the enclosure fell silent.

That night, the Wisdom was nowhere to be found amongst the prisoners. Klaus closed his eyes and tried to cast his mind forward into the desert, and felt nothing – absolutely nothing, so that he wondered if that extra sense had ever been there at all. Perhaps bitterness had twisted his mind and opened a window onto madness. When sleep cut his consciousness, Merik's face filled his dreams again, broken and white with dust.

37

Sea Without Shore

FOR THIRTY DAYS AND NIGHTS THE HEAVENS WEPT,
UPON THE FALL OF ANSOVALD STURMSINGER. AND EVERY BLADE
OF GRASS SHRIVELLED, EVERY FORGE-FLAME DIMMED,
FOR THE FALL OF ANSOVALD STURMSINGER.

SONNONFER: THE PASSING OF ANSOVALD STURMSINGER

It was difficult not to lose track of time. Little distinguished each day from the next, other than the whisperings of assorted horrors that crept between enclosures like a bad smell the pirates couldn't contain. Klaus forced himself to count each day so the monotony didn't consume him entirely.

The foreman who'd arranged Merik's murder had taken a particular disliking to Klaus, seeking to torment him whenever he could. He ensured Klaus worked in the least sheltered parts of the quarry, under the intensifying gaze of the early spring sun, which had also lengthened their day's work. If Klaus picked up another prisoner's fallen load, he was made to do the work of both men. Once, he had to carry a prisoner who he'd helped up after a stumble. The man died later anyway, a bundle of skin and bones who didn't wake the following morning. Klaus thought twice before favouring or aiding others, lest it marked them for punishment. Eventually he kept his distance from everyone but the Wisdom.

While they were lax over some things, the pirates were meticulously cautious with others. After almost five weeks in the camp, Klaus still had no clear idea of where they got their water. The water carriers were usually children, and always accompanied by a guard. They changed regularly – likely to prevent them from getting too familiar with the routes to the well. Gonsar claimed the pirates killed them every fortnight to protect its location. This seemed improbable, but if it contained even a grain of truth… *How many children are here?* Frustratingly, Klaus was collecting more questions than answers.

Prisoners were herded in and out of the camp by the same route, so they saw little of their prison. The ironstone they mined was loaded onto wagons driven by pirates, and no one knew where it was taken or what happened to it. Klaus was certain he'd heard the familiar din of a forge drifting from the eastern side of the camp, and occasionally he smelled sulphur. But a true forge required great furnaces and more fuel and water than the pirates appeared to have. Not once since his arrival had Klaus seen the night sky, always leaving the enclosure at dawn and returning before dusk. Any opportunity for estimating his location based on his rudimentary knowledge of the Derindin constellations was denied.

They had robbed him of the stars, and his mind still could not touch the land.

The Eh Menishian often visited the mine and the pits. Klaus tried to study them without looking. They watched, said nothing and left. He was digging in the pits one day when an unmasked Eh Menishian arrived with the black-helmeted guards.

This Eh Menishian was a wiry man wearing a long green-golden kirtle and a burnished breastplate, an ornate blade at his belt. He was taller than the Derindin but not as tall as an Invelmari. His dark, glossy hair was braided over his skull and cropped short over the sides of his head, falling in a thick ponytail to his waist. But, like his companions, the most striking thing about him was his face: heavy-lidded eyes made darker by the pallor of his sculpted cheeks.

The foreman hurried over, bowing stiffly.

'Didn't know you'd returned, Lord Renegash...'

Klaus' ears pricked. The Eh Menishian ignored the foreman, speaking with his guards in their language.

An Eh Menishian guard addressed the foreman, gesturing to Klaus. 'He is Invelmari.'

Again, Klaus couldn't place his accent.

The foreman was growing tense. 'Well, yes –'

Renegash spoke again to his guard. Klaus glanced at them once between swings of his pickaxe. Something about the Eh Menishian unsettled him.

'He was sent to the mines,' the foreman began. 'Sharlo thought –'

Renegash and his Eh Menishian guards turned away without another word.

The foreman grumbled under his breath once they were out of earshot, snapping at the prisoners. 'Back to work, or I'll keep you out here into tomorrow night.' He glared at Klaus but left him alone, making Klaus uneasy rather than thankful.

That night the sentries were back on form, as though Renegash's return had rejuvenated the pirates. The prisoners ate in silence. Then the lanterns were put out. Sometime during the night, Klaus awoke, convinced Merik was in the enclosure. Sure enough, there was someone chained next to him where Merik used to sleep; but how could that be? Merik was dead … Klaus looked again, and the sleeper's bruised and broken face turned into Elodie's, her cheeks kissed with white dust and her golden hair adorned with pieces of rubble, her big brown eyes staring sightless into the night…

He awoke for real with a great jolt. He lay still, heart pounding. The enclosure was quiet. A soft snore came from the entrance. The sentries had fallen asleep.

Klaus waited for his eyes to adjust to the dark and realised the Wisdom was sitting beside him.

Relief washed over him. The Wisdom's wrists were chained as though he had always been in the enclosure, though Klaus had not seen him for some days. Klaus decided not to question this. Was he not the Wanderer? Instead, Klaus had hoped and waited, like Nerisen waiting to stumble across a rare species of flower. The Wisdom was a bridge to the world outside the camp, and to something else beyond – a serenity that seemed not part of the world altogether.

'It was a dream,' said the Wisdom quietly, once Klaus' breathing grew even. 'That is all.'

It *was* a dream, but night always lent a clarity to his mind that he found at no other time, endowing him with fears that his Form normally quelled by day.

Klaus whispered, 'Will you teach me how to reach the land again?'

'If you will take the remedy from me.'

Desperate and hopeless and determined all at once, Klaus nodded.

The enclosure was dark, but the Wisdom's eyes shone silver, as though they had captured an invisible moon.

'There is a doorway to what you seek that can be opened in every heart,' he said. 'But I told you: first the heart must be polished, for only the purest mirror can reflect shadows of the Unseen world...'

'But it's my own thoughts that I use to summon –'

'You summon nothing. Not yet. It is the earth that reaches out to *you*, drawn to the ilnurhin that resides within your fifth chamber. And it is that chamber to which the land responds, not to your mind.'

Klaus was transfixed. What the Wisdom shared next became a balm gliding over every aching part of him in both flesh and mind. As he listened, the enclosure fell away, the Plains fell away, and the night became a sea without shore from which he never wanted to emerge. Later, he wouldn't remember what exactly had passed, but he was sure that though the Wisdom had spoken in another tongue, Klaus heard him in Invelmen, and what he remembered of the Wisdom's prescription was also in Invelmen: a litany the Wisdom made him repeat, over and over until he memorised the words.

'Guard it in your heart even when your tongue lies still,' the Wisdom instructed. 'But speak the words each day twice, at the rising and the setting of the sun.'

'Why then?'

'That is when we are closest to the Great Sentience, for that is when the Veil between the worlds is thinnest. In that hour, particles of ilnurhin can bridge the Veil.'

He couldn't remember falling asleep, but there was a respite from dreams, and when he awoke the Wisdom was gone from his chains.

*

Not long after, a strange little man visited the enclosure. It was the first time Eh Menishian had entered the tent. Three of them flanked the creature – for that was what came to Klaus' mind when he saw him. It wasn't because he was deformed, with unequal bulbous eyes, a torn upper lip and a spine both twisted and shortened in length. Klaus had seen many infirm and crippled people on his travels, but his garb set this man apart. He wore the spotted fur of a great wild cat. Chips of bone and ivory pierced his ear lobes with more hanging around his neck, and symbols daubed his forehead. His deformities made him difficult to place, but he looked neither Derindin nor like the Eh Menishian who towered over him and whose skin was palest white-gold by comparison to his sallow cheeks. The watery blue of his eyes did not dim the intelligence within them.

A hush fell over their evening meal. The man raised his hand, and his Eh Menishian guards stopped at the entrance. The pirate sentry looked queasy.

The man walked slowly along the rows of chained prisoners, his eyes sliding lazily over them. He stopped in the middle of the enclosure, his gaze spreading like a cold slime.

Klaus suppressed a shiver.

The man shook his head and rejoined the Eh Menishian. He spoke in their hissing tongue, glancing back at the prisoners. His eyes fell on Klaus.

It lasted only a few seconds, but Klaus felt his gaze for much longer, latching onto him with chilling closeness. They left the enclosure.

'Who was that?' Spaero whispered, shaken.

'A shaman.' Gonsar scowled, making the Derindin symbol of the Great Sentience over his forehead. 'I've seen him before ... if he's looking for someone, I pity them.'

'What's a shaman?' Spaero drew closer, one eye on the sentries.

'A holy medicine man,' another prisoner replied.

'A witch, more like,' said Gonsar distastefully. 'Like a sorcerer, or a spaewife. Them that does horrible things and claims it lets them talk to spirits.'

'What does he want here...?'

The shamans Klaus had encountered in the Zmerrudi Part and along the road to Semra were secretive creatures, revered in lonely temples, often shunning human contact.

He guessed what the shaman was looking for the next morning, when word spread of another foiled escape: a group of prisoners had plotted to play dead so they could be put out in the carcass wagon. The story arrived with the boy who delivered their water. He was slightly older than the other water carriers, his upper lip beginning to bear fine hair. Klaus had seen him running errands. It was the first time he'd brought them water.

Klaus listened to the water carrier's story. The pirates didn't normally allow the water carriers to speak to the prisoners, but the sentries had ignored the boy's gossiping.

'Then was the shaman looking for the men hoping to escape?' said Spaero fearfully after he left.

'No,' said Klaus. 'If they were, they would have just sent guards.' What could a shaman identify that a soldier couldn't? 'Did that boy say how the men planned to pass themselves off as corpses?'

'A sickness,' Gonsar replied. 'Though what sickness can make a man look like a corpse without making him one, I don't know. Big risk, if you ask me ... if the pirates thought they were dead, they could have just as easily fed them to their dogs. Those monsters take a lot of meat.'

'If they believed the men had been killed by disease, they wouldn't risk their dogs.'

Gonsar nodded at Klaus. 'Sharp one, aren't you?'

The tale did not sit well with Klaus. He had an inkling that the shaman had been looking for whatever the men had used to make themselves fall ill.

'Don't speak to that water carrier,' he warned his companions. 'And don't make any suggestions when he asks what you think.'

Gonsar waved a hand. 'He won't be back. They don't let the same ones keep fetching the water.'

But Klaus was certain that he would, and sure enough the same older boy continued to bring them water for the next few days. He remained more talkative than the other water carriers, and though the pirates pretended not to notice him loitering, Klaus was unconvinced.

When the prisoners were next all summoned after the day's digging, they went with foreboding. They knew what a gathering meant.

This time they assembled in a clearing in the outskirts of the camp. A pyre had been built in the centre. Four men were tied to stakes upon it. A strong smell of lamp oil sharpened the air. Dread weighted down the dusk.

Klaus searched for the Wisdom. Some four hundred prisoners had assembled, and almost double their number of pirates. Many of the women, grouped to one side and surrounded by guards, were with child. They looked better fed, which did little to reassure him.

Renegash stood at the head of two dozen Eh Menishian, the little shaman beside him. The lord of the camp was dressed like his soldiers today, but the black markings on his helmet were painted over burnished brass.

Renegash walked to the pyre with one of his guards. His pirate translator followed. The hapless victims were around Klaus' age or a little younger. Their faces were clammy, and one had a blotchy red rash. *They must be the would-be runaways.* However they'd done it, they had succeeded in making themselves ill, though not ill enough.

The Eh Menishian didn't need to call the Derindin to attention. The clearing was absolutely silent.

'Our men tell us you are ill by your own choosing, and that you hoped death would deliver you,' said Renegash through his translator. 'But it seems death has not come soon enough.'

Spaero inhaled sharply; Klaus squeezed his forearm in warning. Spaero hadn't spoken again of his idea to poison the water supplies, but his fear would be enough to betray him.

'The Great Sentience have mercy upon them,' he breathed.

Klaus fixed his eyes on their terrified faces. 'Tell me their names.'

Renegash circled the pyre. Again, Klaus noted how unfamiliar his speech sounded as he spoke to the translator; quite unlike any language he had studied or heard anywhere in the Parts.

'Do you know what we do to the sick?'

A pirate handed Renegash's guard a torch. One of the men began sobbing. Renegash nodded, and his guard threw it onto the pyre. Its base went up in flames.

Klaus would have closed his eyes. Not to deny himself the sight, but to safeguard himself a little from his rage, and summon the place to where the Wisdom had taken him. But the pirates would be watching. The Eh Menishian didn't flinch, faces hidden behind their helmets except for the shaman. His deformed face was alive with a glow akin to pleasure, mouthing something as he watched.

Nothing could safeguard their ears.

Revulsion shuddered beneath Klaus' Form. Invelmar did not burn living flesh. That was the way of Far Northern savages.

Paralysing rage surged in his breast, like the heat of the burning pyre. He clamped his Form around it. Still it smouldered until he feared the rage would finally break over him again in a violent flood – *no, no, it will keep me blind – I must regain the land* – he clutched at reason; if he lashed out now, the pirates would kill him and his entire mission would be for nothing ... but rational thought was no match for his anger. He reached further still and found the Wisdom's litany. He heard-spoke-felt the Wisdom's words, over and over, dimming the smell of burning flesh, dimming screams.

Slowly his body relaxed. Now the men were dead. Their bodies burned on, but they were gone, and the suffering now belonged to the living.

Around him, prisoners caved to varying degrees of distress. The pirates cracked whips to contain the crowd, felling more than one prisoner turned reckless by fury. Klaus looked for the Wisdom again to no avail. They were forced to wait until nothing remained of the victims but blackened suggestions of human forms, twisted and smudged by the flames. Sweet-acrid smoke cut through the stench of vomit. The prisoners' anger condensed into a sullen silence, lined with horror and fear and loathing. Klaus spotted the young water carrier who had told them of the failed plot of the now charred men. His face was ashen.

The pirates were reassembling prisoners to lead them back to their enclosures when Renegash beckoned a pirate to him. They spoke through his translator, and the pirate turned and looked directly at Klaus. Within moments, several pirates surrounded Klaus and marched him into the clearing.

It was Lord Wintermantel's voice that rang in his ears then, not Master Arnander's.

'A warrior must know fear. Without it, he cannot see the limits of himself. And then he will never be forged.'

They brought Klaus to the Eh Menishian. Renegash sat flanked by his black-helmeted guards. At his shoulder, the shaman watched Klaus with those watery, bulbous eyes. Klaus gazed into the eye slits in the painted brass hiding Renegash's face.

Renegash spoke in his own tongue to the pirate translator.

'He asks if you are a Northman.' The translator paused, correcting himself. 'He asks what a Northman is doing in the Plains.'

Klaus spoke directly to Renegash. 'I came to sell my sword.'

The brass face considered him. Then Renegash spoke again, and the translator repeated after him in Invelmen.

'He wants to know how long you have been here. And what you have been doing.'

Klaus schooled his face into the void of an Intelligencer's bare-faced mask. These were things Renegash could easily learn from the pirates. He had seen Klaus working in the pits for himself only a week before.

'Some seven weeks,' Klaus replied. 'Your man Sharlo put me to work in the mines.'

The prisoners followed this irregular exchange curiously. There was no sign of Sharlo, but a couple of other pirates began fidgeting.

'You did not carry Invelmari steel when you came,' the pirate translated after another exchange with Renegash.

Klaus remained silent, staring into those eye slits. Renegash knew what he and every prisoner had brought or not brought to the camp – unless it had been stolen by the pirates.

After a moment, the pirate translated again, this time sounding uncertain. 'He asks that you prove why you came.'

'Tell him to unchain me.'

Renegash nodded. Two pirates stepped forward, one holding the key to his cuffs; Klaus recognised him from the cave-in that had killed Merik. His face was full of such hatred as he freed Klaus' wrists that it made Klaus feel Invelmari again.

As soon as the click of the key had sounded, Klaus caught the chain linking his loosened cuffs and twisted it around the pirate's neck in a lethal throttle. The second pirate froze for one heartbeat. It was all the time Klaus needed to deliver a short sharp kick under her chin, instantly breaking her neck. In one fluid motion, he grabbed the falling pirate's spear, turned and vaulted it into the stunned crowd of prisoners.

The boy who'd been their water carrier fell forward into the clearing, skewered.

Shouts erupted. Renegash raised his arm, ordering his guards to subdue pirates and prisoners alike.

Klaus straightened. Renegash's own guards hadn't moved an inch. The shaman's face was alight with a troubling smile.

'Man, woman or babe.' Klaus gazed into the brass face. 'I've no need of Invelmari steel to claim my quarry.'

The pirate interpreter began to translate, but Renegash raised a hand to silence him. He addressed Klaus directly in thick Invelmen.

'What payment do you seek for your services?'

The translator gaped; the other pirates were also taken aback. The foreman who'd arranged Merik's murder pushed his way over. 'My lord –'

'Silence, worm.' Renegash said something in his own language. The translator he likely used out of sheer disdain for speaking to the pirates himself relayed Renegash's order to disperse the crowd. As they were herded away, Klaus felt hundreds of eyes cutting into his flesh.

Renegash rose. 'Let us speak away from here.'

Klaus followed him into one of the great tents, conscious more than ever of the pirates. He may have been freed of his chains, but the pirates were perhaps more deadly to him now.

A different world waited inside the tent: ebony furniture inlaid with mother of pearl, richly coloured rugs, lavish cushions. Silk-and-pearl hangings adorned the walls, depicting ships with distinct sails. An ornate brazier generously filled with coals provided more warmth than Klaus had felt for weeks. The oil lamps hanging from the beams boasted coloured glass framed with gold. The Eh Menishian were wealthy and wished to display it. A sweet spicy incense burned; it wasn't one Klaus recognised amongst either the exotic scents Invelmar imported, or the royal gifts sent to Dunraven.

Four other Eh Menishian joined Renegash in his tent.

'Be seated.'

Klaus was happier standing but knew this made him more threatening. He sat on a cushioned seat across from the Eh Menishian. A Derindin slave girl entered the tent with refreshments, then silently helped remove the Eh Menishian lord's helmet. Renegash's face was as Klaus recalled: pale, sculpted and striking.

'We welcome you late here.'

'And yet we met once before,' Klaus reminded him. He made his voice cold and imperial.

Renegash was unabashed. 'My men have watched your work.'

'And?'

A smile teased the corner of the Eh Menishian's lips. 'What is your price? I am told Isarnanheri do not leave the North lightly. Are you Isarnanheri?'

Klaus returned an empty stare.

Renegash nodded. 'They told me you will guard your tongue against your brethren. But there are no Northern spies here to hear you. Spies shrivel like weeds without water.' His smile grew at some secret joke.

'I offer my services as I am, no more, no less.'

Renegash seemed to have been expecting this. 'These men are mostly weak and unruly.' He jerked his head towards the tent entrance, where pirates waited outside. 'Some of them have skill, others fit only to herd slaves. I ask you again, what is your price?'

Klaus considered. 'What will you require of me?'

'For now, to oversee this rabble. But in time we will need more slaves, and better fighters to acquire them … in time we will need to defend this base. In time I will need one who can deal with my enemies.'

So this is only the beginning.

'Gold,' Klaus said finally. 'The measure of which is to double each moon. And passage east, in time, to Semra.'

Renegash didn't mock his demand. In fact it wasn't Klaus' eye-watering price he latched onto, but the condition of his departure from the camp. 'When?'

'When the work for me here runs out.'

Renegash leaned back in his chair. 'I could just kill you. Sharlo seems to think this is safest.'

Klaus spread his hands, heart racing deep beneath the colossus of his Form. 'Then you would also be the loser.'

Renegash's smile widened. One of the Eh Menishian raised the curtain over the entrance, and the shaman entered.

'Krevkatt was the one who first noticed you among the slaves.' Renegash nodded at the grotesque little shaman. 'He has an eye for such things. Long before yesterday and well after tomorrow, his eye can see.'

The shaman's gaze was almost hungry. A shaman would be of great standing amongst his people. Klaus rose to give him a deep Northern bow that he hadn't offered to Renegash.

'Your asking price is bold,' Renegash mused.

Klaus threw his dice. 'It's hardly worthy of a son of the Forge. And I may yet ask for more.'

Renegash laughed, pleased by such high-handedness. *He is arrogant, and is impressed by arrogance.* He expected Isarnanheri to be haughty and aware of their own worth. It was a flaw the highborn nurtured everywhere, mistaking imperious disdain for power.

'Very well,' he said. 'You will have private quarters, a mount and slaves, and your gold.'

Klaus waited a moment before he nodded.

'Shame about that boy.' Renegash shrugged in fleeting regret. 'He was useful.'

Klaus kept his face empty, relieved he'd been right about the water carrier. 'Not even a babe in arms will escape an Invelmari's strike if its time has come.'

Renegash seemed satisfied. He gestured towards the tray laden with wine and sweetmeats; Klaus shook his head. Renegash complained again about the pirates' incompetence, and announced the expected arrival of more captives. Sometimes he switched to his own tongue to speak with Krevkatt the shaman, who watched Klaus unwaveringly. Two pirates were summoned to escort Klaus to a tent of his own, in the midst of the great tents and apart from the pirates' quarters.

Alone in his new prison, Klaus finally breathed deeply.

Relief ebbed away fast.

They hadn't yet returned his weapons, and he was certain he would be under close surveillance He would have to avoid anything that might arouse suspicion. For now, at least, he would be bound to do whatever they asked. And he had seen what they were capable of.

His tent was much smaller and less lavish than the one he'd just left, but it was comfortable. Another thick rug hid the ground, and a beautiful hanging stretched across the wall over a low bed littered with soft cushions. He peered through a gap in the curtain flap over the entrance.

Outside he had an Eh Menishian guard of his own.

A slave girl brought water for the wash bowl, and clean clothes and tooth saltbark and scented soap. A tray of food followed. He took a bread roll and gave it to the girl before sending her away. Her eyes widened with gratitude rather than fear, so he decided it was safe to eat. *Besides, if they wanted to kill me, there are more showy ways to do it than with poison.*

Because that was the way of the Eh Menishian, he decided as he began cleaning weeks of dirt from his skin. They revelled in the fear with which they shackled prisoners and pirates alike. The sight of the captives writhing as they burned tried to visit his mind's eye. More chilling was the echo of their screams in his ears. That was always the way: however much the mind recoiled from horrors, it could not resist reliving them, renewing rage and revulsion. But it was the shaman's face that stayed with Klaus longest: enraptured as he watched the pyre, his mouth muttering unheard words, and, later, the cold and hungry slither of his watery eyes, like a hunter studying its prey.

Outside, the smell of burned flesh lingered long after day had faded into darkness, defiant over the light in unholy triumph.

*

In the morning they did return his knives and Rasan's sword, but an Eh Menishian guard kept to his side – for his own protection from the pirates until they were accustomed to his new position, Renegash claimed. It was no less than Klaus expected.

'I have no need of another guard to oversee the slaves in the mines,' Renegash told him. 'But the pirates lack discipline, and some of them are unreliable. Keep them in check.'

And the pirates rewarded Klaus with plenty to keep him occupied, so he didn't have to turn his attention to the prisoners themselves. On his first day in the mine in his new role, he rooted out a makeshift brewery where some of the pirates had been fermenting precious derina water to cider. Soon after that, he found one of Renegash's slaves, a young Derindin woman who'd been missing for a week and was presumed to have fallen down a mine shaft, hidden away in a tunnel by a handful of pirates, shackled and battered. Klaus was wracked with guilt, delivering her from the lair of one monster to another's. *At least in the camp she will be fed and cared for by the other women.* Renegash allowed him to punish the culprits as he saw fit. Klaus executed them himself.

The pirates accepted his new status very quickly after that.

His mind was finally free to machinate. He rode with the Eh Menishian to the mine without a blindfold, memorising the routes. He was better positioned to explore why a pirate kidnapper and then an assassin had been sent after Verdi, but he was also keen to study the Eh Menishian. Fortunately, Renegash was no different to every tyrant Klaus had met, and tyrants couldn't resist talking about themselves.

'You have perhaps never encountered our people,' said Renegash. The Eh Menishian seemed to hold Invelmar in high regard, and thus Renegash often invited Klaus to his tent.

Klaus confessed, 'I have not.'

'That is no surprise. The Isarnanheri do not travel much through the West. But then neither does anyone else.'

Where in the West could possibly be home to these people? The Black Lava Plains were more barren than Derinda's desert, and Klaus hadn't heard of Eh Menishian in the lands further west. *Of course, he might be deliberately misleading me.*

'Invelmari soldiers travel to serve, not to adventure,' Klaus reminded him, neither refuting nor encouraging Renegash's assumption. Better for the Eh Menishian to believe he was Isarnanheri. 'The war contract must come first.'

Klaus' indifference only served to encourage Renegash. 'Our home is a glorious place. Rich and abundant both in the belly of the earth and above it, though cooler in clime than this wasteland … with rivers that never quieten and mountains that reach the gods.'

'It sounds far more pleasant than here. In your place, I wouldn't leave such a home.' Klaus feigned a sip of wine. 'Though sometimes a bounty is so great, it should be pursued to the ends of the earth.'

'To the ends of the earth,' murmured the Eh Menishian lord in agreement.

But Klaus soon realised that though Renegash delighted in thinly-veiled vanity, much of what he said was inconsequential. How and why the Eh Menishian had come to the Silfren Part to mine this presumed bounty, Klaus could only guess. Neither did he understand how they'd gained the loyalty of the pirates, who they controlled without challenge, and who, for the most part, seemed devoted to their mysterious masters beyond the pull of gold.

Slowly, over the coming days, Klaus finally obtained an impression of the entire camp. It was larger than he'd suspected. The base was loosely divided into four areas; prisoners, pirates, Eh Menishian and stores. The prisoners' enclosures were to the north. The sounds and smells of the forge came from the east; this was the only place he had no business to go, and he resolved not to venture there uninvited lest he aroused suspicion. In the stores they kept horses and wagons and several chariots, some cattle for the Eh Menishian, and a granary. Their food stuffs, other than exotic dried fruits and sweetmeats and a bittersweet wine of deep amber, were all Derindin. Looted by pirate raiders? Purchased from traitors on a black market? Then there were the comforts the Eh Menishian brought with them. How far had they transported them, and by what means? And from where?

The Eh Menishian didn't speak of how many prisoners they kept or how many pirates served them, and Klaus didn't ask. These he could estimate. He observed that only a small proportion of the ironstone was taken to the forge, while most was transported to the east of the camp, heavily guarded by both Eh Menishian and pirates. He didn't ask what they intended to do with it. Just as they guarded their water source, the Eh Menishian were careful to send the prisoners of each enclosure to work only in one location, so that none discovered the true extent of the site. Little by little, as Klaus rode to other parts of the mine, he formed an idea of the territory the Eh Menishian had claimed as their own.

They'd dug a series of disconnected mines and quarries, rather than concentrating their efforts on a single site, suggesting their discoveries of the ore had been piecemeal and less than methodical. Anyone else might have expanded one mine. *Perhaps their time here is short.*

Klaus considered the land through the lens of the Septentrional Scrolls. That fateful passage turned over in his thoughts daily now: '*Ansovald encountered a stone brother in the west who gazed upon his little sister in the east. Each reached out to embrace the other but were always denied, though there was scarcely a wolf's howl between them, and in their reaching arms rocked the Selvaran Cradle...*' Two siblings; two mountains. On a clear day, he could see the Mengorian mountain range hulking near the westernmost quarry. But the Mengorian range was still too far west for the mine to be the site of the Selvaran Cradle, and he couldn't make out the smaller Ilmaz mountain range at all. *They're digging too far to the east.* But the dig was now also extending west. It would only be a matter of time before they would encounter the Selvaran Cradle, the rock that had bewitched Sturmsinger and his company.

The source of their water, the lifeline of the camp, proved to be the most difficult to investigate. Water was the Derindin's greatest weakness, and the Eh Menishian guarded their secret accordingly. All Klaus could discover without enquiry was that the Eh Menishian guards themselves escorted blindfolded water carriers in and out of the camp, passing through the Eh Menishian's quarters. Which meant it came from somewhere even further to the east; somewhere too far east of the Selvaran cradle, by Klaus' estimations. The location of the sealed spring wasn't as well described in the Scrolls' forbidden passages as the mine, and he could only pray the Eh Menishian and the pirates knew no more than he did. *After all, the prisoners had extracted rumours of an excavated well, not a spring.*

Everywhere Klaus went in the camp, he sought the Wisdom; to his disappointment, he was in none of the enclosures. He couldn't risk asking after him openly, especially not with an Eh Menishian constantly over his shoulder, and began to wonder whether he hadn't imagined the man entirely in the sheer desperation of starless nights. But the litany the Wisdom had gifted him was very much real, coming alive when Klaus spoke it at sunrise and sundown as instructed, so that it was more spirit than words.

Even if he found the Wisdom, there would be no way to speak with him now, for Klaus' time was still not his own. His hours were more or less the same as they'd been in the enclosure; he oversaw pirates by day and returned to his tent at dusk, and had no cause to venture out at night. Sometimes, he was invited to take refreshment with the Eh Menishian over his reports; there was no opportunity to stray from these short walks. There were other lesser lords besides Renegash behind those black-painted helmets, most of whom didn't speak Invelmen. Slowly, Klaus began to learn more about them. Questions had to be very carefully forged. If the Eh Menishian suspected him, he would be lost. So when Renegash first solicited Klaus' opinion of the mining, he initially declined to offer one.

'I am a blademaster,' he said. They were dining on spiced smoked meats, fresh cakes made from derina flour, and the preserves of fruits Klaus hadn't sampled before. 'Not a smithy.'

'But you must have some knowledge of metalwork,' an Eh Menishian insisted. 'Invelmar's mines are legendary.'

Eventually, he allowed himself to be implored to comment on the subject. 'I merely wield of what my people forge. In the North, there are great fire-mines and gas vents and wind-furnaces. The process by which the ore is treated is as important as the quality of the ore itself.'

Even with the language barrier, he could sense the Eh Menishian's frustration with their own experiments with the ore, whatever these were. Yet they didn't take Klaus' lure to discuss the ironstone they were mining.

The shaman Krevkatt was sometimes present at these gatherings. He said little, sitting alone over a curiously marked table, casting runes or studying writings. As Klaus suspected, he was of some importance to the Eh Menishian, for Renegash and the others always spoke to him with deference. Klaus made sure to pay him silent respects whenever they met. Krevkatt spoke no Invelmen, hence there was no other exchange between him and Klaus. But Klaus often felt the touch of his watery gaze, or the latch of those bulbous eyes. Krevkatt had been the saviour who had lifted him out of the enclosure, but he worried Klaus more than the Eh Menishian company altogether.

And so his fortunes at the camp came to change.

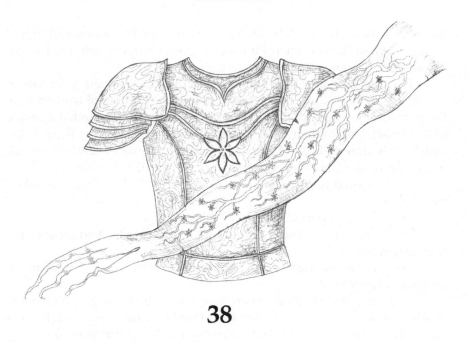

38

The Wolf Howls

LONG DID THEY SEARCH, HIS FAITHFUL EALDORMEN, FOR THE PLACE
WHERE HE FELL. ONLY HIS BLADE DID THEY FIND, BROKEN IN ITS GRIEF
FOR THE PASSING OF ITS NOBLE MASTER. FOR ONLY GRIEF
COULD SHATTER THE STEEL OF STURMSINGER.

SONNONFER: THE PASSING OF ANSOVALD STURMSINGER

There was no keeping Verdi in Samsarra for long. He was determined to
see his father again, perhaps all the more so as even *his* hopes for Klaus'
return wavered, and not even Arik could talk him out of it.

'The harder you try, the further away you'll push him,' Arik warned
Alizarin. 'Let him go.'

Grudgingly, Alizarin had conceded.

'This time I'll ask him about Murhesla,' Verdi vowed as they rode
to Romel. 'I'll have more answers for when Klaus gets back.'

'How are you going to find him?' Arik asked. Klaus had been gone for almost six weeks; Arik had very little hope for his return. But they'd barely reached Romel when innkeeper Riorga himself delivered Verdi a note from Sassan.

That was how they found themselves in a tavern, waiting for Sassan to arrive. Arik was struck by the disproportionate number of women here. Derindin brothels were outlawed in several clandoms. He spotted a couple of Invelmari, both in their latter years and evidently enjoying them in the South. Arik doubted the Murhesla spent much time in brothels, which meant the distraction hadn't been meant for Verdi or Sassan...

Verdi waited until Arik's kahvi had arrived. 'Marcin ... he asked me to go alone.'

'What? Are you mad?'

'He's my father.' The fool had already decided. 'And he sent me Murheslan escorts.'

Two would-be merchants, sand-masks loose around their faces, took the adjacent table.

Arik clenched his teeth. There was no use being angry. Normally, Verdi's instincts were sharp, not least thanks to his oceloe – who was helpfully nowhere in sight, but he seemed to have stumbled into grey when it came to his father. And there was no Klaus to anchor him. Arik didn't just mistrust Sassan Santarem. He didn't trust Verdi either.

A comment caught Arik's ear through the sordid medley of smoke and false feminine laughter. He made up his mind. 'Where do you want to meet afterwards?'

Verdi's shoulders relaxed. 'Riorga's inn.' He offered Arik a limp grin. 'Look, you can keep Ravi until I return.'

'I'm not *that* worried about you.' Arik looked the waiting 'escorts' up and down. 'If you're not back tonight...'

'I will be.'

A moment later, the three of them disappeared.

Arik pulled up a chair at a table piled with dirty crockery but within earshot of the voice that had distracted him.

'Four thousand men!' The Babble shook a fistful of bells, repeating his story. 'Amassed near Eisnach. Far Northern raiders burned five villages to the ground. They say Isarnanheri have been pulled back to Invelmar from contracts in Zenzabra and the Aurelian Part for the first time in a century. I tell you, war's coming.'

'None of this is news. Far Northerners have raided the Northern front for centuries!' This was the voice that had captured Arik's attention: crisp, native Invelmen.

'This new Far Northern warlord has done what no other warlord managed,' the Babble insisted. 'Quietly won over enough tribes to command a massive army. And he's taken control of a karrionhjord.'

Then the conversation drifted out of the inn, and Arik couldn't risk following it.

A serving girl stopped at his table. 'A drink, sir?'

She served him a smile that was meant to make him forget, at least for a while. In Dunraven he might have offered her surrwyrte and taken her above stairs. But this was not Dunraven.

He left the tavern. *Have I lost my senses?* He'd let Verdi go with no idea of where they would take him. But Verdi wouldn't be contained, and Romel was now either the best or the worst place to allow him some air. The main square was busy with market cries and the turmoil of trade. An Invelmari could disappear more easily in Romel than in Samsarra. The thought summoned Klaus and a pang; Arik brushed both aside for now. He raised his hood, wishing to be alone with his worries, and waded through the busy streets.

A small darting movement caught his eye in the thick of bartering: a grubby hand that vanished behind a sack of apples at a fruit stall, leading to a small scruffy head...

'*Fibbler!*'

The little boy jumped at his name, but his alarm was washed away by relief when his eyes landed on Arik. He dropped his prize and scampered to Arik with unrestrained delight.

'Fibbler, how on earth did you wind up here?' Arik took in the dark circles around the frightened aquamarine eyes; the thinness of his arms. 'What in the Part happened to you?'

*

Heart hammering in his ribcage, Verdi followed the two Murhesla. He regretted leaving Arik the second he was out of sight. But his father had been constantly in his thoughts.

The Murhesla trod lightly through Romel's streets. They moved like oil on leather. Within twenty minutes, he was once again in the underground labyrinth of passageways burrowing beneath the citadel.

This time Sassan was not hidden in a cloak, but wore an embroidered tunic and an intricate silver armlet that extended from his shoulder to his elbow. A midnight-blue cloak draped over his other shoulder. He spread his arms, embracing Verdi. When he released him, Verdi's escorts had vanished.

'Welcome back, my son.'

My son. Verdi thrilled each time Sassan spoke those words.

Sassan led him into a richly furnished chamber. How *human* his father was, compared to most Derindin – especially his uncle, who was so devoid of emotion that at times he seemed lifeless.

'I would have come sooner, were it not for the raids,' said Verdi. 'I'm afraid they'll only get worse.'

'You have a good heart, like your mother,' said his father. 'That is why the pirates concern you. The men and women of the Plains have been corrupted from within. It's their own doing that pirates came into being at all – cast-outs, exiles, misfits for whom no clan could spare a place. Now they've chosen to take back some of what was denied them.'

'What do you mean, "take back"?'

Sassan laid a hand on his shoulder. 'Come. You wished to return to the timevault.'

For the first time since meeting his father, Verdi felt uncomfortable. But he didn't want to examine this dissatisfaction too closely. He followed Sassan to the place where the memories of Derinda went to be forgotten. There were many questions he'd prepared about Lorendar, but really his curiosity burned elsewhere.

'How did you become Murhesla?'

'It was the only solution I could find to a problem I couldn't escape.' Verdi latched onto his father's every word. 'There is much unfinished work in Derinda. As your Northern guard will tell you, a heart is never satisfied until it finds its way safely home. One day, this land will once again quake with the march of war. I wished to be amongst the prepared.'

Hope-dread-excitement stirred in Verdi's heart. 'War against the pirates?'

'The pirates?' Sassan looked bemused. 'Murhesla only fight for a worthy cause, Viridian. The pirates are not our fight.'

'But the damage they're doing ... even now they may be on the brink of taking a citadel!'

'It is not for us to intervene if Derindin tear themselves from within,' said his father. 'We are the spirit of Romel. It is far more than just a citadel. Our purpose is to protect it until *its* purpose is fulfilled.'

'Then which war do you mean?' Verdi frowned. 'Merensama?'

'Neither is Merensama the concern of the Murhesla.' Verdi's mouth had already opened for the next question when his father interjected: 'You've not yet asked about your mother.'

All other matters evaporated instantly. Verdi hurried to keep up with Sassan's stride.

'No one seems to want to speak of her.' Verdi hesitated, afraid to lose the moment. 'I was worried you wouldn't, either.'

His father paused. A wall lamp cast deep shadows over his face.

'Your mother died because two clans fought over water-rich land that neither could bear to concede. They fought until one clan finally dried out the other. She and many others drank from a sick well in desperation. Only a mile away from the siege that incarcerated her caravan, springs gushed and irrigated fields of almonds bred for Northmen and market town traders.' Something savage rose to Sassan's surface. 'That was the will of your clan, of Elendra. They had to teach Voista's water-poachers a lesson. Oh, they're not the only ones – many innocents have suffered at the whims of their Elders. To them, people are nothing more than pawns on a gameslab.'

His words were crushing. The flash of Sassan's grief was raw, but Verdi was more deeply cut by the jagged verge of his anger.

'We Murhesla will avenge her, and everyone like her.' Sassan Santarem's face smoothed again, eyes now as calm as lagoons. 'And then we will replace this chaos with justice. Is that not a cause worth fighting for? Justice, upheld by her husband? Her son?'

Sassan had already resumed walking when his meaning hit home.

'*Me*? Join the Murhesla?' A confusion of panic and possibility clouded Verdi's mind. 'But – I already made a promise … I don't know anything about the Murhesla…'

'But you have not yet taken Lorendar's oath.'

They had arrived at the timevault. In every direction were passageways that led to books, tablets, artefacts. The remains of a damaged suit of armour was displayed behind glass nearby. It boasted a faint sheen that shifted at different angles of light: finest Invelmari steel. Keen and yet loathe to change the subject, Verdi walked to the display case. The crest on the battered breastplate caught his eye: the six-petalled starblossom; the ancient sigil Klaus had dissected from the Murheslan tattoo.

'What's this?'

'That is the armour of Ansovald Sturmsinger.'

Verdi's mind sharpened immediately. It shouldn't have been surprising to find a token of Sturmsinger in the Plains; he had ravaged the South while his armies began building the Ostraad. But the armour had been tended with care, bearing not a single spot of rust.

Verdi murmured, 'I would have thought anything of his would be shunned.'

Sassan shook his head at the twisted metal. 'If we erase those parts of the past that dismay us, we have only ourselves to blame when they come revisiting.'

Klaus had been very preoccupied with the finding of the six-petalled starblossom in the Murhesla's emblem. *I'm not going to get a better chance.* 'What *are* Murhesla?'

'Perhaps it's better to ask how one *becomes* Murhesla,' his father replied, walking past artefacts. 'Most people think only tumblers join our guild, and then either become initiated as Murhesla or leave the path.

That was true once, when Murhesla first liberated Romel from warlords. But we are thinkers and artisans as much as warriors now. Any who can dedicate their lives to our creed are permitted to remain amongst us. In return, we reward them with the means to master whatever skills they choose to commit to our guild.'

'I thought all Murhesla had to be warriors.'

Sassan smiled. 'I would not invite you to our ranks if that were true.'

Verdi blushed, but Sassan's voice held no criticism. Now the vault was a warren, as convoluted as an anthill. Verdi couldn't remember the route his father had taken, just as he had steered Verdi's thoughts.

'What's this?' Verdi stopped by a curious mask; a dented brass helmet with narrow eye-slits, painted in black lacquer. From it hung what looked like a dark tail decorated with colourful beads. Verdi realised this was human hair, likely torn away when the helmet had been detached.

'A trophy,' his father replied. 'Now it is a testament. It was said that Lorendar came across a herding tribe with strange powers during his rampage in the South. They spoke Derindask, but he believed they were demons. He feared they would threaten his precious alliance. So he killed them all.'

The torn tail of hair made Verdi shiver. Half-thoughts nagged him. Taking a gamble, he touched the six-petalled starblossom worked into the pin on his father's cloak; the emblem of the Murhesla

Tentatively he said, 'I've seen this before...'

'Of course you have.' His father looked pleased. 'It is the rarest species of thrift-daisy to grow in the Plains, now extinct. But when it grew, its sap yielded a powerful antidote to scorpion venom. You must be well-studied in medicines indeed to have recognised it.'

This time Verdi couldn't ignore the nagging. Because he'd paid attention in Maragrin's lessons, he knew there had been no such things as Derinda or Derindask during Lorendar's time, when the Ninvellyn still ran thick through the South and the desert was as green as the North. Derinda was a name that took hold like a thuggish weed long after Sturmsinger's Second Redrawing, when nothing was left of the Southern kingdoms but warring clans forced to subsist on drought-safe derina. Perhaps Sassan had not expected him to know.

Then there was the matter of the six-petalled starblossom; Sturmsinger's abandoned sigil. Verdi knew very well where it had come from; it was not a thrift-daisy and it had nothing to do with venom. Why would his father conceal these truths from him?

Why would he lie to me?

His heart grew heavy.

*

Fibbler finished one bowl of stew, then another. Arik stopped him from wolfing down a third.

'Give yourself time to breathe.'

Eventually he regained a little colour, and his head began to nod.

'You're exhausted.' Arik wrinkled his nose. 'And filthy. What in the Lifegiver's name have you been doing with yourself?'

Fear jerked Fibbler alert. 'Are you sure he won't find me here?'

'Who?'

'The Babble...' His eyes darted to the window. 'I pinched something from him. He was so friendly when he asked if I wanted to go with him – to do a proper job, not just run errands like I was doin' in Samsarra. So I said I'd go, but I thought we was coming back in a day or two.' Fibbler drew his knees up to his chest. How long had his feet been bare? 'At first he gave me errands, messages to deliver. Nothing important like he promised. Then a few days ago, we left Romel to collect a letter from a man ... the man gave the Babble the letter, but then he tried to take me with him. And the Babbler didn't stop him.'

'The man tried to take you from the Babble?' Arik frowned. 'What did you do?'

'The Babbler told me the man had more messages I needed to collect and deliver to him in Romel,' the little boy said. 'So at first I went with him. I had a bad feelin', but I didn't want the Babbler to think ... I heard all these stories about people and children bein' taken but it wasn't like that, the Babbler told me it was important I bring back the man's messages. He said I had to prove I could do it on my own, without his help. We rode a few hours in this man's wagon and then his horse threw a shoe. When he stopped to look, I ran away...' Fibbler's eyes filled with tears. 'I think he was a pirate.'

'You came back to Romel on your own?'

'Lucky we was still close to the citadel when I escaped. A caravan heading back there picked me up.'

Arik exhaled through his teeth. He had no doubt Fibbler had been kidnapped by a pirate.

'Which way was the man going?'

'Border towns. We didn't make it very far...'

North. 'Where's the Babbler now?'

Fibbler shook his head. 'I dunno, but I'm ever so scared, Mister Marcin. If he finds me he'll kill me. There was summink different about this Babble. He was ever so clever in Samsarra, and I'd never met him before this summer. I been back for two days and I've not seen him again in Romel, but he's bound to be looking for me...'

'But he gave you to the pirate – well, to the man who took you out of the citadel.' *Who's probably been paid for you already.* 'Why would he still be looking for you?'

'Because I stole his letter.'

The little boy produced a crumpled envelope from his ragged coat. The nondescript seal on it was unbroken.

'When I saw he was going to leave me with that man, I was so angry I picked his pocket.'

He handed Arik the envelope. Arik broke the seal. The note inside was short.

'The wolf howls now in the South. He will guide you to the bloodstar. Await my signal.'

Arik read it twice. Lead filled his stomach.

'What is it?' Fibbler fidgeted anxiously with his empty bowl. 'Did I do wrong?'

'No, Fibbler. You did nothing wrong.' Arik folded the parchment away. 'Except for leaving Samsarra with that worthless Babbler,' he added severely. 'I would tell you I'll have your hide, only I know Mayda's looking forward to it.' Fibbler stiffened in fleeting alarm before his eyes narrowed, preparing his defence. '*She'll* kill you first. And then if there's anything left of you, you can worry about the Babbler.'

But Arik couldn't admonish him for long, holding him tightly in a bear hug into which he disappeared altogether. A tension he had buried behind his Form finally eased.

'Tell absolutely no one about stealing this letter, Fibbler. It could do a great deal of harm. Do you understand?'

Fibbler nodded.

'Good. I'll have some hot water brought up. You're to have a good wash and then get into bed. Else Ravi won't come anywhere near you.'

'Is Verdi here, then?'

Arik managed a brittle smile. 'He will be.'

When Alizarin returned to the inn after his business in the citadel, he wasn't so certain.

'Sassan Santarem is *not* to be trusted!'

Arik had never seen him so angry. Alizarin raked his hair, pacing their quarters.

'You're his sworn guard,' he fumed. 'The *one* thing you had to do –'

'Sassan won't harm him.' Arik could barely believe *he* was the one sprouting this madness. 'And right now steel is no longer the protection he needs.'

Alizarin exhaled, forcibly reclaiming his composure. 'I presume you mean from his father.'

'If you're not careful, you're going to lose him for good.'

The door swung open. Verdi's head appeared sheepishly around it, Ravi around his neck.

Arik sprang to his feet. 'I *am* going to kill you.'

Alizarin could have been relieved. He could have even chided Verdi, for that was a sort of attention. Instead, he stood. 'I've wasted our tumblers' time enough here.'

Before they could come to blows, Ravi shot from Verdi's shoulder to the table, whiskers twitching. Arik caught him before he darted towards the adjoining bed chamber. He kicked his furry legs, hissing.

Verdi relieved him of the struggling oceloe. 'Whatever's the matter?'

'Fibbler's asleep in there and I don't want him woken up.'

Verdi's mouth fell open. 'Where did you find him?'

'In a street market, half-starved. I've been waiting for you ... I think there's a spy in Romel sending messages about Klaus through the Babble.'

The colour drained from Verdi's face as Arik repeated Fibbler's story to them both.

Fierce as bloodlusting wolves, and teeth as sharp... The Wintermantels had never been able to shake off the dark reputation that overshadowed their house, however cold and collected their Forms became. Lord Wintermantel's father was not so long dead that the memory of his rages could be so soon repressed. *So Klaus is the wolf.* But for the life of him, Arik couldn't make sense of 'the bloodstar'. He was no scholar, but he knew the Sonnonfer well enough.

'Whoever wrote this knows Klaus was an Ealdorman,' said Arik wearily. 'And the Wintermantels are the only people who have any reason to think Klaus might still be alive.'

Alizarin read the stolen note again. 'There's no mention here of you.'

'That makes me even more suspicious that whoever wrote it is working for the Wintermantels, not the court. If they thought we might still be alive, the court would be hunting us both. The Wintermantels just want to bury the evidence of their guilt.'

The wolf howls now in the South. Did that mean Klaus' arrival in Derinda, or his recent departure southward? Was he being followed even now by the Wintermantels' spies to the bottom of the Part, where he would be truly alone? Verdi looked up from the dreadful words. The fear that paled his face was framed by exhaustion and the beginning of despair.

'Klaus risked everything to help clear your path,' Arik told him quietly. 'Between your father and news from the Far North ... we've each grown distracted.'

'I'm sorry.' Verdi sat heavily. 'I shouldn't have lost sight.'

Alizarin had the grace not to intrude on their shame.

'That Babble who lured Fibbler away was working out of Samsarra,' said Verdi. 'He's bound to go back there sooner or later. If he sees Fibbler, he might guess his message has been intercepted.' He looked at his uncle. 'Can you have him arrested if his returns?'

'There's also the small matter of him likely selling a child to a pirate,' Arik added. 'I'll wager my sword it wasn't the first time, either.'

'I can order his arrest if he sets foot in Samsarra.' Alizarin paused. 'Though it might be wiser to watch what he gets up to next.'

'But then we'd have to keep Fibbler out of sight,' Verdi said doubtfully.

'Mayda will see to that,' Arik replied drily. 'Regardless, the damage is done – Klaus has been tracked. If we want to protect him from spies, we ought to say he's been killed.'

Verdi's face fell. 'No.'

Why not? It's probably true. Arik smothered the spiteful voice. 'Let the Babble think there's only one Invelmari left in Samsarra. It could buy him some time.'

Alizarin held out a hand to Saya, who darted onto his shoulder. 'It would certainly stop the Elders asking where he's got to. Or suggesting he was a spy all along.' He ignored Verdi's resentful look. 'Then it is settled. I will see to it that news of his death is spread.'

'I'm not lying to Fibbler,' Verdi warned.

Alizarin paused at the door. 'Can you trust him to keep his mouth shut?'

With that, he left them alone.

'I don't trust your father,' Arik told Verdi bluntly, too uneasy to soften the blow. 'I don't think he's telling you the whole truth.'

Verdi slumped in his chair. 'I know.'

*

Late the following morning, they returned to find a sea of wagons and tents around Samsarra.

Verdi's heart stumbled. *The citadel's been taken!*

Alizarin gazed through his eyescope. They were not pirates.

He stopped a patrol of tumblers as they approached the gates. 'What's going on?'

'They want refuge.' A tumbler grimaced at the makeshift camp. 'Started arriving yesterday by the dozen. Travelled together for safety. We've not been bothered by pirates, and this is as far as they can get from the West…'

The new arrivals were mostly nomads, cattle herders and wild horse tamers. Though they hailed from all over the Plains, Verdi glimpsed the same demons in all their faces: fear; desperation; uncertainty. Children darted-scampered-fluttered like bright-winged birds, ragged but still easily delighted. Fibbler, who was sharing Verdi's saddle, squirmed.

Verdi hissed into his ear, 'You promised to stay out of sight!'

He would have liked to have delivered Fibbler to Mayda himself, but instead accompanied his uncle to the Chieftainess' house, where a heated discussion raged, Nerisen in its midst.

'Most of them have been travelling for days, Ahena,' Nerisen told the Chieftainess. 'The Plainswalkers are distributing as many supplies as we can.'

'We can't play host to every stray and deserter,' Fenral exclaimed. 'Another hundred arrived this morning – who knows how many more will come? Order them out!'

Verdi knew he ought to wait, but he couldn't help the pounce of his outrage. 'You can't refuse them entry!'

A metallic silence rang through the chamber, and his stomach clenched.

'Glad to see you've returned, Master Viridian,' Maragrin said mildly. 'I didn't receive a note excusing you from your class.'

Alizarin ignored Verdi's outburst. 'What's happened?'

'Our alliance with Voista has evidently made us the safest clandom in the Plains.' Unabashed accusation laced Fenral's reply; Alizarin's hand in the alliance had not gone unsuspected.

'But that's true, isn't it?' said Verdi. 'So what's the problem?'

'The problem is they're demanding refuge but not offering fealty, Master Viridian.' Tourmali rubbed his eyes. 'They wish to remain on our lands under our protection, but don't want to pledge clanship to Elendra.'

'Aren't most of the clandoms open to nomads?'

'Nomads, yes. *These* people mean to stay, at least for now. And if they keep coming, the strain on our water supply will be immense. This is the largest pasturing clandom in the Plains. But our granary is stocked for Elendra's winter, not Elendra and all her guests.'

Verdi looked around the chamber. 'How do you hope to ally *all* the Derindin for Merensama if you can't even cope with just a few?'

'*This* isn't an alliance,' Fenral retorted. 'An alliance means pledges, taxes – taxes that feed and irrigate and armour the whole clan as it grows –'

'Calm yourself, sister.'

The Chieftainess was composed but resolute. 'Things have been set in motion that are now beyond our control. Rumours are spreading that we're preparing to challenge the West. Those rumours may well provoke Baeron and Hesper against us, or else attract pirates hoping to find us stretched. Our alliance with Voista is untested. We've sent them tumblers, but have not yet called upon them for help in return. Spring's only just arrived; more windstorms are on the way. Even a modest strain on our resources now could leave us very underprepared for a disaster.'

It was a painful summary. But Verdi imagined the caravaners outside the citadel being rounded up and captured by pirates. Nerisen began to protest, but Verdi was louder. 'This is the wealthiest clan in the East.'

Fenral reddened. 'They have no business here. And if we encourage them, we'll attract every beggar and vagabond in Derinda.'

'Beggars? Have you been out there for yourself?' Verdi's pulse raced recklessly. 'They're desperate. Some of them are survivors. Who knows what raiders have taken from them? Or are people nothing to you until they choose the shackles of your rule?'

Her jaw slackened with outrage.

Cutting in before it spilled over, Arik bowed to Emra. 'Ahena, amongst the men and women out there will be skills, experience; even tumblers. If you offer them protection in exchange for their aid, rather than clanship, you'll earn their trust and their gratitude.' Fenral threw her hands up. 'It's not Elders you must win over now, but the ordinary folk who fill the Plains. When the time comes and you call the clans to Merensama, they will give you their allegiance.'

Emra listened silently. Verdi couldn't guess his uncle's mind. He never knew what Maragrin thought about anything, and Tourmali, often the most agreeable of the Elders, seemed torn. For once, Nerisen's eyes betrayed her, juggling hope with resignation.

'They shall stay in exchange for whatever assistance they can provide,' Emra said at last. Her eyes slid to Alizarin. 'For now, mind. And you'll have to ensure that none take advantage of our generosity.'

'Without pledging to the clan?'

'Without pledging to the clan.'

Fenral stood up. All trace of her rage had vanished. 'I cannot stay, Ahena. I will not serve in a council where a Northman's voice has more sway than our own.'

Emra's reply was swift. 'Then go.'

Fenral left at once, closing the heavy doors behind her.

The quiet grew stony. Arik didn't look the least bit sorry. Verdi wished he had an ounce of his resolve.

Tourmali sighed, possibly with more relief than regret. 'Shall we at least impose a curfew for our visitors?'

'Yes. Have the gates locked earlier and double the patrols around the citadel.' Emra paused. 'Master Marcin, your friend chronicler –'

'– is dead.'

A palpable shock jolted through the room. Verdi couldn't meet anyone's gaze, because suddenly in his heart it was true.

He heard Arik say, 'Killed by pirates.'

When he blinked hot tears away, the Elders had gone. He couldn't bear the compassion in his aunt's face.

'My dear –'

'No.' Nerisen pointed to Emra, tight-lipped with anger. '*You* should know the truth.'

Arik had more presence of mind than Verdi. 'Nerisen –'

'The chronicler wasn't "killed". He left to find the pirate camp four-and-a-half weeks ago.' Her voice rang louder in the emptied chamber. 'I followed him to Kastava's Summit. I saw the pirates take him captive.'

It was the first time Verdi had seen his aunt look shaken. She looked at Alizarin.

Alizarin didn't flinch. 'His mind was made up, and it was a good plan.'

'For who?' Verdi snapped. '*If* he's still alive and *if* he finds out what the pirates are up to, he's got no hope of getting back.'

Emra pressed her temple. 'Is that all?'

Nerisen was already expressionless again. 'There's a clanswoman of Baeron outside who came with the caravans. I convinced her it would be safe to speak with you.'

'Bring her in.'

The tumblers admitted a finely cloaked woman. She walked with the sort of pace Verdi had often hurried to keep up with in the palaces of Dunraven.

'Ahena, my name is Reska Velgara. This Plainswalker spoke well of you.'

Emra dismissed the tumblers. 'Then I hope you shall not be disappointed. You may speak freely here.'

Reska was probably in her thirties, her dark hair drawn back from a handsome face.

'I wish to renounce my clan, but before you question my sincerity, let me give you my reasons. My husband is Agatin Sarskinder, envoy to Baeron. He has clashed with your nephew many times.' Reska's gaze slid to Alizarin; Verdi thought his eyes widened a fraction. 'I left him and my clan a fortnight ago. There was no more hiding the news of raids and abductions, even rumours of slave camps.' Her voice was even, confident. 'I'd heard the stories and was appalled. But my husband put my mind at ease. Like you, we've had no raids on our clandom. None of our Elders were concerned. Then three weeks ago, returning from Romel, my suspicions were confirmed.'

She faltered.

'I discovered that for over a year, my clan has sold grain, milled derina and oil to pirates. Caravans pass through our eastern territory, travelling south – carrying slaves packed like cattle. Chieftain Voldane turned a blind eye to them. I have ridden past them with my husband and heard their screams.' Briefly, her eyelids fluttered closed. Verdi's breath caught, his imagination filling in what she left out. 'I couldn't ignore what I knew any longer. I only regret waiting as long as I did to leave.'

So Klaus was right. They're building a stronghold there. But any triumph Verdi might have had was crushed by the reminder that Klaus had walked right into it.

Emra's gaze was unwavering. 'What would you do with this knowledge in my place?'

'That's not for me to decide, Ahena –'

'Decide.'

Reska hesitated. 'Tell all the clans. I would have it known from Akrinda to Fraivon that Baeron has fattened the scourge now slaughtering and enslaving our own blood and flesh.'

'And you'll stand beside me to bear witness, will you, before every Chieftain and Elder at the Assembly?'

The faintest blush coloured Reska's face.

Emra didn't press her. 'You must be tired, sister. I'll not keep you from your rest.'

Nerisen glanced at Reska. 'She's risked her life to come here. She can't stay outside the citadel.'

Emra raised her eyebrows. 'So I will have to bring in a noblewoman and keep her under a roof with a guard at her door while the peasants remain encamped in the wind outside?'

Now faint rose tinted Nerisen's cheeks.

'Of course she cannot stay outside the citadel.' Emra smiled at Reska. 'There is as much desert between us and Baeron as there can possibly be between two clans, but you've forsaken a great deal to follow your conscience. We won't put you at more risk in return.'

Verdi couldn't get away fast enough from his aunt's house after that. He had no appetite for her unfinished sympathy. He'd wanted to see Rasan before news of Klaus' 'death' found her first, but there was one more matter to attend to. He and Arik found Mayda rubbing Fibbler's head with a towel, having wasted no time getting him into another washtub.

'You wicked boy,' she sobbed. 'Oh, you wicked, wicked boy.' But she enveloped him in floury arms before pulling away to scold him again. 'I ought to send word to Terim, I shouldn't wait until he brings the herd in. We'd all but given up hope…'

'I can run and find –'

'You absolutely will not,' Verdi warned Fibbler. 'Remember what we agreed. You're to stay indoors with Mistress Mayda unless you're with a grown up. And if you can't, you'll have to be imprisoned like a troublemaker.'

Ravi gave him such a fierce glare that he nodded meekly, fidgeting under his towel.

'Whatever happened to you?' Mayda clucked. 'Why, there's barely half of you left. No, never mind, you drink your soup now. You can tell me later.'

She followed Verdi and Arik out of the house, shutting the door. 'Is it true, what they're saying about Master Tristan?'

A pang stabbed through Verdi. *Word really does get around fast.* She took their silence for confirmation, knuckling her forehead, then her heart. It was worse than any wail of mourning.

'The Great Sentience knows, all young men think they're immortal,' she said softly. She grasped their hands. 'That's twice now that we'll never be able to thank you enough.'

They hurried away before more questions came, and before the probable truth of their lie could once again overwhelm him.

*

Alizarin assigned tumblers to watch for the return of the Babble who'd lured Fibbler. He ensured that word of Klaus' death was circulating the taverns. Then he assigned a spy to monitor the renegade Baeronian clanswoman. He'd learned to listen closely to his aunt – to every word. Finally, when he could no longer contain his thoughts, he rode to the Arboretum.

East of Samsarra, he could almost imagine he was up near Noisy Tree, where the world was green.

The patrol had barred the refugees from camping there, not least because fires were strictly banned. Alizarin sank into the grasses and closed his eyes. Their slender blades whispered around him with desiccated voices, their words unintelligible.

When he opened his eyes, the world hadn't budged.

He rode on to the laboratorium, where Meron needed his approval for extensions to an aqueduct. A churlish wind was trying its luck with the afternoon, slamming shutters against windows frames. When he arrived, it wasn't Meron awaiting him, but Nerisen.

'Back to work so soon, Nerisen?' The Plainswalkers were a law unto themselves, like Murhesla. If Alizarin had had any idea of her mad plan to follow Klaus, he would have had her detained. He was sure Rasan was to thank for that. 'Do you have the blueprints ready?'

'Do you believe Viridian is the man who'll die twice?'

His smile vanished. Her face was empty, but there was fire in her eyes.

There was no point dancing around how she'd learned of his dream. 'We can't be guided by prophecies.'

'Really? Because it's thanks to a prophecy that there's any hope at all.'

'Merensama is far more than a prophecy,' he said, losing patience now. 'Whoever came up with the legend, in practice it will be a contract like any other.'

'Legend? *Contract*?' Nerisen shook her head. 'Elders' contracts and negotiations won't force people together. You're lucky Lorendar's followers don't know how you really feel.'

'And you're lucky to be alive. What possessed you to go off chasing a chronicler and his foolish impulses across the armpit of the desert?'

'He's not foolish, he's braver than all the clan councils put together,' she retorted. A little too quick, a little too scathing, with a hint of red in her cheeks. It was enough to set Alizarin's teeth on edge. *No, he's far worse.* The blasted intelligencer disturbed the balance of things wherever he went.

'Have a care, if the Northman makes it back alive,' he told her tonelessly. 'Don't trust his face.'

Alizarin left to find Meron, shaken. What did he believe now? Each time he recalled either his dream or the sage's explanation, doubt and conviction still grappled in his heart.

It was much later that Alizarin finally admitted to himself what he'd known all along, since that very first meeting in Noisy Tree. This time he had no need of a sage to explain. This time he understood for himself.

*

This time when Verdi pressed the gnomon into the ground, it was waiting to greet him.

He hadn't been expecting it. The sun had finally set on this terrible day, and his mind was far from the device in his hands. *Klaus is dead. That's what they're saying in the taverns now. And it's probably true.*

He stared at the earth around the gnomon. In the absence of daylight, the long edge of the sundial wasn't visible. *It's just a metal stick in the ground.* Verdi sat against the wall behind Thillaina's house and mourned.

How dare the Elders consider driving the refugees out? Anger consumed all manner of fears, stripping his hesitation away. Klaus was gone; Verdi no longer had to worry about suddenly having to follow him out of Samsarra, if the Wintermantels came after him. But even if Verdi left, there was no way he could forget the Derindin now.

When he looked again, the gnomon had cast not one but *two* new white shadows on the ground: slivers of light slicing through darkness.

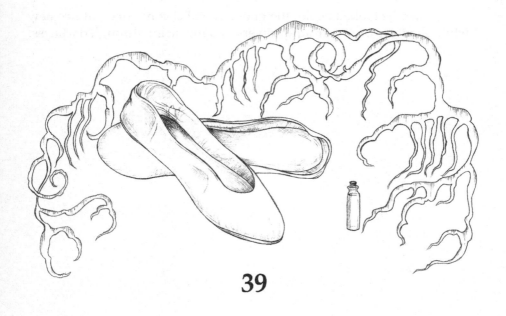

39

Smokeleaf and Surrwyrte

NORTH HIS CHILDREN JOURNEYED TO MAKE A SHRINE IN HIS
FAR NORTHERN BIRTHLAND. BUT THE TRIBE OF STURMSINGER
HAD NOT FORGIVEN HIM FOR ABANDONING THE WAY OF THEIR
FATHERS, AND CONSPIRED TO EXTINGUISH
THE BLOODLINE OF STURMSINGER.

SONNONFER: LAMENT FOR THE HOUSE OF STURMSINGER

The next time Klaus saw Spaero and Gonsar was a week after his
unexpected promotion, as he patrolled the mine where he himself had
been put to work. It was a cool day made colder by a modest but relentless
wind that scattered sand and heavy dust. An older man had collapsed
working in the quarry. The foreman didn't see him at first, and Gonsar
stopped to help him up. Two idlers didn't escape the foreman's notice
for long.

'Back to work,' the foreman bellowed, storming over with his whip.

But the man remained on the ground, and Klaus knew what this would mean. The foreman had begun to threaten the fallen man when a loud crash came from the mine. Both the foreman and the Eh Menishian at Klaus' side stepped away to investigate the source: a small cave-in, damaging a cart but little else. While their backs were turned, Klaus joined Gonsar and the ailing prisoner.

'If you don't get up, you won't see the enclosure again.'

The man didn't even look up, overwhelmed with exhaustion. 'Then my prayers will have been answered.'

'Not like this. They'll leave you alive in their dog cages.'

Both prisoners shuddered.

Gonsar gazed at Klaus with open hatred that would have made another man flinch. 'What's it to you if he lives or how he dies, child slayer?'

But Klaus' warning had the effect he'd intended; the man forced himself up with Gonsar's aid, picking up his pickaxe.

'Work over there, where the rock is looser,' Klaus told him. He paused by Gonsar. 'The boy was an informant. He was the one who betrayed the men they burned at the stake.'

He didn't wait for a reply, knowing little acts of mercy would not go unobserved. He would have to turn his attention to the prisoners soon, or the Eh Menishian would notice he only punished the pirates. The Derindin were as desperate as they were resilient. Not long after the burning, there was another attempted escape, this time more desperate and daring – two men picked the locks of their cuffs and slipped out from an enclosure at twilight. They'd barely been gone ten minutes before a pirate sentry raised the alarm.

'Get the dogs,' an Eh Menishian ordered in coarse Invelmen. But the dogs were sickly.

'All of them?'

'The shaman's been tending to them since morning.'

'It'll be pitch black soon, and it's completely dry out there for miles,' a pirate began. 'They'll pray for capture just for the hope of a drink before death. There's nowhere for them to go, my lord –' He earned himself a slap that split his lip.

'Fool,' the Eh Menishian guard snapped. 'Do you want others to follow? If even one prisoner gets away –'

He stopped himself. Klaus glanced at the sky. 'We're losing light.'

'Then we follow them,' said the Eh Menishian.

None of the pirates dared refuse. But though twilight played tricks with the eyes, the escapees were soon visible on the horizon.

'Run them down,' roared the Eh Menishian.

Klaus pulled up his horse. 'Give me your bow.'

A pirate laughed, then realised he was being serious. 'It's too dark.'

It wasn't too dark for the student of an Ummandiri bowmaster. Klaus' heart squeezed painfully as both his arrows swiftly found their targets.

The Eh Menishian guards ordered the pirates to retrieve the prisoners' bodies. The pirates scowled at the growing dark, but obeyed.

'Rarely is a reputation surpassed by the reality of which it boasts,' Renegash told Klaus on their return. 'The Isarnanheri are truly exalted. But your sentence was too swift. You should have made an example of them to the rest.'

Confidence wasn't enough; Renegash expected arrogance. Klaus shrugged. 'They'll know now that even the desert night will not hide them.'

Of this, Renegash approved. Klaus recalled the fate that had befallen the last escapees. Who knew what horror the Eh Menishian might have conjured for these men had they been caught alive? This didn't lessen his guilt. Still, mercy had to be disguised.

'What have the dogs been fed?' Klaus asked Renegash.

'Slaves, once they can no longer work. And they eat derina, but fresh meat is best, and meat is dear. We need workers, but after a while all men must break.'

'Did the escapees have any recent contact with the dogs?'

They had not.

'These men had help.' Klaus watched the pirates drag their bodies away. 'Your dogs didn't all fall ill on the same night of their escape by accident. Someone incapacitated the only thing they thought could hunt them down. The prisoners know the weakest slaves are fed to the dogs. If someone's poisoned another prisoner, knowing this...' Understanding dawned in Renegash's eyes. 'There you will find the true culprits.'

And so Klaus was awarded the task of rooting out the perpetrators who had indirectly poisoned the dogs.

He walked through the enclosures the following day, surreptitiously counting prisoners.

'If any of you know something you wish to disclose, you may tell me in confidence.' The prisoners were silent as stone. 'On this matter, or anything else. If the culprit isn't found, Lord Renegash will start choosing healthy offerings from amongst you for his dogs.'

Everywhere there are maggots. It wasn't long before Klaus began to draw the maggots out. No one had anything of value to disclose about the ailing dogs, but they had other tales to tattle.

'A youth in our enclosure often speaks with a water carrier,' one man told him. 'He's still small, so he blends in with them out in the mine. I'm sure he's going to help some men escape.'

'Have you seen him with the water carrier?'

'Oh yes, sir. More than once.'

'Tell me his name.'

One Derindman claimed a fellow prisoner was exchanging food rations for smuggled kahvi beans. Another accused a retired tumbler of stirring up a rebellion in his enclosure.

'Most of them are trying to curry favour and have nothing of import to say,' he told Renegash over refreshments in his tent. 'How are your dogs?'

'Recovering, though Krevkatt hasn't yet discovered what ails them.' Renegash scowled; he had underestimated the Derindin.

Two of the informants were genuinely malicious. An aging prisoner, harmless and more than a little unhinged by the camp, came to Klaus' tent to rant one evening. All his fellows were scoundrels but he loathed one in particular; a man who repeatedly stole his water.

Klaus diverted him from petty complaints. 'What do you know of a man named Zolstan?'

'Another scoundrel,' the old man muttered. 'Man of no clan. Used to sell smokeleaf to pirates at the waterholes, until they snatched him along with his smokeleaf. Tells that story every night.'

Zolstan was a prisoner who often spoke to Klaus on his patrols. He chatted elegantly and with calculated ease, repeating so many of the rumours reaching Klaus from a variety of prisoners that Klaus wondered whether he wasn't the source of most of them himself. One such story was about the boy swapping kahvi beans for extra food. Klaus had few concerns about the boy, but summoned him to his tent.

'What's your name?'

'Helan,' the boy stammered. A few hairs clung to his upper lip, but he was very much a boy.

'How long have you been in the camp?' Only two weeks; he'd arrived after Klaus' promotion. Recently enough that he might still have a smuggled supply of kahvi. 'And where were you captured?'

'Carnelian Wells,' said Helan miserably. *Not far from Cora.* And Nerisen had taken back only one thing from there: highly prized kahvi.

Klaus glanced over Helan's head at the tent entrance. 'How did you hide your beans?'

With trembling hands, he showed Klaus the seams of his tunic and coat, into which beans had been individually sewn. Having been his currency, most of them were now gone. This was something he'd been doing long before pirates had captured him.

'Now,' said Klaus, the soft slope of an Intelligencer's voice slipping into his command. 'I want you to name everyone who's exchanged something for one of these in return.'

And one person had taken most of Helan's beans: Yergan, the other informant who'd prickled Klaus' senses, and who'd reported the youth colluding with the water carriers.

Klaus fingered a bean. 'Can these be eaten as they are?'

Helan shook his head. 'They're for brewing. But for kahva, they've got to be diluted first. These were smoked over efeshyun ashes. Make you see things. I dunno, maybe someone got desperate and tried to eat one.'

'You will say nothing of this to anyone,' Klaus told him in the voice that had been a hair's breadth from the Wintermantel throne. 'That's the price for keeping your life.'

Next, he cornered the youth who reportedly consorted with the water carriers. Too old to be a water carrier but younger than Helan, he was mulish in a way that reminded Klaus with a pang of Fibbler. *They pick on the weakest of them.* Klaus cornered him in the mine, and he adamantly refused to answer questions about the two dead runaways – until Klaus sprung him with a question on whether he had ever been a Babble.

Even in the lamp-lit darkness, his eyes gave him away.

'Babbles hear rumours,' Klaus said softly. 'And sometimes they say careless things which cost others their lives – even earn them an arrow in the dark.' The boy's eyes widened at the prospect of sharing in any guilt for the runaways' deaths. 'What *news* have you been retelling?'

'It didn't have anything to do with those men who escaped,' he said stubbornly. But a note of panic shook his voice. 'The other Babbles had boring stories, and I got hold of a good one. That man who likes to talk to you in the mine – he was a smuggler...'

The only informant who spoke to Klaus publicly in the mine was Zolstan, who likely regarded his growing relationship with Klaus as something to use to his advantage against his fellow prisoners.

'The man who smuggled smokeleaf?'

'Not just smokeleaf. He brought the pirates children, to go down into the mines.'

'How do you know?'

Helan's face became stony beyond his years again. 'That's how I ended up here.'

There were other slave sales, too, before Zolstan was finally captured himself, most likely to silence him once he knew too much about the pirates' activities. Several enquiries later and after much scratching beneath the surface, the web began to form. The two escapees Klaus had shot dead were no strangers to Zolstan, and hadn't been long at the camp before attempting their escape. And they had recognised Zolstan as the smuggler rumoured to lure children to the pirates.

A dangerous past for a prisoner to have amongst Derindin slaves.

When Klaus summoned Yergan, he arrived looking prepared to provide more information – until he saw the pirates present.

This time Klaus didn't toy with him. 'What did you do with the beans?'

He left the pirates to get Yergan talking. If Klaus were right – and the possibility he might have been wrong didn't torment him much – Yergan had much to answer for. His tongue soon loosened; he'd left the beans he'd obtained from Helan in a derina gourd hidden in a hole in the wall of a latrine. This was shared by two enclosures, one of which sheltered Zolstan, the child-smuggling smokeleaf merchant.

Klaus made sure word of Yergan's arrest was widely circulated. After that, it didn't take long for Zolstan's panic to show, for the two men were brothers. It was the smokeleaf smuggler, with his intimate understanding of the desert's vices, who'd known that a concentrate of the efeshyun-smoked beans stored in water in the gourd and kept warm buried in the ground would first make a hypnotic, and then an intoxicant. It had been easy to slip this into the food of a hapless prisoner who couldn't be woken from his deep sleep the next morning. And, of course, the Eh Menishian knew little of kahvi, and of its toxicity to animals even in small quantities, and fed the drugged man to their dogs. Once the sick dogs were confined to their kennels, Yergan had convinced the two newcomers to attempt an escape that he knew was doomed to fail. Once they were executed, Zolstan's child-smuggling past would remain hidden from the camp's prisoners.

There would be other agents, for someone had monitored the dogs' progress and informed the escapees once it was safe to make a run for it. But Klaus had no need nor any appetite to cast his net wider.

He delivered his report to Renegash without the smallest grain of guilt.

'What do you wish to do with them?'

'Even criminals should have a clean death.' That was Master Arnander, and it had surprised Klaus at the time. A former Spyglass was surely the least likely vessel for clemency. Thus, Klaus had asked why that was so; he had been very young. *'Who do you really harm with cruelty?'* Klaus could recall the reply as though Master Arnander were standing at his shoulder still. *'Every cruelty that you qualify as well-deserved punishment is born of nothing more than your lack of control over yourself. Nothing more than a toast to your lowest nature. And a man who has no control over his base self can never have true Form.'* With Master Arnander, everything came back to Form.

Lord Renegash's reply was predictable. 'The dogs will be in want of good meat as they recover.'

Klaus had no objection. *They fed a poisoned man alive to those same beasts.* And all to conceal the fact that at least one of them had smuggled children to the pirates.

'With your permission, my lord, I will make their crimes known. It benefits my work if the prisoners know there can also be justice here.'

Renegash agreed. He was vastly amused at Zolstan's motives. 'So he wished to conceal his smuggling activities from the others.'

'He feared the other prisoners would kill him once they discovered what he'd been doing before he was captured.'

'That should not be what he fears most here.'

It was amongst the most ominous of Renegash's remarks. This time, when the prisoners were gathered, the mood was different, for they knew the sentenced pair were traitors. Klaus gazed across the Plains as the revived dogs tore the two men to living shreds. Master Arnander remained at his shoulder. *Even criminals should have a clean death...*

Krevkatt the shaman was especially pleased with his findings. Klaus gave him the confiscated smoked kahvi beans to examine. The following morning, the Eh Menishian guard at Klaus' door vanished.

He had finally earned the trust of the lords of the camp.

That evening Klaus left his tent and looked up at the night sky for the first time since he'd arrived. He had not dared to do so under the watch of his escort, lest he betray himself.

It was glorious: a roofless eternity in which the Wanderer's words danced and shimmered even more brightly than the stars, for their syllables flared in his mind as he gazed into the heavens. The moon was an empty cradle. Impossibly, the Far Southern sky seemed even larger here than anywhere else in the Parts. Too many of these stars were still strangers and so his navigational estimations were rudimentary, but he was sure his tally had been correct: he had been at the camp for seven weeks.

It was in this camp that Klaus began to truly know the Derindin – here, in their enslavement. They were brave, fierce and loyal. He took great pains to learn the name of every captive he encountered, living or dead. The desert had prepared them well for the camp's conditions. It only strengthened Klaus' resolve to serve them. Despite what he had told Renegash, he had always detected further strength in Invelmari steel when it was wielded with conviction – such as an Invelmari's faith in Sturmsinger's Blood Pact. Here, Klaus felt that conviction again. He hoped Verdi had found it, too. *Here is a thing worth fighting for.*

If only he knew what they were fighting.

It was clear the Eh Menishian had no intention of confiding in him. Not once did they hint that they were searching for anything other than ore, let alone a skydisc. They said little of their home and nothing of their plans. When two more Eh Menishian joined the camp, none mentioned how they'd arrived. Groups of pirates came and went often, and Klaus became convinced that only a small proportion of them were stationed in the camp. *Surely they must know the clans may attack.* But the camp was a long way away from the clandoms, and there was no water but what the Eh Menishian guarded.

Still, he had stolen into Renegash's vain heart, and though the Eh Menishian would never fully trust him, they had too much use for him. Slowly, painstakingly, Klaus earned more degrees of freedom – though it was more a lengthening of his leash than true freedom. He was careful not to overstretch this leash. Liberty was a cloying honey that grew stickier the more he took of it, drawing him ever closer to the centre of a deadly web.

Their hospitality remained lavish. Klaus accepted the delicacies they gifted him but preferred to eat derina, for it afforded almost as much nourishment as meat, rebuilding the strength he'd lost in the enclosure. He excused himself from their wine, declaring that it hampered his work. Soon after the execution of the treacherous brothers, Renegash held a banquet in Klaus' honour, where he presented a slender woman.

'A gift.' Renegash pulled back her hood. She was Eh Menishian, barely older than Elodie. 'Long overdue, but the Derindin she-slaves are only fit for producing more slaves. We do not touch them. This one is unsampled. She will be honoured to serve.'

She kept a pair of dark and lustrous eyes cast down. She was beautiful, and he was horrified.

'You are gracious.' Klaus inclined his head appreciatively. 'Although I should warn you I've no intention of being tied to one tree.'

This produced hearty laughter from those who understood Invelmen.

'Have no fear. She will be the first of many.'

Sure enough, she arrived at Klaus' tent with refreshments and a bottle of surrwyrte, known by Southerners as verembet. Klaus recognised it immediately; the coveted green liquid was officially forbidden to Ealdormen, for it was treason to prevent the birth of a royal child. In Invelmar it was also forbidden to common women who had not borne at least one child to serve the Crown, so Klaus had confiscated plenty of it over the years. Good concoctions cost almost as much as Invelmari steel. The generosity of the Eh Menishian was grotesque.

She gripped the bottle tightly. 'I am to deliver this to you.'

'Your masters are thoughtful,' Klaus murmured. He tilted the vial once by the lantern. It was counterfeit; surrwyrte transilluminated in the light, while this was opaque. *There's no way they don't know this is fake.* The notion that his hosts wanted to trick out of him a progeny of Northern and Eh Menishian stock troubled Klaus deeply.

His thoughts raced. 'What if I wish you to drink it tonight?'

His guess was confirmed in the struggle that surfaced in her dark, rounded eyes; she had no wish to carry a child but every instruction not to prevent it.

Klaus put a finger to her lips, sparing her a reply. Alarm bells rang in his ears. Of all the threats to his subterfuge, this was the most dangerous. He couldn't afford to be distracted in the arms of a woman, but neither could he offend his hosts – or arouse suspicion by refusing their gift.

He gestured to the decanter of wine she'd brought. 'Pour yourself a glass.'

It would be easy to use a concubine to my advantage. But he recoiled from the prospect. Ealdormen were sworn to purity out of wedlock, for it was also treason to produce a royal bastard – not that this stopped a fair few of them, hence why the Ealdormen secretly hoarded confiscated surrwyrte. *But you are not an Ealdorman,* a little voice reminded him. He thought of Gerlinde, but the thought was forced. Besides, what did he have to be faithful to – the memory of a noblewoman who'd spurned him and who was now truly out of reach?

Dear Sturmsinger, let there be a place for me at your table even now.

She filled the glass. Perhaps he could make her drink herself into confusion.

'What is your name?'

'Gainshe.' At least she looked him in the face now, although she remained demure. *They sent me one who can speak Invelmen.* In their place he wouldn't have done that – or else done exactly that. Most of the Eh Menishian and even the shaman couldn't speak his tongue.

'Where do you come from, Gainshe?'

'Only a little village.' She moved closer to help him unfasten his belt. *Perhaps not so demure after all.* Her dress was almost sheer, doing little to mask the contours of her body.

He teased, 'And why was I denied the sight of you until now?'

'I was not here, my lord.' The deftness of her fingers was at odds with those downcast eyes. But her back was rod-straight. She may have been taught how to please a man, but her spirit hadn't been broken yet. 'My ship arrived only a week past…'

The words died in her throat as she realised her slip. He pretended not to notice, cupping one hand to her face and brushing silkily over the moment. *Ship*, his mind repeated. *Ship…*

But he couldn't follow the thought, for Gainshe drew closer and without warning the blood rushed to his skin; her hands were hurrying over his shirt, and a hesitant eagerness dawned in her eyes that caught them both unawares, and his body clamoured for what his rational mind forbade. *Gerlinde!*

It was Nerisen's face that his desperation summoned, and clarity was restored.

He gripped her waist tightly, inching her away from him. 'You forgot the wine.'

An alarm sounded outside. He pushed her aside and reached for his sword.

Gainshe crouched back, a shy girl again. 'What's that?'

Klaus recognised the eerie cackle of hyenas tumbling through the night. Many of them, and close.

'Something else to deny me the taste of you.' He pulled the curtain flaps aside. Outside, several guards were running towards the cackling. 'Can you find your way back to your quarters in the dark?' She nodded. 'Go now, you'll be safer there than here on your own.'

There was already a group of Eh Menishian guards leading pirates towards the advancing pack. At least fifteen animals, lean and starving, larger than the Eh Menishian's dogs. By the time they killed them all, one Eh Menishian was wounded and several pirates dead.

Renegash surveyed them with cold fury. 'These animals do not attack without invitation.'

This was true; something had drawn them into the camp. There was probably no food for miles; it wouldn't take much to lure them. The now-recovered dogs quickly found the source: rats, two dozen of them at least, recently killed and shallowly buried in the middle of the camp.

'Bait,' said Renegash softly.

He summoned Scaffal, the pirates' leader, to his tent.

'I wish to know how prisoners are able to bury carcasses in our midst, unobserved.'

Klaus had had few dealings with Scaffal. He was made of sterner stuff than most of his men, but apprehension hunched behind his Derindin expressionlessness. *I bet there's a Murheslan tattoo on the back of his shoulder.*

Scaffal held his nerve. 'They can't, my lord.'

'No? Then it can only have been one of your men.'

The pirate opened his mouth, then thought better of it.

Renegash leaned forward, ignoring his translator now. 'You will find the perpetrators and bring them to me. If you do not, I will do to you what was done to those rats, and our agreement will end.'

The pirate bowed; a very unDerindinlike thing to do. What was the Eh Menishian's hold over the pirates?

After he left, Renegash turned to Klaus. 'Tomorrow, you will begin your enquiries.'

Klaus nodded. He did not bow, though it *was* a very Invelmari thing to do. 'My lord, someone needs to check the girl got back safely to her quarters. There was no time to escort her.'

Renegash sent one of his men immediately. *They're protective of their own.*

'Worthless fools…' Renegash's displeasure was severe, and for a moment Klaus thought he might drop his guard and confide in him. 'If I cannot trust my soldiers, then I have no use for them.'

'This I can well understand.'

That seemed to remind Renegash of Klaus' presence, and the moment passed.

'I will have the concubine sent back to you at once.'

'Not yet, my lord. If I had been faster to my blade tonight, you might not have lost so many men.'

For tonight, at least, this was sufficient. But he would have to prepare for the next time – and he was sure there would be a next time. The guard at his door had been exchanged for a temptress. The Eh Menishian had sent him a snake whose venom was intended to intoxicate, but not kill.

Klaus left and cleaned his sword. The air of the camp buzzed: the red thrill of fear and fighting and death. And something else, too, that had been absent so long he had almost abandoned hope of feeling it again: the heart-lifting awareness of the land.

There it was, just on the edge of his mind, like a rising mist.

It trickled away again, like the last of a desperate man's water. But there had been a drop.

Buoyant and awash with relief at its return, Klaus returned to his tent. The untouched refreshments were still there, as was Gainshe's scent and the vial of false surrwyrte.

He pocketed the little bottle and began to think.

*

'Lotrapa greyskin. A blue-green herbaceous perennial with hairy leaves and poisonous berries. All green parts are safe to harvest and preserve in dried or even pickled form.'

'Very short season', Verdi added in the margin. *'Key properties: blood-warming, circulatory dilatation, ease of breathing. Note headaches.'*

But he couldn't concentrate.

It would be another hour at least before Arik went to bed, and before Verdi could test the gnomon again. Each time he anchored it in the earth now, the new dials appeared – sometimes one, sometimes two. By day it continued to show the single bold edge of the sundial. But by night – by night, the device transformed before his eyes.

One, which he was almost certain was the moondial, now appeared consistently. This one was a crisp slice of light as thick as his finger, like light slipping through a door cracked ajar. Light, not shadow. *How?* It was always accurate, no matter the moon's phase – *which makes no sense*. An ordinary moondial accurately told time only when the moon was full.

The second dial was more skittish, visiting whimsically. Its whiter, fainter edge was a mystery. Verdi had no explanation for it, or for its movements

He'd stayed up long enough to discover the moondial migrated through the night, accurate to his pocket-clock. The second dial – the *spectre*, as he began to think of its fickle, flickering form – was unpredictable. Sometimes it moved at its own secret pace; others, it hovered as a white flame on the ground, an inconstant lick of light.

Two dials of light, defying all reason. He would not have believed such a thing possible had he not seen it himself, night after night.

Verdi was sure of one thing, however: he wasn't ready to share his findings.

They might not even believe me. He would graduate from ignoramus to lunatic. Klaus would have believed him, though. *And Klaus is probably dead.*

In these quiet hours, an impossible serenity soothed Verdi as he huddled in his cloak outside Thillaina's kitchen. But morning always arrived with fresh worries. However was he to make sense of his discovery? How could either dial determine the Merensaman phase of the moon?

And so it was that his head began to nod during Maragrin's lessons. Maragrin mistook his somnolence for sullenness. Verdi hadn't forgiven Maragrin for white-washing Lorendar's glories. But he'd curbed his questions, and they no longer came to blows over the darker corners of Lorendar's past. This had an effect that Verdi couldn't have predicted.

'The sheep-herders of Carnelian Wells have still not forgiven the purging of their ancestors,' Maragrin lectured today. 'But for fifty years they held the Qinnamon Road, and fixed the price of wool every winter to more than what most people could afford. When they refused to stop, Lorendar warned he would take their land. Yes, Lorendar raised swords against them when they refused to go. His army tore children from mothers' arms and then set fire to all those who refused to leave their houses.' Maragrin paused, defiance yet peppering his admission. 'But no more did the folk there freeze to death in their beds for want of warmth after that.'

Maragrin's stabs at honesty about Lorendar's methods ought to have helped. They didn't. Verdi had no idea who to trust now.

Besides, the Elders weren't the only ones who worried Verdi. *'It is not ours to intervene if Derindin tear themselves from within.'* His father's words wormed tunnels of dismay into his heart.

Surely the Murhesla won't stand back and watch the clans destroy each other. That couldn't have been Sassan's meaning. Surely...?

One evening, Nerisen delivered Verdi a note. 'From Master Meron.'

She visited Thillaina's house most evenings now, collecting donations for the refugees outside the citadel. Ravi always grew shy in the presence of Onax, her sleek panfarthing. She watched Verdi open the note. He sat bolt upright, startling Ravi from his hiding place in the crook of Verdi's elbow.

Within thirty minutes, he was outside a doorway in a quiet street in the Alchemists' Quarter, too eager to await Arik's return from the training ground. *Besides, my father always keeps watch over me now.*

Barrels of herbs flanked the physician's door; sage, early mints, budding lavender. Verdi was about to ring the bell again when a man opened the door.

'Yes? What is it?'

He held a poker in one gloved hand, and his spectacles were askew.

'Where's the patient?' he demanded, looking up and down the street. 'You look rather well. Where's that maid? Drat!'

'Sorry to disturb you, sir…' Verdi steadied his voice, holding out the note. 'Master Meron – I asked Master Meron for … are you Master Fresmo?'

The physician glanced at Meron's note and then at him.

'Ah.' He adjusted the spectacles on his nose. 'Ah.'

Verdi had hoped for a chance to demonstrate his learning – perhaps a trial of sorts. He had expected to be told there were no pupillages available. What he hadn't expected was a thorough reprimand.

'Please explain, young man, what you mean by this?' The physician brandished Meron's note at him. 'An *"apprenticeship"*? Don't you have work enough to do, striving for your ancestor's great destiny? Why are you not spending day and night preparing to revive Lorendar's will amongst these sheep? Or decoding his moondial? Why do you seek any other work? What need have you of *my* work, hmm? Perhaps you don't realise what an undertaking either path entails, which can only mean you must be a very foolish person.'

Horror rooted Verdi to the spot. He almost hoped the physician would slam the door in his face, but realised the man was actually waiting for a response.

'I meant no harm –'

'Ha! So has many another foolish person said before you.' Evidently not *that* keen for a response. 'You neglect the greatest of duties. And your neglect will bring war upon us. The greatest selfishness I have ever seen. And there is no room for selfishness in a physician's soul. Now be off with you.'

He did finally slam the door, leaving Verdi's ears ringing.

The street was still empty, but Verdi was too numb yet even for humiliation. Dazed, he returned to Thillaina's house.

Arik was waiting to berate him but stopped short. 'What's the matter?'

Too crestfallen to explain, Verdi shrugged and flopped down at the kitchen table. Ravi was finally lured out of his pocket by the leftovers on Arik's plate.

Arik flicked a crumb of bread at Ravi. 'Have you eaten?'

'I'm not hungry.'

'At least leave word. I only guessed where you'd gone because I saw Nerisen before she left. You probably think your father's got eyes looking out for you everywhere, but don't be so trusting.'

Verdi nodded. He wasn't ready to admit just how right Arik had been about Sassan. One disappointment at a time.

*

In the days that followed, more Derindin *did* arrive outside Samsarra. They didn't come wholly unprepared, bringing the last of their winter stocks with them. But some had fled burning hamlets, or had been robbed of last summer's earnings. Plainswalkers distributed food and water, blankets and lamp oil, condolences and sympathy.

Keeping her tumblers at a distance, Emra ventured into their midst. She followed Ayla to where a party of Baeronian defectors had pitched their tent.

Several men and women were finishing a meal. They'd not been expecting a journey so far from home, and their caravan had known better days. It had to have taken a great deal to drive Baeronians here.

Chaaro, the man who spoke for them, was wary but also driven to desperation. He answered Emra's questions guardedly at first, unravelling when she didn't interrupt him. He betrayed his former clan reluctantly, which was honourable. But like all things, even loyalty had to be kept in balance.

'When the pirates first attacked, we thought help would come from Taur,' he said of Baeron's citadel. 'Our fields in Draal draw water from two good springs, west of Romel. When the winds are calm, our crops are plentiful. Maybe that's what kept attracting the pirates. We waited … but no help came.'

Chaaro stared at the ground.

'After the first raids, we sent messengers to Chieftain Voldane in Taur. My brother was certain his council couldn't have known of the attacks. There was no reply. Wave after wave of raids came, stripping our entire hamlet bare. Then at last we saw tumblers passing during a pirate raid. We thought they were coming to our aid – but they rode on to Taur.' Anger mixed with disbelief on his face. 'They looked the other way.'

'How did you escape from Draal?'

'We finally challenged the pirates ourselves, and it was they who told us that we were *"the price"*.' Chaaro's face twisted. This wound was very much raw. 'Baeron's Elders gave the pirates permission to raid our land. Some of the other villagers wouldn't believe it, they're still there waiting for help – if the pirates spared them. But we couldn't deny what we'd seen. Voldane's council was allowing pirates to come – was feeding and watering them with the fruits of our labour.'

'Too busy,' a woman snarled. 'Too busy grabbing Periam to look out for the likes of us.'

Fury darkened their faces. They had made their pledges and paid their taxes to their clan, and their clan had abandoned them.

'Do you know if this is happening elsewhere on Baeronian land?' Emra asked.

'On the fringes of the clandom. In several of Baeron's eastern hamlets, where the springs are strong.'

Prime land, then. Emra combed her memory. A Chieftainess had to always hold in her mind the fragile web of bonds made and broken in the Plains. 'Was Draal not once part of Fraivon's clandom?'

'Over a hundred and fifty years ago,' replied another villager. 'Even after Baeron took it and renamed it, my grandfather never called it anything but Lairat. That's what it was called on Fraivon's maps. Refused flat out to shift allegiance. It was shift or leave. Luckily for him, he was too old to live long enough to be forced out.'

A woman hissed. 'It's Baeron's now.'

'Is it?' a man replied bitterly. 'Maybe in their eyes we never stopped being Fraivon's.'

Emra's seed had germinated fast. Their betrayal was very close to the surface, and made for a rich broth. 'The pirates who raided you … did they take their loot north or south?'

'Both.'

Now Chaaro trod cautiously. 'We heard you were building an alliance, and that we would be welcome…'

Emra exchanged a glance with Ayla. Were they truthful because they were desperate, or were they lying because they had nothing to lose?

'Your clan deceived you,' she said, coaxing her seedling. 'They demanded from you an oath of fealty and denied you the rights they promised in return. They did not wish to spare soldiers to defend a hamlet when they had their sights on a greater prize in the West. They might as well have robbed you of your taxes. In Baeron's eyes, your homes will never be as dear to them as their ancestral lands. *You* have never truly become part of them, after they conquered your lands from Fraivon and forced your ancestors' allegiance. So it was easy to sacrifice you to the pirates. And just as they have betrayed you, so they will betray Periam in time to come.'

But for what purpose? Neither Baeron nor its close ally, Hesper, had openly declared support for the pirates.

Sour whispering rustled through the tent.

'Will you send us back?' Chaaro asked.

'To death and starvation?' Emra raised her hood. 'No. While you are on our territory you shall have my clan's protection if pirates come, and food and shelter while you are without. I do not ask that you swear fealty to Elendra.' Eyes widened all around her. 'I only ask that you offer whatever services you can as we prepare for war, if that must come.'

Hope is a strange thing, she thought, striding out past murmurs of suspicious gratitude. In the South, it was armoured with layers of disbelief, then doubt, then mistrust. But still it was there in the tender pulp of the soul, fearful and trembling.

'What will you do?' Ayla asked when they returned to Samsarra's gates.

'Even Baeron can't escape the fury of the Plains,' Emra replied. *The scorpion must be over a rock, never under it.* Though they clung to ghabala, the Derindin loathed such deceit. The desert's tenets were few, but as old and precious as ambergris. 'If they've been fattening up the pirates, they've a great deal of blood on their hands. *Everyone's* blood. And in two weeks, that's what we will remind Derinda at the Assembly.'

Baeron and Hesper had betrayed *every* clan, including their own. Their flagrant ambition was frightening. The rest of the clans couldn't risk standing alone against another monster in the West. And through Viridian, the East could provide a solution to pirates and monsters both. *If only he can guide us with the gnomon. If only he can find the Merensaman phase of the moon.*

It was working, the Northerner's suggestion to extend an umbrella of protection to the Unsworn and the refugees at their door – to build a fortress that swelled between the grasses. Marcin had been right. Tourmali was grumbling about the injury to their coffers, but once again it was a Northerner's vision that proved the clearest.

*

Nerisen watched the departing Chieftainess. She'd finished distributing derina flour for the evening. Her heart tightened with worry. Donations had been generous, but generosity had its limits. What she saw in the faces of these newcomers would call upon her later, when she lay awake in the pit of night: a fragile gradient between hope and hardship.

Yet another arrival stopped her as she made her way back to the citadel.

'Is it true?' These western defectors had kept to themselves, and had been shunned by most of the other refugees. Even now, a great deal more than a common enemy was needed to break old bonds. 'Has the Seed of the Limolan returned to Elendra?'

They waited for her reply. They were tired and dirty; their clothes torn, their knees and knuckles bloodied.

'I didn't think there was much regard for Merensama in the West,' Nerisen replied.

But they insisted, and she told them it was true. What was there to lose? They neither hissed nor sang for joy. They returned to their caravans with their heads huddled together.

Perhaps even the oldest of bonds were ready to unravel in the right amount of light.

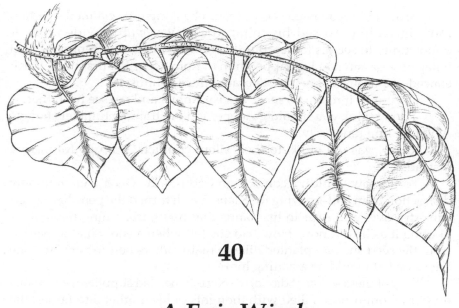

40

A Fair Wind

AND SO IT WAS THAT STURMSINGER'S HEIRS, YET PUPS, WERE SLAIN
BY THEIR FAR NORTHERN BRETHREN. EVEN A QUEEN AS VALIANT AS
DAGMAR COULD NOT BEAR SUCH BRUTAL PARTING, AND DIED OF HER
GRIEF BESIDE THE LAST BLOSSOMS OF STURMSINGER.

SONNONFER: LAMENT FOR DAGMAR, QUEEN-OF-THE-HEARTH

Verdi arrived at the barracks to find Rasan saddling her stallion.

'Where are you going, Rasan?'

'The limolan tree in Romel.' She checked her water carriers. 'I make pilgrimage to the shrine whenever I can.'

Arik dismounted. 'Tell me something. If you're so religious, how come you didn't join Mantelon?'

'Lorendar's heir is in Samsarra, not Yesmehen.'

Ordinarily, Verdi might have cringed. But something else twisted his insides.

'Can I go with you?' he asked, immediately uncertain of himself.

Her smile was all the more radiant for its scarcity. 'Of course.'

Arik's eyes narrowed. Verdi would be lying if he claimed a certain thought hadn't crossed his mind; the visit *would* provide another opportunity to see his father. But things were much different now than when an assassin had kidnapped him in Romel. For the first time, Verdi conceded a desire to see the celebrated tree for himself.

Of course, it made no sense to visit Romel and *not* see his father.

'I don't think you should go alone, and I'm training tumblers today,' Arik told him tonelessly.

Rasan was oblivious to their silent conflict. 'I can go tomorrow instead.'

Tomorrow couldn't come soon enough. It was a welcome new distraction from half-grieving for Klaus. Verdi turned the pen-that-never-runs-dry over and over in his hands that night, imagining his mother holding it as he did now. How had she felt when a shoot had appeared from the seed she had planted, like so many others before her? Had she known what would be awaiting him?

Four of them set off at dawn, for Nerisen needed supplies from Romel for her laboratorium. Filled with thoughts of his mother and father, the gates of Romel seemed much nearer than Verdi remembered.

When they arrived, Rasan dismounted in the Poets' Quarter. 'From here we go on foot.'

It was a quiet part of the citadel that had a *forgotten* feeling, thanks to the silence of ancient houses, and cobbles worn smooth underfoot, and interlacing capillaries of passages bridged with arches. The empty streets were swept clean and lined with planters of spring flowers. Verdi raised his hood over his head. He wondered if his father already had eyes on him here, and, if so, where they could possibly be hiding.

They passed through an archway into the courtyard of a temple. Shallow steps led down to a raised garden. A fountain bubbled amongst flowering shrubs.

Arik hung back, eyes scaling the walls of the temple surrounding the courtyard, perhaps also wondering whether they concealed watching Murhesla. There were three or four other visitors. The quiet magnified Verdi's self-consciousness. He could feel Nerisen's eyes. Rasan walked down into the garden. Mouth dry, Verdi followed.

Beyond bushes of bay and laurel and fragrant mounds of salvia and sage was a round pebble-ringed bed from which rose a great tree, underplanted with herbs. Its heart-shaped leaves were the juvenile yellow-green of tender spring. Here it was, the only tree from which the sage-bird could eat – though it had never flowered.

Rasan gazed up at the only living limolan in the Plains. 'I wish Tristan could have seen it before he died.'

Verdi's fingers were trembling; he hid them in closed fists. He had expected a slender sapling. Why was that? After all, he was a child no longer. The limolan had had twenty-four years to grow.

'I feel as though I've been here before.' It was bizarre and impossible, but for the first time in his life he felt a delightful comfort in his middle: the warmth of being *home*.

'You have,' said Nerisen over his shoulder. 'Your mother would have come here, carrying you.'

For a shining instant, he imagined a young woman kneeling under the tree, slender as its youngest branches, wondering what the seed she had planted would become. He blinked, and she vanished.

Rasan knelt to murmur a prayer before retreating to sit on the steps. An older couple sat on a stone seat nearby, their lips moving in silent prayer.

Verdi had forgotten Ravi until he darted out of his pocket. He started after the oceloe.

'Ravi!'

But Ravi didn't disappear into the bushes for his favourite game of hide-and-bite. Instead, he paused underneath the limolan, tail twitching. Then he scuttled up its into its branches.

The limolan tree shook. Verdi hid his crimson face with his hands. He stepped under the tree and whispered heatedly, '*Down*. You come down *this instant*, you little rascal!'

Arik had no sympathy. 'You didn't have the sense to keep hold of him?'

After a barrage of angry threats trimmed with insincere pleading, Ravi finally relented once Verdi deployed a stick of sugarcane he'd been saving for his horse. Verdi scooped him up by the scruff of his neck. Nerisen stifled laughter; Onax hadn't budged from her shoulder. Rasan ignored the disturbance, eyes closed. Not so the elderly couple.

'This is a sacred place!' the man admonished. 'Not a playground.'

'The creature can't help himself,' said his companion gently, laying a hand on his arm. 'Besides, a young man can do as he pleases when he is home.'

The man looked as astonished as Verdi.

'I felt you coming when you crossed the gates.' Tears shone in the woman's eyes. Her smile was radiant. 'Hope is a garden that must be tended as dearly as all that drinks from this spring … perhaps one day soon we may even see the sage-bird.' She touched Verdi's cheek. 'We will follow you to the end. We have not forgotten.'

The commotion had drawn the other pilgrims. A man embraced Verdi; another pressed a paper-wrapped sweetmeat into his hand. These were not zealots. Theirs was a tranquil belief.

'Have you come to take the oath?' another woman asked. Anxious suns rose in their faces.

'No...' Verdi faltered, acutely conscious that he was poised above the fragility of their dreams. 'First – first I must be deserving.'

It was the wrong thing to say; their smiles became dazzling to behold.

'There's nothing more that can prepare you than what you already possess.'

This was Rasan, watching from her step. The pilgrims nodded to each other.

'The land's already chosen which seed to nurture,' said the woman who had recognised him. 'It is never mistaken.'

'Deliver us,' a young man urged. 'End ghabala. We'll come to your aid. Give us your word.'

'We've not forgotten. We'll follow you to the end.'

The pilgrims echoed each other. *To the end ... we have not forgotten.*

Later, long after the courtyard had emptied, he returned and sat on the steps deep into dusk, listening to the limolan leaves sighing with the wind. He couldn't imagine the self-righteous brutality of a man like Lorendar producing tranquillity such as this. *'Is there no provision for redemption, Master Viridian?'* Maragrin's reprimand blew in with the wind. It was this that loitered longest in the darkening sanctuary: the sweet remorse of a spirit finally relieved of its burdens.

Perhaps Sassan had been mistaken about Lorendar.

What would Klaus tell him now?

Arik waited on the steps. Verdi confided very different things in Arik than he did in Klaus. He longed to test the gnomon here under the limolan tree, but he had left it in Samsarra. And he wasn't ready to share the moondial just yet.

Arik nudged him. 'We should go, if you want to see Sassan.'

But Verdi didn't want to dilute this discovery with his father's cynicism. Tonight, he would safeguard the pilgrims' faith from the tarnish of doubt. Rasan stayed to keep vigil in the sanctuary. Nerisen had already gone to see to her errands. They returned to Riorga's inn alone; two old friends and a sleeping oceloe.

*

The unsigned note was burning a hole in Arik's pocket. Innkeeper Riorga had no idea who had delivered it, but it had been waiting when he and Verdi arrived at the inn. Arik waited until Rasan returned from the sanctuary. He left her at Verdi's door and slipped downstairs.

'A drink, Master Marcin?'

Arik shook his head at Riorga. He needed his thoughts to remain clear.

It was early yet, for scoundrels. Although Riorga's was an Elendran inn, it welcomed all manner of visitors. Arik noticed the woman not because she was beautiful, though she was very much so, but for her gliding walk between tables. She moved like a snake.

Murhesla? But her dress bared most of her back; there was no tattoo on her shoulder.

Arik lit a cigar. He fixed his eyes on her until she was forced to notice him. A half-smile toyed with her mouth. She left her table and crossed the tavern to join him.

'Is it a good evening, Master Northman?'

Arik knew that kind of smile anywhere. And yet he was certain she wasn't a whore.

Eyes holding hers, he turned his head to exhale his smoke. 'Not yet.'

The woman sat without invitation. Her skirts could hide a modest weapon. Dark hair framed her cheeks, just grazing her shoulders, but most of it was pinned up in an intricate braid at the back of her head. Her eyes were darkest blue.

She leaned across the table. 'Without a drink, I see.'

Maybe she *was* a whore. But something about her was as dangerous as it was seductive.

'It's not drink I'm looking for.'

Another inch closer; a crookedness to her lips. 'Perhaps I can help?'

Arik put out the cigar. 'I'm looking for surrwyrte.'

It lasted barely a second, but he caught her startlement. She recovered quickly, throwing him a glittering smile.

'Verembet? But of course.'

She stood. After a moment's gamble, he rose and followed her out of the inn.

Her name was Rovena. The crowded tavern to which she took them was of a much different kind, throbbing with music and laughter. A noisy high-stakes game of cards reigned centre stage. The current eye-watering wager was only an appetiser, Rovena confided. She was familiar enough with the proprietor that even in this crowd he found them a table and brought them drinks unsolicited.

The sight of a Northerner here barely drew an eye; in fact Arik spied two other Invelmari, twice his age and grown leathery with sun and sandy wind, drunk on Derindin cider. Rovena got up to dance, her eyes latched onto Arik over the shoulders of her string of partners. The card game was followed by another. Rovena talked, laughed, drank, and always kept one eye on the door. After an hour of pouring Arik wine that barely passed his lips, Rovena smiled at the arrival of a Derindman supported by a crutch.

She grazed Arik's arm with the back of her hand. 'As I promised.'

The Derindman who relieved Arik of his gold – an apothecary, he guessed – asked no questions. To Arik's amusement, the surrwyrte was of good calibre, and better than some of the stuff he'd risked using in the past. He was in no hurry, but though Rovena seemed happy to drink and talk, none of what she said was useful – just like everything else she'd told him for the past two hours. He let another hour pass, allowing the appetite to ripen behind the claws in her eyes. When he finally took her upstairs, she was hot skin and smouldering hunger, eyes darkly-knowing and flesh sweet.

He latched their door. Rovena was readily pleased, purring at his touch. There were no weapons under that dress. He raised her wrists above her head, nuzzled her neck.

'No surrwyrte, then, Master Northman?'

He didn't reply. The slightest alarm flashed in her eyes. She shifted slightly beneath him. *Shame; she would have been deeply satisfying.*

'What d'you want, Rovena?'

Another flash, this time of fear. His hands tightened around her wrists. Gripping them both with one hand, he drew out a long thick pin from the braid behind her head, holding it between their faces.

She clung to her half-smile, unrepentant. 'I didn't think I would have to instruct you.'

There must have been a sheath for it within that braid, for it was razor-sharp as he drew it lightly down her neck. Panic flushed away all playfulness.

He nuzzled her neck again. 'I know you're here because of the jemesh.' She had looked at the little bone hanging around his neck only once, but the deliberation with which she had avoided looking at it again had given her away. 'If you tell me from whom you were hoping to claim your reward for finding me, I might let you live.'

'We're in Romel,' she whispered; half scorn, half disbelief. 'You wouldn't dare.'

Form filled his smile with frost. 'You should have known I had no intention of bedding you when I didn't give you the surrwyrte to drink.'

She froze, then feigned a loud scream of pleasure. A plunge of the pin cut it short.

Arik got up, throwing the discarded dress over her nakedness. He'd barely removed any of his own clothes. Blood spurted from her neck to the floorboards, then quickly stopped. He put out the lantern, unlatched the door and waited for whoever had been awaiting her signal.

Moments later, the door clicked open. Silence hovered uncertainly on the other side, testing the darkness. A masked Derindman slipped into the room, briefly visible in the strip of light outside.

He was alone. Arik hooked one forearm across his mouth, pinning him with the other.

He waited until the man stopped struggling. 'Who else was hoping to share your reward for finding me?'

The Derindman, a youth with more ambition than skill, glanced over Arik's arm at the bed. The light of the street lamps silhouetted Rovena's limp stillness. His eyes widened. Arik lowered his forearm across the man's neck, uncovering his mouth.

'The Murhesla will...'

Arik pressed against his neck. 'I'm losing patience.'

'Wait! Downstairs, running the game, there's a man...' He faltered. 'Who?'

'A poet...' His eyes flickered towards the bed again, terror swallowing his words. Arik shook him to attention.

'You're doing this on a *poet's* bidding?'

'He keeps the wagers – all wagers in the citadel, they must go through him –'

His voice crested in fright. Arik covered his mouth again and waited for the panic attack to subside.

'Go on. Is he a pirate?'

'He's the intercessor –' The intruder began hyperventilating. 'Everyone knows about the jemesh and the reward – oh God, oh God oh God –'

There was no getting sense out of him. Arik twisted his neck. He fell lifeless to the floor.

Arik went downstairs. From the bottom, he had a good view of the table where the card games had been played. Wrestlers had now replaced the cards, ringed by a larger and rowdier crowd.

He spotted the 'poet' at once: a man sitting between the wrestlers but watching neither, facing the staircase instead. Waiting.

A great grin spread across the man's face as Arik descended, as though he'd been expecting him. The intercessor rose and waded through the crowd. Behind him, an explosion of cheers and frustration erupted at the close of another round. He raised his voice so Arik could hear him.

'I warned them they'd set their sights too high.' He was middle-aged, finely attired, trim-bearded. Whatever he mediated, it was not poetry. 'They even wagered against their own success. No surprise, no surprise.'

Arik stared down at the so-called poet. The poet wasn't fazed.

'Master Invelmari, I invite you to my table. You will surely win more gold than these fighters all.'

'Do you think I'm interested in gold?'

The intercessor's eyes narrowed playfully. 'No? Then I'm sure I can offer you a better prize.'

Arik fastened the clasp of his cloak. The intercessor's voice became silken.

'Surely there must be something that will tempt a Northern warrior?'

'Do you know anything about the jemesh?' Arik asked. The poet's smile became fixed. 'Then no. That's my price. I want to know who sent it, and why. If ever you can offer me what I'm after, send word to me again when I'm next in Romel. I'll be waiting.'

*

Verdi lay awake all night at the inn, acutely aware now of the nearness of the limolan tree. Of his connection to it. Like the gnomon, it exerted a pull on him, but its lure was warm, comforting.

Its sanctuary housed the Book of Oaths. He would need to sign his name in its pages to fulfil the second of Lorendar's conditions. But the mere thought was terrifying. *I could never leave.* Now that Klaus was gone, he could dare consider staying. Still – he wasn't ready, wasn't right for this; perhaps he might never be. Why couldn't he have been more like Klaus? *What would Klaus have done?*

By morning he was exhausted. Now that he'd seen the limolan, leaving Romel was laced with dread, as though that tender connection would be severed as slyly as it had formed. Their return journey was quiet, each keeping to their own thoughts. A few hours later, Samsarra's gates were in sight.

Nerisen surveyed the sea of tents outside the citadel. 'Is it so terrible, to be a beacon of hope?'

The most terrible thing of all. Hope was a perilous road, and often without destination. Wars were fought with steel and sinew, not hope.

*

Fifty-seven days since Klaus left us. Verdi closed his notebook, unable to concentrate.

Waiting for nightfall to study the gnomon again was proving torturous now. Studying was poor distraction. Even the Arboretum provided little respite. And, after his last meeting with Sassan, he was as afraid as he was keen to discover more about his father.

From between the pages of his book, he extracted a drying leaf from the limolan tree, papery and worn with the worrying of his restless fingers. The Derindin despised amulets, but the leaf seemed to hold some of the sanctuary's tranquillity within its fibres.

He went for a walk, taking the uphill path from the laboratorium to the olive press to collect pomace oil for Master Meron. The kindly scholar supplied Verdi with just enough errands to provide him with a tenuous link to the school, though he wasn't a student. He passed through evergreen olive groves, some already heaving with fat green fruit, and young orchards bridal with spring blossoms. Briefly, the barrenness of the Plains was erased.

Half a dozen Derindin were already working the press, turning grinding stones over the earliest olive harvest. Others passed pulp into large discs of sandwillow fibre and hemp that was pounded to extract the oil. Zoraya the press master filled a generous bottle of the cloudy green oil for him. Verdi climbed the grassy dunes to admire the groves and the school buildings nestled against the Arboretum.

He wasn't alone. A frail man, snowy white of hair and as gnarled as the oldest of the olives, sat on the grass beside a handsome staff.

'Seven years, at least, and well worth it,' said the man, nodding at the bottle of oil under Verdi's arm. 'A long time to bear fruit. But the noblest of fruits.' A gentle twinkle entered his eye. 'And yet not so long or as noble as a limolan.'

'So I've been told,' Verdi replied cautiously. The limolan tree's branches had carried nothing but delicate leaves. 'Perhaps it doesn't flower or fruit all, like the wild olives.'

'Ah, that may be true. But it may well simply not have been rightly nourished. Even a tree as precious as a limolan can starve or sicken.' The man winked. 'Although I am certain that fruit it will.'

More misplaced Derindin hope. But there was something heartening about this gentle stranger's encouragement. For the first time, Verdi was briefly freed of thoughts of Klaus' 'death'. To his astonishment, Ravi crept onto the man's knee and pawed insistently at his chest for attention.

'What would Lorendar do to revive the limolan?' Verdi asked.

'Does it matter? He was a man who didn't succeed. The tree *he* planted grew but never fruited. Why on earth would anyone do as he did? Return to what you were first, young man, before you ever heard the name of Obsidian Lorendar. You've no need of anything else for your own tree to fruit.'

This was contrary to everything Verdi had been told. The man chuckled at Verdi's silence, scratching behind Ravi's ears. The oceloe curled up into a blissful ball in his lap and settled for a long nap.

'Now. Will you run an errand for an old man and take a message to one Master Fresmo?'

He drew out a corked bottle from his garments, small enough to fit in the palm of his hand and dark green to protect its contents from light degradation.

A snake twisted in Verdi's belly, shattering the tranquillity. 'I don't think Master Fresmo would be pleased to see me anytime soon.'

'Oh, he's in need of this too much to protest. Tell him the olive keeper would remind him that the roads of men and women are drawn by a far more discerning mind than his own.'

'Is that your message, sir?'

'It is.' He leaned heavily on his staff as he rose, but then straightened as tall as the trees. Ravi jumped down petulantly. 'Well met, young master.'

When Arik came to accompany him back to Samsarra, Verdi reluctantly asked him to wait at the top of the street in the Alchemists' Quarter and made his way again to the physician's door. His heart thudded awkwardly. *I must be mad.* This time, the maid answered and kept him waiting so long he almost turned away.

'You again?' Fresmo's eyes fell on the little bottle Verdi offered, eyes rounding. His scowl disappeared. 'Ah...'

Fresmo considered him, then glanced up and down the street, looking straight through the warrior waiting on his horse. Verdi glanced curiously at the bottle, offering it again to the physician.

'This is –'

'– for you,' said Fresmo. 'I received mine many moons ago, when I could still not tell a citric gum from a smelling salt, and sought a pupillage of my own.' He seemed to gather himself together. 'Well, Master Santarem. When do you wish to begin?'

*

For several nights, Nerisen had not slept, tossing and turning in her bed. By day, her studies and visits to the refugees left little time for worrying. But night was inescapable. Onax was as restless as she, scurrying about until he became insufferable.

After the third night, she saddled her horse as soon as there was enough light in the sky and rode east out of Samsarra.

She had tried to find the Wisdom twice before, and the only time she had succeeded was in the company of the Northman, when she had *not* been seeking him. It was difficult not to be irked by this. She took Tristan's compass with her, for it was remarkably fine and – though she was furious with herself for such superstition – perhaps somehow held a little of his uncanny waymaking in its lodestone... But for the first time in her life, the road to the sacred olive grove came easily, and she wasn't even within sight of his house when she met the Wisdom himself, striding out through the twisted olives to meet her.

'Turn back, daughter.' He was as old as the trees, but she had seen for herself the solid strength in the deceptively frail trunk of him. 'There's no time to lose.'

'But –'

The Wisdom stroked her horse's head, whispering in her ear. She neighed, her muscles tense as a coiled spring. Onax finally settled on Nerisen's saddlebag, watching the Wisdom.

'I came to seek guidance,' Nerisen said breathlessly. 'About the one who they say will succeed Lorendar –'

'Will you follow ilnurhin to its source no matter where that leads, daughter of the Plains?'

She was wholly unprepared for his question.

'Can Viridian rid us of the pirates?' she demanded. 'Will he find the phase of the moon that will bring Merensama? Will it be worth it, even if it means war?'

'There's nothing on earth that will give you the assurances you seek.' His eyes grew steely. 'What hopes and doubts you have, you must reconcile for yourself. I ask only whether you will go.'

Heart racing, she nodded.

'Then turn back and make for Ahravel. The Northerner who serves the fruit of the limolan will need help.' She had a split second for astonishment to register, then another for a mountain in her heart to shift – which it did, with sweet and sudden certainty. 'Waste no time. Do not worry, you will be safe – as you have always been, a daughter of the Plains. A caravan will cross paths with you as soon as you leave this clandom and keep you company as far as a small village of Fraivon. When you get there, trust your horse. She will know where to take you. Go now...'

She was already steering her horse around.

'And Nerisen –' She looked back, for the Wisdom's voice had become stern. 'Sometimes there is only a hair's breadth between ruinous pride and greatness.'

He's alive. She rode back to Samsarra.

*

If it were at all possible, the pirates had grown even more resentful of Klaus.

Sharlo, who oversaw the enclosures, was extremely disgruntled when Klaus began his investigation of the hyena attack with a search of the pirates' quarters. But the Eh Menishian had given Klaus a free hand.

Sharlo watched him open a wooden chest. 'You'll find nothing here.'

Privately Klaus agreed, but it was too good an opportunity to waste.

'I crossed paths with another Invelmari. The one with a bounty on his head.' Klaus rummaged through clothing. 'A Northerner who wears a little bone around his neck. A jemesh. Has the reward been claimed yet?'

Sharlo's eyes narrowed. 'What do you know about that?'

'Those Romelians must have told the story a thousand times over. He'd killed that pirate weeks before I set foot in Romel and they were still telling it. With a reward like that...'

'It will be claimed.' The pirate spat in the sand. 'We've all eternity to wait.'

'Eternity, eh? Seems an awful lot of time to waste on a woman long skewered.'

Such hatred filled Sharlo's eyes that Klaus thought he had finally found something the Eh Menishian wouldn't be able to subdue. *Even pirates mourn their lovers.*

Klaus searched a stack of bedding. 'I would have brought you the Northerner's head and the little bone around it, but he'd already moved on from Romel. Still, it's a decent amount of gold. Maybe I'll go after the jemesh for you if I leave.'

'Just the Northman,' growled Sharlo. He jerked his head towards Renegash's tent. 'Jemesh's theirs. We don't want it back.'

He spat again and left.

The Eh Menishian had sent the jemesh! Klaus could well imagine it between Krevkatt's fingers. It seemed as distasteful to Sharlo as it had been to other Derindin. Then had the *Eh Menishian* sent Sharlo's lover to capture Verdi? *And why? Why put up the reward for Arik's capture?*

Klaus would have dearly liked to dig more, but this might invite fatal suspicion. He returned to the matter at hand. The pirates' quarters were larger and more comfortable than the prisoners' enclosures. It was day, and they were empty but for sleeping night sentries. His main findings were things the pirates had likely looted: a broken bracelet bearing an inscription in Orenthian; a promise-ring; a smokeleaf case. The case was most interesting; solid gold, engraved with a snake entwined around an axe: the crest of clan Hesper. He left as few of these behind as he could.

In another tent, Klaus discovered a water barrel hiding a burrow in the ground. It led into a short tunnel, the bottom of which was blocked with broken crates and sack cloth. It was too small to admit a man, but could fit a woman or a child.

He found Renegash on the hill overlooking the largest quarry. A turbulent wind had been prowling the desert since morning.

'It is a plague in this land,' muttered Renegash, and Klaus took him to mean the wind. 'A terrible sentence that was prophesied to pass, and so it has.'

By whom, and in which scriptures?

'I've heard many stories of deadly windstorms ransacking the South, but never heard them described as a sentence.'

'A prophecy.' Renegash seemed distant, half-listening. 'One that has been long fulfilled.'

When the Eh Menishian said no more, Klaus broke the silence. 'Have winds disturbed the camp before?'

'Once, causing considerable damage. But the ore was safe. Everything else is dispensable.'

Including the prisoners and the pirates.

'I found something in one of the pirates' tents that I believe you should investigate.'

Renegash listened in silence to his report of the hidden tunnel, gazing over the Plains, where the dark figures of men moved like overgrown ants. Clouds dimmed the sunlight to a dirty yellow-grey, and the wind carried a sound Klaus hadn't heard in weeks: bird cries, long and low-pitched. A feathery explosion of birds shook the clouds; they circled above several times before flying west. Coaren's words came to Klaus' mind: *birds are the first to know when something's afoot.*

'Perhaps they are quicker to learn than I thought,' said Renegash at last.

Klaus didn't know what he meant, but was disquieted. The sky was growing dark as well as turbulent. 'If I'm not mistaken, that looks like a storm...'

'We will have to halt the work and recall the slaves for the day.'

'Can you afford to lose the yield of a day's work, my lord?'

'There may be no choice in the matter.' Renegash fell silent, still watching his men. 'You have never wished to know more about the ore?'

'I chose the way of blades, not metal.' Klaus made his voice neutral. 'An Invelmari warrior should focus only on his own business, lest he becomes divided from it. I have kept to mine, and I don't begrudge that you keep to yours.'

Though he'd said the right words, this time he wasn't sure Renegash was convinced. Klaus felt the ominous ruffle of the shadow-wing that folded around an Intelligencer's heart at the intangible stirrings of danger. The disquiet swelled between his ribs.

'It'll be too windy soon to work, my lord,' he said briskly. 'What will you have them do?'

Renegash called off the mining. He didn't give Klaus any instructions for what to do next about the hidden tunnel in the pirates' quarters.

The prisoners walked back into growing wind blowing in from the east, sometimes pushing against it. A storm would bring a welcome reprieve from their back-breaking work. Pirates inspected their enclosures, ensuring they were secure. The wind persisted all night, howling through the camp like a tormented beast in the early hours when Klaus woke to speak the Wisdom's litany before dawn. By morning, the storm had only worsened.

Pirates inspected the camp again, checking and reinforcing the tents.

'The mining's been called off again,' a pirate shouted over the wind.

Klaus walked to the perimeter of the camp, from where he could see the open desert. Guttural gusts of wind tossed sand and stones about, gathering into a dusty wavefront. The sky was overcast and grey. He returned to his tent to find Renegash had sent yet another tray of sweetmeats. *So I am to keep to my quarters.*

He lay awake for much of the night. For the first time since losing the connection with the land, he dared reach out with his mind to the desert, afraid of meeting silence.

He would have been happy to sense even just a shadow of it again. To his delight, it was as though he'd stepped off a precipice into a deep green valley: his mind plunged into a wide tranquillity far removed from the storm seething around him, where the consciousness of the land saturated his senses.

This awareness was more defined than it had been before it was severed. For a moment, he thought it would speak. It didn't, but something streamed like a river between the heart in his breast and the heart of the earth…

Relief stung his eyes with tears. He slept at last.

A second day of high winds brewed a different restlessness in the camp. Spring did not soften the storm's blow. The Derindin knew these storms well; the Eh Menishian had less experience of them. Between the anxiety of the pirate guards, the dread-filled *rebellious* excitement of the prisoners and the impatience of the Eh Menishian, a palpable turbulence crowded the air. Klaus patrolled the camp, ensuring this nervous energy didn't spill over into skirmishes. Once again, there was no invitation to the Eh Menishian's quarters for supper, but to his dismay he returned that evening to find Gainshe waiting in his tent.

She wasn't attired for a storm. 'Lord Renegash has been indisposed and sends his apologies.'

Klaus wondered whether this time his luck had run out.

'Aren't you cold?'

'No, my lord,' Gainshe replied, shivering. He drew his cloak around her bare shoulders, trapping a sleek fall of dark hair. She really was exquisite.

Dear Sturmsinger, let me stay in the light.

Klaus pulled out a chair. 'Here. This wind isn't going anywhere.'

It would have been cosy, with the tent keeping out the worst of the wind while letting in its hollow howl and the coals glowing warm in the brazier. He was reminded of mountain wolves and log cabins buried deep in dark forest, summoning a pang of sadness more powerful than the pull of the girl in his quarters. Gainshe raised graceful arms to help remove his coat. Her orders were plain. More worryingly, this time Klaus was sure she'd been sent as a distraction while the Eh Menishian kept their own counsel. She added more coals to the brazier and sat beside him.

'We should try to know one another, Gainshe,' he said. 'I wish you to be more to me than a common whore.'

Whatever her instructions, she was all too happy to talk. What the Eh Menishian had not anticipated was the spell he would weave over her with his stories: of valleys that had no bottom and others filled with fire or forest; supple rivers that entwined and quarrelled and embraced again like lovers in myriads of watery circuits; meadows of wildflowers, the might of steel, the cold Northern moon. He played with her fingers and noted what made her eyes widen with wonder, or her pulse quicken in excitement. Thus he learned she was intelligent and admired exotic beasts, and hid behind those downcast eyes a wilful spirit that thrilled in the discovery of shieldmaidens. She fell under his spell in spite of herself.

Hours passed in this manner until it was almost morning. Tonight he had triumphed.

'You should go back,' he told her, and she pulled away reluctantly from the crook of his arm.

The third day's winds brought flying rubble to the camp from the mines.

Klaus didn't envy the pirates sent to check the mines, or the water carriers now making just one trip for water by wagon. His horse, a young yellow mare, wouldn't settle in the stables. The prisoners remained confined to their enclosures, their water rations cut.

This time, when Gainshe slipped into his tent he was almost glad of the company. She brought a jug of water, more prized now than wine, and yet more smoked dry-meats. Shyly, she pulled out a pendant from the folds of her kirtle.

'What's this?'

'An amulet from my home.' She laid it on Klaus' palm. It was a trilogy of trinkets secured to a golden ring: a blue-veined rock, a leaf preserved in resin, and a tiny claw. Klaus had seen something similar in Nékke, where folk believed amulets warded off evil spirits. 'You told such wondrous stories of your home, I wanted to give you something of mine in return.'

She must have taken a great risk in showing it to him, because Klaus was certain the Eh Menishian had ordered her to be as evasive about their homeland as they.

'You must be tired today.' He stroked her cheek.

She lowered her eyes, blushing. 'They were glad I stayed with you all the night.'

Again, Klaus grew uneasy. Why were the Eh Menishian so desperate to station Gainshe in his bed with false surrwyrte?

She settled herself on the rug at his feet. 'I want to know more about shieldmaidens.'

'If you like. But first tell me why you like to hear about them so much.'

Gainshe considered. 'I didn't imagine a girl could grow so strong. The women of my home plough and dig with the men, but that is their lot. Men have many wives, and wives worship their husbands.' She frowned. 'But then the men pray to she-idols...'

'In Invelmar, we pray to the Lifegiver.'

'Only one?'

'Only one. And some Invelmari honour spirits from a time before Invelmar, inherited from ancient tribes who came from the Sterns.'

'Has anyone ever reached the top of the Sterns?'

'The very tops of the mountains are so high that in Invelmar we say they've left this world altogether. The peaks are known as the Dreamers, dipping into the heavens. They've no time for our goings-on below, and we've no means to climb them.'

She gazed into an invisible distance. 'Where I come from, nothing is too high to reach. Or too deep.'

'No mountains?' *No sea?*

'Very few. But my people dig, as they do here. We are no strangers to digging. For us, it is the road.'

A very meaningful look refocused her eyes. Klaus stowed her words away.

Despite her orders, once again she was all too happy to listen to stories rather than seduce him. Gainshe might have even enjoyed his attentions now if he took her, but he sensed she'd once had dreams of her own, and she probably hadn't dreamed of becoming a Northerner's concubine.

The winds outside had only grown in ferocity. It was not yet fully dark.

'You should go,' Klaus told her. Wind shook the tent. 'It might be too stormy later, and the bigger tents will provide better protection than mine.'

'They won't object if I stay with you.'

Only modesty moderated the tiny pleading note in her voice. What fate had Gainshe been threatened with, if she failed?

'I do not resist you still for lack of want, Gainshe,' he said gently. 'An

Invelmari must have honour. I would elevate yours, not steal it from you.'
He paused, calling on all the subtleties of his Form, making his words a
brush of lips. Now he was the seducer, to something else altogether. 'You
have dreams. In your heart, you've no wish to be bedded by a stranger.'

Unshed tears shone in her eyes; his aim was true.

'There is no dreaming here, only duty,' she whispered.

Klaus got up to find the vial of surrwyrte. 'You have my permission
to make whatever claims you need. But you'll need this if you're going
to convince them.'

Three particulars about his body he told her, flushing her cheeks
crimson. He uncorked the vial. The false potion mimicked the smell of
surrwyrte perfectly: aniseed and liquorice root.

He held out the vial. 'Don't worry, it smells strong but it's quite safe.'

She drank it reluctantly. The scent was only added to common
stock, to help identify its consumption and illicit smuggling, and to
prevent merchants from dodging payment of the hefty tax on its sale.
Unscented surrwyrte made for a mighty dowry in and of itself. Then he
tore the fastening of her dress. He hoped she was resourceful enough to
contrive the rest.

'Be careful,' he warned. 'If they suspect you of lying…'

The smell lingered on her breath. She donned her cloak, pausing
at the tent flap.

'When they first told me I was to come to you, I was very much
afraid. I had heard of Northern mountain warriors, and they sounded
brutal and heartless.' She hesitated.

'What is it?'

'You have been kinder to me than anyone here, my lord.' Fear lurked
in her rounded eyes. 'I must return your kindness.'

Klaus lowered his head to catch her whisper over the quarrelling
winds.

'They have been debating your fate ever since you found the tunnel
in the pirates' quarters.'

'Why?'

'They are afraid you will realise how we came to this place.'

We are no strangers to digging…

So that was how the Eh Menishian moved through the Plains:
through the earth.

It would explain their unlikely presence in the desert, the sudden
arrivals of goods and concubines, and possibly the fate of the mined ore.
It was such a fantastic feat that Klaus hadn't considered it possible.

But where do they come from? The Zmerrudi Sea, on ships like the
one that had brought Gainshe? Now Klaus understood Renegash's only
response to his discovery of the pirates' secret tunnel: *'they are quicker to*

learn than I had thought.'

'When the storm passes, pretend you've forgotten about the tunnel,' Gainshe urged. 'Or else tell them it's probably of no importance. Krevkatt will argue that you suspect nothing.'

'The shaman?'

'He takes a great interest in you. He questions me each time I come here. He says –' She blushed again. 'He told me I must do my duty.'

Klaus' thoughts were boiling over. 'Go back before the storm worsens. Thank you, Gainshe. I'll remember what you said about the tunnel,' he added, and she looked somewhat appeased.

He knew what he had to do.

But not long after she left, there was a lull in the wind, and the flying dust settled, and the air even stilled such that he feared the storm was finally retreating. After the wind's incessant wailing, the calm was eerie and insincere and almost dreamlike.

And then the heart of the storm arrived in the camp.

*

Klaus raised the lantern high over the pirates crouching on the ground working. They'd splinted a broken beam in one of the enclosures and packed earth around its loosened supports. Even after this, it creaked ominously. There were more repairs, but the storm was peaking.

'Tent's too big,' a pirate shouted. 'There's a reason folk here keep their tents small!'

They kept close to the enclosures and out of the path of a wind that bellowed with sand, lashing back at the camp with the entrails of the nearby mines: a grey rubble-laden dust that had already torn away a pirate tent and swallowed some of the livestock.

Renegash and two of his guards appeared through the curtain of flying dirt, their shoulders hunched against the storm.

'Almost all the enclosures have been seen to, my lord,' Klaus called.

Renegash nodded. 'Double the guard at every post. No – empty the pirates' quarters, they can rest when this is over. I will take no chances tonight.'

He had barely spoken before metal screeched: the wind had dragged a long bolt out of the earth. The walls of the repaired enclosure ripped away from the ground.

Pandemonium erupted in the dismantled enclosure. It was the one in which Klaus had himself been held prisoner not ten weeks before. Prisoners huddled together for shelter while others strained against their chains, some tearing them free from the ground. Oil lamps smashed or flickered out, and sudden darkness descended.

'Surround them!' roared Renegash. One of his guards blew a horn to raise the alarm. 'None must escape!'

Klaus and the pirates fanned out around the prisoners, marked now only by their shouts in the dark. One by one, the guards' lamps went out in the wind. Klaus kept his lantern close before him, riding carefully to avoid trampling on prisoners. He spotted Spaero and leaned forward in his saddle out of the lantern's light.

'Take this.' Klaus slipped the empty surrwyrte vial into Spaero's hand. 'You'll need something to collect that brush-snake venom ... if ever an opportunity arises. Keep it buried in the sand.'

Spaero squeezed Klaus' arm before he rode on.

Lanterns were finally relit. Pirates contained the prisoners. Klaus rejoined the Eh Menishian, heart racing hard.

'If you wish to redistribute these prisoners, I can have space cleared in the other enclosures,' Klaus shouted, and Renegash signalled his consent.

Pirates scattered to continue repairs. Lanterns, while they lasted, bobbed in the turbulent dark. The flying sand made it almost impossible to see beyond the span of his arm. Head down, Klaus rode through sheet after sheet of biting wind, making straight for his tent.

He'd packed everything he needed as soon as Gainshe had gone. He had no bow, but he had his knives and Rasan's sword.

Klaus blew out his lantern.

When he stepped out again, the sharp-toothed night chafed without mercy. The sky was the colour of steel and wholly blinded the stars. But the land beneath him spoke in his heart with a voice no shrieking storm could drown out.

He followed the pull of the desert, navigating with nothing but what he borrowed of its consciousness, and rode with the westerly wind.

41

Pearlberry Ivy

FOR WEEKS INVELMAR MOURNED ITS FATHER'S PASSING, HIS THRONE
WAITING EMPTY. FOR WHO COULD BEAR THE TERRIBLE HONOUR
OF THE STATION OF ANSOVALD STURMSINGER?

SONNONFER: THE PASSING OF ANSOVALD STURMSINGER

He threw himself where the land took him. At first he rode hard, trusting
his earth-sense, almost blown away from the camp by the wind. It was
the darkest night he had known in the Plains. Had he not tested the
land's silent command before, he would have dreaded unseen rocks or
treacherous sinksand. But he resisted fear, itself a sinkhole once indulged.

Trust me, he felt the desert say. *I know.*

So he gave himself to it completely.

Klaus had already estimated the Eh Menishian's camp was too far
east of the Selvaran Cradle. Now his suspicions were confirmed, for the
land steered him west. He listened for the Eh Menishian's dogs or horses,
but the wind muffled his ears, and in any case it would be a while before
he would be missed. Besides, who in their right mind would attempt to
navigate this storm and this darkness?

514

Lend me of your strength, dear Sturmsinger... He found himself breathing the Wisdom's litany as he rode, praying he wouldn't lose his restored sense of the land, for it was all that kept him from being lost in the black sea of sand.

Eventually, he slowed to a pace his mare could maintain and rode through the night.

Renegash was ruthless. He would send guards after him as soon as the storm settled. So when morning brought a relative calming of the wind, Klaus paused only long enough to refresh his horse, for her comfort was more important than his. The air was still yellow and torrid with dust. The spring sun's baleful eye glared through the haze. He rubbed his mare down and gathered his bearings. The larger mountains that had been to the west of the camp now lay ahead of him, and he could also make out the smaller Ilmaz range behind him, to the east. A thrill warmed his heart. *I should be near the Selvaran Cradle.*

If he continued west, he should eventually arrive in Baeron's clandom. Further north-west would be the S'beyan Strip, the tongue of land Sisoda guarded from its neighbours. He could veer north towards Ahravel, but feared the Eh Menishian might expect him to pursue this shorter road. Klaus cast his mind back experimentally, as he'd done with Nerisen. The land he had left behind felt more disturbed than the desert ahead, and from this he inferred that the storm was still very much alive over the camp.

He tried to grasp the particles of this bond; interrogate them to gauge whether he could sense the impact of a horse's hooves disturbing the land's surface. But these finer details were swathed in grey, beyond his reach.

Feeling the land's voice was not without cost: a fatigue as wearying as miles of hard road. Sword resting against his chest, Klaus closed his eyes in a brief and shallow sleep, trying not to think of the prisoners he had left behind.

*

The volume of anatomical verse Physician Fresmo had gifted Verdi lay face down on his lap, and Ravi snoozed under the hollow of its spine. Noise had never stopped Verdi from reading, and there was plenty of it in the barracks' cantina. But noise wasn't what hampered his concentration. His shortsword lay beside him, abandoned; he only really still bothered to train to please his uncle, who was never satisfied with anything anyway.

Sixty-three days. No word; no rumours of a Northern mercenary working for pirates. Even Verdi had to admit they were unlikely to see

Klaus again. Already the news of his death had been replaced in the taverns by talk of Sisoda's impasse, Baeron's ambition, and brewing war in the North.

His fingers itched to write to Elodie again. Arik would say it was reckless, and he was probably right. The letter Fibbler had stolen from the Babble verified Elodie's warning that a spy had caught their scent. It was too risky to correspond. But he missed her beyond all belief. Arik would approve of this even less.

Ravi emerged from under the book, wide awake. Verdi looked around, spotting Saya perched on the rafters. His uncle appeared a moment later in the entrance of the cantina.

Verdi turned his book face up again.

'Still sulking about the Northerner?'

Verdi swallowed back the angry torrent that refluxed into his throat. What was the point?

Alizarin sat beside him. He tugged the book from Verdi's hands.

'"The Vessels of the Organs of Man."' He set it down on the table. 'Congratulations. Fresmo is a formidably selective teacher. He will keep you so busy, you'll have no time to spare for anything else.'

'At least he'll teach me something useful.'

Silence.

'No one's going to show you what to do with the gnomon, Viridian. The truth is they don't know. Would you rather they created a mould for you to fill?'

Verdi searched his uncle's face, where a door was perhaps ajar. 'Isn't that what the Elders are trying to do?'

'Some of them, yes. But this is a path you'll have to fashion for yourself.'

Verdi generally had either comfortable confidence or crippling confusion about most things in life. Derinda was no exception. None of what he'd learned about Lorendar felt like it had anything to do with *him*. Until he'd stood beneath the limolan tree, at least ... and even that had coloured his uncertainty with guilt. But, echoing the olive keeper's encouragement, Alizarin's words lifted a curtain in Verdi's mind.

Though he wasn't feeling generous enough to admit this.

'What about all the things I *don't* hear about Lorendar?' he said rebelliously. 'Or am I supposed to pretend they didn't happen?'

'And childish behaviour is not how you're going to convince anybody.' Alizarin was once again a sour, distant stranger. 'If it's confirmation of whatever your father told you that you want, I could have provided that long ago. I have no illusions that Obsidian Lorendar was a saint. But the key to our victory is buried in his prophecy. The faithful will whitewash the past however it suits them, if that's what it will take to unite the clans.'

Verdi oscillated between anger and surprise at his uncle's frankness. 'So I'm to inherit lies and spread them too, *if* that's what it takes. Maybe even repeat his crimes, if necessary.'

Saya jumped down to Alizarin's shoulder, as cold-eyed as her master. 'Our duty is to ensure the right thing is done.'

'You don't even believe in Lorendar's promises, do you?' Verdi marvelled at his own stupidity for not having seen this sooner. 'You don't have any faith in prophecies. You're just using them to get what you want.'

'What we *need*,' his uncle corrected.

'You're just as much a fraud as I am.'

Now Alizarin's eyes were fire and ice. Verdi stalked out of the cantina before either of them could say something regrettable, leaving Arik in the barracks.

He returned to Thillaina's house. Angry and bewildered, he sat at the kitchen table and buried his head in his arms. His ears buzzed with thought-midges. The guilt always seemed to win: guilt over his inability to help the Derindin; guilt that he could make no sense of the moondial. Guilt for bringing Klaus here, for keeping him in Derinda despite Elodie's warning of a spy on the prowl ... guilt for writing to Elodie, probably attracting the spy himself. Elodie, an impossibly stupid dream. Arik wouldn't understand; he passed through lovers as leaves changed with the seasons.

'You're trembling like a newborn colt, dear.' He hadn't heard Thillaina enter. 'So's your little friend. And you're cluttering my table. What's the matter? I'll get some kahva brewing.'

Verdi wanted to be alone, but accepted a cup without protest and found himself grateful for it. Setting her basket of needlework on the table, she sat across from him and waited.

'I don't know what I should be doing.' Months of confusion tumbled out of him. 'I've heard so much about Lorendar, and some of it ... I've had that prophecy recited at me a hundred different ways. But it can't be about me, I'm no fit for whatever they're planning.' Verdi wanted to go on, to air his fears about his father, but he couldn't bring himself to hear them aloud.

'You've been surrounded by too much yapping, that's all.' Thillaina patted his hand. 'They all yap like a bunch of old widows, and I'll be the first to say it. What you need is a bit of peace and quiet.'

With that, she returned to her work. Her words were unexpectedly bolstering, the way Elodie used to put him at ease with little effort. Perhaps it was because he was thinking of Elodie, but his eyes latched onto a fold of brocade in the basket Thillaina had left behind.

A bolt of ice seared through him.

Verdi stared at the brocade. It bore a pattern he had seen countless times in Sunnanfrost, the Wintermantels' palace in Dunraven.

Fingers trembling now, he pulled it out of the basket and studied the unmistakable pattern of tiny pearlberry-laden ivy leaves favoured by Lady Wintermantel.

It was a new and unfinished work, the embroidery needles still threaded with silk and neatly pinned into the edge of the fabric. Thillaina had been working on it for weeks herself. *Why didn't I spot it sooner?* Had he not folded away countless errant shawls embroidered with these leaves; even seen them draped around Elodie's shoulders? Lady Wintermantel periodically ordered the fabric, made especially for her, the pearlberry ivy copied from a drawing she'd made herself as a bride. What was it doing in Thillaina's house in Samsarra?

Verdi dropped it as though it had caught fire. Then he refolded it and returned it to the basket, praying the old widow wouldn't notice.

'Oh.' A rush of fear swept all his other anxieties aside. 'Oh no, Ravi … oh no.'

When he finally stopped shaking, he went back out to find Arik, and to be anywhere but Thillaina's house.

*

'Are you absolutely certain?' Arik demanded.

Verdi nodded, deathly pale.

'I made lace for the queen herself … there's not a better bit of brocade to be found in all the Plains than Thillaina's.' The widow's own proud declaration echoed in Arik's ears.

Not Adela. Not this queen, but the next.

Arik sank onto a bench in the barracks. *So that's how word of us reached the Wintermantels so soon after we got here.* All this while, they had been sleeping in the snake's own nest.

He exhaled through gritted teeth. 'We have to tell your uncle.'

'Why?'

'First, he can arrest her and block more messages to the North. Klaus thought Elodie was warning us about only one spy, but we don't know who else might be helping. And second, if the Wintermantels decide to send Isarnanheri after us, he should at least be warned.'

Now Verdi looked queasy. 'The message Fibbler stole … could she have sent that too?'

Arik's head began to thump. *It was foolish to think no one would track us here.* 'Let's hope so. If that wasn't her, then more than one person is after us.'

'Do you think she's told Adela as well?'

'Just assume anything's possible.'

They found Alizarin in his study at the Arboretum. Even he was lost for words.

'I've known Thillaina since I was a child.' His knuckles were white, gripping his pen. 'She may be happy to take payment for informing on Klaus, but she won't draw Invelmari soldiers to Samsarra...'

'Can you arrest her?' Verdi asked anxiously.

'My priority is to protect my clan, not your friend. I warned you of that when you came.'

Arik couldn't begrudge him this. *In his place, my priorities would be the same.* 'Can you at least stop her from doing more harm?'

'Arresting her will be difficult to explain – and may alert any accomplices that you've found her out. That could trigger an alarm ... escalate matters further. Even confronting her is dangerous.'

Verdi's shoulders slumped. 'Then you won't help?'

Alizarin ran a hand roughly through his hair, as though raking his thoughts.

'Carry on as before, but be on your guard,' he told Arik finally. 'After all, they've had months to come after you and Klaus. There must be a reason why they haven't.'

It wasn't a solution, but Arik saw the sense in this. The thought of leaving Derinda in hope of a fresh start elsewhere was only fleeting. *I can't drag Verdi away from here now.*

'It's no good. We'll just have to be careful.' Arik glared at Ravi. 'Fat lot of use that oceloe and his "instincts" turned out to be. Little traitor worships her.'

Hearts heavier each day, they rode back to Samsarra.

*

It had been twenty-four years since Alizarin had last sat here by Thillaina's empty hearth, awaiting her return. Her seamstresses had left for the day, her maid had gone to bed, and Tenken was keeping Viridian and Arik at the tavern as instructed.

She returned alone. Her eyes found Alizarin as soon as she lit the oil lamp, as though she'd been expecting him.

Alizarin usually sieved practical matters from the nuisance of emotions. *She was spying on Northerners for Northerners. No crime against our clan.* But if she were capable of that, what other trusts had she betrayed?

'It's generally considered polite to enter a house *after* its owner's returned to it, young man.' She moved more slowly than he remembered. 'Well? What is it this time?'

'Why did you have me send Viridian to the Wintermantels' house?'

Surprise sparked in her eyes for just a second, but he caught it. He would never forget that night, in the black days after Yirma had died. The bundle of a boy suddenly left in his arms had been the heaviest weight he'd ever had to carry. Thillaina had known what to do. He had been desperate, and she had insisted.

'What does it matter now? His mother wanted him to be sent away. You wanted him to receive a good upbringing somewhere safe. That's exactly what he got.'

'Why the Wintermantels?' Alizarin pressed. 'You even led me to believe it would be Derindin settlers in Dunraven who would actually take him in, not Ealdormen.'

He had never forgiven Thillaina. She had known Viridian's lineage, when Alizarin had sought her help. Were it not for her, his nephew would never have ended up in an Ealdorman's house. She'd been widowed for some time and had already made her fortune in Dunraven, and turned a great wheel of far-flung acquaintances. *No one was better placed to help.* But until Viridian's discovery, Alizarin had never realised Thillaina's close connection to the Wintermantels.

Had she known about the false Wintermantel prince? Viridian and Klaus were only a couple of years apart in age. *And if she were an accomplice to the Wintermantels' treachery, and one day leads the wrath of Dunraven here…*

Her eyes sharpened, melting away some of her age. 'It was the safest place.'

I can't expose the bloody Northerners. That would risk drawing Isarnanheri to Samsarra in pursuit of them. So he couldn't ask her the real questions burning his mouth.

'He'll never be anything more than a follower of masters now,' he said harshly instead. 'He was raised a servant and it's all he knows. That's your doing.'

The ice cracked at last. 'Given half a chance, he may well surprise you,' she snapped. 'I dare say he's been more downtrodden here than he ever was in Dunraven.'

Later, when the lava of anger cooled and facts crystallised into recognisable forms, Alizarin would find himself more perplexed than ever. Of Thillaina's deception he now had no doubt, but it went against the grain. Her reverence for Merensama betrayed a devout faith – or at least, superstition – that had always struck him as being at odds with her clever and practical mind. *What's she up to?* Even now he couldn't see where she hid her sting.

Or else she had once again simply got the better of him.

*

Three days after escaping the camp, Klaus' water ran out.

The storm had finally dwindled to a middling wind that thankfully still covered his tracks. A hazy sun even scowled in the sky. Daytime was growing warmer, magnifying thirst. He'd found derina once, the tubers small and yielding very little milky water, most of which he gave to his horse. *I bet I'd find more if Nerisen were here.* Derina seemed to find its way to her hands as the road snaked towards his feet.

He descended into a hollow basin and realised what it was: a desiccated riverbed. Gooseflesh tingled on his arms. *This is where the Ninvellyn once ran.* Sturmsinger and his men had stopped here, and become 'enchanted' by the rock they found along the river's banks.

This must be the Selvaran Cradle. Somewhere beneath his feet was the main body of the mine.

And nearby: the hidden spring that could reshape the fate of a desert.

I can't lead them here. I can't be found. Whatever the Eh Menishian were digging up, either they'd started too far east, or else the mine extended from the Selvaran Cradle all the way back to their camp. They could yet dig in this direction if they followed the ore. Then they'd be sure to discover the spring. He couldn't risk drawing them here.

And yet if there really was so much water nearby, why was there no derina?

Klaus rode on towards the mountains, hoping to find a stream. How long could a man and his horse last without water? The Eh Menishians' gifts provided sustenance, but it was drink they needed. He saw wild birds, but they could fly far for water. Still no sign of an oasis, and still no derina.

'If they run south, they'll pray for capture just for the hope of a drink before death.'

He blotted out the pirate's words.

By the fifth day, when his head throbbed with thirst and strange pictures shimmered in the air, and he had milked the last measly derina tuber dry, he began to fear the dry riverbed was to be his grave. *And it would be a fitting end: to desiccate beside the severed lifeline my people dammed. It would be justice.*

He had been mapping as he followed the tug of the desert. He no longer knew where the land carried him now, giving himself up to the will of the Plains. Dimly, he was aware that his faithful yellow mare was gently ascending the mountain, picking out a path that had forgotten the footholds of men altogether. Gaps appeared in his consciousness. Figments of Dunraven tortured his waking eye. Sometimes, a pair of green eyes filled his mind, bottomless as a Northern river in the sun, salting his wounds. He could not know how the desert steered his horse into a deep crevice in the mountainside; how the dunes shifted in their wake so that their path disappeared behind them without trace. Then there was tawny silence.

When he came to, it was to a sound so familiar that at first he thought he was in the Helftads back in Invelmar: the hollow-bodied slow-dripping of water.

Something licked his face. Klaus opened his eyes; it was his horse. She was much refreshed, nose damp and nostrils flaring with curiosity. There was a throbbing ache in the side of his head where he had hit the ground, and beneath him was solid rock, wet and cold and slimy.

Klaus sat up cautiously and still saw explosions of stars.

He was in the mouth of a cave. A thin lip of light crept in through its slit-like entrance. That was probably where his horse had wandered in. The ceiling rose, opening abruptly into a cavern that vanished into darkness. Cupped between the rocks was the dark glint of water.

He crawled deeper into the cave and drank in sips to avoid the shock. It was the most delicious thing he would ever taste in his life. Then he drank more deeply.

He stretched his limbs; everything worked. He risked standing. The cave entrance opened like a keyhole into the mountain's flank. Outside was a narrow pass between two walls of the mountain. To the north, the pass led down into dunes; to the south, it climbed towards cooler peaks. His horse seemed happy outside the cave entrance, where she nibbled at arrowgrass growing between the rocks. She stood flicking her tail in the sliver of sunshine filtering down into the pass.

Klaus returned into the cave and drank again of the cold, crisp water. He lay on the ground until his pulse slowed and his eyes acclimatised to the darkness. Further into the cavern, water dripped more resonantly, as though falling onto deep water. A thrill of excitement shivered through him. He reached out with his mind into the earth.

It sprang up towards him, lithe then soaring, as though awaiting his summons. He was on the edge of the western Mengorian mountains, the *big brother* he'd seen from the camp. The cave burrowed into its north-eastern skirt. Further south, the Mengorian and Ilmaz ranges moved closer together until they merged. And beneath the ground, extending both south and east with staggering reach, he sensed a rocky labyrinth akin to a honeycomb buried in the earth: a series of caverns.

That's why the spring is hidden. They would have to bring down the mountains to find it in these caves.

But Ansovald Sturmsinger *had* found the spring. And however he had 'sealed' it, Klaus had found it too, and so could the Eh Menishian. He had to retrace the warlord's footsteps to the water caverns and guard the Derindin's buried treasure, or else the South would be lost to whoever got there before him.

*

'The citadel of Pir Sehem is under siege.'

It was the news Ayla had dreaded ever since the first raids on Sisoda. She had never seen the Elders so stunned. Still shaken herself, she understood. *Of all the clans to fall to pirates, Sisoda!*

'And Yodez?' Tourmali asked.

'Chieftain Yodez's forces were driven west into the S'beyan Strip, but they're his last hope for taking back the clandom. He won't keep them there long.'

'We can't lose what's left of the West to the pirates,' said Emra. 'We have to help Sisoda defend their clandom.'

'It's a twelve-day march to Pir Sehem from Romel, and we've already sent tumblers to Voista,' Tourmali pointed out. 'And we've no idea how many pirates we'll be up against. Evidently enough to take a clandom.'

He was right. The raids on Sisoda's land had begun weeks ago; there was no telling how many pirates might have infiltrated the clandom by now, and they could be as hidden as sand amongst stones.

Maragrin arched his eyebrows at Alizarin. 'This can be the first test of our new alliance with our northern neighbour.'

'How many tumblers can we afford to send to Pir Sehem?' Emra asked.

'Fifteen hundred,' Ayla replied. 'No more. Not if you wish to secure the citadel and the Arboretum, now that the Plains are turning up at our door.'

'Alizarin, send word to Navein and Chieftain Ilgarz of Voista. Request whatever tumblers they can spare.'

Heart quickening, Ayla left with purpose in her step. Months of uncertainty and inaction made soldiers restless, fostering an idle tension in the barracks. She knew she ought to brief her own deputies, but it was the Invelmari she went to first.

She found him in the sparring ring, disarming a tumbler who spat on the ground behind him.

A jeer rose from a handful of the new arrivals encamped outside the citadel; untried volunteers. Marcin ignored both affronts.

'Master Marcin.' Ayla's greeting cut through their mockery. 'Seems like some of these ill manners have gone unpunished.'

'They're not my soldiers to discipline.'

She looked around the yard. 'If they're to fight under you when we march on Pir Sehem, you had better see to it that you do.'

Tumblers fell quiet across the ground. Marcin turned his attention to his next student, and animated chatter filled the barracks as her news spread.

Gerit appeared at her shoulder. 'They'll begin to ask questions if you elevate a Northman above them, however deserving he is. We need them united, not resentful.'

Ayla watched the Invelmari warrior correct Rasan's form. Gerit was a seasoned soldier and a good man, and she knew he didn't speak from a place of envy. 'When they can fight as he does and save the life of Lorendar's heir several times, then they can ask questions.'

Nonetheless, she knew she was taking a risk. When the tumblers stopped for water, Marcin joined her on the balcony of the watchtower overlooking the barracks.

'Sisoda's citadel has been taken, then?'

'The pirates have it surrounded. If it isn't, it will be soon.'

Marcin shook his head. He didn't look surprised.

'I want you to lead a battalion when we march into Sisoda's clandom,' she told him. 'General Sarak of Mantelon and I will take the Cinnabar Road to Pir Sehem. Once we know how many swords Voista will send, we can devise our attack.'

There was no masking his hunger. 'Are you sure they'll follow me?'

'They'll do as I ask.'

They watched tumblers resume sparring below.

She chose words carefully. 'Is Tristan truly dead?'

There was no reply from the warrior.

'Well, at least that's not a lie,' she said.

Marcin gazed at his tumblers. She wondered what he actually saw. 'I don't know if he is, or where he is now.'

'Then he's alive.'

He met her eyes then. 'What makes you so certain?'

It was the starved shadow of hope in his question that convinced Ayla he *was* being truthful, whatever else he was holding back.

'Because I do not think the pirates are any match for Isarnanheri.'

There was no one within earshot, but he glanced around anyway. 'We are not –'

'Do you take me for a fool, Master Marcin?'

Again, there was silence. He rejoined the tumblers. She gazed across the yard, where Alizarin's nephew sat with a book.

No, Viridian was no soldier. That would have been too convenient. But the Great Sentience made no mistakes. Viridian was a banner, and that was enough.

*

Thankful for the flint he'd pilfered, Klaus fashioned a torch from some deadwood and ventured into the mountain. The ceiling glowed faintly, studded with an astonishing array of crystal growths shimmering with blue-tinged fluorescence. Still pools of water formed in bowls of rock; stony palms cupped in liquid prayer. The silence grew deeper as he went, and the air colder, and the world more peaceful.

He glanced back over his shoulder. Thanks to the crystal-glow, darkness rather than daylight now marked the way back. He memorised how the lie of the rocks *felt* in his mind and went on.

Once or twice he almost slipped on wet rock, and every so often he dipped his hand for a drink of the glassy water. How long since it was last disturbed? The cavern expanded around him, hung with shards and spears of gently-pulsating crystals. When his torch flickered out, he hardly noticed. The water pools grew larger and deeper. Soon the cave joined its cousins, and he found himself in the heart of a honeycomb of cave-chambers, just as his reading of the land had shown him.

Klaus stopped and made sure he could place himself, fearing he might not be able to contain this myriad of routes in his mind. Where crystal-light became scant, he relied on his sense of the land again. The caves began to ascend. A familiar sound hummed ahead, a *woosh* that grew louder as he ventured deeper and higher into the mountain. He continued for what might have been hours, stopping once for a bit of dried derina; something pulled him on, overriding all other urges. The cave narrowed and darkened again, his path tapering into a passage so small he had to crawl for a few moments in the dark. Then the *whooshing* became a roar that he recognised before standing up again on shaking legs…

From an unseen mouth above, a great fall of water cascaded into darkness. It had been so long since he'd seen such water that it seemed otherworldly. The ceiling of the cavern vanished into shadow, such was its height. A few feet ahead of him, the ground gave way to a sheer drop into foaming, bottomless water.

A light shone across the watery chasm. At first Klaus thought he'd imagined it, but then he saw it again: brighter than the humming glow of the crystals, like a subterranean star. *It's coming from behind the waterfall.* A ledge of rock surrounded the waterfall in a crooked ellipse. He inched along it around the chasm, feeling his way with his hands as well as his mind. The ledge continued into the waterfall itself. Extending one toe, he felt for solid ground on the other side of the freezing water. After a moment's hesitation, he followed the inexplicable tug and stepped sideways through the watery wall.

Cold assaulted him cruelly. His feet found firm footing in another larger cavern. And standing amongst the crystals – crystals now taller than Northerners, with the girth of ancient tree trunks – was the beacon that had drawn him: a lantern held by a woman.

She was as old as the crystals and yet her skin was smooth. Her frame beneath a grey shift dress was slight, but her *presence* eclipsed the might of the mountain. And her eyes were dark as steel and full of thorns.

'Why are you here, son of the North?'

Drenched and freezing, Klaus gaped. He curbed his questions, bowing low.

'Forgive the intrusion, I came – I was looking for this place...'

'Why?'

He waited for his teeth to stop chattering. 'I wasn't certain it was real. Others are also seeking it, and I – they mustn't find it.'

'And why should *you* find it? What right have you to decide who should?' she demanded. 'None. Why are you here?'

Klaus tried again. 'I promised to help a dear friend. Do you know of the pirates? They're looking for something –'

'Why are you here?'

He wrapped his arms around himself, shivering violently now, abruptly overcome with weariness. His eyes burned with fatigue accumulated over weeks in the Eh Menishian camp, and then a journey that had leaned heavily upon his perception of the land.

'To know,' he said finally, and only then understood what she asked, and realised what she was. *The Hermit!* Of course she was the Hermit, here in this lonely wilderness. His heart spread fresh wings, exhaustion extinguished. 'To seek wisdom wherever I find it, even in this cave.'

She was unmoved.

'None of your kind has listened before. Why should I waste words on deaf ears?'

And she turned and began walking away into the cavern.

'Wait!'

He started forward, and she looked back warningly. 'You are uninvited and unwelcome, like the one who came before you.'

'Please –' Klaus stopped. 'Has someone else been here? When?'

A reflection of the pale green crystals flickered in the Wisdom's eyes.

'Long ago,' she said, in a voice as deep-reaching as the tunnels. 'Only one: a man who came here and tried to bury his crimes, thinking a seal on the mountain would keep them hidden. But a man cannot be so easily renewed.'

Klaus' heart raced, thoughts sprinting. Slightly breathless, he told her, 'I came to bear witness to the crimes of Ansovald Sturmsinger.'

She considered him so long that for a moment she seemed to disappear amongst the flickering crystals.

'Knowledge is a great burden,' she said at last. 'That is why ignorance is so comfortable.'

'I understand.'

'You don't. But you may come with me.'

42

Sedad and Serasu

NOT ONE OF HIS EALDORMEN WISHED TO FILL SUCH A VOID,
BUT AN EMPTY THRONE IS A BECKON TO MISCHIEF. FINALLY
THEY FORCED THE THRONE UPON HOUSE WINTERMANTEL,
THE FIRST VASSAL TO PLEDGE TO ANSOVALD STURMSINGER.

SONNONFER: THE STURMSINGER CHAIN

The Wisdom led him past rockpools and twisted pillars of crystal. She
moved lightly, a wisp of shadow, disturbing nothing. The cave narrowed
into a passage again. The rock underfoot formed a crude stairway, with
metal handholds along the walls. Others had indeed been here before.
Klaus felt the faint stirring of wind; there was an opening somewhere
close. After a while, during which he focused on where he put his feet
rather than his questions, the stairs opened into another cavern.

'Rest.' The Wisdom pointed to a sheepskin by a wall, and he was
too exhausted to resist.

When he awoke he had no way of knowing how much time had
passed, and whether it was day or night. A small fire crackled, a pot

bubbling over it unattended. He sat up feeling the worse for wear. A wide pool of shallow water trickled quietly into a crevice between the rocks at the back of the cave. He couldn't see the source that kept it filled. He refreshed himself with the ice-cold water, but the reappearance of the Wisdom from the depths of the cavern jogged him more sharply to his senses.

'I don't know your name,' he said. None of the Wisdoms had named themselves to him.

'Eat.'

The derina porridge in the pot filled him quickly. Klaus looked into his bowl.

'I began to doubt whether this spring ever existed. I thought perhaps the Scrolls had got that part wrong. The Derindin said derina grows towards the water, but there was no derina...'

'Little derina grows here. Not for lack of water, but because of the ore in the earth. It forms a salt that is too acidic for the tubers to thrive here.' The Wisdom cleaned the empty pot. 'The Derindin have become narrow-minded, unlike the enquirers who fathered them. *They* built devices that could interrogate the speech of the different species of particles that reside in matter, or translate wind currents into predictions of the earth's shaking long before the strike of a quake.'

Her words were loaded with contempt, and when she sat on a rock to survey him, he felt uncomfortably exposed to her disdain.

'You are further from your home than ever before,' she remarked.

Klaus opened his mouth to correct her and stopped. It was true; no matter how remotely he had travelled, he had never felt as far from his old life as he did now.

'I want to help Elendra destroy the pirates,' he began. 'The Eh Menishian –'

'First you must help yourself.' She pursed her lips. 'But you have the impatience of youth. What have you learned of the man they called Sturmsinger?'

He wasn't prepared for her question. 'The Sonnonfer is rich in praise of him. As for the Septentrional Scrolls, I don't know how reliable they are –'

'The Scrolls led you here, didn't they?' she interrupted. 'It follows they must contain at least a kernel of truth, however much the North has cursed them.'

'I suppose.' Even this admission summoned a bilious revulsion in Klaus' gut. 'Although the Scrolls said little of how Sturmsinger hid all this water ... another deathblow he dealt to the South.'

'Deathblow? No. The seal on this mountain was not one of his crimes.'

'Then why did Sturmsinger conceal the water in these caves?'

'To repay the terrible debt he incurred with his war.' The Wisdom looked through him. 'Every drop of blood shed from the Sterns to this mountain was spilled in his name. When he journeyed south to expand his new kingdom, his armies butchered whole cities of men and women without mercy; watered their land with blood and fertilised it with their ashes. It was on his order that the cursed dam was raised. By the time he knew remorse, his sins were too great to atone for in the short lifetime of man. Too many wronged, too many wounded.'

Klaus recoiled. 'He travelled south to eliminate any threat to Invelmar, not to "expand" it.'

The Wisdom's laugh raked talons through his Form. 'So has many a conqueror told himself before, to soothe the burden of his guilt.' Her eyes found Klaus again. 'But even a conqueror can be crushed by guilt – if he is fortunate. Sturmsinger *was* fortunate; he learned remorse. When Sturmsinger discovered these caves and the ore in the earth, he knew his Northern allies would massacre every Southerner living if necessary in order to possess them … generations more of war yet to come. So he placed a seal on this place until the balance in the Part was restored.'

Klaus leaned back against the damp rock. This time, his Form struggled *against* him, shrieking back everything he had ever known. Ansovald Sturmsinger was a rightful victor, unvanquished by men or mortal regrets; the beloved defender of the North. Victory was necessary to diffuse centuries of Northern wars. His conquests were crucial to safeguard his newborn peace in the North. For the sake of peace, compassion had never held him back.

Resist. More than a little doubt crept back.

'What kind of seal keeps such a treasure so well hidden, all this time?' *After all, I managed to find it.*

'Not a seal of locks and barricades. He sealed it with words: a vow, made with the Creator Himself. In his desperation, Sturmsinger struck a bargain with the Great Sentience.'

Klaus shivered. 'What did he promise?'

'To know that, you must ask a descendent of Sturmsinger.'

Now Form riled with contempt. *See? This is the reward for treachery: folly akin to madness.*

Klaus clung to the comfort of disbelief. 'Sturmsinger died heirless. His wife Dagmar and his children were slain by barbarians when he didn't return home to the Far North. His sword lies in shards in the Silfrenheim in Dunraven. None of his kin lived to claim it.'

'A lie,' she replied. 'He was killed, but not in battle. His Far Northern brethren did not betray him. His only two children became hunted by his own allies in the North, to end his line and his claim to the throne of Invelmar. So the queen he left in the Far North fled with his children;

disappeared into hiding. And so a branch of him lived on, preserved by the Great Sentience and guarded by secret-keepers – thanks to the bargain Sturmsinger made, though that bargain would become a blight on the bloodline of Sturmsinger.'

Klaus shook his head. His hands were shaking. 'He ended the bloodshed that plagued the North. He forged Invelmar from nothing. Why would his allies have wanted to deny him the throne?'

'Indeed, and yet how else could the Northern tribes of his alliance claw back power, had he been allowed to rule his new kingdom? How else, but to kill him?'

Klaus struggled through the Wisdom's blows.

'*But alas, he did not return to rule the kingdom he had made ... in honour of him the Sturmsinger Chain was created, and thus the Ealdormen of his armies swore by the Blood Pact, entrusted for all time with its preservation...*' He had recited those passages of the Sonnonfer all his life. The very suggestion that – *absurd, preposterous!*

But the Wisdom was as merciless and serene as silence itself. 'Sturmsinger was betrayed by his own allies, killed to end his claim to the throne. They knew their people would have wanted no one else crowned.'

'No.' He resisted her with every fibre of his Form. 'He was their marrow...'

'He was Far Northern by blood, who chose a Far Northern woman-of-the-hearth for his wife, and his allies never forgot that. He sent back word to halt the construction of the dam he had ordered, and his fate was sealed.'

Again, Klaus shook his head. But he had no proof that she was wrong. No one had ever claimed to know where exactly the father of Invelmar had died. His tomb had never been found.

'I told you truth is a great burden,' said the Wisdom. 'And it has many parts. But the rest, you must see for yourself.'

She pointed to a passage leading out of the cavern.

'There lies a tomb that has long awaited a visitor.'

Still reeling, Klaus got up and picked his way through rocks and rivulets, taking her lantern with him. The passage ascended to another rough stairway hewn into the rock. His mind boiled, his heart raced: was he about to find the resting place of Sturmsinger himself?

He couldn't say how long he climbed, such was the frenzy of his thoughts. Soon he emerged into a large, round cave.

A small lake filled the centre of the cave. A great rock rose from the middle of the lake. Something stood on the rock; *this must be the tomb*. He removed his boots and waded through the lake, the cold water biting his calves, and up the smooth steps to the tomb.

He stared down at the recumbent effigy over the tomb. An eruption of dizzying shock rooted him to the steps. There was indeed a monarch buried in the cave, but it was not Ansovald Sturmsinger.

*

'We march on Pir Sehem after the Romelian Assembly,' Arik announced. 'One last attempt to rally more clans to Sisoda's aid.'

Perhaps the timing wasn't so bad. Verdi's lessons with Fresmo had only just begun. The physician was crabby but excellent, and Verdi was keen to make a good impression – with the gnomon as well as his studies. *I'll show him I can do both.*

Now the prospect of returning to Romel summoned longing not just for his father, but the limolan tree. There would be another chance to open the Book of Oaths. Perhaps this time he would.

The air in Samsarra was different, and not because winter had retracted her claws to make way for a cautious spring. Preparations for the two-week-long journey west had kept the citadel continually on edge. Anxiety and anticipation were palpable in the streets and squares. Verdi knew this air; it was the breath of coming battle, sharp and metallic. But in the North, it had fanned much less fear in his heart.

They saw very little now of Thillaina, returning late to their rooms only to sleep. Once or twice they stayed in the tumblers' barracks; less suspicious than quitting her house altogether.

'There have been quarters for you in your great-aunt's house since the day you arrived,' Alizarin reminded Verdi unhelpfully, cornering him in the tavern where he and Arik spent most of their evenings. He raised one arm and his unbelievably well-mannered tigon stepped onto it, disappearing into his breast pocket. Ravi followed her every move; half curiosity, half grudging awe. 'Another Chieftainess might have been insulted at the snub.'

'A seamstress' rooms are good enough for me.'

Alizarin pulled up a chair. Verdi closed his book.

'If you're to take up this mantle, Viridian, you must behave like a noble.'

'I thought I'd left all that behind.'

He was testing his uncle's patience now, but he couldn't stop himself.

Alizarin didn't take the bait. 'I've not seen you studying the gnomon much.'

Admitting his progress with the moondial might get his uncle off his back, but the last thing Verdi wanted now was to share it. He shrugged. 'It's a moondial, it works by night. I'm hardly going to bring it to the tavern.'

'Whatever their loyalties, every Derindin from the Ostraad to Kastava's Point is waiting for a sign of Merensama.'

'I've already pledged to this clan, isn't that enough?'

Alizarin drummed the tabletop. 'The Assembly is almost upon us. It's a chance to unite the clans, to propose an alternative to the suzerains in the West. But no one's going to take us seriously if you've not at least taken the oath. We are speaking of war and famine, Viridian.'

How dare he suggest that I don't care! It was enough to set Verdi's teeth on edge. The glimpse he got of his future through Alizarin's eyes was suffocating – and far displaced from the tranquillity of the sanctuary where pilgrims gathered around the limolan tree.

But his uncle didn't stop there. He lowered his voice. 'You can't wait for him to come back and tell you what to do.'

Verdi's face was roasting now, as much with humiliation as with anger. But it was true; he *had* been waiting for Klaus.

I'll be waiting forever.

How could his uncle think so little of him?

Verdi's back straightened for the plunge. 'There's no point putting off the oath any longer, then.'

But his uncle was far from pleased.

'Signing the Book of Oaths isn't like pledging to a clan.' Alizarin seemed to grapple with himself for a moment. 'You will be the seal that stamps every treaty between clans, the one who people curse when the price of war bites. The wind in their sail. If you set yourself on this course only to abandon it...'

'You don't think I'm cut out for it.' Verdi's cheeks flared. 'Father was right, the whole idea is a sham.'

'Your *father* is filled with poison of his own,' Alizarin snapped.

They glared at each other.

Alizarin exhaled through his teeth. 'He tells you only what he wants you to know. Just like the Elders.'

Thrown at this concession, Verdi listened.

'Your mother wasn't the second coming of Lorendar, but she had a portion of his gift for truesight. Visions.' Alizarin looked away. Verdi held his breath, afraid he would stop. 'Her gifts warned her that the limolan seed she planted for you in Romel would be the last of its kind – that the land would never again sprout another limolan.'

A chill thawed Verdi's excitement. 'What does that mean?'

'It means your mother believed the path to Merensama would take a blood price from you,' said his uncle quietly. 'Lorendar swore to restore the limolan. If you commit yourself to fulfilling Lorendar's promise, his line will end with you. The limolan will steal your life.'

The world came to a halt. The tavern disappeared around them.

'She couldn't rejoice with everyone else when the limolan seed sprouted. She wanted nothing more than your safety – why else would she wish you to be sent away, denied a great destiny?'

Bruising. This was a bruising shock. He'd always assumed it had been Alizarin or his great-aunt who'd sent him North.

'But why did she believe that? Did she tell you what she saw?'

'No.'

Verdi slumped back in his chair, too tired to feel bitter or betrayed. 'Do the Elders know this?'

'Yes.'

A small furry ball appeared on Verdi's forearm; Ravi, nuzzling his wrist.

'I did not wish to call you back from the North.' Alizarin's words were barely audible over the roaring in Verdi's ears. 'Many have prayed for your return, but I would that you have the freedom your mother wanted for you. If she had lived, she would have banished you forever.'

'Was she ... certain?' Verdi hadn't imbibed the superstitions of the South. But he imagined his mother, sick and alone, her arms newly filled with a helpless creature, having to rewrite his fate with her gift.

'I never had the chance to ask. But as Derinda celebrated her seedling, she mourned.'

Silence stretched between them. Sometimes truth had an odd way of unravelling gently, when least expected. Merensama had softly usurped Verdi's heart – but it had been safely in the distance.

It loomed much closer now.

'You should have told me sooner.'

'That would have also robbed you of the freedom to choose.' Alizarin became a fortress again. 'Who are we to believe we know the future? If there's any mercy in the world, we can appeal against destiny itself. I would have held my tongue, but I had to honour the promise I made to my sister. She would have wanted you to know the price of this path.'

'You don't believe her vision, then?'

Alizarin stood. 'What I believe doesn't matter. The rift between the clans will never close until we atone for the violations of Obsidian Lorendar.' Unexpectedly, Alizarin squeezed his shoulder. 'I fear your task will be much greater than the Elders imagined.'

Verdi felt the weight of his hand for a long time after he departed.

*

Klaus stared at the effigy on the tomb.

It was cast in pure gold, chiselled with exquisite detail. The features were unmistakable: high forehead over rounded eyes, straight hair, long nose. In life, he was certain the darkness of the hair and those eyes would have been borrowed of night. It could have been Gainshe's face.

The woman buried in the tomb was Eh Menishian.

He raised his lantern. The cavern was hung with reliefs and writings: a geometric alphabet not dissimilar to the markings on Krevkatt's tablets. He saw soldiers wearing black-painted Eh Menishian helmets, and kaftans adorned with feathers and scales. Around them swarmed beasts he couldn't name, and long ships sailing behind them. And beside a likeness of the buried Eh Menishian woman, now crowned and carrying a sceptre in her hand, was the carving of a Northerner: armoured and far taller than she, boasting a six-petalled starblossom on his breast.

'This is where Sturmsinger buried Sefta,' came the Wisdom's voice from the edge of the lake. 'The Eh Menishian queen who landed on our shores fleeing war and who smelted his iron heart.'

Klaus barely noticed the freezing water now. He walked around the cave, following the story etched into its walls. Even without the Wisdom's quiet narration, he deciphered most of it for himself.

Here was Sturmsinger, rampaging through the Silfren Part, offering Sefta and her people refuge in the Southern citadel he had conquered. The Eh Menishian queen kneeling before him, ensnaring him with her beauty as she pleaded for clemency. The handfastening ceremony in which he had taken her for his second wife. Sturmsinger, the penitent king, defeated by this woman even as his armies began building the Ostraad far away in the North.

And here ... the army of Northerners that would take him captive. A river swollen with corpses, both Southern and Eh Menishian, Sefta amongst them. A royal funeral procession for a murdered queen.

The lantern shook in Klaus' hand. Many more chapters awaited – but there was no sign of the warrior king's fate after his betrayal by the North.

'This is why the Eh Menishian are here,' he breathed. 'They remembered this land.'

They certainly remembered Sturmsinger's discovery of a sacred rock between the mountains.

Klaus returned to the scene of Sefta's death. Eh Menishian fell under the longswords of tall broad-shouldered Northerners; Northerners sent by the other five tribes of Sturmsinger's alliance. *By the Ealdormen.*

'Yes, here they are,' said the Wisdom. 'The first Ealdormen. Sent to kill Sturmsinger and his army, once his invasion of the South was complete.'

Along with the new ally they found at his side. Klaus traced the starblossom on a broken breastplate. 'And now the Eh Menishian have returned to seek Sturmsinger's rock.'

Dread chilled his marrow.

The pirates were cruel, but they were scattered outcasts; challenging but not indomitable. But the Eh Menishian – skilled descendants of an imperial force, wronged and vengeful, cruel as the masters of the pirate stronghold…

And yet he couldn't help but feel the sorrow sleeping in the cave for Sefta's plight.

'Where do the Eh Menishian come from?'

'We know only why they came to this Part,' said the Wisdom. 'They were driven out of a southern land that they had themselves conquered centuries before.'

And before that?

Klaus longed to see Gainshe now. *'Where I come from, nothing is too high to reach. Or too deep.'*

The pirates were seeking a skydisc, a celestial map. Klaus had assumed this would encode the location of these caves, this wealth of water. To the Derindin, water would be a treasure indeed, but the Eh Menishian? Had they really come all this way just for a mine?

And yet Sturmsinger himself had been bewitched by the land here, before he met Sefta. Perhaps the ore he'd found *could* yield a metal as valuable as the sacred steel of the North. *And perhaps the Eh Menishian believe that.* Avarice was a powerful spell indeed.

Klaus waded further around the lake. A breeze sent ripples across the water. He found more tombs, set back from the water's edge: warriors guarding Sefta in death, Eh Menishian and Northerners alike. Sturmsinger's warriors, bearing his six-petalled starblossom.

But Sturmsinger wasn't buried with her.

Klaus craned his neck; the ceiling vanished into darkness. Something else was carved high into the cave's walls: High Invelmen letters, the height of a Northerner, as familiar as the lines of his palm: *'Cometh the fall of the kingdom of destruction made if its fate is bartered for blood…'* The oath that had anointed every prayer Klaus had ever made, cushioned every sacrifice and bandaged the cracks in his conscience. *'To the dead we are bound and by our grace are the dead repaid.'*

'But they kept this.' Anger warmed his freezing calves. The Ealdormen had kept his Blood Pact. The only part of Sturmsinger they didn't dare erase, lest their new kingdom fall around them.

'Even the corrupted heart may recognise truth, before it buries it away.'

Klaus fingered a tablet of flowing script resembling the inscription at Ilaria. 'Orenthian?'

'Early Orenthian, predating the First Redrawing.' The breeze tossed the Wisdom's voice around the cave. 'This place is much older than Sefta and Sturmsinger. Orenthians passed down the safekeeping of this cave to locals before the First Redrawing.'

A thrill ran down Klaus' spine. 'Did Sturmsinger take the mountain from Southerners?'

'Not by force, but by cunning. Sturmsinger was shrewd; he feared his allies may betray him once he ordered the building of his dam to be halted. He smelled treachery even before his murderers arrived under the pretence of bolstering his forces.' The Wisdom drifted away from the lake. 'He saw that the people of this mountain had guarded it for centuries. So he asked them to guard his secret here, in exchange for sparing their lives.'

The Wisdom stepped out of the light; Klaus shifted his lantern just in time to see her vanish into a passage. He hurried after her, wondering how she managed to see in the dark. *Perhaps she senses the passageways and the past as I sense the land.* The breeze grew stronger, and within moments he stepped out through an opening in the mountainside…

He stopped, astonished. Dawn hovered on the horizon, and ghosts of stars glimmered in blushing sky. They were standing on a ledge high on the southern face of the mountain. From here he could see – and feel – the crescent shape of the mountains, its concavity facing south. The Mengorian range towered in the west to his right, while the smaller eastern Ilmaz range lay to his left. The ruins of two citadels clung to the southern face of each range, built into the mountains. Great mounds of rubble marked where both citadels had tumbled down to earth.

'Look upon the remains of the twin cities of Sedad and Serasu,' said the Wisdom. 'They were the eyes of the mountain, once. It was to the eyes of the mountain that Sturmsinger entrusted the cave.'

'What happened to them?'

'They fell into decay. The people of Sedad and Serasu cut down every tree for grassland to feed their cattle, and the hooves of their horses churned the ground to dust. When there was finally no more forest to protect the mountains, a great storm swept in from the sea and crushed them. They thought themselves safe in their towers in the sky.' The Wisdom's contempt was scalding. 'But they kept their oath to Sturmsinger until they fell … perhaps the only saving grace of Sedad and Serasu.'

Klaus sat on the ledge. His head grew light, and not with the thinness of the air. Ahead of him the Plains stretched south. To the south-east, he thought he could see the ancient riverbed where the Ninvellyn once ran down to the sea, before Sturmsinger throttled it with his dam. He closed his eyes and beckoned forward, reaching for the shore, but he was exhausted in mind and flesh, and couldn't grasp the beyond.

He abandoned his efforts to wonder instead. Dawn spilled into the world, gilding the morning. He leaned back against the brow of the mountain and fell asleep between its eyes.

43

The Final Wisdom

HEEDFUL OF THEIR LIEGE LORD'S WARNING, THEY STAYED TRUE
TO HIS BLOOD PACT. THEY SERVED WITH HIGHEST FIDELITY,
AS YOU MUST NOW, O INVELMARI. AND THEY DECREED THAT
EVERY ONE OF YOUR SONS BELONGS TO THE CROWN.

SONNONFER: THE STURMSINGER CHAIN

Without meaning to, Alizarin once again found himself at Thillaina's door.

He felt as lost as he'd been that first night he had come here, though this time he had not the raw grief of Yirma's death.

All these years, in spite of himself, he'd been clinging to one enduring hope; a boyish vision, a sage's words. Yet he knew now that Viridian was not the one who would die twice.

In a few days they would leave for Romel where Viridian might yet sign his name in the Book of Oaths, delivering the future Yirma had sought to prevent. How could he betray his sister?

And then there was Klaus.

Surely that had been a matter of unhappy chance.

He found the old widow alone in her parlour by the fire, nursing a fruity cough and a streaming nose. The maid was also coughing in her bed. The errand boy who let him in was off home with his week's wages.

Thillaina seemed thinner wrapped in a heavy shawl, and her usually sharp gaze was in want of whetting. 'Such attentiveness to an old woman.'

'Why did you send Viridian to the house of the Wintermantels?'

'This again,' she grumbled. 'You asked me this question only the other night.'

'And you never gave me an answer.'

'What makes you think there was much choice in the matter?'

Alizarin sat down. 'I don't believe you've ever lied to me before now. Concealed much, but never an outright lie.'

He was toeing a dangerous line. But Alizarin knew he was close.

'I've never lied to you.' She blew a red nose. 'There *was* a Derindin settler in Dunraven who agreed to take your nephew in. A horse trainer, of good standing. But his master was in search of a companion for another child close in age, and offered the best education and a good living. His master wrote to me himself with many assurances that there would be no better place in Invelmar for your nephew.'

'His master?'

'The man who was in the employ of the Wintermantels, when their boy was still an only child of two. A man called Florian Arnander.'

*

The smokeleaf was intoxicating. This particular blend was a rare import from Tungstaa. Adela was a little too fond of the stuff. Every few weeks now, Klaus was summoned to her chambers and deftly dissected. It was the only time he took smoke, hoping it would lend him the appearance of ease.

'You understand, don't you, Ulfriklaus, why it is better this way?'

She had a way of looking lazily at things even as she stripped them to their bones. He wasn't fooled by the soft heather of her half-gaze through the smoke. He knew the briars of the blackberry eyes waiting beyond.

'I wish to serve however I must.' He had to reach very far into Afldalr for this.

She smiled slightly. 'They have trained you well, my dear. I would never have known how deeply you've mourned my orders had I not been told otherwise.'

He bowed low, an Ealdorman's bow to his Queen.

'I hope you shall forgive us in time, Ulfriklaus.' He had always admired her ability to disarm with apparent sincerity. Adela needed no one's forgiveness. 'You would have been wasted in the judiciary. You were born wearing an

Intelligencer's mask. But you have a good heart. That is why you are drawn to the dispensing of justice.'

'I am,' he confessed, because it was useful to garnish his performance with just the hint of vulnerability.

'It loses its appeal quickly. In the end, you would have found it a terrible incumbrance. Far better you followed in your father's footsteps. That is why you will join the Eye.'

He started inwardly, deep within the confines of his Form.

'You bestow upon me the greatest honour, my Queen. But I've not yet completed my training. Isn't it too soon?'

'Florian doesn't think so.'

Adela exhaled a wandering stream of smoke.

'Ahh, Ulfriklaus. So many of my Intelligencers die in service much too soon … alas, I fear one day the Eye of the Court shall become blind. But it is necessary. We could take what we seek with steel, but soldiers trample all over the true treasures of this world. They do not know how to guard themselves from scrutiny. So I must take what I want with stealth, and hence lose Intelligencers like the passing days.' She gazed over the citadel below with genuine regret, but it was packaged in unhesitating resolve. 'It is necessary, my dear … some secrets are too great to be shared.'

Klaus awoke with a start from deepest sleep. Sweat coated his skin, and his heart jumped loudly under his ribs.

'When did the dreams begin to plague you?'

The Wisdom was tending a small fire. He hadn't seen her eat, or drink, or rest.

'I was a child at the time. Perhaps eight.'

She handed him a cup of a hot liquid. It smelled savoury.

'There is something you keep in your heart with a door that is closed. So long as this is shut, you will neither be free of the dreams, nor will you awaken the senses you need to gain the Unseen World.'

When he realised she meant Afldalr, he was filled with horror at the thought of ever having to be without it. Averting a reply, Klaus tasted the soup. It was good, but he had little appetite and set it down

Absolute silence stretched behind the gentle flicker of flames and the soft whistle of a thin mountain breeze. The quiet of the desert held a magnifying glass over his thoughts, drawing them out of him, making their torment inescapable.

The Ealdorman betrayed Sturmsinger. Invelmar was raised on lies, the Blood Pact looted and exploited.

'It isn't too late to turn back,' said the Wisdom.

But it was already too late. She had been right; this truth was a great burden indeed.

His heart hammered. 'You are the mirror I was promised.'

The Wisdom nodded. 'Have you chosen your road from here?'

The road home, his heart cried. *The road to my real parents!* Not even Afldalr had vanquished the ache to discover how he had arrived in the lap of the Wintermantels. But he had seen the heart of the caves, and assassins were seeking Verdi, who was still surrounded by puppet-masters in Samsarra. Once again, he needed to recalibrate his course.

The Wisdom watched him keenly, and again Klaus feared she skewered his very thoughts. 'The heart must be whole if it is to nurture a connection with the land.'

Klaus shivered, recalling that severance of his bond with the desert in the camp. 'I know.'

You could stay here, a voice whispered. *You have been freed of the Sturmsinger Chain.* Still smarting with the Ealdormen's betrayal, perhaps he was now ready to be free even of the Blood Pact. Childish dreams of roaming the Parts on voyages of delight and discovery would be poor sustenance now.

Klaus rose to look down over the Plains from the mouth of the cave. Somewhere to the east, the Eh Menishian still enslaved hundreds of Derindin. Pirates were holding and harrying many more elsewhere. Wild tribes gnawed Invelmar from the Far North, Adela's iron rule stifled the North, and shanty towns starved in the shadow of the Paiva. But here, he could finally disappear.

He turned back to the Wisdom. 'I would be content to stay here and learn whatever you teach me.'

She frowned. 'That is not your path.'

'When I left Invelmar, I had hoped...' Words choked around a painful lump in his throat. Now his heart was an eel, slipping from every attempt to grasp it. 'I used to have so many dreams.'

The mirror tilted. 'You wished to become something more,' she said. 'Not even the North gave you this. You longed to travel in search of the unknown, but had you roamed to the edges of the earth, you would not have found what you sought.'

'What do I seek?'

'The Unseen World that waits beyond the Veil – greater, undying. You wished for a road without end, Master Invelmari. Yet all things are finite in this realm – except for ilnurhin. That alone is borrowed from the Unseen World, boarding in the fifth chamber of the sound heart. And the sound heart is the looking glass into that undying world beyond.'

A road without end. Every needle of his being aligned in perfect symmetry to this.

Her words filled the vessel of night, once again swollen into a sea without shore in which he would have happily drowned. The land filled his mind unsummoned. *Come with me.* It flowered into the collective consciousness of every crumb of earth, every pebble and grain of dust, mingling with each particle of life sleeping in its womb. *Come with me.*

His voice sounded as though from a distance. 'I would pass through the doorway tonight if that world is where it will take me.'

The Wisdom frowned. 'You would choose death? While there is work to be done here? No. There are many paths through the Veil, but an idle death is not one of them. The Unseen World must be earned, and it has loaned you a great gift to use to that end, not squander.' Now she was stern. Perhaps it was a trick of the low light, but the contours of her shimmered. 'A gift not bestowed upon any other for moons beyond counting, not since the last Simyerin. The Simyerin harnessed slight matter to serve the land. If you wish to gain the gifts of the Unseen World, you too must serve in the realm of the living.'

'I know nothing about the Simyerin,' he said, feeling terribly foolish. 'I wasn't taught anything about the Lost Sciences or Orenthia –'

'Do you think scholarship is how you stirred slight matter?' The Wisdom shook her head. 'The Part has seen hundreds of scholars come and go. Most of them too clouded by the trappings of this world to truly know it, let alone cross into the Unseen World. *This* realm is all they see – the world of touch and feel and taste. True knowledge of the worlds resides in the fifth chamber, and it can only be opened with soundness of heart. There are no books or scrolls that will teach you this.'

'What must I do to gain the Unseen World?'

Now the Wisdom's skin was smoother, her eyes warmer. 'I can merely show you what you are now. Once you have resolved your self, you can build your own bridges there.'

The thought of knowing what the Wisdom saw in him was terrifying. Pulse galloping in his neck, Klaus nodded.

'You thought you were special. Gifted, strong, lettered – you believed these things would arm you for anything, even all the roads of the world. Vanity is an insidious disease.'

He quelled the indignant swell of his ego. In Invelmar, he had become invincible.

'What else?'

'Have you accepted now that you will not be known?'

I never wanted to be king. Was that not so? But hidden in Afldalr was an ugly truth ripened by the hardships of the desert. It ought to have been much easier to part from the crown he had been promised. *Of course I wanted to be king. And they took that from me.*

Bitterness gazed back at him in the mirror.

'Entitlement is the crutch of vanity,' said the Wisdom. 'The prestige you expected would have crowned you with shadow.'

Warm with shame, he nodded. 'I will begin here.'

'But you cannot stay in this cave. Humility is forged in full sight of the living.'

'What about the Eh Menishian? They may yet dig their way into this mountain and find it, just as I did.'

'I told you, it is protected by the oath Sturmsinger swore. How else do you think it has been safe for a thousand years? It is only open to all those who serve the way of Sturmsinger.'

Klaus shook his head. 'I left that path in Invelmar.'

'Your mother has not.'

He stared at the Wisdom. Time stumbled.

My mother!

'You were only able to enter the mountain because your parents are amongst the last of Sturmsinger's secret-keepers, like the Southern guardians who once preserved this cave. Now only his secret-keepers know that any of his descendants survived.'

'Then have my parents been here too?'

'No, but the truth was carried North – though very few survive who remember it. And you were turned out of your birth cradle because your parents feared their secret had been discovered.'

He was trembling now. 'Did *they* give me away?'

'To protect you from their fate: a lifetime of being hunted by those trying to bury the past.'

Was she beginning to fade at the edges?

'Are they still alive?'

'Yes.'

The heart threatened to beat its way out of him. 'Do you know where...?'

'A place that would take you far indeed from the road you have chosen.'

Klaus closed his eyes. *Of course.*

So he was always going to be a fugitive.

This fork in the road was more than he could bear.

The Wisdom waited. It was the longest moment in his life.

'I have to get back to Samsarra.'

When he blinked tears away, the Wisdom was smiling. 'If you wish to return, time is short. Your friend will need your sight.'

Her voice had definitely thinned. Klaus feared she would vanish altogether.

'I can't harness slight matter alone.'

But her smile bloomed. 'Patience, Master Northman. I did not believe such a vessel for ilnurhin could be fashioned once again by this world, and I am glad I was mistaken.'

She put the soup in his hands again and made him drink it. It expanded his belly, leaving him comfortably full. His eyelids grew heavy; his tongue leaden.

'After you've served your friend, go to the market town they call Tiptoe that lies at the foot of the Paiva.' Her voice ribboned with the breeze. 'Follow my token. She is sure of wing. She will show you your mother.'

My mother!

Hope thrashed against exhaustion, clamouring for a foothold.

You know where I came from. Tell me about my parents! Tell me my name!

He succumbed to her dram.

When he awoke, midday sunlight filled the mouth of the cave. At first, he thought he'd fallen into another dream. But the Wisdom's lantern still flickered in the cave. He bolted upright.

There was no sign of the Wisdom, and he sensed this time he was alone.

His heart pattered on clumsy feet. *There will be a road to my mother.*

What was the Wisdom's token, and when would he find it?

'*Patience, Master Northman.*'

Whatever had been in that soup, his aches had vanished. Klaus picked up the lantern and returned into Sefta's cave, circling the lake again. Now that the Wisdom had gone, a thousand questions exploded in his mind.

Beyond Sefta's tomb, he found more Orenthian treasures from a time before the First Redrawing. Alcoves hid capsules and scrolls, some ruined by the damp air. There were etchings and enamelled reliefs of fantastical towers and gardens and domes, birds of every kind, blueprints of machinery, detailed star charts – a civilisation he could scarcely believe ever existed in this southern reach of the Silfren Part. A lifetime of discovery awaited. He could stay right here and explore that lost world, safe from the Wintermantels at last.

What about the living?

Klaus spotted a crude map of the Seven Parts, depicting a trail of longboats crossing the North Zmerrudi Sea to alight on the southern shores of the Silfren Part … he frowned. He had never seen the like of the Eh Menishian in the Zmerrudi Part. Who had driven them away, and from which Part? Where had they next made their home, after escaping these shores?

The oil in the lantern was dwindling. The walk back out of the mountain would take several hours, and then he would be once again at the mercy of the desert. Klaus returned to the cave mouth to gaze down across the Plains, and upon Sedad and Serasu. There was no sign of life on the dunes and the rocks below, but something fluttered softly to his right.

He threw himself back into the cave.

A grey-spotted white peregrine landed on the ledge, majestic and as tall as his forearm was long. She cocked her head to gaze directly at him: the Wisdom's token, stern as the Hermit herself.

'Hello,' he said quietly.

The peregrine half-spread her wings and settled them again, eager to depart.

But still he didn't want to leave. He returned to Sefta's cave and waded into the lake. He sat beside the tomb and studied Sefta's golden face, and imagined. How must it have been for Ansovald, flushed with the success of his victory only to be conquered by this queen who had bewitched him…? The sledgehammer of remorse that had moved him to halt the building of the Ostraad dam; the treachery of his allies in the North. The desperation in which he had promised the Lifegiver to repay his debt. What had Sturmsinger promised?

Klaus trailed his fingers along the tomb. Its smooth stone became irregular beneath the surface of the water. He felt again: letters, each filling the span of his hand. An inscription was engraved all the way around the tomb, submerged in the lake.

He shivered in excitement: *these* letters were High Invelmen. He traced them with freezing fingers. It took several turns around the tomb to decipher the inscription:

· WITHOUT HER I AM A SHIP SAILING THE STARLESS NIGHT ·
THE STORM HAS PASSED BUT IN DARKNESS I AM FOREVER
DROWNED AND LONGING IS MY ONLY MOORING ·

An unspeakable ache came over him.

He knew then with certainty that Sturmsinger had not died with his queen. He had been alive to bury her. Who else would have imparted such anguish so lovingly onto her tomb?

His eyes fell on the buckle of Sefta's belt. It was the only part of her effigy cast not in gold but in iron, shaped oddly like a large, spoked wheel. He touched the circle and nearly jumped when it turned with a gentle click; first clockwise, then anticlockwise, and clockwise again, rising slightly with each turn until it came away altogether in his hand.

Klaus brought the lantern closer. A flat round piece of metal lay in a hollow over Sefta's womb. Carefully, he teased it out and looked down at the skydisc.

So this was what the caves guarded.

It was bigger than his palm. The markings upon it were too small to see in the dwindling light. What did they encode that was so valuable that the Eh Menishian were trawling the desert for this skydisc? *He placed it in her tomb.* So its secrets were likely Sturmsinger's, and not Sefta's. What did Sturmsinger possess that the Eh Menishian might now want?

His stolen kingdom, near indomitable... His steel; well, they were trying their luck with this southern ore. His Form... Klaus froze. *His Form.*

'*A cloak cut from darkness, that he purchased from shadow and donned to blot out the light.*'

He had banished that troubling passage from the Septentrional Scrolls into Afldalr. There, it couldn't torment him with a growing fear: that Sturmsinger had created Form through monstrous means ... Form animated by a far more sinister mechanism than rigorous training.

Was Form part of the bargain that Sturmsinger had struck with the Great Sentience?

Shivering now, Klaus pocketed the skydisc. He replaced the iron buckle over the compartment in Sefta's effigy before wading out of the lake on numb legs. He looked back at her tomb one last time; a small island of grief. As though she knew he was leaving, the peregrine fluttered into the cavern like a great pale moth in the dark.

Klaus rubbed his legs until the blood returned to his feet. He tipped water out of his boots and began the long walk back to where he hoped his horse was still waiting.

44

The Poet of Rogues

THE EALDORMAN LAID DOWN THE LAWS OF THEIR SUCCESSION,
LORD STURMSINGER'S BLOOD PACT IMMORTAL IN THEIR HEARTS.
EACH HOUSE MUST FOR THREE GENERATIONS UPON STURMSINGER'S
THRONE REIGN, TURNING AN UNBROKEN CHAIN TO PRESERVE
STURMSINGER'S SACRED PEACE.

SONNONFER: THE STURMSINGER CHAIN

It was hours before Klaus reached his horse. The return was more challenging, as though the Wisdom's absence deepened the darkness. He remained orientated only by constantly probing the earth, and at times the white shadow of the peregrine alighting on rocks ahead was all that distinguished his path from a deep crevice or still water. Though it was almost night when they were reunited, his horse was restless and wouldn't settle.

Klaus stroked her nose. 'We're better off waiting until morning. I'm tired. It'll be no good if I sprain an ankle or you throw a shoe on those rocks.'

But her impatience was catching, making him just as anxious to be gone, and it was barely false dawn when he saddled her, unable to wait any longer.

Here was the difficult part. Did he go north-west into Baeronian territory, and then pursue a longer route east to Samsarra through less arid terrain? Or should he retrace his footsteps eastward back towards the Eh Menishian camp but gain the shorter road through Fraivon's land?

Instinct tugged him towards the latter, though it would bring him dangerously close to the camp. He filled his water skins and left the safety of the mountain for a slightly north-eastern road.

For three-and-a-half days, he saw nothing but cottonwood trees and dry shrubs, and even a thin bush of derina that provided welcome nourishment. He ate it raw. What would the Derindin have done, without this defiant crop?

It should have been a long and lonely road. Thoughts full of his hours with the Hermit, it was far from it. How many of the Ealdormen knew of Sturmsinger's fate? Had the Wintermantels known that Klaus' parents were amongst Sturmsinger's secret-keepers, when they had chosen Klaus to raise as their own? Had he been forcibly taken from his family, or offered? He tried to imagine his parents, weary with living in fear of discovery, wishing for him a life free of the burden of truth.

Or perhaps Lord Wintermantel had deliberately chosen Klaus, hoping to use him as a lure to draw out Sturmsinger's secret-keepers. *That's what an Intelligencer would do.* Soon he might be finally free to trace his mother to Tiptoe and find out.

But not yet. Not while slaves toiled in the camp and the Eh Menishian planned a slow erosion of the desert, and pirates roamed free to reach again for Lorendar's heir.

Two weeks passed like prayer beads through the fingers. He would have longed to share this quiet road with Nerisen. He rode more by night than day, honing his ability to navigate the desert in darkness, and saw no pirates. Derina and waterholes cropped up more often as he neared Fraivon's clandom. And then, when Fraivon's south-eastern boundary was perhaps within another day's ride, he caught the glint of sun on steel in the east, and a cloud of dust appeared on the horizon that grew larger however fast he rode.

Pirates. Eh Menishian.

They probably had eyescopes, spotting him from afar. And this time he had no bow.

Heart sinking, Klaus brought his mare to a halt. They'd had little rest and nothing but derina for days. But there was no point trying to outrun them now. He chose his position behind a great dune amongst the rocks and waited to meet them.

*

Fera was old enough to remember being allowed to play in the dunes around her village late into the evening, when the sun wept coral tears on the sand and countless little scuttling night-creatures awoke amongst the rocks. But for two summers now her brother was sent to fetch her indoors hours before sundown, like all the other children. Since the pirates had started coming, no one could boast of being allowed out beyond their bedtime, and woe betide those who snuck out anyway.

She even knew a boy who was taken, a few months ago. His mother's eyes were still often red with weeping. The whole village had trawled the desert for days looking for him, even as far out as Ahravel. Each night they'd return empty-handed. She'd stopped protesting the daily homeward march after that.

But for now, it was still early enough for a game of slaves and pirates, and she was hiding from a bandit who was sure to sell her at Baeron's slave markets. Her brother claimed slavery was outlawed by all the clans, but the captives had to go *somewhere* if their bodies were never found, and she was sure he was wrong.

The dunes were always shifting, and here so far south where the rocky ground dipped this way and that like the shrivelled skin of a dried derina tuber, the hiding places changed each day depending on the wind. Fera could hear pirates shouting nearby as they found another victim. Finding a good spot between some rocks and a sandhill, she settled in the shade and waited.

Soon their voices moved further away, not closer, and a grin spread across her face. The last slave to be found walked free and got to skewer a pirate with great ceremony and took their evening's share of sweet-meats besides; that was the deal. Moments passed. It was colder than when they'd started their game. The shadows of the boulders over her hiding hole loomed longer on the sand. Her eyelids grew heavy.

When she came to, she was immediately afraid, for it was almost twilight and she had never been out here alone so late before, not even before the pirate raids had begun.

Quietly, she crept out from her nest between the rocks. All around were waking stars and the gentle hooting of the wind. Little legs hurried. The scuttlers became fierce scratchers; the dunes and rocks and sand-mounds became the shoulders of giant daysleepers bearing vicious clubs.

'Reman!' Surely by now her brother or the other children would have noticed she was gone. Might they have given up the search already?

'Reman!'

A noise came; a horse. Her heart clapped in relief – Reman and her father would come. Wait – it came not from the hamlet but from the opposite direction, away from the village, where they were never to go. Then the sound took form: a yellow horse with a big dark shape on its back –

Fera didn't wait. She turned, stumbling on stones her feet normally knew without looking, and ran wildly towards the village. And then she gave a great big sob of relief, for that *was* father on his black stallion riding towards her with their dog Bral at his side. There were several men with him carrying lanterns and Reman looking very shaken. Her father shouted; Fera couldn't make out the words through her tears. He dismounted and scooped her up, hugging her tightly as he bellowed, but she didn't care.

'Go back, Father,' she sobbed. 'Before they get here –'

'What are you jabbering about, child?' He frowned, then stiffened. 'Reman, take your sister home. Bolt the doors and tell the villagers to go to the bunkers –'

But he stopped short as a *thud* sounded behind them. The men turned with raised spears, her friend Malina's father's sword drawn (he had been a tumbler once). Fera watched fearfully from the clutch of Reman's arms as they lowered their weapons in astonishment.

'Is he alive?'

'Seems to be...'

Uncle Osringen uttered a word she wasn't to say. 'Why, that's the Invelmari chronicler!'

He knelt down beside the man who had fallen from his horse. She craned her neck; he was the tallest man she had ever seen, and his head was more gold than brown. His eyes were closed and he was very pale. The flanks of his yellow mare had dark stains that ran to her hooves, and she looked not much better than her master.

Uncle Osringen looked up. 'He needs a physician.'

'There'll be no one now but Kaska on the way to Ahravel.'

'That'll take too long.'

Her father glanced up at the sky warily. 'It's almost night.'

Uncle Osringen stood. 'This man saved my hide and downed every other pirate who raided Alizarin Selamanden's caravan into Romel. I'll take him to Kaska alone in the dark if I have to.'

Fera gasped. It was the first thing everyone learned – *never go into the desert at night!* – but Uncle Osringen was determined, and after a row, two others agreed to go with him with lanterns to light the way. First, they carried the unconscious man to the village. Her mother screamed at the sight of her and pulled her from Reman's arms, and Fera's eyes filled again with quiet tears and her body trembled from head to foot.

'Look!' Reman pointed to the sky.

A great spotted bird circled over their heads, uttering a long piercing cry that raised the hair on Fera's arms.

'Take her inside, Lenat,' she heard Father tell Mother. 'She's falling asleep on her feet.'

But Fera wasn't too sleepy to see the young woman tearing into the village on her dun mare; a raven-haired woman with a sleek black panfarthing at her throat. She rode straight to the men who were lowering the unconscious man to the ground. Then Mother insisted on going inside and grew cross at Fera's protests, and she followed meekly or else risk a sore ear. The last thing Fera saw was the woman tumbling down from her horse to check the strange man with fierce eyes and frantic hands.

*

Tristan stirred with a groan. He rose on one elbow, opening unfocused eyes. The tawny hair Nerisen had shorn before they had parted had regrown and was thick with dried blood.

Relief made her voice quaver. 'Lie back.'

His eyes latched onto her in recognition. There was a wildness about them.

'Nerisen,' he whispered hoarsely. He licked his lips and fell back.

A villager brought a flask of water; he gulped at it once. They helped him into a house where a warm hearth drove out most of the cold. One of the men returned with a midwife who looked old enough to have birthed every child in the Plains.

She shooed away everyone but the master of the house, Khandal, and his wife, before she looked over Tristan. 'He'll be well enough.'

'He's not spoken more than three words together and he's covered in blood,' said Khandal doubtfully.

'Most of it not his own, it seems. Let him rest. And fetch me more water.'

But Tristan shook his head. 'I have to get back to Samsarra.'

Nerisen was aghast. 'Are you mad? You're not fit to sit on a horse, and it's a fortnight's ride even by the fastest road.'

He was growing more lucid by the minute. 'There are things the council needs to know, urgently –'

'You'll have to wait. Pirates are on the brink of taking Pir Sehem. When I left Romel, the Eastern alliance was preparing to drive them off … I don't know when, I left Samsarra before the news came from Sisoda – Elendra will probably make their bid at the Assembly –'

He gripped her arm. 'When's the next new moon?'

Within moments he was outside, looking for his horse.

'Tristan, really –'

'The pirates are just puppets, Nerisen. They have masters who are far more dangerous than they and who've no love for any of us, neither your people nor mine.'

Around them, the villagers gaped. Nerisen stared at the Northman. Always so sure and so profoundly in control of himself, his agitation now shook her.

Khandal led a dark stallion out of his stable. 'Take this one. Your mare needs a good rest, much like you. But I see you won't be stopped.'

Still shaken, Nerisen helped Lenat refill their saddlebags and waterskins. A makeshift package was tied to Tristan's saddlebag, wrapped in rags stiff with a dark stain – was that blood? The hair rose on her arms. The villagers urged them to wait until morning. A peregrine's shrill cry cut through the twilight, silencing their warnings. Nerisen looked up but saw only the pale smudge of great wings against the dusk.

'I brought your compass.' She returned it to Tristan, though there was little light left to see by. He didn't open the golden case.

Nerisen's mare pawed the ground nervously, unaccustomed to riding blind. Night was now pitch black and mercilessly infinite; a menacing bowel waiting to ingest them.

Tristan mounted the stallion. 'Stay close.'

Close she stayed, following him on the wings of night.

*

Emra arrived in Romel a few nights shy of the new moon marking the Assembly. The citadel swelled with arrivals and anticipation, inhaling long and slow before the great roar that was sure to follow. Half-uttered fear stumbled through the streets, fuelled by facts and rumours alike. Not here in the sanctuary of the limolan, where a handful of worshippers knelt in prayer in the temple below.

'None of us wanted a battle,' Emra told Navein. 'I don't hold your resistance against you.'

'Resistance? Two thousand of my tumblers will leave Yesmehen tomorrow. Meanwhile, Viridian's name is still missing from the Book of Oaths. I hear he is now dispensing medicines around Samsarra like an errand boy.'

'That is where his heart is.' They spoke quietly. They were alone on the balcony leading up to the stargazers' tower, but their voices would carry far. 'Do you not remember when my nephew wished to follow the astronomers, and instead I urged him to continue our family's work so that the blueprints of the aqueducts would remain safe amongst us? Now his heart is hardened like the stones he assembles, and he barely believes in anything he can't calculate. I'll not make the same mistake again.'

'That is wisdom indeed, Chieftainess.'

They turned at the soft interruption. A man garbed in the grey robes of the temple attendants stood on the narrow staircase behind them, lowering his hood.

Emra's voice sharpened. 'Perhaps Murhesla don't feel compelled to announce their presence in the citadel, but I would hope they've courtesy enough to do so when they wish to share the conversation of others.'

Sassan Santarem's smile was neither sincere nor malicious but empty, like his eyes.

'Good evening to you both, Chieftain, Chieftainess. I hope we will always meet in good fortunes and the best of health.'

Navein nodded curtly. 'Master Murhesla.'

'I wouldn't dream of prying. Only I'm as concerned as you are for the welfare of my son.'

Navein's eyes flashed. 'His future was written in the heavens. You ought to consider yourself the most honoured of fathers in the Part.'

'Be that as it may, Ahen, it was not the future he had intended for himself and nor I for him, when he was taken from his crib and kept from both himself and his father.'

This was a guilt Emra had resolved long ago. 'The barracks of a shadow guild which reduces a man to a secret and blinds him to the world beyond its gates is no future for him.'

Frost glinted on Sassan's smile. 'So to become the tool of Elders is a better life for him, then?'

Navein's brow darkened. 'Viridian has a great legacy that even your poison can't spoil.'

'Then you'll stand aside if he claims it, will you, Chieftain? If he rallies all of Derinda to him, will the Elders step aside and let him lead?'

'Lead? He's barely discovered himself.'

'But that *is* what a Custodian's meant to do, is it not?'

A drift of prayer song tempered the silence. Emra glanced warily at her old ally. Their disagreements had always extended to this.

'Ahhh,' said Sassan softly. 'Now we come to the pith of the matter.'

'The future is unknown,' said Navein shortly.

'Moments ago you assured me it was guaranteed.'

The two men held each other in a deadlock. Civility turned cold.

'Perhaps I'll warn him he'll be a puppet, nothing more than a banner in the wind when the time comes,' said Sassan. 'As his father, I will see he does nothing he will regret. Good night to you both, Chieftain … Chieftainess.'

*

It had taken Nerisen some two weeks to reach Tristan from Romel. Night was no barrier to him now, and they covered nearly half that distance in little over a week. Conceding only a few hours' rest during the coldest portion of night, he guided them through star-studded eternity, attuned to every invisible boulder and ridge and sinksand. He'd sensed the scuffling of sand by a thick rattleserpent one night and the approaching sandslide of a crumbling dune, altering their course often.

Nerisen battled with quiet awe.

His stories of the camp kept her awake long after their fires went out. Then he retreated into weary silences. As they neared Romel, his head began bobbing towards the end of each day's ride. Whatever was directing him, it was beginning to take its toll.

'We need to rest longer tonight,' she warned.

He gazed into the darkness to their right, as though a beacon had signalled on the horizon.

'We're nearly there. The new moon's only three nights from now. We need to arrive before the Assembly.'

But when she awoke a few hours later, he was still lying under his cloak.

'Tristan?'

False dawn tossed a little silver to the sky. Tristan's face was grey, and dark circles ringed his eyes. He was murmuring fitfully in his sleep. Was it a prayer he was repeating between broken words and gibberish? He wasn't feverish. But when she shook him, he didn't stir.

They'd camped under some sandwillows that would at least give them cover, and there was a promising bush nearby that might be derina. Onax curled up in the shade of the trees, too wary to sleep. An hour later, after she'd fed the horses and dug up a few fat tubers, Tristan still hadn't woken.

Nerisen considered the grey morning. She was exhausted. *Maybe I should rest too.* They were close enough to Romel that they might intercept a caravan. But there was a waystation nearby which might draw travellers for water. Travellers – and pirates. Perhaps she would lean against this tree, keep watch over Tristan and the road…

…when she opened her eyes it was still dawn – no, dusk! – and there was a smell of burning firewood.

Nerisen sat up with a start, stiffness burning her side. A man knelt over a small fire, crumbling something into a smoking pot. Tristan lay quietly asleep beside him.

'Are you rested now, daughter of the Plains?'

He was middle-aged and slight, his smile distant. His horse stood beside their own, as contented as her master. Onax was finally asleep by his fire.

Nerisen stayed back. 'Are you travelling alone, sir?'

'Is that not what you do?'

He poured tea into three small gourds, offering her one. He took the other to Tristan, whose eyes opened at the man's touch. He had regained his colour.

'Something to restore your strength.'

He'd also cooked the derina. Darkness fell as they ate. Tristan seemed much refreshed.

Nerisen sniffed her empty gourd. 'Where did you pick this honeysage? It's difficult to find now.' For two seasons, Meron had tried to propagate their dwindling stock without success.

'And a pity, for nothing's as good for soothing the stomach. When you have wandered the Plains as I have, all manner of hidden things are recovered.'

The man was a fellow escapee from the pirate camp. But he was not weary; in fact, he possessed a soothing serenity. The only other time Nerisen had felt this way had been in the olive keeper's grove. Tristan, too, seemed calmer in his company, the fire that had propelled him burning down to its embers. Nerisen listened with a heavy heart as they revisited the prison they had shared, talking in low voices late into the night so as not to wake her. But sleep remained just out of reach.

'Not once did they discuss the ore,' said Tristan. 'But they weren't satisfied with whatever they were doing with it.'

'Perhaps they don't fully understand it.'

'And yet they've gone to all this trouble to find it. Breeding Derindin slaves...' Tristan paused. 'There's something dark about them.'

'Something that bothers you, Master Invelmari?'

'They tried to mate me with a concubine. What would they want with a child?'

'Curious indeed. Did they succeed?'

'No.'

'Are you certain?'

Her eyelids were finally growing heavy. She dreamed of men and dogs in cages, and black ash-clouds from a hundred fires engulfing hamlets across the Plains. In the morning, she was finally rested and the man was gone.

*

Verdi spotted his father waiting in the crowded market square as soon as they crossed Romel's gates; a solitary pillar of stillness.

Arik saw him too.

'I'll deal with your uncle.' He took Verdi's reins. 'And I'll keep watch from a distance.'

Verdi slipped away, hood raised and head lowered against a sandy wind.

Sassan embraced him tightly. 'Let us walk.'

So they walked through the darkening streets past Romelians hurrying to shutter shops and close up stalls, fearful of the threat blowing in on the wind. Eyes glided over the two of them without pause. When he was with Sassan, Verdi felt he no longer had to hide in his cloak, as though a little of his father's aura swathed him as well.

'Have you given my offer any thought?'

Verdi's heart skipped. He chose words carefully. 'You've still not told me much about Murhesla. I've no idea of how the Guild will bind me. It's like walking into shadows.'

'Isn't that precisely what you're doing, taking Lorendar's oath?'

This was a little too on the mark. 'Merensama is a worthy cause, though I don't know I'm up to the task.'

'Of course you are,' his father replied. Verdi glowed. Sassan stopped; to Verdi's surprise they were outside the temple of the limolan tree. 'But I fear your good nature has been abused already, Viridian. The Elders need you, but only so much. They will sharpen you for their war, then keep you on puppet strings. Once their treaty is signed, you'll be nothing more than the banner that flies over their triumph. Is that what you want?'

Again, his father's words resonated with Verdi's own fears far too well.

'I won't let that happen,' Verdi told him, convincing no one.

'You could choose now,' said Sassan. 'Do not imagine Murhesla are bound only to serve Romel. A man does not satisfy the hopes of thousands without power. I can give you that.'

'Why not help *us*?' Excitement made moth wings of Verdi's breath. 'Help me? In two days, Elendra will appeal at the Assembly for help breaking the siege on Pir Sehem. Imagine what the Murhesla's strength could bring. And not just against the pirates. The desert could be such a better place.'

'But we *will* build a better place,' his father said gently. 'What if fruit is so rotted from within that all its flesh is tainted? Consumed, it ails even the healthy; ignored, its rot spreads to its fellows. Is it not better to discard it and begin again?'

Verdi froze. 'You don't mean ... the Murhesla wouldn't *destroy...*'

'No. But we can contain the filth as best we can. You have a good heart,' his father repeated. 'You do not know the corrupt core of this land. You may not even believe it if I showed you. The slate must be wiped clean before a better chapter can be written. Until then, the Murhesla must wait.'

'Wait for what?'

'A great purge after which we can start anew – build one great nation in its place.'

Verdi stifled a shiver. *A purge is long overdue ...* that had been Rasan, hadn't it? Was that, then, the will of the Murhesla?

Hope tumbled down around him, replaced with dread. He stared at his father, who seemed unaware of how greatly they had each misjudged the other.

'In the end your goals are the same, you and I,' Sassan told him. 'Only our methods are different.'

Verdi waited until he was sure his voice wouldn't shake.

'I can't join your guild,' he said. 'I'm glad to have found you. But I made a promise, and now I must keep it.'

*

'Don't take your eyes off him for even a second,' Arik told Rasan at Riorga's inn, where another note had been waiting for him.

He left her with Verdi and the rest of their caravan. Verdi had returned terribly distracted after his time with his father. He was perhaps even more vulnerable than the first time he'd been taken from this very inn, though it wasn't abduction that Arik feared now.

But Arik had work to do.

The citadel was bursting at the seams with visitors arriving for the Assembly. Arik found the gamblers' tavern easily enough. The intercessor was waiting for him. His name was Fro Tarka, and he beamed as Arik entered.

'Master Marcin, I see you received my message.' He spread his arms wide. 'Well?'

'Not a bad offer,' Arik replied. 'If payment is guaranteed. My terms haven't changed.'

'But of course. And if you lose?'

Once again, he was impeccably dressed, moustache pencil-sharp, single gold earring furnished with a blood-red ruby. *He likes his riches.*

'Invelmari gold. I'll double whatever odds you lose against all bets placed in my favour.'

If Fro Tarka grinned any more broadly, it would have split his face. 'Come on in, Master Marcin, come on in.'

He ushered Arik in with a deep Invelmari bow. The tavern was full, and wagers had been renegotiated several times over.

The fights themselves were easy. Only two of Arik's opponents were Derindin, both tumblers. There was a man from Morregrat and a Pengazan – wrestlers who earned their bread from these games; the latter most likely tricked with drink into taking part. There were even a couple of Invelmari again, one of them almost certainly an exile. Only the Pengazan and the exile presented Arik with any challenge. Several barrels of cider and wine later, the tavern was filled with sweat and smoke and the cheer of those who'd bet on his victory.

Arik allowed himself a swig of the cider and exchanged his shirt for a clean one. Cheers faltered as the jemesh swung into view on the cord around his neck.

Fro Tarka extracted himself from his clientele. 'Our champion tonight!'

More cheers. Fro Tarka assigned a pair of broad-shouldered Derindin to the matter of payments. He nodded at Arik before disappearing into the back of the inn. Arik followed.

'Over here, Master Marcin.'

He led Arik into a store room full of crates. Arik kept one hand on his sword and both eyes on the Derindman. To his surprise, Fro Tarka produced, of all things, paper and pen.

He crouched down and wrote on the paper, straightening to hold it up.

'The necromancer whose name is "the Bloodstained". All things of the hallowed ice are sacred.'

Arik stared at the page.

What the hell does this have to do with where the jemesh came from?

Fro Tarka waited patiently. All trace of showmanship had vanished here, the lines of his face taut. 'I obtained this from a renegade who'd escaped the Murhesla's guild.'

'A renegade told you this willingly?'

'Hardly. A little powder in his drink, a big debt to repay … many have a debt to repay to Fro Tarka.' His glamour glimmered again. 'Regrettably, this one was a great loss to my arsenal, too. A very profitable debt, it was. Better to call in debts only when all other options are exhausted.'

Arik raised an eyebrow. 'I've made you a fortune tonight.'

'Indeed you have. If you are satisfied, I will take that back.'

Arik returned the paper and they went back into the tavern. Fro Tarka lingered by the fire just long enough to ensure the paper he'd dropped into the flames was consumed. He clapped Arik's back.

'Good night, Master Invelmari. My doors will always be open to you.'

Arik returned to Riorga's inn where Saarem and Broco had waited up for him, just in case. Riorga's doors had closed for the night and they were alone. A sleepy maid was drying the last of the dishes, and the fire burned low. A crooked smile woke her up, and she was all too happy to bring Arik a pot of kahvi.

Arik pulled up a chair. 'What d'you know about Fro Tarka?'

'A right rascal.' Saarem cocked an eyebrow. 'Never took you for a gambling man, Marcin.'

'Depends on the prize,' Arik murmured. 'He's been very useful.'

'I'm sure he has. Wagering's only what he does to sniff out every weakness in Romel and get a foot in every doorway that'll give him a look-in. He collects holds on as many poor bastards as he can.'

'What for?'

Broco waited for the maid to pour kahvi. 'Better stop smiling at that girl, Marcin, or she's going to trip onto her face. Romelians call him the Poet of Rogues.'

Arik sipped the bitter kahvi. 'He prefers his work dirty, then?'

'Blackmail, heists, forgery – you name it. From the shadows, of course. But it's common knowledge. Watch yourself around him, Marcin. He's more dangerous than he looks.'

That night Arik re-wrote Fro Tarka's message to himself in the Prosperi cipher. This sort of thing was better left to Klaus, but there was only one place Arik knew made of ice. Necromancy was a nonsensical ambition of distant Ungal … and the Far North.

How can the jemesh be remotely related to the Far North? The possibility was as troubling as it was unforeseen. There had been genuine relief in Fro Tarka's eyes when the paper had been safely incinerated. As though he'd been afraid he might have bitten off more than he could chew by sharing it. What could frighten such a man?

Arik didn't yet know whether the message had been a satisfactory return on their bargain, but that look in Fro Tarka's eyes told him two things: these words were of enough value to erase a great debt, and there was no chance Arik would secure another such payment again from the Poet of Rogues.

*

Romel's taverns were heaving. The rise of the new suzerainty in the West, an alliance in the East, the siege of the most battle-hardened of the clans… all this promised a perfect storm of an Assembly tomorrow. Merchants and farmers speculated hopefully and anxiously by turns as they caught the unmistakable current of war and wondered to each other whether the whispers of Merensama had more substance to them yet than Babblespittle…

Verdi was impervious to all of this.

He sat as though he had no business but his own and none of it very important, eventually disappearing into his hood. Rasan had stopped trying to get him to eat. She finally left him to the book now neglected before him, though he could feel her watching him from the fireside where the tumblers played a game of cards.

'You couldn't have chosen a better moment. The clans will carry the news home to every part of the Plains.'

Verdi hadn't noticed Alizarin arrive. He'd been staring at a wood carving mounted proudly over the hearth; a leaf from the limolan tree. He hadn't known what it was before.

Fear nudged between his ribs with cold fingers. What would Klaus tell him now, if he knew why Verdi's mother had sent him away?

The questions never changed and only seemed to multiply.

Verdi met his uncle's eyes. 'Is it true Voista's theft of Elendra's water caused the drought that killed my mother?'

The look in Alizarin's face confirmed the answer.

'They will keep you on puppet strings…'

Verdi swallowed. 'How could you bear allying with Voista? Letting me help seal the deal, like a fool?'

Rare compassion thawed Alizarin's eyes; or pity, perhaps. 'If we always keep those who've wounded us at bay, we never move forward. Sometimes our own wounds must be set aside.'

And sometimes they eclipse everything. Each time Verdi salvaged a little more of the life he ought to have had here, anger pushed him away again.

'I'm not taking any oath,' he said. 'Not yet.'

*

Arik crossed the courtyard and sat by Verdi on the steps overlooking the limolan tree. Late spring still coaxed young yellow-green leaves from its branches. Bulbs extended shy stems through the warming earth. Verdi had come here every day since they'd arrived, though not once had he set foot in the temple.

'You're sure, then?'

'Yes.'

'What are you waiting for, Verdi? You like it here. You have kinship with these people, this place.'

Eventually, Verdi replied, 'Not yet.'

Pilgrims had taken to hovering about the courtyard whenever Verdi visited the sanctuary. Rasan said they were hoping to be there when he signed the Book of Oaths. Arik grimaced. *They'll be waiting for a long time.*

'Verdi...' Arik summoned Form. 'He most probably isn't coming back.'

Despite the shield of his Form, hearing it aloud still wrenched his gut. Anger ignited in Verdi's eyes, but it was dimmed with tears.

They sat in silence. There was perhaps no better place than this haven to digest reality. The scent that drifted from the limolan – subtle, halfway between a Semran tuberose and bergamot – loosened the tightness in Arik's throat.

'I'm afraid of the Murhesla,' said Verdi, barely audible over the breeze.

Good. Sassan Santarem was best handled with caution. Later, he'd ask Verdi what he meant. For now...

'Mourn him if you must, Verdi, but remember you still have a life to live of your own.'

Arik touched the jemesh through his shirt, thinking again of Fro Tarka's payment. For the first time since he'd received the jemesh, foreboding flared at its touch, and it had nothing to do with its pact with death.

Form contracted around this fear. For now, he too would mourn.

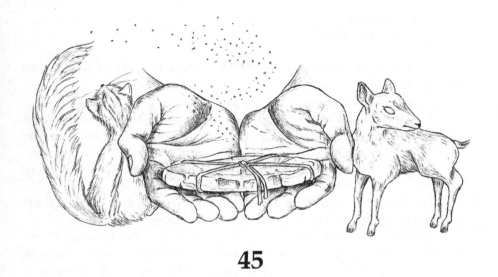

45

A Necklace of Names

WITH THE STEELCRAFT OF STURMSINGER, THEY FASHIONED THE FORM OF
BLACKSMITH: TEMPERER OF STARBORN IRON;
MIGHTY FIST OF INVELMAR.

SONNONFER: ON THE FOUR NOBLE FORMS

'Brothers and sisters, I bring forth a charge.'

The Chieftainess of Elendra stood on the dais at the Assembly. A hush fell over the crowd squeezed into the great chamber; the largest in Alizarin's memory, spilling out into the streets. Outside, the sky held the darkness of foul-tempered rain, though such a rain had not pelted Derinda in living memory. But for the notable absence of the Sisodans, every Chieftain was present in anticipation of a coming storm.

'You are the dagger of this gathering,' Alizarin told his nephew. Tension had recast Viridian in iron. In fact, since Klaus had gone he had lost his fidget. 'Hold your nerve.'

'But first,' Emra continued, 'I shall remind you all of what goes on while we slumber. Hundreds captured or murdered, homes robbed or ruined. Trade routes paralysed, cutting off hundreds more from food and shelter all winter. Men and women and even children enslaved – yes, enslaved!' Emra raised her voice over the first protests. 'Now a citadel has fallen to pirates. Pirates have besieged the jewel of Sisoda, and by all accounts are gathering to break Pir Sehem's defences as we speak.'

Eskandan, the Periami Chieftain, wasted no time currying favour with his masters in the West.

'Long have the Eastern clans conspired to cast chains upon us free Derindin! They want to remake the old kingdoms, where kings and their cronies grow fat off our toil. Already they've ensnared Voista. This fearmonger claims that bandits have made slaves of us – what proof does she have?' A few cheers lauded him. 'Or has this Assembly no more weight than the muttering of Babbles?'

Emra waited for quiet. 'What does Eskandan tell his clansmen when their loved ones are taken, but their bodies never found? Perhaps he doesn't care.' More protests. 'Elendra has welcomed a survivor of your clan who was herself captured, along with many others. We believe the captives are being held in the South, beyond all our borders.'

Alizarin stifled a groan; the outpouring of mockery that followed was no less than he'd expected.

'Ah, yes, we've heard these rumours you've spread of a pirate stronghold in the Far South.' Soft-spoken Voldane stifled the commotion effortlessly. 'A barren place – beaten down by deadly winds, so dry even derina won't grow. Can the Chieftainess explain how these hundreds of slaves could possibly survive in the wastes there?'

Emra ignored the jeers punctuating his words. 'With your blessing, Chieftain. With the permission you've given pirates to raid the edge of your own clandom for supplies. With the safe passage you've granted them through your lands, so they can smuggle slaves while you look the other way.'

Pandemonium erupted around the dais.

Voldane barely stirred. 'Without proof, Emra Selamanden, this is slander of the highest order.'

'Scores of refugees driven out from Draal are encamped outside Samsarra right now, Chieftain. Including the wife of your own envoy, Reska Velgara.'

It was the first dangerous moment of Emra's plan. Both Fraivon and Lebas' councils bared their fury. The cry of *'Traitor! Traitor!'* rose from Baeron's ranks at the mention of Reska, but the damage was already done – the crowd's wrath swelled. Behind Voldane, one face was livid: Agatin, Reska's husband.

Watershin shot Alizarin a dark look. Voista hadn't anticipated nosediving into war with Derinda's most powerful clans when they'd agreed to an alliance. *Perhaps Baeron won't risk open war. They know the sentiment is building against them.*

Just as Emra won the balance of the crowd, she stepped back to make way for Maragrin on the dais. The chamber fell quiet again for the oldest of the Elders, leaning on his stick.

'I've been alive long enough to have witnessed the last rain we had over the Plains, and seen dozens of Chieftains replaced.'

Voldane bowed his head. 'And long may you live to watch over us all.'

'And yet I've not before witnessed a clan offer up their own folk as payment to pirates. Those fortunate enough to escape your clandom were driven out by pirates roaming unchecked. Do you deny it, Chieftain?'

Voldane waited for a renewed furore to fizzle out. 'I swear to you and before all the clans that not one Baeronian sword has been raised against Derindin.'

'Liar!' came a cry from the crowd. The chant was taken up eagerly.

He's probably telling the truth, the bastard. Silent fury roared in Alizarin's blood. *Baeron didn't have to lift a single sword if pirates are doing it for them.*

'While the Plains burn, these agitators stir up war with the West for their own gain!' The Hesperi Chieftainess Qoris was a bear of a woman; densely built, with a voice that came from her guts. 'No one knows how many pirates there are, but these scaremongers claim they'll conquer us all. How do we answer?'

Navein's deep voice carried over hers. 'The pirates have taken Sisoda hostage. If we don't stop them, who'll be next? Brothers and sisters, while we bicker, they grow stronger!'

'And once the pirates are defeated?' Eskandan demanded. 'We all know what you're really after, scheming for your alliance – plotting to impose Merensama upon us. Do you think we're stupid enough to take your bait?'

It didn't take much to tip the simmering chamber to boiling. Elders rowed, sworn enemies and fervent followers of Lorendar alike. They flung accusations across the dais until Alizarin feared that not even hatred for the pirates would be a strong enough contender for the confusion the Plains felt for Obsidian Lorendar.

'Peddlers of false prophecies!' shouted a Periami Elder. 'Lorendar was a butcher – and his heir sits right there, plotting to drag us back into darkness!'

He raised his arm and pointed at Viridian.

Alizarin felt his nephew shrink beside him. But the attack had been misjudged: most of the chamber cheered. *Too many people cling to dreams of Merensama still;* a gamble Alizarin had never been prepared to take. Elders gave up trying to subdue their clans.

Tourmali shook his head. 'These people won't be helped.'

'It's not the people,' Emra replied, waiting to regain a foothold. 'Listen to them – they're angry, afraid. But they don't know where to turn.'

They'll turn upon themselves. Alizarin curled a wary hand around Viridian's forearm. Tumblers spread around the dais uneasily. Murhesla were woven into the very air of Romel, but in a hot moment the enraged beast of a mob might forget this. But the momentum stumbled: there was a commotion across the chamber, then gasps. The crowd parted around a tall figure. They shrank back to let him pass, for he was menacing to behold.

Alizarin froze: Klaus, bedraggled and covered in blood.

He heard a sharp intake of breath beside him, and grabbed Viridian's arm.

'Wait...!'

The Northman strode onto the dais. A majestic peregrine crowned his left shoulder, a grey-spotted white of a variety Alizarin had not seen in life.

'And now we're a mouthpiece of Northerners!' cried Eskandan. 'Not even at the Second Redrawing did our enemies darken this stage! What's the meaning of this impudence?'

Klaus stopped in the middle of the dais. He carried something in one hand and held his other arm now bearing the peregrine awkwardly, less accustomed to the great bird than it was to him. Even in his dishevelled state, he radiated imperial authority. He summoned quiet to the chamber before speaking a single word.

'I am not your enemy.'

Quiet deepened to silence.

'I'm not your enemy,' he repeated. 'But I have been to the pirates' nest, a camp south of Kastava's Point where they keep hundreds of your kin prisoner. Slaves of every age, bred like cattle to make more –

'Lies! There's no such place!' Voldane bellowed. 'He's in the pay of the agitators, hoping to scare you into joining their alliance!'

'– tortured for dissidence, culled if they are sick or injured, raped to raise a new class of slaves...'

The crowd strained to listen, paralysed by the need for news of their missing. The Northman knew this. And he was spellbinding: towering, the peregrine standing tall on his forearm in complete trust, its gaze uncannily knowing. Alizarin reckoned Voldane might have pulled him down from the dais were it not for the magnificent bird.

Klaus ignored the Elders, circling the stage like a great cat and seeking out the anxious faces behind them: tear-stained, pain-stricken, eager to know more of those they had lost.

'Shall I tell you their names?' He could have whispered, and he would have been heard across the chamber. 'Shall I begin with the names of the dead, or the living? Gheld Ottovar, Fargo Ranse, who became dog-food and pyre-wood … Piri of clan Periam. Merik, carpet-weaver of Lebas, snatched on the Qinnamon Road with five of his kin … your wife Saffa, Elder Harid, kept as a brood mare. I stole from them her promise-ring. Gesun Lannindar… Saepo, Periami tanner…'

The hair rose on Alizarin's skin. He spared no one, filling every corner of the chamber with confirmations of their worst fears.

It's his Form. Even knowing the source of the Northman's spell, Alizarin couldn't resist feeling what he compelled them to feel. *Surely this is magic.*

'Where is Colihm of Fraivon?' Klaus pulled something from his cloak. 'A token from your Helan. He said he was the last of your house.'

He stooped past Fraivon's Elders to pass a braided ring into the crowd. The peregrine's wings ruffled slightly, adjusting to his movements. He paused for Colihm's stricken cry.

His aim was true. *It always is.*

Qoris rose, flushed. 'Do you expect us to believe bandits have been able to do all this?'

'The pirates have fooled you. While you've been bickering they've found favour with a far more dangerous enemy, worming their way into your land from the sea.'

Jeers showered him, and the quiet crumbled into confusion and sneering protests.

Klaus untied the bundle he carried. The peregrine half-spread her wings twice, unsettled; Alizarin grew uneasy. Klaus dropped the cloth, revealing a grisly sight: the head of a man.

He raised it high. 'Look upon the Eh Menishian.'

The cold desert wind had dried and hardened the skin, like a curing meat. In death, the pale face was almost alien. Alizarin had never seen its like.

'Great Sentience,' breathed Tourmali to his left.

'They came from far beyond this Part, and it's their gold that has united the pirates against you.' The jeers vanished. 'They're still coming. Mercenaries and Unsworn flock to serve them. Their way is one of terrible cruelty. And they're stealing the desert from under your very feet.'

Alizarin was rooted to the spot. Even the Elders were speechless. Klaus circled the dais, holding out the half-rotted head. Alizarin caught a whiff of its stench as he passed. He couldn't tear his eyes from the contorted face: sallow and high-browed, the long dark braids by which Klaus carried it woven with coloured beads.

'It's not just for Derinda that I fear,' he said. 'What I have seen makes me fear for this Part.'

He set the head down on the edge of the dais, to face the clans of Fraivon and Lebas.

Alizarin released a breath. Emra was pale. Elders whispered urgently amongst each other.

'Why should this Northerner be trusted?' Qoris shouted. 'We've never forgotten who dammed the river!'

'If my people built the dam, yours were its architects. This land fell long before the North took it. Shall we judge your fathers by your own laws?' The sight of the severed head still held his audience captive. 'Your land is for the taking by anyone who can defend it. You live and die by this – by ghabala. Brother may slit the throat of brother and usurp his birthright. Your fathers made those laws to feed their greed for more land, and mine took it from you. So far, no laws broken. Usurpers, that's what you became. And what are you now?'

He lashed at them with cutting disdain. Form flared again, flogging them with shame. Even Alizarin felt it; *my own shame,* he realised, *coaxed to the surface, like river scum.* The peregrine cocked her head, her gaze pitiless.

'What are you now? You share your very name with a plant that grows like a beggar in wretchedness, scrounging in the dirt for its nourishment. Is that how you want to remain, in the face of another conqueror?'

There was no furious backlash from the crowd. The Northman had bewitched them.

'But you are men and women of honour.' Klaus paused by the sundial. 'The Seven Parts over you have been called Oathkeepers. The wisdom of your ancestors once had the reach of the skies. Go back to what you were first. A young man sits between you who can restore balance to this land.' Klaus reached out a hand to Viridian. 'Gather behind him not just for pirates or Merensama. Gather behind him for the sake of Orenthia.'

The roar that spilled into the chamber shook the dais.

Alizarin trembled. He saw at last with certainty the man who had died twice: *first in the North, and again in the Far South…* The peregrine took off from Klaus' shoulder, the span of her wings as wide as a Derindman was tall. Klaus stooped down and pulled Viridian from his seat, and Invelmari and Derindin embraced as thunder spilled around them...

*

Klaus managed a smile at his oldest friend.

'I knew you were still alive,' Verdi said hoarsely. 'You look terrible…'

Cilastra laid the first knife at the base of the sundial. 'Mantelon will be proud to follow the heir of Lorendar!'

The jostling resumed around the dais. But the will of Elders no longer reigned; there was too much fire in the grasses now. Emra's shrill cry rang out through the confusion.

'Brothers and sisters! The hour is already late. We march to Pir Sehem. Brothers and sisters! We will free Sisoda, and then we'll reclaim our prisoners from this new invader. Who'll pledge to an armistice? Who will march with us?'

Derindin shouted, clapped, rapped the wooden benches. They would not be ignored.

Elders embraced Verdi. Men and women stretched forward to touch him for luck. Klaus slipped down from the dais, leaving Verdi behind.

He glimpsed Arik, but there was no way through to him. Klaus pushed his way through the crowd back to Nerisen. Her eyes were red-rimmed, her face pale with exhaustion.

'My arm's aching again,' he told her. His head was also spinning. Derindin touched him as he passed, blessed him; pleaded for more news, more names.

She threatened, 'You can't fall over now.'

He didn't fall but he did sway as he followed her out, grateful for her attention though he knew she would just as willingly help any wretch in need. For now, he was glad to be a wretch. Out in fresh air and quieter streets, he slipped out of consciousness by the side of a road.

*

By the time Arik had safely detached Verdi from the mob, Klaus was already sound asleep in Riorga's inn, succumbing to the physician's draught. Cleaned up, he looked less battered. Arik watched as Sonru, the physician, cleansed and re-dressed a wound on Klaus' arm.

'Will it heal in time?'

'If you mean for battle, yes.' She rinsed a bandage. 'He's exhausted and still recovering from the toll of thirst. But I know he'll not rest.'

Fallen comrades came and went like winter's snowdrifts. If he'd mourned them all, Arik would have been buried under a mountain of his own despair. Now he was numb with relief. Lisbeta would have berated him. But what was the point of struggling if there was nothing to struggle for?

Klaus tossed again, muttering fretfully.

'It's not strong enough, whatever you've given him,' Arik told her. Sonru prepared another draught. Verdi returned with the herbs she had requested.

'Has the wound festered?' Verdi asked as Klaus' unintelligible rambling grew louder.

'No, but he has a chemical weariness.'

The second draught still wasn't enough to dispel whatever disturbed him. Hours later, after Arik had nodded off and woken again, he realised Klaus was finally quiet.

Arik sat up, managing an uneven grin: Klaus' eyes were open. 'You took your time.'

'Where's Verdi?'

'Asleep in the next room. Don't worry.'

'Has he taken the oath?'

'Not yet. I think he was waiting for you. And then his father went and upset the milk pail.' Klaus blinked, confused. 'Klaus, his father is Murhesla.'

Klaus rubbed his eyes. He seemed agitated, his mask slipping. 'Did Nerisen give you the package?'

'Yes.'

'Open it.'

Arik retrieved the small parcel. His breath caught at the heavy disc inside.

'Is this...?'

'Yes.'

So this is what the pirates are looking for. 'Do you know what it's for?'

'Not yet.'

'Any ideas?'

But Klaus was barely listening, distracted. This crack in his Form made Arik uneasy.

'We've been such fools, Arik. To have ever believed a word of the Sonnonfer...' Arik flinched, glancing at the door; it was shut, but tumblers were stationed outside. 'The mine's exactly where the Septentrional Scrolls promised. The spring is hidden in mountain caves. And the Eh Menishian won't find them.'

He talked. Sometimes he rambled, straying into avenues of bitterness, but he was no longer delirious. Later, Arik would look upon that hour as perhaps the first waking moment of his life.

He heard himself ask again, 'Are you sure?' The machinery of a Warrior's heart was ill-equipped for catastrophic recalibrations. 'Could you have been mistaken?'

'Arik, Sturmsinger's guards are buried in that cave ... side by side with Eh Menishian. There's more – much more than I had time to see.'

His first instinct was to storm out of the inn; to shut his ears and his heart. But this was Klaus, not a Babble, so Arik remained rooted to his chair, listening stupidly. Outrage simmered slowly, metallic on the tongue and hot in the veins.

'We can't let this go, Klaus. We should go back and expose them.'

'The Chain's kept Invelmar safe.'

'Built on betrayal, perpetuated by lies. The Ealdormen are *traitors*!'

'And ousting them could break the Blood Pact.'

Arik was shaking now, from head to toe. His Form could barely contain this anger.

'Believe me … I've had plenty of time to think about it.' Klaus squeezed his arm. 'Besides, how do we make anyone believe us? We'd be branded heretics and be put to the pyre.'

Silence, long and hollow.

'It was Eh Menishian who sent kidnappers after Verdi, not pirates,' said Klaus. 'Maybe they consider him a threat to whatever they're planning … and you along with him.'

Arik's fingers drifted towards the little bone hanging around his neck. 'But the jemesh is Far Northern.' He told Klaus about Fro Tarka's payment for his little contract. A terrible foreboding lurked beneath his Form. 'How did it wind up in the hands of these Eh Menishian?'

They talked late into the evening of the mine and the worrying prospect of ore superior to Invelmari steel, and of the Eh Menishian. He didn't tell Klaus about Fibbler's stolen note, or about Thillaina. There would be time enough to burden him yet.

*

When Klaus next awoke, Arik's chair was empty. It was night, and the oil lamp had burned out.

Something warm nuzzled his side; he twisted to find Ravi had burrowed into his bedding.

'Really sorry,' Verdi mumbled, sitting up and yawning across the room. 'Gave up trying to keep him away.'

Klaus stroked Ravi's soft head, teasing out a happy purr.

'How do you feel?' Verdi took the empty chair. 'You've been asleep since noon.'

Had the Assembly only been yesterday? Klaus felt as though he might have been sleeping for days.

'Fine, and that's enough about me. Any progress with the moondial?'

But this wasn't what Verdi was itching to share. 'My uncle finally told me why he sent me away to Dunraven. It was my mother's wish.' His fingers plucked at each other in his lap. 'She had visions, and she was convinced Lorendar's successor would be the last of his line…'

'Ending with you?' Klaus finished.

Verdi shrugged helplessly. Klaus had never seen him look so conflicted. 'My own mother would have told me to turn away from all of this. She believed I wouldn't survive.'

And my mother sent me away to spare me the burden of becoming Sturmsinger's secret-keeper.

'Perhaps sometimes mothers are blinded by love.' Klaus thought of the Wisdom's peregrine hunting outside with a thrill of both fear and excitement. He would have traded every privilege of his royal childhood in Dunraven for the suffering of a lifelong fugitive, for the chance to have known his family and a place to call home. 'What does your uncle think?'

Verdi snorted. 'I don't think he knows.' He paused. 'I reckon he'd sacrifice me like a Far Northern virgin at midwinter for Merensama, if he wasn't so guilty about betraying my mother.'

Death is the doorway. A Derindin saying, but Invelmari were raised striving to earn a place at Sturmsinger's table. A pact with death from the cradle.

But Verdi was not Invelmari. Klaus trod carefully.

'Few of us are fortunate enough to choose our meeting with death, Verdi.'

Verdi's shoulders sagged. 'I didn't want any of this. I was just following you.'

'I know, and I'm sorry.'

A drum began beating in celebration outside; a distant pulse counting their sorrows.

'I don't know what to do.' Verdi slumped back in the chair. 'What do I do?'

Only days ago, I asked the same question of the Wisdom. Why was it easier to guide the paths of others while one's own way was lost?

'You have the chance to make a difference. But only you can set the price on that. And you might still fail. Is it worth dying for? You can't lean on other people's belief as a crutch.'

'You did many things for Adela and the Spyglass that you didn't believe in.'

I was following orders. I had to uphold the law. I had to bide my time for my own day on the throne.

Instead, he replied, 'I know.'

The door opened, and Sonru entered, trailed by Arik and Rasan. Klaus' pulse skipped; Nerisen hovered by the door, carrying the physician's case. He longed to thank her, to fall asleep again under her eye.

'Good, you're awake.' Sonru lit a lamp. 'You can drink this.'

Klaus took the glass she offered. 'I'm indebted to you a second time, mistress.'

'Stay here in Romel, you need sleep and nourishment. One man's absence will make no difference to the battle. Now let him rest.' She shook her head, leaving with Nerisen.

'All the clans except Periam and the West have pledged tumblers to march with us,' Rasan told him. 'These Eh Menishian...'

'There'll be plenty of time for all that later,' Verdi interrupted.

'They're formidable warriors,' said Klaus. 'Clever and without remorse.'

'How many of them were there?'

'Only two dozen, but their ships are still arriving to the Part.' Klaus found Arik's eyes. 'I believe more will come. And they've bewitched thousands of pirates with gold.'

'What do they want?'

'For now? They're digging for ore. I think they come by tunnels. Under the sand, from the shore? Or from the west? Who knows how long their plans have been in the making.'

'You should rest.' Verdi picked up the lamp. 'We're leaving Romel soon.'

Rasan pulled out his sword from under her cloak and knelt solemnly by the bed. Klaus sat up, and the room swarmed.

'Get up, you're not a Northerner.'

'It's a Northern sword.'

She offered it laid across both her palms, unwittingly so reminiscent of the ceremonial exchange between Isarnanheri that his heart ached. He grasped the scabbard, knuckles white.

They left him alone with the fierce joy of reunion. *For the steel, or a bridge to vainglory?* He gripped the blade across his belly. Sonru's draught kicked in, leaving him with tattered memories; the warm bed, a sour tonic, an interval of green eyes. Later, he would swear that sometime in the night, he woke to find pale lanterns upon lanterns hanging from the rafters, bathing the world in a hue of golden blue. He would marvel, then slip gently into a sleep of the kind that only came after the deepest exhaustion, entirely undisturbed by dreams.

*

Finally, it was night. A thousand hours might have passed since the Assembly, not merely one triumphant day. Talk of tumblers and horses and spearhands between the six clans who'd pledged to an armistice continued until Riorga declared he was out of food and drink. It was too late now to pledge tumblers to defend Pir Sehem, but they offered gold for more supplies. Buoyed, the citadel celebrated the remembrance of hope.

Alizarin wasn't ensnared. He escaped down an alley behind the inn to be alone with his stars, only they were veiled by clouds.

A few moments later, Emra joined him.

Alizarin looked away from her patient eyes. 'I'm sorry I didn't tell you his plan.'

'On the contrary, Alizarin, I'm glad you had faith enough to let him go.'

Something inside him snapped at such misplaced generosity.

'I knew who he was,' he whispered harshly. 'I *knew*, and yet I put him in the path of danger – so that we almost lost him. I escorted him from Samsarra myself. All my life I'd been preparing to recognise him instantly, and when I did I averted my gaze.'

When he finally met her eyes again, they were still too full of understanding.

'Pride is the serpent,' she said. 'It has never changed its nature. But we can change ours. When it whispers, we can choose not to listen.'

He *was* listening now, and all he heard was his own bewilderment.

'What about Viridian?'

'Even Lorendar needed help. He had the sage-bird. Why should Viridian not have help?' She paused. 'We fell too deeply into the future we imagined to see it clearly now.'

A pale shadow passed overhead. It might have been a great spotted peregrine.

'Do you believe what they're saying about him?'

She knew he didn't mean Viridian now. Emra gazed into the night. He wished he knew what she saw.

'I believe what I feel about him. Perhaps there are things we have understood wrongly.'

For a few minutes more they savoured this tranquillity, for they knew their victory was a tender fledgeling and must soon be anointed with blood.

46

The Nightcrossing

WITH THE SACRED STEPS OF STURMSINGER, THEY FASHIONED
THE FORM OF WARRIOR: GUARDIAN OF THE WARDANCE OF JARNSTIGA;
DEFENDER OF LAND AND LIEGE.

SONNONFER: ON THE FOUR NOBLE FORMS

Klaus rode back to the tumblers' tents, grateful for the weight of his crossbow across his back.

Ayla had ordered them to make camp a few hours' ride from Pir Sehem, where the desert afforded generous dunes and good derina. Two days earlier, Klaus had mapped this terrain and shown Arik.

'What do you mean, there's *going to be* a sinksand over there?'

Explaining his gift to Arik proved harder than Klaus had reckoned. In fact, part of him feared Arik would feel betrayed. Worse, that it would drive more distance between them.

'When I navigate, I feel the lay of the land. If I listen…'

'*Listen?*'

'It's how I got out of the camp in a storm; how I found the caves.'

574

It was the first time in his memory that Arik had struggled to take his word for anything. But Arik had no other maps to follow. The war council had been debating Arik's proposals since.

Now Klaus saw the land with his eyes. As he'd predicted, to the east the desert rose to a great rocky ridge that marked the eastern border of Sisoda's clandom and shielded the camp from the pirates' eyescopes. Beyond the ridge, a rock-strewn valley surrounded the mount on which Pir Sehem stood. The ridge curved around the northern side of the citadel mount and sloped gently down into the valley, making it Pir Sehem's most vulnerable aspect.

By noon, Ayla, three generals and the two Elders were still at a deadlock.

'They haven't left that tent,' Arik told him.

'We've only enough water to sit here for three days. They'd better decide soon.'

'Are you sure about the terrain?'

Arik had seen for himself the accuracy of Klaus' predictions so far. The question *behind* his question was much harder to answer.

'Yes.' Klaus wished he could explain better. Arik was a Warrior; Warriors relied on steel and solid numbers. 'The desert is … sentient. It has a voice that I can translate into navigations.'

'How?'

Klaus trod cautiously. Arik was really trying.

'Because of slight matter.' He regretted the words as soon as he'd spoken them; this was another forbidden subject. 'The same force that pushed up Verdi's sapling, maybe. Whatever it is, it's never been wrong.'

Warriors did not have masks. Klaus watched Arik wrangle with his Form.

He resurfaced a long moment later. 'You're starting to sound like Lisbeta.'

Knowing precisely what Arik thought of his Form Mistress, this was a blow. But there wasn't time for insecurities; Ayla pulled her tent flap aside. They rejoined the war council.

Rahdib Loosebelt, the Voistan general, was the first of their problems. A tall man with the silver fur and lean flanks of a wolf, he had proven unexpectedly likeable and terribly practical.

'Master Marcin. The scouts estimate five thousand pirates are camped east of Pir Sehem beyond the valley, and that only accounts for what we can see by eyescope. It would be madness to divide our forces and lead only three thousand tumblers against this number. And greater madness still –' he eyed Klaus '– to take the rest *in the dead of night* to ambush the citadel from the north, however vulnerable it may be there. Guided by a *chronicler*.'

'But if it works and we divide their forces, our chances of taking the pirate camp look much better,' Cilastra insisted.

Despite her own reservations, Ayla had been the most willing to consider Arik's proposal without immediately lambasting Klaus' part. *Cilastra and Ayla, fervent followers of Lorendar.* Klaus wasn't sure their support was much of a measuring stick.

'The first attack *has* to begin at night,' Klaus repeated. 'They'll be watching the citadel all day. Otherwise you might as well sound our arrival with a trumpet.'

'But to split our strength?' Rahdib repeated. 'We don't know how many more pirates might be stationed around Pir Sehem.'

'The bulk of their forces *must* be stationed where our scouts saw them south of the citadel, because that's where the main water supply to Pir Sehem runs.' Tourmali proved to be the second of their problems. Though he was less dismissive of a nocturnal assault from the north, he'd flat out rejected the key part of Arik's plan. 'They'll stay close to the spring.'

Arik asked, 'What about the spring to the north of the citadel?'

'Poisoned.' Alizarin pointed to a dead lizard on the ground. 'Suman's falcons brought in a few of those from there this morning.'

'Are they really stupid enough to slash their own water supply?'

'It puts pressure on the siege and leaves only one spring for them to watch. The short term gains must have been irresistible.'

'But it does suggest they've not got enough pirates to watch both springs,' Cilastra pointed out.

'And then there's this additional *third* battalion you wish to march to the southern arse of the clandom.' Rahdib turned back to Arik. 'Yes, it would be great to intercept pirates fleeing south towards Baeron. There'll be nowhere else for them to run – Black Lava Plains to the west, and miles north before they'd reach Hesper. But you'd need at least a thousand swords, and that would shrink the army we'll have left for the main attack.'

'We're aiming to be rid of these pirates, General, not to sweep them from one clandom into another,' said Alizarin.

Sarak, the Mantelonian general, shook his head. 'It's tempting, Master Marcin – to divide the pirates with twin attacks. But I stand with the Voistan. The success of this entire plan hinges on a thousand tumblers getting to the citadel mount at *night*. If that fails, we'll be left with a paltry army to take on the pirates we can actually see.'

'Then send fewer tumblers for the night assault,' Klaus replied. 'A few hundred will be enough to distract them and split them up.'

'In the darkness.' Rahdib's voice climbed. 'You want me to follow your directions in full *darkness*. I will not lead my tumblers on a suicide mission. Voista's soldiers will join the main attack.'

'Very well.' Ayla's patience was fraying. 'Tristan, take my tumblers by night. And some of Mantelon's, if General Sarak will permit it.'

There was a terse silence. Sarak looked down again at the map; the map Klaus had drawn three days before they'd arrived, capturing the terrain so intimately. His struggle was plain. His eyes dropped to the gauntlet now adorning Klaus' left forearm, thick to withstand the claws of a great bird.

'Those amongst my tumblers who volunteer themselves may join you,' he said at last.

Cilastra's shoulders relaxed. 'Master Marcin, is it really wise to pursue three battles and risk losing them all?'

Arik had thankfully withheld his own scepticism from the Derindin. 'We don't know how many more pirates are waiting in the villages. Even if we win the citadel, we'll have to reckon with them later – when we'll be tired. Better not to stumble at the finish line.'

'It's a hard journey to the southern border,' Tourmali warned. 'The descent south from the ridge is steep, the crossing through the valley short but full of rocks. You'll risk running out of water. You'll be exhausted when you arrive.'

'Then the third battalion should leave earlier, to allow time for rest,' said Klaus. 'Set off a full day before General Ayla attacks the camp.'

Cilastra stood. 'Leave us.'

It was hours later before Ayla found them by a cook fire.

'They've agreed. Marcin will lead a small battalion to Sisoda's southern border to intercept fleeing survivors. You'll leave at dawn.'

Arik was triumphant. 'And the rest?'

Her gaze slid to Klaus. 'If you wish to take a decoy army north to the citadel mount, Master Tristan, you'll have to lead them yourself.' Her eyes were guarded. 'They've allowed you only six hundred swords. If you leave at dusk tomorrow, you'll be there poised to attack just before daybreak. I'll wait until dawn to take my army across the valley, after your attack. Once we cross the ridge, we'll be in plain sight of the pirates.'

Klaus bowed. Hers was a quieter faith than Suman's or Navein's, but at heart Ayla was just as hungry for Merensama. He wondered if her conviction had clouded reason this time.

'Don't hide away,' Klaus told Verdi that evening. 'They know you're not a soldier, but you give them – you *remind* them of hope. Better for them to die with hope than in despair.'

But Verdi's frown only deepened. 'Their hope is what worries me.'

Ravi darted from his collar towards a cook fire.

'That blasted oceloe,' he roared to a round of laughter. 'Well, I can entertain them, if nothing else.' He stomped off after him.

'He should stay with the sick tents tomorrow,' said Arik, watching

Verdi run in one direction and Ravi another. 'What next, assuming we free the citadel and leave alive?'

They'd never looked too far into the future. Verdi's position was still far from secure.

Klaus lowered his voice. 'The Eh Menishian were massacred by Northern armies. They have every reason to hate Invelmar. Sacking the South might be just the beginning. We could be more useful to Dunraven right here in Derinda.'

Arik didn't meet his eyes. Now more than ever, Klaus feared the Warrior's severed ties to the court would yet reel him back north.

At least I'm free of that. Never again would he feel the kinship he once knew with the biggest traitors in the Seven Parts.

But Arik was far from free. 'Maybe we could go back and seek clemency. Tell them about the Eh Menishian...'

'Not while the Sturmsinger Chain holds. They built the Blood Pact on betrayal, Arik. How could we serve the Chain, knowing that?'

'But for a thousand years of peace –'

'A thousand years of lies. My parents are being hounded for protecting Sturmsinger's descendants. Somewhere out there is a rightful bloodline. We can't forget that now.'

He could almost see Arik's Form thrashing to contain this struggle. 'You realise we won't be safe in Derinda forever? Sooner or later, we'll draw the Spyglass's attention.'

Of course Arik was right. In Dunraven, Klaus had been led to believe that Spyglass Adelheim refused to waste good Intelligencers on the Derindin. *All the while, he was ferreting around here himself.*

Klaus wished this was something he'd dared address with the Hermit. 'If the time comes when we must leave...'

'What about Verdi?'

'This is his place in the world.' The admission drew daggers in Klaus' chest. 'We'll stay long enough to convince him.'

'And if he doesn't listen?'

'He's free to choose. After all, I thought the North was my place, once.'

'Well, we've got to choose somewhere,' Arik replied. 'Ealdormen might get wind of us wherever we go. We can't spend our lives waiting for them.'

Where was the furthest they could go? Klaus smiled to himself. *Ummandir, and make the return Kelselem never did – a trade of two oathkeepers.* But it was an unthinkable distance from the Silfren Part.

'Maybe nowhere's far enough,' said Klaus. 'Maybe I'll settle down here, take a wife.' A name spoke itself in his heart. Reason extinguished it, but not before the shiver of possibility taunted him with fleeting delight.

Arik snorted. 'We can ask those Eh Menishian. They seem to know a thing or two about moving on.'

'Who's moving on?'

Rasan arrived with bowls of stew, trailed by Nerisen, who grasped a wriggling Ravi. Rasan handed them the bowls. 'You're not leaving after the battle?'

Arik snatched his stew out of Ravi's reach. 'There's plenty of work here for us for now.'

'There you are!' Verdi hurried back. Nerisen deposited Ravi on his shoulder and left.

'No one's leaving,' Klaus reassured Rasan, watching Nerisen's retreating back. 'Not yet.'

Perhaps not ever.

*

Arik's battalion left first.

The two Invelmari parted as they had done many times before; without ceremony, and with Arik's crooked smile: 'Bottoms up.'

His tumblers began their march at sunrise, following the ridge south towards the sandy grassland that might soon become the pirates' escape passage to Baeron's land.

'That's the happiest I've seen him since we left Invelmar,' said Verdi sadly.

But Klaus understood. His own heart soared as he prepared to lead his own small company to the citadel mount. He briefed them an hour before dusk.

'Most of you will have to leave your horses behind,' he warned. 'We go without lanterns. Never fall outside of an arm's reach of the tumbler ahead of you, beside you, behind you. And keep your silence; I'll need my orders to carry.'

These are the faithful. The ones who believed in the prophecies, who needed little persuading despite the half-promise of death. Klaus was as glad as he was surprised to discover Alizarin amongst their ranks, his blazing eyes overcast.

Verdi kept busy preparing poultices and tonics for the physicians, more at ease with the business of war than his own quandaries. After all, how many times had Verdi seen him off to battle, often accompanying him to its very edge?

Klaus squeezed his arm. 'Don't stray from the sick tents. They won't be empty for long.'

A crack appeared in Verdi's composure. 'I'm sorry. I wish I'd never suggested running away to Derinda –'

'And winding up tangled in all this?' Klaus rummaged a smile for his former servant. 'I'm the one who should be sorry, dragging you back to a door you never wanted to open. Would you have ever come back here were it not for me?'

'One day, maybe.'

They both knew it wasn't true.

Klaus embraced him. 'Don't forget that door is still waiting.'

He counted the minutes to sundown eagerly, finally climbing into his saddle. The peregrine returned from hunting as though called back. Across the sea of wagons was one with a broken shutter and a jade-painted door, behind which Nerisen would be settling for the night.

They'd barely spoken since the Assembly.

The earth was waiting; its particles ribboned through him, shaping themselves in his mind into every twist of the road ahead. The desert clamoured with hunger.

His last glimpse was of Ayla, clinging to her faith in the face of years of well-honed instinct.

'Don't stumble,' she said.

*

Night fell greedily and clung to the land with a cold and callous grip.

'Stay together,' Saarem roared through the ranks, kneading them back into one dense unit. Klaus set a slower pace. More than once someone stumbled in the dark; arms reached out and steadied a tumbler whose nerves had faltered, or whose feet had tripped on loose rocks. It was still but overcast, robbing them of the comfort of stars. Dense cloud hid the young moon.

'It's better like this,' Klaus told Alizarin, who searched the starless sky incessantly. 'Even a little light might give us away.'

Alizarin only grunted in response.

Even for Klaus, this darkness was dizzying. He focused on the road ahead, warning of the approach of abrupt descents or jutting boulders, or a treacherous wrinkle in the rocks underfoot. The sentinel tumblers he'd stationed in every third row carried back his instructions. They crawled through the darkness like a centipede, over hours that were multiplied by the monotony. Yet something mollified the tumblers as night marched on: a wonder at their own daring, averting every sudden dune and sinkhole; perhaps the white shadow of the peregrine soaring silently overhead.

Klaus stopped every two hours to relieve their minds as much as their legs. Eventually, the wind blew onto his face, and he knew the end of the ridge sheltering them was close. The valley beckoned.

Klaus ordered them to stop just shy of the ridge's descent into the valley. He felt forward into the darkness. There was Pir Sehem's northern perimeter, the land beneath it compressed by its weight. Torchlight twinkled on Pir Sehem's walls. An open palm of valley was all that remained between them and the citadel.

Now they were suspended in the ethereal silence that crouched between dawn and the tail of night, infinite in spite of its fragility.

'If they see us crossing the valley, we'll be carrion meat before we reach the mount.'

Klaus couldn't see the tumbler who'd spoken, but he heard his fear.

'Down there is the old riverbed where the Ninvellyn once ran,' he said. 'It is dry now, but the Ninvellyn is not. Be the river. The water must disturb everything as it charges home.'

Behind them, the blood-red line of dawn dissected heavens from land. Klaus signalled their descent down the ridge in the dredges of the dark, slowly and deliberately, feeling first for loose stones that might tumble underfoot.

He'd been worried about crossing the rocky valley, but the slow pace and hours of practice rewarded them with more stealth than he'd dared to hope for. Now the first few hundred men had crossed the valley, ascending the gentle slope up to the mount. A dozen tumblers had already scaled the citadel's north wall when rocks crashed down into the valley behind them: a tumbler had fallen with his horse.

Lights flared on the citadel wall. Shouts raised the alarm.

'Now!' Klaus cried, and a volley of arrows darted overhead from the mounted archers behind him.

Pandemonium exploded. His tumblers broke over the mount; an overspill of rage churned up from the dormant riverbed. He raised his blade and raced forward to bring in the morning.

47

For Sisoda

WITH THE CUNNING OF STURMSINGER, THEY FASHIONED THE FORM OF
INTELLIGENCER: SHADOWSPUN AND FAR-SEEING, SO THAT INVELMAR
NEED NOT RELY UPON STEEL TO VANQUISH HER ENEMIES.

SONNONFER: ON THE FOUR NOBLE FORMS

The wind struck at dawn, quite suddenly and without warning.

Ayla's voice was hoarse. Her eyes stung with sand. Even with her sand-mask on, she was spitting out its grains. The morning rolled on, and there was no sign of the storm letting up. They'd been forced to wait behind the ridge. Tristan and his company should have long crossed the valley, expecting Ayla's forces to follow.

I've sent them to their deaths. I agreed to this.

The sand-laden wind blinded their eyescopes. They should have marched to Tristan's aid over an hour ago. How many pirates had his ambush diverted to the north of the citadel mount? How many of his

582

company were still alive?

It was a full two hours after dawn before the storm finally calmed enough for them to continue. There was no time now to scout the pirate camp ahead. The two Elders began preparations for the aftermath, tight-lipped.

'We'll lose tumblers crossing the valley,' Rahdib told her as they took their positions on the ridge. What cover pre-dawn would have given them was now lost. At least the air still buzzed with sand. It shimmered like coarse smoke and shrouded the bottom of the valley, and would obscure them until they neared the mount. And the ill-fitting joints of the wind would groan over the rumble of their march.

Ayla lowered her helmet. 'There was always a valley to cross.'

They swarmed into the valley in waves, crashing over the eastern citadel mount.

*

As soon as the wind-gauges began spinning, Arik knew something was about to go badly wrong.

They'd not yet reached the southern border of Sisoda's clandom. They'd marched along the ridge, the valley running to their right, but the visibility Arik had hoped to gain from this higher ground was denied by the approaching storm. As Klaus promised, the ridge levelled out to gentle dunes, where they would be more vulnerable on lower ground. It was almost noon; Ayla should have attacked the pirates' camp. Yet there was no sign of fleeing pirates.

Who else had the wind crippled?

'Shouldn't we have seen a pirate or two by now?' said Starra irritably. Arik's fist of tumblers had all joined his battalion. They were growing restless.

'We're only two hours' ride from the border with Baeron,' Rasan told him. 'There's a wood over the next hill. Where do you want us to take our positions?'

Arik watched the sky. The storm clouds were moored back north, perhaps over the battle itself.

'We won't stay,' he said finally. 'We'll backtrack north-west, towards the citadel. Then we might intercept them.'

It would leave them far more exposed, both from any reinforcements the pirates might summon to their aid as well as from those fleeing the citadel. But the storm clouds smudging the horizon cooled Arik's blood. Something was terribly wrong, and waiting only fanned his foreboding.

*

By the time the wind finally settled, Ayla's battalion had wreaked devastation upon the camp. Tumblers swarmed over the citadel mount on the hem of the wind, replacing the storm with death.

Among the pirate mercenaries and common cut-throats were well-trained fighters, and – of this Ayla was now certain – ex-Murhesla. There were enough of the latter that an overall inferiority had not undermined the pirates' number. So the fight was uneven, their adversaries unpredictable.

Ayla felled another pirate and paused for breath. Rahdib had forced the pirates back against the eastern citadel, where besieged Sisodan tumblers were scaling the walls from within to lend their swords. Sakar had splintered the southern bulk of the pirates' camp, aiming to secure the spring before the pirates could contaminate their only remaining water supply. For now, they were evenly matched, which meant a substantial number of pirates had been diverted north around the citadel by Tristan's attack at dawn.

She circled her spear high in the air. 'To me!'

They carved a bloody path around the mount, aiming north. But the pirates anticipated her target, for a shrill cry ordered a volley of arrows that downed several of her tumblers.

She screamed, 'Onward! Onward!'

They pushed forward, out of the range of the pirates' arrows. Now the main battle was behind them. A faint din buzzed up ahead. It grew louder as they rounded the northern citadel wall and reached the battle raging in the shadow of the ridge.

Cold gripped her heart. The ground was dark with the fallen. Swathes of pirates pressed around the last of Tristan's tumblers. Something came from their midst; a cry that held all the savagery of a wild beast and raised the hair on Ayla's skin, and which set a feral pacemaker for the beating of her heart … with a chill, she recognised the battle cry of Isarnanheri.

He's alive.

She unleashed her tumblers onto the pirates to tear down their triumph.

*

Arik's biggest worry was that they would intercept not stragglers or deserters, but fresh *reinforcements*

The scouts saw them first, racing back to where they'd paused for water.

'At least a thousand, heading northwest – probably back to Pir Sehem. Our paths will cross.'

A thousand pirates. They might be evenly matched in number for now, but how many more such reinforcements might come their way? They'd already dispatched several waves of fleeing pirates – and not without some cost, thanks to their poisoned arrows.

'We'll meet them here,' said Arik. 'It might stretch us, but they mustn't reach Pir Sehem. Whatever damage we can deal here will help break the siege.

Fear rippled through the reassembling tumblers. By Arik's reckoning, it was not unwarranted.

At least they've had a drink.

*

It was well past noon now, and visibility remained poor. Nerisen lowered her eyescope. Physicians and Plainswalkers hovered behind the ridge, wagons ready. The wait for a signal to cross the valley was longer than she could bear.

Viridian sat atop the ridge, watching the citadel mount. He'd been surprisingly composed all morning, but tension now stiffened his stillness.

She filled two gourds with tea and joined him. 'You've done this before.'

He accepted one with a watery smile. 'I've spent plenty of time in the Far North.

Nerisen sipped; the tea was flavourless, made with stale derina water, but it was hot. 'Is it always like this?'

'What is?'

'The waiting.' She struggled to ascribe words to this sickening fear, laden as it was with uncertainty.

Viridian blinked. 'I thought the clans fight often enough.'

'This is different. At least clans know who they're fighting...' He was paying close attention now, and Nerisen wished she hadn't spoken. She *ached* to ask about the gnomon, and whether he'd unlocked the moondial that would guide to a victorious Merensama ... supposedly. It felt wrong to ask; too intimate. But finding the Merensaman moon phase wasn't the only condition he hadn't yet fulfilled. 'Do you mean to take the oath?'

He spluttered on his tea. Ravi squealed indignantly as a coughing fit expelled him out from under Viridian's collar. Nerisen leaned down to catch the oceloe before he got too far.

His voice was hoarse when he got his breath back. 'I don't know.'

'At this point, it's just a formality. Most of those tumblers are here because of you. When they die, their loved ones will console themselves that at least it will have been for Merensama.'

'But it's not, it's to break the siege –'

'Not anymore.'

He pointed across the valley. 'I can't lead a battle like that.'

'Why do you need to lead it when you can be here? There'll be just as much for us to do when the fighting's over.'

He really was an open book, confusion and compassion naked in equal measure.

Of course, it would be then that Elendra's horn sounded across the valley. They sprung to their feet and hurried to the wagons.

*

The second wave of pirates was larger, and came soon after they'd crushed the reserves arriving from the west. Fortunately, these were deserters fleeing the citadel, already tired and wounded. But they were soon followed by a third wave, and a fourth.

Arik moved seamlessly in Jarnstiga. He kept his shield arm raised against poisoned arrows. Amongst the pirates were more seasoned fighters; likely ex-Murhesla. They weren't as skilled as Ayla, but they still outclassed the rest. His fist of tumblers fought savagely. *A good cause is more deadly than good steel,* Lisbeta had insisted. If he were to die in this valley, these Derindin would not be unworthy company.

It was a grim but timely thought. Pirates now numbered almost twice his soldiers, and the last wave brought mangonels launching flaming missiles. Most of these were now aflame, but the damage had been done.

'Bring the last one down,' he roared to the archers firing torched arrows.

They'd remained in the peripheries of the storm: winds that littered the air with grit and waylaid the mangonels' missiles. But now his eyes were raw with dust, and his throat was sore from inhaling mouthfuls of toothed wind, and his arms were growing heavier as he swung his way through yet more pirates.

A pirate caught his eye in the thick of the fighting; he wore a black armguard and a strange painted helmet. He commanded the pirates around him from a great bay stallion.

'On me,' Arik shouted hoarsely, gathering a fist of tumblers behind him.

They hacked their way through the battlefield. Soon they were no longer merely in the outskirts of the storm, but within its path. The wind gasped unevenly, sand rising and falling in erratic currents. The helmeted pirate had seen their approach, summoning pirates to him.

They kept shields raised against a rain of arrows. One of Rasan's knives flew past Arik's shoulder; the bay stallion collapsed with a violent neigh. Tumblers and pirates collided.

Arik spun around, seeking the painted helmet. Sand and grit hummed angrily in the air like swarming bees, now accompanied by a heavy odour, sweet and cloying... Arik's head began to swim. The clashes and cries of battle faded in his ears...

...*there!* The painted helmet, not a few paces away. But the pirate wearing it was much larger now, twice the height of an Invelmari – *impossible!* The centre of him blazed, like the heart of steel thrown to the furnace before it became molten... His helmet grew to monstrous proportions and became cruelly horned, and his blade was alive with blue fire and venom... Every fibre of Arik's aching body screamed at him to turn away, but he was arrested by this demon –

'*Upon your head it will be.*' Arik *felt* as much as heard the rusting thunder of the demon's voice. '*The dead wolf whose name cannot be again spoken –*'

Confusion threw a lifeline to his Form. He heard himself snarl through the wind: '*What* will be?'

'*By his hand, the fall of all you hold dear – at last, the demise of the North –*'

He couldn't possibly mean Klaus. *How can he know about Klaus?* It was no time for reason, and reason seemed beyond him altogether.

'*What say you to the breaking of the North?*'

How? But Arik could no longer summon his voice. He no longer saw soldiers around him, but shadows moving as dark plumes of smoke. There was such a sickly smell, a horrible smell – *how?*

'*For the sake of the North, he must be extinguished. I will tell you all. Let me live to tell you.*'

Arik had no idea if his lips moved – if there was anything there of substance that could even hear him – but he heard his own thoughts whisper back into the smoke. *If that's the price, the North isn't worth saving.*

Something terrible happened then; Thunraz became a dead weight in his hands, and when he swung it he felt as though he were wielding the weight of a felled tree. Cold, clammy fear broke over him; he was powerless without his sword here. Then the moment passed, and Thunraz was moving again. An instinct as primitive as blood wrenched him back to himself, and he summoned the icy stillness of his Form, and his blade swept through the smoke, splicing the speaker in half.

The demon spoke no more, though Arik was certain he had seen yellow eyes glow through the haze before he expired, crowning a triumphant smile.

The sickly sweet smell still lined Arik's nostrils, like the sooty residue of a fire. But with that deathblow, the battle re-erupted into his consciousness, and he gave himself to his blade.

Hours later, their swords finally fell still.

Arik walked through the dead. The storm still fizzled. A few stragglers crossed their path, but nothing challenging. His heart dragged. Barely a third of his battalion was left.

Gonsar asked, 'What about the survivors?'

'We didn't come to take prisoners.'

The wind finally fell silent for the execution of the remaining pirates. Arik combed through the valley. It was growing dark; he picked up a torch. There was the downed bay stallion, Rasan's knife deep in its flank. He pulled it out and wiped it clean on the grass. He searched for the painted helmet. Soon his torch picked out the glint of painted metal...

The pirate's remains lay near his horse. *Just a man after all.* Whatever he had professed to know, no one else would hear it now. Arik removed the helmet; it was not Derindin, but the pirate was. There was no tattoo on his shoulder blade, but around his neck was an assortment of trinkets, and figures were cut into both his cheeks, and feathers were woven into his hair.

'Master Marcin?'

Gonsar and Rasan joined him. Arik returned Rasan's knife. She leaned forward to peer at the dead pirate.

'This one doesn't look like any Derindman I've ever seen.'

'Hard to believe he is,' Gonsar muttered, examining his adornments. 'I've heard of these types, but not in Derinda – *shamans,* I think they call them. Didn't Tristan say he met one in their stronghold?'

Arik stared at the mutilated face. From what he'd seen in the other Parts, shamans came in all varieties. Perhaps this one was an initiate of the Eh Menishian.

Rasan was watching him. 'Is something wrong?'

The sickly smell still clung to Arik's nostrils. 'He did something to me.'

'Something? What?'

'A vision ... an illusion of some kind...'

Gonsar prised open the dead man's hand. There was a pipe in it; not the sort the Derindin favoured for their famed smokeleaf, but one with a very long shank. Charred contents filled its bowl. Gonsar sniffed at it, wrinkling his nose.

'Efeshyun.' He straightened. 'Strong mix, by the smell of it.'

'What is it?'

'A herb. Some use it for a dirty high and a trip to the faeries because it's cheap and grows like a weed. But this is a lot more concentrated.' Gonsar pulled a face. 'You've really not come across it before, Master Marcin? It probably affected you more, then. Most of us have had a whiff or two of efeshyun. Effect wears away after a bit.'

That evening, when Arik had finally stopped for a bite, Rasan came to find him again.

'There's another one of those shamans amongst the prisoners.'

This one had arrived with a group of reserves marching to Pir Sehem. And he was alive.

He was younger than the pirate Arik had killed. Rows of rings and piercings adorned his ears, nipples, nostrils, belly; white feathers were tied into matted hair. Blood and bruises obscured the symbols daubed on his chest in black and ochre ink. Again, familiar enough to Arik but alien amongst the Derindin. He wasn't going anywhere on the two broken legs still trapped under his fallen horse, and these were the least of his injuries.

Arik told Rasan and the two tumblers standing over him, 'Leave us.'

They glanced at the pirate curiously, but obeyed.

Arik knelt down beside the pirate. He opened one eye. The second eye remained closed, the empty socket covered by a sunken fold of skin that had once been his eyelid.

'Now *you* are Derindin,' Arik told him. 'And yet this –' He picked up one long feather-pierced coil of hair, trailing a string of wooden dice. 'This is not.'

Most of the pirate's teeth were bloodied or missing. 'And you're a filthy Northman,' he croaked.

Arik leaned closer. He smelled dirt and approaching death.

'Not just a Northman,' he said softly. 'The Arm of the Court reaches very far indeed.'

He let Form creep into his eyes. The pirate had strength enough for fear, and hatred was close on its heels.

'It was a Northman who took my eye,' he spat. Then he laughed. 'Did him no good for that missing ear.'

A shaft of ice skewered Arik's heart. 'What did he want? When?'

The pirate laughed again. Arik drew a knife. A moment later he was ready to talk.

'In Romel,' the pirate gasped. 'A year ago – I was just a tumbler then... He knew about the digging, tricked me into thinking he was recruiting for them, the bastard –'

'What did he look like?'

'Northern ... young ... older than you – redheaded, Northern –'

'What did he want to know?'

'What they're doing –' He choked; Arik loosened his grip on his throat.

'I know this man, and I mean to do to him what he did to you,' he told the pirate. 'Do you want to die knowing you'll be avenged? Tell me what you told him. Did he know about the mine?'

The pirate's breath came in gasps. 'He knew.'

Arik waited again as the pirate coughed, choked on bloody secretions, coughed again. Then he realised the pirate was laughing.

'It was already in Invelmar,' he said, laughing until he wheezed. 'What they're looking for, all of them … and he thought it was just the ore they wanted! The bonemaster knows…' He stopped, wheezing, staring at Arik with wild eyes. 'You promised.'

Laughter exhausted the last of his breath. He slipped out of consciousness. He would die an hour later, secure in the vow for revenge.

Arik let him go. In the torrid storm of his thoughts, one shard of clarity stabbed as suddenly as a knife.

One-eared Clevenger Eldred is Adela's Spyglass.

Who else would be so deeply entrenched in dark intelligence, working quietly alone, unless their secrets were too great to be shared? He *must* have been secretly appointed as Spyglass after Adelheim's death.

Even a Warrior's blood chilled at the notion of a Spyglass scouring the Plains.

And I've just promised to kill him.

He rejoined the Derindin. For all their faults, they seemed more wholesome to him then. They buried their dead late into the night. Then, because even the Derindin had no objection, they left the pirates for carrion.

*

Ayla had not yet slept.

She rode around the liberated citadel, reviewing the destruction. The dead littered the Plains, pirates and tumblers alike, and nowhere more so than north of the citadel mount.

Tristan's tumblers *had* broken up the pirates' army for the rest of them, and most of them had paid for it with their lives. Soon she would know the full scale of their losses, for in the last hour a falcon had brought word from Marcin, and there was time yet to lose more tumblers if he met more deserters on his return along the ridge. Thus, Ayla had no appetite for the strangled cheer that spilled from Pir Sehem when its gates finally opened.

This was the true taste of victory: choking and bilious.

Sisodans brought out their dead as Plainswalkers entered the citadel with food and medicines. Ayla returned to the sick tents erected outside the gates. It was easy to pick out the one sheltering Tristan; every so often, the spotted peregrine circled the sky above it. Ayla was not superstitious, but she had her beliefs, and they were deeply rooted.

He was still under the effects of the sleeping draught. His face was grey, but the physician said exhaustion was his greatest injury. Beneath the fine layer of Invelmari steel chainmail shirt that few Derindin would even recognise for what it was, he was bruised but not severely wounded. She had fingered the curiously shadow-sheened, blood-spattered metal herself, examined its fluid joints and links. *It is still only of the earth*; only as strong as the soldier it protected. But this Northman was no mere soldier. Of this, she was sure. Already, the tumblers moved around him cautiously, reverently.

Elder Tourmali watched from the shadows of the tent. Viridian, to his credit, had not lingered long by Tristan's bed, tending the wounded elsewhere.

'We are playing with fire, General,' said the Elder. 'We've only just begun to garner support. How long before it turns against us for making a crutch of our oldest enemy?'

Ayla bit down on a slew of choice replies. There *was* substance to his fear. The shadow of the North still loomed longest over the Plains. Had she herself not felled an elite Northman for each of her wings? And yet without these two Invelmari, she might be amongst those lying in stony graves at the bottom of the valley. She might not have ridden to Sisoda's aid at all.

*

A tattered cheer greeted Arik and the remains of his battalion when they reached the citadel mount. His armour had grown impossibly heavier in that final hour, and every bit of him ached. It was well past dusk.

Someone crashed into his side; it was Verdi.

Relief washed over Arik. 'How's...'

'Alive. But his company took heavy losses. The sand storm delayed Ayla, and they were on their last leg by the time she reached them...' Verdi's face fell. 'So few have come back with you.'

He led Arik into a tent and went to fetch water. Arik sat down and loosened his armour. A gash to his left arm most likely needed cauterising. A residue of that sweet smell clung to his nostrils still.

...the fall of all you hold dear ... at last, the demise of the North –

He looked up at the distant sound of his name. Nerisen held out a cup of water.

Arik's head swam, the smell pulsing stronger in his nostrils; he almost looked around for the painted helmet. She was helping him now with his armour, then the sleeve over his wounded arm. The touch of her hands cleared the clouds a little. His head hadn't felt completely his own since the efeshyun smoke; even his Form had been sluggish.

He managed, 'Where's Tristan?'

'Resting. How long has this been bleeding?'

A physician seared his wound, leaving Nerisen to dress it. *The dead wolf whose name cannot again be spoken* ... Arik's head throbbed. It was hardly coincidence – Wintermantels, wolves amongst Ealdormen, their first heir dead ... *how did he know about Klaus?* And how could *Klaus* be such a harbinger, how could he possibly – the entire notion was unthinkable.

Or was it? The oily little voice prising at the joins of his Form was as greasy as the residue of efeshyun. *He's already begun to change ... does he not already have every reason to seek vengeance for what was done to him?*

Is he not the child of Ealdormen's enemies?

Furiously, Arik summoned Form again, quashing the voice again, dizzy again.

'Nerisen, what do you know about efeshyun?'

He realised he'd interrupted her. He hadn't even heard her speak. She didn't reproach him, peering at him instead.

'It's a potent hallucinogen, toxic in large amounts. Plenty of fools make a tea of it when they can't get enough of its smoke, and choke in their sleep. Why?'

Arik described the pipe-blower in the pirate's hand. 'It was as though it had stolen my...' *My Form.* The thought made him sick. 'My strength. Can it make ... could it have controlled me through the hallucinations?'

'That's beyond the power of science and sounds more like superstitious nonsense.' Her crisp confidence was just what he needed. 'Sounds like you had a bad reaction. Not everyone has fun with efeshyun.' She tied the final bandages. 'In any case, it'll wear away soon enough, more slowly since there's more of you.'

Arik was *not* superstitious, but it hadn't escaped him that the pirate, a Derindin, appeared to have been initiated in the ways of a shaman – perhaps an Eh Menishian shaman. Arik had politely sneered at the shamans of Ungal and Zenzabra, but he'd nonetheless been wary of their eery otherworldliness.

Perhaps she's right. He'd reacted badly to a drug. Arik decided he was satisfied with this.

'Thanks, Nerisen,' he said, feeling more like himself. Enough to appreciate her startling eyes, and the way her braid coiled over her shoulder to fall between her breasts.

'Who's Elodie?'

The smile creeping across his face turned wooden. 'That's a name I've not heard in a long time. Where did you hear it?'

'Tristan mentioned it several times when he was with fever.'

'Probably delirious.' Jerked fully back to clarity now, Arik held her gaze innocently. 'Though a man leaves behind many names when he travels so far.' He garnished this with a rogue's wink. 'Speaking of the devil, I'd better go and find him.'

*

Bells rang throughout the citadel. Alizarin walked through the lower quarter, his good arm resting on his sword hilt. The other was in a sling after Viridian had reduced his dislocated shoulder. People wandered around, dazed. Others put out the last of the fires; when the pirates sensed defeat, they began burning whatever they could. The cleanup would continue for weeks, but tomorrow there would be a celebration of their victory, bittersweet as it was, before Sisodans began the slow and painful repair of the clandom.

He returned to the tent where Klaus was finally awake. Alizarin hung back; Arik and Viridian were already there. He was about to leave when a voice behind him demanded: 'Where is he?'

It was Yodez, newly returned home from the S'beyan Strip. Tourmali hurried in after him.

The Sisodan Chieftain looked the worse for wear, a bloody bandage around his chest and a crutch keeping the weight off one leg. He limped inside and pointed to Viridian.

'I charge you, fruit of the limolan, to raise Lorendar's banner and renew his holy war. For this, Sisoda will join your alliance.'

A hush greeted the first pledge to Merensama itself.

Viridian paled. 'Thank you, Ahen. Though I can't accept your pledge before making my own.'

'Then sign your name in the Book of Oaths,' Yodez replied. 'The first token of our allegiance will be a confession. The pirates didn't choose my clandom for their first conquest at random. A month ago, we captured a pirate who confessed allegiance to tunnel-makers working in the shadow of the Mengorian range. He was a pitiful creature. We dismissed his claims as desperate lies, because there's not enough water to piss in that far South. Now I hear of these *Eh Menishian* digging in the Waste.'

Klaus sat up on the makeshift bed. 'Did he say anything else?'

'He claimed more of them were camped on the edge of the Black Lava Plains, further west still. I erred: I sent spies to investigate. They never returned. Now I believe it was his confession to me and the spies I sent that marked our clandom for destruction.' Yodez grasped Arik's forearm. 'All of Sisoda salutes you, Masters Invelmari. I will lend whatever support you need to hunt down these brass-faced men.'

Tourmali was aghast. 'What could there possibly be in the Black Lava Plains that they want?'

Yodez's face hardened in grim determination. 'I intend to find out.'

Alizarin's heart plummeted, further than ever from triumph.

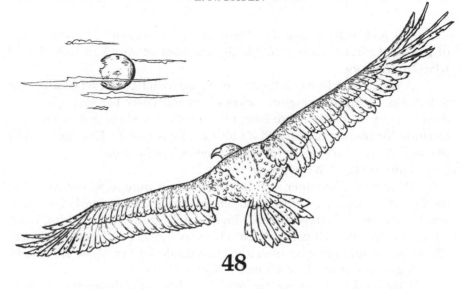

48

Aftermath

Smokeleaf burned, cider flowed. They'd buried the dead. Pir Sehem's dungeons were full of any loose tongues that might yet wag some more. Another toast raised another cheer in the Chieftain's hall.

Klaus sent a serving boy on his way. His cup had not gone empty all evening. He was growing tired of tipping it out.

Arik wasn't drinking much, either. Klaus had never seen him less pleased to be at a feast. They'd finally escaped to a corner of the hall.

Arik whispered despite the cover of music. 'You agree that pirate crossed paths with Adelheim's squire, then? That he might even be Adela's *Spyglass* now?'

Arik had been on edge since the whiff of the efeshyun. His description of the dead pirate-shaman invoked a memory of Krevkatt that chilled Klaus to the bone.

'Adilmar said that Adelheim – well, the merchant who I believe was Adelheim – caught sfarsgour sickness several years before he actually died in Dunraven. But there hasn't been a case of sfarsgour sickness in Derinda for two centuries, and it kills fast. I wonder if Clevenger hadn't planned Adelheim's death for some time before he died.'

'Planned to *kill* a Spyglass?'

'Why not? Clevenger's an Intelligencer. A quiet one, not raised to the Eye. Adelheim was difficult to rein in, and the Lifegiver knows how much intelligence he'd gathered. Maybe Adela grew weary of him. What better way for an Intelligencer to earn his way into her highest confidence? Clevenger would have been an ideal candidate for Spyglass, after that.'

A grimace soured Arik's face. 'Eisen's blade...'

'I think I'd rather spend the rest of my life in the desert flirting with *tesh* than go back to that again,' Klaus murmured. *Those days are over now.* But they would haunt him always. 'I'd rather get lost in the sand.'

'From what they're saying, that's not likely to happen.'

A wary edge gilded Arik's voice. They never spoke of slight matter in Dunraven. Not just because it was the most forbidden branch of the Lost Sciences; the only alchemy that had ever interested Arik was the guarded science of making Invelmari steel, and Arik had relinquished that curiosity when he chose the Form of Warrior over Blacksmith.

Klaus said nothing.

Unmistakable panic crept into Arik's question. 'Do you really not want to see the North again?'

'Perhaps one day when Elodie is queen.' Yearning stabbed Klaus. 'Does it matter? With my parents being what they are ... I can't go back now, even if I wanted to.'

'You don't know anything about them yet for certain.'

Arik was still resisting the version of the world sealed in Sefta's cave. Klaus couldn't begrudge him this. *His betrayal is more tender yet than mine.*

'The only thing my family left me came from Ettsrakka in the Sterns.' Klaus' fingers hovered over the weight in his pocket. 'Ealdormen massacred Far Northerners there. Doesn't it seem strange that no one knows where Ettsrakka is? The Ealdormen don't just forget their battles, the Sonnonfer records everything. Unless they never wanted the bloodland found.'

'Why would the Ealdormen conceal it? They won their battle there.'

'It wasn't so long after Sturmsinger's death. Maybe Ettsrakka was the last enclave of those loyal to Sturmsinger – like my parents. Maybe some even knew the truth about his death.' *Why else would my parents choose this weight to leave with me?*

'There'll be Ealdormen who want a place at Sturmsinger's table much more than the throne, you know,' Arik insisted. 'They'd support the truth, if they knew it.'

'And the rest? Adela wouldn't spare her own mother and father if she caught them betraying the Chain. Why would anyone believe me, anyway?'

'What if you're actually a nobleman?' Arik suggested. Perhaps anything was better than the truth. 'The Wintermantels might have just looked for an heir closer to home, rather than put a commoner on the throne. Maybe some Ealdorman's bastard. Wolfram's, even.'

Klaus didn't bother reminding him that royal bastards were killed in their cradles. 'Nothing will help me win Adela's favour if she learns what my parents are.'

'She ought to be warned about the Eh Menishian, at least.'

'They'll know soon enough. Most likely they already do.'

'Enough of your tear-jerking,' a grizzled tumbler roared across the hall at the bard. 'Let's have a bit of a drum. A drum!'

This was greeted with cheers, and the bard was jostled aside by a player a little too drunk on the wine pilfered from the pirates' supplies. The drums weren't loud enough to stifle the next cheer to erupt when the doors swung open: Verdi, returning with a few Plainswalkers from the sick tents.

'Never known you to talk in your sleep before. Bad habit to pick up now.' Arik jerked his head towards Nerisen. 'She asked about Elodie.'

'What did you tell her?'

'I thought it might do your chances some good if she's a little jealous.'

A sly glint flashed in Arik's eye, but a genuine warning lined his humour.

'You needn't worry,' Klaus murmured. 'If Nerisen had any idea of the truth, she would have drawn a knife on me long ago.'

Verdi spotted them. 'There you are! Hiding in the dark...' His eyes slid to Klaus. 'Almost thought you'd buggered off back to the border already.'

A watery smile was poor disguise for the fear hiding behind his shaky humour.

Klaus trod gently. 'A caravan's travelling to the border towns to restock Sisoda's granary. I'll go with them.'

He glanced up at the rafters, half expecting to see the peregrine still perched there, and suppressed another jolt of excitement. The Derindin were far from ready to lead an army south to the Eh Menishian stronghold. There was time enough to go to Tiptoe at last.

Arik set his cup down. 'I pulled Fibbler out of Romel when you were away –'

'Why've you waited all this time to tell me?'

'– from the clutches of a Babble who we think was smuggling a message about you.'

Looking very sheepish, Verdi gave Klaus a folded note.

'The wolf has flown South. Await my signal.'

He stared at the dreaded words.

The Derindin's world had absorbed him just enough that, briefly, he'd slipped out of the shadow of the Wintermantels. But here it was: all the darkness of the North, still close on his heels.

Arik added, 'The Babble used Fibbler to deliver it to a pirate.'

Klaus stilled. If Form towered any higher around him, he'd lose sight of himself altogether. 'A pirate heading south, to the camp?'

'North. He took Fibbler too. Luckily he didn't make it far before Fibbler got away. We've not tracked down the Babbler yet.'

Every bruise, every cut and scrape and sprain throbbed all at once. 'There's more…'

'Oh good, don't hold back.' Klaus got up. 'This bard's off key.'

Outside were cool dark gulps of night air, still torrid with the ghost of the storm, though finally clear of its debris.

Klaus listened to the rest of their confession without interruption. Of course he knew the pearlberry ivy. He hadn't spotted it in Thillaina's house, either.

He reached out aimlessly into the overcast night. Sickness soured his stomach, and he couldn't touch the desert.

'You've gone very pale…' Verdi guided him to the upturned remains of a wagon.

His head spun as he sat. *It's the exhaustion.* He'd been sitting for hours in clouds of smokeleaf.

'Do you have any recollection of Thillaina in Dunraven?' Arik asked. 'Even a mention of her?'

Klaus shook his head. He'd seen Lady Wintermantel's pearlberry ivy daily, in different forms. He knew that woman's particular fondness for it. But Lady Wintermantel never said more of the celebrated seamstress who had so long retained her custom.

Why didn't I see it myself? He was certain he would have recognised the familiar pattern immediately, if he had. Had Thillaina grown careless, after Klaus had gone?

She was perfectly positioned to send word north. How smug he'd been, thinking he'd sidestepped the Wintermantels. The Hermit's scorn echoed in his ears. *Vanity is an insidious disease.*

Verdi knelt beside him. 'Do you need a drink?'

'A drink?' Saarem appeared at the helm of a handful of Elendran tumblers returning from a watch. 'You're within sniffing distance of one, what are you doing jabbering away out here when you could be in there?'

Moments later, they were back in the midst of the feasting, this time surrounded by Derindin.

'Here.' Rasan pushed a kahvi towards Klaus, herself favouring it over drink. 'You look like you could do with this.'

He took it gratefully.

She remained quiet, apart from the gales of laughter and raucous jokes, periodically pulling her eyes away from Arik. 'Does it get easier?'

'Familiar,' he said. 'Not easier.'

'Where now, mountain legs?' Saarem drew up a chair, setting down a pitcher of wine. 'Not picking up the scent of the next fight?'

'Stay here,' said a Sisodan tumbler. 'You'll be heroes. Only fools would turn your swords away. Then, once the pirates are buried, take some land and a woman to share your bed. You can have your pick of both. It can be a good life.'

For a moment, Klaus glimpsed the world through the tumbler's eyes: the savage beauty of the desert; a lifetime's study of its stars and its ancient wisdom. The warmth of a woman every night who was as fierce as she was tender. Then he returned to the desolate place in his breast that had opened since he'd stumbled into Sefta's cave, and felt the pull of the peregrine hunting somewhere outside.

'Perhaps.'

Rahdib tapped a glass at the Chieftain's table. He was bolstered by a round of banging on tables before the hall fell quiet to listen.

'Derindin!' A cheer rose, and had to be hushed again. 'To the most noble of us all: the fallen.' The quiet softened with echoed murmurs: *to the fallen.* Rahdib raised his cup towards Verdi. 'And to a new dawn.'

Saarem raised Verdi's arm, oblivious to his red face, drawing another cheer. Klaus rapped on the table with the others. Sendar rose beside him as music began playing again.

'Gentlemen, ruffians.' He raised his cup to their small gathering. 'To a Northern wind in the Plains.'

Around their table, cheers condensed to solemn murmurs. Saarem squeezed Klaus' shoulder.

Arik emptied his cup and got to his feet, winking. 'I'm going to find fairer company.'

He left amidst gales of full-bellied laughter. Klaus scanned the hall. Still no sign of Nerisen; probably in the refuge tents, her work barely begun.

Verdi nudged him. 'Call it a night?'

Outside, the citadel was wide awake. A waning gibbous moon grew in the sky. Soon it would be full; Klaus resisted asking Verdi how he was faring with the moondial. Pir Sehem betrayed flashes of splendour: in the silhouettes of castle towers framed with torchlight, and magnificent desert pines the Sisodans had refused to cut down for firewood even under siege. But its streets were strewn with broken wood and twisted metal, stacks of barrels, rubble. Sisodans had barely waited to begin; even now people walked around with torches: inspecting, planning, salvaging. Mourning. A girl touched one knuckle to her forehead as they passed.

Verdi managed to hold out until they reached the makeshift camp outside the citadel. 'When will you leave?'

'Tomorrow.'

There was a world of worry in Verdi's silence.

Klaus elbowed him lightly. 'I mean to come back.'

'Don't go looking for trouble,' Verdi pleaded. 'Don't be tempted…'

'To punish the Wintermantels?' Klaus finished. 'I'm not angry now.' Ironically he was growing grateful for the gift of common blood. *At least now I can try my luck with Nerisen.*

'What about Thillaina?'

'She has no reason to suspect where I'm going.'

They found a lonely fire for warmth.

'I do want to help them, Klaus.' Verdi dodged his eyes. 'To find this phase of the moon they need.'

'I know. And you should.'

The first part of relief finally loosened Verdi's shoulders. 'But not alone.'

'You won't be alone.'

Hope hovered in the smoke.

Verdi cast him a sidelong glance. 'Do you remember when you wanted to travel the Parts, before you settled for your Form?'

Settled. Verdi had that knack; to soften any blow. Time had not dulled the sting of that severance, even though the hunger to roam that had once burned Klaus no longer gnawed. What he wouldn't give now instead to walk Dunraven again, to fall asleep in Longtooth to the howl of wolves.

Verdi prodded his side. 'You're free do that now, you know. Go wherever you want.'

Klaus repeated, 'I'm coming back.'

'Maybe it's not the journey you wanted, but the destination,' said Verdi. 'An anchor.'

But he *had* chosen an anchor. His Form, the Blood Pact, and a place at Sturmsinger's table. Even this had been shaken. Now he was let loose again, new shores in sight.

That night he dreamed of warm desert-kissed skin, and a green-eyed girl in his arms.

The following morning he found her in the refuge tents, preparing rations of food and fuel. She barely glanced up when he entered the tent.

How he would have liked to have been at liberty then to offer her a wreath of the jasmines she favoured.

'Nerisen?'

Her eyes were sharper than a rebuke. 'There are many in the citadel who'll still have nowhere to sleep and nothing to eat by nightfall.'

He held out a fold of cloth. 'I won't keep you long.'

Inside was the resin-leaf from Gainshe's amulet. The rock and the claw, he would give to Alizarin and Coaren.

'The Eh Menishian who gave me this said it was from her homeland. Her people were careful to reveal little of wherever that is.' Her frown vanished; she examined the leaf preserved in resin. 'Will you give it to Master Meron to study?'

She looked up. 'You're not going back to Samsarra?'

'Eventually. I'm going to Noisy Tree with Sisoda's caravan first.'

She touched the bail screwed into the base of the resin-leaf. 'Was this part of something else?'

'An amulet,' he replied. 'To ward off evil spirits. It was very dear to someone, once.'

She didn't ask any more questions. How illegible she could be, like the Southern constellations. It seemed impossible that there had been anything more than this frigid silence between them.

'Thank you, Nerisen.' He bowed as low as he'd once done before Adela. His fingers ached to touch her, even through the steel-laced leather of his gloves. Curling the fist of his Form around this longing, he joined the caravan that would take him back to the North.

*

It was a full fortnight before they pulled out of Pir Sehem. Now that he'd seen the pirates' numbers here, Alizarin dreaded any news from Samsarra. But Emra's falcons had brought no word of opportunistic raids on Elendra, and the influx of refugees had finally slowed. The real gain from those extra weeks in the West was Viridian. He worked tirelessly alongside Plainswalkers, rooting out the weak and wounded under the Sisodans' eyes. They would remember him now.

But not once did Alizarin see him with the gnomon.

An air of expectation travelled with them, simmering to a silent frenzy of speculation as they approached Romel. But Viridian had made it clear he had no intention of opening the Book of Oaths before Klaus' return. Viridian was certain Klaus *would* return; something Alizarin would have once doubted. Alizarin braced himself. Allies lined up with their questions, and Elders were growing restless. *This* was the moment to seal their victory with another step towards Merensama; now, when the echoes of Viridian's name still rang throughout the streets.

Yet Alizarin's thoughts dwelled not on Viridian or even the Eh Menishian, but on the man who had thrust his nephew into the centre of the Romelian Assembly; the man who had died twice.

The Derindin sensed it too. Ilnurhin hovered around Klaus now like a sweet nostalgia. Even if they couldn't name it, those who were perceptive to the invisible currents of it flowing so strongly through the Plains recognised there was something *other* about the Invelmari chronicler – though Alizarin suspected few had any idea of his significance.

Alizarin let the matter of the oath sleep for now. Theirs was a quiet dinner at Riorga's inn. They had reached an uneasy truce. But there were other matters Alizarin couldn't ignore.

'When we return to Samsarra, Viridian, you'll have an ideal opportunity to find somewhere else to live.'

Viridian pushed food around on his plate. 'I suppose.'

Arik was less gentle. 'Horse's arse to that. You can't stay under a spy's roof.'

They waited as a maid collected the remains of the meal. She loitered a little too long by Arik, but Alizarin found himself growing grudgingly glad of the Northman's presence.

'Well?' Alizarin pressed.

Viridian nodded, bottom lip jutting out stubbornly. Yirma had done just the same.

'What will we do the next time she sends a message to the North?' he worried.

'I've placed a watch on her comings and goings, and on the girls who work at her spindles.' Alizarin paused. 'Have you decided where you'll go if you're discovered, Master Warrior? You and I at least can be frank with one another.'

Arik's smile was humourless. 'They need me alive.'

'Thillaina mentioned a name,' said Alizarin. 'Perhaps you know it. She spoke of one Florian Arnander.'

He might as well have thrown a match onto hay. The colour drained from his nephew's face.

Arik's smile vanished. 'In connection to what?'

'He was the one who first sought a Derindin companion for the Wintermantels' child.'

Arik stood up. 'I don't remember this place being so stuffy.'

Saya crouched at Alizarin's elbow, tense as a coiled spring. Alizarin followed them outside. The yard behind the inn was empty.

'Florian Arnander is the Wintermantels' chief spy,' said Arik quietly.

'He was Klaus' Form Master. If Thillaina knows this man, she's more dangerous than you think.'

Alizarin caught his breath. 'Well, if there was any doubt she's working for the Wintermantels –'

'It's worse than that,' Arik interrupted. 'He was the Spyglass at Adela's coronation. The Spyglass is almost always an Ealdorman, an Intelligencer; Arnander was a rare exception – such were his talents. The only reason he isn't the Spyglass still was a fall from his horse that almost killed him. We were children when it happened. Another Spyglass was appointed and Arnander went into the service of the Wintermantels when he recovered. Wintermantel's man he may now be, but whether a Spyglass' loyalties really ever change...'

Something about the Ealdorman's stillness made the hair stand straight on Alizarin's skin.

'I'll have her placed under house arrest. I can find a reason.'

'Why didn't you arrest her sooner?' Fear flared Viridian's nostrils. 'You *want* her to be free, don't you? So she can lead Wintermantel's spies to them –'

Alizarin's anger exploded softly. 'And into Samsarra? At least think before you say the first foolish thing that comes into your head.' Alizarin closed his eyes for a moment. *He's young. It's his fear talking.* 'She'll be prisoner by morning.'

But Viridian kicked a pebble bitterly. 'It's already too late.'

*

Still aglow with their triumph, Klaus found the Sisodans' company easy, bolstering. They were soldiers; simple of purpose, steadfast in loyalty. A welcome waft of the North. Or perhaps it was hatchling hope that buoyed Klaus as they edged closer to the border. For the first week, the peregrine soared high above them, giving cheer to the Derindin.

'Do you know where your bird came from?' asked Klira, a husky-voiced tumbler with an unruly head of curls and a good eye with her crossbolt. She had a few more years of fighting than the others.

'A hermit,' Klaus replied. 'And I don't think I can call her mine.'

'That's wise.' She followed the peregrine's path through the skies. 'The last time a great spotted peregrine was seen this far south, the dam would have been a twinkle in Sturmsinger's heart. They're river creatures, nesting only near water. Now they stay close to the border. Whenever they're sighted, we make a prayer for rain. They're the spirit of the Ninvellyn in the sky.'

Now he understood the wonder in the Derindin's eyes as they watched the peregrine. Klaus admired the span of her wings, wishing he could cross paths again with Niremlal the birdkeeper while the peregrine still kept his company. He would have dearly loved to know Niremlal's thoughts.

'What's her name?' Klira asked.

He reminded her, 'She isn't mine to name.'

The morning she failed to appear, he was filled with trepidation trimmed with joy. *Perhaps she's gone to find my mother.* He couldn't eat for excitement. Would his mother know what the Wisdom's token meant? Would his father be with her?

That first hot desert crossing into Derinda from Invelmar felt like a lifetime ago. Spring was slowly ripening to summer. Time passed fluidly with this smaller caravan, though he still carried as many worries as the miles. A Spyglass in the desert; the mysteries surrounding the Eh Menishian. Pirate disciples to one such as Krevkatt. Once or twice they spotted signs of pirates by eyescope. Perhaps the pirates were still smarting, for they steered well away. The Sisodans awaited them fiercely, daring the dunes to produce bandits that never came.

They joined the Saffron Highway after a second week. Each time Klaus paused to take measurements or consult his compass, the Sisodans waited without complaint. If he commented on the road ahead, they paid close attention. Around campfires they became all the things he'd come to prize about the Derindin: warm-blooded, sincere, passionately alive.

'Come back with us to Pir Sehem,' urged Perlo, a retired captain and de facto leader of their caravan. 'Other Invelmari settlers swear that Sisoda suited them best of all the clans. You've met Adilmar, from the S'beyan Strip?'

'There are a few others, too,' added Kaarl, a younger man.

'The first Simyerin came from the West.'

Perlo bonked his head. 'No they didn't, they came from the Zmerrudi Part, over the sea.'

'Bollocks to both of you,' scoffed another. 'They were given wings, like the sage-bird, and roamed the Plains, seeing everything. No one can prove where they came from.'

'Careful though, Master Invelmari,' Klira warned. 'Some of the Simyerin became mad.'

Klaus savoured his campfire kahvi. 'Why?'

'Driven mad by ilnurhin. Wandering off into the desert, never to be seen…'

'Don't put him off.' Pirlo threw an apple core at her. 'He's only just been born.'

Soon they were all drawn into this surreal debate.

'There've not been Simyerin since the First Redrawing, you dolt.'

'What other explanation is there?'

They began like this, those earliest insinuations. Klaus could scarcely contemplate them. For now, he was content to be a simple chronicler. In this wholesome company, there was certainly no need to be an Intelligencer. Being neither of them but no longer quite apart from them, he found his place with easy affinity. He became less reliant on Afldalr. His wounds were slowly healing, his hope late into its gestation. For those three weeks, he only dreamed once, and it was a strange dream: Elodie, a woman fully grown, her golden hair out of girlish braids, her arms full of something that lit her face with joy. She held out her arms to show him the child, but both vanished before he could see. He woke rested, filled with both her joy and a terrible sadness.

The speckled peregrine reappeared three days before they expected to reach Noisy Tree. Now his heart began beating in earnest.

*

Cheering crowds spilled out of Samsarra to greet them. Someone hung a garland of flowers around Arik's shoulders. If anything, the celebrations deepened his disquiet, like the deceptive lull before a storm. With each victory, the noose seemed to inch lower over them.

Rasan was rarely away from Verdi's side, so they saw a lot of her. She was an excellent guard, but it made it difficult to speak with Verdi alone. Consequently, not much consultation informed what Arik did next.

'Stay with Verdi,' he told Rasan as they made their way through the welcoming crowds.

'There's to be a victory feast,' she reminded him.

Arik slipped away, the distraction serving him well. Hood raised, he took a longer, quieter route to Thillaina's house.

Alizarin would arrive any moment to arrest her. Arik broke the latch on the kitchen door with a practised hand. It was late afternoon, after the girls usually put their looms and spindles to rest. He saw at once that something was amiss; a layer of dust coated everything, and the air smelled stale. Dagger drawn, he stalked silently through the house.

He found the old widow wrapped in a blanket in her parlour by the remains of a fire long burnt out. It had not been relit, though the house was uncomfortably cold.

The back of her chair faced the door. 'If you're going to have me followed, you might have at least had the decency to come sooner...'

The words died in her mouth as she turned. She looked sickly, and had likely been for days: her cheeks were sunken, her lips cracked, and the flash of her eyes, normally matched only by the sharpness of her tongue, had dimmed.

'Ah,' she said, almost a sigh. 'Have you come to kill me, Lord Prospere?'

Though he knew now what she was, cold shock sparked beneath Arik's Form. He forced his hand to remain steady on the dagger.

'How like your father you are,' she whispered. 'Your uncles would be proud.'

He petrified white fury in the ice that he had been taught to embody in the heart of fire, becoming stillness itself. He drew his longsword.

Thillaina's eyes followed his blade. 'Would you not like to listen to what I have to tell you?'

'I don't trust you to speak the truth.'

A noise came from the hallway. Arik had no intention of being stopped. He crossed the room in three long strides –

'Arik!'

It wasn't Alizarin, but Verdi; only this fact spared her life.

'She *does* know,' Arik told him harshly. 'There's no other way to contain the poison –'

'He would tell you to wait. Think of what else she might know...'

Verdi was breathless; he had run here. *I'll deal with Rasan later.* Beneath the death-grip of his Form, Arik was still shaken by the sound of his true name spoken in this house. Had Klaus not been so badly treated by the Wintermantels, he would have silenced her.

But Klaus deserved to find out if she knew how he'd ended up in that treacherous Ealdorman's house.

So Arik stayed his hand.

Trembling, Verdi rebuilt a fire in the hearth.

'You needn't bother,' she said, in a coarse whisper that crackled like the kindling.

'It's not for you,' Verdi retorted.

'Where is he now?' The cough rattled Thillaina again. 'They said he went back north.'

Verdi looked away.

She nodded to herself. 'I knew he would. The slyest of all the houses ... in the end those wolves always have their way.'

Verdi's face drained of colour. Ravi struggled to break free from his clenched fist. Voices sounded in the hall. Alizarin threw open the door.

Arik lowered his sword. 'You took your time.'

Alizarin's voice was cold and even. 'Thillaina Mazdahar, you are under arrest for treason. You're not to leave this house or speak to anyone until your summons.'

Her eyes didn't stray from Alizarin throughout the coughing fit turning out her lungs.

Alizarin stationed three tumblers outside the bolted house, strictly instructing them to admit no visitors.

'She knew he's heading north.' Verdi rounded on his uncle. 'How did she find out, if you've had her watched?'

Alizarin raked his hands through his hair. 'He should not have gone back.'

*

There were no raids, no storms. Beyond the bars of his Form, Klaus was so overwrought when they finally arrived in Noisy Tree, he feared he might unwittingly knock shoulders with an Invelmari patrol. He declined Perlo's invitations to share their lodgings.

'Surely your errand can wait until you've had some rest?' said Klira. 'Sup with us tonight. We'll have a yarn or two to spin at the tavern, and there'll be a hero's welcome.'

But there would be no rest for him tonight. 'When I return.'

'Well, we're only staying a couple of days. Don't get left behind.'

Klaus scarce noticed the verdant shadow of Northern spring, cooler and greener on this side of the border. He rode on alone to Tiptoe, crossing the Ninvellyn by bridge before taking the road around Whimsy. He was glad to put the Ostraad behind him, its shadow odious now. He'd last seen the peregrine three nights ago. *What if the Wisdom was mistaken?* What if her messenger couldn't find her way to his mother?

It was a short ride north to Tiptoe. He didn't dare reach his mind into the earth, this rich green earth. He needed a clear head to succeed, and he didn't think he could bear the disappointment if he failed to make that precious connection here in his native land.

He arrived at the sleepy town before dusk. Later he would recall it was a pretty place, with waterwheels that turned a fat tributary of the Ninvellyn, and a small cobbled market square now quiet and swept clean of the day's debris. The Derindin were closing up their shops and stalls, too weary to spare any salesman's fawn for a passing Invelmari. Klaus kept his hood raised, pausing in the empty square with a somersaulting stomach.

Soft flapping caressed the quiet of the silver sky. Klaus looked up; the peregrine landed on a shop sign, and his heart leapt. The Wisdom's token was not lost.

She took off, alighting again as he followed: on roof, then chimney, then tree. She led him to the lonely fringes of the little town, to a stone cottage set back in its own grove, with a pebble path that would announce the crunch of his footsteps and a light shining in the window.

The peregrine landed on a fence post outside the cottage. His pulse raced when she didn't take off again.

He whispered, 'Am I home?'

She stared back at him with dispassionate intelligence. Klaus dismounted and tied his horse to a tree. His palms were moist, his mouth dry. Neither steel nor Form could armour him for this. Heart hammering, he walked up the pebble path and turned the handle of an unbolted door.

It opened onto a sitting room. An oil lantern burned like a beacon in the window. A generous fire roared in the hearth and waiting in the armchair beside it was Lady Wintermantel.

49

Truesight

'No.'

   'Ulfriklaus –'

   'No!'

He threw himself away from her as though from a branding iron. Ringing filled his ears.

Instinct kicked in; he drew his sword and circled the room, finding only one door that led to a darkened hallway, and from there an empty bedchamber. It was a trap, it had to be. The Wisdom had deceived him, he had been such a fool –

   'Where are they?' He ripped aside a curtain. 'Where are your guards?'

   'There is no one here, only you and me –'

   'That can't be true!' He shook from head to toe, the tip of his sword quivering. 'This can't be true.'

She stood back by the fire, her hands raised, her fingers spread. She was unarmed.

'I am not lying to you now, Ulfriklaus.' Her whisper was tight-throated. Unshed tears glittered in her eyes. 'I swear it – it *is* true, and there are none here but us.'

The strength drained from him in a great eviscerating gush. Klaus sat heavily on a wooden chest, sword clattering to the ground.

'Listen to me.' Lady Wintermantel edged towards him. 'Your father and I had no choice. We knew it from the moment you were born, but I had hoped there would be another way, that with time things would change –'

He barely heard her. His heart was too contracted. Form crumbled, Afldalr spewed: violent eruption of betrayal, of crippling disappointment.

'I don't know what you're talking about.'

'Will you let me tell you?'

He stood up. 'You're right, I don't have to listen to you.'

'You came back to know. Don't you want to know?' She took his hands, entangling their fingers. He wanted to push her away but he couldn't – she was everything he remembered, she *was* his mother – he'd been all the more foolish for ever having believed otherwise...

'Your father married me for love,' she said, beginning quickly. 'But it was not by chance that I was placed in his path. Perhaps there is no better place to begin than that.'

He pulled his hands free and stepped away from her, hovering against the wall.

'When I was a bride, I had a serving woman who was as dear to me as a nonna, and who had the gift of truesight. She had reservations about our marriage. It was only after we wed that she told me what she had seen of our future: the two sons I would bear, and the great burden they would shoulder so long as they breathed the air of Invelmar...'

Though he knew her Form was impregnating her voice with that sap with which she reeled in rebels and envoys, Klaus found himself transfixed.

'A burden, she said, that would either crush them or birth a new moon in the Northern sky.' Lady Wintermantel inched closer. 'I was upset; I berated her. I told your father. *He* was in two minds, because after our wedding night a spaewife had arrived at Sunnanfrost with a wedding gift. A foretelling that I would carry the greatest gift to Invelmar, which pleased him. That spaewife left a piece of iron for my son.'

His heart thudded beneath the weight of the iron disc in his breast pocket.

'But I esteemed the word of my serving woman, and I had never met a spaewife who wasn't seeking a price in return for her foretellings.

And when I fell with child, the spaewife returned and sang my child's praises. She promised our heir would be the moon of the North, just like my serving woman ... but unlike my serving woman, *she* didn't warn of any danger to my son, and that stirred my suspicions.'

Now she was within touching distance again. He hadn't even noticed.

'We began to search for what it was the spaewife really wanted. Your father was reluctant. I insisted. We traced her across the Sterns. That was what drew us to endless campaigns in the Far North, in pursuit of her mischief.'

Lady Wintermantel looked away. Her face twisted into something painful to behold.

'There beyond the Sterns, I made the gravest mistake of my life,' she whispered. 'You were not my firstborn, Ulfriklaus. Him I left in the Far North with a tribe of outlaws loyal to me, in the hope that he would escape the burden awaiting him in Invelmar. I told the court he was dead. I would have done anything to protect you both.'

A sledgehammer rammed him again.

'I returned North and prayed for a daughter. Neither woman had warned of any harm to my daughter. When the spaewife discovered what I had done with my son, her rage exposed her true intentions. At that time I was carrying you. In her fury, she promised that no matter what we did, the son in my womb would die in Invelmar. We discovered then why she and her allies had planted me in the path of Wolfram Wintermantel.'

Klaus clutched at splinters of Form, salvaging coherence. 'Planted? You were the daughter of a Thane. You grew up at court.'

'Not by chance. My mother, your nonna, was smuggled by spaewives into Dunraven from the wrong side of the Sterns. She came from the only surviving child of Dagmar-of-the-Hearth, hidden in the Far North so that there would be no bounty on her head.'

Klaus stared at her stupidly.

'The spaewife took her revenge on us with the truth. Far Northern spaewives have long foreseen that the ascension of Sturmsinger's blood to the Invelmari throne at last would destroy it.'

His mind reeled beyond rescue. *Secret-keepers, sworn to safeguard the truth* ... only Svanhilda Wintermantel was not the keeper, she was the secret itself.

Horror strangled his voice. 'What do you mean, Sturmsinger's blood?'

'What do you think it means, Ulfriklaus?'

That's why I found the caves. She was Sturmsinger's heir.

Queues of questions vanished, erased by dismay. He, Klaus, was sired by the man who had slain the South, dammed the Ninvellyn, secured the Second Redrawing.

'And that's the Far North's great weapon. Since Sturmsinger's death, they have sought to restore his line to the throne, and when your father and I –' Here, her Form stumbled. 'They've mixed Sturmsinger's blood with an Ealdorman's at last, hoping to see Invelmar destroyed.'

How proud he would have been once, to carry the blood of the father of Invelmar. He had prayed for the man all his life. Now he felt tainted, sullied. And unable to see past Sturmsinger's sins.

'That's why you drove me away,' Klaus managed. 'To protect the Sturmsinger Chain…'

'No! We only wanted to shield you both… After we lost your brother, I could never again go through – I could not have given you up for all the Parts, not before the chance to know you.' Her voice trembled. 'The chance to tell you, perhaps – but it would have been a noose hanging over your head, if you had known. Each year we delayed sending you away from Sunnanfrost, from Dunraven … and then suddenly you were a man, and such a man.' Her eyes implored him to believe her. 'The entire tribe of rebels disappeared not long after we left your brother with them. I returned to the Far North and found our child dead in the ice before he knew his own name. Someone had either learned who he was, or else the spaewives found him. I could not bear his fate for you. Every word I ever heard from those two women – for years I have cursed the day I ever sought to know the future before its time –'

'Then why are you here now?' he said harshly. 'What was the point of this whole charade to have me leave?'

'Adela. Adela's discovered Sturmsinger has a living heir. That was what finally forced our hand.'

'Does she know, then?' Now his fury cooled to something excavated from the heart of the Sterns. 'Does she know we Ealdormen assassinated him to steal his throne?'

The blood drained from her face as the sledgehammer turned.

'Very few people know this now, Ulfriklaus. Do not speak it. Can you imagine what the truth would do? How many of the Ealdormen do you think would relinquish their claims to the throne through the Chain and bow to a queen of Far Northern blood?'

'How did Adela find out his heir is living?'

'I don't know, but I'm afraid. For generations my family escaped notice, our line thought to have finally ended … she's ordered her Spyglass to find his burial ground. She believes that will help her identify his heir. Our spies say they need something first to locate it. They're sacking the country looking for it –'

'The Umari instrument?'

'That was a ruse. It's safe in Adela's vault. Her guards are fine-combing the kingdom for something far more valuable under the pretence of looking for the Umari instrument.'

'Then what are they looking for?'

'A compass, of singular properties. That's why every lodestone device of worth from here to Malvern has been confiscated. They will infiltrate these border towns next.'

Klaus' heart thudded. *A compass, or a map?* The skydisc was safe with Arik, miles away in Derinda.

He leaned against the wall and sank to the floor, clutching his head.

Once again, the cage bars shrank around him, built with the same cursed bonds. Stillborn hope fragmented – his promises to Verdi, the desert's beckon, the swarming of slight matter in his heart ... *Nerisen.* Another dream stifled at its first breath. *She will loathe me for being an Ealdorman, let alone for being the spawn of Sturmsinger.* It was this that suddenly cemented his despair.

'I have spent my life gathering whatever knowledge I could find in the Far North,' said Svanhilda. 'I changed Form when we learned the truth, so I could travel unsuspected as an Intelligencer ... but we've not been the only ones chasing this truth. Others have been chipping at the ice.'

Klaus rubbed his temples. 'What does Adela want? To kill the rest of us, like they killed Ansovald?'

She knelt beside him. 'Let us keep you safe, Ulfriklaus.'

'She's circling the truth, and *now* you want to keep me close?'

'I thought you might be safer, away from home. But Adela's cast her net wider. She's going to scour the entire Part. There's no point in you being cut off from us now, from our Isarnanheri.' A sweet tendril of mahonia drifted towards him when she tucked her hair behind her ears. 'I never believed they'd suspect an heir still lived, not in our lifetimes. Your father thought the trail had finally vanished. But I would rather keep you where we can protect you.'

He stared at her, lost between fury and astonishment.

'We've been bred on *lies*. They're traitors, all of them. Do you expect me to go back and hold my nose –'

'The Ealdormen don't *know* of Sturmsinger's fate, Ulfriklaus. Even your father didn't know, until I married him – *I* did not know my own lineage until the spaewife visited us. And were it not for my serving woman's warning, I would never have believed.'

'And yet Father went on perpetuating the lies. He's just as much a part of this treachery, you both are –'

'What would you have us do?' She was angry now. 'We are a nation of millions. The Blood Pact preserves our peace because the Ealdormen are forced to keep it. If they ever learn the truth, even the Blood Pact might not be enough to keep the peace – and then we all fall together. The rumours are true, karrionhjords are shredding the hamlets along the Sterns. The Far Northerners would love nothing better than a crack to appear within our kingdom so they can take it at last, morsel by morsel –'

'The Far North's not the only enemy to worry about now.' Klaus bared his teeth. 'I've seen the tomb where Sturmsinger buried his second queen. Did you learn of her too? Of the Eh Menishian? Our armies massacred her people along with Sturmsinger's army, after they sailed their ships to this Part. Now they've begun to eat into the Derindin. And when they succeed, Invelmar will be ringed with her enemies.'

She froze, for one silver second. Then Svanhilda Wintermantel became an Intelligencer again, shutters falling over her eyes even as she tried to tunnel into his.

'All the more reason why your place must be amongst us now, Ulfriklaus –'

'It's too late for that, everyone thinks I'm dead. Wasn't that your plan – like you planned for my brother?' *My brother!* 'You followed soothsayers instead of giving us a chance. You chose fear. And now you tell me that if I reach the throne, I'll be the ruin of the kingdom anyway –'

'Listen to me, Ulfriklaus. Whatever the spaewife threatened – we should never have listened to the poison, we should have been led by hope –'

'Maybe you're ready to have hope,' he told her coldly. 'Mine's crushed.'

'The throne has never been more rightfully anyone's than it is yours,' she urged. 'An Ealdorman heir of Sturmsinger himself; a union at last of Northern and Far Northern blood, polished by steel and scholarship to take back the kingdom he never lived to rule –'

Fury gathered into a sharpened nib. He *would* write his own way now.

'You should have thought of that before you tricked Elodie into scaring me away.'

'You can't,' she whispered. 'You wouldn't leave –'

'I *have* left, Mother!' He hadn't meant to bellow. He scrambled to regather Form. 'I tore myself from that world. How could I even go back now, when the Ealdormen think I am dead?'

She waved her hand. 'Nothing would be easier – a quest, an accident... Many Intelligencers have vanished before you and resurfaced years later –'

'More lies, then.' Now he trembled with barely-contained rage. 'Did you murder three innocents to account for us when we left?'

'We found dead vagabonds in Yelzberg, mauled by wolves. It was the only stroke of luck we've had. That's why we spread the word that you'd perished in the west, though you left a trail to the border that Ealdwine had to conceal...'

So Ealdwine knows. That night in the Paiva, Klaus had been certain that Svanhilda Wintermantel's devoted captain had looked right into his eyes – and said nothing. *He must have known all this time, watching me grow up…*

He stood.

'I did everything you asked. For the Blood Pact, for Invelmar, not for either of you – and you forced me to renounce it. Now I am unmade.' He picked up his sword. 'Now I'll choose my own way.'

Her eyes shone with tears.

'Come home, my son,' she pleaded. 'Come home to Sunnanfrost and be safe. It was never your sister's place to take up this mantle, her heart is too gentle to balance mercy against justice…'

If he thought of Elodie, it would unravel him yet again. He hardened his heart.

'I want no part in it.'

He turned away from her, and from Invelmar, and the North.

50

The Prayer for Rain

AND THE WILL OF LORD STURMSINGER WAS WITHOUT MATCH, FOR
HE BORROWED A CLOAK CUT FROM DARKNESS ITSELF, THAT HE
PURCHASED FROM SHADOW AND DONNED TO BLOT OUT LIGHT.
FOR THE LIGHT CAME FROM WITHIN, AND DECIPHERED WHAT
HIS MIND COULD NOT, BUT YET TORE A HOLE IN HIS HEART
THAT RIPPED HIS ARMOUR ASUNDER.

SEPTENTRIONAL SCROLLS

Verdi was distraught.

Arik could think of nothing to reassure him. With a fair wind and no
setbacks, the Sisodans' caravan ought to have reached the border towns
now. If the Wintermantels' Isarnanheri were waiting for Klaus, it would
be there, in Noisy Tree, not the desert. There'd been no whisper yet of
mishap, though any news other than by falcon would be slow.

No news is no consolation.

'Where are you going?'

Even without his uncle's nagging, Verdi had been eager to attend that night's vigil for the dead. But at dusk, he set off away from Samsarra's oldest sanctuary.

Verdi glanced back over his shoulder. 'To get medicine from Fresmo. She's sick.'

Arik curbed a wave of anger. But their guest rooms in the Chieftainess' house awaited, and he had no appetite for a private audience with Emra just yet. Verdi collected the herbs, and they walked to Thillaina's house in silence, neither of them wanting to give any more weight to their fears with words.

Thillaina's guards may as well have been Murhesla, for there was no sign of them stationed around her house. Not that Verdi had any intention of being stopped. *Alizarin will have to think of something to explain her arrest.* A journey, maybe; the widow still travelled from time to time. The girls she employed had been idle at home since her illness, which had proven to be a blessing. When Nerisen returned from Pir Sehem, she would be much harder to throw off the trail.

They found her still lying on the makeshift bed in the parlour. A fire was now roaring in the hearth. The old woman looked no better for it.

She didn't stir when they entered. Verdi warmed water over the fire, adding the herbs from his satchel.

'Here.' He kneeled beside her with a full cup. She opened her eyes then, too ill for surprise. 'You need something for that chest.'

She took the smallest of sips. Verdi waited until she had drunk it all. Arik marvelled at his patience. There was an untouched bowl of soup on the table. Verdi picked it up next.

'I'm going to reheat this and you're going to drink it.'

'I recognised you the moment I laid eyes on you.' Her voice was threadbare. Her cough was lighter but her breathing sounded worse, grating and wet in turns as though there was more purification than air in her lungs.

Verdi looked away, pouring the soup into the pot. He didn't notice Ravi sneaking out of his pocket to disappear somewhere under her shawl. The little stinker really was useless.

'And you.' She dragged her eyes to Arik. 'But not the other one. He'd grown so much, like all Northerners ... how did you find me out?'

The nerve of her... Anger threatened to thaw Arik's Form again.

Verdi stared into the pot. 'The brocade. I've lost count of how many times I've seen it.'

'Ahh,' she sighed, bringing on another bout of coughing. 'I made sure to tell you I'd worked for the queen. Only her, mind. I was loyal.'

Emotions grappled with each other in Verdi's face. *Too honest. Needs to be more like his uncle.*

'You should have known better.' Verdi stirred the soup over the fire. 'He might have left the North, but he's still –'

'He can never truly leave,' she croaked. 'Oh, little ones. Do you suppose it was easy, turning your babe out of your arms?'

Verdi gaped at her. The fire hissed as soup bubbled over the pot into the flames.

Thillaina coughed again. 'She couldn't do it, though she tried the month long after he was born. Not after the first time. But I knew the day would come when she'd have to let him go at last, because everywhere there are spies. I warned her it would be even harder, once he was grown. But she wouldn't have any of it, and he was even less willing than she...'

The world contracted to this stale room.

Verdi's hands shook around the empty bowl. 'He?'

'Wolfram Wintermantel. Who else?' The old woman gazed into the fire, her voice another crackle of its flames. 'Wouldn't let the boy out of his sight. Wouldn't let him go.'

The door behind Arik's back felt as wooden as he did. 'You said you were loyal to the queen...'

'Adela?' Scorn reignited her strength. 'I served the queen of all the North, queen even before she was seduced by that sly Wintermantel. Great-daughter of Sturmsinger, in safekeeping all these years until barbarian witches planted her into Dunraven and under his gaze ... of course he wanted her. The most beautiful creature to walk the Part – how could he not have wanted her?'

A terrible cold crept through Arik, and this time it wasn't Form.

'She's delirious,' he heard himself tell Verdi. 'The fever's got to her.'

Verdi gaped at Thillaina. He raised a hand to feel her forehead. Her laugh was a papery creature with feeble wings, plummeting into another violent fit of coughing.

'Listen to me, both of you. Each year fewer people know the truth. Sometimes truesight comes to those who are good, sometimes to those who are crafty. Crafty and ill-intentioned. I can't claim innocence of the first, but I never meant any ill.'

Arik hadn't noticed himself drawing closer. Verdi knelt by the tangle of her blankets.

'The protection on Sturmsinger's children that held for three hundred years is finally broken. Through Svanhilda Wintermantel, Ulfriklaus and his sister are the youngest of his line. Hundreds of secret-keepers have been killed over the centuries guarding that knowledge. The Far Northerners want nothing more than to ruin Invelmar. There's nothing secret about *that* except how they mean to do it.'

She pointed to Arik.

'It was your mother who brought it to the attention of Florian Arnander, before Far Northerners captured her – their great weapon, though they only knew half of it: if Sturmsinger finally sits on the Invelmari throne, his ascension will bring about the ruin of the North. Wolfram Wintermantel's children will deliver the Far Northerners their vengeance. One more turn of the Chain, and the blood of Sturmsinger will finally reign in Dunraven...'

Arik slammed the iron bars of Form around the hammering of his heart. 'Did she ... what's the half they don't know?'

'Could you bear the truth, Lord Prospere?' When her eyebrows rose like that, he was reminded of Lisbeta. 'Your mother did, she died for it. She was the only one I trusted with the rest of what I saw. Take that off the fire, dear.'

Arik became aware of acrid smoke. Dazed, Verdi picked up a rag and moved the smoking pot off the grate, its contents now evaporating into sour fumes.

'He'll have reached her by now.' Weary with talking, Thillaina scraped words together. 'He'll finally know the truth. But not all of it. So you will tell him for me. I might not be able to wait for him to come back.'

Her chest heaved, coughing so forcefully that Arik feared they, too, would be denied it. But Thillaina reclaimed her breath.

'*Only through ruin will come greatness* – but ruin must come. The Far Northerners' great weapon will test Invelmar, perhaps remake it beyond recognition – but not destroy it. They didn't look into the distance deeply enough. The truth is not for carving up to preserve only the parts we wish to see. It must be taken whole.'

She jabbed a finger gently into Verdi's chest.

'It was no coincidence you were taken into the lap of Svanhilda Wintermantel alongside Ulfriklaus. You must both answer for the crimes of your fathers. Yes, Viridian, for you that means embracing Lorendar's path. A great burden for the innocent to endure. You must bear it together. Then the Part might finally know justice, from the Sterns to the sea.'

'Why did you wait until now to tell me?'

'You each had to discover yourselves, didn't you? That wasn't my work. More than likely you would never have believed. The truth must come when it's ready to be received. It was a long time before I saw that. And I've told no one else, either.'

'You mean you didn't tell Lady Wintermantel?'

Thillaina shook her head at Arik.

'Not after how much harm it did the Wintermantels to glimpse the future. Neither of them were ready. The future is best served at the right time, which is perhaps never before its time. I learned my lesson and left Dunraven, though I'm not sure I wasn't half pushed out. Sometimes it's easier to love from a very great distance.'

Verdi shook his head, dumbfounded. 'So many lies...'

'Lies that have guarded the truth. Don't resist it, Lord Prospere.' Arik realised he was trembling. 'Oh, you are loyal. But even loyalty – especially loyalty – is a terrible thing when misplaced.'

Arik found his voice. 'You ought to have spoken sooner.'

'Don't underestimate an old woman's shame,' she whispered.

'We'll go to my uncle at once.' Tears streaked Verdi's cheeks. Arik envied him the ease with which his sorrow came, like all his feelings. 'Have his order reversed, the tumblers removed...'

'Not too soon, dear. I'm rather enjoying the peace and quiet.'

*

The victory celebrations continued late into the night. The Chieftainess of Elendra felt anything but victorious.

Their council was as sombre as the streets were joyous. Even Maragrin had no barbed wire wit in him now.

'These Eh Menishian puppet-masters ... what's their hold over the pirates?'

'Gold,' said Alizarin. 'And fear. Whatever it is, it's enough.'

'Perhaps the chronicler will have more to tell us.'

Dark shadows ringed Tourmali's eyes. 'He's not yet returned from the border. All we can do now is fortify our clandom and build up our alliance.'

'Sisoda will scout the Black Lava Plains as soon as they've regained their strength.'

'Nothing can survive in the Lava Plains...'

Maragrin raised an eyebrow. 'We said the same thing about the Far Southern desert.'

'What about Voldane?' asked Tourmali.

'He wrote to me after the Assembly,' said Emra. 'Probably to all the clans. Even from here, you could slip on his oil. He claims Baeron's deal with the pirates was to secure immunity, lest Baeron's oil wells fall into pirate hands. He'll likely use fear of these Eh Menishian to his advantage at the next Assembly. Offer suzerainty to more clans in exchange for Baeron's protection.'

'And we ought to do the same,' said Alizarin briskly. 'Maybe it'll help Lebas and Fraivon find common ground at last.'

'What about Viridian?' said Tourmali. 'He's not taken the oath. He seems no closer to mastering the moondial.'

'What else would you like him to do?' Alizarin snapped, fatigue baring his irritation. 'Undo the Second Redrawing, perhaps?' He restrained himself. 'He knows what needs to be done.'

Maragrin looked around their faces. 'And the Northman?'

Silence joined them uninvited, riddled with warrens of reluctance. Tourmali was tight-lipped. 'We're in danger of losing focus.'

'It's no good,' said Emra. 'The land remembers him. Wisdoms have marked him. How long can we look away?'

'But to mix up Merensama with an Invelmari...'

'To taint it, you mean?' said Maragrin wryly. 'The time for dithering is over. These are the cards that we've been dealt.'

*

Klaus was cold.

It was a terrible, eviscerating cold. It numbed him to the cooler air of the border towns which carried icy currents down from the Sterns.

The dissociation from his old life had nearly destroyed him. The glimpse of a new one – intoxicating, once he'd finally seen it. And it had all been in vain. Dreams of freedom had as much substance as a mirage of water in the Plains.

No. There's no going back.

'Anger must be your servant. Master it, and it will be the true steel in your scabbard.'

But this was an anger he didn't *want* to master. This was an anger that made him pull his reins more than once, made him turn and face north – north, where Adela was searching for Sturmsinger's heir. North, where one word would secure the spatter of Wintermantel blood on her flagstones.

They would deserve it.

He wouldn't even need to return to Dunraven. A message would suffice. And he might finally be free. For all Adela knew, he was already dead.

And Elodie?

His heart shuddered. These thoughts weren't sane; weren't his. He reached for Form, and it slipped through his fingers. His brow broke out in cold sweat. *Afldalr!* Though it shook with the effort, Afldalr was a brute. Eventually, it contained even this.

He arrived in Noisy Tree in the early hours of morning, finding a bed at the inn where they'd first met Alizarin. Had that only been only eight months ago? This time, the innkeeper declared his best room was vacant, made no mention of the hour, and wouldn't take his silver.

He couldn't remember falling asleep, and woke to a grey dawn and a yawning cavity in his heart.

At least there were no dreams.

Afldalr bottled the rogue darkness. A mercy, because there was work to do. Keeping an eye out for the Guard, Klaus went to find Ristowin at first light.

The metalsmith was already at work. A young accomplice, a boy, worked the bellows in the small forge adjoining his workshop. Ristowin recognised Klaus immediately, setting down his tools.

'Come in, Master Invelmari.'

Klaus bowed. 'If you will permit me, I've something else to show you.'

Ristowin closed the door to the forge while Klaus retrieved a small rock from his saddlebag.

He offered Ristowin the rock. 'You'll have heard by now about the Eh Menishian employing the pirates. This ironstone was mined near the Mengorian range, and may be what drew them to our Part.' The metalsmith's eyes widened. 'I don't know why they want the ore it will yield, but the Eh Menishian have come a long way to possess it.'

Ristowin examined the rock. Klaus hoped to once again glimpse his ilnurhin at work, but he didn't probe it long.

'Do these Eh Menishian think it has some special property?'

'All I know is they've paid the pirates a great deal of gold to mine it.'

The lines deepened in the little Derindman's brow.

'I'll see what I can do.' Ristowin removed his spectacles. 'Where can I send word to you?'

'Thank you, sir. Send word to Samsarra. I hope to hear from you soon.'

'You are not returning to the North, then?'

'My place will be by Lorendar's heir.'

'Have you learned any more yet of that weight?'

The metalsmith's coal black eyes were as probing as searchlights.

'Yes.' Klaus paused at the door. 'No.'

The metalsmith picked up his chisel and returned to work.

The weight dragged like a stone in Klaus' breast pocket as he left. Why had an enemy of Invelmar left him a token from an Ettsrakkan bloodland, of all things? It burned his skin now; a spaewife's gift. *Irrational.* It had been a spaewife's gift that had warned Sturmsinger of the woe destined to befall Invelmar should war consume it again. *Without her, there'd be no Blood Pact; the kingdom would have perhaps already been lost.*

He wondered if his mother was still in TipToe. Wounds too raw for the Sisodans' geniality, he pleaded fatigue and kept to his room at the inn while they restocked their supplies. Or perhaps he couldn't bear even a glimpse of the Ninvellyn, glistening sapphire-grey to gurgle in fateful death throes against the Ostraad; or the deep green smell of petrichor, or the irresistible beckon of clean cold frost whispering in the air from the North.

There will be no going back.

He rejoined the Sisodans' caravan in time to help load their wagons. This time, when they paused on the Limpra Hills to pay homage to the river, he too shared the longing in their lament; the anguish of *sehresar*. His departing back sagged with the reproach of a hundred snow-clad mountainsides and the fleets of Northern stars he was leaving behind.

There would be no going back.

A wail pierced the sky. The sight of the speckled peregrine spilled warmth into the cavity in his breast. *I thought you'd stayed to nest.*

The Derindin craned their heads in admiration.

'If she's turning her back on the river and coming home with us, surely she's claimed you as her own,' said Klira. 'By now, she must have told you her name.'

A knife twisted in his side.

'Namathra,' he murmured, watching until she vanished ahead of them over the grasslands. She led the way south, always south. 'Her name is Namathra.'

Suddenly, he was much less forlorn.

'Three weeks and we'll be in Romel, if luck goes with us,' Perlo told him cheerfully. 'For once, we go with the wind.'

Three weeks and he would be with his friends, the secrets waiting in the skydisc, and Nerisen. His heart leapt eagerly. He steered his horse south and for the first time in his life followed his longing.

*

'Do you think they are rogue Isarnanheri?'

Ayla watched Marcin disengage Pebr in the training ground. Eleven of his fist of tumblers had returned from Pir Sehem. *Better odds than the rest.* He'd ordered them back to their drills after only a week's respite, declaring even that had been too long.

Gerit had remained wary of the two Northerners, so Ayla had taken his objections with a grain of salt. But he was too experienced to stumble on prejudice.

'They're skilled enough,' she admitted. Marcin circled the tumblers duelling within the stingy perimeter he'd marked in the dirt. 'But Isarnanheri don't escape the North. They would have been followed here and destroyed.'

'How can you be sure?'

There were many things about that Gerit didn't know; many things no one knew on this side of the Ostraad. Not even in Romel's catacombs and labyrinths.

'They are not Isarnanheri.'

Ayla had no desire to make her vice general feel excluded from her counsel. Besides, his caution was not misjudged. She chose words carefully.

'The warrior is of noble stock. He's neither coarse nor vulgar. He's seen enough of comfort not to crave it, luxuries don't impress him … at one time or another, he's had everything. And he's been tried beyond his years. The chronicler…' Tristan, at least, was an open book. 'He's as eager as the next man at the promise of meat. Pleased if a plain girl looks at him fondly. He's got nothing to hide.'

And yet he's the eye of night itself.

Her ears still echoed with his battle-cry wrenched from Derindin throats. Not in her wildest nightmares had she imagined she would hear that here in Derinda, and in the Vale of Pir Sehem of all places. *And yet victory was ours.*

'Send a spy to our watcher in Noisy Tree,' she said. 'Find out if anyone saw Tristan and Marcin arrive downriver eight months ago. And scatter a few birds.'

'Where to?'

'Malvern. Ask if anyone's crossed paths with Marcin there.'

Her real question would be flown a little less further north. Alizarin had kept a firm grip on his nephew's time in Invelmar, arguing the fewer who knew of him the better. Perhaps that had been true once, but Viridian was safely back in Derinda now. There must be a shadow somewhere that remembered a Derindin physician's apprentice.

*

It was a month after the siege was broken before Pir Sehem was vaguely habitable. Ash from the pirates' fires still dimmed dawn with a black-feathered wind that breathed darkly over the land before it settled; a shroud seeking the slain. Tumblers continued to round up pirate stragglers, weeding them out from the sand dells and hamlets as they fled. Sisoda's alchemists concluded the northern spring would not be fit for drinking for months to come. And each day there were more dead to bury as the mortally wounded succumbed.

Nerisen took in the desolation slowly. Each day, victory became more bitter than sweet.

The Plainswalkers had stayed behind to do what they could for the survivors. Soon, most would return to their own clandoms. She'd spent the past week in the sick tents, helping reconnect the disabled or the dying with relatives, and home those as yet unclaimed. Of the latter, there were still too many.

One, an aged man already blind in one eye, had lost the other to a pirate arrow. No one had claimed him as their kin. For days he had succumbed to a sleep from which none had thought he would recover. But a few hours ago, he had awoken, dry as a dead well, his words garbled and broken. He had lost the movement of his legs.

She returned to his makeshift bed in the tent with supper, and found his one white-filmed eye open. The other was a bloody mess concealed behind a patch.

'There is water here, Ada.' She spoke softly so as not to startle him. 'And hot stew.'

He didn't move, but the white eye inclined towards the sound of her voice. She helped him sit up to drink, slowly in spoonfuls because his neck was weak. He was as light as a bundle of branches in her arms. *A terrible way to pass through the doorway at last.*

'You have been here before,' he whispered after the water had moistened his mouth. 'A gentle daughter. Many times I have felt you.'

'There are always Plainswalkers in the tents, Ada. Don't be afraid during the night.'

'No, it was you.'

Nerisen had seen many injustices, but something about this old man particularly outraged her. She raised a spoon of stew to his mouth. 'You've not eaten in days.'

He spluttered and almost choked, and she realised his swallow wasn't right.

'Save it for those whose meat it will build,' he rasped. 'My time is nearly upon me, I long only for an end to this thirst.'

She knew what he really meant was release from the pain of his wounds. He was too kind to burden her with his agony, as though she couldn't see it for herself.

'I'll get more opia poppy before nightfall,' she promised. Supplies of the potent analgesic were dwindling.

'You carry something of the mapmaker.'

She froze. *Does he know my thoughts?* Then she remembered the golden-brown pinch of Tristan's hair in her pocket. *But how could he know that?*

'I saw the one who loosened the chokehold around Pir Sehem.' His speech slurred slightly. Nerisen was still deciding how a blind man *saw* when his next words thumped her in the middle. 'Serenity's bane, they called him once … he comes as a defender now, but serenity's bane he will be again.'

'Who?' she asked, though in her sinking heart she already knew. But he wasn't listening.

'He will destroy everything. Remember this, because the old tongue may die out before the true meaning is understood. Some will claim he is the Deceiver, but this is false – it is *one who is cloaked in deception* that the songs said of him. Remember this.'

Stillness had taken the place of the old man's pain; an otherness that was precious and easily disturbed, like a rare bird that would take flight if she moved and never reappear. Breath held, Nerisen waited to hear what he would say next of Tristan. Was this man a sage? Tilmara whispered in her ear: *A blind man's sight is the clearest of all.*

Fearing his reply, she asked, 'Then can he be trusted?'

'He will destroy everything,' the old man murmured again, gazing over her head. Perhaps he didn't hear her question, or perhaps that *was* his reply. 'But what is everything now?'

Then his eye closed and his breathing deepened and he seemed more at ease, so she let him sleep and retired reluctantly to her wagon, hoping the residue of opia would keep his pain at bay.

In the morning, he was dead. She mourned him more bitterly than any of the others she had seen to their graves. She left with the next eastward caravan, more bewildered than ever.

*

'No, Master Viridian, you'll not need your ink today.'

Verdi realised the fire in the tower room wasn't lit, and Maragrin hadn't removed his cloak.

'There is something I have wanted to give you,' said Maragrin. 'I had been waiting … in any case, I believe you'll make good use of it, whatever you decide.'

Verdi braced himself for another row about the oath, but Maragrin drew out a book from his cloak.

'This is not a volume that any will recognise.' It was small, bound in oxblood leather. 'In it, I have compiled whatever records I've found concerning the ninety-nine days that the sage-bird spent in the company of Obsidian Lorendar.'

Verdi's mouth fell open. 'You said all of that was myth.'

'And what is myth but truth twisted by feeble minds in order to make it palatable?'

He stared at the book. 'Did Lorendar keep a diary?'

'No, though his wife did. In her words is a far better account of what I have tried to teach you. Lorendar's wife was nearer to him than his shadow, and shadows swallow much darkness.'

Maragrin watched him examine it. The leather was worn and cracked in places.

'Yes, it is old. Some of it I discovered as a student like you in my youth, some I hunted across the Plains when my travelling days were still with me. And some...' Maragrin paused. 'Sometimes wisdom is a dowdy little creature that doesn't take our fancy at all, until we are forced to listen.'

'Why've you waited so long to show it to me?'

He realised then that Maragrin's glance around the room was furtive, even fearful.

'There are those who would brand me a traitor for some of what is written here.' The Elder touched the book tenderly. 'But the truth is not for us to refashion however we please, and it makes no apologies.'

Verdi took it solemnly. 'I understand.'

'This is to be our last lesson.'

'What? Why? We've barely begun –'

'At the dawn of this alliance, it is important that what you discover in these pages and how you think hereafter are neither influenced by me nor the clan council.'

The sadness that mellowed the Elder's smile made Verdi uneasy.

'I will keep it secret,' he promised.

Maragrin seemed older than ever as he left. Worry nudged Verdi. He'd grown reluctantly fond of the vinegary Elder.

He released the clasp on the buckle binding the leather and opened the book. In truth, a little of him was as afraid as he was curious. The pages were covered in Maragrin's handsome hand; in Invelmen, Derindask and another script. On the first was a title:

'The Untelling of Obsidian Lorendar'

51

The Noblest Fruit

THERE IS A LITTLE-VISITED PLACE IN THE LAST QUARTER OF NIGHT
WHERE WISDOM KEEPS ITS SECRET HEART. MEET ME THERE,
DEAR TRAVELLER, FOR THE PATH TO THE BELOVED
BEGINS ON THAT SHINING SHORE.

SUMMONS TO THE FIFTH CHAMBER

Arik could have picked out the jemesh from a mountain of bones, so often did he study it now.

If it were beginning to have a power over him, this was entirely of his own making. After the payment he'd extracted from Fro Tarka, he could well believe it was a Far Northern talisman. No one was more obsessed with necromancy than Far Northerners. But pirates had told Klaus the Eh Menishian had sent it. *Maybe the Eh Menishian borrowed the custom.* Something they'd learned long ago from Sturmsinger's soldiers, perhaps … after all, Sturmsinger's tribe traced their ancestral home to the Sterns, abandoned for their alliance with the Northerners who would betray them.

Arik suppressed a shiver.

What say you to the breaking of the North?

Shaman's smoke still stole into his thoughts.

Even he tossed at night now, ruminating on Klaus' discovery in the mountain. There was no escape from this betrayal. Bitter, unforgiveable betrayal. It stirred something Arik had not felt since that first exhilarating discovery of his Form; a sense of *purpose* that had faded when his life in Dunraven had grown trite. His road was now clear.

He counted the days until Klaus' return.

How had I ever believed otherwise? Klaus couldn't have been anything other than a Sterns-blooded Wintermantel. Remarkable like his father, subtle as Svanhilda, and more than both besides.

A darting movement at the back of the tavern caught his eye. Arik followed its trail between the busy tables, reaching forward to grab Fibbler's arm.

'Fibbler!' The child looked rightly ashamed. Arik lowered his voice. 'What did I tell you about running around outside? Do you *want* that pirate to find you?'

'I'm sorry!' He was on the verge of tears. 'I've been indoors this whole time, I swear, even missed the feast…'

Arik considered him. Fibbler had no idea why he was in so much danger. He was still only a child. And a free one, too, not an Ealdorman's child raised from cradle to Form. It was neither fair nor realistic to keep him hidden indefinitely. Not idly, at least.

'Do you still want to train, Fibbler?'

Fibbler's eyes lit up. He nodded.

Arik made up his mind. Perhaps it was the lurking beast of his anger; perhaps it was the recklessness that waited in the wings of such betrayal.

'And you'll do exactly as I say?'

Fibbler nodded again.

'Then you'd better get an early night. I begin at sun-up. And in complete secrecy. Any word of what I teach you to anyone, and we part ways for good. Discipline is the Warrior's first shield. Tomorrow, your life starts again. Do we have a deal?'

His hand engulfed Fibbler's, but there was nothing absurd about their solemn handshake. Fibbler darted out of the tavern. This time, Arik was sure of where the child would go.

Was Fibbler so different to what he had himself been before Lisbeta and the Isarnanheri – restlessly young, foolishly eager, incorrigible? If Arik had any guilt over what he intended, it was buried deeply indeed.

It would be a long time now before guilt could torment him for breaking an Ealdorman's vow.

Besides, he had his pick of torments. The maggot of doubt hatched in the efeshyun-haze would find no more sustenance now, denied by an old widow's gift. *'Only through ruin will come greatness'*, Thillaina promised. Klaus' Far Northern blood *would* ruin the North – the North as they knew it. The crowning of a Sturmsinger would surely be the breaking of the Sturmsinger Chain. That was the price of justice for the father of Invelmar, betrayed and buried in the rubble of his own victory. However the pirate-shaman had known this, he was dead.

My mother died for this. Later, when Thillaina was recovered, when he could bear it, Arik would ask her about his mother. For now, he snuffed out the thought along with its unruly fellows: the dead weight of Thunraz in his hands in the efeshyun smoke, the mad ramblings of Lisbeta's ghost, the prowling of a one-eared Spyglass between the dunes. Later, there would be time for fear.

He found Ayla in the General's quarters by the barracks. Rasan had proven herself a useful addition to Elendra's ranks indeed.

Arik closed the door. 'I thought high-ranking Murhesla couldn't leave the guild.'

She stiffened, glancing at the windows; they were shut.

'The same could be said of Isarnanheri and the North.' Ayla leaned back in her chair. 'And yet no one's come to claim you, so I suppose you weren't lying about that.'

'I told you I am not Isarnanheri.'

'Evidently.'

Arik took a gamble. 'Why did you tip me off about the protection the jemesh gives me in Romel if you thought I was lying?'

Ayla was unruffled, making no effort to deny his guess. 'I'd hoped you wouldn't wear it openly, with such a ransom on your head, but I knew you couldn't resist. Better you were prepared for the consequences.'

'Well, I'm very much obliged to you. That exception served me well. Which brings us back to the guild.'

Iron and ice filled her eyes. Arik was reminded of Klaus. He wondered how much more Rasan knew of Ayla's entanglement with the Murhesla.

'I'm not here to pry,' he said. 'But if there's anything you can do about Verdi's father, any strings you can pull...'

'Sassan Santarem is a force beyond us both. But that doesn't mean we can't play his game as well.'

It was something. Of course he wanted to pry, to find out how she had escaped the Murhesla's bonds after rising so high in their ranks. But they each had their secrets, and it was better for them both that these were left well alone.

*

Samsarra was close. Klaus rode not towards it but east, seeking a quiet olive grove nestled at a coordinate that hovered on the penumbra of his awareness. But when he tried to sense the road to the Healer's house, it slipped away like a sand-eel.

No one crosses paths with a Wisdom uninvited.

So he rode instead through the woods he'd shared with Nerisen, resorting to what landmarks he recalled of that sweet day, and to hope.

The morning shone more favourably on this. A few hours later, he spotted the cluster of time-riddled olive trees on their low hill in the east. Namathra flew down to his forearm as he approached the grove.

He found the olive keeper sitting under a half-prostrated mulberry tree by the stream behind the house. The last of the apple blossoms littered the meadow. His ewes grazed nearby.

A smile wrinkled his cheeks. 'You aren't yet recovered, Master Mapmaker. Come and rest.'

Klaus left his horse to graze happily beside the ewes. He offered the Wisdom a little parcel.

'The smallest of gifts. It's not rest that I need.'

The Wisdom's smile broadened on unwrapping the bottle. 'Ahhh, Paivan pine oil. Soporific properties. Very thoughtful.'

Klaus sat beside the Wisdom on the grass. They watched Namathra soar off over the trees.

'Where does the road lead next, Master Mapmaker?'

'You don't think I'll settle here, then?'

'I do not look into the future, Master Mapmaker, but your past. Always, you wished to travel beyond what you know. Always, you sought something to soothe the ache that calls to you at night. But you will not find the answer down a road.' A frown teased his forehead. 'Few know this hunger for what it is – a deficit of ilnurhin. You will never be satisfied until you find peace *within* you, and can carry it everywhere.'

Klaus' heart chafed in its brambles. 'There's not much peace in an Intelligencer.'

'Don't rue your submission to that path. It armoured you well for the fire you inherited from your fathers. It taught you discipline, but only of the mind.'

It was the first time anyone in the Plains had ousted him, but Klaus had no fear of admitting his true name here in this olive grove.

'The Hermit told me I carry something that is closed … something that will stop me from reaching the Unseen World.'

'You already know what this is.'

His heart began to pound in earnest. A wave of nausea rose in his gullet at the thought of being cut off from Afldalr.

'I don't think I can do without it.'

'You mean without it you can't remain as you are,' said the Wisdom. 'Is that what you desire – to remain intrepid and impermeable, tormented by dreams?'

'But would they stop if I...?'

Klaus couldn't even speak the words. Beads of perspiration formed on his brow. He closed his eyes, waited for the nausea to pass. *These are my real chains. The chains I never saw.*

'You dream for two reasons. Acutely present in the waking world, you notice everything. But then you do not let yourself resolve what you see, locking it away instead in this contraption you have made to conceal your depths from yourself. It is the first of the layers around your heart. The fifth chamber cannot be filled with ilnurhin if it is so rigorously guarded.'

Reflexive panic quickened Klaus' breathing. *I can't be without it.* Afldalr was now all that distanced him from his mother's confession. *Along with the urge to rain the wrath of Adela on the Wintermantels.*

The first *of the layers ...* Form was surely another. Even now, it buried the anger he'd cultivated in the camp, cocooned in Form. It was nascent, but it was there. Again the Septentrional Scrolls whispered to him from the bowel of his fears: '*A cloak cut from darkness. Donned to blot out light.*' Form was a shadowy creature he had failed to comprehend; a cage the North had cast around his mind. But if he couldn't do without Afldalr, he would be crippled without Form, and dared not speak of it to the Wisdom, fearing his verdict.

'I've a great deal of work to do before I strip back any layers,' he managed instead.

'I know, Master Northman Near-and-Far. But there is always work to be done. We will pass through the doorway and still the work will remain unfinished. It shouldn't grip us in an eternal chokehold.'

They watched the sun pulse tangerine waves into the sky.

'Perhaps there's a replacement for this shield you keep,' said the Wisdom. 'In place of a closed box, an open sky – a polished mirror that will reflect all the greatness of the Unseen World. The Derindin forgot this: that Merensama must begin within.'

Klaus looked squarely at the Wisdom. He wondered if the Wisdom had always known whose blood he carried; the curse he'd inherited. 'I'll never escape it, will I?'

'This Part will be your prison so long as it is diseased. You will never escape it until the conqueror's crimes are forgiven.'

But how? Klaus could see no release from the impossible burden of Sturmsinger's debt. *So many wronged. So many lies.*

'Take heart, Master Mapmaker,' the Wisdom told him gently. 'From the same sapling that grew this poison will its remedy be.'

He remained only a short while, though he would have ridden day and night for a few moments in the Healer's grove. But he arrived at Samsarra less weary. It was early, and the refugees encamped around the citadel slept. He went to Thillaina's house first, uncertain whether Arik and Verdi would have remained under her roof. He needn't have wondered; Verdi burst into her stables as he dismounted.

Breathlessly, he said, as if it were ever in doubt, 'You came back.'

When they hugged, Klaus was sure he felt the awkward triangle of the gnomon in Verdi's breast pocket.

'You can't afford to lose much more weight, there's barely enough of you as it is,' Klaus teased. 'Where's Arik?'

'Out with Fibbler…'

The sun was far from risen. Klaus eyed Verdi suspiciously. But Verdi was distracted.

'Klaus, Thillaina told us. She was your mother's servant. Your parents – your mother…'

Something prodded at his ribcage; the furious finger determined to thaw the numbness keeping truth at a merciful distance. They went inside, and Verdi made kahvi as the sun dragged a pale rose morning across the heavens.

'I thought you might have stayed with her. With your mother.'

'Don't be absurd, Verdi.'

'You had every right to.'

Klaus stroked Ravi's head while Verdi fussed and mixed him a tonic, drinking it obligingly. Then he steered Verdi with invisible strings to fill the cracks that had formed in his absence: Sassan Santarem, Maragrin's lessons, council news.

'Tell me again what your father said about Sturmsinger's starblossom.'

How he longed to have been with Verdi in those timevaults under Romel. Why did Murhesla pay such homage to the harbinger of the Second Redrawing, burying his sigil in the heart of theirs?

Verdi sat up eagerly. 'I can show you! We can go to Romel tomorrow. But I'm afraid of what the Murhesla might do, Klaus. If they could destroy Derinda and rebuild it anew, I think they would.'

'If they really wanted to do that, they would have done so already,' Klaus reasoned. 'We'll have to find out what's holding them back.' He paused. 'I don't think the timevaults are why you want to go back to Romel, though.'

Verdi fell quiet.

'There's nothing wrong with wanting to stay here in Derinda,' Klaus added gently.

Verdi gripped his hands together in his lap. 'My mother didn't believe I would survive all this.'

'Set aside everyone else's fears. What does your heart tell you?'

'But what if she's right?'

'Even if she were, would it make you any more or less willing to serve the Derindin?'

He almost envied Verdi. To be certain of death – to choose the road there – was a great privilege indeed. For the Northborn, ruled by the Blood Pact, death was the veiled betrothed. Anger sparked beneath his Form. *Enough of foretellings.* It was all too easy to see only darkness from a place of fear.

Quietly, he told Verdi, 'For all its aim, a mother's love can do far more harm than good.'

Klaus busied himself refilling his kahvi while Verdi dried his eyes and clawed back his grief.

'We need to infiltrate your father's guild,' Klaus told him.

'What? You've only just come back –'

'Not me. You.'

Verdi's jaw dropped. 'I couldn't – I'm not an Intelligencer…'

'You have the greatest weapon of all: you're his son. And I'll help you.'

Why would the Murhesla honour Sturmsinger, the oldest enemy of the South? *Honour, or mark for vengeance?*

Weariness overtook him. The tide of questions ebbed. For now, Afldalr remained undisturbed, his lips moving silently around the Wanderer's litany instead. When his eyes grew heavy, sleep-terrors tossed him a moment's pity, staying away. In their place, a sea without shore filled his dreams.

*

When he awoke a few hours later, Thillaina was still asleep. He sat in the shadows of her chamber. The fire crackled. Outside, a soft wind hooted forlornly to long-lost brethren. Every one of his muscles complained bitterly.

Ravi emerged from her blankets. He fixed one green orb on Klaus and disappeared, reappearing on the arm of his chair. Klaus scratched his head.

'You knew all along,' he told the oceloe softly. 'You recognised her from when you were a kitterlat and Verdi a pup.'

She stirred. Klaus crossed the room and knelt by the bed. Her eyes opened.

'I didn't mean to wake you.'

She tutted in feeble annoyance, a world of sadness folded into her smile.

'Your hair was as fair as your sister's, when you were a babe. You won't remember.'

He tried to summon some memory of this woman, of being carried in her arms or her dragon-fire eyes. 'You went back to see Elodie, then?'

'How could I not?'

She tried to sit up.

Klaus held out a hand to steady her. 'You should rest.'

'I've waited a long time to ask your pardon.'

'What in the Part for?'

'Your parents were only trying to avert the future I showed them, and so fulfilled the prophecy they should never have known. That is my doing. Forgive me, child. I am the one who has killed you twice.'

His throat tightened painfully. 'The spaewife would have told them even if you hadn't. And her words would have done more harm had you not tempered them with the truth.'

'But I didn't,' Thillaina whispered. 'Not all of it … I told Viridian and the young Prospere the rest of what I saw, just in case –'

'I know the rest,' he said quietly. 'Verdi told me.'

He couldn't bear the rays of her relief. Perhaps Thillaina's vision of the future he might have had in Invelmar gave her peace; for him it was little reassurance.

There would be no going back.

'Will my mother – would Lady Wintermantel's ascension to the throne not satisfy the prophecy?'

'That was not what I saw. After all, she was not born an Ealdorman. She will be Queen-consort, but the throne will be your father's.'

'Why did it have to be my brother and I?' The more he tried to trap truth into some semblance of coherence, the more he stumbled on questions new.

'Why didn't the limolan tree grow from the seed they planted for Viridian's mother? Or her forebears before her? No.' Thillaina prodded his chest. 'It had to be Yirma's son. It was never merely a matter of blood – there are as many tributaries of Lorendar as there are of the Ninvellyn. So it is for you, who have awoken the sleepers in the sand. A gift – and a curse – bequeathed to the sons of Sturmsinger, Svanhilda's sons. Your sister was always safe.'

For a moment there was nothing but the gentle crackle of the fire swaddling them in its warmth; the most comforting sound in the world.

'What will you do now, dearest prince?'

'Stay here.'

'And your birthright?'

'I'll not rejoin the ranks of liars and traitors, mistress.'

'Not all the Ealdormen are so bad. Yes, you heard me right. Your father…'

'Perpetuates lies, though he learned the truth. He made his choice, and I'll make mine.'

'Indeed he did. Did he not choose to protect the secret of the woman he loved, though he was warned she would be the downfall of his kingdom? By all rights, he should have executed her. He resisted the spaewife's fearmongering.'

Klaus heard her, and resisted also. That door would remain closed. What he felt for his parents now was more than Afldalr could bear.

He repeated, 'I will stay here.'

They shared a companionable silence before the questions gnawed at him again.

'Are they sure … might my brother have survived?'

At the look in her face, he almost wished he hadn't asked.

'Your mother was the gentlest of souls before she saw her child slain. After that … it was only after that that she truly became an Intelligencer. Your sister is just like her, in so many ways…'

Klaus couldn't imagine the sweet innocence of Elodie filling a vessel such as Svanhilda Wintermantel. His mother had more guile than the brush-snake that had poisoned him near Cora.

'I wish they'd sent me away when I was born, like him.' To never have known Invelmar – that would have been a mercy.

'If your brother had remained safe in the Far North, they would have sent you away from your first breath. Years it took, to let you go.'

'Did you tell them to do it?'

Even she was a bit unseated by his bluntness. But she held his gaze.

'I swear to you I did not. But I did worse – I aroused their demons. That drove them to it. And dearly they've paid for it now.'

Klaus rose. The truth was still too raw to bring much relief.

'I know you meant well.'

'The future is a secret that ought only be shared with those who've mastered themselves. Everyone else will just pervert the passage of time, seeking to know what is not yet permitted.' She squeezed his fingers. 'We've all been set on our paths with purpose, dear prince. Don't reject yours. Else you may as well throw a tantrum in the face of the Great Sentience himself.'

'Rest well.' He kissed her head. 'We'll not speak of them again.'

He left, closing the door behind him.

Alone with only an old woman's shame for company, the widow Thillaina did not rest. *The truth must be taken whole.* But not yet; perhaps not ever. Truesight had brought much pain, and this portion of prophecy would only fuel more. No, the final third of her vision would remain in her bosom, safely unspoken.

*

It was sundown before Arik returned. Klaus smiled when his footsteps quickened on the stairs. He raised a finger to his lips as the door flew open; Verdi had finally fallen asleep, worn out with relief.

His embrace was rough. *Perhaps he hadn't believed I would return, either.*

At least Thillaina told them about my parents. He was grateful to be spared that confession.

Klaus jerked his head towards the adjoining chamber. 'Let's not wake him up.'

The nocturnal cold was not so cruel here as in the open desert, though early summer hadn't blunted its edge. A harrying wind split and multiplied to handfuls of knives. They climbed the streets to a quiet square which afforded unbroken views of the torch-lit citadel gates below. Here there were neither trees nor buildings to cast shadows, and its empty corners could not conceal even the likes of Murhesla.

'How's Nerisen?'

'Still not back from Pir Sehem.' Arik shot him a sidelong glance. 'Don't worry, a company of tumblers will escort the Plainswalkers home.'

'Is the skydisc safe?'

'Yes. But we'll need to find somewhere to keep it hidden. I can't keep carrying it around.'

'The whole of Invelmar is looking for it. Mother –' Klaus paused. 'Lady Wintermantel said Adela thinks it will lead them to Sturmsinger's burial ground.'

'Why's she looking for *that*?'

'She and her Spyglass believe it will help them identify his heir.'

How? Perhaps, like Sefta's cave, Ansovald's tomb hid what Adela wanted to find – or conceal.

'But then why do the Eh Menishian want the skydisc? Why are they really in Derinda?'

They gazed over the Plains stretching beyond the citadel, writing its mysteries in myriad grains of sand.

'Sturmsinger offered them refuge once,' said Klaus. 'Maybe they've not forgotten that. Or maybe it's this ore. I left a sample with Ristowin the metalsmith to examine. As for the skydisc ... we'll have to study it to answer that.'

The wind gathered to a whistle, too gentle yet for airborne sand to have sharpened its teeth. For now, it was the invisible wolf of the desert.

'I know about your mother,' said Arik at last.

Just there, in the dusty distance: the Far South, the Eh Menishian stronghold, and the lair of Sturmsinger's secret. Klaus retracted his mind from all this and turned to face him.

Two Ealdormen searched one another.

'I'm not going back.'

'How can you not?' said Arik at once. 'How can there be any justice –'

'Justice will have its day when Adela dies and my mother joins my father on the throne. And then after them, Elodie...'

'But no one will know. They even stole the Blood Pact, Klaus.'

'And it still holds. It's the only part of Sturmsinger they couldn't bury.'

'Then you'll let the lies continue?' Arik's hands curled into fists, suppressing anger to a fine tremor. 'Let your sister shoulder the burden alone?'

'I've not got much choice –'

'We all have a choice!' Anger unfurled. He grabbed Klaus by both shoulders, forcing him back several steps. Fury flooded Arik's dark eyes with stifled thunder.

Klaus absorbed the Warrior's rage into his stillness. Two Forms clashed like silent swords.

'Even the Blood Pact might not be enough to keep the Ealdormen in check if Mother tries to take back Sturmsinger's throne and name it his.'

Now it was his own maggot that Klaus smothered; the miscreant reminder that he could destroy Wolfram and Svanhilda Wintermantel.

I could smuggle Elodie out of Dunraven. After that, a message to Adela would suffice. Wild thoughts spewed from the bed of this ulcer, this seething bitterness –

Klaus ground it underfoot. 'I won't do anything that would threaten the Pact, Arik. The Chain must hold.'

He watched the Warrior grapple with his Form. Then Arik's arms fell away. Bruising pain blossomed over Klaus' shoulders.

Then there was silence.

Smoke whispered across the belly of the moon. Stars winked conspiratorially.

Arik straightened. He drew Thunraz from its scabbard and dropped to one knee in the dark.

Klaus backed away. 'What are you doing?'

Arik grasped his sword by its naked blade.

'I've no choice, either.' He turned the hilt towards Klaus. 'In the name of the Lifegiver, I bind my blood and the children of my blood to the service of the house of Sturmsinger, and to answer without fear the summons of the house of Sturmsinger –'

'The Chain hasn't turned yet, and we're not in the North –'

'– and to avenge and restore the honour of the house of Sturmsinger, those who came before him and those who will follow beyond.' Arik's fingers tightened around the steel, in the binding oath Ealdormen took at every turn of the Chain. 'It was here in the South that he was betrayed.'

Heart rearing against his ribs, Klaus took the hilt he offered. When Arik released it, his palm was covered in blood.

Klaus returned it to him by the hilt with shaking hands.

Arik waited until he'd dried his cheeks. 'At least you know they don't mean to come after you.'

'But Adela will, if she suspects either of us are alive. Which is only a matter of time. They'll come after the Eh Menishian.'

'Then we'd better make use of the time we've got.'

They gazed south. *Always south.* His heart tugged his thoughts over the citadel wall, west where Pir Sehem harboured a jewel beyond measure.

He murmured into the darkness, 'She'll never have me now.'

A soft chitter nipped at the night. Namathra sank gently onto the low wall before them.

'Looks like *she* will, though,' Arik marvelled as she folded her spotted wings.

They returned to Thillaina's house. It was a long time before either of them slept. But when he finally did, Klaus dreamed of rain; cool and gentle and so long absent it seemed an unreality.

*

Alizarin had been taken aback by his own relief. *But how did Klaus cross paths with the Wintermantels again and escape alive?* He pushed his breakfast away.

'We ought to be thankful, nephew,' Emra chided. 'Things are going better than I'd dared to hope. Viridian's changing. The gnomon *will* respond to him, I know it.'

Alizarin scowled. 'Viridian is too much like his mother. My sister was also too easily influenced, too malleable … her heart was for the taking.'

'And isn't that why you loved her more than anyone?'

Alizarin looked away. 'How can he lever the corruption of these people?'

'He may not be the iron fist you imagined, but perhaps what this land needs isn't an iron fist, but a balsam.'

Perhaps. Or perhaps the land responded to the summons of an older power still. Restless, he returned to Thillaina's house, grateful for the unsavoury truth about her dealings with the Wintermantels. Alizarin had never been so happy to be wrong about anything. It never made sense that Thillaina had risked the clan to spy on Klaus. A fortnight after their return from Pir Sehem, she still kept to her bed, though Fresmo said she was better. Better enough to have summoned the girls back to their workrooms. The humming of looms and the creaking joints of spindles papered over the silence.

'Forgive me,' Alizarin told her. 'I ought not to have doubted –'

'You did exactly as you should, and I would have thought less of you had you believed me a traitor and still done nothing.'

She looked ten years older, if that were even possible.

'He's returned,' he said. 'And the Wintermantels must know where he is now. I vowed to keep his secret. But what about when their Isarnanheri lay waste to Samsarra looking for him?'

'Perhaps the Wintermantels have let him go.'

'And let their dirty secret walk the Parts? Never.'

Her silence had a heavier footprint than it ought to have done. *She doesn't seem concerned about Isarnanheri turning up here.* Then Alizarin recalled Viridian's knife. A blade of finest Invelmari steel, gifted by an Ealdorman to a lowly Derindin; a servant honoured for his service to her precious son…

'No,' he breathed. He searched Thillaina's face, knew at once it was true. 'But why? Why would the Wintermantels send their *own son* and heir away from Dunraven?'

'Rest assured the Wintermantels' Isarnanheri won't be chasing him into the desert.'

'Does *he* know?'

'He does now.'

'But how can it be that an Ealdorman…?'

'Will be our saving grace?' There was fire yet in those watery eyes. 'Perhaps we should marvel instead at the wisdom of the Great Sentience, that even the might of the North has been stationed by your nephew's side at the dawn of Merensama.'

'Viridian is callow,' Alizarin grumbled. 'So tender that even the North couldn't harden him. He'll find brilliance under Fresmo's wing, not in a council of clans. He could sign his name in the Book of Oaths tomorrow and it won't matter. The clans need a leader.'

'What rubbish. How is it that men's skulls are so thick?' she scolded.

'Viridian has such kindness that he would tend to an old woman who he'd believed had killed his brother. In *spite* of all he endured in the North. People will answer to him like the desert to rain. He will be greater than all the councils combined.'

She had the same self-conviction as his aunt, the kind that was so deeply rooted it was in danger of becoming a contagion. But Alizarin's regrets were too many to catch their faith.

Thillaina gazed into a far greater distance than he could share. 'They were good children.'

'They're grown men now, with grown men's crimes.'

'That's what *we* and the world have done to them.' Her eyes became scorpions again. 'We were all children once. A woman remembers a child's own nature; what he was first.'

'That's the problem with women,' he murmured, half jest, half rancour. 'They remember too much.'

And thank the Great Sentience for it.

'Their failings do indeed begin with us,' he conceded. 'If I'd never let him grow up a servant in an Ealdorman's house –'

'Are you still complaining? No prince ever had better company than your nephew. The Prospere's a perfect guardian to watch over him. *He* would have killed a sick old woman in her own home where she had once sheltered him, unfettered by mercy. And the other one...'

Yes, the other one. From her sickbed, Thillaina couldn't have possibly imagined the magnetism of Klaus and his Form at the Assembly, or the secret language he shared with the desert as he guided hundreds of soldiers through a Plains night. She hadn't seen the earth stirring to speak to him at the foot of the watchtower of Ilaria.

But hope was a fickle mistress, and Alizarin had not yet found solace in her arms.

*

'Come in, Master Mapmaker. This is your house as much as ours.'

Emra was alone. Her smile was radiant, and Klaus had never felt more undeserving.

He bowed low, because Invelmari habits were difficult to break.

'Don't thank me,' he told her.

'Very well, I'll impose on you instead. I fear for this Part, Tristan. What you have found in our wastes chills me to the marrow.'

He couldn't tell her of what lay hidden in the bowels of the mountain; of the wrongs that had fermented the Eh Menishians' vengeance. 'Then I pray this armistice will buy you time to build your alliance.'

She nodded at the jewel-pin map of the clandoms. 'When my grandfather made this, the territories were not what they are now. Always they are moving. He made it this way in the hope that one day these pins will be taken down, one by one.'

'How do you mean to use Viridian to that end?'

A shadow passed over her face. 'I don't know.'

'Well, at least that was honest.'

'Five clans have pledged to the armistice. Our alliance is newborn, its terms not yet agreed. The suzerainty in the West retracts its fangs for now. Once Sisoda have recovered, we'll prepare for an assault on the Eh Menishian. All this, and Viridian still resists.'

'What will happen to him after he takes the oath?'

She was struggling to hold his gaze now. 'No one knows. And opinion is divided.'

'You're not afraid for his safety, then?'

'Of course I'm afraid. Why else would I have agreed to Alizarin sending him away? He's young and untried ... though he is most fortunate in his friends.' Her cobalt eyes were blue as the Ninvellyn on a summer's day. 'Pledge yourself to this clan, Master Mapmaker. Viridian will need guidance.'

You'll not admit his mother's vision of his fate, then. Perhaps you've even talked yourself out of the possibility it might be true.

'I'll help him however I can, Ahena. But my first bond is to the North.'

'In the North you may have been born, but it is here you've awoken.'

It was Klaus' turn to resist looking away.

'We plan, but the Great Sentience also plans,' she said. 'I believe you possess something not seen since the time of Whisperers. Viridian will need your gifts. There's a reason your lots have been cast together.'

'And I will help him however I am able. But I'm not yet a free man, Ahena.'

And I have never been, and now may never be. The oath Klaus had imbibed in his cradle had taken his mother's voice now. Rebuking, reproaching. *'Cometh the fall of the kingdom of destruction made...'* Afldalr shook in protest. *'To the dead we are bound ... by our grace are the dead repaid.'*

And serve it I will. My way.

Inside his breast, the Blood Pact dug a new claw into his heart.

*

They stopped for a late meal outside Romel and waited for dusk, because

Verdi wanted to slip into the citadel quietly.

So they passed through the gates at twilight as the moon entered its first quarter, when the markets were closing up. Step quickening and eyes bright, Verdi led the way to the sanctuary, where jasmines anointed summer's first breath, and the bougainvillea bloomed with cerise and apricot leaves. If Klaus had any lingering uncertainty about what Verdi really wanted, he shed the last of it then.

It was the first time Klaus had seen it: the large heart-shaped limolan leaves hanging from smooth maiden's-arm branches; the tranquillity pooling around it. He could have stumbled upon it in the thickest of foreign forests and known it was sacred.

'Look,' Rasan breathed. Round buds were nestled amongst the leaves. One had already half-opened; a large flower of ivory white.

And where there is flower, fruit will follow.

The temple was empty. The Book of Oaths lay on a plinth in the middle of the prayer hall. Its pages were smooth, though they testified to hundreds of vows: contracts between merchant houses; marriages made and broken; appointments of Elders and Chieftains; clan pacts, blood feuds … Rasan flicked back to the record of a handfastening twenty-five years before: *Yirma, daughter of Nerinca, to Sassan Efero Santarem.*

Verdi unwrapped his mother's pen with trembling fingers. In the ruby throes of sundown, secretly and without ceremony, he wrote his name at the bottom of the page. Then he turned the crowded page to the next.

'What happens now?' said Arik.

Verdi's hands trembled, wrapping away the pen. Klaus drew an arm around his childhood playmate.

'Now we hope.'

It was only as they were leaving Riorga's inn the following morning that the bells began to ring. First in the old citadel, then the streets, the watchtowers and verandas as word spread. Rasan and Verdi rode a short distance ahead, hooded and sand-masked amongst dozens of other Derindin leaving Romel. Following them, Arik and Klaus drew the whispers and pointing fingers instead. Joyous bells filled the main square as Derindin gathered to exchange the news. Babblers departed like tasselled darts in a jealous race to disseminate word throughout the clandoms.

Namathra circled the sky, ready to leave since dawn. A caravan trooped tiredly into the square, steering wagons past rows of stalls. Klaus led his horse around them. A road-weary mare peeled away from the caravan, stopping at a water trough for a drink. The tired skirts of her rider's coat hung over dusty trousers torn at one thigh, her dark braid unravelling.

A rush of relief swelled in his heart, hope leaping closely on its heels.

He fixed his gaze upon Nerisen until she felt his eyes, turning to return those impossible greens: spring ferns and raw pistachio heart.

He climbed into his saddle and rejoined his friends at the gate, the road rising like an old friend to meet him.

Epilogue

Utter night would reign here for three moons more, cloaked in snow. Darkness held the stars hostage.

So high in the mountains, the air stretched thinner than spaewives' souls, barely aerating the unacclimatised lung. The little creature, so alien in his outlandish furs and the strange symbols that festooned him, breathed raggedly as he broke the seal on the message.

'Ahhhh,' he sighed. Currents of ice crystals hurried around his breath.

'Is it there?'

The creature unfolded the paper and held up a small mechanicontraption, releasing a lever to reveal its contents: a crumb of rock, a scrap of cloth stiff with a dried reddish-brown stain, and a single golden-brown hair.

He fingered these tenderly, for they were sacred beyond all imagining, his face savagely alive in the firelight.

'Well?'

'Yes.' His tongue still moved thickly around their foreign articulations, though they were no longer strangers to him now. 'The weapon is found.'

The distant din of hammering drifted on the wind from the frozen valley below. Truth slumbered in the womb of winter, awaiting her iron dawn.

Dear Reader

If words are a story's oxygen, you are its lung. Without you, this book doesn't breathe.

If you enjoyed my story and would like to support this book and its sequels, I would be truly grateful for your review and your thoughts on Amazon and elsewhere.

I am committed to bringing Klaus' world to life, beginning with his maps. These are available on my website:

www.lnbayen.com

where you can also sign up to my mailing list. Details of book art and map releases, limited artisanal merchandise and sneak snippets will be announced there in the coming months.

Wishing you peace and prosperity on all the roads of the world,

Lamia

Glossary

ADA: 'uncle'; respectful term of address to a man older than one's self. (Feminine: ADDA).

AHEN/AHENA: title sometimes used to address Derindin Chieftains/ Chieftainesses, often through ellision ('Emra-hena').

ANDAERA: Far Northern constellation of stars mentioned in the Septentrional Scrolls and thus little-known outside the Far North.

ANSOVALD STURMSINGER: Far Northern warlord who united Northern and Far Northern tribes to create the kingdom of Invelmar, drove rebels to the Far North, conquered much of the South, and triggered the Second Redrawing of the Silfren Part.

BARRVEGR: Invelmar's network of grain-trading routes.

BLACK LAVA PLAINS: uninhabitable region dominated by basalt plains, volcanic rocky terrain and lava fields which comprise the western Silfren Parts.

BLOOD PACT: sacred agreement enforced upon Invelmar by Ansovald Sturmsinger which outlawed civil conflict following a spaewife's warning that further bloodshed would cause the dissolution of Invelmar.

BORDER TOWNS (Noisy Tree, Appledor, TipToe, Whimsy): four market towns at the border between Invelmar and Derinda; Invelmari by conquest but populated mostly by Derindin of clan Akrinda.

DERINDA: desertified land in the southern Silfren Part comprised of

THE WINGSPAN OF TREASON

autonomous clans.

DUNRAVEN: Invelmar's principal and southernmost citadel.

EALDORMEN: the ruling nobility descended from Sturmsinger's key allies, comprising the five royal houses of Wintemantel, Prospere, Eldred, Haimric and Rainard.

EFESHYUN: hallucinogenic herbal intoxicant, sometimes used recreationally but toxic in high doses, especially to animals.

ETTSRAKKA: bloodland recorded in the Sonnonfer; also the site of an ancient iron mine.

EYE OF THE COURT: the body of highest-ranking Intelligencers, led by the Spyglass

FAR NORTH: region north of the Sterns mountain range. Occupied by the tribes and rebels who refused to surrender to Sturmsinger at the Second Redrawing and who have remained hostile to Invelmar ever since.

FIFTH CHAMBER: Derindin principle; an additional (metaphysical) chamber of the heart generating ilnurhin and hosting spiritual currents, including namathra and sehresar.

FIRST REDRAWING: great period of war throughout the southern Silfren Part which resulted in the dissolution of the former nation of Orenthia, which fragmented into many competing kingdomes. Precedes the birth of Obsidian Lorendar.

FORM: a guarded state acquired and mastered by Ealdormen through rigorous training, taught to royal children from birth. Four varieties: Warrior, Blacksmith, Jurist and Intelligencer.

GHABALA: Derinda's only universal law; decrees that Derindin may invade and retain any land they are subsequently able to defend and retain.

GREAT SENTIENCE (the): Derindin term for God.

GRÍMALÁTA: ceremonial circlet awarded to Intelligencers, masking one 'all-seeing' eye and exposing a second 'impenetrable' eye, symbolising the evasive nature of this Form.

ILNURHIN: Derindask term for 'slight matter'.

INVELMAR: kingdom in the northern Silfren Part, formed by Ansovald Sturmsinger at the Second Redrawing from the union of the North's five greatest tribes with his own. Language: Invelmen.

ISARNANHERI: Invelmar's elite militia, led and overseen by Ealdormen Warriors; loaned throughout the Seven Parts under contracts typically negotiated by Intelligencers.

JARNSTIGA: ancient swordfighting discipline conceived by Sturmsinger and taught only to Ealdormen and Isarnanheri.

JEMESH: human bone sent as a 'death-promise', signalling a vow to kill the recipient. Usually associated with an award to attract bounty hunters; the value of the award typically proportional to the bone's anatomical importance.

KARRIONHJORDE: formidable Far Northern wild-men bred and trained as soldiers.

KAHVI (Derindask: **KAHVA**): coffee.

KALDISTAZVEGR: Invelmar's iron-trading highroad.

LAMH'MET: Derindin travellers' staple food of shaved deer's heart, offal and beans, cooked as a porridge.

LETTERVAULT: library.

LIFEGIVER (the): Invelmari name for God.

LIMOLAN: extinct tree prophecised, once revived, as confirming the arrival of Lorendar's heir.

MERENSAMA: a fabled peacetime sought by some of Derinda's clans; seeks to unite the clans, end the feudal system and abolish ghabala.

MINIBEAST: diminutive animals bred by the Derindin and kept as pets for their highly adapted senses that can guide or assist humans. Examples: oceloes, panfarthings, bearlings, tigons, fox-stoats, wolveri, dart-hares and fruitnoses.

MURHESLA: secretive guild of warriors who control and guard Romel, outlawing any bloodshed in the citadel.

NINVELLYN: great river formed from the confluences of four northern rivers (Laith, Lune, Larin and Lark), and historically the main overground water supply to Derinda prior to its damming at the Second Redrawing.

NAMATHRA: the Derindin prayer for rain.

OBSIDIAN LORENDAR: Southern farmer-turned-warrior who fought back against corrupt kingdoms and united many Southern kingdoms and factions, hoping to revive ancient Orenthia. Became the last Custodian of the South, but was unable to achieve lasting unity across the South before his death.

OCELOE: variety of minibeast resembling a dimunitive cat with a slightly ferret-like body, bred for its ability to detect danger and deceit. Female: oceloot. Young: kitterlat.

ORENTHIA: ancient Southern realm predating the First Redrawing, governed by Simyerin Custodians.

OSTRAAD DAM: strategic dam built by Ansovald Sturmsinger at the Second Redrawing, cutting off the Ninvellyn river to the South and diverting its waters to east and west Invelmar.

PAIVA: fertile valley in southern Invelmar flanking the Ninvellyn. Previously occupied by Southerners. Invaded by Invelmar at the Second Redrawing but still subject to much superstition and thus an uninhabited wilderness.

PENGAZA: kingdom of the Aurelian Part, neighbouring the Silfren Part to the east. Shares borders with both Invelmar and Derinda. Divided from Derinda by the Sourgrass Sea, making illegal entry challenging.

PLAINSWALKER: Derindin desert ranger and humanitarians.

PORT ELLENHEIM: Invelmar's only sea port and main launching site for Isarnanheri and steel exports; close to its border with Pengaza.

SECOND REDRAWING: the second great reshaping of the Silfren Part, led by Sturmsinger's conquests. Unified most Northern and Far Northern tribes to form Invelmar and expel Far Northern rebels north of the Sterns. Absorbed some Southern territory into Invelmar, including the Paiva, and culminated in the erection of the Ostraad dam.

SEHRESAR: the Derindin longing for the river Ninvellyn.

SELVARAN CRADLE: valley between two mountain ranges in the Far South.

SEMRA: kingdom in the Sirghen Part, rivalling Invelmar for wealth and global standing.

SEPTENTRIONAL SCROLLS: the sacred scriptures of the Far North; possession or dissemination of them is forbidden in Invelmar and punishable by death.

SEVEN PARTS: the seven main continents of the known world.

SIMYERIN: the South's earliest mapmakers, who used slight matter to command the earth's elements and justly rule Orenthia. Derindin believe that humanity's corruption caused the Great Sentience to call back all but two elements to prevent them from serving humanity, leaving only earth and iron behind.

SLIGHT MATTER: immaterial sentient particles generated by the fifth chamber of the heart and sensed by all other organs. Perception of slight matter varies between people. Previously obeyed the command of Simyerin to achieve great feats serving humanity; can now only be sensed and interpreted but not controlled.

SONNONFER: the sacred scriptures of Invelmar, recording the life and conquests of Sturmsinger, the birth of Invelmar, the Blood Pact, the rise of Ealdormen and the formation of the Sturmsinger Chain, and Invelmar's laws.

SOURGRASS SEA: grassy plains which give way to salt marshes, forming the boundary between eastern Derinda/south-eastern Invelmar and Pengaza; an effective buffer to most illegal crossings.

SPAEWIFE: Far Northern soothsayer.

SPYGLASS: leader of Invelmar's Intelligencers, appointed by Invelmar's incumbent monarch. Often themselves Intelligencers, but rarely the position is awarded to high-ranking spies who are not Ealdormen (e.g. Florian Arnander). Identity is usually public ('named') but can also be secret and known only to the monarch ('unnamed', e.g. Queen Adela's current Spyglass).

STAHLAZ: Invelmar's greatest steel forge.

STARBLOSSOM (of Invelmar): five-petalled sigil of Invelmar's five ruling

Ealdormen houses. Derived from the more ancient six-petalled starblossom of Sturmsinger, which was abandoned after his death and the fall of his Far Northern army. The sixth petal had formerly represented the Far Northern house of Sturmsinger.

SUNNANFROST: the principal residential palace of House Wintermantel in Dunraven.

SURRWYRTE: highly prized contraceptive. In Invelmar, its use by all Ealdormen is prohibited, and it may only be used by commoners who already have one living child.

TÄNTAINEN: Far Northern warlord with whom Queen Adela brokered a peace treaty, which collapsed following his recent assassination.

TESH: Derindin term for the fatal, maddening thirst which afflicts travellers cut off from water.

THUNRAZ: the sword of Arik Prospere, forged in Stahlaz.

TUMBLER: Derindin soldiers, all of whom are briefly trained by the Murhesla before being released to seek contracts with clans.

UMMANDIR: kingdom furthest east from Invelmar, located in the Ambar Part in the Utter East. Capital: Salussolia. Birth place of bowmaster Kelselem Ousur'had.

VEREMBET: Derindin term for surrwyrte.

ZARROQ'ULLIM (the-pen-that-never-runs-dry): pen bequeathed by Obsidian Lorendar to his successor, with which Lorendar's Oath (in acceptance of his legacy) should be invoked.

Acknowledgements

I've been fortunate enough to have many people to thank and apologise to any who I've missed.

First: Fievel, the furry godfather of oceloes everywhere who was initially responsible for sparking this story. We wrote it together.

My husband, first reader and companion in our sea without shore. Thank you for the unrestrained criticism that seasoned your unshakeable faith in my words.

Katrin Dreessen-Engler, brilliant writer (though she continues to deny it) and my eagle-eyed critique partner. I couldn't have wished for a better writing companion (our coordinates aside) or friend, and I look forward to championing your own stories as passionately as you have championed mine.

Khadija Ahmed, my oldest friend, for supporting this story despite life's many challenges. I will harass you until your own (incredible) story is finished.

Ed Crocker, my proofreader and a literary star in the making; for exceptional attention to detail and endless support.

João F. Silva, already shining with his grimdark stories; for generous publishing guidance and the final little push I needed (the significance of which he was probably unaware).

The wonderful writers who provided feedback on my opening pages: Helen Chester, Thea Lyons, Laura Kohler. Many other generous writers and friends who have cheered me on tirelessly - especially Lily Lawson.

Finally, to you, the reader, for seeing this long road to the end.

The Author

Lamia is a Syrian surgeon living in London. She also writes literary and general fiction and illustrates. This is her debut novel.

Looking for your next read?

Some reading recommendations from fellow authors and from the Secret Scribes.

Ed Crocker
Lightfall (book 1 of *The Everlands Series;* 22 Jan 2025)

Alethea Lyons
The Hiding (book 1 of *The Seer of York*)
Reawakening: A Collection of Short Stories in the Seer of York Universe

João F. Silva
Seeds of War (book 1 of *The Smokesmiths*)
Ruins of Smoke
Thorns of War (book 2 of *The Smokesmiths*)

Maressa Voss
When Shadows Grow Tall

THE SECRET SCRIBES: a collective of fantasy authors writing fresh and diverse stories

Bill Adams:
The Godsblood Tragedy (Passage One of the Divine Godsqueen Coda)
The Tenacious Tale of Tanna the Tendersword (with Dewey Conway)

Tom Bookbeard
The Corsair (2025)

E. H. Bradley
The Ranger

L. M. Douglas
Gharantia's Guardian (book 1 of *Chronicles of the Endless War*)

Gharantia's Fury (book 2 of *Chronicles of the Endless War*)

Bella Dunn
The Dreams Thief (book 1 of *The Otherworld Series*)
Blood and Dreams (book 2 of *The Otherworld Series*; spring 2025)
The Sorrow of the Wise Man (book 1 of *The Eileerean Saga*)

Damien Francis
The Tome of Haren

Dave Lawson
The Envoys of War (book 1 of *The Envoys of Chaos*)

Seán O'Boyle
The Ballad of Sprikit the Bard (and Company)

R. E. Sanders
A Path of Blades
Tann's last Stand
Demon's Tear

R. A. Sandpiper
A Pocket of Lies (*Amefyre* book 1)
A Promise of Blood (*Amefyre* book 2)

Alex Scheuermann
The Odyllic Stone

G. J. Terral
Bloodwoven (book 1 of *The Binding Tenants Trilogy*)
Bloodbound (book 2 *The Binding Tenants Trilogy*)

Made in the USA
Middletown, DE
26 November 2024

65477795R00374